The BELL *and the* BLADE

The BELL and the BLADE

PAULLINA SIMONS

ISBN: 979-8-3372-0742-1

This edition published in 2026 by Open Road Integrated Media, Inc.
180 Maiden Lane
New York, NY 10038
www.openroadmedia.com

To Kevin

U.K
HOLLAND
GERMANY
Antwerp
BELGIUM
Liège
Bastogne
To Normandy
FRANCE
Dordrecht
Oss
Goeree-Overflakkee Island
Schouwen-Duiveland
's-Hertogenbosch
HOLLAND
Breda
Tilburg
Noord-Beveland Island
Walcheren Island
Roosendaal
Goes
Middelburg
Bergen op Zoom
Zuid-Beveland Island
Eindhoven
Knokke-Heist
Terneuzen
Turnhout
Oostende
Maldegem
Vorselaar
Bruges
Zelzate
Sint-Niklaas
Antwerp
Herentals
Olen
Lier
Aalter
Boom
Duffel
BELGIUM
Gent
Mechelen
Tremelo
Diest
Roeselare
Aalst
Hasselt
Jette
Leuven
Kortrijk
Scale
0
50
Kilometres
Tienen
Sint-Truiden
Brussels
To Liège and Bastogne

The BELL and the BLADE

Do not weep, maiden, for war is kind.
Because your lover threw
wild hands
toward the sky
And the affrighted steed ran on
alone,
Do not weep.
War is kind.

Stephen Crane

PART I

La Jonquille est Morte

Omnia Sentiunt
All things feel.

Pythagoras

1

La Berceau

It was a night to forget—or perhaps it was a night to remember.

Charlie gripped the wheel as she drove into Antwerp, heading toward the old docks, her forged papers lying on the seat beside her. She didn't even know who she was hiding from today.

She had become an expert at subtraction. Strip the color. Muffle the light. Remove the name. She reduced herself to mass and motion—steady, silent—a tensile body of a woman who never stopped moving. Her cap was pulled low, her short hair tucked, her coat loose enough to disguise shape and shift. Her pale lips faded into shadow. Her deep brown eyes were lit with watchful fire. But she always felt a fraction misaligned, like a body conducting no heat, or a particle in hiding.

Seamen spilled from the smoke-choked taverns, the clatter of boots and bottles echoing off wet stone. Past the yellowing lights along the harbor, the Scheldt River lay black as oil, slapping the hulls of a thousand ships tethered till morning. It was early June but raining like it was late December. Drunken tempers flaring, men breaking into laughter, falling, calling for their commander. Someone shouted "*Rendez-vous!* Surrender!"

The rain slicked everything but didn't cool the fever. Sailors stumbled against one another, singing, sobbing. One of them grabbed a German *Polizei* by the lapels and shook him. The gendarme shoved him off and kicked him down the cobblestones, almost good-naturedly. *Get out of here, you drunken hoot*, the shiny German boot seemed to say.

Charlie drove her father's flower truck carefully, threading through the clamor, avoiding the roar of wild men who had nowhere to be, as if tomorrow didn't matter.

Or as if tomorrow were all that mattered.

It wasn't normal, this cacophony in the night.

But on Jordaensstraat, by the castle ruins on the edge of the Old City, it was quiet as always. Here, the docks were smaller, older, mostly deserted. The quay was crumbling, and there were no cranes to help with heavy loads. Everything had to be done by hand.

She parked in her usual spot behind an abandoned warehouse by the river. *La Berceau* was the smallest and oldest of her father's trucks, narrow in the frame and wheezy going uphill, but it had one thing none of the others had—a secret compartment underneath a false floor. That's why she had named the truck *the Cradle.* She and her two brothers had installed it with a sliding panel and a hidden latch, using two planks and a prayer.

The wind and the misting rain carried the salty sea into her nose and throat and made her feel as if she were sick or weeping. But she was neither. She was fretful and impatient. Popping the clasp, she released the scrawny boy from the truck's hold.

His name was Zeus.

It had taken her a long time to find him. She'd driven all the way down to Charleroi to retrieve him and his brother from a Carmelite hostel. But Zeus was alone. They didn't speak of it. He just went with her. The child's face was wide and his hair cropped and curly, the kind of hair someone who loved him might want to ruffle. When they first met, he said he wasn't sure if she was a girl or a boy. When she said she was a girl, he puckered his mouth as if he didn't believe her. A precocious child.

"What if they spot your truck here?" Zeus asked. "Won't they get suspicious?"

"*They* don't come back here on Friday nights. Don't worry. We always do it like this."

"Maybe you should park where other trucks are parked," the boy said.

"But then we'd have farther to walk to get to the ship. More chance of getting stopped by roving patrols."

He began to ask another question, but Charlie stopped him. "You're not my first boy, Zeus. And you won't be my last. Trust me. This is the safest way. Now be quiet and come."

"If we're so safe, why do I have to be quiet?"

She observed him warily. Someone should've told her he'd be like this.

A year ago she'd picked the lock on a back door to the warehouse, installed her own, and tonight they entered the vast space easily. They walked to the front, which faced the quay where the old Portuguese ship, the *Serra Nova*, bobbed in the glimmering water.

"Should we open the window?" the boy asked. "So we can climb out quick when the time comes?"

"No, Zeus. I told you—the patrol shines lights in these windows as they walk past. If a window is open, they'll see."

Charlie could tell the boy wanted to take her hand. She wanted to pat him, tell him not to worry, that everything would be okay. But how okay had everything turned out so far? She didn't want to lie. She said nothing.

"When do they come?"

"I told you, at ten."

"I'm ten."

"I can't believe you're ten already, Zeus."

"What time is it now?"

"Fifteen more minutes." She took a breath. "I don't like waiting either," she admitted. What an understatement. "It won't be long."

Charlie knew the captain, Andres Ferrer. They'd been conducting business for two years. Ferrer brought Portuguese olives and cork into Belgium and exported Belgian textiles and beer to Lisbon. Textiles, beer—and small Jewish children. For this, Ferrer got paid, and Charlie got paid. The money funded her resistance work and left her beholden to no one—exactly how Charlie wanted it. To be beholden to no one.

It all flowed easy as olive oil. It was a well-practiced silent pantomime. She had explained it to Zeus, but he was an exceptionally questioning child. She had to tell him over and over. This was why Charlie preferred to transport the children in pairs. You were never as afraid when you had someone with you. "It'll be fine, Zeus," she said. "But be quiet."

"Why do I have to be quiet if it will be fine?"

"Because I need to focus, and I can't when you're asking me a million questions. If I miss the signal, it will not all be fine."

The boy stopped talking, and the two of them stared through the dirty glass. The boy wiped the dust off with his little hand to see the ship better. She waited for the German sentries to make their hourly patrol down Glaskaai. They marched to the walls of Het Steen Castle, then turned around and slowly walked back. As soon as they were out of sight, Ferrer would flash a light—three short, one long—giving her the all-clear. Charlie and her charges would open the window, climb out, and run to the stern of the ship, where a side cargo door would open. They would rumble up the gangplank and disappear inside.

She would say hello to Andres, and settle the child deep in the lower hold, past the barricade of crates and pallets. She'd give him some food, water, a book, a flashlight, go over the passwords, then lock him inside. She'd pay Ferrer, and before she left, they would have a convivial smoke together—another mission successfully completed.

Charlie thought if their time together had been lengthened and the war shortened, Andres might have expressed another, more romantic, interest in her. But who had time for romance these days?

Friday night was a good time for this exchange, because the rest of Ferrer's crew was off at the pub getting plastered. From the flashing signal to the cigarette took seven minutes.

But that wasn't what happened this Friday night.

Because on this Friday night, the men were reckless on the stones and nothing was ordinary and nothing took seven minutes.

Charlie felt the first alarm when ten o'clock came and went, and there was no patrol. She wiped the face of her watch, just in case she'd misread the time, then pried open the window.

"I thought you said not to open the window?" Zeus said.

"Shh, I need to listen."

The German guards were punctual like pistons. Charlie knew them by form and shape, knew their weapons, their purposeful gait, the smell of their cigarettes, the cadence of their chatter. But tonight they were absent, and the strong wind brought not a whiff of the tobacco smoke that signaled their arrival.

She and the boy continued to wait, but her hands started to shake. Something was wrong. She'd been right to note the drunken cacophony when she first drove in. She should leave, run, take the child to a safehouse, and try again another day. But Zeus *needed* to get on that ship. This wasn't for her. It was for him.

From the distant alleys, where the city was still alive, an accordion wheezed a half-forgotten tune, swallowed by night and wind. This part of Antwerp was nothing more than a still painting: the black silhouettes of ships against the maw of the sea, the crumbling stone castle looming over the shoreline, a waxing crescent moon hidden behind silver-black clouds.

The boy whispered, "What is that song?"

She couldn't remember, though she'd been humming it under her breath for minutes.

Finally, it came to her. "*Parlez-moi d'amour.*" *Talk to me about love. Tell me beautiful things again . . . in my heart I'm never tired of hearing it. I love you, but deep down, I don't believe you. Yet I still want you, need you, wish for you to tell me the words of love that I love.*

Briefly closing her eyes, Charlie gave a pained sigh and checked her watch.

It was 11:30. No! That couldn't be right!

And still no patrol in sight.

Maybe the Germans had sampled a little homemade beer and confused the hour? Had Andres gone out for a nightcap—or five—and forgotten to return? Charlie might not have thought much of it had the Germans not been patrolling the outer Scheldt docks with the exacting precision of priests ringing the bells of Saint Waltrude, every hour on the hour from dawn to midnight. Other alarming things were happening, which, combined with the lack of Nazis, added to her panic. Andres Ferrer was missing too. Why had he not flashed the sign at the appointed hour? Could two unlikely absences occur simultaneously for unrelated reasons? That strained credulity.

Something must've happened. Things were happening everywhere. There was chaos in the square.

"Do I go now?" Zeus whispered.

"Go where? No, Zeus." Could she have missed the sign? She did close her eyes for a moment when she allowed a breath of nearly forgotten heartbreak to flow into her chest. But Ferrer would've flashed again. He knew to signal three times more. It had been over ninety minutes.

Intently, Charlie watched the darkened *Serra Nova.*

In the stillness, fear was born. *Serra Nova* was moored in its usual spot on Glaskaai. Normally, the berths next to it were vacant, but tonight, another merchant ship bobbed to its left, heaving against the pilings. It was longer than the *Serra Nova,* slightly wider, though just as dark, just as locked up, just as abandoned. Squinting, she tried to make out the name in faded white across the prow. *La Fortuna.* Reading that name, something heavy and foreboding tolled inside Charlie's chest. She almost trembled.

There was a Belgian flag on her mast, a Portuguese trading flag below it, and below that, a swaying white flag painted over with a narcissus—a daffodil. A bespoke flag of a painted yellow flower seemed odd for a merchant ship, too personal. Almost as if it weren't a flag, but a sign . . .

"Charlie!" Zeus pointed. In the dark, broken only by a flickering gas lamp, a group of black-clad men appeared out of the shadows. She emitted an audible gasp. Quickly they crossed the quay and hurried down the narrow wooden wharf at the broadside of *La Fortuna.*

The interlopers fanned out along the ship's flank, grabbed onto the mooring ropes and expertly wound their way up the rough knotted twine. They looked chillingly professional. On the freeboard of the ship above the waterline, they found ladders and grappling hooks and climbed up the hull like spiders, to the top of the deck, noiselessly vaulting over the railing—Olympic athletes all. The ship's mass groaned against the pilings, but otherwise there was no sound except for the distant whine of the gut-wrenched accordion.

"Charlie," Zeus whispered, "are they coming for *me*?"

Oh my God. She put her arm around him. "No, dear boy," she whispered back. "That's not our ship."

His body was stiff with tension. "Are they Nazis?"

"I don't know—please be quiet." Perhaps they were looking for another Zeus—or many Zeuses? It made no sense. Why would they need to climb in stealth? The Nazis carried out inspections anywhere, anytime, the louder the better.

Charlie heard the intruders trying to pry open the ship's cargo doors. It was so quiet, she could hear their breathing, their muttering in German. *Zum Teufel! Verdammt!* Finally one of the hatches must have sprung open. But there was no relief, only surprise all around: from the men who came uninvited, and from the men below deck who greeted them. She heard one hiss in German, *"Wer sind Sie?"*—Who are you?—followed by a loud response in French, *"Qui diable êtes-vous?"* Who the fuck are you?

The voices carried back and forth in the night air: intense, combative. Interrogative in German. Declarative in French.

Abruptly, the conversation ended. Muffled voices shouted commands, louder voices responded in protest. She heard rushing footsteps, saw shadows of men lunging at each other. Charlie clasped a hand over Zeus's open mouth, but who was going to clasp a hand over her own?

There was whooshing, grunting, the whistling of metal. She heard gasping, and stifled cries, heard the sucking sounds of lethal conflict, of men ordered to make no noise under mortal duress and making noise anyway. The bodies of men fell on the deck. A metal object rolled; there was a stampede to recover it. Blades caught the crescent moon, dull flashes of silver rose—and plunged down. Agony of metal piercing human flesh. Groans that could not be silenced.

Something dark and heavy leapt into the river off the side of the ship. Another thick jump, then a battle in deep water—a breathless, violent, watery commotion.

In the dull cloudy shimmer, there were fewer and fewer shapes of men standing, fighting. Fewer and fewer silver flashes in the moonlit darkness. "Don't make a sound, Zeus," she whispered. "Don't even breathe." She wanted to close the window but knew she couldn't. The window creaked, and she didn't know who else might be nearby. From her low vantage point, she caught the last slivers of men's raised arms, silent blades, the gasping, gasping getting fainter . . .

Charlie gasped herself.

And then all was silent.

The somber bells of the Cathedral of Our Lady began to toll midnight, echoing across the stones and the water.

Zeus's eyes were like moons themselves.

She jumped to her feet. "We need to leave, Zeus."

"What about my passage?" He rose a lot slower than she.

"Zeus, what passage! No captain, no crew, no signal, no safety! And any second this place will be overrun with Nazis."

"Weren't those Nazis?"

"I don't know *what* that was," she said. "We need to go. Before they close all the checkpoints. Hurry." Charlie couldn't hide the fear on her face. She couldn't even pretend for a ten-year-old! She felt shame, but no bravery.

She was about to slam the window shut when Zeus yanked on her sleeve. "Listen!"

Charlie was done listening.

"Do you hear it?"

"No, and I don't want to. Let's go."

"Listen!"

"No!"

Across the cobbled quay, a man's voice was calling softly for help. Charlie saw a shadowy hand reach up from the black water to grab the coping.

"It's a Nazi, Zeus! We must run!"

"Not a Nazi! Listen."

The man was pleading in French. *"Au secours! Au secours!"* A desperate, intimate cry for mercy.

"Zeus, we can't . . ."

But the boy was already climbing out. Well, why not? He didn't have anyone but himself to worry about. Charlie had to worry about him, her father, her mother, her brother, Louise, her entire resistance cell, and dozens, maybe hundreds of people whose lives would be at risk if she and the boy were arrested at this part of the docks they weren't supposed to be near, having witnessed a slaughter they *definitely* weren't supposed to see. That the boy would be shot was self-evident. But she would be tortured first. What did Zeus care for any of that? The boy was leaping out of windows! Charlie had no choice but to climb out and run after him to the waterline. There, a bloodied hand grasped one of the steel bollards. A panting black man hung on, weakly mouthing, *Help me.*

Oh my God, exclaimed a stunned Charlie.

"Told you—not a Nazi," said Zeus.

Her first impulse was to bolt.

Also her second impulse. And third.

"We are in *terrible* danger," the man gurgled.

No kidding, she wanted to say, speechless and motionless.

"I beg you, help me . . ."

"Charlie!" said Zeus, pulling on the man's arm in a futile attempt to drag him out of the water. The boy was pitched so far forward, he was about to tip over and topple in. Instinctively, she grabbed the back of Zeus's jacket.

She was so afraid to be out in the open like this. Afraid, and unarmed. She'd left her Browning hidden deep in the truck in case she was stopped and searched on the docks. It was *verboten* for Belgian civilians to carry weapons in their own country. Instant execution if you were caught with a weapon. She felt danger all around her, a numbing terror.

Without her help, this gravely wounded man would fall backward, bleed out and drown, and then she, Charlotte Fontaine, could walk away, run away, and maybe even try again with Zeus another day, though in her heart of hearts, Charlie suspected that the human salvage business might be done with for good this time.

"I can't," she whispered, tugging on Zeus. "I'm really sorry, but I can't. Let's go, Zeus."

"Please!" said the man.

"Please!" said Zeus.

What could she do? With hostile reluctance, with tremendous aversion to conflict—which perhaps was ironic, given the daily business of her life the last two years—Charlie crouched and, taking a shallow, miserable breath, grabbed the man's waterlogged sleeve.

"Robert Capelle," he croaked. *"Find him in Jette . . ."* His throat stopped forming words. Blood bubbled out instead.

"Who is Robert Capelle?" Charlie cried. "And tell him what?"

"La jonquille est morte," the black man gasped, and lost consciousness.

The narcissus is dead.

2

A Mandatory Morale Event

Three days before the events on the Scheldt River, on the evening of Tuesday, May 30, 1944, *Sturmbannführer* Erich von Rheinhardt sat alone in his office, examining the shipping manifest before him.

Something wasn't right.

Von Rheinhardt was a forbidding man, impeccably groomed and attired. His SS tunic was buttoned to his throat, even when he was sitting. His Luger Parabellum 9mm pistol lay to his right, within immediate reach. He wore his light brown hair neat and slicked back. His ice-blue eyes—small, round, penetrating pinpoints—were trained on the documents.

When something troubled Rheinhardt, he felt it as a cold electric sting under the skin. His fingers would start to throb from the shooting nerve impulses, like static gathering before discharge. His superiors commended him on his otherworldly attention to detail, praised his ability to pry truth from stone. Rheinhardt would thank them for their oily flattery, never admitting that his talent was less genius than a symptom—of acute physical distress.

And so he sat tonight, well past quitting time, his back straight as a marble column, studying the documents on his desk.

He could hear men outside his door, pacing, waiting.

But Rheinhardt wasn't done poking at his suspicions.

The ship was a standard liberty merchant schooner, eighty meters long.

It was named *La Fortuna*.

It had sailed from the Belgian Congo in Africa under the Belgian flag. The goods were more or less standard issue: coffee, tin, rubber, quinine bark, an inordinate quantity of semi-processed copper ingots, and cobalt. When the ship stopped at Lisbon to refuel and resupply, fifty crates of olives, olive oil, cork, and rum were added to the manifest.

Rheinhardt's long-fingered hands lay steady on the cold table. But the hair on the back of his neck prickled with tension.

There was a knock on the door. Hubner stuck his head inside. "Everything all right, sir? They're waiting."

"Did I ask you if they were waiting?"

"I'm just informing you—"

"Yes, of the obvious."

Hubner slid in, closing the door behind him. "Is something troubling you?"

"Clearly something is, Hubner, otherwise why would I be sitting here at nine in the evening, studying the damn papers?"

"I went over the manifest myself," Hubner said, coming around Rheinhardt's desk. "This afternoon, I inspected the ship with three men, checking it off item by item, crate by crate. Everything is in perfect order, sir, I assure you."

"You assure me, do you? Then why do I even need to look anything over, if I've got you vouching for the ship's contents?"

"That's a good question, sir," Hubner whispered in a soothing timbre.

Franz Hubner was a man of medium height, medium weight, medium age, medium ambition, and medium intelligence. He was both pliant and small-minded. The only superlative quality Hubner possessed was the preternatural eagerness to please his commanding officer. Even that, Rheinhardt felt, was both a blessing and a curse.

"Bring me the captain," Rheinhardt said. "And is Silva out there?" Miguel Silva ran the trading company that operated *La Fortuna*. "He always has his hands in something shady. Bring him to me as well."

"He's not here tonight, sir. Just the captain and—"

Rheinhardt turned. Hubner flinched.

"Why haven't you moved, Hubner? Are you a fern? Was my command not clear?"

"It's nine in the evening, sir . . ."

"Oh, you're a clock also? Go."

Five minutes later, Jacques Dufresne, the compact, weathered captain of *La Fortuna*, stood before Rheinhardt. Dufresne was an aging sea dog, in a naval peacoat with tarnished buttons. He wore a black scarf around his neck and a flat mariner's cap, which he remembered to remove a minute or two *after* he entered Rheinhardt's office.

Next to him towered a glistening African man, doing his best to slouch and look tired. He wore a gray work shirt with rolled sleeves, twill trousers, and an oil-stained deck jacket. Rheinhardt recognized a military man immediately. This deckhand almost saluted him.

"Who is this?" Rheinhardt asked the captain.

"Ngomo Kasonga," Dufresne replied. "He's my first mate."

"Military?"

"Not at all," Dufresne said. "Just a simple Congolese seafarer."

"Simple, eh?" Rheinhardt appraised the African man. "Does he speak French?"

"Not well enough to be interrogated, Herr Commandant."

"If he doesn't speak French, how do *you* interact with him?"

"I speak his language," Dufresne said. "Been working merchant ships since 1926. I need to communicate with stevedores, dockworkers, and port agents in Matadi and Luanda. Speaking Lingala is a necessity." Lingala was a melodic Bantu language spoken along the Congo River, used as a lingua franca in many ports in Central Africa.

Von Rheinhardt contemplated both men. "If you've been sailing hither and yon since 1926, why has *La Fortuna* never docked in Antwerp before? Why is this the first time you're in my port?"

Dufresne shrugged. "I go where they send me."

"On *La Fortuna*?"

"On many different ships."

"*La Fortuna* being one of them?"

"I can't recall, but yes, most likely."

"Most likely," Rheinhardt repeated. "Was Antwerp always your final destination or were you headed to Portugal and redirected here?"

"I believe the manifest says Antwerp," Dufresne said. "You'd have to confirm the initial orders with Miguel Silva. The ship is licensed to him."

"Yes, that scoundrel is never around when you need him," Rheinhardt muttered. "Captain, order your first mate to look at the floor and not at me. I don't authorize his prying stare." With that, he turned his attention to the documents.

"Is there a problem, Herr Commandant?" Dufresne asked. "Herr Hubner told us everything was in order . . ."

"Well, he would know," Rheinhardt replied. "Perhaps he's the one in charge?"

Dufresne said nothing.

"I thought so. But I have questions. Curiosities, really. Says here you're bringing in a hundred crates of Arabica coffee beans, is that correct?"

"Yes. They've been thoroughly inspected by your men."

Rheinhardt waved him away. "My interest concerns the beans themselves," he said. "I happen to be something of a coffee aficionado. I'm quite familiar with the varieties grown all over the world." He paused, just in case the effect was not clear. "And I know that the Congo grows *Robusta* beans. Bold flavor. Strong caffeine. Very good in a concentrated demitasse early in the morning."

He paused again, evaluating the captain, whose expression remained neutral. Perhaps it was this very lack of fear that prompted Rheinhardt to remain wary, to continue to probe. "But your manifest"—Rheinhardt stabbed the piece of paper with a manicured finger—"clearly says ninety-seven crates of *Arabica* beans. Those are grown in *Brazil*, Captain. Different country. Different continent, even."

"Ah! Now I understand your concern," Dufresne said with a relieved chuckle. "Let me assure you, Arabica beans are also grown in the Congo. You are most correct, they are not the predominant bean. But they are grown up north, in the Congolese uplands. The winds in the hills affect the bean quite dramatically. The flavor is not at all like Robusta, which grows hot and brutal on the equator. This one is delicate and flavorful, but it's deceptively strong. Perhaps you'd like to try a kilo? My gift to you for your attention to detail."

"The uplands," Rheinhardt repeated.

"Oh yes," Dufresne said in a jolly manner. "In the remarkable Kivu region. It's a higher quality bean than the Robusta. It has a more *nuanced* flavor. I think you'll be happy with it." Dufresne smiled.

Rheinhardt stared down at the manifest. He didn't like being made a fool of. Hubner returned—of course without the elusive Silva—and took his place by Rheinhardt's side.

"Earlier today, I made a visual inspection of your ship, Captain," Rheinhardt said to Dufresne. "It sits unusually low in the water."

"We have a heavy load. Tens of tons of copper and cobalt. And, of course, tin and rubber. The ship is packed to the hilt, sir."

"Even for the declared tonnage, it sits quite low. I've seen ships filled with heavy cargo. The waterline on yours is a half-meter too high. Maybe forty centimeters."

"Forty *centimeters*?" Dufresne exchanged a glance with his first mate. "That doesn't seem like very much. Probably an issue with the ballast suspension. Monsieur Silva did say she might need some minor repairs."

"Probably. Might," Rheinhardt echoed the words with mockery. "There are a lot of conditionals in your answers, Captain."

"We had a slight warping of the propeller blades," Dufresne said.

"Does that cause a ship to ride low in the water?"

"While navigating through the Scheldt narrows, my hull struck a metal piling and listed."

"Your ship isn't listing, Dufresne. It's *heavy*."

"The manifest declares the weight of the ship and the cargo, does it not?"

"I see fifty to seventy ships a week come through this port," Rheinhardt said with irritation. "My ships deliver iron ore, lead, zinc, marble, and mahogany. You're not about to tell me that copper and tin are as heavy as iron and lead, are you?"

"I don't know anything about iron and lead, sir."

"I do," Rheinhardt said. "And I'm telling you—you're riding too low. Do you have the ship's blueprints? I need to take a look at the construction." He watched the captain's face for signs of disturbance or undue annoyance.

Dufresne's face showed none.

But the Congolese man's did. Though his gaze remained lowered, it was so hot it could burn holes through the floor.

Dufresne pointed to the packet of papers on Rheinhardt's desk. "Blueprints are in your hands, sir. Right underneath the last page of the manifest."

Hubner knew enough to say nothing while Rheinhardt was questioning the ship's officers, but as soon as they left, he started sibilating, just as Rheinhardt knew he would.

"What are you suspecting, sir? This is one of Silva's ships. I know you don't care for him . . ."

"I don't care for many people, Hubner," Rheinhardt said, pointedly.

Hubner coughed.

"No coughing!"

"But you know his trading company well. Companhia Transatlantico Comercio is one of the oldest and most respected in Belgium."

"Silva's a crook. I just haven't caught him yet."

"He's one of our best commercial partners, sir," Hubner said cajolingly. "And we need his deliveries. For the war effort."

"My favorite aspect of your personality, Hubner, truly, is you constantly telling me things I already know."

In a soothing voice, Hubner continued. "The crew needs to offload their cargo and leave. We have nearly *seventy-five* ships coming in this weekend, we're at capacity. We can't have him sitting heavy at port, waiting for us to sign off on his legitimate and uncontested documents. You know how Herr Brandt gets, sir, I'm just trying to . . ."

Otto Brandt was Rheinhardt's superior.

"Don't put your nose into what's not your business, Hubner."

"Your safety and security *is* my business, mein Herr," said Hubner. "It's my only business. You remember what happened last time . . ." He coughed loudly.

"I said no coughing!"

". . . And the time before that."

"Get out."

"Exzellenz . . . please."

Rheinhardt swore under his breath. "Out. But don't leave the building."

"Wouldn't think of it."

After Hubner tiptoed out, Rheinhardt smoked one of his thin Black Crown cigarettes and allowed himself a short pour of a strong plum brandy. He sat back in his chair and closed his eyes for a moment, before focusing in earnest on the blueprints of *La Fortuna.* It was nearly eleven when he leaned away from his desk, exhausted and unhappy.

The blueprints were fine.

But his worry about the ship remained.

What was it?

The existential threat of the inexorable Allied invasion is what it was.

It was the end of May, and Rheinhardt, like every German and every Belgian, knew the attack was coming. The entire fortified coast from Cap de la Hague to the Hook of Holland was on daily alert for aggression, though they knew neither the day nor the hour. And if *La Fortuna* was a Trojan horse—stuffed with high explosives, primed to detonate—this is exactly how it would look. An ordinary ship packed with ordinary goods, manned by multinational civilians passing through customs. Getting its bill of lading signed off by SS high command, mooring in the harbor, pretending to need routine repairs.

Hubner was right, Rheinhardt needed to let *La Fortuna* go.

But Hubner being right was unendurable. He might have been right in the aggregate, but he was wrong about *this* ship. For the last six months, Rheinhardt had been on an active rampage, looking for subterfuge in every ship that anchored in Antwerp. Since April, he had ramped up his efforts tenfold.

Hence the two unfortunate episodes the infernal Hubner was alluding to, which nearly cost Rheinhardt both his employment and his reputation.

The first occurred in mid-April, when Rheinhardt had become convinced that a Swedish freighter was smuggling ball bearings in huge vats of whale oil, to be sold to the Belgian resistance to use in their homemade bombs. He had his men drag all two hundred barrels onto the dock, and emptied four at random onto the quay in front of Otto Brandt and Helmut Drechsler, the Wehrmacht commander of Antwerp. It turned out to be nothing more than a fermented batch of herring, left out for days during unseasonably warm weather. Herring spoiled fast, and this batch smelled like a rotting corpse dipped in feces. The stench was so horrific that Otto Brandt puked on the quay, splashing vomit onto his shiny patent leather shoes and perfectly tailored slacks.

No matter how hard Rheinhardt tried to justify his actions, his embarrassment was total. Drechsler was enraged at the disruption of shipping lines with a valuable neutral partner like Sweden, and Brandt was fed up with Rheinhardt's overzealous paranoia.

If that weren't sufficient humiliation, three weeks later came the incident of the nudes. This time, Rheinhardt was certain that a Portuguese ship was smuggling plastic explosives hidden in crates of Spanish sherry. The manifests didn't match the vintages on the bottles, and several of the crates sounded hollow upon inspection. Brandt was in Brussels for one of his gala receptions, Drechsler in Berlin at a monthly gathering of occupation generals—so Rheinhardt had to make the call.

He chose unwisely. When his men raided the ship, they discovered that yes, there was contraband—but it wasn't plastic explosives. They found a surfeit of nude sculptures, decadent paintings, and inappropriate and illegal pornographic magazines, meant for black market sales in Berlin and Vienna. The lower SS ranks had been profiting from the illegal sales of these items, not the Belgian resistance. Rheinhardt had unknowingly exposed a small corruption ring within his own SS!

He'd embarrassed powerful people and made enemies of his men. Twice he'd been made to look like a fool by fish and libertines. There would be no third time. If Rheinhardt was wrong about *La Fortuna*, he'd be removed from his post and reassigned to Tzummarum, up in the Dutch Arctic. Better a firing squad than to be sent there.

Erich von Rheinhardt was a man of exceeding pride—and an even greater capacity for humiliation. Raised faultlessly by a telegraph worker father and a painter mother, he hid the shame of his common birth when he became an adult. Early in his career, someone mistakenly ascribed to him aristocratic beginnings, and Rheinhardt let the misconception stand. He joined the Nazi Party in the mid-thirties and was commissioned into its officer ranks when he was also in his mid-thirties. He'd hoped for a swift promotion but hit a wall in 1939, and had remained at *Sturmbannführer* for all five years of the war.

As the subordinate to the subordinate to the commander of the city, he believed that by his diligence and perfectionism, he would find advancement. He had not.

Six months ago, Rheinhardt overheard Otto Brandt and Drechsler discussing him and learned what had been holding him back.

They hated him.

They found him overbearing and stiff, and the very thing they praised to his face—his obsessive attention to detail—"grated on their tits," as Brandt had put it to Drechsler while sipping an aperitif.

And it was after learning this that Rheinhardt had brought stark proof of malfeasance to his commanding officers, only to be proven utterly wrong—twice.

It was one of the most damning moments of his life. After the herring fiasco, Rheinhardt had thought Tzummarum would be preferable to the lowliness he felt when he was forced to admit his error.

And then, to his utter disgrace, it happened again with the nudes.

The mocking glances at the canteen became so maddening, Rheinhardt had to stop going out in the evening for a well-deserved beer.

"Careful, boys," he overheard one night at the pub, "you know nothing's as dangerous as a marble pair of tits."

"Boys, please tell Herr Rheinhardt that you saw something very suspicious at the docks," another man said. "A French tart with her knickers *on*."

Not to be outdone, a third man, spitting out his beer, joined in. "Now, now, let's inspect these statues thoroughly for Herr Rheinhardt. After all, they might be *booby-trapped*."

They started calling him "Saint Sebastian" behind his back, a sly and vicious dig, for Saint Sebastian was often depicted nude or semi-nude in religious art.

Rheinhardt retreated into his work, pretended he was immune to the whispered taunts, but punished every man who'd dared laugh at him. Men who arrived late to their shift, even by a minute, were immediately reassigned to dock patrol duty, the least desirable of all patrols. Men whose tunics were unbuttoned at the collar or whose caps were askew were docked a week's pay for "presentation violations" and received formal write-ups for "conduct unbecoming a representative of the Reich."

His men grew to loathe him. They stopped speaking as soon as they sensed he was nearby, but late at night, when they drank, Rheinhardt knew the galling insults they must have continued to spew his way.

He could *not*, under any circumstances, make a mistake again.

Rheinhardt knew something was not right with *La Fortuna*, with Dufresne, and especially not right with the Congolese soldier who pretended to be a shipmate, the mute man with the deadly stare.

It's none of my business, Rheinhardt said to himself, drumming on the manifest.

Drumming, drumming, drumming.

It's no never mind to me. I'm not going to win this war singlehandedly. If I'm right, well, then we're all fucked. The invasion is coming no matter what I do, no matter what's on that ship. If I'm wrong, I've kept my mouth shut and no one's any the wiser.

That is what Erich von Rheinhardt said to himself.

And he wished he was the kind of man who could let it go. He really, really did.

His anxiety over being wrong didn't stop him from feeling that there was something rotten in the state of Denmark, and this time it wasn't the fish.

"Hubner!" he yelled. "Get in here."

Instantly his assistant appeared at his side.

"I need your help," Rheinhardt said. These were the magic words.

Hubner lit up before Rheinhardt had even finished speaking. "How can I be of service, sir?"

"You remember what happened last time with the wine, don't you?"

"And the time before that with the herring? Yes, sir. *Viscerally.*"

Rheinhardt rubbed the bridge of his nose. "All right, no need to recount . . . never mind. I can't make such a public mistake again."

"No, mein Herr. Most assuredly *not.*"

"So before I make a formal accusation, I need a group of our finest *Feldgendarmerie* to assist me. I'll pick them from the *Nebelgarde* troops and have them quietly—but *most* thoroughly—search the ship without prying eyes."

"What would they be looking for?"

"Anything. Anything strange, suspicious, irregular." He paused. "Late at night, after curfew."

"But the crew will be on the ship, sir."

"Yes, Hubner. My *Nebelgarde* troops need two hours of uninterrupted time. Your mission is to get the crew off that ship."

Hubner nodded, radiant with purpose. "Leave it with me, sir. I know just the thing."

MANDATORY MORALE EVENT

(Dockyards of Antwerp)

Authorized under Ordinance No. 77-B

Official Notice

Port Authority Commandant-Antwerp Sector

Date: Friday June 2, 1944

Time: 2000 hours

Attention: All foreign vessel crews, merchantmen, supply ships, auxiliary craft

By the Order of Harbor Authority, in cooperation with the Port Security Office, all foreign-flagged vessel crews currently docked in Antwerp are hereby **required** to attend a **MANDATORY MORALE EVENT** at Dockside Canteen No. 4. Complimentary refreshments and entertainment will be provided.

Attendance is **strictly mandatory.**

Failure to comply will result in:

Immediate suspension of shore privileges

Fines against shipmasters

Possible revocation of Docking Licenses

Crewmasters are responsible for **full** attendance.

All vessels must be properly secured before departure.

3

King of the Ring

Three hundred miles from Antwerp, across the rough chop of the English Channel, in a strait called the Solent, two soldiers, a lieutenant and a captain, stood on the upper deck of a US destroyer, smoking and staring into the black rolling water. The ships were packed into the Solent like teeth—destroyers, transports, troop carriers, every last dinghy that could float and carry a soldier.

On the deck of the *USS McCook*, Fletcher Gray stood smoking, studying the phases of the moon and the coming tides, and writing calculations in his little notebook. Lucas stood next to him, also smoking, but visibly less enchanted by the moon and sea.

"Fletch, are you done soon?" Lucas asked.

Fletcher ignored him. He was busy—trying to divine by celestial signs when they would raise anchor and sail to Normandy and the next phase of his life could finally begin.

Fletcher was tall and lean, like a centerfielder. His mother once told him he had an angel's face. Sharp nose, sharp jaw, deep-set, wide-apart eyes, everything in proportion. "Too pretty," Beatrice called him. "Too pretty for his own good." He got his mother's bold color and his father's fine features. Fletcher's temperament, though, was entirely his own.

"If we spend one more minute on this blasted deck," Lucas said, "I'm going to pull rank on you." He outranked Fletcher by a hair, but in life, as on the battlefield, they stood as equals.

Fletcher sighed. They'd been operationally ready since May. Now it was June, and they were still in England, bobbing ceaselessly in the bumpy water. He wouldn't admit it, but he was also intensely tired of waiting. "We're not going tonight, Lucas."

"How the hell do you know? Are you best friends with Eisenhower?"

"The moon's not full," Fletcher said. "And the tide's too high."

Lucas groaned. Though wiry and small, Lucas was the strongest, smartest, bravest of them all. He'd led the Rangers to victory at Anzio, and he would lead F Company again in Normandy—*if* they ever got fucking moving.

"When's the blasted moon full? When's the tide low?"

Fletcher scanned his notebook.

"This Tuesday," he said. "June 6th."

Lucas groaned. "I can't wait that long, man. I'm going insane."

Fletcher wished he could disagree.

The upper deck was quiet, but from somewhere below came the faint sounds of rowdy, happy men: bottles clinking, laughter ringing, raw voices raised in song. Men, slightly unhinged with drink, but united in some earthly delight.

Fletcher glanced at his watch. "It's almost curfew," he said to Lucas. "We should go tell them it's last call for alcohol."

"Good thing you're not running for office, Fletch," Lucas said, perking up. "You'd come in dead last. But yes, let's."

Fletcher bristled. "Someone's gotta tell them." They threw their half-smoked cigarettes into the sea. "We're not going to stay, though," he said.

"No, no, 'course not."

"Lucas, we can't mix with non-coms."

"Fletch, ease up, we're invading fucking France in five minutes."

"Not the *next* five minutes."

"Blow off some steam, why don't you," Lucas said. "Let's see what they're up to, tell them to pipe down, as you suggest, and then we'll come right back here, and resume counting waves and converting inches to kilometers. Whatever you want. But give me one minute in a room with men drinking and stomping and having *fun*."

"I don't know why you'd think *that's* fun," Fletcher muttered.

They made their way below deck to the torpedo maintenance bay and peeked in. Tucked away, metallic, echoey, lit by red emergency bulbs, and hot as a steam room, it was a jam-packed, half-naked circus.

A King of the Ring match raged in the round. It wasn't so much boxing as shirtless, hand-wrapped, drunken brawling. Two rounds until one man fell. The winner stayed in the ring. The loser drank a pint without stopping. If no one fell, they both drank and went again.

Voices rose and fell in a messy chorus—hoots, hollers, fists on pipes like tribal war drums.

"This is allowed?" Fletcher said.

"Allowed?" Lucas pointed. "The captains and lieutenants are next in line."

The officers weren't just looking the other way. They were fully in it.

The cheers were deafening, half laughter, half taunts, while two men sparred in the makeshift ring.

One of those men was Rafael Canario.

Of course.

They'd met Rafael in Tunisia, when he came roaring out of a burning palm grove in the dead of night on a stolen Wehrmacht motorcycle, smoke in his wake and blood on his boots. In Africa, they didn't name him Demonrider for nothing. He was built for fast rides and faster fights.

Tonight, he stood in the round, shirtless, glistening, his broad olive-skinned chest heaving, his black hair wet, his black eyes joyous. He was smoking a cigarette—*while boxing*. He didn't even bother to take it out of his mouth.

Rafael made Fletcher forget every decent thing his mother had ever taught him.

Don't bother dealing with fools; the world is thick with them. *Out.*

Stop comparing yourself with other men.

Don't waste your time tongue-wagging.

Don't lose your head.

Out, out, out.

"Canario! Put your fire out!" Lucas yelled.

Rafael caught sight of them and beamed. *"Lukash!"* he called, using a nickname no one else dared. The gall. "Get over here! Fletch, you too. You're next!" He spoke English in a maddening posh British accent, shot through with Spanish and French, rolling, lilting, insufferable.

"I'm most certainly *not* next," said Fletcher.

Too late. Lucas gave him a shove, grabbing his tunic, nearly tearing it off. His cigarettes went flying, his Zippo—his notebook! Lucas caught it. "Not giving it back," he said, holding it up like a prize, "till you do two rounds with him."

Rafael Canario wasn't a Ranger—by patch or paybook. But with orders in his pocket for the assault on Pointe du Hoc, assigned through the British Commandos, he was with F Company, even here in staging. Still, he moved like an outsider by blood and by badge, like he belonged nowhere, and everywhere.

"Well, we came, we saw," Fletcher said. "Let's go."

Lucas gave him a shove. "No, you idiot. He's waiting."

"No—"

"Shut up. Two rounds won't kill you."

"Lucas," Fletcher muttered, still resisting, "we're officers . . ."

"Fuck that. We're waiting for history to break loose. No one's going to care you sparred with a non-com, I promise. You're just afraid a staff sergeant might kick your ass."

"I'm absolutely fucking not. And he absolutely fucking wouldn't."

"Hey, Gray, I can hear you," yelled Rafael. "Get your ass in the ring and let's see what we see."

"I'm not fighting you, Canario," Fletcher said. "We're not the same size."

Rafael laughed. "Featherweight boy. You may be taller, but you weigh nothing. I'm all muscle."

"I'm no featherweight," Fletcher said. Why was he so easy to rile? Even Lucas laughed at him. He had to stop taking everything so seriously. Damn it.

Rafael passed him a flask. "Have a sip."

"What is it?"

"Opium in liquid form." Rafael grinned.

Don't lose your head to drink, his mother warned.

Right out the fucking window.

Fletcher took a swig, then another. Rafael was right, boxing would be better with whatever was in that flask. He felt warm all over. Lucas helped him wrap his fists.

Rafael still hadn't put out his cigarette.

"Not bad, Lieutenant," Rafael said, looking him over, now that they both were shirtless. "So—you want to be King of the Ring, eh?" He raised his fists. "To win, you've got to be a fighting man *and* a drinking man."

"Fletcher is a thinking man," said Lucas, already on his second beer.

"There's no thinking in the ring, Gray," said Rafael. "No time for that bullshit. Fight, drink, smoke. Sing. Maybe bet a little. You want to bet on yourself? Or you can bet on me." He pulled some bills from his pocket, cigarette still dangling. "How much you in for?"

"Nothing," said Fletcher. "Not one penny. I have no dog in this fight."

"You *do* have a dog in this fight. Your sorry ass."

"Win or lose, it's no never mind to me."

"But what if *I* win?"

"Then you'll have the full satisfaction of victory."

"I don't want satisfaction."

"Then you shall not have it."

"I want your money, Gray."

"You won't have that either."

Bare-chested, Fletcher stepped into the ring. The noise was outrageous.

They bumped their wrapped fists. Someone banged the steam pipe with a wrench—the unofficial bell.

"It's not going to get better than this, Fletcher," said Rafael.

That can't possibly be true, Fletcher thought. He began to bounce lightly, circling Rafael, not just in a fight but in a story. He watched, measured, waited.

Every glancing blow sparked howls and cheers. More sips from the flask, more gulps of beer.

Fletcher bobbed and weaved, sweat dripping, deflecting Rafael's straight rights and looping lefts. He was looking for a gap.

From near the ropes, a sardonic British voice cut through: "Is it too much to ask for one clean punch, Canario?" Followed by: "I've seen more violence at a Latin declensions seminar."

From the rafters came a booming American voice: "Come on, Rider, clock him like he owes you rent and married your sister!"

Rafael grinned, cigarette still burning between his teeth. He lunged, slightly overconfident, just enough to shift his weight forward.

With a calculated flick of the wrist, Fletcher knocked the cigarette from his mouth. The room roared. Rafael didn't have time to move his head. In that half-beat, Fletcher's left jab came from the other side, sharp and fast, catching him flush on the jaw. Off balance, Rafael staggered—and went down.

And for a few minutes, Fletcher was King of the Ring.

Afterward they sat, smoking, drinking, cheering. Inevitably the conversation turned to the only thing on all their minds—the invasion of France. "No matter how low the tide or how full the moon," Rafael said, "the storm-tossed sea's going to reduce us all to vomit husks. Even you, Fletcher. What do you know of angry waters? You're from Wyoming."

"What do *you* know of them, Canario?" Fletcher shot back. "You're from the Pyrenees."

"Water on both ends, thinking man," said Rafael.

Hours passed. They'd fought all the fights, talked all the talk, smoked all the cigarettes. The liquid opium was gone from Rafael's dry flagon, alas.

"Admit this is better than whatever the hell we were doing up on deck," Lucas said, arm slung around Fletcher.

"Yes," Fletcher said. His mother wouldn't have approved—*distracted by fools* and all that—but Fletcher had to admit it was.

Rafael led them slurringly in song, the others joining in.

He could sing too, the bastard.

"In Dublin's fair city, where the girls are so pretty, I first set my eyes on sweet Molly Malone . . . she died of a fever and no one could save her, and that was the end of my Molly Malone. Now her ghost wheels her barrow through streets broad and narrow, crying cockles and mussels alive, alive oh . . ."

And the drunken, collective chorus:

"Alive, alive, oh!
"Alive, alive, oh!
"Crying cockles and mussels,
"Alive,
"Alive, oh!"
It was Saturday, June 3, 1944.

4

The Belle of Bastogne

Late Saturday morning, June 3, Louise biked home from the market in Herentals. As always, she was biking and singing. She loved the arrival of summer in northern Belgium. Everything was blooming. The birds chirped, the sun warmed her face, and the wind made ruin of her blonde, braided hair.

What Louise wanted most in life was for the war to be over. Belgium hadn't asked to be pinned between two enemies who'd spent a millennium spilling blood on her green fields and in her thick forests. But Louise especially hadn't asked for it. She wanted peace back. Spring without fear. It was such a small dream, and yet it often felt the most unattainable.

On warm June mornings, though, she almost forgot.

Almost, except for the part where she spent her days biking to and fro through the countryside, rain or shine. To the market, to the post office, to the church. Picking up packages, dropping off photographs and messages, buying fruit, delivering lunch.

Charlie kept advising Louise to hide the outer woman, but sometimes Louise felt the outer woman was all she had. And Charlie didn't understand that, because all she had was the inner woman. Charlie had never entered a beauty pageant, never won first prize, never been called the Belle of Bastogne. Winning had filled Louise with so much joy, because she thought she was going to have a beauty pageant life.

How was she to know that would be her one and only pageant, at the ripe old age of *nine*!

And here she was, eleven years later, not living in Brussels, not going to university, not dressing smartly, not feted or fashionable or celebrated.

It wasn't Charlie's fault.

It wasn't even Germany's fault.

It was her mother's fault.

After her father died, her mother took Louise and left Bastogne for Herentals.

After her father died, Louise wore his old clothes in grief. He had been larger than life but diminutive in stature, and his trousers barely fit her. Now that Louise was a young woman, her mother occasionally called her generous hips *life-giving*. But had there been any life-giving in those hips? *Nein!* None at all.

"I'm just trying to protect you, Lou," Charlie would say when she urged Louise to wear men's boots, to smear mud on her cheeks. Charlie wanted to show Louise how to be ugly, and couldn't fathom why she didn't jump at the chance.

Charlie knew a lot, but she didn't know some basic things about human nature. About men and women. For example, Charlie didn't understand that the reason Louise could bike around with astonishing ease, zipping across canals and through checkpoints, was because the Germans allowed her liberties no one else got. And they allowed her those liberties precisely because her blonde hair was windswept, and there were flowers in her hands, and a smile on her lips, because she bounced with joy when she biked, and a happy tune lined her path with open gates and drum rolls and larkspurs.

Her mother was home when Louise arrived, a little perspired, carrying the groceries. The first thing Hélène said was, "I hope you're not doing anything that will get you killed, Louise Aubel." Louise cheerfully replied of *course* not, she would *never*. "You're not ferrying illegal documents back and forth, are you?"

"What documents, Maman?"

"I don't know *what* documents," said Hélène, barely listening. Why did it so often seem to Louise that the people in her life were distracted, barely in the conversation? "A messenger's life can be woefully brief, Louise."

"What about a deliverer of fruit? Is her life woefully brief, too?"

"If they find something on you, they could kill you."

Louise opened her arms to display the pink floral dress, the puffy sleeves, her tanned bare arms, the short, empty apron. "The only thing they'll find on me, Maman, is cherries, peaches, and my warm and welcoming heart." She beamed into her mother's churlish face.

"I have no time for your nonsense," said Hélène. "If that terrible girl gets arrested, her dangerous shadow will fall on you."

"Do you mean Charlie, Maman? Why would she get arrested?"

"Because she is a rapscallion!"

Louise stared at her mother with frank affection. "*Avec tout mon amour,* Maman." She hugged her mother and gave her a kiss. Hélène allowed it.

"I wish I didn't love Fitz so much," Hélène muttered. "The fact that his sister is *that* girl really rankles my bones. She's always up to no good, always trying to rope you into her worst devilries."

"You're right," said Louise. "I wish she'd rope me into her *best* devilries once in a while."

"Always scheming, conniving, ugh! She's a real plotter, that one."

"Maman, I don't know what you're talking about. Charlie works for her father, delivering flowers."

"She's up to her muddy neck in resistance mischief, and nothing you say will convince me otherwise," Hélène said. "Children lie to their parents all the time. And collaborators are everywhere, Lou. No one can be trusted."

"Are you saying Charlie is a *collaborator*?"

"What I'm *saying*," Hélène said, "is stay away from her."

"Really? Because that wasn't clear."

"Remember the Boursicots? Arrested last year? Gustave was beheaded at Breendonk. No one ever found out what happened to Leontine!"

"So she could be fine, then?"

"I don't want you associating with Charlotte. Allies of dangerous persons will also be arrested."

"What are you going to do, Maman?" said Louise. "If I marry Fitz, I'll have to associate with her, won't I? She'll be my sister-in-law. *Your* family. You'll have to *associate* with her, too."

A flustered Hélène dropped her napkin and knocked the plate off the table. It hit the floor and cracked in two. "Look what you did!" Hélène said. "Go to your room."

"Gladly," said Louise.

And in her room stood Charlie. Pale, disheveled, unsmiling. Not even sitting, just standing, waiting for Louise. She looked like she'd come in to rob the place and got caught. Baggy trousers, dirty old boots. Her shapeless gray coat looked like it'd lost a fight with a hedgerow. If there was beauty there—and there was—it was meant to pass unseen. She shoved her hair behind her ears in that stubborn way she always did when she was trying not to fall apart.

"Mon Dieu!" Quickly, Louise shut the door. "You look like you crawled out of a ditch. Is that blood on you?"

"Not mine."

"Charlie! Don't let her find you here. Didn't you hear her?"

"No, why?" said Charlie. "Was she talking about me?"

Louise felt a pang of guilt at the words her mother had bellowed. It was instantly replaced by resentment toward Charlie. "Do you wish me dead?"

"*Jamais.*"

"She'll kill me if she finds you here."

"I need your help, Lou," Charlie said.

"And there I thought for a second you came to shoot the breeze," Louise said. "You know, like a *friend*. Whatever it is—no. I'm already late. It's almost noon. I have to bike to Zvart Haus."

"Saul can wait. Please? It'll be quick."

"There's no quick with you. Only years of slow torture. And I told you, Saul doesn't eat lunch unless I bring it."

"Sounds like *his* problem," said Charlie. "Come on. We could be there already." She took Louise's wrist.

"Be *where* already?" Louise pulled away.

"Lou, can you walk *and* talk?" Charlie pointed out the window. "Time's a little bit of the fucking essence."

"What else is new?" Louise said. As if war and urgency weren't always at her elbow.

"I need your help."

"These aren't magic words, Charlie, like you say them and I come running. You always need my help. You should choose a line of work where you need my help *less*. See how I've chosen a line of work where I don't need *your* help at all?"

"That's not true. I bring you flowers. To take to your dumb starving Saul."

"You think Saul cares about your morning glory?"

Plumes of lavender and delphinium lay on the floor of Louise's bedroom, like offerings at her feet. "Not morning glory," Charlie said quietly.

"Stop buttering me up with flowers," Louise said, her tone softening. "You think I'm a pushover. That because I love flowers, I'll do what you ask."

"Pushover? You're tough as nails. Let's go. Please."

Rolling her eyes, Louise had no choice but to acquiesce. They jumped out of her bedroom window and raced for the woods. "I never would've sent you on that fool's errand to Zvart Haus," said Charlie, "if I'd known you were going to turn it into your life's purpose. It was meant to be just a couple of times."

"Mad scientists need to eat too, Charlotte," said Louise.

"And I see you once again failed to mention to your lovely mother that not only are you *not* marrying my brother, but you broke it off with him."

"Why does she need to know every detail of my life?" Louise muttered. She didn't want to talk about it. Fitz was still hurting. "How far are we headed? I really have to—"

"Not far. Just over there."

Inside the woods behind Louise's house, near a boulder on the mossy ground, they came upon a small boy kneeling beside a splayed-out black man, wounded, bleeding, barely conscious. Louise cried out in shock.

"He needs a doctor," Zeus said, lifting his pleading eyes to Charlie.

"I know, Zeus," Charlie said. "I'm trying. Louise, this is *Zeus*."

"Is she a doctor?" Zeus asked.

"No," Louise said, exhaling deeply, staring at the boy. "I'm nobody—not even a nurse."

"He's bleeding a lot," Charlie said. "Please, Lou. Bike to St. Elizabeth's, ask Sister Colette to give you bandages, iodine, maybe a needle and thread? He got knifed. It's going to get infected. Some sulfa powder. Morphine if you can get it."

"Does he need a blood transfusion, too?" Louise said, leaning over the man. She threw out her bare white arm. "Why don't you just siphon my blood straight into your latest treacherous cause?" she said to Charlie. "What are you dragging me into? Who *is* this?"

"His name is Ngomo," said Zeus. "Charlie and I watched him get stabbed to death."

"Not to death yet, little man," Ngomo murmured, blinking at Louise with pain-glazed, ebony eyes. "Not yet."

"Where did he come from?"

"The Congo in Africa," said Zeus.

"Zeus!" Charlie said. "The child is impossible."

"The boy speaks truth," Ngomo said softly. "That's where I'm from."

Louise whirled to a contrite Charlie.

"He survived a massacre, Lou."

"I don't want to know!"

"Help me."

"See, if I help you, it'll become my business," Louise said. "I didn't get this far in the war by getting involved in crazy shit like this. I help you with small things. This is too much."

"Help me this once, and that's it."

Louise laughed bitterly. "Yes, right. Just this once."

"He'll die of his wounds."

"The best thing that can happen to him," said Louise.

"Merci beaucoup," said Ngomo.

Louise didn't mean to sound so harsh. Contritely but resolutely, she dragged Charlie a few feet away. "What's your plan?" she whispered, hissing. "If he survives—God forbid—where are you going to hide him? Whoever tried to kill him is going to come looking."

"They don't know he survived."

"He's a black man in Belgium!" Louise shouted. So much for quiet. "What are you going to do, paint him white?"

"There's an idea," said Ngomo.

"You're sucking me into your insanity, Charlie. I won't have it."

"Lou," Charlie whispered feverishly, "Something *big's* happening! He made me go to Jette to see *Robert Capelle*."

Louise put her hands over her ears.

"Capelle had an *army* of Gestapo trailing him. He must be someone important. He said he'd contact London. He told me to wait for word."

"No. Please no."

Charlie pressed on. "We'll hide him in the woods. I'm sorry, Lou, I wish I didn't have to—"

"If wishes were horses," said Louise, "beggars would fucking fly."

Ngomo spoke. "There's something on that ship the Germans can *never* be allowed to find," he said. "And now it's completely unprotected."

"Like you, Ngomo," Charlie said.

"I don't matter. But we're in mortal danger."

Violently, Louise shook her head. "No. I'm not risking my life for a stranger. Not when we're so close to the end."

"If we do nothing, it *will* be the end," said Ngomo.

5

Two Conversations Between Three Men

Near midnight in London, two hundred miles away from Charlie and Louise's existential angst, a man hurried out of his sparsely furnished rooms in Belgrave Square and sprinted into the blackout streets. Belgrave Square housed the temporary command of the Office of Strategic Services—the intelligence branch of the US Army during the war. The man's name was Jonathan Reed, and he was the American commander in charge of all special missions in Africa, Italy, and, imminently, Europe.

Now in his mid-forties, Colonel Reed was a veteran of the First World War. He concealed his high rank by wearing a civilian suit, almost like a costume. The United States preferred civilians to run their military intelligence.

Jonathan Reed was normally a calm man. But not on this rain-soaked Saturday night.

He sprinted down Grosvenor Crescent, crossed Hyde Park Corner, flashing his identification twice to jumpy MPs, skirted the edge of Hyde Park, and tore up Park Lane before turning onto Brook Street and stopping at Claridge's, utterly out of breath.

He allowed himself a minute to recover, then walked briskly into the lobby and, still panting, asked to see the hotel manager. The manager immediately ushered him up a private elevator past three levels of security, into the large suite of General Leslie Groves.

"Hello, Jonathan," Groves said, stepping into the parlor to shake his hand. Groves was an ample man, expansive in width, girth, and presence. He eyed Reed with wary amusement. "Is everything all right?"

Jonathan Reed, still trying to catch his breath, said nothing.

"Because if not," Groves continued, "about thirty men just saw you race across town and demand to see me at midnight. I'm sure the Nazi spies won't bother mentioning it to Berlin."

"I didn't want to speak by telephone," Reed said.

"Well, that part was smart. Could it not have waited till tomorrow? We're both scheduled to be at the foreign dignitaries' reception downstairs."

"This couldn't wait till tomorrow, no," Reed said.

"You come barreling into my personal quarters," Groves said, "breaking every rule of diplomacy and protocol. I need little else to assure me of the gravity of whatever this is. Where would you like to speak? I trust no men, no walls, no suites, no hotels, no rooms, no balconies. You could pantomime to me. Perhaps, through charades, I'll glean the nature of your emergency. And this *is* an emergency, Colonel?"

"Condition red."

Groves paled, motioning for Reed to follow him. He crossed the parlor and put on Glenn Miller's "Moonlight Serenade," letting the soft music fill the suite, and ushered Reed into the butler's pantry between the study and the dining room. "Let's have it," Groves said without preamble.

Reed replied in kind. "Hubert Pierlot just came to see me at Belgrave Square," he said. Pierlot was the exiled prime minister of Belgium.

"What did he want?"

"Apparently, when King Leopold was selling you *coffee from the Congo*, he decided to take some of this rarefied bean for himself."

Groves went still. "There's nothing left. We made sure of it."

"Yes, well. When there was, he took some."

"How much? A few kilos? You and I thought he might, remember?"

Reed took the deepest breath. "Eighteen thousand pounds."

Groves grabbed the counter. Reed poured the general a glass of water, on second thought gulped it down himself and poured another.

"Reed," Groves said, "*please* tell me the coffee is still in the fucking Congo."

Reed said nothing.

Groves groaned, a low, gutted sound. "Fuck. Christ. Fuck. Where is it?"

"Antwerp."

Groves gaped at him. "Belgium?"

"Yes. There are *eighteen thousand pounds* of Kivu coffee in Antwerp, Belgium."

In their shared shock, neither man spoke for a long, ugly moment.

Groves slumped over the counter, the glass shaking in his hand.

An hour earlier, at Belgrave Square, Jonathan Reed's chief of staff had knocked on the door just as Reed was getting ready to turn in. "Sorry to disturb, sir, but there's a man here to see you. Says it's urgent."

Reed glanced at his watch. Nearly eleven o'clock. "What man?"

"Hubert Pierlot, the Prime Minister of Belgium."

Reed thought he had misheard. "The prime minister of *what*?"

The door opened, and a tall, handsomely dressed man of about sixty strode into the parlor, brushing past his befuddled adjutant.

"Would you leave us, please?" Pierlot said to the chief of staff. It was not a request. He barely remembered his manners, giving Reed the briefest handshake. "I'm sorry to come at such an hour," the prime minister said. He spoke English in a modest tone, thick with a French accent.

Reed waved him toward a chair. "Please, sit. Can I get you a drink, Prime Minister?"

"No, thank you. I'll get right to it. As I'm sure you're aware, Colonel Reed," he said, "your government and my king had entered into several ironclad agreements—for the purchase and transport of certain . . ."

"Coffee, Prime Minister," Reed cut in.

"Yes. Coffee. Very valuable. Of the rarest variety."

Reed tensed. "We have many commercial partners," he said.

"When the King saw the keen interest your government showed in . . ."

"His excellent Congolese coffee," Reed finished grimly.

"He decided to keep a few grams. To see what all the fuss was about."

Reed was silent. He wasn't unduly concerned—yet. The coffee beans were worthless without refinement, and refinement required technology and facilities the Congo didn't have.

"I understand, Prime Minister," Reed said. "Thank you for bringing it to my attention. It is his coffee. Still, the King should not have done this without notifying us. It puts too many men at risk—his and ours. But—as you are well aware—the country of which he is nominally king is not free. And we have more pressing concerns—"

"You think what I'm telling you has nothing to do with your pressing concerns?" Pierlot interrupted. "Or with the coffee extraction project into which you've poured *all* of your intellectual and material resources? It has *everything* to do with it! You're not listening to me."

"I'm listening extremely carefully, Prime Minister."

"Do you think I'd be bothering you if your precious coffee was still stashed away in some forgotten depot in Matadi?"

Reed bolted upright.

Pierlot was right. He had misunderstood.

"Ah, you're catching on," Pierlot said.

"Where is it?"

"This afternoon, I received an urgent message from Robert Capelle. Don't worry, he sent it over two short bursts, and it was received by vetted military intelligence operators, not civilians."

"Prime Minister, how he sent it and who received it is the least of my worries right now. Please continue."

"Count Robert Capelle is the King's right-hand man—"

"I know who he is, Prime Minister! What. Did. He. Say?"

Pierlot produced a piece of paper from his pocket. He cleared his throat and adjusted his glasses theatrically. Biting back a curse, Reed snatched the paper out of the man's hands without apology.

LA JONQUILLE EST MORTE STOP CREW MASSACRED STOP CARGO UNPROTECTED STOP 8MT/60 STOP IMMEDIATE DANGER OF CONFISCATION BY SS STOP

Reed was speechless.

"*La jonquille est morte* is the code phrase," Pierlot said. "Had it said *La jonquille est vivante*, it would have meant that the cargo was secured."

"Jonquille—for *yellow*?" Reed went ashen.

"Of course for *yellow*."

Jonathan Reed could hardly breathe. After a moment, he said, "This couldn't come at a worse time, Prime Minister. I'm being quite literal. This could not come at a worse time."

"The chain of events that led us here," Pierlot said, "was precipitated by the very proximity of the events you hint at—those that loom ahead. King Leopold got wind that invasion was imminent and liberation might soon follow. He wanted his coffee in Belgium before that happened."

"Why?"

"To protect the interests of the country of which he is *nominally* still king," Pierlot replied.

"Instead of protecting Belgium, he has sunk it," Reed said. "You and your deposed king have completely fucked us. Royally."

"I'm just the messenger," Pierlot said. "And not deposed. Detained."

"If only you knew the danger he's put us all in."

"Why do you think I'm here, at nearly midnight, in your private residence?" Pierlot said. "You think I don't know?"

"No, Prime Minister," Reed said, grabbing his coat. "I don't think you do."

A black silence passed between Leslie Groves and Jonathan Reed.

Groves spoke first. "Where is the coffee now?"

"I assume still in the cargo hold of the ship docked at Antwerp."

Groves's face was a grim mask. "We thought we were so clever, Jonathan. Our guards stopped visitors twenty miles from the groves. We stopped them again ten miles away. One mile away. At the entrance, they faced a small army, with police dogs. No one was getting a bean of it. And there was nothing left to get. We had taken everything, blew what was left to hell, secured it, filled it in, built an electrified moat around it, and hired a hundred armed guards to sit and watch a pile of dirt."

"We did think we were clever," Reed said. It was true—Leslie Groves had wielded total control over the Congo claim and its contents. "How were we supposed to know the horse had already bolted?"

"And now what?"

They both needed a stiff drink. Inside the general's study, Reed poured them each a shot of Old Forester whisky. They didn't even clink glasses; they gulped the liquor like men at a battlefield funeral, then sank into armchairs, their bodies heavy with burden.

Groves sat smoking unfiltered cigarettes, anguish etched across his broad face. "Capelle ought to be shot for treason," he said at last.

"Capelle is a servant," said Reed. "The King commands the armies of the land and sea. Leopold demanded it. Capelle complied."

"Who did he even get to help him do it? Fuck. I bet it was his security chief, Ngomo."

"I don't know, General."

"Treason!" Groves barked. "What the fuck would Leopold even do with Congolese . . . coffee?"

"If only we could ask him," Reed said. "More important—what are the Germans going to do with it?" He drew a steadying breath. "*Can* they do something with it?"

"Of course," said Groves. "They have grinders, extractors, purifiers, ovens. If they find it, we're fucked." He looked at Reed, almost pleading. "But they might not find it, right?" The man looked gutted. He grabbed a pencil but snapped the lead by pressing too hard. "Jonathan," he said hoarsely, "I can't figure it out. Is eight metric tons of coffee enough?"

"Of Congolese coffee?" Reed nodded bleakly. "More than enough."

Groves shot to his feet. "Don't just sit there," he said. "Do something!"

Reed took a breath.

"Don't even tell me what," Groves said. "Just *do* it."

"The ship's in the dock," Reed said. "The coffee is hidden. They haven't found it yet. They might not even be looking. We have a little time."

"How much time?"

"A few days. Perhaps a week."

"A *week*!" Groves exclaimed in a stricken voice.

"General, nothing can happen until we're on the other side. Right now, every ounce of our effort needs to go toward making Overlord a success. If we land as planned, the Germans will close Antwerp to naval traffic. The ship will stay docked. That'll be our best chance. Then I'll put together a team of my best men. They will go and secure it."

Groves slumped back into his chair. "Who do we even have that can be trusted with something like this? Our boys are brave and strong, but this?" He shook his head. "No one can comprehend the devastation to come. No one."

"I'll find the men we need."

"As fast as possible."

"Yes. After Overlord." Reed didn't add, *After we see how many men we have left.*

"Jonathan, the Germans *can't* . . ." Groves broke off.

"I know, sir."

"We've spent the entire war trying to get ahead of them. We've sunk thirty billion dollars into this, employed two hundred thousand men, driven the best minds to the brink—all to stop the very thing that's on the verge of happening." He stared at Reed. "Don't tell me we could all be undone by a deposed renegade king."

"Not deposed," Reed said. "Detained."

"Reed!"

"Leave it with me. Do I have your permission to handle it as I see fit?"

"You have my permission to invade fucking Belgium if that's what it takes."

6

One Day in the Life of Kurt Vogel

On Sunday morning, Louise delivered the bandages, the iodine, and a needle with thread, just as Charlie knew she would. They did their best to clean Ngomo's wounds with water from a nearby brook. They even managed to stitch him. Once they gave him morphine, he stopped groaning and fell into a stupor. But the imposing, infected, unhideable problem of Ngomo Kasonga remained unsolved. Where did one hide a large ebony man in ivory Belgium? She had asked Capelle this during their brief exchange at the Bonaventure Market in Jette. *What do I do with the Congo man? Hide him*, he replied. *Hide him so they can never find him.*

So now in the damp moss lay a black man marked for death, shiny with sweat and blood, and beside him sat a Jewish boy, also marked for death.

Zeus posed another thorny problem. His grandparents had paid Charlie a great deal of money to get him out of Belgium, and believed the boy was en route to Portugal. But Zeus remained very much *not* en route, while the money was long gone.

After Louise left, the three of them spent Sunday morning in the woods. Charlie taught Zeus how to change Ngomo's dressing and clean his wounds. But she needed to know what she was facing—and what she was risking. She sat by his head—she on one side, Zeus on the other.

"Everything," Ngomo said. "*Tout*."

"What does that mean? I'm facing everything and risking everything?"

"Yes."

Her bones crackled with anxiety. "What do I do?" Charlie said. "I'm busy with a million things. Do I drop everything else?"

"Yes," Ngomo said. "You drop everything else—for this."

"Tell me what *this* is."

"I was given a very important mission," said Ngomo, "and I've failed. I've placed us all in terrible danger."

"What was your mission?"

The Congolese man shook his head.

"Ngomo, don't be naïve," Charlie said. "If the SS captures me, it won't matter what I know. They'll torture me till I'm dead anyway. You might as well tell me."

"I can't."

Charlie sat back. "Ah, now I get it," she said. "It's *me* you don't trust."

"You saved my life," Ngomo said. "That means something in my country. I won't repay your act of grace by sending you to your death."

"Great, Ngomo. Just great." It had been raining for two weeks straight, and the ground was mud and muck. They couldn't stay in the wet woods, not if they wanted him to survive.

"Where are you taking us?" Zeus said after they managed to get Ngomo back inside the *Berceau*.

"The only place I know that can't turn me away," Charlie said. "Lillehaven."

Lillehaven was silent in the damp June morning. Thick bushes, saplings, hedgerow country, rolling fields. She left Ngomo and Zeus in the truck, parked behind the family barn, a short walk from the farm through a patch of woods. She was glad she did. As she approached her house, Charlie overheard a heated exchange between two familiar voices, and became sure that this time, Kurt Vogel had returned to murder her father.

Charlie was always afraid.

She didn't know how to go on living in a state of such fear. She didn't know if she had always been this way. But she'd certainly been this way since the Germans came to Herentals.

No one else was like this—not her brothers, not the girls she worked with, not her father, not her mother. Not even Louise.

Everyone else seemed either intrepid or indifferent.

For Charlie, it was just layers of terror.

It was small consolation that in these red-alert crisis days there was a lot to be afraid of. Her country had been occupied since 1940.

All their efforts to undermine the German war machine had proved insignificant, mosquitoes to elephants, though at any moment, it was true, England and America were poised to bring the war home to Germany. But even that was a mixed blessing, since they would bring that war to Germany straight across the Belgian rivers and her father's flower fields. And the French would soon join—not just in the obliteration of her farmhouse and what remained of her family, but in the inevitable destruction of her one ordinary life.

And because things were never quite bad enough, the merciless hand of fate had thrown Charlie into a real calamity—witnessing a slaughter on the high seas.

Another secret Charlie kept close to the vest and told no one: sometimes, that suffocating weakness in the form of fear made her do astonishingly stupid things.

Up ahead, in the hazy sunshine, Kurt Vogel and Alder Fontaine squared off in the clearing. The Belgian SS officer's battered hand-me-down BMW motorcycle with a rusted sidecar was pulled right up to the front door. Vogel stood rigid, barking at Charlie's father in the brittle, bureaucratic French of a man who had spent his life filing papers in Brussels and now fancied himself a soldier of the Reich.

If Alder Fontaine knew his end had come, he didn't show it. He stood calmly with his hands by his sides. Nothing in his demeanor said heated, but Charlie knew her father was steamed from the way he enunciated the words "Herrrr Vogel," with a subtle, venomous emphasis on the rolled *rrrr*.

"You have four trucks, Fontaine, yet three of them are not here, and you won't tell me who's driving them or where."

"Why so much conversation about my trucks, Herrrr Vogel?" said Alder. "They're out on deliveries. I don't know if you know what business I'm in—you've only been coming here every week for two years—but in Lillehaven, I grow flowers. And then, when they bloom, I pick them, and I arrange them, and I deliver these bouquets to churches and reception halls. I bring them to German generals and German wives. I deliver them for German weddings—and German funerals." Alder paused for emphasis. "That's where my trucks are. Delivering flowers to the Reich."

"Who's driving them?"

"My daughter. My son. My wife. My hired help."

"I know where your one son is, Fontaine, and he's not delivering flowers. I need to speak to your daughter."

"She's not here," Alder said. "But I'll be sure to tell her you stopped by."

"You know what? I'm going to wait for her. I'm going to sit at your table and have a tall glass of milk until she returns."

"She may be at the Antwerp docks waiting for a shipment of tulips from Maastricht," said Alder. "Go catch her there."

"Oh, she's most definitely not at the Antwerp docks," Vogel said. "There was a terrible commotion there yesterday. Nothing confirmed, of course. We're sniffing around for a four-wheeler that reeks of flowers and is possibly hiding Jewish stowaways. As you can imagine, I immediately thought of you.

And now you're saying your trucks are not here, and your daughter's not here either." Vogel tsked. "What rambunctious little moppets your children are turning out to be."

"Will there be anything else, Herr Vogel?" Alder said. "It's my prime harvesting time, and I've got a delivery today of a thousand tulips to your governor's mansion that can't wait."

Vogel stood self-importantly in front of Alder.

"There most certainly is something else, Fontaine," Vogel said, dropping the pretense of politeness. "It's now against the law to harbor or conceal Jews."

"What does it have to do with my trucks or my flowers?"

"Do you know *why* it's against the law? No, no. Let me tell *you*. You've shot off your mouth enough. It's against the law," Vogel said, "because despite what you think, the Jew is not one of us. He's not one of you or one of me. The Jewish specimen is no lover of water," the Belgian officer went on, with visible distaste. "He is unclean, and his appearance is, to put it kindly, *unheroic*. He has repulsive traits. He is an inferior being. The personification of all evil comes to us in the living shape of the Jew. He poisons our souls like the germ carrier that he is. He is cold-hearted, calculating and shameless. He is a dialectical liar. Nothing he says can be trusted. He is most often a traitor—"

"*He's* the traitor, Herr Vogel?" Alder said quietly.

"Yes!" Vogel went on as if he didn't understand her father's meaning. "A profiteer, a usurer, a swindler. In a world of rats, he is the hydra. When we cut off his head, he grows a hundred more. He is a parasite, an eternal bloodsucker, restrained by no moral scruples, and he possesses no courage, physical or moral. He is part of a brotherhood of evil. Our Führer has done what he can to cleanse our continent of this scourge, but *obviously* more work remains, if a man such as yourself, a true Belgian and a pillar of this community, can't see the truth." Vogel didn't pause, even for breath. "I'm not here to change your mind, Fontaine, though I do wish it were possible. I'm here to *compel* you and your prodigal daughter and your wayward son to follow the law. The punishment for those who harbor criminals is execution."

"This is new," Alder said.

"How would you know?" Vogel said. "Have Jews been seized on your property before today, and you've escaped punishment?"

"No." Alder blinked. "But I know the law."

"The law," Vogel said, drawing out every vowel, "has been changed."

Both men stood in silence.

Vogel stepped closer. "Your daughter's been up to no good. There are whispers about her all over Antwerp."

"Haven't heard a thing," said Alder.

"You do seem to be ignorant on a whole host of subjects," Vogel said. "Except the laws that protect Jew hoarders. On that topic, you seem to be the most informed flower farmer in all of Belgium."

"You're welcome to search my house," Alder said, waving toward the front door.

Vogel threw up his arm in a Nazi salute. "How long do you think she can hide, Fontaine?"

"I don't believe she's hiding, Vogel," Alder said. "I believe she is driving."

"That's it," Vogel said, grabbing Alder by the arm. "I'm taking you to Breendonk. Maybe then she'll finally appear at my quarters." Breendonk, near Mechelen, was a Nazi torture camp, a concrete fortress where Belgian prisoners were starved, beaten, and never seen again.

"Are you looking for me, Herr Vogel?" said Charlie.

The SS man whirled around.

Charlie stood behind him. In her hands she gripped a Belgian Browning 9mm—one of the finest military pistols in the world.

"No, Charlotte!" said Alder.

"No, Charlotte," said Vogel, with an arrogant smirk. "You know what happens to a girl carrying a weapon in Belgium?" He was so full of himself, so confident. "The Germans shoot her dead. Then they shoot five more to make sure the message gets across."

Charlie's hands were shaking. "Who's going to snitch on me to the Germans? You, Herr Vogel? The SS collaborator? But tell me—who's going to find *you*?"

The smile vanished. Vogel lunged for his weapon. But Charlie's Browning didn't need to be unholstered, cocked, or aimed. It was already all those things.

She fired into his chest.

It sounded like a small explosion through the clearing. A startled dog barked in the distance. Birds burst into the sky. Vogel slammed back into the dirt, dead before he hit the ground.

Minutes passed.

Father and daughter stood silent and grim, waiting until the slowly exsanguinating body of Kurt Vogel stopped pulsing.

Only then did Alder speak. "Hello, Charlotte," he said.

"Hello, Vake." Charlie had called her father "Vake" when she was small—a child's mangled mix of "Papa" and "Vader." It stuck. They kissed on both cheeks. Her hands still shaking, she holstered her weapon. Alder pointed to the ground and opened his hands in a mild question. "He shouldn't have come alone," said Charlie.

"Clearly," said Alder. "What was he saying about some chaos at the docks?"

"No idea." She looked away from his questioning gaze.

"Are you involved, Charlotte?"

"'Course not. Where's Fitz?"

"Your brother can't help you this time," said Alder. "He's in jail."

"*Mon Dieu!* Why?"

"You've been gone so long, you don't even know."

"I told you, I had to go to Charleroi—"

It was as if her father didn't want to hear it. "You vanishing is one thing, but you took one of my trucks."

"I took *La Berceau.* As always."

"You know this is the busiest season for me. You haven't made any of your deliveries."

"Father—Fitz?"

"Your brother got picked up for removing the lug nuts from Vogel's Opel Olympia. Herr Vogel barely escaped a fatal accident when both his front wheels popped off." Alder and his daughter stared at each other and, without saying a word, glanced once more at the prostrate body of Kurt Vogel. "So your brother is now in the clink in Herentals," Alder continued, calm about Vogel, agitated about Fitz, "awaiting indictment on vandalism charges."

"Charlie?" sounded a voice behind them. "Is everything all right?"

Propped up by Zeus, a bleeding Ngomo limped out of the sparse woods. Charlie fought the impulse to squeeze her eyes shut—she didn't want to see her father's expression. She really wished they would've stayed put until she had a chance to talk to her father about it.

There Charlie and her father stood, in the clearing at Lillehaven, with a dead Belgian Nazi lying motionless in his own blood, his rusting motorcycle an eyesore beside him, and a bleeding black man with his arm around a Jewish boy at their doorstep. It was not even noon on Sunday.

"What in the world have you gotten yourself into, child," Alder said.

"Nothing, Vake, it's just temporary . . ."

"Life is *temporary*!"

"We heard a sound like a cannon going off," Ngomo said weakly.

"Yes, we thought you might be in trouble," said Zeus, staying close to Ngomo. It was hard to tell who was propping up whom.

"And how were you two planning to help me?" Charlie muttered, bone tired. "Ngomo, Zeus, this is my father, Alder Fontaine." She paused. "It's *Zeus*, Vake," Charlie said with emphasis, giving her father a blinkless stare.

Wincing, Alder barely managed to glance at the boy before looking away. "Charlie. I need to speak to you."

They had to step around the dead Belgian for some privacy.

"In five words, explain yourself, young lady."

"Andres Ferrer didn't show up," said Charlie.

Alder waited. "That's it?"

"You said only five words."

"Perhaps you should have begun with—oh, I don't know—the bleeding black man in my front yard."

"His crew got massacred yesterday."

"By?"

She opened her hands.

"Is that why Vogel was looking for you?"

"Hard to tell. But possibly."

"Okay, that's enough. Stop taking everything I say literally. Speak like a normal human being. Use all your words. Explain yourself."

"I've been hiding them in the woods, near Louise's house. But Ngomo needs to dry out, or he'll die. His chest wound is serious. The boy needs somewhere to stay, too."

"So you brought them here." It wasn't a question.

"I didn't want it to be like this, Vake. I wanted to talk to you first."

"Yes, talking first is difficult when you *first* shoot Nazis in the heart."

"A *Belgian* Nazi, Vake."

"I know who he is, Charlotte! You don't have to tell *me*."

Charlie reached out to comfort her father, but Alder reeled away from her, eyeing Zeus and Ngomo with the look of a man who sees ill omens in front of him and is powerless to stop what's coming. "I had nowhere else to take them," Charlie said.

"So you brought them to *me*? You have a dozen safehouses to choose from!"

"Vake," she said quietly, "come on. Obviously I can't take Ngomo where people will see him."

"What trouble is he in?"

"Don't ask."

"Yes. Better I know nothing." Alder waved his arms toward the chaos in the clearing. "This mess is vast and of *your* making. I told you to stay out of it. But no." He twitched. "Children never listen to their parents." There was real grief in his voice. He blinked hard—then forced his attention back to the clearing. "What do you intend to clean up first? Because Elke will be back from deliveries soon, and she can't see this. It'll upset her." Elke had been working for the family for two years.

"Where's Maman?"

"I haven't seen her in days. Like you."

"What are you talking about? Where is she?"

"Probably in town. At the shop," Alder said, sounding evasive. "You think your *mother* is going to help you with this?" He scoffed.

"Zeus and Ngomo could stay in the apartment above the shop for a couple of days," said Charlie, "while I figure out my next steps."

"And Vogel?"

"He deserves a proper burial, don't you agree?" Charlie said. "Right in the pit where the old outhouse used to be."

"What about his motorcycle?"

"He's not going to need it anymore, is he?"

"It's at my front door!"

"I'll take care of it," Charlie said. "Can they stay here while I go see Maman? Maybe Ngomo could lie down for a few hours? He's in bad shape. And the boy needs some food. After he eats, you can give him my bed."

"Well, why not—you're never in it. They can't stay in the apartment above the shop," Alder blurted.

"Vake! Why?"

"Your mother has moved there," he said, kicking the dirt with his boot. "She says she's not coming back this time."

7

Trail of Blood

A day earlier, on a glistening blue morning mere hours after the bloodshed on the river, Rheinhardt paced Glaskaai like a caged animal, with Hubner fluttering nervously beside him.

The deck of *La Fortuna* wore the violence of the night before like a coat of blood-red paint. Rheinhardt was incandescent with rage. He couldn't even court-martial his men for botching a simple reconnaissance mission because they were all dead! What a monstrous complication.

And yet, through his rising anxiety, a small smug feeling bloomed inside him—a gleaming, self-satisfied *I told you so*. The irrefutable proof that he was right lay in the lifeless bodies of his *Nebelgarde* unit. Elite indeed! They couldn't even eliminate a civilian crew of Congolese tree climbers.

But what if that crew weren't civilians? The thought kept jabbing at Rheinhardt. What if it was all a disguise, just as he had suspected, a decoy, a fraud, and the real answer lay dripping under the floorboards?

He did what he always did when no one useful was available to yell at. He swiveled the cannon of his formidable wrath toward Hubner. "What kind of *mandatory morale* notice is this?" he shouted, flinging the leaflets in Hubner's face. "The crew didn't leave the fucking ship!"

"Sir, I beg of you—it was an extremely successful event, we had perfect attendance, ahem, except for the few people on *La Fortuna*, that's true . . ."

"You imbecile! I should have *you* court-martialed! What the fuck do I care if all of Belgium was drinking at the canteen last night! The only twelve sailors I *needed* off a ship were the ones who *didn't* get off a ship!"

"Yes, sir, that *is* most unfortunate . . ."

"It's more than unfortunate, Hubner. What's going to happen when Brandt or Drechsler discover that on top of the dead civilian crew, a dozen of our own men were butchered? And that I sent them to their deaths?"

"They won't look on it kindly, mein Herr," bleated Hubner, eyes darting like a cornered stoat. "And that's why I will clean up this mess. Clean it up as if it never happened."

"You don't think anyone's going to miss eleven assault troops?"

"We'll say we sent them on a mission to Ghent."

"That's your plan? What about the men mopping up this ghastly mess—you don't think they might talk over a lager next time they're off shift?"

"I have a very good crew, sir, that I trust implicitly and use for all kinds of unpleasant jobs. I've already summoned them. They'll be here shortly. Before we do anything else, we must scrub the ship—remove all trace of . . ." Hubner waved his short arm over the gruesome scene that surrounded them. "Two dozen bodies can't be rotting on a blood-soaked open deck in June during one of our busiest weekends. Word is already leaking out—dockworkers, officers are murmuring about it . . ."

"Yes, Kommissar of the Fucking Obvious." Rheinhardt threw up his hands. "As always—when you depend on other people to carry out your most basic orders, you run into incompetence, overeagerness, complete uselessness, really. Did I tell them to murder everyone on board?"

"Of course not, sir."

"Did I so much as intimate it?"

"Not a breath."

"I was very clear."

"Crystal."

"I ordered them to examine the ship, especially the lower holds."

"I heard you say this myself, sir. There could be no misunderstanding."

"I wasn't speaking in code. I didn't say *go inspect the lower hold* and mean *stab them to death*. How can such a simple order be so *catastrophically* misunderstood?"

"It beggars belief, mein Herr."

"There's no one left alive even to call to account!"

"No. There's no truth to be gotten from the dead," said Hubner, a little too philosophically for Rheinhardt's taste as they paced the quay.

"It's gone completely sideways, and you know the one thing Herr Brandt doesn't tolerate, Hubner, is a debacle."

"Yes, he is most averse to debacles. Also to herring."

Rheinhardt stopped walking. "Is this a time for jokes, Hubner?"

"No, mein Herr," Hubner said sheepishly.

"Go and fetch your cleaning crew. Run!" Otto Brandt was averse to many things—inspections, clearances, honest labor.

Hours passed of grisly work. The crew removed the bodies of twenty men from the ship's decks and holds. A few had to be fished out of the water. Before they bagged them and loaded them onto truck beds, Rheinhardt counted and examined each and every corpse. He was searching for two in particular: Captain Dufresne and his mute Congolese mate. Dufresne's body was found almost immediately. But the other eluded Rheinhardt.

Blood was everywhere, congealing in the seams between the deck planks like caulking. A heap of rope, the color of rusted iron, lay soaked near one of the cargo hatches. The cleanup crew toiled in silence. One man vomited over the rail. Another muttered prayers in Dutch.

While the men scrubbed the sticky decks and dark ladders, Rheinhardt scoured the quay for tell-tale signs of survivors. After an hour of microscopic examination, he found a small something near the concrete bollards between *La Fortuna* and the ship directly to its right, the *Serra Nova*. There, on the coping above the piles, was a sizable smear of dried blood. It had been partially washed away—or wiped away. Perhaps someone had tried to climb out of the water. An injured someone.

Or just perhaps, Rheinhardt thought, kneeling on the cobblestones in his field grays to examine the blood spatters more closely, someone had helped the wounded man. The blood spread outward. There'd been a moderate effort to brush it off the planks, made by little hands, only smearing it more.

Rheinhardt got to his feet and straightened his coat. So. A wounded man, who'd climbed out of the water—or been helped out—wouldn't vanish without a trace or conveniently stop bleeding. Rheinhardt had a hunch the man didn't die, at least not immediately. For one, where was the body? So now he would follow the blood.

A few feet away on the cobblestones, he spotted some blood drops. Again, someone's foot in a small shoe had tried to rub them away. Following each drop, Rheinhardt made his way to the window of an old warehouse directly across the quay. The window wasn't locked. He lifted it and climbed awkwardly inside—like a common criminal.

He found a smear of blood on the sash, the sill, the frame. A large bloody handprint made by a man trying to hold on to the wall, falling, blood following him into the dirt and the straw. Nearby, a few bloodied rags were left behind, prints from various pairs of hands: little ones, and slightly bigger ones. Another hasty attempt was made to cover the blood with dirt. Someone had tried to get the wounded man away from the killing ground—fast. How else to explain so much evidence left behind?

The man, probably barely conscious, needed to be dragged. The blood trail led Rheinhardt to a back door that opened into a small rear courtyard. The door had been carelessly shut. In the unpaved area behind the warehouse, the blood drops led to a dusty rectangle—and vanished. What remained were the four tire tracks of a vehicle that had screeched away in a hurry.

Rheinhardt stood in the muddy lot, his crank-powered flashlight swinging in his hand.

Well, this was curious. He returned to the warehouse and stood by the window with the pooled blood around it. The view was toward the *Serra Nova*, the ship next to *La Fortuna*. He stared at both ships, gathering his thoughts.

Someone had parked a truck in the lot behind the warehouse. For reasons unknown, someone had found a way inside, sat here by the window late on a Friday night, and then just happened to bear witness to a narrow-focus operation that got completely out of hand. This someone stayed long enough to rescue a man wounded in the attack. Rheinhardt knew the man was not one of his. All *his* dead men were accounted for. *La Fortuna* carried twelve crew. Only eleven bodies were laid out on the docks. The mute Congo man who had stared at him insolently a few days earlier was missing.

It was time to find the captain of the *Serra Nova*. Time to question the guards at checkpoints around Antwerp about a small four-wheeler that had exited the city between midnight and dawn. It was a big job—there were nearly three dozen checkpoints. Rheinhardt would investigate each one himself. Yes, there was legwork to be done, but he was certain: the answers would reveal themselves.

And even more important than the dead men—or the escaped man—was *La Fortuna*. Von Rheinhardt would not rest until he knew what was on that damned ship that was worth killing for—and dying for.

8

Marriage

"What, your father didn't tell you?" said Gretchen Fontaine after Charlie barreled into their flower shop in Herentals. "Shocking—you and he never stop the chitter-chatter." The smell of flowers and rising yeast from the baker next door overpowered Zandstraat. "Yes, I've left him, Charlotte."

"Okay, Maman . . ."

"For good this time."

"Okay, Maman."

"I mean it."

Charlie had a pain between her eyes that no amount of rubbing could quell.

"Charlie, the man is inveterately *infidèle*," Gretchen said in a tone of mortal affront. "I refuse to put up with it any longer."

"Maman, we're fighting a war . . ."

"War doesn't mean people should be criminals in their personal lives."

"You're imagining things," Charlie said, the insincerity in her tone evident to them both. "Vake works the fields all day . . ."

"Not by himself, as you well know. He's with that trollop who pretends to tend to his flowers. That's not all she's tending to, obviously."

"Elke? She lives in a shack by the compost heap. She never leaves the fields or the truck, never comes inside, never stops working." Plus, Elke was ordinary and dull-faced, while Charlie's mother was arresting and dramatic. How Charlie might have looked had she been arresting and dramatic herself—instead of inconspicuous and stoic.

"She stopped working long enough to get knocked up, didn't she?" said Gretchen.

"Elke's not pregnant, Maman!" Could her mother be right? Charlie tried to think. Elke toiled like a long-suffering ox in the fields. Please, no.

"Charlotte, don't be naïve. You're going to be twenty-five soon."

It was nice of her mother to remember when Charlie's birthday was. She said nothing. Gretchen also said nothing.

"I must tell you," Gretchen went on quickly, "I admire you for not wanting to find a husband. I used to wonder if there was something wrong with you . . ." Her mother circled with her hand, as if the gesture alone was enough to explain what was wrong with her daughter. "But now I see—you were simply brilliant."

Charlie, who had a million things weighing on her like concrete, forced herself to perch on a stool while her mother angrily pruned and trimmed the bushy tulips. With as calm a voice as she could muster, she said, "Vake is very sorry if he's done anything to upset you, Maman. Could you please come home?"

"What do you care where I go? You're never home yourself."

What was Charlie going to say—because I need the apartment upstairs to hide a stabbed man from the Congo? Also to hide a Jewish boy. Zeus, Mina's nephew. You remember Mina, don't you, Maman? "Tell me why you're really upset," is what she said instead, trying not to sound defeated.

"This is not only about compost heap Elke, Charlotte." Gretchen spoke as if they were discussing the ill effect of cold weather on tulip blooms. But then she said, "Your brother's been taken . . ." Her voice got hoarse.

Ah, finally. So this was the shadow of truth hanging over her mother's eyes. The thing she hadn't been saying.

"Don't worry. It's just vandalism charges, Maman."

A tremulous Gretchen shook her head. "Because he's in jail, he can't work. And because he can't work, they've filed papers to transfer him to an *Arbeitslager* in Germany." It was made compulsory: all Belgian men and women between 18 and 55 who were unemployed would be sent to German labor camps to support war production. "I can't do it again, daughter," Gretchen whispered. "I won't make it. And your father certainly won't."

"It's going to be fine, Maman . . ." Charlie said, her voice catching.

"Now you know why I moved here," Gretchen said, her head bowed deeply into the tulips. "To get away from everything. You gallivanting. Fitz in jail. Elke in the field. I just want to not feel anymore."

"Your mother is *so* dramatic," said Alder when Charlie confronted him upon her return home. "Did you tell her about your Congolese predicament? That might put things in perspective for her."

"You didn't answer the question, Vake."

"I forgot what it was," Alder said. "Do you know why? Because in the two hours you've been gone, and I've been babysitting an injured man and a frightened orphan, I've had four people bike up to this house to urgently tell *me* to urgently tell *you* that you haven't picked up any of your dead drops in days, despite the fact that six different signals have been plastered all over town that you've ignored. *Four people!*"

"I've got a lot to do," Charlie said, remembering Ngomo's words in the woods. *Make this the only business of your life*. She stopped interrogating her father. She had neither the energy nor the ability to solve her parents' problems. She couldn't even solve her own.

"Your evaders can stay here—until you get your drops," Alder said. "The one from the *klokkenmaker* is apparently the most urgent."

9

Omloop

Rheinhardt could not *believe* the lackadaisical approach of the sentries at some of the Antwerp crossings. On the major bridges and on high traffic roads, the checkpoints were buttoned up like coffins. But over the narrower canals and less-traveled footpaths, the indifference to security protocols was astonishing.

None of the guards Rheinhardt questioned could tell him how many trucks they had allowed through on that Friday. They could not describe their size or purpose. They could not corroborate who'd been driving them, what their business was, what they were delivering or picking up. These highly trained paragons of German security acted as if they were hungover.

Two of them mentioned a small truck that smelled like flowers.

But when asked to describe it, one said it was a weathered green, and the other said it was beige or ochre. They couldn't describe the driver. Both agreed it *might* have been a man. One said he was a curly-haired bearded fella about two meters tall, while the other said he was a bald gnome.

Finally, under relentless questioning, a guard remembered a *klokken-maker* driving unusually late into west Antwerp.

Rheinhardt was fed up. "Bring him to me," he said to the man. "I don't care how you find him. If he's not standing in front of me in two hours, then you'll be standing in front of me, awaiting your *Disziplinarverfahren*."

Fear usually worked. A minuscule old man, hunched and listing permanently to one side, was soon brought in, shuffling and sniffling. He suffered from some affliction—a part of him was always in motion.

"Who are you?" Rheinhardt demanded.

"Omloop," the old man replied. "I am Omloop."

"Omloop what?"

"Joris Omloop at your service, Herr *Sturmbannführer*."

The increasingly impatient Rheinhardt learned that Omloop had been taught by his Flemish father, the *klokkenmaker* before him, and he by his father, and so on. Rheinhardt tried to interrupt, but Omloop was on a roll. Recently, all his assistants had quit or died and now repair and maintenance fell solely to him, a man deep in his seventies who looked too weak to lift a hammer, let alone wrestle with a cast-iron bell.

Omloop drove a busted-up truck, and in this excuse for a vehicle he to-ed and fro-ed between Boom and Brecht, forging and fixing the bells of Flanders.

"You deliver bells in that thing outside?" Rheinhardt didn't believe it.

"Oh, yes, mein Herr. I know she don't look like much, she's small like her driver, but I made her mighty. Reinforced her to haul bells. Short in the frame, but strong where it counts."

"Like you?"

Omloop smirked and shook. "Strong once maybe. Not anymore." He had scraggly white hair, wore a patched musty suit, and sported a wide-brim felt hat, which he now held in his quaking hands—revealing a gray silk skullcap that kept sliding off his unruly mane. As he spoke, he shifted from side to side, and forward and back. He was nearly out the door by the time he finished furnishing Rheinhardt with his unwanted life story.

Finally, the insufferable fool got to details Rheinhardt actually cared about. "You were in west Antwerp last Friday night. Why?"

"Oh, not night, sir. During the day. Difficult for me to tend to the bells at night, Herr *Sturmbannführer*," Omloop said. "My eyes aren't what they used to be." He creaked out an apologetic laugh. "I spent the day—did what I could with the old Dominican bell at Sint-Pauluskerk, serviced the brand-new carillon at City Hall, and was on my way." Before Rheinhardt could ask, Omloop offered. "Left around 6:30. No, that's not entirely true. I was done with me work, but I stopped by the De Pelgrim Tavern and had me some dinner, and a stein of brew. Pelgrim has the best cold on tap. After that, I went on me way. No, that's not entirely right, either, mein Herr. I drank me large stein too quick, and had to wait a bit before I could be on me way. But then the tavern got lit up and there was quite a festive air. I stayed probably longer than I should have. I had another pint. And then was *really* unsteady on my feet, if you can believe," said the old man, who hadn't stopped twitching the entire time he spoke. He creaked out another embarrassed laugh. "I crawled into my truck, slept off the beer, and got going."

"When?"

"Later than I should have." Omloop tittered.

"Where was the truck parked?"

"Right where I enjoyed me bitter, mein Herr, outside De Pelgrim."

"What time did you leave?"

"Oh, bless you, I couldn't tell you. The revelry had been going on a few hours, and I slept a few hours. I don't carry a watch and didn't look at the clock in the tavern. I'd say it was somewhere between eleven p.m. Friday and one a.m. Saturday."

Rheinhardt eyed the little man, shaky but resolute, his gaze not firm, but not evasive either, and contemplated him with scorn. "You're the bellkeeper and you don't know what time you're keeping? Aren't these your bells that ring every hour on the fucking hour all over this city?"

"Quite right, quite right, and what beautiful carillons they are too, but when I'm in me cups, I don't count the rings. I can barely keep upright at that point." Omloop gave a sheepish chuckle.

"Are you the *klokkenmaker* or the *klokkenringer*?"

"I can do anything with bells, mein Herr," Omloop said proudly. "I am all things bells."

Rheinhardt fought not to roll his eyes. "Does your work send you to the western part of the docks? Around Het Steen Kasteel on Jordaensstraat?"

Omloop shook his head. Or just shook. "The Het Steen bells have not been serviced or rung for years," he said. "That castle is crumbling stone by stone. I'm surprised any of it is still standing. No, I have no business on Glaskaai, none whatever. Heaven forfend."

"Why heaven forfend? What do you know about Glaskaai?"

"The less the better," Omloop said. "And I know nothing."

Rheinhardt was at the end of his tether. "You fix bells in churches?"

"Of course. Churches are the main source of me business."

"Sometimes they have weddings or funerals?"

"Often. These days probably more funerals than weddings . . ." Omloop muttered. "I mean no disrespect by this, mein Herr, *none* whatsoever . . ."

"Shut up. Have you seen flowers being delivered to these churches?"

"My work takes me up high in the belfries, and flowers, well, they are close to the ground, and me eyes aren't what . . . so no."

"You don't know the names of any flower companies that deliver to your churches?"

"Everyone's growing flowers this time of year, if that's what you're asking." Omloop glanced over Rheinhardt's spartan, document-filled space. Not a single living thing adorned a vase or a pot.

"Omloop, listen to me carefully. Do you know *anyone* who drives a flower truck in and out of Antwerp?"

"A what?"

"A flower truck, Omloop."

"What does it look like?"

"What does a *truck* look like?" Rheinhardt was about to lose his temper.

"Well, wouldn't the truck say whose flower shop it was, sir? My truck has a painting of a bell on it, and my name." He chuckled. "A little bit of self-promotion never hurts. Flower trucks usually have flowers painted on them, almost like an advertisement."

"Thank you for explaining how a business works, Omloop," Von Rheinhardt said, glancing at Hubner with an expression that read, *He's pretty irritating, eh? Remind you of anyone?* Hubner, misunderstanding, smiled warmly.

"If there's no name of the business, sir, how do you know it was a flower truck?" asked Omloop.

"A sentry mentioned a heavy floral scent from one of the vehicles that left the Glaskaai area late on Friday."

"Oh, yes, flowers have the most aromatic scent!" Omloop exclaimed.

"I wish I could say the same for you." Rheinhardt didn't bother hiding his disdain. "Go, *klokkenmaker*. Take your odor out of my office. You've been most unhelpful."

"I've tried to be *most* helpful, mein Herr," Omloop said with a slight bow, backing out of the office and leaving.

"What did you think of him?" Rheinhardt asked Hubner.

"Excruciating," Hubner replied.

"Indeed," Rheinhardt said. "That's going to be *you* in twenty years." Pause. "Probably not even that long."

Hubner swallowed. "Yes, mein Herr."

"Bring me Kurt Vogel, Hubner. Why hasn't he reported to me after his drive about today, as he said he would? Why am I still waiting for him?"

"I'll go to headquarters right away and find out," Hubner said, hurrying toward the door. "I agree—the delay is most unacceptable."

10

Saint Waltrude

Charlie was on her knees in the pews at Saint Waltrude, hands clasped, eyes closed. The church was empty in the mid-morning, except for one or two laity lighting candles and a deacon in the corner, reciting the psalms in the eighth tone. Charlie felt lost. She didn't even know what she should be praying for. *Help me.* But help her with what? *Guide me.* But guide her to what? *Save me.* But save her from what? *Have mercy on me.*

There it was.

Help me, guide me, save me, have mercy on me. Altogether, not a bad prayer.

"Charlie," a voice whispered next to her.

It was Omloop.

Charlie didn't open her eyes. "Can't you see I'm busy?"

"You came to meet *me*."

"*After* this. Not during." She sighed. The moment was ruined. "*The bell rings in the holy place*," she said, to assess the level of danger.

"*And the faithful bow their heads*," he replied, confirming the situation was one level up from the normal *the faithful walk unharmed*.

Opening her eyes, she glanced at the old man resentfully. His skullcap had slipped halfway off his bowed head. His strong, steady hands were clasped together like hers. His spine was straight. His long gray hair was combed back neatly behind his ears, tied with a short length of twine.

"Tell me what you have to tell me," she said.

"You have to pick up your drops, Charlie," Omloop said. "I have things to relay."

"So relay."

"You didn't tell me what a disaster Glaskaai was."

"Yeah, well. I told you enough."

"You forgot to mention the massacre on the docks! Rheinhardt, the commandant of the port, has gone off the rails. I barely got out of there alive."

Charlie didn't know what to say to commiserate.

"Why were they all killed?"

"How should I know?" *There's something on the ship*, Ngomo said. She shivered.

"Do you still have him?"

"Yes. Unfortunately."

"Capelle couldn't take him?"

"While he was trailed by a squad of Gestapo? No."

Omloop squeezed his hands together. "London contacted me," he said. "I don't know what's going on, but . . ."

Charlie's skin crawled with dread and exhaustion.

"Don't go into town anymore," Omloop said. "They're searching for your flower truck."

"Great," she said, lowering her head even deeper. What was her poor father going to do? She had legitimate business in Antwerp—delivering his flowers.

"London said to hold fast. Help is on the way."

"Great," she repeated. *Help me, guide me, save me, have mercy on me.*

"They asked if the man was safe. *Very* important that he is kept far from the Germans, they said."

"Radio them back immediately, Omloop, tell them he's not remotely safe. Tell them he's the opposite of safe."

"Did he tell you anything?"

"He said to find Miguel Silva," said Charlie.

"I know him," Omloop said. "And tell him what?"

"La jonquille est morte," Charlie said.

Omloop was taken aback. "That'll tell Silva what he's supposed to do?"

"Apparently. That's the phrase that's been sending everyone into a frenzy." She couldn't get the image of Robert Capelle's crushed face out of her head when she said those words to him at Bonaventure Market two days ago. Tall, aristocratic, utterly composed, Capelle looked ready to collapse upon hearing those words. *Don't look at me*, he said, turning toward the berry stand. *Stand next to me and tell me what happened.* And after she told him, the only thing Capelle said was, *Is Ngomo still alive?*

"Just hold the line till they get here, Charlie."

"Who's they?"

"Whoever's fixing whatever this is."

"Oh? And when are these fixers planning to get here?"

"After *the thing.*"

She opened her eyes. She and Omloop stared at each other. His gaze was steady and solemn. Meaningfully, he raised his brows—and nodded.

Charlie lowered her head until it rested on the hard wooden pew in front of her. She was so tired. The resistance cells had been muttering about the Allied invasion for months. "And when do you think *that* will be?" she said, barely able to string words together.

"Very soon," Omloop said. "As in *full moon soon*."

Charlie recalled the nearly full moon from three days earlier, before her life had come apart. "When is it full?"

"*Tonight*," Omloop replied.

It was Monday, June 5, 1944.

11

Beauty and the Beast

"Louise . . ."

"Don't Louise me. Did you see Omloop?"

"Yes. I'm so worried about everything."

"Well, you should've thought of that before you saved a black man's life," Louise said. "Next time maybe you'll think before you act."

"Omloop said the Allied team is supposed to come soon."

"Yes, they'll ride in on their white steeds to save us. Wait—what? Did you say *Allies*?" Louise couldn't believe her ears. "So what I'm hearing, Charlie, is you're going to need safehouses for another six, seven, twelve men? Yes, that'll make everything easier."

"Once they're here, *the ship*—and Ngomo—will be their problem. We just have to hang on till then."

"Their problem, I see. And let me ask you," Louise said, "who is going to help *them*?"

"They won't be African," Charlie said guiltily.

"At least your Congo man speaks French," Louise exclaimed. "The jokers who are coming to save the day, are they fluent speakers?"

"Clearly I don't know!"

"Don't get ticked off at *me*, princess," Louise said. "My way, we wait it out, keep our heads down, and then have our lives back. Your way, we'll all be in the tulip fields with the rest. In five minutes, you'll be standing over the graves of the dead."

"At least I won't be kneeling over them," snapped Charlie.

"And won't *that* be a fine difference," said Louise.

A fed-up Louise sped three kilometers down Albert Canal to Zvart Haus to bring lunch to Saul Grunfell.

She had first met Saul a few years ago when Charlie asked her to ferry him letters from his wife. He was detained in a country house in Olen, and the wife, with their two children, lived in a shack in Leuven. While delivering flowers, Charlie would pick up the letters from the wife and pass them to Louise, who would ride her bike to Zvart Haus with a basket of blueberries and fresh bread, the missives from his beloved buried at the bottom.

The letters from the wife got shorter and shorter until they stopped altogether, but the lunch food had become more elaborate. Now Louise brought flowers too.

She smiled at the guards waving to her from the front gate, and biked around the property to the side entrance.

There, two new low-level *Polizei* stood leaning against the posts. While she was waving to the gardener inside and hopping off her bike, Louise assessed the two guards. The younger one was smiling, but the older one was humorless *and* higher ranked—and therefore more dangerous.

"Bonjour, Brigadier!" she said to the younger man, bumping him up a rank to corporal.

He flushed with pleasure. "*Bonjour*, mademoiselle!"

The older guard snorted. "*Brigadier?* Hah! Then, I'm a—"

Smiling guilelessly, Louise interrupted him, bumping him up a rank too. *"Bonjour, Sergent!"*

The guard shut his mouth with an audible click and squared his shoulders.

The young guard turned to his partner. "You were saying, Remy?"

Remy scowled, busying himself with her papers. "You're the Louise Aubel who brings lunch for Grunfell?"

"I'm the one."

Having established the purpose of her visit, he opened the gate to let her through. "You know where he is?"

"Where he always is," she said. "Upstairs."

"He's not always upstairs . . ." the young guard began before Remy elbowed him in the ribs.

"Careful over the cobblestones, mademoiselle, they're uneven near the steps," Remy said. "Would you like me to carry the basket upstairs for you? Looks heavy. What have you got in there?"

She opened it to show them. Wine, a sandwich, potato salad, lemon poppyseed cookies and peaches. "Would you like to try a peach?" she said brightly. "They're tasty. The cookies are even better. But just one each, or our poor Professor Grunfell will have nothing to sustain him."

* * *

"Saul," she said. "Saul."

He didn't hear her, didn't even look up.

Upstairs in the large, disorganized, book-lined room he had fashioned into his study, Saul sat at the table by the window, buried in his notebook, a pencil behind each ear and one in his fingers. In his left hand he held a burned-down cigarette. Louise had never actually seen Saul light it or smoke it. It was always just ash in his blackened hand.

Saul Grunfell had arrived at Zvart Haus in 1941.

He'd been a professor of something or other—possibly math; he told Louise, but she forgot—at the University of Brussels. In 1940, after the Germans stampeded over Belgium, he and other Jewish professors had been relieved of their posts. He wasn't deported out of the country like other Jews. Instead, he and two colleagues were sent here, to a spacious and attractive house in the country.

One professor died of dysentery last year, as though it was the 15th century and not Belgium in the civilized 20th. The other, Henri Weissmann—the senior man at Zvart—died just a few weeks ago, from an "unfortunate industrial accident," as Saul put it without elaborating further. So now only Saul was left, surrounded by four lowly guards and the June azaleas.

Saul was a sullen, deeply internal man. He lived so far inside his head that he paid no attention to his physical appearance or his diet. He lost weight in the time Louise knew him, which made her feel even more guilty for the days she was too busy with her other duties to come. His jackets and trousers, never particularly fashionable, looked especially ill-fitting and crumpled lately. He shaved sporadically and didn't like to cut his thinning hair. Unless he was gripping a pencil, his fingers always trembled slightly, either from stress or an undiagnosed ailment. His hands were a war zone. Blackened at the tips, they showed burn marks and scars.

He had a good face once, Louise thought; good eyes. Now the eyes were dimmed, and he was pale. No healthy glow for Saul. There were days he seemed more ghost than man. Louise wasn't entirely certain the professor was sane. Sometimes he spoke to her in such abstractions, it stymied her natural ability to communicate with him. Louise prided herself on being the kind of young woman that most people responded to strongly and warmly.

Not Saul.

Often when he spoke to her, in a slow, rolling, lecturing cadence, as if explaining difficult things to an idiot, she would just nod and smile, but every once in a while, Saul would adjust his black-rimmed glasses and interrogate her. "What do you think of what I just told you?" he'd say in a voice that suggested he was testing her comprehension.

Today, when she walked into his study and greeted him once, twice, and then a third time, he jerked up, stared at her unblinking for a few moments, then blurted, "There's no such thing as isolation below the Planck length, Louise. Entanglement mocks even the dead!"

She was a beautiful girl living in a mad world.

"The dead are not easily mocked, Saul," she said, setting her basket at his feet because there was no room on the table, and showing him a bright bouquet of yellow daisies. She liked to bring him flowers—not only to beautify his study, but also to mask the brassy smell that seeped into the wood and the furniture, despite the windows being open all day, a smell like metal in sour milk. She looked around for the vase she'd found last week.

"What did you do with the green vase, Saul?"

"What vase?"

"The green one."

"Never seen it."

She placed the daisies into a tall glass instead and set them on the table, shuffling aside his books and notebooks.

"Careful, don't touch anything. Everything is arranged."

She glanced over the far-flung chaos.

"Why are you upset?" Saul asked. This was what professors did. They noticed things. They were observationalists by nature.

"I'm not upset," said Louise.

"You're less smiley than usual. Also, you shouted at me."

"I called your name twice and you didn't answer."

"And you're upset why?"

Louise didn't tell him. Where would she even start? An in-over-her-head Charlie, a heartbroken Fitz, a niggling, needling mother, a mess with Jews and Africans. Saul had his own problems, obviously. No one wanted to hear about other people's.

She served his lunch and sat in a chair by his side, nibbling on a lemon poppy cake while he ate in silence, reading a multi-page precis in tiny type, making minute calculations with his free hand.

"You should go outside, Saul," Louise said. "Look how beautiful it is. Sunny. Warm. It's good for you. It'll bring some color to your face."

"A slowly drowning man cares nothing for the sun or what's good for him," said Saul.

"Why are you drowning?"

"I'm just a rat in a wheel, Louise," said Saul. He gave a brusque, resigned wave. "You don't know what I mean."

"I know what you mean, Saul," said Louise with a faint sigh.

"The wheel is spinning faster and faster," Saul said, "and I can't keep up. Sometimes I don't even want to. It's all so pointless."

"Maybe go out in the sun, Saul," she said quietly. Usually her dazzling smile brought out the best in people. "So, whatcha working on that's giving you trouble?" she asked, trying to take an interest.

"You don't care."

"Of course I do. Tell me. Maybe I can help."

Saul almost smiled at her audacity. "I'm trying to create something. Build something. And I'm failing."

"Build what? A box?"

"Yes, Lou. A kind of box."

In good humor, Louise scanned the room, taking in the overflowing shelves of books, notebooks stacked floor to ceiling, four or five desk lamps, broken pencils across every surface, a half-dozen rimmed glasses, empty teacups. There were no workbenches, no chisels, no mallets, no handsaws, not even a whetstone for sharpening a blade. There was nothing to indicate that any building had ever gone on in this jarringly quiet, slightly malodorous house.

He took in the kindly expression she fashioned just for him. His face softened. "Imagine we're trying to build this box not out of wood or stone or metal," he said, "but out of gossamer thread, like spider webbing, which is thin and fragile and breaks easily."

"Not easy to make a box out of that."

"Some might say impossible. To make it stronger, we lay the gossamer threads one on top of another, nearly to infinity, hoping that the sheer quantity will make the walls of the box sturdy enough."

"I have a question, Saul," said Louise, munching slowly on her lemon cake. She was trying to make it last. "If you really need a box, why don't you make it out of metal or wood? Why do scientists always have to complicate things?"

Saul actually reached out to pat her arm before stopping himself. "The box is an analogy, Lou. It's a magic box. So, let's take it as fact that the box needs to be built out of spider webbing. Do you want to hear the real complication? Imagine that one of these strands takes a single spider hours, sometimes days, to make. And the box we're aiming for must be this size"—Saul held his hands about twenty centimeters apart—"but instead, what we have, after *years* and *years* of effort, is a box about this size." He pressed his thumb and forefinger tightly together and emitted a despondent wail.

"Shh. It's okay," Louise said. "Why does it have to be spider thread?"

"Because spider thread is the only thing in the universe that will build a magic box. Everything else will create a regular box. We have plenty of those. We need a spider box."

Louise paused a moment and then hit herself on the forehead. "I got it!" she said, offering him her biggest smile. "You need more spiders. You're waiting for one spider to spin you a thread at a time. That's the problem. Go get a thousand spiders, Saul. Or a million. Then you'll have your box."

This time, Saul did reach out and pat her arm. "That is *exactly* what I need, dear girl," he said, brimming with impressed affection. "Look how smart you are. A million spiders. And the tragedy of my useless life is I've got just one."

12

Invasion

"Hubner, don't interrupt me when I'm speaking."

"Sir, I have news . . ."

"I don't care what you've got to tell *me*. Listen to what I'm telling *you*."

"Yes, mein Herr, but—"

"I need the ship emptied. Why is that so hard to understand or accomplish?"

"It's not hard, sir, but I have questions."

"We haven't the time for questions."

"That's true, sir, the clock is ticking. But normally the dockworkers remove the cargo from the ships."

"Thank you for explaining to me how a port works, Hubner."

"And then the cargo gets loaded onto trucks or trains and delivered to the people who have ordered it," Hubner said.

Rheinhardt sat. "No, no, you're right," he said. "We have infinite time to ruminate on all stages of port work. Let's discuss the intermediary stage next. What happens to the cargo when it *must* be offloaded, but the trains or trucks aren't ready?"

"It's transferred into company warehouses."

"Very good, Hubner! Do that."

"The cargo has been contracted by Miguel Silva's company, sir."

"And I care about this why?"

"Silva has skipped town," said Hubner. "He hasn't answered his phone for two days, so I drove to his office this morning with a contingent of Gestapo officers, and found it padlocked. The note on the door said: 'Away on urgent business. Back in six weeks.'"

"*Six* weeks! He employs no one else?"

"Also gone. The two warehouses he owns on Bonapartestraat are locked—

and full besides. No room in either of them to transfer the contents of *La Fortuna* to."

Rheinhardt spun a pencil between his fingers. "How many crates on the ship?"

"Seven hundred and ninety-four individual crates spread across fourteen categories."

"Total value of insured goods?"

"Five million, four hundred thousand francs, mein Herr."

Rheinhardt shrugged. "Hubner, I'm not saying we shouldn't be holding daily conferences on how to resolve Silva's cargo fiasco. What I'm saying, and I don't know if I can be any clearer, is—*it's none of our fucking business!*" Rheinhardt's booming voice made Hubner jump.

"Here is where it becomes our business, mein Herr," Hubner said, standing firm. "Seven hundred and ninety-four crates must go somewhere. And if they're not leaving the port on Silva's trucks, and there's no room in his padlocked warehouses, perhaps his Exzellenz would care to suggest what we're meant to do with them."

Rheinhardt lapsed into a rare silence.

"We can't leave nearly a thousand crates sitting on the docks, mein Herr," Hubner went on. "That's bound to draw the very kind of attention I assume you're trying to avoid. A thousand crates spread out on Glaskaai? Brandt's first question will be about the cargo. If there was no one to take possession of it, why did we take it off the ship in the first place?"

"There's *something* on that ship, Hubner," Rheinhardt said. "And we can't find it with the crates packed into the cargo hold like sardines."

"Is there a chance Silva is smuggling diamonds?" asked Hubner. "They could be easily hidden in the coffee crates. He could've become alarmed by your refusal to sign off on the manifest. And then, even *more* alarmed," Hubner added evenly, "by the subsequent massacre of dozens of men aboard his ship. He took his diamonds and vanished."

"He would've had to collect his diamonds while wading ankle-deep through his crew's blood," Rheinhardt said. "We've had a four-man rotating guard posted at *La Fortuna* since Saturday. No one's getting anywhere near that ship without our knowledge and authorization."

Hubner acknowledged this was so.

"I don't need you to concur with me, Hubner," Rheinhardt said, acutely aggravated. "Do I have to spell out *everything*? Stash the crates in the warehouse across the quay. We know it's empty. Break the padlock. Anyone questions you, send them to me. Leave the cargo there, but spread out, so our men can go through it—crate by crate, if need be."

"But if it's not diamonds," said Hubner, "what are you worried might be on that ship?"

"If I knew what was on that ship," said Rheinhardt, "tell me, would I be risking my position, and yours, and involving Port Authority, whom you know I can't stand, to learn what's on it?"

"No, mein Herr. Of course not."

"No, mein Herr. Of course not." Rheinhardt mocked him. "You really are an imbecile, Hubner. You don't find it at all suspicious that Silva has cut and run?"

"It could be a coincidence . . ."

"Hubner, are you my aide or my punishment? There's no such thing as coincidence. There is only enemy action. Maybe Silva got wind of the impending invasion. No, no—don't interrupt! We don't know exactly where the Tommies are going to breach the Führer's Atlantic Wall," Rheinhardt said. "Could be right here in Antwerp. Why not? Maybe Silva discovered something and ran. Don't shake your head at me, Hubner! It would make a lot of sense. We're a vital port. And we're not prepared. *La Fortuna* could be—I told you, do *not* shake your head at me!"

"Mein Herr . . ." Hubner was whispering. "The Allies attacked at dawn this morning. French coast. Normandy. Not here."

"How do you know this!" Rheinhardt shouted, leaping out of his chair.

"Everyone knows. That's what I came to tell you."

"Then why didn't you lead with that?" Rheinhardt roared.

"We got sidetracked with *La Fortuna*, and—"

"*La Fortuna* is not a fucking sidetrack," Rheinhardt said through his teeth. "It should be the point of your daily existence! Are you sure about Normandy?"

Hubner nodded. "One hundred percent. The Allies are in France."

It's finally happened, Rheinhardt thought, grabbing his coat and cap and bolting into the street, the mystery of *La Fortuna* sidelined for a moment. They had waited on the invasion for so long. Now, at last, the wait was over. The enemy was here. Finally, the war would begin to end—one way or another.

And men like Rheinhardt would decide how it ended.

13

Minus Zero

Fletcher was burning even as he was drowning, drowning in a sea of blood.

Except it wasn't his blood. It was Lucas's. He'd been shot in the throat.

This wasn't Alamein. This wasn't Anzio. Lucas never even got a chance to aim his rifle. He was cut down clutching it in his wet hands, a blade of grass by a scythe. And Fletcher was still hip-deep in the sea.

No drop zones. No flashing lights. No beacons. No guidance. Just the *rat-tat-tat* of gunfire.

They both ran from the landing craft into the low tide, ran headlong into the bursts of flak, Lucas first.

Lucas was always first.

The Germans knew we were coming, Fletcher thought, lying in the cold water as if dead himself, his arm over his closest friend.

Two men, soldiers, Rangers, elite, best of the best. Fletcher and Lucas had been shivering together in the troop carrier for nine hours. The waves were so high, they smashed over the deck from one side to the other, washing away the putrid odor of vomit, though the eye-tearing smell of diesel oil remained. Lucas had been trying not to throw up—again—but it was too late for Fletcher. Everything that was once inside was now outside. He was so sick, he could no longer throw up. They'd been preparing for this moment since Tunisia in 1942, but they didn't expect the seas to be so rough. Maybe Rafael was right. Maybe they should've waited another week, another month. But it was too late now for should've, could've. They were in a steel drum, thrashing from side to side in the roiling dark, spinning clockwise, then counterclockwise. Fletcher listened to the high whistling wind, the water slapping against the sides of their landing craft with every deafening wave.

They were F Company, 2nd Rangers, frontline strike force. Lucas was captain, Fletcher team leader of the 1st Rifle platoon. They were understrength in Company Fuck, only ninety men instead of one-fifty.

Just before they jumped off the boat, Lucas said, *Get going, I know you can*, because Fletcher was having trouble getting going. *Our fate lies across that beach*, Lucas said.

Maybe that was the problem.

Fletcher and Lucas, strapping young bucks. Wyoming, Colorado. Born two months apart, brothers from other mothers. They'd met at OCS, trained hard together, graduated together, got selected into 1st Rangers together, went to North Africa together, to Italy together, Anzio, Monte Cassino, Aquila. Got wiped out in Italy, regrouped to become 2nd Rangers. Travelled to England together, spent months preparing for the invasion of Normandy. Went on liberty to London together, drank together, met girls together. Now they were here. Everything they did, they did together.

Except die together.

Fletcher must've been in shock—what else could explain why the only thing going round and round in his head, as he lay behind the hedgehog being pummeled with fire, was a Creole tune from childhood his mother used to sing to him called "Stella Pellerin." *The bayou always remember, the bayou never forget that her father murdered her mother while Stella Pellerin slept in her bed.*

Fletcher glanced up. Planes overhead. Contrails crisscrossing the sky like chalk lines. Amber lights blinking Morse code through the hulking clouds,

three dots one dash,

three dots one dash,

three dots one dash,

for victory.

14

Lost Hope

"He's not the one," Louise said in the woods. They were talking about Fitz; why Louise couldn't be with Charlie's brother. She'd brought more bandages and sulfa drugs for Ngomo, and with Zeus assisting, the women cleaned and re-taped Ngomo's wounds—a deep one in the chest, smaller ones on the arms and shoulders. She brought the boys drink and bread, and now the girls perched on a nearby stump watching Ngomo gently play red hands with Zeus.

"How do you know? He could be," Charlie said. "I thought I'd met the *one* and look what a flaming disaster *that* turned into."

"It might be too early to tell for me," Louise said. "I'm only twenty, not old like you. Maybe when I meet the one, I'll know. How's Fitz doing? Is he feeling better?"

"He's fine." Charlie didn't want to tell Louise that Fitz was in jail. She didn't want Louise to blame herself, even though it wasn't her fault. "We've got to get Ngomo out of these woods, Lou," she said. "We just have to."

"Why couldn't they stay with your father?"

Charlie didn't want to go into the mess at home. Alder was a good father, but a poor husband. He kept trying to get Gretchen to come back, but she'd dug in her heels and said she wouldn't return until Elke left for good. But Elke was due to give birth, and Alder could not throw her out. There was nowhere for her to go in Herentals, a single unwed mother with a new infant. The Germans could take the child from her and send her to Breendonk for vagrancy and dissolute behavior. Gretchen didn't care. Hence the continued drama—to add to all the other strife.

"I got us into terrible trouble, Lou," Charlie said, her mouth bitten bloody from anxiety. "I didn't mean to. I was just in the wrong place at the wrong time."

Louise shook her head. "Even when you're not asking, you're asking," she said, rolling her eyes. "Go get the *Berceau*. I'll get these two packed up." She sighed. "Don't overreact, but . . . I talked to Omloop. We found a place for them."

"You did?" Charlie jumped up. She wanted to cry. "Where?"

"They can't keep them for long," said Louise. "But once a week, I bring your flowers and my peaches to a tiny priory outside Vorselaar. Onze-Lieve-Vrouw van de Verloren Hoop."

"Our Lady of Lost Hope? I know it. Omloop fixes their bells."

"Charlie, that convent hasn't had bells since the First World War," said Louise. "Omloop doesn't fix their bells, he runs his secret work from there. Ten Augustinian nuns live there like paupers, the youngest of whom is eighty. They're too frail to ring bells. They can barely carry their bibles. But Omloop said there's a little space under the rafters."

Gratefully Charlie hugged Louise. "Loosha . . . you're such a good friend. The best friend."

"Yeah, yeah. I'm a real gem." Louise hugged her back.

The two men were deep in conversation and weren't ready to leave.

"So why do *you* have to be smuggled out of the country like a bar of gold, little man?" Ngomo asked. He looked more spry now that the rain had stopped—*and* he had more morphine. Mostly it was the morphine.

Zeus shrugged. "I don't know. No one ever gives me a straight answer."

"What do they say?"

"Charlie, what did you tell me?" Zeus asked. "She said there were good people and bad people, and the bad people wanted me dead."

"Why?" asked Ngomo.

"Why, Charlie?" said Zeus.

"Because they're bad people," Charlie said, as if it were self-evident.

"That's the whole reason?"

"That's what Charlie says." Zeus slapped Ngomo's huge hand lightly with his own smaller one.

"But why *you* especially?"

"Because I'm Jewish," Zeus said.

"That can't be right."

"That's what I said!"

Ngomo looked questioningly at Charlie. "That's about right, Ngomo," Charlie said.

"We don't have Jews in the Congo," Ngomo said. "I know nothing about this."

"You have tribes in your country, though, don't you?" Charlie said. "Hating each other, warring with each other?"

Ngomo gave a pained, reluctant nod. "Yes, brutal violence in my country too," he said. "Some tribes like to eat people. And the people who don't like tribes that do that go to war and kill them. Some tribes like to pray to a hundred gods. And others, who pray to just ten gods, slice them up with machetes. Some tribes in the Congo still keep slaves. It's not allowed anymore, slavery, so they go up high in the mountains and keep slaves there, and then other people come and kill them—for keeping slaves and eating people and praying to a hundred gods."

"To be honest, Ngomo, some of those things don't sound very good," said Zeus.

Ngomo laughed, grabbing his chest. "Don't make me laugh, Zeus, I have a near-fatal wound near my heart." He patted the boy's hands. "Tribal warfare is not good," he said. "But the weather is hot and sunny. The music is wonderful. The food tastes great. There's strong drink and beautiful women." Ngomo almost smiled.

"Do *you* have a beautiful woman?" Zeus asked.

"I did, yes. A long time ago." Ngomo looked into the moss. "My wife and daughter were members of a tribe that was attacked by another tribe, and everyone in our village was killed." He didn't look up.

Charlie exchanged a mute glance with an equally quiet Louise. She kept watch on Ngomo's bowed head. He had lost everything, and still he spoke gently. How did he do that? She and Fitz had been on a warpath for two years. Did it take a lifetime of violence for Ngomo to become this gentle?

And now, how did she get those two to safety? Did sanctuary even exist for Ngomo and Zeus?

Zeus reached out and took Ngomo's hand.

"At the time it happened, I was far away in Kinshasa, helping the King," Ngomo said. "I was in the royal service, so my job took me away from my wife and family for months at a time."

"You have a king in the Congo? We have a king too." Zeus smiled.

"Yes, Zeus," Ngomo said. Profound emotion seeped into his eyes that Charlie couldn't quite name. Affection, tenderness, amusement? "We have the same king."

"No!"

"Your King Leopold is my King Leopold. I serve your king."

"You *know* King Leopold?!" Zeus gasped.

Well, *that* explained a few things, Charlie thought.

"You're lying to me," Zeus said. "You think I'm . . . what's that word?"

"Gullible? *Naïf?*" Ngomo shook his head. "I'm telling you truth, little man. When the King was still a prince, he spent many years in the Congo, studying, working, hunting, learning how to be king one day. I was chief of his security detail. My job was to protect him."

Zeus's eyes were pools of wonder. "That sounds like the greatest job in the world," he murmured. "What was he like? Did you like him?"

"I loved him," Ngomo said. "Still do."

"But what was he like?"

"He was disciplined and devout," Ngomo said. "He was very strict with himself and he loved God. I haven't seen him in many years. I hope he's still like that."

"Who is Robert Capelle?" Charlie asked.

"Don't ask," Louise whispered. "What if he tells you?"

"Count Robert Capelle is the King's chief of staff and closest advisor," Ngomo replied. "We worked together for many years all over the Congo."

The mystery around *La Fortuna* was deepening.

Zeus pulled on Ngomo's arm to redirect the man's attention from Charlie to himself. "Who tried to kill you, Ngomo?" he whispered. "And why?" He lowered his voice even more. "Because you eat people?"

"Zeus, I told you, don't make me laugh. But yes, yes, I do. Only small people, though. Small delicate Jewish people."

Now even Zeus laughed. Charlie, feeling like a real joy-killer, told them to keep it down, in case there were real cannibals in the woods.

"But *who* tried to kill you, Ngomo?" Zeus repeated.

"I think the same people who want to kill *you*, little man." Ngomo smirked. "You and I have the same enemy now." He rocked his head. "But also . . . who says they wanted to kill *me*?" He gave a small gallows-humor smile. "Maybe it was the other way around."

Zeus never took his wide eyes off Ngomo's face. "Okay," the boy said slowly. "Why did *you* want to kill *them*?"

"Now you're asking the right questions. Maybe because they were busy-bodies, snooping where they weren't supposed to."

"Were you hiding something on the ship, Ngomo?" Zeus smiled.

"I was, yes."

"Was it small boys to snack on?"

"How did you know?" Ngomo ruffled Zeus's hair. "It was some rocks from the Congo."

"They don't have rocks in Belgium?"

"You're good, little man. You're real good."

"Zeus, leave Ngomo alone," Charlie said. "He's exhausted from your questions." Both men ignored her. "*I'm* exhausted from your questions, Zeus," she muttered.

"Charlie doesn't like questions, Ngomo," Zeus whispered.

Ngomo smiled thinly. "I bet Charlie likes answers, though."

Zeus tugged at Ngomo again, eager for more. "Who's guarding your rocks now?"

"No one." Ngomo stopped smiling.

There was a tremble to Zeus's mouth. "What if the bad people find your *trappe secrète*?"

Charlie locked eyes with Ngomo. A shiver ran through her. There was terror in his dark eyes. "Zeus! Enough already. I blame *you*, Ngomo. You allow too many questions. God! Get up. Let's go. Lost Hope is waiting for you two."

15

The Empty Ship

It was nearly two days of frenetic activity after the Normandy invasion before Rheinhardt could convene a crew to offload the cargo from *La Fortuna*.

A thousand new German troops poured into Antwerp to shore up its defenses. All merchant ships coming and going were stopped. Mines were carried to the edge of canals in preparation for submersion, weapons were tested, ammunition delivered.

Rheinhardt's concerns about the ship intensified. Yes, he became less worried that *La Fortuna* might be a bomb in waiting. But he grew more certain there was something *else* on that ship of extraordinary value to someone.

He paced Glaskaai and smoked incessantly, watching the men unload the ship. His field-gray overcoat dragged through the puddles and his porous leather boots seeped wet misery into his cold feet. The stiff SS visor on his head was dripping. He sighed as he squinted through Antwerp's depressing June rain. It never ended.

"There is *nothing* on that ship, sir."

It took all of Rheinhardt's strength to remain outwardly calm as he listened to Hubner's excuses. Now they both paced the top deck of *La Fortuna* after the lower holds had finally been emptied out.

"We counted every crate and checked them against the manifest. We combed every cabin and storage closet. We searched in the engine room. Every nook and cranny on this ship has been thoroughly inspected."

"Did you open every crate?"

"Sir, there are nearly 800 crates!"

"So how do you know there's nothing there, then?"

"Every crate has been checked against the . . ."

Minutes and minutes of this dullard tripe!

"I don't know what more can be done . . ."

"There's always more that can be done, *Kriminalkommissar*," Rheinhardt said with icy contempt. The heavy heel of his boot pounded against the wooden slats of the deck, punctuating every word.

"Please . . ." Hubner said beseechingly. "Don't get yourself into more trouble with—"

"You're not even doing the bare *minimum* of what you could be doing," Rheinhardt continued. "Which is *thinking*, Hubner. *Thinking*. The most rudimentary thought process would get even you to where I've been for days. Have you asked yourself, even once, why twelve crew—sailors, hired hands, usually the least combative men on earth, men who avoid not only conflict but mere *contact* with other men—would be willing to *die* to protect whatever it is on this ship? *Die*, Hubner!"

"I understand, sir, but—"

"You understand nothing! You lack any imagination and all intellect. There is no *but*. There's only the search. And, more important, the discovery." Rheinhardt didn't raise his voice or stop pacing.

"We have—"

"You have *not*. Do you know how I know you haven't? Because you haven't found it." Rheinhardt was on a rampage. "All I'm hearing is explanations and apologies, when what I need to hear is the sound of success. Our Nazi compatriots have been butchered! Murdered in the dead of night on the deck of an ordinary merchant ship waiting to unload its ordinary cargo. Are you telling me that our brave men died just to have you stand here and insist they died for *nothing*?" Rheinhardt's voice rose a quaver at the end. That's how enraged he was.

"No, sir, no, sir, no, sir," Hubner mewled. "Of course. We will not rest until it's found." He paused. "What are we looking for exactly, mein Herr? Just a little detail would be so very helpful."

Rheinhardt wanted to slap Hubner across the face. "Get out of my sight," he said, pitching the butt of his cigarette over the railing. "Clearly, if I want any job to be done—not just right, but at all—I have to do it myself. Go away. I will find it." He pulled open the hatch leading to the cargo hold, threw off his coat, and started down the ladder.

16

D-Day Plus Two

"I'm not *asking*," Fletcher heard a man's fed-up voice say. "A specialized assault unit is what I need, and you'll have to make do without."

His pack and rifle by his side, Fletcher sat on his helmet on the ground, at the rear of a military truck, and tried not to listen to four elevated voices around the corner decide the fate of his life. He hadn't washed the blood off his body, nor changed his uniform, nor cleaned his gun. He couldn't remember having any food since the landing two days earlier. The night before they sailed, each man was offered a supper of his choice. Fletcher asked for a Thanksgiving feast—roast turkey, mashed potatoes, pumpkin pie. It was the last meal he had shared with his friend Lucas.

It had taken seven hours of deafening carnage to stave off death and scale the bluffs overlooking the grayed-out beach. He had a gash on his scalp stitched by a medic, and shrapnel dug out of his shoulder sockets and the base of his neck—hot metal from a mortar shell that came too close. When they summoned him to the makeshift high command briefing, he walked up to the truck on his own two feet, carrying his own weapon. But he wasn't invited in, not yet. First they needed to talk about him without him.

The colonels and captains, and one sergeant major, had draped a swath of camo netting between the truck and a nearby tree—enough for some shade and cover from prying eyes—and had their loud conference under it. The low rumble of distant artillery never stopped. Planes buzzed over Fletcher's head. Everything stank of gunpowder, blood, manure, wet earth. In the near distance, the men who'd made it lay on the grass, dirty, muddy, banged up, exhausted. Soon maybe they'd get some tents.

"Colonel Reed, with all due *respect*," a man said, "where the fuck am I supposed to get you ten Rangers who speak French—pardon my French?" It was Roy Caldwell, the battalion commander of 2nd Rangers.

"I agree with Colonel Caldwell, sir," said Dan Ward, Lucas's replacement.

"I need the team assembled by 2200 hours today," said Jonathan Reed, as if no one had spoken.

"Assembled!" Caldwell spat the word. "I just told you I don't have them."

Stu Granger, the sergeant major, remained as quiet as a sinner in church. A minute later he popped his head out of the loose netting. "Sit tight, Fletch. A few more minutes."

"Take as long as you need, Major Granger," said Fletcher. He had nowhere to be. Sometimes, it all goes well, he thought.

And sometimes it doesn't.

The voices raised higher.

"My orders are to push past the beachhead and get to Carentan!" Caldwell shouted.

"Do what you must," Reed said. "Just without my ten men."

"You mean *my* ten men?"

Stu finally piped up, bless him. Clearing his throat, he said, "The lieutenant out there, waiting to meet with you, speaks French, sir. Fluent."

"Major Granger!" Caldwell sounded steamed. "Colonel Reed, Fletcher Gray is not your man, sir."

"What's wrong with him?"

"Absolutely nothing." He didn't sound convincing.

"Does he speak French?"

"Yes."

"What is he?"

"One of mine. Company F, 1st rifle platoon. I need him."

"So, an elite assault officer fluent in French? Find me nine more. They don't all have to be lieutenants. I'll make do with sergeants and specialists."

"Have. You. Considered. The 101st Airborne?" Caldwell said. "They have some crack professionals. British Commandos too."

A short, weighty silence followed. "I'll tell you what I need from *you*, Colonel Caldwell," Reed said in an icy voice. "Ten men with maximum skills who need minimum training."

"And who speak French!"

"Yes!"

"I lost most of my best men," Caldwell said. "I'd like to keep the few I've got left, if I can help it, *sir*."

"You *can't* help it," Reed said. "You're going to have to lose ten more. Where's Gray's file? This is it? Rather thin, no? Okay, all of you out. Major Granger, send him in."

Before the camo netting was flung aside, Fletcher was already on his feet. *I offer God my contrite and grieving heart*, he thought as he struggled up. *But I feel something more will be required of me.*

"Don't just stand there—go on then, *go*. Do the best you can," Caldwell barked, storming past Fletcher, as if he just *knew* Fletcher's best wouldn't be good enough.

Caldwell was right. Lucas Brady was the best of men, and now he lay dead, and Fletcher was what was left. They were stuck with him. No wonder they were all so hopping mad.

"You got blood on your face," Stu whispered. "Wipe it off."

"What are you, my mother?"

"Should've cleaned yourself up," Stu said, pushing him forward.

"I was busy," Fletcher said, *drowning, blood, deafening fire, explosions, mud, vomit, death, Lucas*, the images flashing behind his unblinking stare. Fletcher did look ghastly. "Next you're going to tell me to be myself."

"No, no," said Stu, "whatever you do, Fletcher, *please*—don't be yourself."

Fletcher stood at attention, wary and dog-tired, caked with blood and grime, in front of a colonel sitting on an ammo crate with Fletcher's file in his hands. The officer's uniform was spotless, his jaw clean-shaven. He was dropped in from a different world. Jonathan Reed studied Fletcher's papers as if he were grading a medical exam. Eventually, he raised his eyes and studied Fletcher. Reed's expression was one of desperation and intensity. That was unnerving in a ranking officer. Usually they tried to maintain calm at all costs.

Fletcher hoped he was standing straight. When not muddy and gross, he presented better than this.

"So what's wrong with you?" Reed said. "Don't bullshit me."

"Colonel Caldwell is correct, sir."

"Not what I asked."

"If I said anything in my defense, I'd be branding my commanding officer a liar, and I won't do it. Sir."

"Ah, so you've got a mouth on you," Reed said, appraising him.

Fletcher hated to be appraised. He really picked the wrong profession to be in, didn't he? In the army, they examined your rectum through a microscope before issuing you a fork.

"You fought in North Africa?"

"Briefly, yes."

"And Anzio?"

"Yes."

"Anzio was a good op. Successful."

Fletcher paused, the corner of his mouth twitching.

"What, *not* successful?"

"Anzio is why we no longer have a 1st Ranger battalion," Fletcher said. "But successful in the first wave, yes." Only thirteen killed on the beach at Anzio. The men called them the unfuckinglucky thirteen. Not like Omaha, where thousands lay dead. No, not at all like Omaha.

"You're not dead," Reed said, as if saying something remarkably astute.

How to respond to that? "Yes, sir," Fletcher said.

Reed bent over his file. "Says here you were born in Thermopolis, Wyoming. Father Gideon Gray. Mother Beatrice Gray. One brother, one sister. French is listed under your skills, but not under your background. Why?" Reed raised his eyes.

"Probably just a miscommunication, sir."

"Uh-huh. So how does a small-town Wyoming boy speak fluent French?"

Fletcher weighed his words. "My mother is French."

"Why'd that take so long?"

Fletcher had no response he wanted to give.

"Soldier, speak freely," Reed said. "What am I missing? Just tell me what I don't know but should know."

"I'm just silent, sir. Taking it all in."

"Silent, yes. But also reluctant."

"Yes, sir," Fletcher said. "Silent *and* reluctant."

"Why?"

"Tell me what the mission is, sir. I'm ready to do what's necessary to help my country."

"But reluctantly."

"And silently," said Fletcher.

"Where's your French mother from?"

The only sounds were the planes overhead, the banging of canteen pots, an occasional *fuck*.

"New Orleans. A small parish in the bayou near Lake Pontchartrain."

"Huh," Reed said, his eyes gleaming with interest. "What's your full name? The French Catholics from Louisiana love to give their offspring elaborate names."

A beat went by. "John Fletcher Beauregard Du Soleil Gray."

Reed nodded approvingly. "Much better. Now *that* fits into what I understand, Lieutenant John Fletcher Beauregard Du Soleil Gray." He got up off the crate to stretch his legs. "So how did a French New Orleans woman get to Wyoming to meet and marry a rancher?"

"Not rancher. Trapper."

"Yes, by all means, correct me, Lieutenant."

Fletcher became argumentative when he was anxious. He over-compensated by lowering his voice and speaking slower and clearer. "People come from all over," Fletcher replied tersely.

"Nope, that's not it," Reed said.

"This is not a mystery to uncover," said Fletcher.

"I disagree, *mon ami*," Reed said. "Disagree most strongly. Rather, this isn't *the* mystery. But as you yourself just admitted, it may be *a* mystery."

Fletcher's inscrutable stare was his only reply. Jonathan Reed laughed. "Thank you for that, Lieutenant Gray," he said. "I haven't had a laugh since this fucking debacle began a week ago. Whatever else happens," he added, "it's obvious I've found my man."

Fletcher's face must have been a masterpiece in hesitation, because Reed quickly lost his good humor. "Look," he said, "I have zero fucking time to decide if you're right for my mission. You don't seem to think so. Caldwell doesn't think so. But I'm out of good options."

"In that case, sir, I'm *definitely* your man."

Reed tapped Fletcher's file, hard. "Be straight with me."

"I don't know how to be anything else," Fletcher said. "That's why I'm not usually choice number one for clandestine missions."

"On paper, you seem like an exceptional soldier."

Fletcher's face froze into a flat blank. Exceptional, he says, and I nod like I know who that is, like I know that man, the one who didn't crawl through a surf full of teeth, who didn't see a helmet with a head in it float by, who didn't count breaths and cartridges and arms without rifles and rifles without arms, who didn't lie there wondering if the sea could drown you faster than the Germans could kill you—

"May I speak freely, sir?"

"You must. At ease."

Fletcher put his hands behind his back. "The reason I may not be the ideal candidate for secret missions," he said, "is the same reason I've never been the ideal candidate for frontline assaults. I work best when there's time to plan, to prepare, to think." He hesitated. "I'm a chess player, sir. I won the Wyoming state championship seven years in a row—not that it matters here, but it explains a lot. In controlled situations, where I can contemplate the board, I can be extremely effective. That's not self-praise. It's a limitation. In fast-moving environments—when things go wrong—I'm not the one who acts first. Or best." Fletcher fought the impulse to lower his head. That was always Lucas. Lucas, who saw the shape of the battlefield—beach, mountain, meadow—before anyone else. Lucas who moved first, while Fletcher counted rounds and wounds and fallback positions. Together, they'd been a whole soldier.

"Lieutenant, I hear you," Reed said. "I also know that two days ago, on Omaha, despite what you must perceive as your failures . . ."

They'd landed four miles too far east! Lost fifty men out of seventy.

Pointe du Hoc had been secured, yes—but not by him, not by his men.

"Soldier," Reed said, almost cajolingly, "you were blown off course by heavy surf. You can't blame yourself for that."

Company Fuck, 2nd Rangers. Not Pointe du Hoc—Pointe du Fuck. *Company Fuck, fall in, if you're still breathing!*

It was a cruel joke, bleeding out on the wrong fucking beach.

Lucas never even made it out of the water.

Full moon, low tide, rough seas. All that training. The prep, the discussion, the anticipation—for what? Fletcher's lip trembled. Grief and guilt were so utterly invalidating.

His agonized face must have given him away.

"Here's what you did," Reed said. "You covered your wounded on an exposed beachhead. You charged the hill. You forced your way into enemy bunkers, you laid the thermite where it needed to be. You disabled their anti-artillery weapons the way you were commanded to. Not on Pointe du Hoc, no, but right here, above Easy Red."

Reed flung his arm toward the sea below the bluffs. "And let me tell you, Easy Red was the heart of the bloodiest part of Omaha. For hours, Easy Red was hell itself. Yes, Captain Lucas Brady's company sustained massive casualties, including him. But you returned to the beach after breaching the shingle and dragged your wounded comrades to safety. You're about to receive the Purple Heart and the Bronze Star. That doesn't seem like a small thing or the wrong thing, Lieutenant Gray. It's precisely the thing I need."

It had rained all day. A cold fog hung dreary and low; it hadn't lifted since dawn.

Fletcher hadn't taken off his boots in three days.

"Caldwell's not going to help us, that's for fucking sure," Reed said, as they meandered among the soldiers lying every which way on the headlands above the English Channel. "We'll have to build your team on our own. I've got briefs here on 140 men from your battalion. Another thirty from the Provisional Engineer Brigade—demolition maniacs, all. And fifteen from the Big Red One." Reed patted his leather satchel. "Let's sort through them, and you pick me nine more of the best."

"Sir, I'm not even the best."

"By all means, Lieutenant—pick nine men better than you."

They planted themselves on a stump, lit a smoke, and Fletcher leafed through the files, studying the names, ranks, skills, and records. Someone shot a squirrel out of a tree right above Reed's head. The rodent fell nearly on top of the colonel. Fletcher shook his head. Hawk. Had to be. Who else would be so ballsy and cavalier?

Reed watched Fletcher work. "So, not only are you an overachiever, Lieutenant Gray, you're an overthinker."

"You're just repeating back to me what I told you about myself, sir."

"I don't want you to love them, for God's sake," Reed said. "You're not picking a fucking bride!"

"I'm trying to find men who can get the job done."

"Scout, sniper, medic, fighter," Reed said. "That's how you select them and remember them. A pair of each. Two more for the just in case. How hard can it be?"

"Nearly fucking impossible—sir," Fletcher said. "For starters, many of the men in your files are dead." He pointed to the thick pile he'd thrown in the dirt. "And second, no one speaks French."

"Are you telling me, except for you, in the entire battalion of highly trained professionals, you don't have a single other soldier who speaks even basic French?" Reed was incredulous.

"We *had* a corporal who spoke French," Fletcher said.

"He's no good to me dead!"

Fletcher was thoughtful. "You've got many skilled fighters left," he said. "Demolition guys, mine defusers, master sharpshooters, assault raiders, world class navigators, doctors."

"They'll be dead in five seconds if they're stopped and can't utter a word in French, bomb skills or no."

Fletcher furrowed his brow, building contingencies in his head. "On the other side, will there be partisans to help us?"

"MI6 assures me yes." Reed sounded neither confident nor convinced.

Fletcher waited. "Um, is that it?"

"Yes. Oh, and—you're wheels up in forty-eight hours."

"Forty-eight hours!" Fletcher lowered his voice. "I don't have a team. You've got no one but me."

"You should get cracking on that," Reed said, waving his hand over the discarded briefs. "Seeing as all ten of you are airborne on Saturday."

"Maybe we need two of *me*, sir," Fletcher said after three cigarettes.

"Ahh, he jokes," Reed said.

Fletcher wasn't the least bit joking.

"I know a man who might be able to help us." He spoke with overwhelming reluctance. "Not only does he know everybody, he may also speak French, though I don't vouch either for him or his language skills."

Reed snapped alive. "Who is it?"

"Rafael Canario. Assault Commandos No. 12."

"Ah, yes! He's one of Gordon Firth's guys? The Butcher's Dozen?"

"Hmm."

"Excellent. Quick, let's go find him. Gordon owes me a favor anyway. What? Why are you shaking your head? What's wrong with Canario?"

"What isn't wrong with him."

"I just heard the same about you. And look how well you're shaping up."

17

Ashes

Across the bluffs, through the mud and grime they traipsed. There was no need for formalities—not when both colonel and lieutenant were ankle-deep in sludge. Reed's uniform was no longer pristine. He fit right in.

"What are we calling our mission, sir?" Fletcher asked.

"How about Operation Santa Fe."

Fletcher nodded. "Santa Fe like the capital of New Mexico? Or *Santa Fe* like holy fire?"

"Yes to both," Reed said. "And more like *un*holy fire."

"Understood. Is New Mexico significant for reasons that aren't immediately clear to me, Colonel?"

"Yes. You're asking good questions, soldier. Keep going."

"When will I know what's required of me?" Fletcher asked as they made their way between splayed-out men, stepping over limbs and gear, searching for Rafael. "What's my objective?"

"To save the world?"

"Well, sure," Fletcher said, responding dry and in kind. "But *after* that?"

Reed stopped walking. Fletcher, taking his cue, stopped too and turned to face him. He could see the difficulty with which Reed was weighing his words. Conflict distorted his face.

"There are sixty barrels of dangerous explosive, hidden aboard a ship that's docked at Antwerp," Reed said, each word delivered with slow precision. "They were supposed to get offloaded and secured without incident, but . . ."

"There was an incident?"

"You could say that. A Nazi assault team got suspicious and decided to investigate. The crew squared up and—everyone was killed."

"Everyone?"

"Except for one crew, which is how we learned anything about it."

"When was this?"

"Last Friday."

"A week ago? So what is my mission?"

"I need you to drop into Belgium, sneak into Antwerp, and secure those barrels."

Fletcher waited. "Secure them how?"

"However you see fit," said Reed. "Your prerogative."

"Is the ship guarded?"

"Probably."

"Am I supposed to engage the Germans?"

"You do whatever needs to be done."

"Do you want me to sail the ship out of the harbor?"

"I don't know if that'll be possible," Reed said, glancing around at nothing Fletcher could see. Maybe searching for a way to explain the unexplainable. "These barrels of explosive cannot get into German hands," Reed said. "How you accomplish that is up to you. Full field discretion, Fletcher. It just has to be done."

"Maybe detonate it?"

"No." That *no* was so adamant, Reed accidentally woke two corporals lying dead asleep on the ground nearby. "They won't explode," Reed said, clarifying something and nothing.

"Explosive that doesn't explode?"

"More like starter for an explosive."

"Sixty barrels of starter?"

Reed nodded. "Think of it like iron ore. A pile of rocks isn't going to cut you up. But smelt it, forge it, shape it, and you can make a blade sharp enough to split a human down his spine."

"Are these barrels heavy like iron?"

Reed rocked his head from side to side. "Much heavier," he said. "Twice as heavy."

"Twice as heavy as *iron*?" Fletcher was astonished.

Reed patted him and slowly resumed walking. "Son," he said, "strap in. The weight is the least shocking fact about this whole fucking thing."

"What does each barrel weigh?"

"Probably 300–350 pounds."

Fletcher whistled. He did a quick calculation in his head. "Eighteen *thousand* pounds?"

"Eight metric tons, yes," Reed said, casting Fletcher an impressed glance.

"Sir . . . what the hell am I supposed to do with eighteen thousand pounds of bomb?"

"Not sure. And not bomb. Bomb starter. Figure it out when you get there—where's this Canario fella?"

After asking around, they learned they were a half-mile from the British encampment and headed there through the mud. Fletcher was grateful for the time; he had questions. Reed, however, seemed deeply averse to answering them.

"Sir, you said the cargo was hidden?"

"I hope so."

"But there's a chance the Germans have already found it?"

"Why would they find it?" Reed sounded truculent.

"I don't know, but . . ." Fletcher hesitated, choosing his words carefully. The mission sounded insane. The cargo wasn't even explosives! So what if the Germans found it? And besides . . . "Correct me if I'm wrong, Colonel," Fletcher said, "but aren't the Germans making V2 rockets? Those are some motherfucking badass rockets. Each payload carries like a ton of TNT."

"And your point?"

"My point is maybe we should let sleeping dogs lie," Fletcher said. "Sixty barrels of starter doesn't sound like much. How many possible bombs could they build with that?"

"One."

"One bomb?"

Reed's face was grim. "Fletcher, there are things in this universe you will never understand," he said. "And that's okay. Smarter men than you and me are unable to understand them. You'll have to take my word for it. This is *nothing* like the V2 rocket."

"*More* incendiary?"

"You could say that."

"How much more?"

Reed stayed silent so long, Fletcher wasn't sure he'd heard the question.

"A V2 rocket levels a building," Reed said. "This bomb flattens a city. And then burns the rubble to cinder. Instantly."

Fletcher gave a skeptical smirk. Reed didn't stop walking when he spoke. "I know it doesn't seem real. But the thermal pulse at ground zero of a bomb made from this starter, if you will—in the core of the explosion—is several million degrees Celsius."

Fletcher assumed Reed had misspoken. "*Millions* of degrees?" he said lightly. "I think that may be hotter than the sun."

"It *is* hotter than the sun."

The smirk was erased from Fletcher's face. "You're not serious."

"Unfortunately, Fletcher, I most assuredly am," said Reed. "The temperature of this bomb if it explodes is hotter than the fucking sun. If this thing detonates, you don't burn—you vanish." He shivered. "You're instantly vaporized. Nothing of you will remain. Maybe a shadow on a wall before the wall itself is blown apart by the shockwave, but that's it. You'll be turned into carbon dust in a fraction of a second."

"That doesn't sound plausible, Colonel," Fletcher muttered faintly, feeling his nerve endings go cold.

"I wish it weren't," Reed said. "Can you even imagine a war waged by the Nazis with a weapon like that? Securing the cargo is the most important mission you and your men will ever undertake. Your best efforts are the minimum requirement. You have only one objective. To stop the Germans from getting their hands on these barrels. Whatever you can do, you must do. Whatever sacrifices are required must be made. If we fail, it's not the end of a thousand men—it's the end of mankind."

18

Coffee from Kivu

Rheinhardt searched once, searched a second time, and now was below deck again, in the forward hold, searching a third time for a groove, a dent, a metal ring—anything that would indicate a false floor. He left the flashlight in the corner and crawled along the planks, feeling around with the tips of his fingers. Whatever it was, it resisted discovery. As if it had a will, as if it whispered *don't* to anyone who came near. But Rheinhardt would not be deterred—

And finally—

There it was.

After grueling hours of creeping, he found it: the slightest raised groove, nearly imperceptible even to his bare palms.

He wedged his military knife between the boards and, with some effort, popped up the hidden hatch. What relief he felt, what vindication. Down below lay a small secret compartment toward the bow of the ship. It was pitch black inside. There were no windows, no light of any kind.

He grabbed his crank-operated flashlight and, holding the handle in his teeth, carefully descended the short ladder into the crypt below. It almost didn't matter what was down there. The most important thing was that there *was* a down there. He wasn't delusional. His senses and deductive powers had not failed him. How cleverly they'd built and concealed it! Behind steel panels, sealed with rivets, disguised as a single ballast block on the blueprints. So easy to miss.

At first glance, the vault looked empty. Rheinhardt spun around and bumped against an immovable object. He thought it was a dividing wall. When he shone his inadequate light on it, he saw rows of short stocky barrels, neatly arranged. The casks weren't much bigger than cremation urns. They sat silent and squat in the bowels of the gloomy darkness, packed tightly together. Each row had twelve barrels, stacked two high. There were five rows. A quick calculation told him he was looking at sixty barrels of whatever it was, hidden in a windowless tomb.

The cylinders were made of a heavy metal alloy and had flat clamp lids and recessed side handles. He tried to move one. It was like trying to move an ocean liner. It didn't so much as wobble. Forget about moving it, he couldn't even rock it. Was it his imagination, or did the barrel feel warm to the touch? From the look of the anodized steel, he was certain he'd feel a still, deathly coolness. Instead it was warm.

That was deeply unsettling.

He climbed out of the hold, ascended the stairs and smoked two cigarettes on the rain-slicked deck, trying to get his bearings. It was Friday, June 9, exactly one week since the ill-fated morale event that ended in the deaths of two dozen men.

Rheinhardt almost didn't want to open the barrels. He spent a few extra minutes on deck cranking the flashlight to full power, delaying his return below. He almost—not quite, but almost—didn't want to know what it was.

Back downstairs, he took off his black leather gloves and pressed his bare palm against the barrel. It was definitely warm. He ran his hand over the adjacent ones. They were all warm.

Rheinhardt was not a man easily shaken, but this shook him. The number of the barrels, combined with their inexplicable weight and warmth, sitting silent and menacing in the entrails of a merchant ship, was something neither his brain nor his heart could process.

Carefully, he unclamped one of the lids with his knife, pried it open like a paint can and trained his flashlight on the interior. For a long moment, he stood staring.

The compact metal barrel was filled to the brim with rocks. Jagged, non-uniform, packed to the top. At a casual glance it looked like coal, except the rocks weren't quite ebony.

And who'd want to hide coal?

Rheinhardt reached in to feel them. Involuntarily, his hand snapped back. It was as if some charge had leapt from the stones into his palm, heated his blood, and sent hot particles of unease through his very heart.

What was this?

For a moment—a moment was all he could stand—he switched off the flashlight and, in the dark, stared into the open barrel as if gazing into the void of space. Did the dark stones give off an eerie glow? Faint, almost imperceptible, but *yes*. Some internal illumination emanated from a pile of rocks, so heavy and dense it took steel canisters to bear their weight.

He flicked his light back on. The rocks gave off a troubling warmth, a peculiar near-glow. Some of them were marbled with long glossy veins of gold and orange, as if they had been painted from within in tiger stripes of flaming gamboge.

It looked like fire in solid form.

There was something ancient, terrifying, and hideous about them. He reached out, then stopped. After a moment, he pulled on his gloves before lifting out one of the glittering black stones.

Could they be *radioactive*?

Was that even possible?

Could this be . . .

Uranium?

PART II

La Ligne

"I have a rendezvous with Death,
At some disputed barricade."

Alan Seeger

19

Gray Ghosts

Briskly, Fletcher walked through the mud alongside Reed, trying to keep up. He was no slouch in the height department, and he was younger than Reed by probably fifteen years, but the man walked with a pace that bordered on the abnormal. He could outrun a pronghorn.

Reed walked and talked. While maintaining the Olympic pace, he leafed through the stack of damp dossiers. “It’s quite ironic,” Reed said, “how this morning I was shouting up and down the bluffs for ten men who spoke French, and now I’m just praying for ten men who have a pulse.”

“Nine men, sir. I still seem to have a pulse.”

They were building a team out of the wreckage of D-Day, one man at a time.

“So what’s wrong with Rafael Canario?” Reed said. “You think he might be dead?”

“No, he’s alive.”

“How do you know?”

“Because he’s got the luck of a jackrabbit in a minefield,” said Fletcher. “But he and I . . . I don’t know if we’re a good fit, sir.”

“Why?”

“We’re not compatible temperamentally.”

“Why?”

Rafael always acted first and thought second. And Fletcher was just the opposite. A terrible combination.

“He’s headstrong,” Fletcher said. “Impulsive. Loud, brash, full of himself.”

“But he speaks French,” Reed said.

“Yes, he’s a slightly obnoxious French-speaker.”

“But a good soldier?”

“Yes, sir.”

"Just insufferable?"

Pause. "Yes, sir." What made matters worse was Rafael's reaction when Fletcher and Reed finally found him, sitting cross-legged in the mud, pitching cards into a tin bucket. When he saw Fletcher, he leapt to his feet, cigarette in mouth, cap on the ground.

"Fletch!" he yelled—and ran over as if he'd found a long-lost friend. He pumped Fletcher's hand, bear-hugged him, and saluted Reed, unfazed by the seniority, grinning like the world belonged to him. "Good to see you still kicking, buddy," he said to Fletcher. "How've you been?" The reckless glint was back in Rafael's eyes—not even the carnage of D-Day could burn it out for long. The mud and a week-old black beard carved the strong lines of his Basque face deeper, setting off the black eyes that missed nothing and had nothing to hide. Despite the blood and dirt, Rafael was still every bit himself—rakish, brazen, disgustingly good-looking.

He wasn't tall; that was the only mercy.

"Staff Sergeant Canario, we've been looking for you," Reed said, glancing at Fletcher as if to say, *What the hell, Gray? Look at this guy. He's fucking awesome.*

Yes, yes, Fletcher wanted to say. *Everybody thinks he's awesome. That's what's wrong with him.*

"You were looking for me?" Rafael grinned. "Uh-oh. What did I do? I mean, what did I do now?" The splendid teeth were on full display, the dark eyes burning, alive and bright.

"Button your tunic, soldier, tie your boots, doff your cap, and come with us," Reed said. "You have two minutes to get yourself together. We'll wait." As Rafael raced off, Reed turned to Fletcher. "I don't understand your hesitation, Lieutenant. He seems to think you're the best of friends."

"Understanding human beings is not his strong suit, sir."

Reed laughed. "We don't need his psychological insight, Fletcher. We need him because he can blow shit up—and get shit done. In French."

Without knowing, caring, or even asking about the objective of the mission, Rafael heard the words "Belgium," "elite team," "who's still alive?", and immediately fired off a dozen names for Reed to choose from. The nerve. Fletcher wanted to point out that he didn't need help selecting his own crew. Except he did—which only made him resent Rafael more.

Scout. Sniper. Medic. Fighter. "I've got a great medic for you, Fletch," Rafael said.

"I have my own medic, thank you very much," said Fletcher.

"We need two medics, Lieutenant Gray," Reed said before leaving to find two close-combat fighters Rafael had suggested.

"Let me tell you about mine," Rafael said, lowering his voice and leaning toward Fletcher. "He's been with my unit since Tunisia. You sure you haven't met him?"

"Haven't needed him," Fletcher said.

"Good thing, too," Rafael said, cheerfully chewing a wad of gum. "Listen, I won't sugarcoat him for you—"

"What's wrong with him?"

"He's a bit of an asshole. No other way to describe it."

The medic sat under a ragged scrap of canvas pitched over a supply crate, shading him from the sudden, too-bright sun. He was a slim man in his early thirties, with light brown hair plastered to his forehead and the pale, academic expression of someone who belonged indoors. His sleeves were rolled with surgical precision, and a battered pair of wire-rimmed glasses slid halfway down his nose. He was perched, a Latin book of proverbs balanced on his knee, cigarette burning low, looking for all the world as if he were enjoying a civilized afternoon instead of performing triage at the end of the world. When Rafael said, "Knock, knock," the medic didn't even look up. He merely lifted a finger to shush them, as if Rafael was nothing more than a fly buzzing past.

"Lieutenant Belvedere, eyes up," Rafael said. "I have Lieutenant Gray with me."

Belvedere somehow managed to roll his eyes without lifting them from the book. "What is it now, Canario?" Belvedere said, in clipped British exasperation. Sighing theatrically, as if already fed up with whatever stupidity was about to unfold, he said, "Don't tell me. You need me for a mission."

"Yes," said Fletcher. "We need you to come and meet my commander, Jonathan Reed of the OSS. Immediately," he added when Belvedere didn't move.

Finally Belvedere glanced up, eyeing Fletcher as if he were diagnosing a skin rash. "So, I must meet not only with *your* approval, but also with the approval of another Yank who outranks you?" Belvedere's disdain could not have been sharper. But at last he got up and followed them.

"Told you," Rafael said as they walked across the headlands, Belvedere trailing at a distance, clutching his book. "The guy's an absolute wanker. But when shit goes down, trust me—there's no one else you'd rather have in the field."

"Rider," Fletcher said, "you're not thinking this through. We have to be close to this guy for . . ." He didn't actually know how long. "However long to achieve our objective."

"What objective would that be, Fletch?"

"Not to be an absolute bloody idiot," Belvedere said crisply from behind them.

Fletcher stopped walking and slowly turned around.

"Excuse me, Lieutenant Belvedere . . ."

Belvedere corrected him. "Actually, it's Leftenant. British rank—just under captain, *Lef*-tenant Fletcher."

"My mission, *my* command,," said Fletcher. "Otherwise, ask Colonel Reed to put you in charge."

"Technically, that's *Lef*-tenant Colonel Reed," Belvedere muttered.

"I didn't hear if we were all clear, *Loo*-tenant Belvedere," Fletcher said.

"We're *all* clear, *Lef*-tenant Fletcher," said Belvedere.

"Oh, this is going to be fun," Fletcher muttered, moving off again. "Thanks, Canario. I don't remember *asking* you for a medic recommendation."

"I'm a giver," said Rafael, clapping Fletcher on the back.

From behind them, Belvedere spoke again. "It's only polite to be more courteous to those who saved your sorry ass."

"What's he talking about?" Fletcher said.

"Belvy, shut the fuck up," Rafael shot back. "Or I'll tell your commanding officer what your full name is."

"Do it if you want a bayonet butt between your shoulder blades."

"What's his name?" whispered Fletcher.

"Enobarbus," said Rafael, already laughing. "Enobarbus Percival Belvedere."

Fletcher blinked. "Wow."

"Rider!" a big brutish man scooped Rafael off his feet. "How you been, my man?"

"I been well, Briggsy, you?"

"Can't complain. You pegged me for this thing?" When Rafael nodded, Briggs shook him again. "That's great. That's fuckin' awesome. Where are we going?"

"No one's telling," Rafael said. "Strictly need to know basis."

"I need to fuckin' know," Briggs said.

Reed and Fletcher watched on.

"What do you think of him?" Reed asked quietly.

"Bill Briggs, technical sergeant, demolition and tactics from the Provisional Engineer Brigade," Fletcher replied. "Tough guy. Plus he's alive."

Reed stayed silent.

"Do you have reservations, sir? Is he a bit . . . *loud* for a clandestine mission?"

"Yes," Reed said. "But you do need a wrecking ball. Canario and Briggs seem to know each other well."

"I told you, sir, Canario knows everybody. Like Briggs, he's also not the most subtle of men. Why? Are you reconsidering him too? Wise choice. He's an absolute maniac."

Reed turned to Fletcher with an amused half-smile. "So no Canario, no Briggs, no Belvedere. Who *are* you recommending, Lieutenant Gray? The soft-spoken and courteous medic Howard Miller?"

"Yes," Fletcher said. "He's excellent for a stealth operation, sir. Besides triage, he's got many other skills. He's an engineer. He can fix, hotwire, or sabotage vehicles in a million different ways. And for the sniper, I'm recommending Laurence Turner."

"Who?"

"Hawk Turner. The man who shot the squirrel above your head while we were going through the papers. He's the best shot in Normandy, and therefore the world. Plus, he hardly ever speaks."

Reed smiled. "Fletcher, we can't have an entire team made up of people like you!"

Why not, Fletcher wanted to ask. Quiet, polite, pensive men who got the job done. What was wrong with that?

Fletcher found "Hawk" Turner sitting by himself, cleaning his spotless rifle. The Sniper Springfield had a black matte finish, a custom scope, and looked brand new. It was some weapon. Hawk was blond with elegant bones and a pianist's long, slender fingers. His hazel eyes were so eerily light, they looked pale gold in the sun. That was probably why Hawk didn't make eye contact with strangers. He barely even glanced at people he knew. He nodded to Fletcher, but ignored Rafael, which in Fletcher's book was a plus, but clearly not in Rafael's.

"I don't know about that guy," Rafael said after meeting him.

"Right man for the job. Trust me," Fletcher said. Hawk required minimal explanation. You told him he was needed, and that was that. He didn't ask why or even where. Fletcher found Hawk's acute lack of curiosity extremely appealing. But it bothered Rafael.

"He didn't even ask where we were going!" Rafael said.

"Neither did you!"

"That's because I already heard you and Reed talking. You only thought you were being quiet. I heard every word. Operation Santa Fe. Plane, drop, Antwerp, barrels of something or other."

"What the fuck?" Fletcher muttered.

Rafael grinned. "Got hearing like a wolf's. So don't talk shit about me, because I hear everything."

Fletcher thought back to the hundreds of times he'd talked shit about Rafael.

Rafael raised his eyebrows and nodded. "I hear fucking *everything*," he whispered with a good-natured grin.

After an exhausting day of nonstop interviews, by Friday night, 24 hours before takeoff, Fletcher and Rafael reported to Reed that they couldn't find a tenth guy to complete the team. It had taken some hard digging to scrape together even the nine.

Reed took stock of what they had. "We've got you two, the two medics—Howie Miller and this Percival Belvedere fellow with the bedside manner of a vulture . . ."

"Enobarbus, sir," Rafael said. "Percival's his middle name."

"Dear God." Reed went on. "For fighters we've got Brian Green, a heavy weapons corporal from Second Commandos, and Arthur Brown from the Fourth, a stealth specialist." Reed looked up. "You vouch for them, Canario?"

"Yes. Brown especially. He's a close-quarters combat genius."

"Okay," Reed said. "And we've got another fighter, Bill Briggs, that's three, but only one sniper, the rodent shooter Hawk Turner."

"Can't find another sniper, sir," said Fletcher. "But the rest of us can shoot."

"You're not snipers!" Reed looked down at his notes. "And you've only got one scout, this Wolski guy from the Carpathian Unit. If you lose your sniper and your scout, then what?"

"We've got Canario for the fighting, and me for the sniping and scouting, sir."

Reed shook his head, slapping shut the dossier. "You go in with what you've got," he said. "What choice do we have." He didn't look optimistic.

"What we've got is a stew of not great," said Fletcher as he and Rafael started toward their temporary camp near the makeshift airbase.

"Speak for yourself. Briggs, Brown, Green, they're the best."

"Maybe," Fletcher said. "But your Belvedere is a pompous ass. A lot of pomp and ass for such a diminutive man."

"He's also the best."

"And you? I suppose you're also the best?"

Smile ear to ear. "Hey, but look, you got us Hawk and Miller. They're pretty good, right?"

"Hawk is the best," Fletcher said. "What about this Wolski guy?" Janusz Wolski was from the Independent Carpathian Brigade—formed in Syria in 1940 and made up mostly of Polish exiles escaping Soviet occupation. They fought with the British Commandos in Africa—Tobruk, Gazala, Tunisia. "He's Polish, you said? Does he speak English?"

"I thought you wanted him to speak French?"

"*Does* he speak French?"

"Don't think so."

"Rider!"

"Don't yell at *me*. You wanted the best navigator. I got you the best. This guy led us out of the fucking desert when for a hundred miles in every direction there was nothin' but sand. One hundred miles of sand, and Wolski pointed north like Moses. You have no idea what he can do."

20

Contact Points

"Girls, girls! Pipe down," Charlie said. "This isn't a cotillion."

She had hastily called in her team for an emergency meeting in the Lillehaven glade. London was sending in a unit in less than 24 hours, and her women weren't informed or ready.

Charlie was pacing, while the others lounged on the grass: Louise, of course. Brigitte, Mireille, Hildimar, and the twins Margot and Maxine. It was a crisp Saturday morning. In the breeze, white cherry blossoms floated like cotton. Charlie tried to get her girls back on track—to the paramilitary details. But the day felt too enchanted for war, too soft for what lay ahead.

"How many men did you say are incoming?" said Brigitte, big, blonde, and beaming.

"Not men," Charlie replied. "*Soldiers*. In a war. In occupied territory. Near a militarized seaport."

"Of course, Charlie," Brigitte said. "When did you say the soldiers are being dropped in?"

"Tomorrow. At dawn. Eighteen hours from now. The insertion point is five kilometers from here. And we have a lot to do. They all need fake papers, civilian clothes, a place to stay. Weapons, possibly—more weapons—and other logistical help."

"*La Ligne* is here to help, make no mistake about *that*," said Brigitte. She could lift a barrel and still bat her lashes. *La Ligne* was the name of Charlie's partisan unit—a tight-knit cell of women who ran intelligence, moved supplies, and carried out covert orders for Omloop, who ran the larger resistance. They were unseen, unsung, and essential.

"Charlotte, you forgot to answer Gitta's question about how many soldiers are incoming." That was Mireille, willowy and patrician, who always looked as if she'd just wandered off the stage at the Paris Ballet. Poised and overdressed, Mireille removed her white gloves before she spoke, which for her was tantamount to disrobing.

"All of you, eyes on me," said Charlie. "Something urgent and grave is going on. An SOE operative from MI6 is running point on this thing, so it's as secret and high up as it gets." The Special Operations Executive was the most covert division of British intelligence. "And I don't have to remind you," Charlie added, reminding them anyway, "that Antwerp blackshirts are knocking on every door looking for an African man and anyone who might have helped him escape."

"Which would be *you, Shar-lee*." That was Hildimar, grave and gaunt, with the voice of a church bell.

"I'm not pointing fingers, Hildi," said Charlie. "I'm simply sketching the outlines of the gravity of our operation."

"We hear you loud and clear," Brigitte said. "Right now we're gathering important information, so we know where to focus our energies. Which is why we keep asking how many soldiers are incoming."

"Yes, Charlie, it's not like we're asking for their names," piped up the sunny Maxine, she of the identical Martin twins, whittling something with her knife and pretending not to smile. Next to her sat her sister Margot, who wasn't whittling or smiling.

"How would Charlie know their names?" Margot said. "*Think* before you speak, Maxi."

Charlie had known these women since girlhood—before the curfews, before the armbands. Since the occupation, they'd been brilliant: testing the vigilance of checkpoint guards with forged papers and plastic charm, slipping notes into flowerpots, photographing Nazi troop carriers from second-story windows. In April they spent two days scrubbing grease-caked ball bearings clean of herring rot—an incredible op that had slipped past the Germans in plain sight. They'd done everything she asked. And here they were, on the surface all business but underneath like seminary girls who'd been told the fencing team was coming to town.

"We're serious, Shar-*leee*," said Hildimar. "We need more information." If Hildimar was saying this—Hildi, the most solemn not just of Charlie's women but of all the women in the world—you knew the mission objectives were slipping away from the unit leader.

Only Louise sat quietly, like she was lost in thought. "Are we done soon?" she said. "I have to make my stops."

"Saul?" said Charlie.

"And Fitz," replied Louise. She'd found out Fitz was in jail and looked miserable about it.

"Lou, can you bake something to welcome the troops to Belgium?" said Brigitte.

"Now we're the welcoming committee?" said Louise. "They'll be lucky to get a hunk of dry bread and a bar of soap."

"It won't hurt to offer them one of your lemon cakes, Louise," said Mireille in a prim tone.

Quietly, Charlie said, "Actually, Mireille is right, Loosh. If Saul gets them, why shouldn't the brave Allies be offered a tasty treat?"

"Oh, not you too, Charlie," said Louise, pressing her palm to her forehead.

"Lou, bake, don't bake," Brigitte said. "Let's return to the matter at hand. Charlotte, don't you want us to prepare for the men's arrival? We don't want a situation in which twelve men might be dropping down, and we're not ready."

"Twelve men!" Maxine exclaimed. "That seems so many." The women were no longer lounging but sitting upright, at attention.

"Max is right," Margot said. "I don't know if we can collect a dozen outfits by tomorrow."

"And without Fitz, we can't get the forged documents," Louise said. Fitz was Omloop's forger.

"Omloop has extras," Charlie said. "We'll be fine." Louise was right, though. One way or another, they had to get her brother out. Her mother was losing her mind with Fitz in jail.

"How much food do we need to get?" Brigitte said. "Are we going to need some black market supplements? If yes, who's paying for that? These are important details, Charlie. To feed six men is one thing. To feed a dozen is quite another."

"And where are these dozen men going to stay?" Mireille said, fanning herself with one of her gloves. She suddenly looked quite perspired.

"Two in each of our houses?" Brigitte said.

"Yes, sure," said Louise. "My mother the alderwoman is going to let me bring *two soldiers* into our house."

"Well, then, Marg, you and I will have to take four," said Maxine.

"Pipe down, sister," Margot said. "No one is giving us four men."

"I'm just trying to be helpful," Maxine said. She was the optimistic one.

"No matter how helpful you want to be, we're not getting four men," said Margot, the *not* optimistic one. "We'll be lucky to get one."

Charlie raised her arm to calm her crew. "Who said anything about twelve men?" she said. "From where in the heavens did you get that number?"

"Well, you didn't present us with another number, Charlie," Brigitte said solemnly.

"Because I don't know!" Something stirring was creeping into the glade, and Charlie didn't know how to nip it in the bud.

"Did you say they're flying in *tomorrow* at dawn?" said Hildimar. "That's not enough time to prepare. Why are we lollygagging? There's so much to do."

"Girls, I can't call them and tell them to come a few days later because we're not ready to receive them," said Charlie. "They're coming when they're coming. And we've got to be ready, that's all there is to it. We need to stop everything else and focus only on this." She shuddered.

"If that's what's required of us," said Brigitte, all bloom and no shade, "then as patriots and partisans, that is what we'll do." She saluted Charlie.

"Save it for the parade, Gitta," Charlie said under her breath.

"Don't worry, Marg and I will get the clothes sorted," Maxine said. Their mother was a seamstress.

"How can we sort it if we don't know how many are coming?" cried Margot.

"Charlie," Mireille said, "Didn't you say you're driving to a Brussels market today? Can I come with you? I need to pick up a few things."

"For the soldiers?" Charlie was planning to go to Jette. She wanted to let Robert Capelle know what was happening.

"Not exactly for the soldiers," Mireille said. "I need a new hat."

"You might as well get two hats, Mireille," Brigitte said. "One for me."

"I don't need a hat, Shar-lee," Hildi intoned. "I'm going to go sharpen my knives. Do you think the soldiers will need knives? I have plenty."

"I think they're bringing their own, Hildi."

"Who's going to get them the ammo they need if Fitz is in the clink?" said Hildi. "Knives are better than nothing."

Louise pulled Charlie aside. Charlie was glad to focus elsewhere for a moment. "I went to Lost Hope," Louise said.

"Did you get the Eureka?" The Eureka was the ground-based transponder Charlie needed to signal Rebecca, the airborne receiver, to guide the plane to its drop zone in the darkness. Omloop stashed many of his resistance supplies behind the walls of the belfry at Lost Hope. He didn't like to secrete anything in their home church, in case the Nazis came looking. The decrepit monastery with deaf ancient nuns was ideal for concealment.

"Yes, I got the dang thing," Louise said, "but I wish you'd told me how heavy it was."

"How would I know? I've never seen one."

"But while I was in Lost Hope, I went to visit our friends . . ."

"And?" Charlie held her breath.

"They're hanging in there. But the crows came knocking the other day at dawn. The nuns didn't let them in, of course, but Ngomo grabbed the boy and they fled into the woods. Calm down—I found them and brought them back, but Ngomo doesn't want to stay there anymore. And the nuns are jumpy as hell. Last thing they want is Nazi trouble."

The men couldn't get here fast enough, Charlie thought, so Ngomo could become their problem. But Zeus still remained hers. What a nightmare it all was. She just couldn't get ahead.

The girls were calling them back to the meeting, ablaze with questions.

"How many of us did they request?" Margot asked.

"They demanded—all my boots on the ground," said Charlie.

"Well, lady warriors, that sounds like a *platoon* of men," exclaimed Brigitte. "Get me a hat, Mireille. And Louise . . ."

"Yes, yes," Louise said. "For the war effort, I'll make some lemon cakes."

"I promise you there are not going to be enough men," said Margot.

"You're such a doomsaying thundercloud," said Maxine to her twin. "You announce a sunrise and manage to sound like you're reporting a funeral."

"Trust me, sister," said Margot, "not enough men will feel *nothing* like a sunrise."

"Girls, girls," Charlie muttered, but she was out of fight. And next to her Louise whispered, nearly inaudibly, *Leave them be, Charlie. They'll do what's required of them. They're just starving for life. They want to feel alive, if only for a moment.*

21

Photograph

The pounding of his heart was so loud, Rheinhardt thought the ship's engine had turned on. He stood frozen, staring into the dark hold, considering the possibilities.

Before today, Rheinhardt had only read about such things in books. He was born and raised in a small alpine town near Salzburg and educated in Berlin, where he completed a doctoral thesis in naval engineering at Humboldt University. Before joining the Nazi Party in 1935, all Erich von Rheinhardt ever wanted was to design warships. He loved their weight, their symmetry, the predictable action of steel under great tension.

Being third in command at a busy port in an occupied territory was as close as he was ever going to get.

But this—this was something else entirely. He had lived and studied in Berlin during the years when atomic science caught fire in lecture halls and laboratories across the nascent Reich. In those Berlin days, his circle included physicists and chemists who debated neutron capture and decay as easily as others spoke of politics or sport. Rheinhardt himself found chemistry and physics too messy. He preferred the order of ship design: ballast and balance, steel and seaworthiness.

Yet, as a boy, Rheinhardt had for a time been obsessed with stories of the Polish woman scientist who made rocks glow in the dark. *Madame Curie.* That same thrill gripped him now. Whatever was in these barrels wasn't coal, or tin, or iron.

It was power.

Wrapping one of the heavier stones into a handkerchief, he slipped it carefully into the large front pocket of his overcoat and slammed the lid shut. Before climbing the stairs, he stared at the five dozen sickly black barrels, pressed silently against one another.

He sped down Glaskaai to his office at Baert Haus.

Everyone else in administration was headquartered at Antwerp Port Authority—the sprawling modern brick building in the center of town. Not Rheinhardt. That multi-story stone edifice was staffed with insufferable clerks and bureaucrats.

Instead, he found himself a tiny wooden outpost on a side street off Napoleonkaai. The street was called Madelievenlaan, or Daisy Lane. It was no more than an alley, close to the main docks of the Scheldt, tucked behind a row of buildings and shaded by some half-dead poplars.

Sitting low and crooked, the house itself was a two-story timber cabin. It had been built in the nineteenth century and was historically used as the home of the harbor overseer. The last overseer was named Bartholomew Baert, and so the place became known as Baert Haus. Rheinhardt claimed the vacant house as soon as he laid eyes on it. He had the windows fixed, the floors redone, some other structural work performed—and moved in by Christmas 1940.

Behind the house stood a detached brick shed, obscured by birch and blackthorn and grayed by time and salt air. It was called *"der Raum"* in whispers. It had no windows, one large lock, and a drain in the center of the floor. Rheinhardt used it for *special* interrogations.

Hubner worked in the front room of Baert Haus, near a closet that contained the current year's shipping records. The rest of the files, three years' worth of manifests, were stored upstairs, where Rheinhardt could keep them close.

Rheinhardt strode past Hubner, barking that he was not to be disturbed, and slammed his office door, locking it.

Carefully he took off his coat, eased the wrapped stone out of the pocket, and sank into the leather chair behind his massive desk, holding the rock in his lap.

He looked around, as if wondering what to do next. He took in the coat stand, the maps on the walls—of Antwerp, of Belgium, of Germany, of Europe, and of the little town in Austria where he was from called Bad Vigaun. In his locked desk drawer was a pair of binoculars, some morphine, and interrogation records from the last four years. From underneath the records, he pulled out an old photograph. It was of his mother and father flanking ten-year-old Erich during their one and only trip to the Berchtesgaden Salt Mines in Bavaria. It was the only photograph Rheinhardt had of himself as a child. His father, a telegraph clerk, was a deeply serious man, not prone to such whimsical things as photography, and his mother, a painter, held photography in high contempt.

For many minutes Rheinhardt sat, lost in thought.

At last he got to his feet, placed the stone carefully on the desk and emptied the drawer of its contents. He returned the photograph to the drawer, placing it face up. Tearing a sheet from his shipping manifest logbook, he placed the blank paper on top of the photograph. Unwrapping the warm rock, he dropped it into the corner—being careful not to touch it with his bare fingers—and shut the drawer.

For five minutes he sat on his hands—and then opened the drawer.

The paper was still blank. The rock was still warm. Rheinhardt slammed the drawer shut.

He put on his coat and turned off the light, preparing to walk home, but reconsidered. Instead, he lit a cigarette and sat in the visitor chair, dragging it as far away from his desk as possible. He sat in the corner, near the small closet which hid an exit door—in case Rheinhardt ever needed to sneak out of the building without confronting anyone in his reception area.

When Hubner checked on him an hour later, he was still in the chair in the corner, the unsmoked cigarette burned down to ash in the tray.

"Mein Herr, is everything all right?"

"Yes, it's fine," Rheinhardt replied. He asked Hubner for a fresh pot of coffee, said he had some urgent work to complete, and told him to go home. "I'll see you in the morning, Franz," Rheinhardt said. "And thank you."

The alarm on Hubner's obsequious face was palpable. "What's wrong, sir? What did I do? I promise you, whatever it was, my intention was and remains always to serve you and the Reich."

"Why are you acting like a flustered damsel, Hubner?"

"You have *never* called me Franz," Hubner replied. "And you have never thanked me."

Thoughtfully, Rheinhardt lit another cigarette. "That sounds like it's my deficiency, not yours, *Kriminalkommissar*," he said at last. "I shall try to do better."

Shaking with unrelieved anxiety, Hubner went home.

For the rest of the night, Rheinhardt sat in his office and waited. He tried to read, but no words got through. He attempted to do some administrative work—the kind of tasks that he usually felt were beneath him—but even mindless bookkeeping was beyond his abilities tonight.

He sat, staring into the darkness. He knew that when the time came and he opened that drawer, either he was going to change his life by being the hero that Hitler desperately needed, delivering a miracle in a barrel, a God-given miracle straight from heaven—or he would be exiled or shot.

There was no in between.

And there was no going back to the way things were either. He had ordered the murder of a ship's crew, which resulted in the death of a dozen Nazi soldiers. Even in a tribunal sympathetic to the cause, the order on paper remained: no harm would come to anyone in the occupied territories by the Germans unless they broke the law. And Rheinhardt couldn't really argue that twelve people who weren't even Belgian, getting ready to turn in for the night, had been breaking any laws.

Well, *eleven* people. A man had been lost in the shallow waters near the southern docks. And that vanished black man was the only other person who knew about the contents of those sixty barrels. Where was he?

All in good time.

It took all the willpower Rheinhardt had not to open the drawer to reveal his fate.

22

I Can't Say

On Saturday night, Fletcher and his cobbled-together, spit-and-shoe-polish eight-man team sat around the fire—mere hours before takeoff—and got to know each other. Fletcher was lost in thought, trying to find a way to tell them about the parameters of the mission without flagging the stakes, just as Jonathan Reed had instructed him to.

It was a warm, muggy night. Belvedere was sipping tea from an old tin cup with dramatic disgust, muttering to himself.

Fletcher tried to stare him down, but the man was impervious. Fletcher stared Rafael down instead, who sighed theatrically loud himself. "Belvy, why does everything have to be a Shakespearean tragedy with you?"

"I studied medicine at Cambridge for this?" Belvedere said. "Drinking lukewarm ditchwater out of a sardine can?"

"Would you prefer your ditchwater boiling hot, Enobarbus?"

"There must be something in the Geneva Convention prohibiting this kind of torture," Belvedere continued, taking another sip and grimacing. "This isn't just underbrewed. I'm fairly certain this cup was a field latrine in its past life."

"*Past* life?" Rafael said. "I pissed in it just yesterday."

"Sergeant Canario!" That was a fed-up Fletcher. How did Rafael always manage to make matters worse?

"So tell us, Lieutenant," said Bill Briggs, the demolition man, "where are we headed at midnight tonight?"

"I can't say."

"How long will it take us to get there?"

"Not sure."

"How will we know where the drop zone is?"

"Either flares or a radio signal. Not positive."

"Are we dropping into an ambush?"

"I want to say no."

"Is it just nine of us, or will there be more on the other side?"

"Hard to say."

"Who's meeting us? Civilians? Soldiers? Trained? Untrained?"

"All good questions, Sergeant."

"Will there be enough of us to accomplish our mission even without the extra help?"

"Hard to tell."

"Why is *that* hard to tell?"

"The parameters of our mission will be field-determined."

"Okay . . . so, what's our mission?"

That, Fletcher could almost answer. "Some cargo on a ship needs to be offloaded and secured."

The men were quiet. "They don't have dockworkers for that?" said Belvedere.

"Secret cargo," Fletcher said. "Classified."

"Where's the ship?" Briggs asked.

"Moored somewhere."

"In enemy territory?"

"Of course."

The men sat up straighter, leaned in, focused.

"Is the ship guarded?" Rafael asked.

"Most likely."

"How much cargo is there?"

"A fuckload."

"Aha! Is it a fuckload of heavy cargo?"

"Yes. A fuckload of *very* heavy cargo, Sergeant Canario."

"The heavier, the fucking better," Briggs said. "Bring it on."

"Are nine men going to be enough to offload it?" asked Rafael.

Fletcher grimaced. "I can't say." Eighteen *thousand* pounds! A hundred men might not be enough. "Too late to back out now, Canario."

"Wouldn't dream of it. And after we offload it, where do we put it?"

"I can't say." Fletcher couldn't say because he didn't know. He didn't want to tell his men that Reed himself didn't know.

"Is there a warehouse we can use?"

Fletcher hedged. "Probably we'll need to find a location other than a warehouse." From what Reed had told him about the cargo, they needed to find a mine and drop it a thousand feet down the empty shaft, and still they might not be safe.

"And how do we get the cargo to this other location, Lieutenant?"

"I can't say."

"And if we do find another location and secure it there, will our mission be complete?"

"I can't say." Fletcher didn't want to tell them they had no way of getting out of Belgium.

"Does anyone here speak German?" Rafael asked.

Wolski said he spoke a little German.

"Oh, yeah?" Briggs said. "What can you say in German?"

"I surrender," Wolski said, who, as it turned out, spoke accented but nearly fluent English. "Please don't shoot. I'm here to see my mother."

"Those are your three fucking phrases in German?"

"What can I tell you?" said Wolski, grinning amiably. "Germans love their mothers." He had a broad calm Slavic face. He was rugged, balding, heavily stubbled, and constantly smoking.

Briggs turned back to Fletcher. "Do we need any equipment to move the cargo? Will we have access to winches, cranes, dollies?"

"Can't say."

"Are you not telling us in case we get caught, or because you don't know?"

"I can't say."

"Fuck me!" said Briggs. "This is just a bunch of horseshit, if you ask me."

"State your question, Sergeant Briggs."

"I'll state my fucking question," said Briggs. "What kind of a crazy-ass suicide mission is this?"

"I can't say," said Fletcher.

"Do we have any known parameters you can actually tell us?"

"I can't say."

"Can you at least say how important it is if we succeed or fail?"

Fletcher didn't answer right away. He stared at the fire. "I can't say," he said quietly.

"Aha! So, it's very important we succeed!" exclaimed Briggs.

"I can't say," Fletcher said, lowering his head.

"Right, so nothing less than the fate of the free world depends on us accomplishing the impossible and doing this thing that can't be done and can't be spoken about, is that right?" said Briggs.

"I can't say," Fletcher said, nodding vigorously.

23

The Golden Apples of the Hesperides

Rheinhardt paced in front of *La Fortuna*, smoking, his metal-reinforced heels scraping across the ragged cobblestones. When he turned, Hubner stood in front of him. His face showed worry, anxiety, confusion. Rheinhardt knew he must be a sight. He met his aide's inquisitive frown with a glassy, vacant stare.

"Mein Herr . . . is everything all right?"

"Yes, of course." Rheinhardt deepened his voice, attempting to sound officious and nonchalant. "Why do you ask?"

"It's Saturday morning, sir. I left you late last night. You haven't shaved. You haven't changed your clothes. Baert Haus wasn't locked, yet the door to your office was—with a bolt from the inside. Did you go out the closet door, by chance?"

"Don't go into my office, Hubner."

"I understand, sir, but . . ."

"Don't step into it. Not one foot."

"Of course. What's *wrong*?"

"Nothing. Nothing. Nothing." Rheinhardt got stuck on the word. He couldn't stop repeating it.

"I got it, sir. Nothing's wrong," said Hubner. "Would you like to come back to the office with me now? We must finalize the port status report for Herr Falkenhausen in Brussels."

"I know," Rheinhardt said, in the tone of a man who had absolutely no idea what the words even meant.

"Port Authority told me last night that Falkenhausen's courier will arrive at eleven o'clock sharp to retrieve the report, and we haven't even begun."

"A status report on what, Hubner?"

Hubner stammered in response. "On *what*, sir? Guard rotations, breaches, disturbances, areas of vulnerability. We compile one every week."

"We do? I mean—of course we do."

"Every week for four years, mein Herr . . ." Hubner was trembling. "Are you sure you're all right?"

"Hubner," Rheinhardt said, pointing to the four guards standing at attention in front of *La Fortuna*, "why are there four guards here? Speaking of guard rotations."

"You told me to put four guards here. You insisted, sir. Two days ago, on Thursday. Right after we emptied the ship. Would you like me to remove them? I'll see that it gets done at once."

"Remove them? No. I meant to say—and as always, you didn't let me finish—why are there *only* four guards here?"

"Only?"

"Yes, Hubner. Yes. It's imperative, absolutely mandatory, that we have a platoon stationed here round the clock. Twelve men. At least. Fully armed. The best, most highly trained SS guards we have. If I could get some Waffen-SS men to guard this ship, I would. In their absence, pull them from our *Totenkopfverbande* units. You have my full authorization. I need to see them stationed here on the quay by noon today, is that clear? Twelve men."

"Perhaps—"

"Oh, and another question. Do you know anyone on staff at the university here in Antwerp?"

"I know a few people, yes, sir. Are you looking for—"

"Anyone in the physics or chemistry departments?"

"Uh, I don't personally know anyone, no."

Rheinhardt stared off into the Scheldt.

"Is there . . . anything *I* can help you with, sir?"

"You? No. Just get the armed guards here. Immediately."

"Yes, sir. Under reason for the enhanced security, shall I say . . ."

"Potential sabotage threats on Dock Sector Seven, near Het Steen Castle."

"Yes, sir."

"We can't be too careful, Hubner," Rheinhardt said, intensely but absent-mindedly. "We simply can't be careful enough."

"Of course." Hubner started for the office then glanced back. Rheinhardt was still staring at *La Fortuna*.

"Are you coming, sir? Herr Falkenhausen's report . . ."

"You go on—get started on it, Hubner."

"Some of the documents I need are in your office, sir . . ."

"Do everything else. I'll get them for you when I return."

Rheinhardt didn't even turn to his adjutant when he spoke. "I have full confidence in you." He took out his Black Crowns and a matchbook. His eyes remained on the ship.

Even before he touched the rocks in the barrels, he knew. His team of trained soldiers had been slaughtered by men who looked like civilians but fought like samurai. The barrels were hidden so thoroughly that it took him three days of assiduous crawling to find them. They were buried in a secret grove, like the Golden Apples of the Hesperides. Guarded by Ladon, the hundred-headed dragon, the fruit promised to grant its owner immortal life.

He had known it in his heart, even before he opened the drawer.

The old photograph of himself with his mother and father had ghosted onto the blank ledger paper in his drawer, the faces faint but unmistakable. Not a perfect copy, but something deeper, a spectral echo. Just as Marie Curie had once shown, radiation alone—without light, without contact—seared an image from one surface to another.

And it had taken less than six hours.

Uranium.

What other element on earth could radiate so fiercely?

What sorcery was this?

He knew. And yet, there was so much he didn't know. Was it the right kind? Was it enough? Was it too late? Did it mean nothing—or everything? Before he ruined himself before Heinrich Himmler, Rheinhardt had to be sure if this was merely radioactive—or revolutionary.

Was it fool's gold or Promethean fire?

24

The King's Request

Fletcher felt like a beast of burden—every limb weighed down. The main chute was strapped to his back, the reserve chute lay across his chest. His M1 carbine. Two pistols, two knives, ammo, grenades, an extra scope, and morphine. Canvas bags, drop bags, a radio pack. Crank generator, compass, map kit, mess kit, binoculars, first aid. Everything secured with straps, buckles, tape. He sat on the ground, not far from the runway, tightening and checking the straps. He wasn't sure he could get up without help.

It was 11:00 p.m. on Saturday night. They were leaving at midnight. Their plane, a C-47 Skytrain troop carrier—the Dakota—stood nearby on the tarmac of a hastily constructed runway at Saint-Pierre-du-Mont, right next to Pointe du Hoc, where Fletcher was supposed to land four days earlier—and didn't.

Dressed in black battle fatigues and black combat boots, he wanted to stand up on his own steam. He wanted a smoke but couldn't find the Zippo in his pocket, so he sat there, yoked by the present, an unlit cigarette in his mouth. He refused to think about the future—the jump and all beyond it. That was one way Fletcher had learned to control his fear—by focusing only on the now. This required an extraordinary effort for the seven-time chess champion of Wyoming, for he had built his entire identity on learning to think five moves ahead.

Earlier he'd splashed some water on himself from a rain barrel but hadn't bothered to shave. In his hands he held a small tin of boot polish. He was about to blacken his face when a shadow fell across the grass, and he sensed Jonathan Reed standing over him. Fletcher looked up. Reed sported a spectacularly anxious expression.

Politely refusing Reed's proffered arm, Fletcher hauled himself upright without a wobble or a stumble. "Just finishing my gear check, sir," he said, removing the absurd unlit cigarette from his mouth.

"Of course. You're doing well." Reed offered his Zippo, and Fletcher lit up gratefully. "Tell me," Reed said, "why didn't you join the Airborne?"

"I'm afraid of heights," Fletcher replied dryly, taking a long, satisfying drag. "Also not a fan of water."

Reed looked distinctly unsettled. "Can you walk with me, soldier?" He looked Fletcher over, strapped down with steel and canvas and the whole damn war. "If you can manage it. Just a quick stroll. A smoke. I have something to discuss."

Fletcher was puzzled. "Something *else* to discuss?"

"Yes." Reed sounded exhausted and resigned.

Fletcher unhooked his rifle from the leg harness and laid it on the tarmac. Reed lowered his voice as they strode away into the dark. "Operation Santa Fe *is* your top priority, Fletcher."

"Got it," Fletcher said. He took another drag. "Am I getting a secondary priority?"

Reed swore under his breath. "This isn't coming from me. But I have superiors too, and they've handed down new orders. We need you to ensure safe passage for the Congolese colonial officer."

"Fuck."

"I know, Lieutenant."

"Who is he?"

"Ngomo Kasonga. The one who survived the massacre."

"Passage to where?"

Reed shrugged, not meeting Fletcher's eyes. "He can't remain in Belgium. He's not safe, and no one who hides him is safe. The Nazis are searching for him. If he's captured . . ." Reed stopped short. Gritting his teeth, he said, "This man means a great deal to the King of Belgium. The King personally appealed to Churchill. And Churchill, knowing what's at stake, asked my CO. Who asked me. And now I'm asking you."

Fletcher stared into the dark. The way Reed wouldn't meet his eyes—wouldn't even look toward the plane—told him there was more to this. Something he wasn't being told.

"Am I cleared to leave my unit to escort this man to another location—even out of Belgium?"

"Yes," Reed said. "Anything you need."

"Sir . . ." Fletcher hesitated. "Aren't most of the other countries in Europe occupied by Germany?"

"At the moment."

Fletcher tilted his head in question.

"Do your best," Reed said. And then added, "Ngomo Kasonga can *never* be captured by the Germans. It's imperative that you understand this."

"I got it." Fletcher let the pause stretch. "Because the King of Belgium made a personal request, correct?"

"Yes," Reed said heavily, staring as far away from Fletcher as he could. "He was never supposed to leave the Congo. Now he's in Belgium—*where he's not safe*. He knows too much. He knows everything."

He can't be captured suddenly acquired a whole new meaning.

That didn't sound like a secondary objective.

That sounded pretty fucking primary.

It wasn't just a recovery mission.

It was containment.

Fletcher finally understood.

"Are we clear?"

"Loud and clear, sir," Fletcher said quietly.

Quickly they tried to move on to other things. Reed handed Fletcher a small waterproof pouch. Inside, he found cash, gold coin, and a fistful of rough diamonds. "Here's your field fund," Reed said. "Forty thousand francs, ten gold sovereigns, ten rough-cut diamonds. That should be enough for emergencies."

"Well, sir, it's been an honor," Fletcher said with a mock salute. "But I'm going to need a head start." He slipped the pouch into the cargo pocket of his battle fatigues. "You didn't see me. I was never here."

Slowly, they started back to the plane.

"Where's he now, the Congo man?"

"Not sure," Reed said. "You'll need to find him on landing. He'll help you secure the barrels."

"So use him first. Good thinking."

They both lowered their heads.

Back at the Dakota, Reed's composure was evaporating before Fletcher's eyes. "You remember the password?" Reed asked.

"Of course, sir."

"And the name of the man you're meeting?"

"Omloop, right? Who'll take me to Charles. His partisan cell is *La Ligne*."

"Very good. I told Dorsey to fly over the sea to avoid Antwerp. Don't let him cut across to save time—you'll get shot down."

"Will do, sir." Fletcher had no idea how he was supposed to tell a captain who outranked him where to fly.

"And keep an eye on Frobisher."

"Who?"

"Clyde Frobisher, Dorsey's flight navigator."

"What's wrong with him?"

"He's coming off a dozen missions over France. Might be a little high-strung. Did you bring a map?"

"I did. But I'm not the one flying the plane, sir."

"Just follow the flight path. You'll be fine."

"Yes, sir." Again, Fletcher was at a loss as to how he could keep an eye on the navigator, in the cockpit, behind a closed door.

"And leave no footprints," Reed said. "Don't make noise when you land. Don't engage your peashooter. We don't want the Krauts to know you're in Belgium."

"Got it."

"And keep your eye on the King's man."

"Will do."

"Are you happy with your team?"

"Best men I could ask for."

"And Canario?" Reed tried to smile.

"He's growing on me," said Fletcher.

They both drew a breath.

"Tell me it's going to be all right, Fletcher," Reed said.

"I can't do that, sir," Fletcher said. "But I'll tell you what my grandfather once told me. He said he'd do everything he could to make sure the worst that could happen didn't happen."

"And then what happened?"

Fletcher shrugged with pretend indifference. "The worst happened."

Shaking his head, Reed pumped Fletcher's hand and clapped him on the back. "Never underestimate the strength of your enemy," he said. "On D-Day, we misjudged the Germans—and paid a heavy price. We thought they'd be caught by surprise, be unprepared, and maybe they *were*—a little. Imagine how much worse it would've been if they'd actually been expecting us. Whatever you do, soldier—let your enemy underestimate *you*. Fool him into thinking you're the fool."

Fletcher saluted him. "You won't be disappointed, sir."

25

Frobisher's Twelve Missions

Just inland from Pointe du Hoc, Fletcher and his eight men took off in the Dakota and headed north over the English Channel, through the Dover–Calais narrows and across the sea.

The plan was to fly as far west over water as possible, bypassing Antwerp, and then to slow down and return to the shoreline of the Dutch archipelago. Just above Antwerp, they were to count the jutting islands of the Zeeland Delta that marked the coast north of the Scheldt River. First landmark: the dim town of Westkapelle at the tip of Walcheren Island; then, a few miles north of that, the smaller, rounder Noord Beveland; and finally, the tiny, craggy Goeree-Overflakkee.

After passing "Overflake," as they called it, they would fly fifteen miles over the Haringvliet Estuary until they reached Willemstad, where they would adjust southeast for fifty miles toward Brecht, Malle, and finally Herentals.

The distance from takeoff to Overflake was around 220 miles. The time was just over two hours. From Overflake to Herentals was another sixty-five miles, or about forty minutes. They lifted off just after midnight for the 3:00 a.m. drop.

They flew low, and a mile offshore, to avoid the radar near Bruges and Antwerp, and to spend the shortest time possible over land. The designated jump zone was in an open field near Landendonk, northwest of Herentals.

For two hundred miles, the flight was uneventful. The men sat in semi-darkness strapped in the troop bay, their faces and necks blackened, weapons at their sides like third legs. They chatted, joked, even sang a bit. Rafael wouldn't shut up about Hawk's gold eyes blazing out of his blackened face like beacons. "You want some boot polish, Hawk, for them eyeballs? Those things are glowing in the fucking dark."

Hawk didn't speak much, but he spoke then. "They're not glowing," he said. "It's bloodlust."

"Ah, the apex predator speaks! They're shining like a goddamn bird of prey's!"

Only Wolski and Fletcher—sitting closest to the cockpit—didn't participate. Fletcher, because he was the jumpmaster and was trying hard not to think about the jump, much less what awaited them beyond it.

And Wolski, because he was buried in his map. Somewhere around mile two hundred, he yanked off one of his leather gloves with his teeth, fished out his tiny buzzer light, and hunched over the field map, examining it like a jeweler.

"What's there to see, Wolski?" Fletcher said, glancing out the small boxy window by his elbow. Honestly, he couldn't see shit. It was black outside, already 2:30 a.m. The barest glimmer of the moon broke through the cloud cover, lighting the sea in brief flickers.

"We fucked. They going wrong way," said Wolski, who didn't believe in definite articles but was wholly confident in his powers of navigation.

"Like north instead of south?" Fletcher was joking. But Wolski didn't so much as snicker. "They overshot islands."

"How do you know?"

Wolski hit himself in the chest. "I know. I feel flight time and speed in my gut. Go—tell them they going wrong way," he said, tacking on a perfunctory *"sir"* at the end.

"I don't know you, Wolski," Fletcher said, struggling to his feet. "Rider better be fucking right about you."

"If he told you I'm best, then he right," Wolski said.

Fletcher shambled a few steps to the cockpit door and pulled it open.

Immediately, he knew Wolski was right. Dorsey and Ainsley, the pilot and co-pilot, were arching toward the bowed windshield like cranes, trying to see through the darkness. Frobisher the navigator—hunched in the jump seat behind the pilot—was buried in his own map, much like Wolski. Except Frobisher was cursing. "No, we're good, we're fine," he said to Dorsey in a voice that was anything but reassuring.

"Did we miss the turnoff to land?" Fletcher said.

"We didn't miss the turnoff!" Frobisher said. "Go sit."

"That's it? That was your whole involvement?" Wolski said when Fletcher returned to his seat.

"What did you want me to do, wrestle them?"

"They missed all three islands!" Wolski said. "We near Hook of Holland, we on way to Monster and Scheveningen—beach suburb of Hague."

"We *cannot* be that far north already!" Fletcher said.

"We are, Commander." Wolski sounded unshakeable. "They can't see it through cockpit glass, but I see it. Coast is dead straight. Look yourself. No islands or estuaries here."

Fletcher heard Frobisher's voice from the cockpit. "We're fine!"

Wolski got up and wedged himself into the narrow cockpit door.

"We're between Dunkirk and Bruges," Frobisher said. "First island landmark coming up shortly."

"Bruges? You left Bruges behind," said Wolski. "You between Hook of Holland and Hague."

"Who the fuck are *you*?"

"Corporal Wolski, British Commandos, Carpathian Unit."

"Well, Corporal Fucking Wolski," Frobisher yelled, "meet your pilot, *Captain* Dorsey, and your co-pilot, *Captain* Ainsley, and me, *First Lieutenant* Clyde Frobisher."

Wolski barely nodded. "Captains, Lieutenant—you overshot your turn. Human error. Understandable. Too far west over North Sea. You forgot to take into account high tailwind. You fly too fast. You didn't turn back to shore until you already passed our three islands. You need to recalibrate."

"Who the fuck do you think you are?" said Frobisher. "I do this for a living!"

"I also do this for living," said Wolski. "I wouldn't say if I wasn't hundred percent sure."

"Well, I'm a hundred percent sure you're wrong," said Frobisher. "We just passed Bruges. We're fine. Go sing a song."

"Bruges gone bye-bye. You headed to Hague. You want to pop into Hague for pastry and tribunal?"

"Captain, don't listen to this man," yelled Frobisher, "he doesn't know what the fuck he's talking about."

"Where did you learn to be a tracker?" asked Ainsley, studying the instrument panel.

"Carpathian Mountains," said Wolski. "You have straight shoreline to your right, and you suppose to have islands. This shoreline between Hook of Holland and Hague looks exact same as one between Dunkirk and Bruges. Bad mistake but easy mistake too."

"You know what *is* clear?" Frobisher said. "I didn't fucking ask you!"

"You fly too fast. Do the math."

"I've done the fucking math. Below us is Bruges."

"Below us is Hague Beach, seventy miles north of Bruges," said Wolski. "You're in Nederland."

"We didn't miss it! But we will if you keep yapping at us! Get the fuck out, that's an order!"

"Cloud cover, estuary fog, poor visibility. You can't make out curve of land," said Wolski. "Oh, look, you just passed Hague. Now you headed for Amsterdam."

"Stand down!" yelled Frobisher.

"You missed it."

"I didn't miss it!"

"Next stop, Amsterdam, boys," said Wolski, turning to the soldiers in the cargo bay. "I hear tulips lovely this time of year."

"If he doesn't go sit down, I will throw him out of my plane," shouted Frobisher.

"You upset I'm right?" said Wolski.

"Close the cockpit door, *Corporal*," Frobisher said. "Behind you."

"Will do," Wolski said, "but when we hit Bremen in Germany, will you admit then we overshot?"

"Shut the fuck up!"

"Enough, Corporal." That was Captain Dorsey. "Leave it to us. We'll figure it out without you." But he slowed the plane to barely a hundred miles per hour.

"No visibility plus high tailwind," Wolski said. "Recipe for error. Heavy fog from three estuaries blocked your marks. It's okay to make mistake."

"Will you *ever* fucking shut up?" Frobisher yelled.

"We're not going back and trying again tomorrow," Wolski said. "Whatever happens, you're bringing us to Herentals."

The tracker sat back down next to Fletcher, who said nothing, studying his watch and peering into the night. He knew Wolski was right, but he also knew that Frobisher was digging in out of pride, rank, and flustered nerves. The man was running on pure caffeine and doomed confidence at this point. Reed had told him: Frobisher had just flown twelve missions. He was exhausted, overloaded, and was flying blind. Recovering from D-Day made him prone not only to mistakes but also to staggering stubbornness.

"Ask him to check coordinates for Herentals, Commander," Wolski said. "And coordinates of where we are right now. By my calculations, he's at least seventy miles too far northwest."

Fletcher didn't need to verify coordinates. It was past astronomical dawn—3:40 a.m. They were forty minutes late for their jump and nowhere near Herentals.

The cockpit door remained open. Another minute or two passed, first of silence, then of light muttering before Fletcher heard a defeated: "There's a small chance we could've missed it, Captain . . . Fuck."

"Are we still over water?" Dorsey asked.

Fletcher exchanged an incredulous look with Wolski, who put a finger gun to his temple and pulled the trigger. "I see trees below us, Captain!" Wolski yelled into the cockpit. "Are there trees in *water*?"

Three voices responded in unison: "Shut the fuck up!"

Another minute of stressed muttering went by. The co-pilot motioned Fletcher over. "Lieutenant," Ainsley said, "I'm afraid we did miss the turnoff."

A miserable and sullen Clyde Frobisher, hunched over his map, said nothing at first. "We can turn around, try to find the islands again," he said, quiet and uncertain. "But with the fog, I don't know if . . ."

"My advice is to return to base, Lieutenant Fletcher," Dorsey said. "Try again tomorrow night. We'll get it right next time."

Eleven men looked to Fletcher for answers. He was crippled by indecision. What would Lucas do? *Help me, Lucas.* He tried to remember the most important thing. What was it? To secure the cargo. But no one told him how to react if they missed their turn by a hundred miles and their eventual drop time by 90 minutes.

Fear sharpened. Dawn was coming.

The landscape was ominous, dark, about to shift.

Astronomical dawn had come and gone; the first faint blue color on the horizon.

Nautical dawn was fast approaching: 4:10 a.m., land and sea separated by deep dark blue.

Civil dawn wasn't far behind: 4:55 a.m., pink horizon, pale sky.

Sunrise: 5:21 a.m., Central European Summer Time.

Time wasn't stopping for them, no matter where they were.

There was no going back.

The only way out was forward.

Fletcher gave the order. With Wolski wedged in the cockpit door, peering at his map and directing, they made a sharp right at Noordwijk and flew inland for thirty miles, passing over Utrecht before turning south.

But flying southeast from the northwest wasn't the same as flying south from the north. Instead of flying a tight seventy over an estuary and land, they now had to meander a hundred miles over land, using only speed, compass, and the distance to Herentals from Utrecht as their guides.

Because they came at it sideways, they missed the town and the belltower and the flashing signal.

Dorsey made three runs around but couldn't find the D-zone. He dropped to 600 feet and slowed nearly to a stall as he and Ainsley hunted rivers and roads by the shape of the blue darkness.

Fletcher sent out a Rebecca ping when Wolski thought they were maybe ten miles away and immediately received a Eureka response from the ground. But as they flew toward it, the signal faded and then stopped altogether. Fletcher glimpsed a church steeple below, but no one could be sure if it was the Herentals church or some other spire. No flashing signal came from the bell-tower to help them. After missing Herentals, the Dakota banked east, trying desperately to correct.

It was 4:25. Sunrise in one hour.

Fletcher knew the silhouette of their blacked-out plane could be seen from the ground against the lightening sky. He glimpsed a sporadic green flash from below—from the woods, not the church. It could've been anything. It wasn't part of the plan. And the Eureka was silent. Perhaps because they were over the destination? Eureka couldn't be heard if you were flying directly above it.

Fletcher had no more time to think.

Up ahead, between low dense trees, was a marsh or a meadow, a swathe of flat land. He told Dorsey to aim there for the jump.

Fletcher unstrapped and clumsily shuffled across the aisle to the paratroop door. The fifty pounds of main and reserve chutes made him feel like a claustrophobic turtle. He couldn't lower his head, couldn't see over the reserve pack on his chest, and couldn't drop his arms to his sides. He pulled the heavy latch.

The door swung open and slammed against the fuselage with a metallic bang. Frigid air blasted into the cargo bay, the wind chill biting, even in June. His eyes watered. He couldn't wait to get on the ground.

He flicked on the green light and bellowed the signal to his men over the deafening roar of the plane. "Stand up, hook up—let's go!"

No time to think. Barely time to cross himself. Certainly not enough time to dwell on the fact that in all his elite commando training, the one thing he had never done was actually jump out of a plane.

Fletcher jumped first.

26

Eureka on the Ground

Louise was murmuring, whispering in her soothing voice, about flowers and cookies and boys, but nothing could calm Charlie's nerves. They'd been in the black woods since two in the morning, waiting for the landing. Charlie spent hours pacing like a wolf, praying no one would be captured or killed. Not even Louise could talk her down, and she was usually so good at it. Not even praying to Saint Hubert, patron of hunters and forests and hopeless causes, could comfort her. *From snares unseen and evil unspoken, deliver us, O Lord.*

Intermittently, Omloop would flash his light from Saint Waltrude's belfry, but the German DF trucks kept rolling through town, their whirling antennas sniffing the air for middle-of-the-night radio signals, and he had to stop. Once they left, he flashed again, but into empty skies. Charlie had no idea what was wrong, why the soldiers were so late. Maybe they crashed somewhere. Or got shot down. Or got lost.

She barely blinked, her eyes fixed upward for the signal from Rebecca in the sky. Just like she once waited for Andres Ferrer's from the *Serra Nova.*

"They'll be here," Louise said. "You just hate waiting."

It wasn't the waiting, Charlie wanted to say. It was the not knowing. The agonizing limbo where she'd hung suspended so many times before. Sometimes it all went well. And sometimes it didn't. Sometimes your best efforts were enough. And sometimes they weren't.

Sometimes the boy got off the train.

And sometimes he didn't.

She wanted to scream.

For seventy interminable blackout minutes, the signal didn't come.

Finally, at 4:16 a.m., she got a Rebecca ping—and nearly threw herself at the Eureka set. She sent the reply back immediately.

And then they waited. And waited.

"Did you get another ping? Did you get it?" Louise kept asking.

They heard the plane before they saw it, but it wasn't coming from the right direction. It just flew casually overhead, low and slow, missing her and the field and Herentals entirely. Where the hell was it going? Brussels? Bruges? Fucking Waterloo? It meandered over them like it had no idea where it was, or where it was meant to be.

"*What* are they doing?" Louise whispered, looking up, befuddled.

Charlie guessed Waterloo was *not* going to be the plane's final destination, because a few minutes later she heard it coming back—but not toward Landendonk. Obscured by a wide patch of woods, the field was impossible to spot from the west side. The plane didn't slow down for the jump until it was already well past it. Charlie cursed in Flemish, in French, even German.

It was ridiculous, but also deeply concerning. Leaving the heavy Eureka transponder in the moss, she sprinted like she was at the races, motioning for the girls to follow. Across meadow and glen they ran, through another wood, stopping at a field near Saint Lament.

She lunged just inside the tree line, flashed her small green signal skyward, and prayed for a better outcome. The plane must have seen it—there *was* a God!—because finally the cargo door slammed open, its deafening metal clang echoing over three sleeping towns. One by one, the pale parachutes flared against the sky and drifted down. But they didn't land in the perfectly secluded, flat, empty field in front of Charlie.

No. They landed as far away from the field as possible, in a swamp. Near a base full of Wehrmacht soldiers guarding a main road into Antwerp.

Bravo, she thought, shutting her eyes for a moment. Well done.

"What a fucking disaster," she said, watching in disbelief as the melee of men fell across the marsh, groaning, crashing, losing their weapons, their wits—maybe even their lives. These couldn't be the top-tier soldiers sent on a make-or-break mission. They simply couldn't be.

"Should we go help them?" Louise asked.

"What are *we* going to do?" Charlie said. "How are we going to help men who can't help themselves?" If the Germans woke up to this rambling fiasco—and how could they *not*?—the last thing Charlie needed was to have her brave tiny cell of friends and fighters be identified and shot for aiding a bunch of morons who couldn't land quietly in an open field before dawn.

"But isn't our objective to help them?" said Hildimar, clutching her long, sharpened knife. "Isn't that why we're here?"

"Hildi's right," said Louise.

There was no point flashing the green signal again through the fog. Across the wet field, grunting confusion reigned. Two or three times, they heard silenced fire. Cursing American voices. Low British ones. And one frantic German yelling, *"Schnapp's dir! Schnapp's dir!" Grab it!*

"Are we going to help them *now*?" said Louise.

"Shh, Lou." Charlie looked calm. Inside, she was a hot knot of boiling fear. Her grip tightened on her beloved Browning, loaded and ready, just in case. This wasn't the plan. A firefight with Nazis in her own village? *Merde!* Why didn't Omloop suggest a drop somewhere else? Somewhere *not* in her hometown.

Slowly, the fields and forests returned to dripping silence.

"What's happening?" Louise kept pulling on Charlie's binoculars. "Show me. What is it?"

"It's quiet now. That's a good sign, right?" Maxine said, ever hopeful.

"It's a bad sign," said Margot, never hopeful.

"It's bad either way," Charlie said. "If the Germans are dead, we all get searched and investigated. Arrests, interrogations, Breendonk. If the Allies are dead, then it's all been for nothing." She tried to keep her voice from breaking. She didn't want it to be true, even now at her bleakest.

If the men were gone, then Ngomo was still *her* crisis. *Don't tell anyone about him*, Robert Capelle had warned. *You will never be safe.*

Charlie's pistol was still cocked in her grip when, through the mist in the meadow, a Greek phalanx emerged—black-clad men in black helmets and boots, faces blacked out, rifles in hand—striding toward her through the foggy glade.

Behind her, Margot muttered, "Told you there wouldn't be enough men."

"Six is a *lot*, Margot," said Maxine.

"It's a lot if there are only six of us. But we have seven."

"Louise is with Fitz," said Maxine. Next to Charlie, Louise made a low negatory sound. Maxine went on. "And Charlie—she's never been into that sort of thing. Now's definitely not the time to start. So if you take that away, there are five of us and six of them. Welcome to paradise, girls."

"Shh," said Louise. "They're coming."

"They most certainly are," said Brigitte.

27

Rebecca in the Sky

Patchy farmland. Canals. Hedges, small ravines. An abandoned barn. An unlucky bunch of Nazis, sleeping off their Saturday night.

Fletcher and his men dropped out of the indigo sky in a fractured fall. They plunged over the wrong bridge, into the wrong glade, the wrong forest, the wrong ditch, the wrong house.

They fell into trees, crumbling farmsteads, a canal—and the enemy.

Fletcher hit the ground in a skid, crashing into a mudflat between the trees. All around him came the sickening sounds of soldiers tearing through elms, glass, through sharp metal spikes.

Airborne Rangers. Assault commandos. Sergeants, corporals, lieutenants—a kaleidoscope of war. They were cobbled together and hobbled. Trapped and stuck and impaled. Fletcher didn't know how many Germans were inside the farmhouse, but there was a Wehrmacht light truck outside, and *fifty* boots and two dozen packs arranged by the back door.

"Here we go, chaps, everybody sound off," Fletcher whisper-yelled to his men.

There was no response.

"Come on, lads, call out, let me hear you. Everyone okay?" Silence. "If you're alive, say yes!"

"Rider by your side," Rafael said quietly, unhooking his harness and pulling his Tommy gun out of the snaps. "I'm going inside to pay the fuckers a visit before they start shooting."

"No," Fletcher said. "Holster your weapon. Find our guys first. I told you—no shooting. Men—sound off!"

"Why are you shouting?" Belvedere said, behind him. "No one can hear you." He was instantly off, to search for the rest in case they needed help. In case?

The assault force suddenly didn't seem so mighty.

Rafael found explosive charges in the shed. "Let's blow everything up and run."

"No," said Fletcher. "I told you—no noise, no fire, no grenades, *nothing*. No one can know we're here."

"Then why are you fucking shouting?" Belvedere called out, boots squelching through sodden ground.

Briggs was hard to miss. "Holy fucking moly!" he said, soaked in mud, M1 and all. "Were we *supposed* to drop on a fucking house?"

"By all means, Briggs, be louder," Belvedere said, his back to them, strolling away, med bag in hand, as if he were heading into a London clinic after a leisurely lunch.

"Did you ever see an op go this fucked this fast?" Briggs said. "First we fly all the way to fucking Holland. Then we miss the DZ, and now we're stuck in this boggy fuck—what a shitshow."

"Louder, Briggs!" Belvedere said. "The Germans across the field didn't quite catch that."

"Let's find the rest of our men, Briggs," Fletcher said. "Now's not the time for a fucking debrief."

The four of them searched as quietly as they could.

"All those fucking Nazis whose boots are outside the door are about to wake up," said Rafael, "and find us prancing around in their yard like we're on tour at the candy factory."

Just then, Fletcher heard the unmistakable sound of a silencer go off inside the house. Ah, so Hawk was still breathing. Good. As soon as Rafael heard the Welrod, he drew his knife and tore into the house. "Don't follow me," he said to Fletcher. "I'll be quiet. You go save Green, the poor bastard." He pointed to the greenhouse.

Brian Green, the close combat specialist, had crashed into a roof made of glass. How was anyone still sleeping after such a racket, Fletcher wondered, as he and Briggs climbed up the broken wooden frame.

"The Krauts have a greenhouse?" Briggs said. "What the fuck kind of war is this? We've just come out of a fucking sea of blood at Omaha, and they're growing tomatoes in Belgium?" They tried to extract and wake the unconscious Green. But he was stuck good and proper.

From the top of the busted roof, Fletcher sighted two more of theirs. The combat engineer Arthur Brown, whose task was to clear any barbed wire from their path, had landed *in* the barbed wire—and was now the very obstruction that needed clearing. And Fletcher's chosen medic, the soft-spoken Howie Miller, who should've been providing medical assistance to barbed-wire

Brown, had hurled himself into the well in the side yard and was dangling eighty feet above the well floor. Only his parachute kept him from dropping straight to the bottom, and that was in danger of tearing any second.

Fletcher sent Briggs to free Brown while he ran to Howie. But Howie's parachute ripped just as he got there, and the medic plunged to his death, the parachute falling on top of him. *Oh, Howie, you poor bastard.* Fletcher exhaled a terrible sigh of failure and frustration. How did Jonathan Reed know to give him two of each? They'd barely thrown off their harnesses and were already down one medic and two combat specialists. At this rate—having lost forty percent of his men at jump—there might not be anyone left to meet their contacts.

Belvedere ran up. "What did you do?" he said, peering inside the well. "How can I fix him where he's down there?" He tossed a pebble into the dark shaft. No splash. "I don't know how you Americans do it," said Belvedere, shaking his head. "Leave it to a Yank to find a well with barely any water."

To Fletcher it felt like an hour had passed, even though it had probably been no more than two or three minutes. They had to lock it down and get out—fast. If those fifty boots on the ground woke up, they wouldn't stand a chance. And it certainly wouldn't stay even this quiet.

"Green?"

"I'm afraid the greenhouse got the better of unlucky Green," said Belvedere. "Slamming into a glass roof will do that."

"Fuck."

"Yes, just a flawless landing, Leftenant. Right over a cottage where the Nazis are slumbering. Shall we aim for a minefield next?"

"And Brown?"

"Briggs is cutting Brown out from the barbed wire," said Belvedere. "But you're about to have more trouble—" Before he could finish, a German soldier staggered out of the house, machine gun dangling, hand pressed over a spurting puncture hole in his throat. He crashed onto the front walkway. Behind him walked Hawk Turner, his Welrod silencer in one hand and a blood-soaked stiletto knife in the other.

"Rider and I could use some help, Commander," Hawk said in a soft Southern drawl, pointing behind him with the dripping knife. "There's a few of them left, and they're headed out back for their boots and weapons—boots first, I'm hoping."

"Sweep and clear—then lock it down," Fletcher said, yanking out both of his knives. "Silent kills only. But no stragglers. Go."

Even Belvedere dropped his bag and grabbed his commando dagger as they ran into the fray. They could've really used greenhouse Green, who knew how to fight at close range. Briggs got Brown free, and they were already inside—just in time for doomed disoriented Brown to get stabbed to death by the one German who could fight drunk.

Fletcher's men were outnumbered, and the Germans would've been a hard fight, but they were still plastered from the night before, and extraordinarily slow. Hawk used his silencer pistol, but even the suppressed shots were too loud. Fletcher told him to stop, but Hawk pretended he didn't hear. The rest of them made do with knives and garrotes.

"At least it was quick," Briggs said after it was over, bloodied and knifed in the arm, but otherwise in one piece.

"Quick, you say," said Belvedere. "Given that the Krauts were tanked, asleep, and didn't know you were coming, it wasn't quick enough, frankly. How'd you get a knife slash if they were sleeping is what I want to know."

"Are you going to fix it or just yap about it?"

Belvedere pushed Briggs away. "I was done with your scrape before you started your battle summary."

Briggs glanced at his arm. "I'm not even *bleeding* anymore?"

"I went to medical school, Sergeant Briggs. Not gym class," Belvedere said. "And you're welcome."

"Rider," Fletcher said to Rafael, "stop being such a fucking maniac."

"Somebody's got to be first into the breach, Leftenant," said Belvedere, closing his medic bag.

"Shut the fuck up, Belvy!" said Rafael.

"You're not expendable, Canario," said Fletcher.

"You know who's *not* expendable?" Rafael said. "You. Because you're the only one who knows what the fuck we're doing here, and how to get it done. If anyone needs protecting, it's you, Commander."

For a breath, Fletcher was rendered mute by Rafael's war logic. Then: "We've got to clear out. Like we were never here. Who's left?"

"Just us five," said Rafael. "You, me, Belvy, Briggsy, and Hawk, the apex predator—who, by the way, killed like twelve fucking Krauts all by himself—"

"Yes, with the Welrod I told him not to use," said Fletcher.

"I didn't hear you, Lieutenant," said Hawk, motionless like a statue. "I thought I heard you say you needed them silenced."

"I said silent kills only!"

"Shit, where's Wolski?" said Rafael.

They looked around.

"Oh, no," said Fletcher. Without Wolski, they could've never gotten here. "Wolski!" he shouted in a whisper. "Wolski!" *Please God, no. I can't lose* four *fucking men before I've left the drop zone.* "Wolski!"

"Eyes up," said Rafael.

Down the lane, Wolski dangled upside down, trapped in the thick, leafy branches of a white cherry tree. His harness must've gotten stuck. His shredded parachute blended in seamlessly with the ghostly white flowers. Fletcher heard the gentle flapping of the torn silk, lit silver by what remained of the D-Day moon. "For fuck's sake, Wolski," Rafael said as they ran up to him. "I recommended you! Don't embarrass me like this. Why didn't you cut yourself loose?"

Wolski pointed to the ground, where his dropped knife lay.

"Fuck, Wolski!" Rafael said. "I said *don't* humiliate me!"

They cut him down, and then all six ran around, hurrying to clean up the mess they had made.

A green light kept flashing from a dense line of woods across the grassy meadow. A low flickering light, brief and carefully shielded.

"Is that for us?" Rafael said when they were done burying Brown and Green.

"I hope so," said Fletcher, "because if it isn't, we're done for."

28

A Kiss on the Hand

He walked toward her with the rifle in his hands. He stopped a short distance away and stared at her with a blank, blinkless, war-weary gaze. He was tall and thin, bloodied, disheveled. His face was camo'ed with soot and dirt. There were no insignia on his shoulders, no markings on his black helmet. She couldn't tell anything about him except that he stopped in front of her.

His eyes zeroed in on hers, like scopes. There was confusion on his face, almost as if he were looking for someone else but found her instead. There was anxiety and uncertainty. He said, "Are you Omloop?" But his expression told her he wouldn't be satisfied even if she said she was, and that he had questions that went far beyond it.

"Do I look like Omloop?" Her tone was rough, unkind.

He blinked, and his gaze hardened. "Yes," he said. "That's what you look like. Now answer my question." He spoke to her in strong, passably fluent French.

"Clearly, I'm not Omloop," she said, irritation prickling every word. "He was the one signaling you from the north side of the belltower, risking his life to do it. You must've missed it, seeing as you came around three times, from every direction *but* the north."

"We just dropped from a fucking plane," said the smaller man beside him—smaller, but instantly more annoying. He also spoke French—with a rolling Basque tilt.

"How do I know where you dropped from?" said Charlie, barely glancing at him. "How do I know who you are? I was told a team of elite professional soldiers, not—" She waved her disdainful hand over whatever *this* was.

Surrounded by what was left of his men, Fletcher stood at the edge of the woods and eyed the moss-maidens sitting on the rocks and stumps in front of him. Some were leaning against the trees. They weren't armed.

They were all women, every last one of them. The one out in front was clearly the leader, because she carried a Browning and also glared at him as if she was about to yell bloody murder. This confused Fletcher even more. He scanned the treeline, wondering if they'd followed the green light to the wrong location. These could have been milkmaids at dawn, or migrants moving from one town to another. Fletcher opened his mouth to issue the password challenge, fully expecting blank stares in return.

But before he could utter a sound, the woman with the Browning said in French, "No, no, please, take your time, there's no hurry. By all means—make slow and steady the order of the day."

He blinked. "Are you talking to me?"

"You see any other foot-draggers here?"

He exchanged a glance with Rafael, who stood by his side, appraising the silent women.

"La jonquille est vivante," Fletcher said, speaking the challenge. *The narcissus is alive.*

"Mais son ombre est mortelle," the woman responded. *But its shadow is deadly.*

So they'd come to the right place, but with all the wrong facts. Were they always meant to meet up with *women*? Reed hadn't said a word about that.

And why was this woman so upset?

"I'm looking for the *klokkenmaker*," Fletcher said in French.

"Pourquoi?" she said.

"Omloop," Fletcher said.

"Why?" she repeated.

Rafael stepped forward. "And who are *you*?" he asked impatiently, also in French.

"Who are *you*?" returned the woman. Behind her, the others didn't utter a sound, staring at the men with intense curiosity.

"We're looking for Omloop and his group of Belgian partisans called the . . ." Fletcher struggled to remember. The adrenaline of the battle and the angst-ridden flight before it had fried his memory. Come on, Fletcher, he told himself, do better. Just. Do. Fucking. Better. "*La Ligne*."

"That's us," said the woman.

"We're looking for Charles."

"No Charles here," she said. "Do you mean Charlie?"

"You're Charles?"

"I'm not Charles. I can't be clearer. Charlotte Fontaine. Charlie."

"And your entire team is women only?"

"You are wonderfully observant."

"Something's not right," Fletcher said. "Where's the Eureka?"

"Where's your Rebecca?" she shot back.

"Up in the fucking plane," replied a fed-up Rafael.

"And my Eureka's in the fucking woods," Charlie responded in kind. "Where *you* were supposed to land. A kilometer away."

"This can't be it, Fletcher," Rafael said, stepping back. "No. We can't be here under these circumstances. Reed wouldn't do this to us. I won't believe it until we see Omloop. He'll get us to the right people."

"Where's Omloop?" Fletcher repeated.

"Probably asleep in his bed," Charlie said. "He was awake at three when you were scheduled to drop by. Nearly *three* hours ago."

They moved inside the tree line, away from the open fields. Briggs carried a helmet in his hands, overflowing with the cigarettes he'd filched from the Germans. Relaxing slightly, the men shouldered their rifles, lit up, and leaned against the trees, eyeballing the women.

"I don't know who's navigating your planes," Charlie said, "but he ought to be dismissed from duty. Possibly court-martialed."

"That's what *I* said!" said Wolski.

But Rafael, clearly rubbed the wrong way by Charlie, jumped to Frobisher's defense. "Yes, excuse us that while flying by dead reckoning in darkness with nothing to tell water from land, and no signal flare from the church spire, we missed your tiny blot of a village next to a thousand other tiny villages with church spires."

"Oh, Omloop signaled," said Charlie. "But to the north, where you were supposed to be flying from. Not east, like you came the first time. Nor south, like the second time." She shook her head. "What was the plan—land, then start punching Nazis?"

"What were we supposed to do?" said Rafael, continuing to argue.

Fletcher was unable to intervene; he was still too astonished at being met by women. This wasn't the plan. He struggled not to feel demoralized. He knew how punishing the road ahead would be. "Is Omloop a woman too?" he asked. He wasn't sure of anything anymore.

"Do you *need* him to be a woman?" said Charlie.

What we need you to be is men, Fletcher wanted to say. *With muscles and guns who can fight and carry heavy things and run.*

What he felt must have been plain on his face, because Charlie smirked. "Be careful what you wish for. He's a man, all right. But he's seventy."

Rafael groaned. Fletcher suppressed a groan.

"You didn't answer my question about the Germans," Charlie said. "Was that always your plan—to engage them?"

"What do *you* care about dead Germans?" said Rafael.

"I care nothing for them dead," said Charlie, "but *you* should. What do you think will happen when their bodies are found? Did you lose any of yours? Ah," she said, "I see by your faces you have. The Gestapo is going to search every home for fifty miles, until they find you all." She looked so pissed off.

"Maybe if we got the help we needed," said Rafael, "we wouldn't have landed on top of the fucking Krauts."

"We did help you. By signaling you from the tower. Which you ignored."

"Not ignored! Didn't see!"

"Rider," Fletcher said, in a low warning. He faced the woman. "Where's Omloop?"

"Why do you keep repeating his name like a magic spell?" she asked. "Omloop was going to bring you to *me*. But look—you made it. You're already in front of me."

"Aren't we the lucky ones," said Rafael.

"Aren't *we* the lucky ones," said Charlie.

Another young woman spoke up. "Charlie, Charlie," she said in a soft voice.

"Not now, Louise."

"We need to get out of here," Louise said. "It's past dawn. The patrol trucks are on the road. We still have a long way to walk with them. Come on—goal, not process, remember? It's done, they're here. There's so much to do. Why argue?"

"I'm not the one arguing!"

"Uh-huh, fine," Louise said. "Let's go." She rose from her rock and stepped forward.

And as she moved, so did every man in Fletcher's squad—toward her. As if caught in a magnetic storm, they drifted to her like shrapnel to a blast site. Only Fletcher stayed put.

It was remarkable to witness. This young woman was covered head to toe in dark garb, as all the women were. Barely a strand of her blonde hair was visible. All that showed were her blue eyes, her nose, some of her mouth, and the apples of her cheeks. She was shorter than Charlie, and fuller-figured. Her voice was high, but not soft. Her hands were in dark gloves. There were old boots on her feet. And yet . . .

As Fletcher watched, Rafael, who a second earlier had been so hostile toward Charlie, stopped speaking as if his tongue had been cut out. He opened his stance, straightened out, and squared his shoulders—as if to prevent the other soldiers from getting near her.

And then Rafael smiled.

He unleashed his full, high-wattage, Basque-born-and-raised, Pyrenees smuggler, dazzling movie-star smile. "*Bonjour*, Louise. I'm Rafael." He yanked off his glove and extended his hand to the woman. "We should be properly introduced since we're going to be working together."

"Did you properly introduce yourself to me?" said Charlie.

It was as if Charlie stopped existing. Louise rolled her eyes, but she took off her glove and gave Rafael her hand. He bent down theatrically, like a beret-clad Frenchman, and kissed it, pressing his lips to her bare flesh. "*Enchanté, mademoiselle, très enchanté*," he murmured.

Louise smiled back! She didn't slap him, or push him, or swear at him, or do any of the things Fletcher imagined a woman might do if he or any other filthy, muddy, bloody, sweaty stranger—all his easy charm and good looks blacked out by war—tried to ingratiate himself into her good graces in such an obvious and unsubtle manner. Instead, the woodland creature called Louise pulled the hood away from her face and regaled Rafael with her own movie-star glaze.

Perplexed, Fletcher stared at the enchantress, and then slowly returned his gaze to Charlie. *This* woman—unassuming, straightforward, exasperated, serious—was the only thing that commanded Fletcher's attention. But he had other imperatives too—six armed soldiers needed to get off the road and into somebody's bunker. The adrenaline draining away, Fletcher felt the first ache of the full-body collapse that always came after endless days of too much war.

"What's happening?" he said quietly to Charlie, gesturing to the *frisson* next to him.

"Beats me," Charlie said, eyeing Rafael with scorn and Louise with weary impatience—as if it weren't the first time this had happened, but the millionth. "He's *your* soldier." And then, louder, "Lou! I thought you said we needed to get going."

"I did say that, didn't I?" Louise murmured.

"Well, let's go then," Charlie said sharply. "Let's get going."

"Can I have my hand back?" Louise said to Rafael.

"If I said no, would you be upset with me?" He tilted his head.

"Yes," she said. "*Beaucoup*."

Was it Fletcher's imagination or did everything and everyone else in the woods fade a little?

Charlie had planned it different, imagined it different. And her girls had too. They had discussed it, apportioned it. Everyone was going to take a boy, like a package from the post office, and stash him for a day or eight until the men made a plan. But Fletcher shot that down immediately. Like he was the one in charge. "No," he said. "We're not getting separated."

And that was that.

Brigitte tried to argue. "But we all live close by," she said. "We're just a few minutes on bikes away from each other. It won't be a problem." She flashed a smile in Belvedere's direction.

Belvedere glanced behind him, to see who she was smiling at.

Fletcher shook his head. "No. We stay together. I can't have my men getting drunk at alehouses and frolicking in the meadows. We're not on furlough. What if we need to act instantly, and they're indisposed?"

"Indisposed how?" said Charlie with her most unwelcoming frown.

"Yes, indisposed *how*?" said Brigitte, but in her smiling suggestive mouth, the phrase sounded different.

Fletcher didn't reply, as if he'd said all he was going to say on the subject.

Only he and the Basque spoke actual French. Wolski spoke Polish, which wasn't as helpful, and a mishmash of French, Italian, and German.

After brief introductions that sounded more like roll call than friendly exchanges between young men and young women who'd just found each other in the trees, they began to trek away from the drop zone, through field and forest. Louise pulled Charlie aside. "So where are we taking them?" she whispered.

"Why, what are you offering?" Charlie said. "To take them to your mother's?"

"You know I can't! I'd love to—but I can't."

"Well, you heard the man, Lou. He said they must stay together. Why don't we go ask Hélène how she feels about that. Maybe they can sleep on the grass in your garden."

"Just *talk* to him," Louise whispered. "And not like you've been talking to him. Nicer. See if you can persuade him. Use your wiles, Charlie. You keep telling me you have wiles. So use them. Tell him it'll be much better if we each take a soldier with us."

"You're going to bring that rogue home to your *mother*?" Charlie didn't know whether to laugh or gasp. Was Louise joking?

Before the conversation devolved any further, Fletcher called her to him, as they crunched through the forest. "Where is the man from *La Fortuna*?"

"Why?" And then, "What man?"

He didn't respond for a few moments. "Where is he?" he repeated. "Hidden? We need to get him today. As soon as we're settled."

From behind, Louise hit Charlie in the back. *Leave me alone*, Charlie wanted to say. *All of you. Just leave me alone.* She was so tired. "Oh, sure," Charlie said, replying to Fletcher. "Is that before or after I get your clothes and papers and feed you, and find you a spacious enough accommodation?"

"During," he said. "I need to speak to him right away. To know what we're up against."

"You want to know what you're up against?" Charlie said, as hostile and afraid as she'd ever been. "You don't need Ngomo to tell you. *I'll* tell you. You don't have enough men. You don't have enough weapons. You don't have any transportation. Half your men don't speak French."

"Did I ask you?"

"I'm giving it to you straight."

"I didn't ask you. Just bring the man to me."

She tightened her mouth. "He is not alone," she said. "He's got a small Jewish child with him."

"Why?"

"I don't know why." What a question! What nerve! "Because."

"I don't understand. Is it his child?"

"Of course not."

"So what's the problem, then? Just separate them."

"Maybe I didn't make myself clear," Charlie said. "The Congolese man and the Jewish child travel as a pair."

"Why?"

"Will you stop with the why!"

"Answer me and I'll stop. How old is the child?"

"Ten."

"Fine," Fletcher said. "When we sleep, you go get them."

"Why?" said Charlie.

And Fletcher almost, not quite, but very nearly, half smiled.

"They'll stay with us, until—" he began, but she cut him off.

"Oh, so *more* people to stay with you? Where do you think you'll be staying, the six of you together, with Ngomo and the boy?"

For a minute or two they walked in silence. They had another three kilometers to go, but she didn't tell him that. He looked like he might not make it. They all did. Walking next to him in the woods, seeing how drained he was, she regretted her lack of manners. He cleared his throat. "I admit," he said, "I was expecting a different group of partisans."

"Is that supposed to be funny?" said Charlie. Why did she do that? Instantly on the attack.

"Maybe a little bit," said Fletcher.

"Who were you expecting, Lieutenant Gray?"

"Men."

"You *had* men," Charlie exclaimed. "You came from an encampment of half a million men. Why didn't you bring some of them with you if you needed more? Why'd you only bring five, one of them a medic?"

"Actually, he's a board-certified surgeon with the Royal Army Medical Corps," said Fletcher. "And I came with eight men. Lost three."

"Lost three already?" Charlie blinked through her conscience. "You should take better care of them," she said. "Seeing as you have so few."

He looked so devastated when she said this, she wanted to nail her mouth shut before speaking again. What was *wrong* with her! "Did you bury them?" she asked, much quieter.

"Yes."

"They'll look for them," she said. "They dig up everything."

"They'll find nothing," Fletcher said. "No dog tags, tattoos, papers, clothes. They're known only to God."

Everyone has their reasons, she heard her father say in her head. In the past she found succor in those words. The saying helped her understand, allowed her to let things go. But now she wondered if her father would be quite so understanding today. Last week, Alder had turned away one man and one boy. Now there were six! Lumbering, stinking, bleeding, starving, wary, wet. They tried to be quiet as they pushed through the brush, but each of them carried sixty kilos of bulky, unwieldy gear—almost the weight of an extra man.

A platoon of vagabonds needing a place to hide until they figured out how to accomplish what Charlie and Omloop knew to be impossible. Hiding Ngomo was a fool's errand, as was getting anywhere near *La Fortuna.* So naïve with their little hopes and dreams, Charlie thought, as they walked. So childlike.

And yet, like children, they were counting on *her* to take them somewhere safe, where they could regroup and eat. Wash up, bandage wounds, clean their weapons. Talk like normal men, as they forged plans to go into the heart of darkness.

What a burden it was to be counted on.

So arrogant, so demanding, so unapologetic.

Fletcher was saying something to her, but she didn't hear.

"What?" It came out as a bark. *Geez*, Charlie!

"I *know* we're a terrible burden," said Fletcher. "We're asking a lot of you. I'm truly grateful."

Flustered and tongue-tied, she couldn't think of a single thing to say in return.

"Does anyone call you Charlotte?" he said.

"My father, when he is livid with me," she said, cringing.

"Charlie it is, then," said Fletcher, facing ahead.

Louise wrapped her knuckles into Charlie's back. "You didn't even try!" she whispered from behind her.

"How the hell did you want me to finesse that one?" Charlie hissed back. "You heard him. We stay together."

Charlie was headed to the only place she could go, the only place she knew she couldn't be turned away from. She took Fletcher and his men to Lillehaven.

29

Saint Lament

Hubner entered—and stood like a dolt in the middle of the office.

"I'm not done yet." Von Rheinhardt was staring blankly at the walls, not attending to the dozen pieces of urgent paper on his desk. They were so behind on the work, they had to come in on Sunday.

"Did you have a chance to approve the new colors for the camouflage nets?" Hubner asked. Berlin had mandated stricter camouflage standards.

"Remind me—what were my choices again?"

"*Dunkelgelb*, Panzer Olive, and Reed Green."

"Let's go with Panzer Olive."

"Very good, sir. Did you sign off on the photographs?"

"What *photographs*?" Rheinhardt screeched.

". . . Uh—for the weekly flagpole inspection?" Hubner looked frightened.

"Oh." It was a Saturday morning ritual. The Nazi flag was raised undamaged and saluted at dawn, and photographs had to be taken of the process every week. "Yes," Rheinhardt said, composing himself. "They're somewhere on my desk. I'll get them to you." He'd never even glanced at *those* photographs.

"Did you have a chance to review the disciplinary procedure for the *Feldgendarmerie* who urinated on a statue?"

"Not yet," said Rheinhardt, "but I did look over the other one, the *Kommissar* caught bartering his wife's nylons for some chocolate on the black market."

"He said it was their anniversary, sir."

"Give him 24 hours latrine duty and wish him a happy one, Hubner."

"Will do."

"Oh, and please revise the Herentals church bulletin before it's printed and distributed. In it, they're asking for prayers for 'liberation.' Are they joking? And they're writing in some detail about the Allied landings. That won't do.

Is that Omloop's doing, do you think? Didn't he say his shop is right by the church? You think he messes with the bulletins?"

"I don't know if that man can read and write, sir, but that reminds me—I overheard some news."

"I don't have the time or the inclination for any more news, Hubner," said Rheinhardt, sounding completely depleted even though it was barely noon on Sunday.

"This morning I was delivering Form 27-B to the Port *Polizei*, to get a sign-off from a junior clerk on that enhanced security augmentation you requested for *La Fortuna*, and I heard some interesting chatter."

"He tells me anyway," Rheinhardt muttered. "This is important to me why?"

"There was a raid on a local army garrison."

"Where?"

"Off Saint Lament, near Vorselaar."

"Not familiar with it. A raid by who, the partisans?" This wasn't unusual. The Belgian bastards were constantly disrupting army operations. Rheinhardt took a breath. Why did everything irritate him these days? "You know what? Don't tell me. It's none of our business. Seriously, Hubner—we've got trouble aplenty without worrying about fisticuffs on the outskirts of town. Was it our men? No. Was the fight inside Antwerp? Again no. The perimeter of my authority is clear. Why are you bothering me with this?"

Hubner lowered his voice. "Sir, you know I'd only bring it to your attention if I thought it might be useful."

"That's not true, Hubner. You constantly bring to my attention the most idiotic facts, and you regale me with them until I'm ready to bite down on a cyanide pill. You're like the *klokkenmaker* Omloop—but a lot less entertaining."

"Yes, sir," Hubner said, and proceeded to speak in rapid-fire German, to get his words out. "I overheard them saying that all our soldiers were killed, mein Herr!"

Von Rheinhardt stared at his twitching and angular lieutenant. "How many killed?"

"Two platoons. Two dozen men."

"All dead?"

"Yes, sir."

"And why would this be of interest to me?"

"The manner in which they were killed, mein Herr, closely resembled what happened aboard *La Fortuna*."

Rheinhardt waited. "Continue," he said.

"Most of them were killed at close range, the *Polizei* said. Looked like military close-quarter combat. Some were garroted. There were no grenades thrown, no demolition charges. No audible fire. And all their weapons and cigarettes were filched!"

"When did this happen?"

"Not sure, sir. Last night some time. The milk delivery van chanced upon a corpse at seven this morning." Hubner was nearly whispering in anxiety and excitement.

"Their corpse or ours?"

"Ours, sir. We're still searching for any of theirs."

Late afternoon, Hubner knocked again and, shutting the door behind him, rushed forward. "Sir, there've been developments!"

"Speak to me calmly like a Gestapo *Kriminalkommissar*. Be worthy of your rank. Now—what developments?"

"They found two men buried in the freshly dug ground!"

"Calmly, Hubner. Ours or theirs?"

"Theirs!"

"Only two?"

"Yes! Apparently, they were naked, with no marks on them—no papers, no weapons, no dog tags, nothing!"

Von Rheinhardt sat mulling.

"As if someone was trying to hide their identities in death, sir!"

"Yes, Hubner, thank you," Rheinhardt said. "Where would I be if you didn't explain the most basic things to me."

"They were wrapped in silk rags, sir."

"*Silk* rags?"

"Yes, cut-up silk material." Hubner widened his eyes. "Like maybe from *parachutes*."

"Aha."

"That's interesting—right, sir?"

"It's not *not* interesting," said Rheinhardt, appraising his lieutenant.

"The worry at headquarters is that maybe some Allied soldiers dropped down for port disruption or reconnaissance."

"Hubner, think about it. Why would the Allies need to land here for recon? The Belgians are doing all their dirty work for them. Our mission is to apprehend and discipline the Belgian saboteurs, not to look for side trouble." Rheinhardt got up and grabbed his cigarettes.

Hubner watched him. "Where are you headed, sir?"

"I'm going outside for a smoke—right on Daisy Lane. Is that all right with you? Do I have your permission?"

"It's a little unprecedented."

"Unprecedented things are happening everywhere, Hubner," said Rheinhardt. "I need to clear my head." He stopped. "Oh, by the way, I looked over your report on the weekly morale questionnaire post invasion." He clicked approvingly. "Your summary of the soldiers' state of mind was a masterpiece of evasion. You managed to turn operatic despair into cautious optimism. Well done. Goebbels himself would be proud."

"I'm pleased you're pleased, sir."

Rheinhardt stopped at the front door and turned around. "Out of an abundance of caution, go ahead and put eight more men on the *La Fortuna* detail."

"You want me to—" Hubner blanched. "Sir, you'd like *twenty* men on Sector Seven out of an *abundance of caution*?"

"After what you just told me? Absolutely," said Rheinhardt. "One can never be too careful, Hubner. Look what happened in Saint Lament."

30

Lillehaven

On Sunday afternoon, after the morning masses, when Saint Waltrude was mostly empty, Charlie waited in the pew, but Omloop walked right past her without stopping. She knew what that meant. To assess the level of danger, she said to him sideways, *"The bell rings in the holy place."*

"And the faithful kneel in prayer," he replied.

That was just below the drop-everything-and-run-because-they're-coming response: *And the faithful pray for mercy.*

Omloop walked on, slow and steady. When she rose a few minutes later to follow him to the confessionals in the nave, her legs were shaking.

He went into the priest's box, and she slipped into one of the penitent stalls.

"Got them?" he said.

"Yes. They're at the barn. He needs to see you. Can you come?"

"No," Omloop said. "I'm being followed. Not safe for him—or even for you."

"What am I supposed to do?"

"Bring him here if you can. Tomorrow afternoon maybe."

"Do you have papers for him? For the others? There are six altogether."

"I've got two sets," he said, pulling some documents from his tunic. "I'll get you the rest tomorrow. Keep them close, don't let them wander around."

"Where are they going to go? He won't let any of them out of his sight."

"Good. What about your two *packages* from Lost Hope?"

"He needs them. Immediately."

"I don't know what you plan to do," Omloop said. "All the area checkpoints now have dogs sniffing through the trucks, looking for that one hidden . . . *package* from equatorial Africa. New procedures."

Charlie was splintering from anxiety. "Who's after you?"

"Dory," Omloop said. "He volunteered. That's how I know. They put a tail on me after our little interview last week."

Dorian de Smet was Fitz's friend and their partisan plant at the Belgian *Polizei.*

"I mean . . . who hired Dory?"

"Who do you think? Rheinhardt, of course."

"Personally?"

"No—Hubner, his fucking aide." Omloop crossed himself. "Forgive me, Father," he muttered, "for my coarse language in Your house. I shall never say the adjutant's name again."

"Is it going to be safe to bring"—she checked the fake identity papers—"Florent here tomorrow for a visit?"

"Am I a soothsayer? I don't know. Don't dress him too clean."

"Oh, not to worry," Charlie said, recalling the state of the soldiers.

"Holy, holy, holy," Omloop said, signaling the end of the conversation.

"And the earth is full of His glory," Charlie murmured in coded reply, but Omloop was already gone.

"They're dead," said Margot, summarizing the situation in her inimitable style when Charlie returned to Lillehaven. "It's been over twelve hours, and they haven't stirred." The women peered at the soldiers through the broken slats of the decaying barn.

It was true. They'd dropped where they stood, still in their tactical gear, dirty and soot-covered, and passed out. Now, it was eight in the evening—almost sunset, and they were all still out.

The girls had gone home and returned in the late afternoon, freshened up and dressed in their Sunday best. Charlie and Louise brought food and drink, some bread, a bit of cheese. Charlie found them some smoked sausage from one of her black market vendors. Now that they knew how many were here, Margot and Maxine collected civilian wear for the men, shoes, caps, belts, and placed them silently by each soldier's head. Mireille and Brigitte laid a bar of soap on top of the clothing piles as a reminder of what to do first.

Louise made them her mini lemon meringue tarts. She took her lemon obsession and made it into a showstopper. She scraped every rationed egg white to do it. What a wasted effort it was. The men never woke. After it got dark, the girls finally dispersed, and Charlie curled up in a corner of the barn, her Browning hidden in the straw by her hand, and fell into a dead sleep herself.

When she woke up at six on Monday morning, she was covered with one of the extra tunics the twins had brought. All the men were gone.

They appeared back in the glade so quietly, not a crunch, snap, or rustle announced their return. So, they did have some skills after all. All six men—scrubbed, shaved, and wearing civilian rags—looked like different humans, though none of them seemed comfortable in Belgian clothes. The pantaloons and tunics hung unnaturally on their bodies. They all looked like concrete blocks in burlap sacks, stiff and awkward. They returned carrying their wet combat gear which they'd washed in the brook Wolski found and hung them out to dry on rafters inside the barn. Briggs said he would dive back into his combat garb as soon as the clothes were dry. Fletcher translated for her, and it took him a good few minutes to explain that Briggs was joking.

Of all the men Charlie didn't recognize, she didn't recognize the man named Fletcher the most, except for his height and his violet eyes. She wanted to warn him not to stare at people—the brown-gray neutral garb would be all for naught if he allowed the enemy to catch the color of those eyes. No one could forget them. Grudgingly, she had to admit the rest of Fletcher was also unnecessarily attractive. He had a strong neck, a defined jaw, a prominent Adam's apple. He had a mustache and under it a proportioned, perfectly formed mouth. There was simply no reason in the universe for his mouth to be that appealing.

"I did a poor job of shaving, didn't I?" he said to her, catching her gaping at his chin and throat. "I didn't know the facial hair norm for men in Belgium."

Recovering, she quickly composed herself to hide her embarrassment. "Clean-shaven is good," she said, clearing her throat and regaining her solemnity. "Mustache is also good." She wanted to ask if he was the one who had covered her up, but didn't—just in case the answer was no.

The men demolished their bread and sausage as if they'd never eaten before and might never eat again. Everything she and Louise had brought them, they devoured, including the day-old meringues. Charlie had to fetch more milk and pull more carrots from the garden. The food was meant to last them a week.

The other five weren't hard on the eyes either. Briggs was enormous; the Belgian clothes looked like they were being punished for trying to contain him. Wolski had the sturdy, familiar face of men Charlie had grown up with, solid and smart-eyed. Belvedere looked like a worn-out professor at the end of a particularly disappointing term. Hawk Turner never spoke and never looked at her. He was gaunt, almost spectral, a beautiful blond wisp of a boy—and absolutely petrifying. Was it her imagination or did he have gold-colored eyes, like a tiger? She tried not to stare. No, not a tiger. A hawk. *Faucon.* Of course. That only made her stare at him harder, and him turn away from her even more.

Rafael was a different story. Her ill-will toward him was so strong, it actively obscured his dramatic features. She knew he was handsome, but her mind rejected the fact. While the others had been vastly improved by soap, water, and the miracle of dry clothes, she thought Rafael looked about as good clean as he did covered in muck. For some reason he decided to address her. "Shar-*leee*," he drawled, "why are you the only one here? Where's the rest of your splendid crew? Any chance you could collect the lovely Louise and bring her back for a visit? Or does she live close enough to bike here?"

"Rider, read the fucking room," said Fletcher.

"What? I'm simply expressing a guest's curiosity about one of our gracious hosts," Rafael said with a clipped smile. "Though none, of course, as gracious as *you*, Shar-lee."

"Do you think we've been sitting around waiting for you to fall to us from our skies?" Charlie said.

"Yes?" said Rafael. "Or was that a rhetorical question?"

"Do you think my girls have nothing else to do? You know, because of you, we can't tell the British—for whom we've been working all these years—why we're suddenly unable to deliver photographs of troop positions, or tell London the Germans have increased Belgian production of coal and copper, or that they've ramped up production of electricity near the Olen corridor—for inexplicable reasons." Charlie kept her voice level. "My brother was arrested two weeks ago on vandalism charges. He's now sitting in the local jail, about to be shipped off to Germany. And I can't figure out a way to get him out, because I'm here watching *you*." She scanned all six of them with open judgment. "And I promise you," she added, "you want him out because you're going to need his help."

"Where is the Congolese man, Charlotte?" said Fletcher. "We agreed that you would bring him to me today."

"What's his name again, Fletch?" Rafael said. "Ngong?"

"His name?" said Charlie, her voice dripping with derision. "I'll tell you his name. Molotov cocktail in a barn. Walking wildfire. The reason we'll all be burned to the ground—civilians, partisans, guilty, innocent—all of us reduced to ashes. *That's* his name. Take your pick."

"If only you knew how right you are," Fletcher said grimly.

"Charlotte!" a voice bellowed. Everyone jumped, even the hardened soldiers. Alder came crashing through the woods, rounding the barn, with a look of dismay that bordered on horror. "Oh my God, child, what have you *done*?"

"Charlotte!" Fletcher whispered. "You didn't tell your *father* you were bringing us to his barn?"

"Well, you know what they say," Charlie muttered, stepping forward. "Better to beg forgiveness than ask for permission. Vake!" She motioned for him. "I'd like you to meet some people."

Alder was incensed and didn't care who heard him. "They can't stay here, Charlie!"

"Well, hang on, Vake . . ."

"No, no, no, no, *no*. Find them another safehouse."

"Vake, there are six of them, and they must stay together."

"Where are they from?"

Fletcher began to speak, but Charlie shushed him. "America. France. England. Poland. Allied soldiers, Vake."

"Elite of the elite," Rafael offered in French. "Rangers, technical sergeants . . ."

"I don't give a fuck if they're Eisenhower himself!" shouted Alder. He was so loud that he had summoned Elke with his earsplitting wrath. She waddled out of the woods, arms outstretched, tumbling toward Alder in a panic, crying, *"Aldeke, Aldeke!"*

"Your mother is pregnant?" Fletcher said sideways to Charlie.

"She's not my fucking mother. *Shh*."

He widened his eyes and stopped talking.

"Elke, go back to the house. I'm fine, stop overreacting, Go." But Alder himself did not calm down. "The Allies are the sworn enemy of the Reich!" he resumed yelling as she tottered off. "It's execution for us all if we get caught."

"Jews or Allies—what's worse, Vake?"

"It's all just degrees of catastrophe!" Alder was red in the face.

"What about Congolese men? Are black men the enemy?"

"We are all enemies of the Germans," Alder said through his teeth. "Us, Jews, Africans, collaborators. But Allies, being the actual enemy, are the ones they will hit hardest."

Rafael began to speak, but Fletcher stepped forward, cutting him off. "Charlotte," he said formally, "may I speak with your father in private?"

"No, Fletcher." Don't do it, she wanted to add. There's no point. You're not going to talk him out of his feelings. He's going to feel what he's going to feel, and that's that.

"Lieutenant Fletcher Gray, Monsieur Fontaine," Fletcher said, as if Charlie hadn't spoken.

"Call him Alder," she said with a sigh. Was it barely morning of the first day? *Mère de Dieu*.

"Call me what you like," said Alder, "but you can't speak to me in private. What are you going to do? Try to persuade me in your broken French that *your* mission is the single most important operation of the war?"

"He speaks fluent French, Vake," said Charlie.

"He could be Voltaire for all I care!" Alder hollered.

Fletcher stood his ground politely but firmly. "Just over there, Alder."

They walked a few meters away. Charlie joined them, but she didn't stand beside Alder. She stood with Fletcher, across from her father. Fletcher held out his closed fist. Inside were two large rough-cut diamonds. Alder stared at the stones in incomprehension. "Is this a joke?" he said. "What am I supposed to do with those?"

"Anything you want," said Fletcher. "Go anywhere, buy anything, start over, hide, pay off whoever you like. Take them. They're yours."

Alder's hand didn't move a centimeter forward. "What good are they to me?" he said. "This is my home, my work, my life. Where the *fuck* am I supposed to go?"

"I know you're afraid," Fletcher said.

"Oh? What gave that away?"

"It's not going to be for long," Fletcher said. "We'll stay here only until we achieve our primary objective."

"And when is *that* going to be?"

Primary? Charlie wanted to ask, frowning. There was more than one?

"We'll be quiet," Fletcher said. "We'll leave no footprint. If they come snooping, we'll hide. But this is the most important—"

Alder cut him off. "I've heard it *all* before. Vital, you say. Essential. Like the package I was supposed to transport to a man in Bruges?"

"What package?"

"Like the message about bells I was supposed to relay to a journalist at *La Libre Belgique*?"

"What message?"

"Like the flowers hiding forged papers I was supposed to deliver to a woman in Mechelen?"

"What woman?"

Alder blinked.

Charlie blinked.

Fletcher took a breath in the sudden drop in pressure in the clearing.

"Do you think I'm new to this?" Alder continued. "I've been doing this nonstop for four years!"

"You don't sound like a civilian to me," said Fletcher. "You sound like a soldier who's been fighting a long, hard war and you're tired. I'm asking you to find it in yourself to fight one more battle."

Alder jabbed a finger hard into his chest. "I *know* in my heart," he said, "that this is the most dangerous operation of all." He was panting. "I'll lend you my trucks. I'll give you my flowers. I'll ferry your messages, but you can't bring the war to my door."

"Understood."

"Lillehaven can't be the place of your battle against the Wehrmacht."

"It won't be."

"And you can't use your radio equipment to communicate with anyone from here."

Fletcher paused, glancing at Charlie.

"Father is right," Charlie said. "That you cannot do."

"Do you know why?" Alder said. "Because there's nothing for a kilometer around me. They pick up a signal, they'll know it's from my farm. And then we're all belly up."

"Fine," said Fletcher, sticking out his hand. "You have my word."

Alder said nothing more. Charlie reached for her father, but he staggered away, looking spent and deflated. "I can't believe you're doing this to me again," he said to her. "My children will be the death of me."

Turning, he stumbled back toward the farmhouse. Charlie waited a few beats, then motioned for Fletcher and the rest to follow her. Vake would recover, Charlie knew. Somehow, he always did. And though the men didn't know it, her father wanted to make peace. He knew there was no other choice. She led, and they fell in behind her as they passed through the last line of the trees.

The woods gave way, and Fletcher stepped out into a parade of color. The fields at Lillehaven were in full bloom, row after row of red, gold, blue, violet, pink, and yellow. It was color so loud it felt like sound. Like fireworks at the fairgrounds, only exploding in broad daylight instead. A stir of wind rushed in and caught him mid-breath, sweet and thick and overpowering. Lillehaven ambushed his senses. He had to stop walking.

"What? You like?" said Charlie, coming to stand beside him.

Fletcher nodded. "Not even Solomon in all his glory was arrayed like one of these," he said quietly.

"Yes," she said. "It was a nice home for us once."

"No wonder your father's upset. Look at all he's risking."

"Yes," said Charlie, taking a breath. "It's coarse to admit it, and Father won't say it, but unfortunately, the occupation, though very bad for life, has turned out to be *very* good for business."

"Really?" Fletcher muttered, staring at the fields.

"As you can see," Charlie said, waving her arm over the flowers. "Who knew how much the Nazis enjoy fresh flowers in their vases every morning, as they eat their breakfast and plan the devastation of Europe and the extermination of the Jews." The words caught, and she stopped speaking.

Alder emerged from the house with a tray bearing a jug and eight mismatched glasses. "Homemade plum brandy," he said, pouring. "*Slivovitz.* Let's raise a glass to all the impossible things we don't want to do."

"Hear, hear," said Rafael.

"It's not for drinking," Alder added. "It's for surviving."

Briggs took a swig and coughed so hard he had to sit down. "Jesus!" he said. "What the hell is this? It could pickle a live pig."

"Eau-de-vie-de-prune." Water of life from plums. Alder raised his cup. "*Proost.*"

"Proost," echoed the others.

Charlie and Fletcher clinked glasses. Belvedere swigged, muttering, "Well, that was medicinal." The brandy was syrupy sweet at first taste. Then came the fire, scorching Fletcher's throat. He could see Charlie was used to it. But determined not to show her how it affected him, Fletcher took another long swallow, even as his eyes watered.

"Yank's got something to prove, as always," Belvedere said, pouring himself another.

"Me, I got nothin' to prove," said Wolski, holding out his cup. "Just keep it coming."

Charlie gave Fletcher a quick once-over. "Easy, soldier. Maybe your men can be three sheets to the wind, but you're about to meet Omloop—your favorite Belgian. You'll need your wits about you."

"His wits went the way of the Slivovitz," said Belvedere.

31

The Klokkenmaker's Apprentice

Omloop was standing in the courtyard of Saint Waltrude, smoking, when Rheinhardt pulled up on a brand-new BMW motorcycle, with Hubner crammed into the sidecar. The adjutant climbed out and headed straight for the rectory to interrogate Father Bavo, the parish priest, about the inappropriate items they had found in the latest church bulletin. Rheinhardt veered toward the smoking *klokkenmaker*.

"To what do I owe this unexpected visit, Herr Rheinhardt?" said Omloop, trying not to drop his cigarette.

"We have business with the priest," Rheinhardt said. "But I haven't seen your truck around Antwerp recently. Thought I'd check in."

"How kind of you to inquire after my health, mein Herr," said Omloop. "You're right, I've not been at my best. The arthritis, I'm afraid."

"What's with the shakes?"

"I don't know, sir. But I agree—it's a growing problem." Omloop smiled faintly. "Still, I have been to Antwerp. Our paths haven't crossed, but rest assured, I'm working harder than ever."

At that moment, three direction-finding vans screeched into the church courtyard like hounds on a scent. The first slammed to a stop, and a sweating *Funkabwehr* signalman jumped out, still wearing half a headset, trailed by a corporal scrambling to keep up. "We got a spike, Herr *Sturmbannführer*!" the technician panted. "Brief burst—definitely interference—somewhere near the—uh—spire? No, maybe the crypt. Possibly the roof. It's always a damn farm or a steeple, sir. But something hit."

"Could've come from down the street," said the operator in the second van, waving a clipboard. He didn't bother getting out. "You said farmhouse last time, and it was a shoe shop."

Casually, Omloop pointed, his arm shaking. "I'd try the woods over there. Perhaps the cellar. There's no one in the belfry, I assure you—no one except my grand-nephew Florent."

"Who?" said Rheinhardt, as the signalmen and the Gestapo hurried around the corner, out of view.

"Florent, sir. He's helping me to restore the steeple bell mechanism."

"I thought you worked alone, Omloop," Rheinhardt said.

Omloop showed Rheinhardt his trembling fingers. "I'm having a bit of trouble with the fine work, sir," he said. "He's come from Bruges for a few weeks to help out—till I'm back to speed."

"What if you never get up to speed, Omloop?" Rheinhardt said. "Where is this nephew? Call him down here at once."

The wooden stair-turret door creaked open, and a tall, limping man hobbled into the courtyard, wiping his hands on a grimy cloth. A brown cap was slouched over his brow, and a short file was clutched in his right hand. Grease streaked his tunic sleeve, and his face was smudged with soot. "Uncle," he said, approaching Omloop and ignoring Rheinhardt, "it's not good."

"What is it, Flor?"

"The second clapper linkage is fused with verdigris," Florent said. "I scraped off most of it, but the counterweight's still unbalanced."

"Yes, I been having problems with it meself," said Omloop, looking into the dirt.

"We're going to have to file the gudgeon, or she'll never strike true at quarter-past," Florent said. "Do you want me to do that?"

"Well, hang on. Did you oil the yoke?" Omloop asked.

"Lightly. Too much and you know she'll pitch forward."

"Eyes up," Rheinhardt cut in. "Who are *you*?" His French wasn't good enough to evaluate anyone else's, and besides, the Belgians in Bruges spoke a dialect so garbled, even other Belgians had trouble understanding them.

"I told you, mein Herr," said Omloop, "that's Florent, my nephew."

"I need him to speak for himself, bellmaker."

"Say hello to the *Sturmbannführer*, Flor. The esteemed Erich von Rheinhardt, Commander of Antwerp."

The man raised his chin and tipped his cap. "*Bonjour*." He didn't look directly at Rheinhardt, keeping his eyes hooded.

Rheinhardt flared his nostrils and narrowed his gaze. Up close, the bellmaker's nephew reeked of the unmistakable, cloying scent of homemade alcohol. Disgraceful. "Your papers," Rheinhardt snapped.

Sticking the sanding file under his armpit, the scruffy apprentice rummaged awkwardly in his pocket.

"Flor's my cousin's husband's nephew by marriage on his mother's Flemish side." Omloop chuckled, while Rheinhardt inspected the documents. "I can barely keep it straight myself, mein Herr."

Rheinhardt had to cut through Omloop's verbal muck or he'd never get any answers. "Why isn't he conscripted like everyone else?"

"Oh! But you can see for yourself why—he's lame, mein Herr. Just look at him. His one leg is shorter than the other by five centimeters. Fell out of a belfry when he was twelve. Never quite recovered."

Florent slumped to one side, shuffling his feet. With a subtle wince, he shifted his weight, as though his limp were something ancient and bone-deep. "Also, Uncle, one of your smaller bells has a hairline crack on the soundbow," he said. He was all business. Rheinhardt wasn't used to this lack of deference. Well, drunks and eccentrics were often like that—unpredictable. And this man appeared to be both.

Florent went on speaking. "It's going to lose resonance soon if we don't pull it down and reforge the shoulder." His attention remained solely on his uncle. "Want me to carry it down?"

Omloop patted his arm. "Maybe tomorrow you can help me with that, Flor," he said. "You've done enough for today."

Rheinhardt appraised both uncle and nephew. He remained wary—but then, he was always wary these days. Deciding to be satisfied for now, he handed the papers back to the younger man, and said, "You keep close time, young Florent."

"Close is the only way I know how to keep it," the cripple said. His eyes flashed violet—brief and strange. Wiping the file on his trouser leg, he limped back to the stairwell without waiting for a reply.

Fletcher was pulling the wooden planks out of his shoe when a huffing Omloop appeared at the top of the spiral staircase in the belfry. "Did you send your message before the trucks came?" he asked. "That was close. We can't do that again. It's all over for us if we get caught."

"Yes," Fletcher said. "I'm a little rusty on the keys. I need to type faster. But it went out."

TEAM ON GROUND STOP SIX ACCOUNTED FOR STOP FIRST OBJECTIVE UNDER RECONNAISSANCE STOP SECOND OBJECTIVE FLUID STOP WILL REPORT FURTHER ANON STOP

"The Rheinhardt man is dangerous."

"Tell me about it."

"He doesn't miss much, does he?" Fletcher said.

"Actually, he misses quite a few things," Omloop said, "because of his astonishing arrogance. But forget him for a sec. Tell me how you did that."

"Your voices carried. I heard you, knew there was a problem. I stashed my radio in the wall like you showed me, broke off a piece of railing, stuffed it in my shoe, and headed downstairs."

"That's not what I meant."

Fletcher picked up his two packs, radio in one, crank generator in the other. "What do you want to know? How I got the *klokkenmaker* details so tight?" He smiled lightly. "My grandfather was a *klokkenmaker* in New Orleans. Best there was—no disrespect intended. Even in Wyoming, he still forges a bell or two for the local churches. And he taught me. You could say I was his apprentice." His voice was full of affection.

"He taught you well, young Florent," said Omloop.

"Yes, he lived through many things." Fletcher lost the casual tone. "Where can we go to talk?"

"Talk here. Just keep it low. Like you said—voices carry."

Once he heard Fletcher's mission objective, Omloop was not encouraging. "You may be excellent at bells and lies," he said, "but what you want to do can't be done. You have failed before you've even begun."

Fletcher appraised him. Omloop was probably older than his grandfather, but boy, did this man have some verve and life in him. "Why don't you wait to hear how I want to do it before you trash my plan."

"I may not know why the Allies had to send a half-dozen of their best to secure some cargo off a trading vessel, but here's what I do know." Omloop stared directly at Fletcher. "The man you just met downstairs—he knows what's on *La Fortuna*."

"No, he doesn't," Fletcher said, feeling himself pale slightly. "He can't."

"He *knows*," Omloop said in the low, calm tone of someone who could not be argued with. "And the reason I *know* he knows is because five days ago, he barely had one patrolman posted at the dockside. Three days ago, he had twelve. And this morning he had *twenty*."

A skeptical Fletcher became less patient. "You're exaggerating."

"You don't think I can count to twenty?"

"Are they armed?"

"To the gills. Automatics, semi-automatics, a surface-to-air gig on the quay, a crateful of grenades."

"When do they go off duty?"

"Never."

Fletcher stopped talking.

"Erich von Rheinhardt knows what's on that ship," Omloop said. "And he values it just as much as the United States Army."

"I don't believe you," Fletcher said. He said it, but inside, he deeply feared Omloop was right.

"Florent, my dear nephew, what do I care what you believe?" Omloop said. "My only stake in this is to protect my own people. I don't want you to use my precious women—and men—for a suicide mission."

"Is Charlotte's brother Fitz one of your people?"

"Who wants to know?"

"She says he's in jail. She wants him out."

"She always wants something. It's not so easy to spring him. Everyone knows who he is and where he lives. If he runs, they'll come for Alder. She's not thinking straight."

Fletcher studied Omloop, chewing his lip. "How big is the town jail?" he said. "How many holding cells?"

"Three, I think. And one drunk tank. Why?"

Reaching into the inner pocket of his tunic, Fletcher pulled out a pouch and produced a thousand Belgian francs.

"You want me to bribe the guards?" Omloop scoffed. "A thousand francs won't do it."

Fletcher told Omloop his idea.

Omloop narrowed his gaze, eyeing Fletcher more closely. "Who *are* you, kid?" he said with a whistle. "That's not bad. Give me another two hundred and I'll see what I can do."

"Can we get back to *La Fortuna* now?" Fletcher said, handing him a few more bills.

Omloop shook his head. "No money in the world's going to fix that one for you, *mon p'tit*."

"Tell me why I can't take the ship out to sea and sink it."

"More reasons than there are hours in the day," Omloop said. "The egress to the sea through the Scheldt River is nearly twenty kilometers." He shook his head. "And before you suggest it, no, the river isn't deep enough to sink a ship. Even if you did get past the sentry or cast off without anyone noticing that the ship they're supposed to be guarding has gone missing, you'd be moving at barely two knots through the narrows. That's some stealth operation, Florent—taking five or six hours to trudge to open water. No, no, I'm not done," he added, cutting Fletcher off before he could speak. "Ships aren't allowed to move at night, so your derring-do, peanut-the-speed-demon mission would have to happen in broad daylight. And just in case you're *still* entertaining this fantasy, after your Normandy invasion last week, *no* ships are allowed in or out of Antwerp. Not merchant, not medical, not even German vessels. The port's locked down. In sum"—Omloop looked down into his weathered hands—"*La Fortuna* cannot be moved."

Fletcher took barely a breath before he said, "*If* you're right . . ."

"I'm always right," said Omloop.

"If you're right," continued Fletcher, "and Rheinhardt knows, then why hasn't he offloaded the cargo and taken it elsewhere?"

"I'm not privy to the workings of a Nazi heart, Florent," said Omloop. "What do you care what he does with it?"

"Because once he transfers the cargo onto trucks," said Fletcher, "it could be our chance to act."

"And do what?"

"Take it from him, obviously."

"And do *what* with it?"

Omloop was impossible. "That's a bridge too far for me at the moment," Fletcher said. Baby steps.

"Everything's a bridge too far," said Omloop.

"Do you have eyes on him in Antwerp? Can you find out what he's planning?"

"Are you giving me directives, Florent? Commanding me?"

"Yes, dear uncle. I am. On behalf of the most worthwhile cause—the unconditional surrender of Nazi Germany. And thank you."

"Before or after I deal with the Fitz fiasco?"

"During."

"Holy, holy, holy," muttered Omloop in disbelief and dismissal, gripping the railing to begin his descent.

Fletcher had no idea what that meant, so he replied with the only thing that came to mind.

"The earth is full of His glory," he said.

32

Racial Properties of Belgian Clay

After returning from Herentals, Rheinhardt sat alone in his dark, locked office, seething.

He didn't know how to free himself from the quagmire he was in.

He didn't know how to find the answers he needed.

Above him was military pomp and bureaucratic uselessness.

And below him was nothing but Hubner.

Sabotage lurked around every corner. Rheinhardt was the only one down in the shit and the dirt and the mud, the only one driving around to barbaric outer villages like an errand boy, mocked by lesser men and his own commanders alike.

The rot wasn't just on the outside.

It was within.

Take Otto Brandt—an SS-*Standartenführer*, a full colonel, always with manicured hands and sleek hair, always lathering on too much cologne and puffing the most expensive cigarettes. *The garden-party Nazi* is what Rheinhardt called him.

Brandt had given himself the additional title of SS Liaison for Civil Shipping Operations in Antwerp—a moniker both meaningless and grandiose. The new title allowed Brandt to avoid any real work, yet to skim off every manifest Rheinhardt brought to him for his careless signature. Often the man wasn't even at headquarters, but instead attending luncheons and black-tie galas in Brussels. Rheinhardt was left in the dirty port to do the actual work, and was rewarded with vicious mockery when he on occasion became overenthusiastic about details.

All three of them, Rheinhardt, Drechsler, and Brandt, viewed Antwerp as a backwater post that no one cared about, a stepping stone to a more prestigious transfer. And yet it was obvious that this transfer would never happen. The stark fact that Rheinhardt had to drive to a parochial fringe like Herentals to interview a pathetic, twitching *klokkenmaker* and his souse of a nephew proved his point. There were no more good men left, and victory was by no means assured. Rheinhardt was a touch skeptical about the veracity of the glowing reports from Berlin.

He knew that both Brandt and Drechsler were utterly disconnected from the realities of war, and why not? In the four years they'd been stationed in Antwerp, hardly anything of note had happened. Oh, there were minor hiccups—black-market smuggling, wrong quantities of basic goods, occasional odd shipments of raw materials such as beryllium, which no one had ever heard of—but mostly it was just sparkling receptions for Antwerp's high command and unremitting slog for Rheinhardt.

But finally, *finally* there was a sliver of light, and for the first time, that light shone on him. Except nothing came easy. Even the tiniest chance to thrash his way out of obscurity was filled with pitfalls and craters.

Rheinhardt stormed across his office, flung open the door and barged into the reception area. Hubner staggered into his chair as if blown back by a gale. "Did you find me someone at the university?" Rheinhardt loomed over Hubner's small desk. As always, when there was no one *up* to yell at, he yelled *down* at Hubner.

"University?" Hubner repeated dumbly. "No. Was I supposed to?"

"Hubner!"

"Perhaps the *Sturmbannführer* with his keen insight could remind me what I was supposed to—"

"The physicist, Hubner! The chemist!"

Hubner was speechless. "Was I supposed to do that, sir?"

"Hubner, if this is one of your jokes, I'll have you in the brig by nightfall."

"Sir, if you recall, I told you that I didn't know anyone there."

"And you thought that was the *end* of your duties? I wasn't having a conversation with you! Clearly your directive was to find someone!"

"I badly misunderstood, sir . . . it wasn't clear . . ."

"You thought I was just shooting the shit? Making small talk?"

"Absolutely not, sir. But you gave me no direct order . . ."

"Your boss needing a physicist wasn't enough of an order for you?"

"It absolutely—yes, sir."

"Get out. Don't come back without one."

Hubner fled. He returned four hours later. "I'm afraid I have bad news, mein Herr," he said.

"I've had enough bad news to last me till the end of the fucking war," said

Rheinhardt. "The only thing I want to hear is, 'I have your man, and he's waiting outside.'"

Hubner began to stutter in his anxiety. "There are no physicists left at the university, sir! I was as shocked as you! I spoke to the dean and to the provost. Apparently, they've all been removed. The last one four months ago."

"All of them?"

"Yes, sir. Most, *most* unfortunate."

"*Verdammt nochmal!* Not one professor left in either physics or chemistry?"

"Unbelievable, sir, I know."

"Then what the hell are they even teaching over there?" Rheinhardt said, working hard to keep his voice low. He wanted to throw something, break something.

"Well, they still offer the languages, mein Herr—history, other humanities. There's a wonderful course on art appreciation." Hubner smacked his head. "The Chair of Agricultural Heritage is teaching a seminar himself this upcoming term—Introduction to Germanic Soil Analysis: The Racial Properties of Belgian Clay. Perhaps he can be of service—" Trembling, Hubner broke off. Rheinhardt felt himself going dark in the face.

"Hubner," he hissed. "You imbecile! The Racial Properties of Belgian Clay? Am I enrolling in fucking night classes?"

"No, sir . . ."

"Tell me, have you made any progress on locating that Belgian weasel Vogel? Or his Portuguese counterpart Silva? Has *he* returned?"

Hubner shook his head.

"Have you made any progress on finding the survivor from *La Fortuna*—you know, the *African* man who's impossible to hide, Hubner—*that* man? Or the person or persons who helped him escape?"

Hubner didn't and couldn't answer.

Enraged, Rheinhardt swept the papers off his aide's desk. "You are such a disappointment to me, Hubner."

"I do apologize . . ."

Rheinhardt stormed out of Baert Haus. He went to the only place where he could still think, the place with the only sliver of light shining on his future. *La Fortuna*.

33

Sequoia

There was a time when the Lillehaven barn had been whole and looked like a place where rebels might hide with their bombs and their guns. It was secluded, separated from the main house by a wood, a glen, and a narrow creek bed. But then Vogel began showing up twice a week and hunting through every needle in that haystack. So Alder and his children took the barn doors off their hinges, knocked out the windows, and tore off part of the roof. They wrecked the barn's exterior to make it seem derelict and discarded, and it worked. Vogel—a man who judged everything by appearance—stopped searching it.

Once the barn was safe from his random inspections, Charlie and Fitz dragged in an old rickety wooden picnic table and set it in the overgrown clearing. They cobbled together splinter-filled benches, so wobbly they'd collapse if you looked at them wrong. It gave them a spot to hold meetings in the dell, and it meant Mireille didn't have to sit in the dirt in her elegant dresses. Though, judging by the reaction Mireille was having to the barbarian Briggs, Charlie wondered if in the dirt wasn't exactly where Mireille always wanted to be.

Charlie would've thought that Briggs and Brigitte were the obvious match, both stitched from the same cloth. Loud, boisterous, unapologetic, utterly tactless—and physically imposing.

But no.

For reasons known only to God, Briggs gravitated toward the pristine Mireille, and she, the woman who wore white gloves to wash fish guts off ball bearings, gravitated right back. She shaved Briggs barehanded, cut his hair, let out the tunic the Martin twins had brought him, and burned a fresh notch in his belt so his trousers would stay up. As if planning for the long-term, she began teaching him French—with varying degrees of success.

Charlie found this exquisitely amusing. Mireille, the soft-spoken, no-nonsense accountant, who tracked every franc *La Ligne* spent, going soft on Briggs, the human avalanche who'd never balanced a thing in his life, except maybe a crate of explosives. Briggs, in turn, spent the afternoons teaching Mireille how to land a punch. He was gruff but patient, nearly saintlike, while she tried to explain in French that ladies didn't clench fists or throw punches. From Rafael, Briggs learned how to say *fight*, and used it as both instruction and lure.

"Bats-toi, Meer-WAH!" he kept saying, unable to pronounce her name. *"Bats-toi, Meer-WAH!"*

Instruction as conquest.

Meanwhile, Brigitte developed a full-blown fixation on none other than Belvedere, a pencil sketch of a man, while Brigitte herself was an oil painting. Flamboyant, expressive, voluptuous, she floated after the medic, flooding him with questions in French he couldn't answer. She would point to his black boxes of metal plates, his pouches of black powder, the tinctures he was trying to make, and chirp, *"Qu'est-ce que c'est?"*

"Qu'est-ce que c'est?" Belvedere would repeat, dumbfounded.

"Oui, oui, mon petit docteur, qu'est-ce que c'est?"

"What does this impossible woman want of me?" said Belvedere to Rafael. "Please inquire, as civilly as you can, what, for the love of all that is holy, she would like."

"She wants to know if you have a wife, Belvy," said Rafael. "And if not, why not."

"I can't have this in my day, Canario," said Belvedere. "I'm too busy. You swagger about like you're on leave at the Riviera. I'm preparing for the four horsemen. I can't be distracted by this nonsense."

Rafael turned to Brigitte and said in French, "Bree-*ghee*-tah, Belvy is overwhelmed by your attention."

She giggled. "Oh, that lovely man must be used to it, especially from women."

Rafael turned back. "She says if you're too busy for a real wife, how about a wife for one night?"

Charlie watched Belvedere blanch. He opened his mouth, closed it, and stalked off, muttering something about sterilization protocols. Brigitte glided after him, humming.

"Yes, we're still close," Louise said to Rafael in reply to a question Charlie didn't catch. "But lately we've drifted apart. We want different things. Right, Charlie?"

Charlie was sitting apart from them by the tree line. "I'm not listening." She was teaching the mute and riveted Hawk how to make a bouquet of wildflowers. He watched her hands like she was defusing a bomb. She wasn't going to lie, his intensity was a little scary. "You want to try?" she asked, handing him a handful of buttercups.

Hawk fiddled with the twine, concentrating intently. When he was finished, he showed it to her.

"Um . . ." she said, looking around for Fletcher. But Fletcher was engaged in an animated discussion with Wolski and wasn't paying attention. "That's pretty good," Charlie said. "No, it is." She hoped Hawk wouldn't sense her hesitation. "But . . . I showed you how to make a bow, *Faucon*, and you made a noose. Around the buttercups. Not that the noose isn't well made—it is. A perfect hangman's knot. *Nœud du pendu*. But maybe . . . not quite the sentiment we're going for? Shall we try again?"

Hawk nodded vigorously.

Nearby, Louise continued her oration. "Charlie has a death wish," she said to Rafael, "and I don't. I want to be happy—and she doesn't. She prefers to suffer, but I don't, and she can't make me. You see? Different things."

"Is that true, *Shar-lee*?" said Rafael. "You prefer to suffer?"

At that moment, Fletcher turned his gaze away from Wolski and toward Charlie, his violet eyes pausing on her, deepening, as if waiting to hear her answer, too.

"I'll tell you what's true," Charlie said, forcefully winding the twine around the daisies. She was psychologically incapable of small talk, of teasing, of flirtation. "There's a fucking war on. We're in the endgame. Time to pull our heads out of our asses. If it matters whether we win or lose, then it's time to act like it, not pretend it's business as usual and twirl our hair and bring lunches on bicycles to our exiled professors."

"Like I was saying," said Louise with delighted self-satisfaction.

"Nœud du pendu," Hawk said, nodding at the bow holding together the bouquet in Charlie's hands.

"Charlie," Fletcher called, "can I speak to you a moment?"

She stormed over to him by the bushes. "I don't want to talk about it," she said.

"Fine. I'm changing the subject," Fletcher said. "When we first landed, I asked you to bring me the Congolese man, and you said you'd do it, and yet, here we are, days later, and we are still Congo-*less*."

Oh, he thought he was so clever. So very clever. "It's not so easy as you saying and me obeying," said Charlie. "I told you many things too. Like how my brother's in jail, and needs to be sprung. How's that going?"

"I'm working on it."

"What, from here in the dell?" Charlie hoped her skepticism and fear and worry weren't as apparent on her face as they were on his. "Omloop's being followed, so he can't get Ngomo, and my *Berceau* gets crawled over by dogs every time I leave Lillehaven. For the time being, he's cloistered where he is. What's more important, Ngomo or your mission?"

There was a pause, a blink, a deflection. "Mission. But he's part and parcel. There are things only he knows, only he can help with. Is he safe where he is?"

"He's not safe anywhere in Belgium, you know that," she said.

"Why's he not safe at a monastery?"

"Because the nuns at Lost Hope have turned the Gestapo away twice already. Next time they're bringing a warrant from the Military Commandant, citing state security—harboring fugitives, hiding subversive materials, both of which are true—and they'll take apart that tiny priory until they find them."

Fletcher became agitated. "We have to go get him immediately. We can't risk him getting found."

"Them. Ngomo and the boy."

"Okay, *them*."

Charlie opened her hands. "What would you like me to do?"

He stalked off into the woods for a smoke, while she went and perched next to Wolski, who was buried in a topographical map of north Belgium. "Wolski, do you see Rafael over by Louise?"

"Oui, oui," said Wolski, not looking up. "He's in fine form."

"How well do you know him?"

"*Bien.* I follow that man anywhere." He corrected himself. "*Je le suivrai.* I *would* follow that man anywhere."

"Pourquoi?"

"Because Rider always runs first," Wolski said.

"To women?"

"Ha! Yes, to women *aussi*. But I mean, to trouble. If there's trouble, he gets to it first. More trouble, faster he runs."

"Sometimes women are trouble," Charlie muttered, watching Louise.

"Sometimes?" Wolski laughed. "You mean *toujours*." He went back to tracing the map with his fingers.

Meanwhile, Rafael was drawing heavily on his considerable repertoire of wiles to charm the summer dress off Louise. Charlie almost wanted to tell him he didn't have to try that hard. Louise was trying not to laugh as Rafael whispered in her ear, engaging her while she gazed away. She looked exceptionally beautiful that morning, her hair silky and shining, freshly braided, and pleated loosely around her head. Her peach country dress barely contained her hips and breasts, and her pink lips were constantly smiling. She was so welcoming. Who wouldn't love her? Who couldn't love her?

Charlie looked away, pushing her own hair hard behind her ears, trying to find something else to stare at instead of those two agents of chaos cloaked in beauty. They willed their power of enchantment so utterly, so effortlessly. They simply were—and the world bent to their will. There was nothing Louise could ask of others that they wouldn't do for her.

It was almost like sorcery.

And when two sorcerers met, it wasn't chemistry. It was alchemy.

Look at him, Charlie thought, with his louche multilingual seduction, and her with her radiant beauty. He lit her cigarette, and Louise forgot to tell him she didn't smoke. Charlie watched in amazement as she accepted the Molotov cocktail from his hands, took a puff or two, and handed it back. He put it in his mouth and inhaled it, as if he were inhaling her.

Yeah. No one in this clearing was making it out unscathed.

"Wolski, I don't know what this infernal woman wants from me," Belvedere said, calling the corporal over because Rafael was too busy with Louise to translate. "Tell her, if madam needs to leave, she's free to leave—by all means." Brigitte was leaning over him, watching him cut up gauze into squares.

"He says don't go, Bree-*ghee*-tah," said Wolski.

"Tell him I'm *mademoiselle*," Brigitte said, batting her eyelashes. "I've *never* been married. *Jamais.* Tell him, and then ask him if he's been married."

Wolski looked woefully unprepared to be the middleman in this game of cat and mouse. He caught Charlie's gaze and pleadingly motioned her over. She shook her head, biting back laughter. She couldn't remember the last time she laughed out loud.

"Marié?" Belvedere said, understanding that one word. "I don't see how my marital status is pertinent to our action here."

"*Non*, Brigitte," said Wolski. "*Belvedere n'a jamais été marié.*"

"Tell her," Belvedere said officiously, "that I'm very busy. *Je suis très occupé*," he said directly to Brigitte, knowing just enough French to say that. "I have no time for nonsense—*none* whatsoever. We came here on a mission, and it has *nothing* to do with—"

"He thinks you very beautiful, Brigitte," said Wolski. "*Magnifique et très belle.*"

"He does?" said Brigitte, making melting eyes at the mirthless Belvedere. "Please tell him I also find him charming and delightful."

Wolski to Belvedere: "She says she finds you charming and delightful."

"Bullshit," said Belvedere.

"I swear to you on my holy mother from Zakopane, that's what she said."

"I've had enough," said Belvedere, grabbing his gauze squares and his surgical scissors. "What did you tell her *I* said, you bastard?" He moved to leave. "No words I spoke had *magnificent* or *belle* as their meaning."

"Oh, I *strongly* disagree, *mon ami*," said Wolski. "Most strongly."

"This is completely unacceptable, Corporal," said Belvedere.

"But so, *so* funny, Leftenant," said Wolski.

Brigitte got up and ran after him. "Belvy," she cooed, "where are you going? Can I come?"

"How do you speak German so well?" Rafael said, his entire being inclined toward Louise like a willow to water.

She didn't back away. She was so used to men flirting with her, most of it no longer registered. But this Basque man was magnetizing! She didn't back away because she didn't want to. "My mother's family is German," she said, trying not to return his ridiculous smile. "I was born and raised in Bastogne, down south. My father was mayor of Bastogne for a time."

"Oh, yeah? And you? What did you do in Bastogne?"

"Well, I was nine. So, nothing." She paused. "I entered a beauty pageant once."

"No kidding. Did you win? Do I even need to ask?"

"I did, sort of, yeah."

He burst out laughing. "Of course you did. Well, I'll be damned." Rafael's smile was so wide, it was like he was placing the crown on her head himself. "So is that what they call you nowadays? The Belle of Bastogne?" His black eyes roamed her face. "The Beauty Queen of Belgium?"

"No one really calls me that," she muttered, disconcerted by his flagrant attention. "Not seriously."

"The other day I heard Charlie call you something as you two were getting our meal together. What was it? I could barely catch it. I meant to ask you about it."

"So why didn't you?"

"I'm asking you now." They were sitting in the most ridiculous of positions. She was perched on top of the table, legs crossed, her bare foot on the bench. He was straddling the bench, his body facing hers, pressing against her leg and looking up at her. She leaned slightly forward, resting an elbow on her knee. Her gaze was downward; his, upward. His eyes were level with her overflowing bosom. "What did she call you, Louise?" he repeated huskily.

"Loosha," said Louise. "It's a Flemish endearment for Louise. Spelled *Loesje*. Hideous, right? You'd think it reads like *low-ess-juh*. Or *lodge*. Yuck. But no. It's pronounced *LOOsha*."

If Rafael's smile got any bigger, it would leave his face. "Loosha," he said caressingly in his beguiling Basque dialect. "*Loosha*." He took a deep breath. "That is the sweetest-sounding nickname in all the world," he whispered, his voice thickening.

Louise didn't know where to look. In her captivated embarrassment she glanced away and caught Charlie with her arms crossed, glowering at her from a nearby bench. *Really?* Charlie was mouthing. *You've got to be kidding me.*

"What?" Louise called out. "What did I do now?"

"You're going to let *him* call you *Loosha*? A total stranger?"

Rafael groaned. "Isn't there something else for her to do other than watch you? Who does she think she is, your chaperone? There's no dead drop she can pick up? No lengthy message she can decode?"

"Why are you bristling, Charlie?" said Louise, pulling up the hem of her long dress so her bare calf could press against Rafael's bare perspiring forearm. "He can call me whatever he likes. What do you want me to do, police his speech? Who am I, the Gestapo?"

"Look, *Shar-lee*," Rafael said, pointing to Fletcher. "Lieutenant Gray is scanning the clearing for you. He wants to interview you too. He's already dealt with Hildi and Gitta and even Mireille. It's your turn. Aren't you the lucky one. Go." He shooed her forward with a flick of his hand. "But careful, Charlotte," he said. "You only *think* he's all business. But he's wily. Any minute you could end up in his hammock." He laughed uproariously.

Fletcher really was looking for her, calling her over. Rafael hadn't made it up. Charlie blushed, mildly annoyed, mildly curious. Primly and professionally, she strode across the grass, and she and Fletcher ambled into the wildflowers to have a cigarette and an interview in the shade.

To be clear:

In Louise's corner, the Basque smuggler was caressing Charlie's closest friend with his words and his hands, electrifying her with his every breath. In Belvy's corner, Brigitte was helping the doctor cut up gauze squares while singing to him in French. Mireille and Briggs were giving each other French and fighting instruction that looked a lot like lovemaking. Wolski was showing Maxine and Margot how to travel by map. Hawk was teaching Hildimar how to strangle buttercups with slipknots. While in Charlie's corner, this is what passed for subliminal seduction:

"I'm going to have Wolski go get him—them," said Fletcher.

For a moment, Charlie's mind blanked. "You mean—my brother, I hope?" When he didn't reply, she shook her head. "Ngomo? You're—no. No, that's a bad idea."

"You have a better idea?"

"Leave them!"

"I can't."

"If *I* can't drive there, *Wolski* can't drive there."

"Correct. He's walking."

"He's walking," she repeated, like she'd just learned to speak.

"Yes. It's thirteen kilometers. Not even ten miles. Practically next door."

"Walking—and then what?"

"Walking back, I suppose," Fletcher said.

"With a large injured black man and a small child?"

"Well, he's not traipsing down city boulevards if that's what you're asking. He has a map. He's pretty confident."

"It's a terrible idea," said Charlie.

"I wouldn't do it unless I had to, believe me."

"*Must* you? Ngomo's up in the rafters! He's wounded! He's had less than two weeks to heal. Why can't you leave him be?"

"Because he can't be found," Fletcher said. "And you know this. Besides, no one but Ngomo can tell me what I need to know about the ship, the cargo, and numerous other logistical impossibilities I can't overcome without him. It's the only way—*Charlotte*." He was prim and professional too.

"It's not even *a* way," she said, motioning Wolski over. "You don't know where the monastery is," she said brusquely as he approached.

"I do. Here." Wolski tapped his head. "And here." He patted his map.

"You don't know which way to go when you leave here," she said.

Wolski told Fletcher to translate. "I see sun, I have compass, map, gun in my hands."

"What are you going to do when you get to one canal, and then another?"

"I'm going to cross them."

"Over a bridge? Over a checkpoint? Your French is not good enough!"

"Merci beaucoup, mon amie," said Wolski.

"And the child?" Charlie said. "The small boy? Zeus is my responsibility. Is he going to swim the canals too?"

Wolski smiled. "Charlotte Fontaine," he said, shaking his head. "Fletch, are you translating? Tell her that she may be great courier, good fighter, capable *Eureka on ground*. But explain in bluntest terms that she knows nothing, literally *nothing*, about boys. Tell her. I'll wait."

"Why don't you give me the rest of it first," Fletcher said, eyes twinkling ever so slightly.

"Tell her there isn't boy in any country on this planet," said Wolski, "who wouldn't think it was greatest adventure of his life to be told that for next thirteen kilometers by day and by night, he must evade bad guys over land

and sea. That he must run through woods and hide in ditches, cross dangerous rivers and keep silent. That he might have to carry knife and be stealthy and strong. There isn't male soul on this earth who wouldn't be first one out monastery door."

Fletcher turned to Charlie. "He says he'll be back with the two of them tomorrow."

34

Cyrano

And he was.

Wolski returned to Lillehaven early on Thursday morning, exhausted but in one piece. Ngomo and a thin wary child named Zeus were with him. Fletcher had seen a lot of fighters in his life but never one like the Congolese warrior named Ngomo. He was a mountain of a man, and just as still, with shoulders as wide as a doorframe. What German could possibly best him? Fletcher thought. No wonder he killed them all and survived. He looked impossible to hide, yes, but also impossible to capture. "*You* dragged him up from the river?" Fletcher whispered to Charlie, while Ngomo was being introduced. "I don't believe it."

"How else is he standing in front of you, cowboy?" Charlie said. "Did he fly here?" She paused. "Zeus helped."

Little Zeus stood encircled by six army men who towered over him. He stared at them in amazement and reverence. "So, you're the famous Zeus," said Fletcher, coming over. "We've heard a lot about you."

"I'm not the god Zeus, if that's who you mean," the boy said solemnly, as if he couldn't understand why they would've heard about *him*.

"No?" said Fletcher. "Could've fooled me."

Belvedere squinted at the boy with clinical disapproval. "Fletcher, the child is vitamin D deprived. Tell your idiots to stop crowding him—you're blocking his sunlight. Canario, tell Louise when she gets here, the boy needs a peach or a plum. He's low in vitamin C, too."

Brigitte brought warm bread from the Herentals bakery. Louise arrived soon after with two jugs of fresh warm milk, which she somehow ferried on the back rack of her bicycle without spilling.

Zeus drank nearly the whole crock by himself and then spent a half-hour recounting his adventures in the woods. "It wasn't all woods, Charlie, there was a river and we had to climb a tree, and I even had to pretend I was a tree stump and not move, and we slept in a ditch! Yanush dug it, but I helped him, didn't I, Yanush?"

"You sure did, buddy," Wolski said.

"He let me carry his knife and I cut a whole vine of sugar snap peas and we had them for dinner and we milked a goat and ran down a ravine, oh, and I banged my shin on a river rock and bled! You can't see it now because we washed it off. I swam in all my clothes but Ngomo carried my shoes and I have twenty-seven mosquito bites and I walked the whole way by myself except for a little bit when Ngomo had to carry me. We didn't shoot anybody but it was still good."

Without saying a word, Wolski and Fletcher trained their self-satisfied gazes on Charlie. "There is nothing I hate more," she said, "than men being right. Because they love to rub your nose in it."

"Probably because it happens so rarely," Fletcher said.

"Speak for yourself, Lieutenant," said Wolski. "I'm always right."

"We almost ran into a patrol," Zeus said. "But they were looking in the wrong direction." He grinned. "I wanted to shout to them—we're this way, you fools."

"But he didn't," said Ngomo, ruffling the boy's head. "We got lucky. If the wind had blown north instead of east, we might not be here."

Ngomo was reserved and not particularly talkative. Just as Fletcher was contemplating how best to pull him away from the others for a debriefing, Belvedere drifted toward the Congolese man. The medic didn't touch him, just circled him, skeptically appraising.

"You've got a wound on your chest that's infected," he said.

"I do," Ngomo replied—in English! "It's not doing well."

"How old's the injury?"

"Friday, June 2nd. Almost two weeks."

Fletcher furled his brow. "You speak *English*, Ngomo?"

"I do. Limited to military intelligence and port communication."

"What else is there?" Fletcher muttered. Ngomo's English was clipped, tentative, like he was first translating from French and Lingala in his head. The hesitation gave each stretched-out word weight—it had to be earned before it was spoken.

Belvedere tutted, pushing Fletcher out of the way. "Lieutenant Gray, excuse me. I'm trying to evaluate the patient. Injured two weeks ago you say? All right. Tunic off. Let's take a look."

Brigitte hurried over, fitted blouse, flared skirt, full of purpose. "I'll help you, Belvy! I'll be your *infirmière*."

Belvedere didn't look up. "Leftenant! Translate before I throw myself in a well. What fresh torment is this woman offering me?"

"The kind lady is volunteering herself into your medical services," Ngomo translated.

"We're doomed," said Belvedere. He peeled back the bandage on Ngomo's chest and studied the swollen wound. The skin around it was still hot and red, with dark pus clinging to the crude black stitches. He reared back as if the wound offended him. "God in heaven, who stitched this? A drunk with a fishing hook? Why did you let someone butcher you like this—Ngomo, is it?" He poked at the edge of a suture with the tip of his tweezers and made a noise like he'd just found jam in a knife wound. "Knots, asymmetrical. Spacing, erratic. Needle depth? Did someone stitch it during an earthquake? This one is looped twice—why?"

No one spoke.

"It's not a stitch job, it's a war crime."

Charlie crossed her arms. "*I* stitched it."

"Should've known."

"And I helped her," said Louise.

"And you did a wonderful job, Louise," said Belvedere, immediately softening. He adjusted his gloves and straightened his back. "Well," he said crisply. "Not terrible—under the circumstances."

He removed the old stitches one by one with tweezers and surgical scissors, grumbling under his breath. Zeus stood like a floor lamp by Ngomo's side. "Does it hurt, Ngomo? Does it hurt? It'll be over soon."

"I'm fine, little man. The kind doctor is helping me."

From his bag—which Brigitte held open for him—Belvedere pulled out a black tin, a silver tin, and a Zippo lighter. "The Zippo is the one thing the Yanks invented that's actually worthwhile," Belvedere said, laying out the items on the picnic table.

"What about the jeep, the M1 rifle, and the U-boat radar?" said Fletcher. "Those not count?"

"Ah, yes, the holy trinity of American ingenuity," Belvedere said. "A lawnmower with wheels, a gun that jams, and a glorified bat detector."

While Brigitte held a small bucket of water, Belvedere cleaned Ngomo's wound. He scanned the gawking group around him. "This isn't a teaching hospital," he said. "Don't you have some eggs to fetch or someone else to mutilate?"

No one moved.

Opening the silver snuff box, he took a pinch of thick black powder and packed it inside and around the wound. A fascinated Zeus stood so close that Charlie had to pull him back, lest Belvedere start yelling.

"*C'est quoi, ce truc noir*, Belvy?" asked Brigitte. She also stood close, pressing her body against Belvedere's elbow. Fletcher smirked. Belvedere was encircled by humanity. It must've been galling him.

"Leftenant, tell her it's my Stitchless Seal."

"It's Saint's Spit," said Rafael. "*Crachat du Saint.*"

"What the hell is that?" Briggs said. "Belvy, are you packing the poor man full of ash?"

With a long-suffering sigh, Belvedere said, "If you must know, it's a powdered clay coagulant. A hemostatic agent. It will be followed by a thermal cauterizing component."

"Just coagulant, he says," said Rafael. "At Kasserine Pass, I watched him use it to stop a full femoral flow that should've killed our guy in four minutes. Instead, the man was back out in the shit inside a tight fifteen."

Everyone huddled closer, looked even more impressed.

"What's in it?" asked Fletcher.

"Smells like sulfur and croissants," said Wolski.

"You're not far off, Corporal," said Belvedere, taking out a small metal plate and flicking on his Zippo. "It's kaolin clay, sphagnum moss, wood ash, dried oxblood, a sprinkling of copper sulfate, just to kill what doesn't belong, and a whisper of saltpeter—all crushed together and milled into a fine powder."

"Did you say saltpeter?" said Fletcher. "Like . . . *gunpowder* saltpeter?"

"That's the one. Shrinks blood vessels almost instantly. Stops the bleeding."

"Is this standard issue?" Fletcher asked.

"Standard? Oh, no, no," said Belvedere. "It's probably banned by every military medical board from here to Madagascar."

"He came up with it in Longstop Hill," said Rafael. "When we were getting butchered and ran out of gauze, morphine, and hope."

"Why are you heating up that plate, Belvy?" asked Briggs. "Looks like a branding iron."

"Precisely what it is. I've created a glorified mud pie. Ready, Ngomo? It's going to burn. Don't move—and no one else speak." Holding it by the edges, Belvedere pressed the hot metal plate to Ngomo's wound. Ngomo didn't make a sound, or change the expression on his face, but he went rigid, his jaw locking in full body silence. Closing his eyes, Belvedere began to recite words in Latin under his breath. "*Quinque . . . novem . . . duodecim . . .*"

"Is that a prayer?" Fletcher asked.

"Yes," Rafael said, grinning. "The prayer of Saint George, the dragon slayer. Belvy's just counting to twelve. In Latin."

Belvedere opened his eyes and pulled the plate away. "You're all done," he said to Ngomo, and, "I thought I told *you* not to speak?" to Rafael. "Any longer than twelve seconds and it's what you Yanks call a barbecue. Any less, and you've just got hot wet flesh—and no friends."

Ngomo's gash was blackened, sealed with ash and heat. The skin around it was red and tight, the edges puckered. A hard crust of clay and blood covered the cut. It looked ugly, but clean.

Ngomo pumped Belvedere's hand. "I feel better already," he said, though Fletcher thought that Ngomo carried himself like a man who was beyond all earthly suffering.

"Right. Well. Try not to get stabbed again," Belvedere said gruffly, closing up his medic bag. "Go lie down. Your body can't heal if you don't sleep."

"Belvy," Fletcher said, "the counting to twelve—how'd you come up with that exact number?"

"Trial and error," replied Belvedere, a glint in his eye.

Zeus, Ngomo, and Wolski crawled into the barn to sleep, and Fletcher busied himself with the loose tangled twine, while waiting impatiently for Charlie to return from the flower fields. She'd promised to take him to *La Fortuna* today. He and Louise sat off to the side, working the rope, away from Brigitte and Belvedere, who were once again locked in their maddening push-pull attempts at foreplay. This time, they'd secured Rafael as their translator. Brigitte wanted to know Belvedere's story. Rafael agreed to play along.

Belvedere: "Tell her I went to Eton College. Studied Latin, Natural Philosophy, and Medicine in Translation."

Rafael translated in rapid French. "He went to Eton College but was kicked out for forging a note to skip a math test and misspelling the doctor's name."

Belvedere waited. "Did you tell her Medicine in Translation and Natural Philosophy?"

Rafael: "He studied Medicine in Translation because he couldn't pass it in English. And Philosophy so he could lose arguments with himself."

Belvedere: "And Latin?"

Rafael: "And Latin so he wouldn't have to talk to people in English."

Belvedere: "Why did you repeat *English*?"

Rafael: "The French word for medicine sounds like English. Go on, Belvy. I don't have all day to be your Cyrano."

Belvedere: "I won 'Most likely to Perform Surgery with a Fountain Pen.' Twice."

Rafael: "He won 'Most Likely to Tourniquet the Wrong Limb.'"

Belvedere: "Twice."

Rafael: "*Deux fois.*"

Belvedere: "I went to Magdalen College, Oxford. And then did four years of

Clinical Training at Guy's Medical School, one of the most prestigious teaching hospitals in England."

Rafael: "He worked at Magdalen College—polishing lecterns and refilling inkwells in exam rooms. And then he worked at Guy's Hospital, sorting tongue depressors by size."

"Vraiment?" said Brigitte, gazing at Belvedere.

Belvedere nodded solemnly. "*Oui*."

Rafael also nodded solemnly.

Belvedere went on. "I specialized in trauma and thoracic surgery. My father was a renowned thoracic surgeon, legendary for keeping calm under pressure." Belvedere smirked. "I wanted to be just like him."

Rafael: "He says he attended veterinary school but lost a goat during a live birth and had to withdraw. His father sold umbrellas."

Brigitte: "Lost, like—*killed*?"

Rafael: "No, no. The goat wandered off. Never found it—or the goatlings."

Belvedere nudged him, whispering, "Tell her about my father . . ."

Rafael: "His father did sell umbrellas."

Brigitte, to Belvedere: "*Les parapluies, c'est très important*."

Belvedere, "*Oui*." And to Rafael: "Did you tell her I wanted to *be* like my father?"

Rafael to Brigitte: "He says he wanted to sell *les parapluies* too."

Belvedere: "Like my father!"

Rafael: "*Comme son papa*."

Belvedere: "I was second in line for a surgical post at St. Thomas' Hospital. I could've been Chief Surgeon by now if I hadn't volunteered for active duty like an idiot."

Rafael: "He was nearly offered *un poste de prestige* sterilizing scalpels at St. Thomas, but the Royal Army Medical Corps needed *des idiots* with a steady hand and no future, so they trained him to be a medic."

Brigitte touched the top of Belvedere's hand. "He's got the steady hand, that's for sure."

Belvedere: "My father was one of the best—inside a hospital. But I studied how soldiers die, and I learned how to keep them alive—not on the operating table, but in the fire of battle. Which is why I'm here." He smiled wanly. Brigitte beamed back at him.

Rafael smiled too. "Belvedere says his father was a great umbrella salesman. But he himself wanted to be in the rain and the mud and the blood with dying men, gross, dirty, drinking tea out of tin cups. That's why he became a combat medic. The *best* in his field."

Brigitte gazed at Belvedere. "Tell him I adore him. *Dis-lui que je l'adore*."

"You *do*?" said Rafael.

"Complètement."

"You don't have to translate, Rider," said Belvedere, reaching for Brigitte's hand. "I understood."

Fletcher stood next to Louise, both of them listening to Rafael's *translation*.

He shook his head. "That sabotage was disgraceful."

"I think I love him," said Louise, gazing at Rafael.

"You weren't outraged?"

"What's the opposite of outraged? Oh, yes—enthralled. *Ensorcelée.*" She sighed, her hand on her heart.

"It almost made me feel bad for Belvedere," Fletcher said.

Louise gave him a sardonic slap on the back. "Fletcher Gray, you've got a lot to learn about women."

His hackles rose. "I don't know what you mean."

"Oh, I know you don't." She pointed to Belvedere and Brigitte, who were now sitting close together, cutting apart flowers—not for bouquets but for medicinal essence—and communicating wordlessly through smells and smiles.

Muttering under his breath, Fletcher busied himself with untangling the twine.

Louise nodded toward the rain barrel where Charlie stood, about to dunk her arms into the water. "Look who's back. Go tell her what you just told me. How disgraceful Rafa's been."

"Why would I do that?"

"You want someone to agree with you, don't you?"

He brightened.

"Yes—because *she* knows nothing about men," Louise continued. "You two are perfect for each other. Rafa—wait!" She ran off to catch up with Rafael, while Fletcher stood, dumbfounded. The scent of summer was in his nose, and Charlie was across the clearing, leaning over the large barrel as she soaped pollen and weeds from her bare arms. She was lean, purposeful. Even the way she wrung out the rag was swift and deliberate. She wore a sleeveless fitted dark green dress and combat boots. He just figured it out—she was a woman who looked and moved like a soldier. It hit him in the gut.

A sunlit, bare-armed, soap-slick soldier. Putting on his military face, he marched over, stood behind her for a moment, and loudly cleared his throat.

Calmly she turned around, her arms still wet. "Why did you make a sound like a depth charge going off?"

"I wanted to alert you to my presence. I didn't want to startle you."

She smirked, and shook her arms to dry them, flicking drops of water into his face. "You think standing behind me like a post is going to startle me,

Lieutenant Gray? Welcome to the war, *mon ami*. You're going to have to do more than that."

Like what? he wanted to say. They both stood like posts. And then they both cleared their throats! God. Was Louise right about him? Was he terrible at this? "Yes, well, um—are you ready to go?"

"Now? It's so early."

"It's not early, Charlotte," he said. "It's very late. It's the eleventh hour."

"You said you wanted to talk to Ngomo first."

"Belvedere ordered me not to wake him."

"You take orders from your medics, Lieutenant?"

"Belvy said he needs sleep to heal."

"Will you be allowed to talk to Ngomo when we return?" Charlie asked. "Wait, let's not jump ahead. We'll check with Belvedere when the time comes. See if he'll give his okay."

He blinked. "Are you ready to go, or. . . ?"

"Yes, Lieutenant. Did you say you wanted to bring Hawk for the just in case?"

Like a glassy apparition, instantly Hawk appeared out of nowhere and stood beside them, the sniper rifle in his hands.

"No, it's not that kind of an excursion, Hawk," Fletcher said. "It's more like recon."

"I will be quiet."

"Quiet? You're bringing a rifle with a custom scope!"

"I will recon them quietly."

"No, Hawk. I need you to stay here and supervise the rope braiding and knotting operation. Charlie tells me you're very good with knots."

Hawk almost smiled.

"Perfect," Fletcher said. "While I'm gone, I'm placing you in charge of getting the rest of the men to braid and knot all the remaining loose rope. This is a very important job. There might be heavy lifting ahead. And that means we need braided twine with lots of knots. Make sure the men get it done. Discipline them as you see fit."

Charlie yanked hard on his sleeve. "I'm just joking, Hawk," Fletcher said. "You knew I was joking, right—about the discipline part?"

A half-second of silence followed. "Yes, Commander."

35

Het Steen Castle

Charlie took Fletcher the back way into Antwerp, across a poorly monitored canal bridge. Fletcher hid in the false floor of the *Berceau*. Dressed in a splendid red coat and fancy hat, she showed her fake papers to the Nazi guard and pointed to the back of the truck. "Delivering peonies to the Cathedral of Our Lady," she told him. Once inside the Old City, she parked by a row of stables off a rarely used alley and threw off her flame-colored outer garment, revealing the green dress underneath, a brown cardigan thrown over her bare shoulders. She hoped the combination would make her blend in like a deer against the bark of the trees.

Fletcher watched her without speaking.

"What?" she said. "You wear the coat to deliver the flowers. You take it off to disappear."

"I get it."

Was it her imagination, or did he look like he wanted to say he liked the green dress even more than the red coat? Ridiculous. It was the drabbest thing she owned. Except it was sleeveless.

They went the rest of the way on foot, meandering more than two kilometers through the narrowest parts of historic cobblestoned Antwerp, away from the boulevards and the crowds.

"You really know your way," he said. "You're like Wolski."

"Unlike him, I only know Antwerp," she said. But she did know it well. She could walk these winding streets in her sleep.

They climbed Het Steen Castle like casual tourists on a quiet Thursday and hid high in one of the distant battlements. Fletcher crouched near a broken merlon, one of his boots planted on a weed-choked stone.

The whole dockyard unfurled from here—Glaskaai, the long warehouses, the ship, the guards, the bend of the river. For several minutes, Fletcher didn't speak, peering through his binoculars.

"I don't get it," he muttered. "You can command the whole quay from this tower with a single rifle. Hawk could zero half the port from here. He'd call it target practice."

Charlie leaned against the wall beside him. "Yeah, that's what the Germans once thought, too."

"Then why isn't there a Nazi up here?"

"Because in '41 a corporal fell through the crumbling floor behind you and snapped both his legs. They brought in a fancy Wehrmacht engineer to give them a structural report. He called it a medieval coffin with a view. Said it was a deathtrap; the whole place could collapse if you tripped over one of the stones. It was too cramped for barracks, too ancient for radio lines, and too far from the new docks. So they let it rot."

Fletcher ran his hand over the weather-eaten parapet. "Lucky for us."

"Hardly lucky," Charlie said. "Instead there's an army below, where you need to be. The ship's not here, Fletcher. It's there." *La Fortuna* swayed in the open water, its three flags fluttering in the breeze.

They spoke in whispers, leaning in close to be heard. Their heads were almost touching.

Charlie had never been this physically close to Fletcher before. In the Lillehaven glade they stood politely apart to smoke and to talk. Being this close to him unsettled her nerve endings, made her heart unsteady, brought shallow breath to her throat.

Fletcher sighed. "I really hoped Omloop was wrong," he said, his brow knitted with worry.

"Infuriatingly, that man is rarely wrong," said Charlie.

"He said Rheinhardt knows about the cargo, judging only by the number of guards and how armed they are. He's right. They're fortified here almost like they were at Omaha." Fletcher shuddered.

Charlie didn't know where Omaha was, and this didn't seem like a good time to ask.

"Barely any foot traffic down there," Fletcher said. "Is that normal?"

"This side's always been slow," she said, "even before you boys landed in Normandy. No cranes, cheaper docking fees."

"A crane might've been nice," said Fletcher.

"What do you need a crane for?" She arched a brow when he didn't reply. "Before the crane, Lieutenant Gray, what do you propose to do with the SS troops in front of the ship?" When he didn't reply a second time, Charlie exhaled in disbelief. Did she need to remind him that there were only five of them, plus a board-certified surgeon?

"Here's the thing, *Shar-lee*," said Fletcher. "Once you understand that we *must* secure the cargo, everything else becomes detail."

"Detail, eh? Like the walls of Troy were just detail?"

"Exactement."

"It took the Greeks ten years to get inside!" She remembered *ses humanités* well.

"*Did* they get inside or didn't they?" Letting the binoculars dangle against his chest, Fletcher pulled out a small notepad and a pencil. He spent a long time studying Glaskaai, a pencil to one eye, marking distance, examining the cobblestones, muttering, making calculations.

He studied the Germans, while Charlie sat on the ground, her back to the fucking Germans, and studied him. He had such an unusual combination of features for a man. His soldier's body had substance—not bulk but grit, like a runner, not a bricklayer—while his face was all elegant refinement. Nothing looked soft, but it wasn't coarse either. He had a long, lean nose, a defined chin, a well-formed, unsmiling mouth. Stubble shadowed his jaw.

Fletcher must have felt her scrutinizing him, for he looked away from his notepad and stared into her face, questioningly. There was an angular intensity to him, a grave seriousness in his mystifying eyes. The inner ring of the iris was rose gold; the outer, indigo; and between them, a muted wash of gray-blue. In dusk, they looked deep violet. During daylight, like now, they were lavender.

"Everything okay?" he said.

"Of course." Charlie raised the mask back to her face. "What are *you* doing?"

"Figuring things out."

"What things?"

"How far everything is. How big the ship, how long the wharf. Where the warehouses are. I'm measuring, counting."

"Why?"

"So I'm prepared. Have some control. I don't like surprises."

What kind of a soldier carried around a notepad and wrote down things about cobblestones and wharves? She wanted to ask if he'd brought a notebook with him to Normandy, but the joke got caught in her throat. Besides, what if he said yes? Or worse, told her instead about the real horrors he must've met with there? She'd lived through some horrors of her own. No notebook could've helped her with those.

"What's on the ship, Fletcher?" Why did she blurt that? Just to change the subject. Louise was right. Some things were better not to know.

He took a breath. "A bomb, Charlie."

"Don't the Nazis have bombs? I read somewhere they might."

"Not *this* kind of bomb."

"Why would Ngomo bring a bomb to Antwerp?" Charlie said, frowning. "Was it part of the invasion plan? Was the King trying to help the Allies?"

Fletcher shook his head. "Just the opposite. He didn't mean to, but he's made things worse. Believe me, this definitely wasn't an authorized action."

"And now you want to blow it up so no one gets to use it?"

"I wish I could. It would make our life so much simpler. No. I need to take it and hide it."

"Hide it where?"

"Don't know yet," he said. "When's their shift change?"

A gull screamed somewhere above the water.

"How would I know?" Charlie said. "Assuming a Nazi level of slavish devotion to schedule, the shifts are probably seven a.m. to three p.m., three to eleven, and then eleven at night to seven in the morning. So three o'clock would be the next one."

It was 2:00 p.m. "We'll wait," Fletcher said.

"We're just going to sit here for an hour and stare at some Nazis?"

"Why, what do you propose?" he said, almost without inflection.

The blood rushed to Charlie's face. "I'll leave if that's how you're going to behave," she said—but her skin flushed hot.

"I don't know what you mean," he said, with the faintest curve at his mouth.

They sat in silence for a few minutes.

"How old are you and your boys?" she asked, to pivot, slightly.

"Rider, Briggsy and I are all 24," he said. "Hawk is 22, Wolski 30. Belvedere, the old man, is 33."

"When's your birthday?"

"End of September. When's yours?"

"Mid-September." She flinched, but then quickly recovered and even managed to grin. "I'm older than you, Lieutenant."

"By what, a week? And this brings you glee why?" he said with a twinkle. "What about your other girls?"

"We're all the same age," Charlie said. "Born after the other war ended, in 1919. We grew up together, went to school together. Except our baby Lou. She'll be 21 in October."

"But you're closest with her?"

Charlie nodded. "She hung out with me and my—me and my brother. Since she was ten. She's like my sister. Tell me about your boys. Hawk first." She got comfortable on the hard ground against the cold stone. "He follows you around nonstop."

"He doesn't want to miss any action." Fletcher smiled. "Hawk's a funny one. His real name's Laurence Turner. His mother still calls him Laurie—something he'd rather die than admit. He became Hawk to erase it. He is a classically trained pianist." Fletcher nodded into Charlie's incredulous expression. "He's quite a character. He was studying to become a concert maestro—then went to war and became the quietest, deadliest man on the battlefield."

"Why's he so protective of you?"

Fletcher shrugged. "He's from Louisiana, he thinks we're blood brothers or something. Now do Hildimar."

Charlie chuckled. "Hildi's like Hawk, but without the piano or the sniper skills."

"What's left after that?"

"Hildi's what's left. She works in a chemical factory. Steals all kinds of acid for the resistance. And she loves her knives. Went on a few raids with Fitz—really got the taste for it. What about Wolski?"

"He's Rafael's guy," Fletcher said. "I don't know him well, but if we ever need to get somewhere, he's our Northern Star. Stubborn as hell."

"Who isn't," Charlie muttered. "Maxine and Margot have taken quite a shine to him. Maxine's the bigger twin—born first—and Margot's never forgiven her."

"Explains everything, really." Fletcher smiled. "Briggs talks too much. Always narrating our doom at full volume. It's his way of processing stress. Tough as balls, though—excuse me. As a wrecking ball, I meant to say."

"And to think my number cruncher Mireille is sweet on someone like him," Charlie said. "She wears high-heeled shoes to weed the garden."

"Yeah, she always looks dressed for church," Fletcher said. "And talks low, like she's in one."

"Belvedere, I know," Charlie said. "Say no more."

"I'll tell you a thing about Belvy," Fletcher said. "He can't see shit without his glasses but refuses to wear them."

"We can skip Rafael," Charlie said. "Should we skip Louise?"

Fletcher agreed. "Except Rafael is always first into the fray. You should know that about him. You want to hear what Louise said about you?"

Charlie sighed. "I guess."

"She said you were the most serious, sober, practical, careful person she knew."

Funny how that worked, Charlie thought. Because those were the exact words she would've used to describe the man sitting next to her.

And yet she knew Louise's description wasn't the whole of her. Not by a long shot.

Did that mean that her assessment of Fletcher was also wrong?

"So who's Zeus?" he asked.

"Um, the boy Wolski brought back with Ngomo from the priory," Charlie spoke slowly. "You met him this morning, remember?"

"Witty. Sharp. I *mean* . . . who is Zeus to *you*?"

She stared at the guards below. "Just one of the boys who came through CDJ." She'd worked with Comité de Défense des Juifs since 1942.

Fletcher didn't say anything. His binoculars were trained on the ship, but she knew he was waiting for more. She just didn't want to give it to him. "I wish I could've gotten him on that ship," she said quietly.

"Where's the rest of his family?"

She shook her head. "Just his grandparents waiting for him in Lisbon."

Fletcher stared at her with sympathy—far too close. She wasn't used to a male expression of warmth and pity in such proximity. It disoriented her, made her wobbly.

"No wonder Ngomo feels responsible for Zeus," he said.

"You have it backward," said Charlie. "Zeus feels responsible for Ngomo."

They sat in silence.

"Are you going to tell me what you're planning to do with Ngomo?"

He turned away from her to the Germans. "No," he said. An even heavier silence followed. After a while his gaze returned to her.

"Why are you looking at me like that?" she asked.

"Like what?" he said. "And I'm not. There's something behind you that caught my eye."

She nearly glanced over her shoulder to check.

"You're the only woman I've met here who keeps her hair so short," he said quietly. "Everyone else folds it, braids it, twists it."

"If I did that," Charlie said, "half my day would be spent thinking about my hair. When to wash it, how to dry it, how to brush it out. I'd have to braid it and pleat it and tie it back, and if it got loose, I'd have to take it all apart and start again. I don't have time in my day to do the actual things I must do. If I had to take care of my hair, too, I'd go mental."

He nodded with an ironic smile.

"It's a war thing," she said. "You boys keep your hair short."

"Hygiene and efficiency," he said. "But we're not women."

I'm not a woman, Charlie wanted to say. *I'm a fighter in the resistance.* She paused, thinking. "What about the girls in Italy? How did they keep their hair?"

"I don't know," he said. "I never noticed."

"You're such a liar."

"I didn't notice their *hair*, Charlotte. How is that a lie? I'm not saying I didn't notice other things."

"That's more like it," she said, averting her gaze. His expression overwhelmed her. Empathy, amusement, something more intimate.

"Why do you sleep in the corner of the barn?" he asked. "Every morning I find you there in the straw. Why don't you go back to the farmhouse, sleep in your own bed?"

"Because," she said starchily, trying to hide her vulnerability, "my orders were clear. No one knows when the hour will come. What if you need something? I'm like Hawk. At any moment, I must be ready."

He continued to stare, the soft purple haze twinkling in his eyes.

"Are you the one who covers me every morning?" She couldn't believe she was brave enough to ask.

"Of course I am," he said, nearly in a whisper. "You look so cold, uncovered."

She had been fighting for such a long time. Sometimes Charlie felt so tired of it, and from it. *Don't make me soft, Fletcher*, she wanted to say. *You can't afford it, and I can't either. I'm here as your asset. The moment you see me as a woman, I stop being useful to you. I become a liability.*

As if reading her mind, he said, "You're invaluable to us here, Charlie. Truly. We couldn't do this without you." He took a breath. "*I* couldn't do it without you."

She was flustered and flummoxed. She wanted so much to have this private moment with him, but now that it was here, her throat was closing up. To ease her nerves, she desperately needed a smoke. But when she pulled out her cigarettes, he said no. They'd smell it down below. He started to tell her a joke but she stopped him. "No jokes," she said. "If I can't smoke, you can't joke. What if you're actually funny and I laugh? They'll hear that."

"Not to worry," Fletcher said.

She almost laughed.

That was a good hour she spent with him, sitting on hard ground against cold stone, high in the castle above the river.

The 3:00 p.m. shift change came much too soon.

During the changing of the guard, a uniformed SS officer emerged down Glaskaai like a blade unsheathed. His field-gray greatcoat was crisp, its belt cinched tight at the waist. His boots shone like obsidian. A black visor cap sat low on his brow, silver piping gleaming above his eyes, which were the color of ice, even from a distance. Standing at attention from across the gangway, the officer observed the new guards as if inspecting a firing squad, his posture ramrod straight, his presence chillingly still. Charlie stared at him from her perch at Het Steen, but it was he who looked like the sentinel.

After the shift was in place, he lit a cigarette. When he finished smoking it, he lit another. He paced in front of the ship, his boots clicking on the cobblestones with the metronomic finality of a funeral march, paced a slow, stalking circuit, never looking away from *La Fortuna*. Even without the cigarettes, he burned with a kind of restless calculation. After fifteen minutes, he lit his fifth cigarette. The tip flared red against the gray stones. Charlie watched him, a cold draft in her spine. Fletcher's face, when she turned to him, offered no reassurance.

"That must be him," she whispered. "Erich von Rheinhardt."

"It's him," Fletcher said, his brow tightening over his uneasy gaze. "Unfortunately we've met."

36

Male Pattern Baldness

Late Thursday afternoon, after an hour of pacing and smoking, a jittery and queasy Rheinhardt returned to Daisy Lane. When he marched inside Baert Haus, he saw that in his haste to leave he'd left his office door wide open. He found Hubner inside, staring at him from behind his desk with an expression of deep concern.

"Get away!" Rheinhardt said. "What are you doing there?"

"You forgot to shut your drawer, mein Herr," Hubner mumbled. "I was just . . ."

"Snooping?"

"No, sir. You left all your interrogation files on top of your desk and your drawer open. They're such sensitive files, I wanted to organize them for you . . . put them back in the drawer maybe."

"There are other things in that drawer now, Hubner."

"I see that, sir . . ." His aide's face was so pale and troubled that Rheinhardt knew he couldn't leave the contents of the drawer unexplained.

And yet he couldn't explain it.

Inside the space lay at least two dozen copies of the photograph of young Rheinhardt with his parents. Each copy was a ghostly image of the one before it—a thick stack, like haunted animation cels, frame by fading frame, repeating forever.

The two men stared at each other in the sunless office.

"Is everything all right, sir?" Hubner whispered.

"No," said Rheinhardt. He couldn't explain to Hubner the chilling of his blood when he thought of spending hours and days in his beloved office, sitting so close to the *thing* in his drawer.

And yet he couldn't bear to be away from it.

From the *thing* in the corner of the drawer that kept ghosting his image in infinite regression. It seemed alive to him, rising in both temperature and threat. Even imagining it tucked away near him filled Rheinhardt with an irrational dread.

It wasn't the dread of death.

It was the dread of annihilation. His fear was so great, he thought the rock might set the desk on fire and with it, bring down his whole house of sticks.

Rheinhardt couldn't confess any of this to Hubner.

He turned and fled into the street. A frazzled Hubner followed him.

Once he was outdoors on Daisy Lane, Rheinhardt calmed down enough to speak. "Hubner," he said, "do you remember a few years ago, or maybe a year ago, we had some guards who got sick?" He paced so fast along the street, Hubner could barely keep up.

"I don't recall, sir . . ."

"Because you're answering instead of thinking, Hubner. Don't reply like an automaton. Think first! We had a few sick officers sent off to recuperate. When they got better, we transferred them to Leuven and Mechelen."

"I don't remember such an event, mein Herr . . ."

"Where were they stationed is what I want to know. Were they guarding a chemical factory and were inadvertently poisoned? I don't recall, but for some reason I feel like it had something to do with the Jews." Rheinhardt rubbed his chin. "Doesn't everything? The posting was somewhere outside Antwerp, and it was a revolving position. After they got better, they asked to be transferred elsewhere—anywhere but there, as I recall—and we obliged at first, but for some reason no one else wanted to go in their place."

"Sir . . . I don't . . ."

"Yes!" Rheinhardt was on a roll, dredging up fragments of memory from the cold deep. "They had to be literally *forced* to return to that post, under penalty of execution. You don't remember this?"

"No, sir, I'm sorry."

Rheinhardt wished he had paid more attention himself. Vaguely he remembered Otto Brandt telling the story of the poisoned guards over an after-dinner drink, but Rheinhardt had always been such a reluctant social participant, and his estimation of Brandt was so low, that he often completely ignored the man's inane banter. The one thing Rheinhardt did remember was Brandt saying: *"The fool would rather take a bullet to the head than return to . . . and I told him that could be arranged—and then it was!"*

But return to where?

Rheinhardt turned his cold gaze on Hubner. "How could you not remember this? You remember everything! Some of them began to lose their hair."

"Ah," Hubner said. "*That* I remember. And they vomited for a few days."

He shrugged. "We thought they had food poisoning." Hubner paused, as if figuring out how to stay respectful. "It seems unrelated, mein Herr."

"You have no idea if it was related or not. Do you remember where the men had been stationed?"

"When they vomited?"

"*And* lost their hair, yes."

"I don't know if I've ever known that, sir."

"Hubner, I need to know what those men were guarding when they became ill."

"Are you—are you feeling ill, mein Herr?"

"This isn't about me!" Rheinhardt yelled.

Hubner blinked several times. "You would like me to look into an intestinal episode experienced by half a dozen men from two years ago?"

"Yes."

"May I ask why?"

"You may not. Just do it, Hubner."

Hubner coughed up a storm before he managed to ask his next question. "Forgive me, sir, for my ignorance, but do the vomiting men have anything to do with your current, pressing scientific inquiries that have not been answered?"

"Today is not the day you will have your answer. I need today to be the day *I* get answers."

Hubner, even in his fear and deference, stood his ground. "If I may be so bold, sir, as to suggest a slightly . . ."

"You may not."

". . . different path," Hubner continued.

"No."

"Sir, I want to help you. Please let me."

Rheinhardt waited. "I'm not hearing any suggestions, Hubner. I'm hearing a lot of breathing and cracking of knuckles."

"Sir, do you remember how over the past four years, we've had a few supplemental manifests that had segregated delivery authorizations? We couldn't put them through our normal customs procedures and were ordered to use vague approval codes. Some were routine classified, some were Code Red, but all were cleared by Herr Brandt's office, not ours."

"Yes. So? Sometimes they were marked as 'incomplete audits,' other times with 'War Essential' priority stamps."

"Exactly! Marked 'mining research,' 'metallurgical research,' 'special projects,' and 'special protection.'"

"I'm not impressed you know *this* useless fact, Hubner," Rheinhardt said. "So what? You think those incomplete manifests can help me now?"

Fervently, Hubner nodded.

"How? Because you think a local metallurgical facility might have participated in some scientific studies that caused a chemical reaction that could have made our guards sick? And that if I find the address of such a facility, I could approach them with my questions?"

"Something along those lines, possibly . . ."

"That's a clever way of backing into the information I asked you for, Hubner, and it fascinates me the lengths you'll go to, to avoid doing any actual work. But it's a dead end. Good try, though."

Hubner was quiet.

"It's a dead end," Rheinhardt said, "because those special manifests weren't ours. They weren't under my authority. After clearance, they were checked off and rerouted straight to Herr Brandt's document storage facility at headquarters."

"Indeed, sir."

"Talk about picking a raindrop from the sea, Hubner. How many such manifests are we even talking about? A few dozen over four years?"

"One thousand, five hundred and eighty-four, sir," said Hubner. "Give or take."

Rheinhardt stopped walking. He stood completely still.

Speechlessly, he took in Hubner's averted gaze, his pale expression, his tense pulsing fingers.

"Hubner, what did you do?" he whispered.

"Please, sir, don't be upset with me. I've worked for you for a long time. And you've always been clear how you want things done. By the book, methodically, meticulously, properly."

Rheinhardt was without words.

"But sometimes I do things in a slightly different way—to protect you, mein Herr! I take full responsibility for anything that wasn't done precisely in the way you require."

"What did you *do*, Hubner?" Rheinhardt cried.

Hubner lost his ability to speak.

Widening his eyes, Rheinhardt took a step back to see his lieutenant in a new light. "Hubner," he said in a low, astonished voice, "tell me you didn't keep a copy of every questionable manifest."

"I—really—"

"*Did* you?"

"I may have, sir—for the just in case!"

Rheinhardt grabbed Hubner by the shoulders and shook him. "This *is* the just in case, Hubner," he said. He almost wanted to embrace him.

"Don't be angry with me, mein Herr," Hubner whispered. "I did it to protect you—and didn't tell you to protect you. If there was any investigation into the irregularities, I wanted to make sure you could never be blamed."

"I can't believe what you've done, Franz. You didn't just protect us. You've saved us." He squeezed Hubner's shoulders. "Let's go get those documents. At once." He headed back to Baert, nearly running.

"There's no light in the attic, sir."

"Then we'll bring the files down—into the light."

Rheinhardt was stunned by the staggering scope of Hubner's meticulous effort in illegal document preservation. And this on top of all his other duties too! There were at least twenty thick piles concealed with a "Reich Research Council" stamp, or "Scientific Matters" or "Special Orders." He leafed through them quickly, astonished at the volume of classified manifests that had been approved either by Brandt or by the SS command in Liège and passed through without any scrutiny.

Hubner had painstakingly kept carbon copies of every one of them and filed them away under innocuous names.

"Material Transfers."

"Delivery Note Duplicates."

"Civilian Priority Shipments."

"Internal Review Only."

"Receipts without Customs Stamps."

It was late at night. They locked the door to Rheinhardt's office, drew all the curtains, turned on the lamps and spread the manifests across the massive desk. Before they got to work, to show Hubner his appreciation, Rheinhardt offered him one of his Black Crown cigarettes. "Are you sure, sir? These are precious. My Revels are fine for me."

"Revels are factory sweepings," Rheinhardt said. "You deserve the best today." From his private crate, he produced a bottle of Remy Martin Louis XIII cognac—ultra-premium, ridiculously overpriced, and utterly over the top. Despite Hubner's protestations, he poured them each a generous measure. "Tonight I raise a glass to you, Hubner. These are words you don't often hear me say."

"If ever, sir—and I'm so grateful."

"You truly surprised me with your daring initiative. *Zum Wohl.* To your wellbeing."

Hubner stood straight, his pale face flushed with pleasure. His chest swelled so visibly, it was as if he might float off the floor. "I just hope we find what you're looking for, sir," he said, looking every bit the man who would dredge the Scheldt with a teaspoon, if Rheinhardt gave even half a word. "Shall we begin?"

Sipping their brandy and smoking their cigarettes, they spread out the files and examined them thoroughly. Rheinhardt didn't realize how many manifests he'd been ordered to authorize without question. Germany was at war, and many projects were above his clearance. He'd thought nothing of it then, but he was thinking about it now, as he leafed through ledger after ledger in the "Special Scientific Projects" folder. Materials for advanced metallurgy. Communications research. Chemical warfare. R&D. Shipments authorized by direct orders from Berlin. Classified Reich Projects. Looking through these, Rheinhardt was reminded how often he had felt like nothing more than a bureaucratic cog. Nothing but a rubber stamp on the shady activities of people more important than himself.

He'd been correct to feel that way. Look at the mountain of metal his mandated signature had rubber-stamped for passage. He checked and rechecked the various delivery addresses for some of the shipments coming from Sweden, Norway, Spain. Many were initially approved for delivery to the Union Minière Metallurgical Plant in Olen.

But some of them, in small print, usually handwritten in pencil and signed off with an illegible signature, were afterward rerouted to a private residence nearby—to a place called *Zvart Haus*.

37

Dorian

Charlie and Fletcher returned to Lillehaven early Thursday evening. Only Ngomo and Zeus were by the barn. Everyone else was at Alder's house, "celebrating," Zeus said.

"Celebrating?" said Charlie. That was a word she hadn't heard in a long time.

Zeus shrugged. "They cooked a chicken and everything."

"Why aren't you there?"

"There's people there we don't know," said Ngomo. "Not a good idea to be seen."

She and Fletcher hurried through the woods. *People?*

Charlie nearly stumbled in the doorway when she walked in and saw her brother sitting at their kitchen table.

"Fitz?"

"Charlie!" he said, not raising his face from his plate. He was ravenously shoveling soft-boiled eggs into his mouth.

The siblings embraced, though Fitz barely stopped eating. Fitz Fontaine was lanky, freckled, and curly-haired—younger than Charlie. You'd never guess from the innocuous, clean-cut look of him that he'd spent years terrorizing the Germans. He looked like a librarian's assistant, even fresh out of jail. Next to him sat Dorian, one of Charlie's least favorite people. She introduced both men to Fletcher, and turned to her brother.

"Does Maman know you're out?"

"Of course. We swung by the shop to visit her first."

"How'd you get out?"

Without looking up, Fitz flicked a hand toward the corner, where Louise and Rafael huddled on the wide windowsill. "You can thank *them*," he said. "They came to get me. Together. The two of them." He glared at Charlie.

"Nothing to do with us," Rafael said. "All the commander's doing. Talk to him. Lou and I were just following orders."

Charlie's face must've shown the acute relief and grateful incredulity she felt, because he shrugged and said, "No reason to make a big thing out of it." He sounded embarrassed. "Omloop did all the work. I just made a suggestion."

"What suggestion?"

"And gave him all the money," said Rafael.

"The *suggestion* is everything," Briggs said.

"What suggestion, what money?" said Charlie. "You never leave the barn, how could you suggest *anything*?"

"I told you I was working on it, didn't I?" Fletcher said, and smiled.

"Get some food, you two," Alder said. "Have the chicken before it's all gone." He kept refilling Fitz's plate and topping up his cup. "My son is home," he said. "I'll worry about everything else tomorrow." Alder was so ecstatic, he let the soldiers into his house and fed them everything he had. He even killed one of his precious chickens!

After a little prodding, Fletcher explained. He'd given Omloop a stack of cash to bribe some indigent locals desperate enough to earn a few francs by getting themselves arrested. Within forty-eight hours, the jail was overwhelmed by a rash of petty offenders charged with vagrancy, hooliganism, public drunkenness, defacing government property, desecrating church steps, stealing tires, and more. The police station had to process more than thirty arrests.

With the jail flooded and no official paperwork prepared to transfer Fitz to the German labor camps, the warden had little choice but to release him to make room for the new arrivals. Louise and Rafael went to fetch him.

Charlie was impressed. "That wasn't a bad plan, Fletcher," she muttered. She couldn't believe he managed to get her brother out.

Fitz, however, looked like he might cry—not grateful, not delighted.

"Your brother looks pretty miserable for a free man," Fletcher murmured to Charlie as they helped themselves to the potatoes and bread from the stove—and what was left of the poor chicken.

"Because you understand nothing," Charlie said. "Fitz and Louise were an item," she whispered. "It only just ended—in May. But he was about to ask her to marry him. He gave her a bag of nuts, that's how serious it was. And now there's *this*." She stabbed her finger toward Louise, laughing softly with Rafael by the window.

"A bag of *nuts*?" muttered Fletcher.

"I've said all there is to say on the subject," Charlie said, grabbing her plate and joining her brother at the table. "Vake, you gave them your large truck?"

"To free my son from jail? I'd have given them half my farm."

"And you should've seen the sergeant drive!" Louise said, bubbling with delight. "He threaded the truck through the trees like it was a bicycle! Took a hairpin turn on the wheels and said, 'Lean left!'—and I did, like my life depended on it. I didn't know trucks could do that!"

"I'm surprised he didn't flip it for fun," Fitz said, scraping his fork back and forth against the plate.

"Flip it for fun and land in the sewer!" said Dorian, grinning—trying to riff off Fitz, and slipping on his own punchline.

"How is that funny, Dory?" said a frowning Louise. "I was in the truck, too. You wanted *me* to land in the sewer?"

"Geez, honestly, shut up, Dory," Fitz said. "Has Vogel been by, Vake?" Alder shook his head. He didn't even blink in Charlie's direction.

"Must be out sick," Dory said. "He hasn't been at headquarters either. He always walks past my desk to say hello. I can let you know when he's back."

"Yes," Alder said evenly. "You do that, Dory. And thank you."

Dorian de Smet was dough-like, despite the war privations. His face was doughy: puffy cheeks, puffy lips, a puffy nose, a puffy double chin. His trousers were belted unnaturally high—not under his doughy belly, but over it—nearly to his ribs. His *Polizei* tunic was tucked into this high-waisted ensemble, making him appear even more rotund than necessary. With his tight shirt, high pants, and baby cheeks that barely took a razor, Dory looked like someone placed a buttered boule of dough in a cold oven and forgot to bake it. That was Dory, Charlie thought unkindly. Pasty, soft, and unbaked. She had never liked him. She didn't like the insincere way he sucked up to her brother.

Dory worked behind a desk at the *Polizei* station in Antwerp, though he told everyone he was actual Belgian *Polizei*. His duties were filing reports, taking notes, and distributing memos. This was not how Dory described his job to Fletcher, who listened politely while he ate. They hadn't even issued Dory a weapon, Charlie wanted to say. He wasn't permitted to patrol or book prisoners. Some *Polizei*.

For years, Dory had been nothing more than a glorified filing clerk—stamping forms for bicycle headlamp infractions and plate violations. But after D-Day, the SS was so short-staffed that he was pulled into the SS headquarters at Port Authority to provide "enhanced administrative support." He was reassigned to the "Temporary Fuel and Transport" department. Now he processed fuel vouchers—the grunt behind the third carbon copy of every requisition slip.

What bothered Charlie was how Dory constantly inflated his role—his importance, his access, his supposed usefulness to the resistance. To Fletcher, he made it sound like he supervised all SS transport in the Antwerp district, instead of being one of ten low-level clerks, furiously churning out fuel paperwork for the command office.

Dorian was a self-important little boil. But her brother tolerated him, and Omloop found him occasionally useful for sniffing out German raids and transfer orders. It was Dory who told Omloop he was being tailed. Charlie learned to bite her tongue—and did so again tonight.

Yes, unfortunately, Dory was the reason Fitz was successful. And Fitz was the reason *La Ligne* had anything: clothes for the evaders, food to barter, supplies to feed Fletcher's boys, liquor to bribe the guards, ammunition, and even medicine when it couldn't be sourced elsewhere.

And half of everything Fitz did, all the bravery and the recklessness, Charlie knew, he did for Louise—so she would love him.

Only four people understood this bitter truth.

Fitz. Louise. Charlie.

And Dory.

38

Second Objective

After Dory left, and Lillehaven was secure once more, Charlie and Louise took Zeus into the fields to pick peonies before sunset, while Fletcher finally had a few minutes alone with Ngomo. They walked and talked among the poppies.

"How are you feeling?" asked Fletcher.

"Better now that I've slept and had Alder's plum juice," Ngomo replied with a soft smile. "Took some of my cares away."

"It's a panacea for most ills—sleep and the water of life."

Sunset in the Lillehaven fields was stunning. The flowers were on fire. Fletcher watched Charlie and Louise bend to Zeus, their hands on his shoulders. He took an aching breath, for a moment almost forgetting why they were all here and what they were all doing.

Ngomo was not forthcoming—either with small talk or big talk. In many ways he was like a mountain. He wasn't going to come to Fletcher.

Fletcher would have to come to the mountain.

He decided to open with a story. "My commander, Jonathan Reed," Fletcher said, "once told me that Neville Chamberlain offered Hitler the Belgian Congo as compensation for the African colonies Germany lost after the First World War. He made that proposal at least three times—and Hitler refused."

"They call that irony where I'm from," said Ngomo.

Fletcher laughed, despite himself.

"Jonathan Reed is a good man," Ngomo said. "I know him well."

Fletcher worked to mask his surprise.

"I am to the King," Ngomo said, "what Jonathan is to General Leslie Groves."

Fletcher nearly groaned. "You know who Groves is, too?"

Not a feature twitched on Ngomo's proud, impassive face. "There is a world beneath the earth you don't know and cannot know, Lieutenant Gray. You think this story began with the murder aboard *La Fortuna*. Me? I've lived inside it for many years. And before me, my country lived with it for a hundred more. I don't even know if I'm in the last act yet." His black eyes locked on Fletcher's—unflinching, unwavering, unafraid. As if to say: *I know why you're here. So go ahead. Come and take me.*

Fletcher felt cold in his bones. Some orders you carried like a coffin on your back.

"Groves and Reed must be livid with me," Ngomo said after a few moments of stilted silence.

"I would not call them ecstatic, no," said Fletcher.

"Is that why you're here?"

"I'm here to secure the uranium you smuggled to Hitler's door—and left at his feet," Fletcher said.

"Yes," Ngomo said, hanging his head. "I should've known better. Back home they say, *When a man travels by map, the river forgets its course.*"

They lit another cigarette and strolled on. "Can I ask, what was your plan before Rheinhardt changed your course? I assume you didn't sail all the way from the Congo to get butchered."

"No, that wasn't my first objective," Ngomo said. "If it weren't for that lizard-hearted Nazi, everything would've gone the way we set it up. We had eight hundred crates of real merchandise, authorized to be delivered to Miguel Silva's warehouses in Beveren, west of Antwerp."

Fletcher smoked thoughtfully, listening for a move, an opening, an opportunity.

"Could Silva's warehouses still be a possibility?" Ngomo asked.

Fletcher shook his head. "Omloop said no. Dismantled. Boarded up. Taken over by the Nazis, searched, looted. Guards posted. In any case, that would be the first place Rheinhardt would search." He took another drag. "We have no way of getting them there anyway."

"Silva has trucks," Ngomo said.

Fletcher shook his head. "All confiscated."

"And Silva himself?"

"In the wind."

Ngomo nodded slowly. "I'd like to be in the wind," he said in the tone of a man who didn't believe that would ever happen.

"Yes, wouldn't we all," said Fletcher.

"The barrels are hard to recover," Ngomo said. "They're extremely heavy and buried several levels down in the bow of the ship."

Fletcher lowered his voice, quiet enough that even the birds couldn't hear.

"So your plan was to leave *eight tons of uranium* in Silva's warehouse in the middle of occupied Belgium?" He couldn't keep the judgment from his tone.

"Hidden behind a thousand other crates."

"Until when? And what if the Germans win the war?"

Ngomo took a long breath. "I didn't think that would happen," he said. "I watched the Americans treat this rock as more precious than the earth's most precious stone. I've never in my life seen the vigilance they exerted to extract it, to protect it, to make sure not a scrap of it got into the wrong hands." His shoulders pulled inward. "Is it possible to get word to the King? To tell him how truly sorry I am for this debacle?"

Fletcher stared at Ngomo, baffled. "I'll be sure to let Jonathan Reed know how sorry you are," he said coolly. "As for your king, I was told that after the invasion, the Nazis relocated him, his staff, and his family to Germany—very much against their will."

Pain distorted Ngomo's normally inscrutable face. For a few moments, he couldn't speak. "What about Robert Capelle?"

"I don't know, Ngomo. He was still here a week ago. But just to recap our current predicament—we have no trucks, no warehouse, no stevedores, and no safe passage. We can't sink the ship, or sail it out of the harbor, and we can't offload the cargo because we have nowhere to take it and no means by which to get it there. Also, it's being guarded by Hitler's seventh army. Do I have it straight? And of course, you yourself can't be seen, can't be housed, and can't be safely moved. Yet your king has pleaded for your safety to none other than Winston Churchill himself. I just want to make sure I haven't omitted anything in this parade of disasters." Though he did omit that one little essential thing—his second objective.

"I can't believe after how I've failed him, the King has asked for my safety," Ngomo said. And then he wept.

39

Charlie and Her Lovers

Charlie had four lovers in her life, though only one could be called a true love affair. The first one had been a boy of nineteen, a child, an absolute child. They were together a year, but what he needed was a mother.

The second one broke her heart. There were days when she thought she might never recover. He couldn't even keep the few promises he had made when he was drunk. She loved him, but he didn't love her. That's all there was to it. Her anger at him and love for him took a long time to die.

Anger longer.

The third one was a rebound, a colossal mistake.

The fourth, and last, was the illegitimate son of her very own father. Blessed be the Lord and all His angels that she found this out *just* before, and not right *after*—which would've necessitated either a swift relocation or a loaded pistol.

She got together with him at his house in Eindhoven, just inside the Dutch border, and in the briefest flicker of foreplay—when he should've been doing anything other than talking (though in retrospect, thank God he was)—he asked where she was from. When she said, "Herentals," he followed with, "Huh. Mother says that's where my *vader* lives." And before Charlie could speak, her heart seized, as if she already knew the truth. In this casual stranger she saw it—the most unwelcome resemblance to her out-of-control father. The length. The slimness. The solemn nose.

All her innocence went up in smoke that night. She put away her childish things, understanding something she wished she never had to. Your parents were as lost as you. They weren't gods, or magicians—or saints.

"Don't tell your mother," was what Alder said when Charlie confronted him upon her return to Lillehaven.

"You know," Charlie said, sharply recalling the unexplained yelling, the nonstop fights, the tearing of hair and the breaking of dishes, "something tells me Maman already knows."

That was almost three years ago. Charlie never saw the boy again. The Germans fell in love with Alder's prize-winning peonies. Father and daughter rebuilt their bond, one flower delivery at a time, one partisan mission at a time. They were too busy to grow apart. And when Alder once asked why she didn't have a fella like the rest of her friends, she replied that she didn't know, geographically, how far away she'd have to go to find a decent one.

Leaning into the joke, Alder said France. "No, wait," he added. "Spain—just to be safe."

That was back when her father still made jokes, like a regular human, before war and grief gnawed away at his humorous bone.

Point was, Charlie had since remade herself into someone too busy and too serious for love. Love was for people with no responsibilities, no war, no outrage. She rebuilt her present life around risk, movement, peril, to keep any hopeless insanity from invading her heart again. One wrong unrequited man was enough for her.

Which is why the ridiculous trembling she felt when Fletcher was near infuriated her.

Charlie both admired and resented Louise's uncanny ability to push away the worries of war by smiling wide and flirting wildly as if their lives weren't encircled, both geographically and emotionally, by ruthless killers. While Charlie kept everyone at flower fields' length, Louise brought everyone within a breath of her sumptuous breast.

But lately, what made Charlie's white-knuckled forbearance easier was the realization that Fletcher somehow remained uniquely immune to Louise's preternatural powers. He did *not* follow her with his eyes. He didn't tilt his head when she spoke, or fawn over her, or grin idiotically each time she passed by.

That alone would've been enough to endear him to Charlie. But to add to her existential confusion, Fletcher acted as if it was *Charlie* whom he wasn't immune to!

Charlie, who made his head tilt.

Charlie, whose voice he heard above all others.

Charlie, whose rare smile he returned with his rare own.

He was always by *her* side, listening to her, asking if she needed help, trying to joke with her. And this was as mystifying to her as Louise's breezy way of surviving the war.

Charlie wanted to ask Louise—an expert in all things men—for advice. She didn't for two reasons. One, she didn't want Louise to discover there was a solitary man in Flanders who wasn't rendered stupid by the sight of her—lest she decide to do something about it. And two, Louise herself had become oblivious to everyone but Rafael. Louise was making jokes to make *him* laugh. Acting as if Rafael was her Charlie.

Loosha was acting as if Rafael was *the one*.

Charlie was on her own, trying to unravel the mysterious state of Fletcher Gray's heart and his true disposition toward a young woman who'd lived camouflaged for so long, she'd forgotten she was even a woman.

During their few private moments, when it was just the two of them, Charlie told Fletcher a few stories about Louise. "A few years ago, after Lou turned eighteen, we'd get dressed up and go dancing sometimes." She said *a few years ago*, but what she meant was *in another life*. "Often we'd be wearing the exact same dress. Maxine's mother made them for us from one roll of fabric. We'd be surrounded by a bevy of boys, and they'd all say to her, *Oh, you look so pretty in that dress*. And I'd be standing right there, wearing the exact same dress! And was completely ignored."

"Yikes."

"And after we formed *La Ligne*, we'd meet up with other cells my brother worked with, and some guy would ask, *So what do you do for the resistance*, and I'd tell him how I stole guns or raided ammo dumps or made bombs, and he'd half listen, and then turn to Louise while I was mid-sentence and say, *And what do* you *do?* And she'd chirp, *Oh, I go to the market and buy plums*, and he'd go, *That's so fascinating! Tell me all about it*."

"Wow. That's almost funny," said Fletcher.

"Yeah," said Charlie. "Almost."

She made it sound like a joke. She loved Louise and didn't begrudge the way her friend's otherworldly beauty pulled everyone into her orbit. Charlie had stood so long beside the sun, she stopped wondering if there might be any reflected light left for her.

What she begrudged—especially now that Fletcher was in her life—was that she herself was invisible.

And worse—that she was the one who had made herself invisible.

40

Protected Resource

"Hubner, get us a car from Motor Pool immediately," Rheinhardt said on Friday morning. "Something not too flashy. Respectable. Four doors. Decent speed—maybe a straight six. Smooth ride. Good for long trips. Maybe an Opel Admiral Sedan?"

"For us, sir?"

"Of course for us, Hubner. I'm not going to drive myself, am I? There's rain in the forecast, and I'd rather not arrive soaked on your precious motorcycle."

"Very well, sir. How long should I get the car for?"

"Make it two days, to be on the safe side."

"Of course. And where are we going?"

"Have you been paying any attention at all, Hubner? Zvart Haus, of course. I need to confirm that I'm correct before moving forward."

"Confidence in your course of action is very important," Hubner said, coughing lightly. "But in the specific instance of Zvart Haus, may I inquire what exactly we are confirming?"

"You may not. I just need to be one hundred percent sure about something before we head to Berlin."

"Berlin!"

"Yes. Wear your best attire, Hubner."

Rheinhardt was trembling with anticipation. In his coat pocket, wrapped in plastic, paper, cellophane, packing tape, and even aluminum foil for good measure, was the Stone of Doom.

They had hours of stultifying administrative business to attend to—wallpaper permits, confiscation tallies from Jewish homes in Antwerp, and missing signatures on execution receipts—and didn't set out for Zvart until midday.

While Hubner drove, Rheinhardt rolled down his window to have a smoke.

It was raining, and the rain reflected off the damp gray stone. Even the sky was the color of dull chrome. The buildings, the factories, the plants, the electric grid, all of it was sinking into the flat, endless mud of Belgium, where the ground seemed almost lower than the sea. The whole earth lay half-drowned in the shallow, dirty waters. The smell of metal was everywhere.

Plumes of smoke from factory chimneys rose like clouds up into the mist, and the power generators with their high-voltage lines loomed over the squat, low-slung factories. Everything was low to the ground, except the latticed skeletons towering over the grime below, humming like mechanical beasts. Their substations were fenced off with electric and barbed wire to prevent sabotage, but it looked as if the substations themselves were in prison, complete with concrete towers and metal walls.

Flat swampy lowlands spread out in a gray fog. Rheinhardt had grown up in the valley of the foothills of the most beautiful mountain range in the world, the Bavarian Alps. Being partial to beauty in his surroundings, he couldn't help but judge harshly this nation of puddles, sparse trees, rivers that looked like canals, and canals that looked like drainage runs. Industrial advancement was everywhere. Germany used and depended on Belgium to supply its war machine, but this did not make Belgium more attractive in return.

Rheinhardt sat in the back seat, the stone in his pocket eating away at all his good senses. He wanted to roll up the window to push the smell of smoke and steel out of his nostrils. But rolling up the window would mean being in a confined space with the warm, pulsing beast in his overcoat.

"So, tell me, Hubner, if the house is just a transit station for Jews waiting to be sent to points east, why did they need four metric tons of sulfuric acid delivered to them just four weeks ago?"

"I don't know, sir. Is that a rhetorical question?"

"Just drive, Hubner."

"Yes, sir."

A few minutes passed.

"Hubner . . . without your initiative, we never would have found this Zvart Haus. I owe you."

"You owe me nothing, sir. I live to serve."

That Friday morning at daybreak, Rafael asked if he could accompany Louise to Zvart Haus to bring Saul his lunch. "It's going to be an awful day," he said from inside the barn. "Look at the rain. Let me ride next to you. I'll hold an umbrella over your head."

"You're going to hold an umbrella over my head while riding a separate bicycle?" Louise wanted to kiss him. "Silly boy."

"I'd be happy to ride on your handlebars, if you prefer."

Louise said no to everything, but wanted to say yes—to everything. Rafael must've seen her ambivalence, because he resumed his sweet talk. She had to leave quickly, before she lost what little resolve she had. This lack of resolve was why she hadn't been to see Saul in nearly a week, ever since Rafael dropped out of the sky like manna from heaven.

She biked home from Lillehaven, where she exchanged loud words with her mother over Charlie. Hélène Aubel was on her way to work, but, as always, was able to find time to stop and berate Charlie for a few minutes. Louise wanted to say, *Maman, I promise you, you're worrying about all the wrong things. Because perched on my handlebars is a powder keg of lust and desire that would make a harlot blush. Charlie is the least of your concerns.*

It was too wet to go to the market, so Louise rummaged through the war larder and baked some dry muffins with a few carrots and barley flour. She changed into a pair of slacks and a white blouse and felt immediately self-conscious in the snug top. Her breasts looked too conspicuous for lunch with Saul. She threw on a cardigan, cobbled together his lunch, pulled a slicker over her shoulders, and set off when noon came.

She rode past the low brick substation with the two leaning pylons and the drooping line of barbed wire along its fence. Every few meters, the tires sprayed her ankles. Despite the overflowing ditches and the warm drizzle, Louise thought about nothing else but Rafael on the way to Zvart. She could hear his voice in her head. *"Who'd want to think about anything else but me? I'm adorable."* Followed by, *"It's true, there's nothing about your breasts that's appropriate, Loosha."* Her smile for the Belgian guards was more radiant than ever. Even their damp "Heil Hitler!" couldn't bring her down as she pedaled past.

Was it her imagination or was Saul thinner, more shrunken since she saw him last? He looked so alone sitting upstairs in his study, his head buried in his notebook, writing down his indecipherable numbers, whose meaning and motive she couldn't begin to grasp. She felt awful that she'd brought him only one peach and the carrot muffins. Those impossible troglodyte soldiers were devouring all her fruit, all her sweetest desserts. She made a mental note to get some more sugar from the black market and to double her recipes next time she baked. Saul needed to gain a few pounds. He looked sick.

"Look, I brought you hydrangeas," she said. "Aren't they nice?"

"They're nice." He didn't look up.

"How's your box going, Saul?" Louise asked quietly. "Making progress?"

"Progress is the last thing I'm making."

"Can't get any more spiders?"

"Not only can I not get more spiders, Louise, my dear," said Saul, "but the one I've got is getting old and slow." He looked so forlorn. Today wasn't a great day, Louise had to admit. It was drizzling outside. She still had to bike back in the rain. Her clothes, her hair would be all wet when she returned to Lillehaven where Rafael was waiting for her.

And look at *that*. Not even the crummy weather could keep the smile off her face. She felt anything but unhappy.

It must've showed in the flush of her skin, because Saul blinked at her warmly, and his mouth turned up. "Why are you all sunshine?" he asked. "Or is it just the contrast with the gloom outside?"

"What else could it be?"

"Many things," Saul said. "You could be in love."

Louise giggled. "Oh, Saul. Don't be silly. It's wartime. In love with who?" But even that rhetorical flourish gave her away. She inflected her voice so high on the last part that *in love with who* soared up the mountain, to all the doves in the sky.

Saul nodded. "That's nice, Lou, good for you," he said. "Who is he?"

Her skin reddened. Her mouth parted. Louise didn't know desire could be so physical. She hadn't experienced that before. Oh, she'd seen it in the boys who had clung to her over the years. But she hadn't felt it inside herself. It was making her light-headed. She wanted to say his name out loud, *Rafael, Ra-fa-EL*, but didn't dare. "Just a boy I know. No one special." Rafael was the name for desire in Louise's heart.

Saul appraised her approvingly. "Is it that Fitz you've been telling me about?"

She shook her head. "I love Fitz. But it's not the same . . ."

Saul sighed. "It's nice to be young," he said. "I used to be young once."

"Young and in love?" She smiled.

"Maybe not quite like you, dear girl," Saul said. "But I used to be a man. Until I ceased to exist, the day they stripped me of my chair at the University of Brussels."

"You're still a man, Saul," Louise said gently. She didn't know what else to say. She couldn't even offer him a tasteless muffin as cold comfort.

He shook his head. "Nowadays I'm nothing but a protected resource, sealed under lock and key at Zvart Haus."

"Who's protecting you?" Louise whispered. "The bad guys?"

"My potential value even to the bad guys, as you call them, is diminishing daily with the ebbing life of my spider, Lou," Saul said. "When it goes, so do I—just like that lowly *Spinnentier*."

41

Zvart Haus

They passed Olen where the sprawling metallurgical plant and refinery of Union Minière of the Belgian Congo lay vast along the wide industrial Albert Canal.

"I didn't realize the Congolese mining works are so close to Zvart Haus," Rheinhardt said.

"Does it matter?"

Rheinhardt wanted to say it didn't. But he didn't believe in coincidences.

As they were nearing their destination, they nearly crashed into a girl on a bicycle who was blithely cycling in the middle of the road, making figure eights in the rain without a care in the world. Hubner smashed down on the horn. The girl waved happily and pedaled away.

"They're crazy around here," Rheinhardt said. "Not only do they have a death wish, but they're biking in the driving rain."

"I wonder if she lives at Zvart," Hubner said. "According to my map, it's just around the corner."

"Why would she live at Zvart?" Rheinhardt said. "Did you see her? She was blonde. I don't care for your musings, Hubner. We have urgent business here."

Zvart Haus was nothing like Rheinhardt had expected, yet everything like he expected. After the dismal gray of their hour-long slog, Zvart Haus looked like a bucolic oasis, a tall, stately mansion, shiny in the rain.

The first bit of irony: the house wasn't black but pristine gleaming white. The window frames were new, the roof was slate, the front walkway was meticulously masoned cobblestone, and the grounds surrounding the main house and its several adjacent buildings befitted landed nobility.

Bright flowers in large planters lined the walkway, and hundreds of white cherry trees, their blooms heavy and fading, bordered the edges of the large property. The grass was freshly cut, the bushes trimmed and neat. On the far side of the house red roses and yellow ragwort lined the stucco wall separating the front lawn from the rear yard.

Hubner stopped in front of a tall wrought-iron gate with dual swinging arms. The princely gate was flanked by thick dense shrubbery—instead of a real fence, a hedgerow. *Interesting*, Rheinhardt thought, getting out of the Opel. *Fascinating.*

He and Hubner huddled for a moment before approaching the sentry.

The adjutant shook his head. "We may have made a mistake," he said quietly. "This doesn't seem like the right place at all. Perhaps there's another Zvart Haus that's actually black?"

"If it's not the right place, then why are the gendarmes guarding the shrubbery?"

Hubner's face was pensive. "Factories that spit out chemical fumes are difficult to hide," he said, "as we've just seen. Yet look at this white estate. I wonder if we should step back and confirm our information? Maybe pop into one of the Union Minière plants across the canal, speak to the floor manager?"

"You're being cautious," Rheinhardt said. "Afraid I'll be wrong again?"

"Most ardently, sir."

Rheinhardt buttoned his coat to his throat and straightened his SS visor. "Well, we're in it now, Hubner," he said. "No courage, no glory. Let's see it through."

With Hubner trailing behind, carrying a thick sheaf of papers, Rheinhardt marched up to the corporals at the gate.

"I am SS-*Sturmbannführer* Erich von Rheinhardt," he said to the men. "I'm deputy commander of the Port of Antwerp and the chief of SS security forces for the region. Open this gate." It wasn't a request, and the guards had no choice but to comply.

"We are investigating a misallocation of resources," Hubner told them, launching into a detailed explanation about the copper wire that might have been erroneously delivered to this address.

Rheinhardt saw that Hubner was wasting his breath and cut him off. These brainless peons knew nothing. They stood silently, as if they'd forgotten German. Belatedly, Rheinhardt realized they weren't German—they were Belgian Gestapo and spoke mainly French. Hubner's exquisite detail of wrongdoing fell, quite literally, on uncomprehending ears.

"Who is the commanding officer on the premises?" Rheinhardt said. "I need to speak to him at once."

The guard said there was no commanding officer. Zvart Haus was secured only by Belgian police.

"Why is the house guarded at all?"

"I believe there are Jews detained in the house under the 'valuable resource' command from Liège, sir," the other guard said. "Under the directive from the Reich Main Security Office on Scientific Matters. But we never see anyone coming in or out. All deliveries go to a separate entrance in the back. We have nothing to do with it, Herr *Sturmbannführer*."

Rheinhardt stood composed, though his mind was reeling. "Who in this farmhouse signed off on thousands of tons of copper, Corporal? I need to speak to *that* person."

"Oh, you must mean Henri Weissmann," the guard said.

"Who?"

Hubner tugged lightly on Rheinhardt's sleeve. "Sir, Weissman is just the man you need," he whispered. They stepped away from the guards for a moment. "He's a very famous Belgian physicist. One of the leading minds on theoretical fission research and radioisotopes." Hubner smiled. "I went to one of his public lectures in Berlin right before the war. He was brilliant."

Rheinhardt walked back to the guards, filled for the briefest moment with hope that this Weissmann might finally solve the riddle of the rock that was burning a hole in his life.

"I need to speak to Henri Weissmann immediately."

The guard shook his head. "I'm afraid that's impossible. He died a month ago."

Rheinhardt wanted to curse. How could this be? What rotten, cosmic luck! "What did he die of?" he asked the guard, glaring at him as if it were his fault the man was dead. "Male pattern baldness? Excessive vomiting?"

The guard was stumped for a reply.

"Is there anyone left at Zvart we can speak to?" asked Hubner.

"I don't know if he knows anything," the second guard said, "but there's a man always hunched by the open window." He pointed to the upper floor of the house, where a form of a man could indeed be seen behind the billowing curtain.

"Should we leave?" Hubner whispered. "Try Union Minière next?"

"Don't be foolish," Rheinhardt said. "We're not leaving without speaking to someone." It was either this man, or Heinrich Himmler in Berlin, and Rheinhardt wasn't ready to blow up his life and career by appealing directly to Himmler.

Breaking both protocol and training, neither guard walked Rheinhardt and Hubner to the front door. "We're going to remain at post," the first guard said.

"Yes, just go knock on the door," the second guard said. "If no one answers, walk right in. It's unlocked."

They knocked, waited a few moments, and when no one answered, they pushed open the door and stepped into the hallway. Hubner began yelling for someone to come to the foyer, while Rheinhardt looked around. The house looked both vacant and lived-in, dilapidated and comfortable. The furniture was high quality but the candlesticks were gone, and the tables had no coverings. The heavy curtains were partially drawn, but the windows were open. It looked like a place where people had lived in comfort and relative luxury for years and then suddenly left. Everything was still in place but stood inanimate. It was like a body whose soul had fled. Rheinhardt felt a small chill at his own analogy.

It also had a faint metallic smell, a cold, sour sharpness. Rheinhardt recognized it—he'd been inhaling it the whole way here, a wet rust odor that assaulted them as they drove by the industrial factories. *How peculiar*, Rheinhardt thought, as he finally heard voices from the kitchen.

He banged on the parquet with his long umbrella.

"SS officer in the front hall!" he yelled. "Come at once!"

A moment or two later, three small children tumbled into the entryway, stared at the two men and ran away. A moment after that, a woman appeared, walking toward them, wiping her hands on a towel.

"Who are you?" Rheinhardt said in French.

"I'm Katrisse," the woman replied in German.

"You're German?"

"I'm the hired help. Who are you here to see—Saul?"

"Saul what?"

"Saul Grunfell?"

"Is he a professor or a scientist?"

"I don't know what he is," Katrisse said. "He lives here. I just work here."

"Are those his children?"

"No, they're mine," said Katrisse. "Saul!" she yelled up the stairs. "People are here to see you!"

"Not people," Hubner said. "The SS deputy commander of the Port of Antwerp."

"SS and his aide are here to see you!" she yelled in French.

The three of them waited. Katrisse said, "Will that be all?"

"He's not here, so no, that will not be all," said Rheinhardt.

"He gets lost in his work," Katrisse said. "And he's eating his lunch. Saul!"

A few more moments ticked by. Just as Rheinhardt's patience was wearing thin, the stairs creaked and a man came down, wiping his mouth with his hand. He was a thin, crumpled, badly dressed man of indeterminate age. He may have been forty, but he looked sixty. He was unshaven, his trousers were wrinkled, and his shirt was untucked and stained. His skin was sallow, like that of a man who did not see the sun, even though he was surrounded by nature. Also, he was patchily balding, Rheinhardt couldn't help but notice with some unease. What was left of his dark graying hair was long and stringy. In his hands, he held his black-rimmed glasses. His fingers were stained with ink and nicotine and cut in a half-dozen places.

He looked like what Rheinhardt expected a mathematician to look like. Imagine choosing this for your life's work, he thought remorselessly. "Are you Saul Grunfell?"

"I am, yes," the man said. "Who are you? Did Krieger send you?"

"Who?"

"Two of you already came—four days ago. I told them then, and I'm telling you now, I'm *working* on it. Weissmann left piles of paper chaos, I'm sorting through it. It's slow, but it's coming along. No, I don't need anything else . . ." He trailed off. "Well, what I need, you can't get me. But I'm working with what you did give me, and it's going as well as it can."

"I don't know this Krieger," Rheinhardt said. "I'm *Sturmbannführer* Erich von Rheinhardt, the deputy commander of the Port of Antwerp."

"Oh," said Grunfell. "What do *you* need?" There was a clipped emphasis on the word *you*, the tone full of indifference and exasperation.

Rheinhardt didn't bother introducing Hubner. There was no point. Unfortunately, Hubner still believed they'd come to Zvart Haus to requisition copper wire from a jailed Jew. He started reading through the manifests, about to make some pointed inquiries of Saul. "Herr Hubner," Rheinhardt said, interrupting him, "why don't you go to the kitchen and ask that fine woman Katrisse for something to eat and drink. It's bad manners to refuse a host's welcome."

Hubner glanced at the thick folder he was holding.

"Leave it with me," Rheinhardt said, grabbing the papers from his aide's hands. He turned to Grunfell. "Is there somewhere private we can talk?" For some reason, this request seemed to stump Grunfell, as if he didn't know where to take the German officer for a discreet conversation in a house that was large enough to host a Party Congress. "You must have a study or a library in this big old house?"

"The rooms on this floor are all open, as you can see," Grunfell said. "Do you wish to talk here in the formal sitting area?"

"I do not. Do you have a small lab we can use?"

"I do, but . . ."

"Let's go there."

Grunfell shook his head.

"You came from upstairs," Rheinhardt said.

"Yes, I have my private study on the second floor, but . . ."

"Perfect. Lead the way."

Reluctantly, Grunfell trudged upstairs. He took Rheinhardt to an overflowing room that once must have been a master bedroom. The space was filled floor to ceiling with books and papers. Heavy tomes, loose manuals, thousands of volumes were stacked in columns against walls and shelves, collapsing over one another. The only aesthetically pleasing—and therefore incongruous—thing in the room was a large vase of freshly picked blue hydrangeas on a low planter table by Grunfell's chair. Rheinhardt appraised the interior critically before occupying a nearby stool by the open window. He didn't bother taking off his greatcoat. There was nowhere to hang it. "How can you find anything in a room such as this?" he asked Grunfell rudely. "Is this how your people treat valuable documents?"

"*My* people are theoretical physicists," Grunfell said, replying in kind. "Everything is rigorously organized." He slid some notebooks from the table and pushed aside a plate holding a half-eaten sandwich and a glistening peach pit. "I can find you a pamphlet on proton separation from 1916 if need be."

"No need." After that, they were both silent.

Grunfell spoke first, to Rheinhardt's surprise; Rheinhardt himself was still gnawing over the best way to approach his delicate questions. "If not Krieger, then who sent you?"

"No one sent me."

"Then what do you want?"

Again, rude. Rheinhardt's brows furrowed. But he found himself in an unusual position. He was the one who needed something from Grunfell, and not the other way around. Rheinhardt said nothing for a few more moments. He opened the folder and pretended to look into it.

"Here's a question, Grunfell. Are you a doctor or a professor?"

"I'm both," Grunfell said. "I'm no longer a professor, obviously. But I'm still a doctor of experimental and mathematical physics."

"What are you by birth?"

"You know what I am," said Grunfell. "I'm a Belgian Jew. Born and raised in Brussels, educated in Berlin."

"Berlin—you don't say," muttered Rheinhardt. Were they the same age? Could they have attended university together? He strained to remember if he'd ever heard the name Grunfell before. He never forgot a name or a face, but he couldn't place him. Still, remarkable. "A math teacher, living in a mansion in the country, under house arrest," Rheinhardt said. "Unusual, no?"

"Not a math teacher—a doctor of experimental and theoretical physics,"

Grunfell corrected Rheinhardt, as if *that* was the deepest thorn in his ego. Now it was Rheinhardt's turn to sneer. Five minutes in, and he'd already zeroed in on a stranger's fatal flaw: incandescent pride. He chuckled inwardly in a rare moment of self-awareness. Let those for whom pride *isn't* the fatal flaw throw the first stone, he thought.

"Do you even know the difference?" Grunfell asked.

"Between arithmetic and experimental physics? It's just a matter of degree, Grunfell."

"Particle accelerators, quantum mechanics, advanced equations—"

"Like I said, math," said Rheinhardt. "But I don't have time for your detailed educational biography. I'm sure you're quite clever. But not so clever as to know why I'm here."

"You are correct, I cannot know what I do not know."

"Let me ask you, are you free to leave? There's barely any security around you."

"Leave and go where?"

"Grunfell, you are an expelled Jew, under an ineffective guard in a manse in the country. You're not in Belzec or Buchenwald, like other Jewish men, even other esteemed physicists. So tell me, what exactly are you doing here that requires kilometers of copper wire?"

"Please direct your questions to Herr Sieg Krieger," Grunfell said. "He's down in Liège. Take a drive in your opulent vehicle. Show him your folder. I'm sure he'll explain the things you don't understand."

"Grunfell, are you . . . dismissing me?"

"Unless you have other questions."

"Copper is critically low worldwide," Rheinhardt said. "At Antwerp, we can barely get enough for our communication grid. How is it that an obscure house in the middle of nowhere is receiving multiple deliveries of this precious commodity?"

"Herr Rheinhardt," said Grunfell, "I promise you, this is *way* above your pay grade. Like . . ." He waved his arm over his head.

"My inspection of this house under the auspices of the security and safety of the Third Reich is above my pay grade?"

Grunfell waved his arm even higher. "*Way* above," he said.

"You're out of line, Grunfell—"

"You have questions, comments, concerns? Take it up with Herr Krieger. Surely, you've heard of Sieg Krieger," said Grunfell. "He's only Heinrich Himmler's second-in-command. He is the Reich Commissioner for Special Projects." Saul paused. "You *have* heard of Heinrich Himmler, have you not? The *Reichsführer* of the SS? The man who answers to Herr Hitler himself? Some even say—not me, but others—that he's the most powerful man in Germany. *That* Heinrich Himmler."

Rheinhardt's steel gaze iced over. "There is absolutely no need for this kind of insolence."

"Oh, I believe there is," Grunfell said. "I report directly to a general who is ranked several orders of magnitude above you. I'm a busy man, and you've interrupted my lunch with your unannounced, and frankly inappropriate, visit."

Grunfell got to his feet. As if their audience were over!

This wasn't going the way Rheinhardt wanted it to go—and needed it to go. Who was this cockroach of a human being? "Grunfell, you are gravely misunderstanding the purpose of my visit—and profoundly overestimating your own position."

"I don't care about the purpose of your visit."

"I also report to Herr Himmler," Rheinhardt said, raising his voice. "I am the commander of a port that's strategically indispensable to the Reich. As director of special projects, Herr Krieger has no authority over me."

"Then by all means take it up with him. Order him to answer your questions."

"What about graphite? Should I take that up with him too?"

"Anything you like."

"What about beryllium?" Rheinhardt said. "Dozens of my manifests show beryllium delivered here—shipped directly from Stockholm. I checked with a few people about this metal, Grunfell. Someone suggested it might be instrumental in bomb-making. But that can't be right—because just across Albert Canal, our V4 rocket factories are churning out bombs and bomb casings around the clock, yet oddly, there are no shipments of beryllium going to them. Zero."

"Sieg Krieger is in Liège, mein Herr," said Grunfell. "Two hours away. He cannot *wait* to explain these matters to you. Please—go pay him a visit."

Rheinhardt had to think on his feet. He'd clearly walked in on something he wasn't supposed to discover. He didn't need a written description of the secret projects the Jewish scientist was assisting Krieger with. All he needed was help in identifying the composition and importance of a small rock.

He tried another tack.

"Where's your family, Grunfell?" he asked. "Are they here with you?"

Grunfell blinked. "Why do you ask, Herr Nazi? Planning to hold my family hostage for leverage? You might want to take that up with Herr Krieger too. I'm running out of relatives for you to blackmail me with."

"I'm trying to understand your situation. And frankly, I don't even need to speak to *you*. I was told there were a few scientists living here, including the renowned Henri Weissmann." Rheinhardt studied his hands. "To tell you the truth, I came to speak to him—because I need help with a small scientific inquiry that probably only he can answer. The delivery of certain metals to this house signaled to me that research might be conducted here, and that he was precisely the expert I needed. You, however, have been nothing but belligerent and uncooperative. I'm done here. Where is Dr. Weissmann? I need to speak to him at once."

Grunfell grumbled, but softened, as Rheinhardt thought he might.

"I'm the most senior scientist here now," Grunfell said. "I'm head of the research lab. Dr. Weissmann unfortunately is dead."

"Oh, that's a damn shame," Rheinhardt said. "Perhaps one of the other scientists, then." He started toward the door.

"If you have a science question, I can help you. You should have said so at the beginning instead of interrogating me about copper wire."

Rheinhardt was caught off guard, unprepared for the opening when it came.

"Your question, Herr Rheinhardt? I really must insist."

The moment had come.

Either this man could tell him, or no one could.

"I have something I'd like to show you," Rheinhardt said, reaching into his pocket and placing his hand over the wrapped warm stone hidden within. "A little while ago, I found barrels filled with a dense heavy rock. They weren't part of the manifest, and they were hidden in the bowels of a merchant ship. Men fought to the death to protect the ship, and I suspect it was to protect this ore. I don't know for sure what it is, but I believe it's radioactive."

"Why?" Grunfell said.

"I performed a simple photographic test on one of the stones," Rheinhardt replied. "Really basic. I put a photograph and a piece of white paper in a drawer, placed the rock near them, and left it overnight. The next morning, a faint image of the photograph had been transferred onto the white paper."

"Do you have this photograph?"

"No."

"So what do you need *me* for? To tell you if your rock is radioactive? Clearly it is, or the image would not have ghosted. Is there anything else?"

"I need you to tell me if this rock is uranium."

"Uranium!" Out of Grunfell's mouth, the word landed like a hammer on glass. Something in him looked like an engine kicking over. "That's quite a leap, Herr Rheinhardt, from radioactive to uranium. Granite is radioactive. So is monazite. Do you have a sample of the ore with you?"

"Yes." Rheinhardt clutched inside his pocket.

Grunfell lifted an eyebrow. "On your person? Clearly you're not that worried if you're blithely carrying it around in your pocket."

"*Should* I be worried?"

"If it's *actually* uranium? Probably. Hang on, let me fetch a pair of gloves." Half a minute later, Grunfell returned with a pair for Rheinhardt too. "You should use gloves if you're going to be handling any kind of reactive ore. Let's see this thing."

Rheinhardt pulled the stone from his coat pocket, carefully unwrapping it—foil, cellophane, parchment—and held it out to Grunfell.

Grunfell studied it without touching it. He looked both animated and unimpressed. Rheinhardt's stomach fell.

"It does look like some kind of uraninite pitchblende," Saul said. "It *is* unusually colored, I'll give you that. Never seen anything like it. Look at these marigold striations. Where did you say you got it from?"

"The ship sailed from Portugal."

Grunfell waved him off, as if he'd lost all interest. "Yes," he said, sitting down. "Portugal is not—"

"But it was mined in the Belgian Congo."

Grunfell shot to his feet, as if he'd been launched out of his chair. Papers scattered across the floor.

"Wait here. I'll be right—" He didn't finish. He bolted from the room.

A few minutes later he came charging back, carrying a heavy square box that looked like a record player. "A Geiger counter," he said, even though Rheinhardt didn't ask.

"I don't know what that is."

"It detects radioactive emissions," Grunfell said. "Each click is one radioactive particle hitting the sensor. The more clicks, the hotter the source." He plugged it in. Rheinhardt heard a low hum and a slight crackle.

"Let's see how much radiation this mystery rock of yours is spitting out. Put it on the table and step back." Saul lifted the probe wand and aimed it at the rock. He was still two or three meters away from the motionless stone when the machine began to rapidly *rat-tat-tat*.

Rheinhardt had never heard this tapping noise before, but it was obvious that Grunfell had. Cautiously, the physicist approached the pitchblende he'd all but dismissed minutes earlier, and from a meter away, extended his arm and waved the wand over the stone.

The Geiger made a noise like a jackhammer tearing through concrete.

"Ah!" Grunfell exclaimed—and dropped the wand. His hands started to shake. "Sorry. Something's wrong with the machine. Something's not right." He was stammering.

"What's wrong with it?"

"It's malfunctioning, can't you hear it?" He went still in a kind of shocked convulsion.

"Are you sure it's just a malfunction?" asked Rheinhardt.

"Yes, it's been finicky. There are only two Geigers in all of Belgium, and mine's up the spout, clearly." The wand lay on the wood floor, twitching, pulsing. The machine continued its gun rattle.

"What if it's *not* broken, Grunfell?"

"The sensor could be saturated," Saul mumbled. "It can't count the emissions fast enough."

"And that would mean *what*?" They were both shouting now, trying to talk over the crackling.

"Possibly, that the sample is extremely radioactive."

"Why can't it be?"

"Because that would mean the ore is"—Grunfell trembled—"hotter than anything I've ever seen outside a reactor. And that's just—not possible." He began to sweat profusely, and appeared to have trouble breathing through his nose. He started to hyperventilate. "No, no—it's definitely the machine," he repeated, gasping for breath. "Something's wrong with it. Something's wrong with me." He clutched his chest. "Excuse me. I'll be right back." He whirled around. "Don't touch anything! Don't touch the machine." He lowered his voice. "Don't touch the *rock*—whatever you do."

"Grunfell, don't you dare leave before you turn that fucking thing off," said Rheinhardt. The relentless hammering of the Geiger was an insanity maker.

Grunfell yanked the cord and fled the room.

Alone, Rheinhardt sat in silence that was so deafening, he thought the machine was still on. All he could hear was the gunfire of the radiation sensor.

Grunfell's panicked demeanor told him that he'd been right all along not to want that thing burning holes in his flesh and his pocket.

But like it or not, it had been burning holes in Rheinhardt's life—before he even knew *what* it was. Before he even knew *that* it was. Even back at the end of May, when he sat innocently behind his comforting desk and stared at the manifest of *La Fortuna*, it was already blasting holes in his entire existence.

Ten minutes passed—an eternity and a second.

Grunfell returned with a large, unwieldy lamp. It was gray outside and miserable; shadowy, even though it was still daylight. There were other lamps in the room, but Grunfell turned them all off and struggled loudly in near darkness with this old lamp, its cord torn at the plug. Swearing under his breath, Saul twisted the frayed wires together over and over. He kept fiddling with them, twisting them. Over and over.

"What are you doing?" Rheinhardt finally said. He'd seen men at the front work rosary beads with more calm.

"This isn't a normal lamp," Grunfell said. "It's a UV light—a black spectrum light."

"I don't know what that is."

"Same function as the Geiger, but silent," Saul said, still twisting. "If the UV light is pointed at an object that emits radiation, sometimes that object will glow slightly."

"Depending on how much radiation it has?"

"Yes." Still twisting.

As he watched Saul wage frantic battle with the cord, Rheinhardt wanted to get up and leave. To walk downstairs, get Hubner, drive away, *never* come back. There was so much to do. He could help Drechsler prepare the port. Even Brandt maybe—that lazy bastard. He was angry at himself. He regretted ever resenting his previously uneventful wartime existence, inspecting ships, signing off on documents, working in the serene seclusion of Baert Haus. It had been so orderly. So peaceful.

Finally Grunfell stopped working the wire. He screwed the plug shut, jammed it into the socket, and switched on the lamp.

The piece of stone on Grunfell's table—a rock that a moment ago had been nothing but warm, inert matter—blazed to life.

It glowed a sickly, otherworldly, demonic green—a color Rheinhardt had never seen.

The entire rock was illuminated from within.

Grunfell's fingers shook like wires in a windstorm as he fumbled for the cord and wrenched it from the wall. The rock stopped burning, but continued to emit a green, pulsing hue, fading, but not quickly enough. Fading like the last light of the day.

Fading like the remains of Rheinhardt's life.

For several minutes, the two men didn't speak.

"Is your lamp also malfunctioning, perhaps?" Rheinhardt said, trying to be sardonic through his terror. "Like your Geiger counter?"

"It's not malfunctioning."

"So I was correct. It is uranium."

Grunfell could only nod. "How much of this did you say you have?" he croaked out in a voice that no longer sounded like his own.

"Sixty barrels," Rheinhardt replied. "Probably around a hundred to a hundred and fifty kilos each."

A strangled groan. "All filled with this?"

"All filled with this."

Grunfell uttered a guttural sound—desperation, thrill, disbelief, terror. "It can't be," he whispered. "It simply can't be."

Once again, he tore from the study, leaving Rheinhardt alone. Just him and his rock. He stared at it from a distance. It suddenly occurred to him that turning off the UV light and switching off the Geiger were just illusions. Sleights of hand. It made it easier to cope with the horror. The light didn't bring the fire to the rock. The light merely revealed the fire to the fool sitting in its casual proximity. The light said, *Here are your invisible, infinite piercing waves. Take a good look. They're washing over you, scorching you, unmaking you cell by cell while you sit and think your grand little thoughts about destiny and war. You're dreaming of immortality, Rheinhardt, while the waves, never flickering, never dimming, consume you from within.*

42

About Louise

"Rider, you have to calm down, man," Briggs said when Rafael returned to the clearing after seeing Louise off.

Fletcher agreed, but he also knew that asking Rafael to calm down was like trying to open an umbrella in a hurricane—pointless.

Right on cue, Rafael said, "I will not calm down." He didn't even rise to the mocking bait. "Why should I? You don't think I know how I feel?"

"We all know how you feel, brother," Briggs said. "The rocks know how you feel. And we have eyes. We're with you. But the girl might not be on your page about this, you get my meaning?"

"Why wouldn't she be?" Rafael said. "What's wrong with me?"

"What if you're not her type?"

"She is *my* type," Rafael said. "And I intend to let her know it."

"Yes, the problem here is you've been too subtle with her," said Belvedere. "You should try a more direct approach."

Rafael took a long swig from the milk jug, followed by a deep drag on his cigarette. His face lit up.

"You're fucking insane," Briggs said.

"Can I help it if she's beguiled me?"

"She's barely said three words to you!"

"Even in silence, she's got a way of jamming all her spokes in my wheel." Rafael smiled. "She's mesmerized me, ensnared me."

"Something tells me, Rider," Fletcher said, "that your spider catches *all* the flies. Not just you. I saw the way all you idiots reacted to her."

"Fine, I agree, she has all the power." Rafael shrugged. "So what? I don't know what to tell you, fellas. She's made me weak."

"And stupid," said Belvedere. "I mean, more stupid."

"I'm going to beg her to love me. On my knees, I will plead for her love. She has compassionate eyes—maybe she'll have mercy on me and love me back." Rafael gleamed, just in the imagining.

And while Rafael spoke, Fletcher's own eyes lay softly and secretly on the girl seated on a boulder three paces from him. Her short dark hair was tucked behind her ears, her intense gaze was on the work of her hands. She was braiding a rope to ring a bell or hold a barrel. She never rested. Her dark, wide-apart eyes carried in them a permanent weary mix of resilience and stubbornness.

There was tension in her jaw even now when she was quietly humming and thought no one was watching her.

Her soft mouth, when it wasn't clenched, was full of expression, but she rarely smiled—and when she did, that smile never reached her eyes.

"I can't let her go," Rafael said, breaking through Fletcher's reverie.

"You don't even have her!" said Briggs.

"I can't let her slip through my loving fingers."

"She will ruin you," said Fletcher, watching Charlie.

"I want to be ruined," Rafael said. "Don't you? Doesn't everyone?"

Fletcher moved away from the others and lit a cigarette, and while he smoked he continued to gaze at the beautiful girl on the rock, braiding the rope and singing her song.

She was always trying so hard not to be seen.

That's what undid him.

Charlie, he wanted to say to her, *don't you know that the loneliest girls are the most beautiful?*

Faintly, in the distance, Fletcher heard a bell begin to toll.

"Charlie," he called out. "Do you hear that?"

"No, what?"

"The bell. Do you not hear? Isn't that Omloop?" He came close to her.

The Waltrude bell tolled, slow and heavy—three times. It paused, then tolled three times again.

"He's knock-knock-knocking, Charlie," Fletcher said, extending his hand. "Omloop is calling for you. Quick. Let's go see what he wants."

Someday, Fletcher wished he could say, *when our work is done, I promise I will find a way to make common cause with you, Charlie Fontaine.*

The bells are ringing, but our time has not yet come.

43

Heavy Water

"Do you have any idea what I've been working on these last three years?" Grunfell said. He couldn't speak without trembling.

Rheinhardt opened his hands, to say, *How would I know this?*

"Zvart Haus is one of a dozen research facilities under Krieger. It was Weissmann's—until he died. Now it's mine. Our charge has been the same for years: isotope separation in general, and uranium isotope separation in particular."

"Separation . . ." Rheinhardt repeated. "You mean like *enrichment*?"

"Yes," Grunfell said. "Our mission has been and continues to be to purify uranium. To make it viable. The work is fragmented, just how Krieger wants it. Some labs focus on theory, others on chemistry, others on the mechanics of enrichment. Here at Zvart we've done a bit of everything. And have tried everything. It's been years of running into walls." He almost began to cry.

"Viable?" Rheinhardt said. "Viable as in . . . have you been making a *bomb* here, Saul?"

Saul scoffed. "I'm not that guy. I'm the guy who's in charge of making *bomb-grade material.*"

"And how's that been going?"

"I've been building equations. Chambers. Failures. That's what I've been building. And do you know why?" Now he really did cry. Rheinhardt, his senses sharpened but his nerves dulled by the rock's lingering chartreuse hum, sat and waited, almost relishing the seconds of relative silence until Saul finished blowing his nose. "They've been shipping me *ore* from a mine in Czechoslovakia." He said it with such ridicule. "It's maybe one percent actual uranium. That's the best they have. Is it any wonder I've been foundering?"

"I don't know," said Rheinhardt. "What percent would be . . . *viable*?"

"More than one fucking percent," said Grunfell.

The unspoken question hung in the air in waves and particles.

"How much is mine?" whispered Rheinhardt.

Emotion choked Grunfell's throat. "Fifty percent? Eighty? All of it?" He sobbed.

Rheinhardt said nothing, trembling slightly himself.

Saul grabbed a notebook and a pencil and for ten minutes didn't speak while he performed feverish, maddening calculations, carrying over tens and sevens, frantically erasing, starting over. Finally he dropped the notebook and stared at Rheinhardt with a face so full of longing, it was as if he was carrying the Golden Apples of the Hesperides home, having attained what could not be humanly attained.

And while he watched Saul, a sensation crept over Rheinhardt like the dam had broken, but the deluge that poured forth wasn't water but fire.

"Listen to me," Saul said, grabbing Rheinhardt's lapels, protocol be damned. "Do you understand what's happening?"

"I do—let go of me." He said *I do*, but he almost didn't.

"You need to immediately get in your car and drive to Liège and speak to Krieger."

"You want me to speak to Himmler's second-in-command without an appointment?"

"Yes! Demand a meeting. Tell him it's a matter of victory or defeat. It's the only language he understands. Everything must be framed in those terms—will it help them win the war or not. Horst, his aide, is drunk on petty power but tell him it's level 'Schwarz Alpha.' He'll know what it means. Krieger and I needed a code to relay laboratory emergencies, leaks, explosions, that sort of thing."

"*Explosions?* In a research lab writing formulas in notebooks?"

"Will you remember or not?"

"*Will I remember?* Who am I, a child?" This lowly Jew barking orders at the Bavarian SS deputy commander would be laughable if it weren't so ridiculous.

"Don't take no for an answer."

"I never do."

"And when you have Krieger's audience, in total privacy—total, you understand—you tell him everything. Don't hold back. Tell him about your extraordinary uranium. Most important—tell him how *much* you have. Tell him Saul said that you have made the single most important discovery in the history of the Reich." Grunfell was overheating. "If he wants me to deliver to him what he needs, he must act at once. How long have you sat on this? Why did it take you so long to find me?"

"Your name wasn't exactly headlining my SS bulletins."

"Did you tell anyone else about this?"

"No."

"Did you tell your aide?"

"No."

"Tell no one. Not a soul. You can't trust anyone."

"Why are you speaking to me like this?" Rheinhardt said coldly. "Don't you think I know? Get yourself together."

"There is no getting ourselves together," Grunfell said. "You should sing and cry." He clenched his fists. "Krieger won't believe you at first. Just as *I* didn't believe you. He'll want proof. Take my Geiger machine with you, so you can show him how real this is. You brought only one sample? A shame, a damn shame. You should've brought two, so I can test it, while you're in Liège." Grunfell shrugged. "It's fine. I know what we've got. You heard the machine. You saw the light!" He teared up. "Krieger is a smart man. He'll give us what we need. You just have to play it right. First thing I need is the entire cargo delivered here, as fast as humanly possible. Krieger will help you with that. You'll need heavy-duty trucks, at least four of them. And many men. Sixty barrels of uranium will be staggeringly heavy. It's probably eight metric tons."

"Well, hold on there, Grunfell," Rheinhardt said. "Slow your horse. Why would Krieger agree to bring it *here*?"

"If he wants *viable* uranium, this is the only place he can bring it," Grunfell said.

"To enrich uranium? Here at Zvart Haus?" Rheinhardt grimaced.

"Rheinhardt," said Grunfell, "the mysteries that lie beyond what you see and what you know are unfathomable to you, I get it. Atoms, neutrons, electrons—particles invisible even to a microscope, yet capable of moving and shaping all things. You're not a man of science, you cannot see the possibilities."

Rheinhardt became defensive. "I was an engineer."

"Well, as an engineer, you'll appreciate this. Zvart is not what it appears to be. Zvart is a facade. It once belonged to a Belgian aristocrat, but was commandeered by the SS in 1940 as a research center. The three of us came here from Brussels—me, Weissmann, and Elias Steinberg. Krieger liked our conclusions and approved the construction of a lab for special projects. We built it in secret, under the auspices of foundation renovation of an old crumbling house. A cement truck, earth-moving equipment, excavation tractors, bricklayers, steel reinforcement. Furnaces. It took us a year. Elias died six months in. Weissmann died a month ago."

The rest of that sentence remained unsaid.

"This lab must be well hidden." Rheinhardt was still skeptical—but less.

"It's deep underground, yes," Grunfell said. "It requires a mineshaft elevator to get down there."

"You built *furnaces* underground?"

Grunfell gave a small patronizing smile. "Furnaces are the least of it, Rheinhardt. Ore crushers, chemical reactors, generator banks, voltage transformers, cooling systems—even a massive electromagnetic vacuum chamber, my *pièce de résistance*. The cyclotron."

"It's impossible. You can't work with chemicals underground. Where does the exhaust go?"

"Subterranean conduits for the fumes."

"I didn't see any smokestacks on the house."

"Hidden, I told you. The exhaust is funneled through ducts, and exhaled far away from here," said Grunfell. "Released with the fumes from the plants and factories along the canal."

"And electricity?"

"Delivered to me the same way. Underground."

Rheinhardt clicked his tongue, mildly impressed, profoundly rattled.

"Maybe when you come back, you'd like to walk through the lab with me, Rheinhardt? The engineer in you will admire it, even if the chemist in you is non-existent. It's a work of art."

Rubbing his chin, Rheinhardt stared out the window at the green wet lawn and the landscaped grounds. "Krieger knows about your lab?"

"Knows? He funded the whole thing, start to finish."

"Is he the one who authorizes the delivery of metals that no one else in Belgium can get?"

"Yes."

"Copper, graphite, beryllium?"

"Yes."

"What's the beryllium for?"

"Come downstairs and I'll show you."

"No, thank you. I should be going. Liège is a ride from here."

"Just remember, if you get any bureaucratic claptrap from Krieger, stay the course."

"What claptrap could you possibly mean, Grunfell? Like where to deliver eight tons of uranium, that little trifle?"

"Weissmann and I built the cyclotron and the lab around it in preparation, hoping that one day we might get the uranium we needed. Until today, I've been working with mere vapors of it, shadows, barely even atoms." Grunfell started to pat Rheinhardt's coat approvingly but stopped himself. He lowered his voice. "I have the only enrichment method in Europe that can actually deliver a final product"—his voice dropped to an intense whisper—"a core of uranium pure enough to ignite a chain reaction. Not a theory. Not a calculation. A bomb. A real one."

"I don't know this Krieger, is he a scientist like you?"

"No one is like me," said Grunfell. "But Krieger is a man of ruthless organization, and yes, some science."

"And you think Krieger is not going to be inclined to move the cargo to Germany instead?"

"That might be his first impulse, yes," said Grunfell. "When Krieger understands what's fallen into his lap, he might want to take the ore to Haigerloch. It's a reactor facility in southwest Germany. I'm not an idiot. I know him. He's under the illusion that heavy water will save him. He thinks he can enrich the ore there, and this is where his limited science keeps failing him. You must disabuse him of this notion, Rheinhardt and tell him—and this is critical—that I am his only hope." He grabbed Rheinhardt's arm. "If you *allow* him to take your precious metal to Haigerloch, you might as well sail that Congo schooner out of the harbor and sink it in the sea, and wave a white flag from its deck as the Allied tanks roll over Germany. This miraculous discovery on your part, your cunning brilliance, your finding me—it will all be for *nothing* if your matchless uranium ends up in that tepid-water teahouse in Haigerloch. They don't have the enrichment facilities, and frankly, they don't have the expertise to put an atomic bomb together." He tapped himself hard on the head. "They don't have the *brains*, Rheinhardt." He sat back, inspecting his nail beds. "You know what?" he said. "If you're not prepared to do what it takes, I wouldn't even bother driving to Liège or speaking to Krieger. There's no point. Your uranium will be garbage, thrown down into the heap of history in that fucking Haigerloch cave, never to be seen or used again. You won't make a bit of difference in anything, Herr Rheinhardt. Just take your rock and go home to Antwerp. Leave it be."

This was it, Grunfell's *coup de grâce*: what he must've thought was a sly appeal to the only thing that truly mattered to Rheinhardt—professional recognition by his superiors in the Reich. But just because Rheinhardt saw through the manipulation didn't mean he wasn't manipulated by it. For a few moments, he stayed silent. He knew he was being played. The same way he'd played Saul earlier when he needed him to look at the stone. He was being worked, yes. But it was working. "How am I going to explain this to Krieger?" Rheinhardt said. "I don't even know what the fuck heavy water is."

"Then let's take five minutes now so you don't sound like a fool later," Grunfell said. "You want to be known as the man who saved the Reich from extinction? You learn about heavy fucking water."

For ten minutes, Grunfell talked—about the difference between heavy water and electromagnetic isotope separation, and about how his cyclotron worked.

"What's in it for you?" Rheinhardt asked when Saul was done.

Grunfell stared out at the gray rain coming down. "I'll be known forevermore as the man who built the first atomic bomb," he said. He no longer looked like the husk Rheinhardt watched trudge down the stairs a few hours earlier, hunched, dejected, humiliated. His chest seemed broader, his eyes sparkled. It was as if a life force had poured back into him the very moment the UV lamp was turned on, exposing the deadly glow underneath.

"I just don't see how you expect me to talk Berlin into using your tiny operation here at Zvart."

The man's face twisted with arrogance and anger. "My operation is not tiny," he said. "To make this work in the shortest timeframe possible, yes, I will need a few additional resources, but I'm the only one who can guarantee success. Guarantee it. I have spent the last twenty *years* of my life in theoretical study, and I know this science cold, like no one else. I know what's possible. Except for the fissionable material, I've had everything else in place. And Krieger knows it—he gave it to me. All I've been missing is your uranium." There was something maniacal behind his smile. "Because of you, I've finally found my million little spiders."

"What?"

"Never mind," Grunfell said. "Bring Krieger to me. Bring Himmler. Bring Hitler. I'll show them all what *can* be done here. What *will* be done."

Rheinhardt shook his head. The man clearly didn't understand either Himmler or Hitler. "By your tone, Grunfell, I fear your intelligence is compartmentalized. Perhaps tragically so." He stood, rewrapped his stone, and began buttoning his coat. "I'll do as you suggest. But what the general does with my discovery is up to him."

"Is that really what you want to do?" Grunfell said. "Hand over the most important decision of your life to permanent bureaucrats?" He fell back against his chair. "I pegged you for a different man than that. A better man."

"I'm not your puppet," Rheinhardt said. "You're overplaying your hand. Stop steering me."

"If I'm right about the quality of your ore, and I'm always right," Saul said, "then I can produce bomb-ready uranium in fourteen to sixteen weeks. Tell that to Krieger. Ask him if anyone else in the world can offer him the same assurance. If the answer is yes, then Godspeed."

Rheinhardt was impressed by how hard the scientist was pressing his own case. That kind of clarity, that kind of drive was admirable. Even in Jews. He felt a grudging respect for the man's unbridled confidence.

Fourteen weeks. Was that fast enough? How long did it take to stop an invading army five hundred kilometers from your border? He woke Hubner, asleep in one of the chairs downstairs, and they climbed into their Opel and took off for Liège.

But the question remained.

Was even three months too long?

44

Krieger in Liège

Rheinhardt and Hubner arrived in Liège just after six in the evening.

Liège was a singularly depressing city. Crouched low along the meandering Meuse River, it lay soaked and sullen in the gray Friday rain. The smokestacks along the river hissed at full throttle, spewing chemical fumes onto slate roofs and copper spires in a town too tired to protest.

Krieger's office occupied the entire east wing of the Palais des Congrès, an imposing structure near the Meuse, repurposed by the Reich and converted to the headquarters of "Special Projects." Rheinhardt ran into roadblocks the moment he arrived. Sieg Krieger, SS-*Obergruppenführer*, in charge of special projects, answered to Heinrich Himmler—and it showed in everything he said and did. Stocky and compact, in his mid-fifties, a logistics warlord in a black uniform, Krieger was a bureaucratic behemoth, overworked and high-clearance, dismissive both to a fault and by default. He had no time for an impromptu meeting with Rheinhardt, whom he didn't know and had never heard of, and refused to make time. "Rheinhardt *who*?" he said to his aide, who was whispering and pointing to the undignified bench in the corridor where Rheinhardt and Hubner sat.

"Tell him to wait," Krieger said, and strode past Rheinhardt, too important to even glance down at him.

They waited. Hubner complained of hunger, thirst, fatigue. But Rheinhardt was aflame with adrenaline. He couldn't have eaten if a fatted calf were placed in front of him. He was close—so close.

"Herr Krieger cannot see you today," the aide said after an hour had gone by. "He has two more meetings before his black-tie dinner honoring the President of Bavaria."

First Drechsler, then Brandt, now Krieger. Nothing but disrespect from them all. Rheinhardt's outer shell stayed icy, but his inner core was broiling.

"It can't wait," Rheinhardt said.

"I'm afraid it's going to have to," said the aide, savoring the obstruction.

The question before Rheinhardt wasn't who lived or died—it was who made the decisions at the crossroads of time that changed history.

Would it be him? Or would it be this venal peon sitting behind his ludicrous desk, filling out forms and ordering pencils?

Rheinhardt waited for the general to finish with the meeting in his office. As Krieger was sweeping past him on his way to the next, Rheinhardt stood and said loudly into Krieger's back, "*Schwarz Alpha*."

Krieger stopped walking and slowly turned around.

"What did you say?"

"Saul Grunfell," Rheinhardt said. "Zvart Haus."

Krieger approached. "What's the emergency?"

"I have a top-secret matter to discuss with you, sir."

"Did Saul send you?"

Oh, so now Rheinhardt was Grunfell's errand boy, too! He kept his degradation hidden. "Top secret. Highest level of classified clearance."

Krieger studied Rheinhardt. His eyes traveled to the floor, where the stolid square Geiger machine sat like a dull brown suitcase.

"You have five minutes," he said, motioning Rheinhardt into his office.

His aide jumped up. "But Herr Krieger!" he sibilated. "Your seven o'clock is waiting!"

"Pipe down, Horst," Krieger said. "This doesn't concern you."

As Rheinhardt carried the Geiger machine into Krieger's quarters, he heard Hubner's voice behind him.

"Yeah, Horst," said Hubner. "Go polish your clipboard."

Krieger's office wasn't like Otto Brandt's—no flowers in crystal vases, no landscapes of Germany, no bar stocked with liquor. Instead, Krieger's office felt like a war general's quarters. High ceilinged and dark paneled with tall windows overlooking the ugly and industrial Meuse, it was dominated by a wide campaign table in the center, and maps and chalkboards on the walls. Technical reports and security clearance documents lay everywhere. A perfunctory portrait of Himmler hung behind the desk, above three telephones, one red, one gray, one black. An entire wall contained a map of Europe crisscrossed with rail lines and coded sites. The room smelled of pipe smoke and fresh carbon paper. There were no medals, no family photographs. Just secrets and war.

As soon as the door shut behind them, Krieger rounded on Rheinhardt and raised his voice. "Who do you think you are to summon me in this manner?

How dare you barge in on a Friday night, acting like I've got nothing else to do but talk to you!"

Without responding, Rheinhardt began searching the room for an electrical outlet. "I'm listening, Herr Krieger," he said. "Please continue."

"I have five factories with partial fuel shortages," Krieger said, fumbling with his cigar and a match. "One of them is meant to be pulverizing a new shipment of ore into fine dust, but it can't, because I'm out of fuel. I'm missing tungsten shipments from Prague, and three dozen of my officers are requesting transfers, for reasons known only to God."

"It sounds like you've got your hands full, mein Herr," Rheinhardt said. Where was that damn outlet? It was time to empty Krieger's hands.

"And to add more insult, you use a *Schwarz Alpha* to get my attention? Do you have any idea what I run here?" Krieger's voice grew louder. "The entire administration for special projects in Germany and the occupied territories! Dozens of ministries and departments all report to me!"

"Yes, you are a very busy man, Herr Krieger." Oh, finally—an outlet, thank goodness. Rheinhardt removed the Geiger from its case and plugged in the cord but didn't turn it on. While Krieger was speaking and pacing, Rheinhardt calmly put on the protective gloves he'd borrowed from Grunfell, took the stone from his pocket, unwrapped it, and laid it carefully on the large campaign table, atop sealed clearance files and a stack of restricted requisitions.

"What the devil is that?" said Krieger. "Damn Grunfell! He's gone too far. I've given that man more money, more materials, more power, more freedom than to anyone! I've protected him from every scrutiny, and this is how he repays me? He's delivered me *nothing* of value, and now he has the audacity to send you—some unknown officer—with a fucking rock—"

Without saying another word, Rheinhardt raised the wand above the uranium and switched on the Geiger.

Krieger was obliterated mid-rant by the machine's over-saturated shriek. He staggered back, caught the edge of a metal chair, and dropped to the floor. His unsmoked cigar rolled under the table.

"What *is* that!" Krieger shrieked.

"By your reaction—and Saul Grunfell's," Rheinhardt said calmly, "I'd say it's witchcraft."

"Turn it off! This instant, Rheinhardt. Off!"

Rheinhardt obliged. The incessant noise stopped, and he could see the mindless relief on Krieger's face. It was astounding to him that someone who was in charge of the atomic program in Nazi Germany—"and all its territories"—could be so ignorant about basic scientific principles.

"I'm sure I don't need to remind you, Herr Krieger, the Geiger is not the problem," Rheinhardt said, trying to keep the derision out of his tone. "The Geiger just measures the problem. Like the thermometer measures the fever. We can throw away the thermometer all we like. The patient is still critical."

Krieger cancelled the rest of his meetings and the black-tie gala with the President of Bavaria. He spent an hour on the secure black phone line with Himmler in Berlin. They never said "uranium" or "bomb" or "enrichment" or "Zvart." They said "birdseed," "the feeder box," "sugar calibration," and "the aviary." A resentful Horst arranged a room for Hubner in one of the guest residences, brought him a full meal and wine, and was ordered "to serve him like a footman" (Krieger's words, not Rheinhardt's). Meanwhile the general and the major dined like kings on china and crystal, drank champagne and pear brandy, and talked late into the night about the future now open to Germany—all because of Rheinhardt.

"Herr Himmler plans to visit Antwerp in the coming weeks to thank you personally, Herr Rheinhardt," Krieger said. "But what you've done for Germany cannot be measured in mere thanks. You are to be promoted—*Standartenführer*. A full colonel. What a triumph you've delivered, with your uncanny attention to detail. If all goes well, what a victory for the Reich!"

"Very good, mein Herr," said Rheinhardt, full of pear brandy and Krieger's praise. "Our first priority is to get the uranium off the ship and to its destination. For that, we'll need reinforced trucks and at least two dozen SS men. We cannot trust the local stevedores. We need strong, reliable men, and absolute secrecy."

Readily, Krieger agreed. "I'll assess how much security we'll need to support the transfer from Antwerp to Haigerloch."

Rheinhardt didn't respond.

"What? You don't agree?"

"I'm no expert, Herr Krieger," Rheinhardt said, "but in my opinion, the uranium should go to Zvart Haus."

Krieger laughed. "I can't do it," he said. "I don't know enough words in German, French, or Hebrew to convince Himmler to hand our greatest asset to a Jew, even one as brilliant as Grunfell. He can't be the lead scientist on this. It has to go to Germany."

"Saul promises the full amount of enriched material needed for an atomic bomb fourteen weeks after delivery of the uranium," Rheinhardt said. "Find me a physicist in Germany who can make the same guarantee, and I'll personally deliver the barrels to him."

Krieger looked thunderstruck. "Is that Saul talking, or you?" he asked.

"How is it possible that Saul, with his shuffling manner and trembling voice, can get men like you and me to do his bidding? He got me to sign over a million marks for a concrete cellar full of magnets. And now he's got you ready to give him the most strategically valuable resource Germany has ever found!"

"He can be quite persuasive."

"Would that I had his powers," Krieger said. "But Himmler will never allow this. Uranium is too important to entrust to a Jew. It must be moved to a secure site in Germany."

"And we *have* a way to enrich the uranium in Germany?" When Krieger didn't reply, Rheinhardt swirled the brandy in his snifter. "I thought the point was to build a bomb."

"Not by a Jew, Rheinhardt! How many times must I say it?"

Rheinhardt's gaze narrowed. He didn't look at Krieger when he spoke. "So I'm clear—we'd rather lose the war than let a Jew help us win it?"

Krieger's voice hardened. Both men had been drinking. "You're aiming above your station, Rheinhardt."

"I'm asking you a question, mein Herr. Do we or do we not have a working method to enrich uranium inside Germany?"

Krieger hesitated again. "We have a program, yes."

"That's not what I asked."

"We're pursuing a reactor-based solution at Haigerloch. Heavy water."

"So the answer is no?"

"We have . . . methods."

Rheinhardt wished he understood more of the science. Grunfell had laid out the principles, but it wasn't enough to argue with strength.

"Sir, why don't you come with me tomorrow," he said. "On the way to securing the barrels, we'll stop at Zvart Haus. You can hear from Saul directly."

"I don't want to speak to him!" Krieger said. "He'll talk me into anything!"

"Saul believes in his electromagnetic method. He says his cyclotron is the only way to deliver what you want."

"Of course he does! Do you hear yourself? He's already using you. He's working on the Reich through you." Krieger lowered his voice, brandy-thick. "I can't stand that arrogant bastard, but . . . unfortunately, he's right. We don't have a completed electromagnetic facility in Germany."

"And the heavy water reactor. . . ?"

". . . Is not fully operational," Krieger muttered.

"Why not?"

"Because we don't have any heavy water."

Rheinhardt fell back against the sofa cushions in astonishment. It was after two in the morning and this was the first he was hearing of it.

"Fine," Krieger allowed, rubbing his forehead. "Maybe Grunfell and Weissmann really did build something extraordinary. The Jews can be damn clever. Practically on his deathbed, Weissmann swore he had the solution—if only I could get him better uranium."

"And now *I* have," Rheinhardt said. "I brought the material and you gave him the tools. Honestly, mein Herr, I don't see the problem."

Krieger snorted. "That's why you're a *Sturmbannführer* and not a *Reichsführer* like Himmler."

"If someone speaks the truth to me, I don't care if he is German or Jew."

"Tell *me* the truth," Krieger asked. "Did his cyclotron *really* make sense to you? I couldn't make heads or tails of it."

"Enough sense," Rheinhardt replied. "I don't know if it's feasible. But it sounded plausible. Just needs a hell of a lot of power."

"And we're already diverting most of Union Minière's grid to Zvart," Krieger said. "Now he wants more? We might have to shut the plant down entirely. We *could*, but—ah, this is sensational, Rheinhardt, I admit it. I will call Herr Himmler tomorrow morning and try."

"Very good, sir. So you and I are agreed on Zvart Haus?"

"What does it matter?" Krieger slammed down his brandy. "Himmler's the one who has to agree, not me. Don't put words in my mouth, Rheinhardt. You sound like Grunfell."

"If you prefer," Rheinhardt said carefully, "I could speak to Herr Himmler myself."

Krieger squinted at him. "What do you think *you* can say that I can't?"

"Perhaps just a new perspective, mein Herr. I might help him see what's really at stake."

"You think Himmler doesn't know what's at stake? God, the arrogance!"

Rheinhardt held his tongue, then made one last attempt to give Krieger the words he would need to persuade Himmler. "General," he said. "The implications here are enormous, as you yourself have said. If this much uranium was shipped in secret, there's likely more where it came from. Possibly *much* more. There could be many mines in the Congo producing ore of this richness. I'd like to think, for Germany's sake, that these barrels are just the beginning." He cleared his throat and paused, letting the idea settle. "But the question is . . ." he continued, low and deliberate, "do the *Americans* know? The Belgian Congo is Allied territory. Have they already mined it? Because if they have, General, then while we're still quibbling about the Jews and delivery locations, they could be halfway to full enrichment."

Krieger's face was a study in shock.

Rheinhardt looked down into his brandy. "If it were me, Herr Krieger, I'd convey that point to Herr Himmler at once. This isn't just about the fourteen weeks or the Allies in France anymore. This is a race to the very finish."

And now he saw it: the words had landed exactly as intended.

In a detonation.

That night, Erich von Rheinhardt could hardly sleep.

45

La Fortuna

There was knock at Rheinhardt's door before five in the morning. The sun was barely up, and Krieger was already standing outside in full dress uniform. "I can't sleep," he said. "This is the most consequential thing that's ever happened to me."

Rheinhardt couldn't agree more.

But there was a lot to do, and they didn't leave Liège until noon, in a convoy of three six-wheeler reinforced steel trucks, and another filled with armed soldiers. Rheinhardt rode up front with Krieger in the general's armored Maybach sedan. Three hours earlier, he had sent Hubner on ahead back to Antwerp in their rented Opel, to ignite the boiler and activate the winch to help with unloading. Few things filled Rheinhardt with more anxiety than Hubner, who stared at him as if hearing a foreign language. "You want me to do *what*, sir?"

"Ignite the boiler. We need an operational winch, and the boiler's the only way. It's going to take five or six hours to get it steaming, so do it as soon as you get back."

"What does that mean—ignite the boiler? Like a stove? Is there a knob?"

"There's no knob. You ignite it—I don't know how I can be any clearer."

"Could you explain it?"

"Do I have to explain everything to you, Hubner?"

"Could you explain just this one thing?"

"You light the coal under the boiler."

"With. . . ?"

"A match, a torch, a flame. And then you stoke it and wait for it to heat up."

"I'm a stoker now?"

"Check the water level first. You don't want an explosion."

"And if the water is low . . ."

"You add some more."

"And if there's no coal?"

"You get some! But don't heat the water too quickly, that's dangerous—you'll warp the boiler plates."

"The what?"

"Ah, hell—just get that two-fingered dock-cart drunk, Firmin, to help you. He's in that shack near Shed 19 by the rail spur."

"Firmin the drunk will help me?"

"He's a former engineer, so yes."

"And if he's . . . indisposed?"

"Figure it out. Just have the winch working before we get there. Go."

As they neared Zvart, Krieger said, "Now listen to me, Rheinhardt," without taking his eyes off the road. "I spoke to Herr Himmler this morning."

Rheinhardt said nothing.

"Thanks to my personal connection with the *Reichsführer*, I was able to clarify the stakes. If the Americans have secured their own supply from the Congo, they may already be ahead of us. Himmler understands the urgency. He's asked *me* to inspect Saul's lab, and if *I* am satisfied and give *my* approval, he'll authorize the full transfer of the uranium to Zvart Haus. But under one condition."

Rheinhardt noted the grammar—*my* connection, *my* approval. Just yesterday it had been all about what Rheinhardt had done for the Reich. And now, not six hours later, Krieger was already writing himself into the story. So be it. The uranium was going to Zvart. The pieces hadn't moved quite the way Rheinhardt had planned. But if you were the one who said *checkmate*, you learned to take the win. "What condition?"

"This doesn't affect anything for the next few months," Krieger said. "But when the time comes, Grunfell's name cannot be associated with this project—no photographs, no documents, no reports. Not now. Not ever. He'll have everything he needs. He can build it. But the Reich will not commemorate a Jew in the forging of its greatest weapon. We'll attach another name at the end. We'll send someone from Haigerloch. Just to formalize the record."

How stupid, Rheinhardt thought. How petty. How monumentally small.

But it wasn't his concern. "Erase him if you must, Herr Krieger," Rheinhardt said. *The bomb will remember.*

"I need your full cooperation on this, Rheinhardt."

"Naturally, sir."

A different Saul Grunfell met them at the door. He was clean-shaven and his stringy hair was trimmed and brushed. He wore a freshly pressed suit, a crisp white shirt and polished shoes that gleamed. He greeted them warmly and led them to the dining room, where sausages, cured meats, cold salads, fresh bread, and hot coffee were laid out for lunch. They shared a convivial meal. Business was kept for outside, over cigarettes. There, Grunfell passionately and clearly laid out his cyclotron vision for Zvart Haus.

Krieger didn't interrupt. When he finished, the general turned and said, "What did I tell you, Rheinhardt? He is very persuasive."

"That he is." Rheinhardt handed Saul the uranium stone and stayed outside in the fresh air while Grunfell took Krieger down to the lab. When they returned, Krieger extended his hand and shook Saul's—casually, as though it were nothing at all for an SS officer to shake hands with a Jew. "Thank you, Saul," Krieger said. "You should see his lab, Rheinhardt. It's impressive."

"I have no doubt," Rheinhardt said, not meeting Saul's eyes.

"The ore will be with you this evening, Grunfell," said Krieger.

"I will prepare my lab to receive it as if it were an honored guest, Herr Krieger. I will begin slowly, as discussed, until our power needs increase."

In the car on the way to *La Fortuna*, Krieger said, "The lab is extraordinary, but I have grave doubts about the security of the house itself. Except for the back, the property's completely unprotected! It doesn't have a fence out front. The morons are guarding a fenceless gate! We're going to need an electrified wall around it. Two sniper towers at least. A hundred men, maybe more. Dogs, too. A dozen shepherds. Just more headache. Perhaps you can handle that while I'm increasing the power supply?" Krieger swore under his breath. "*Verdammt!* As always, everything has to be done all at once."

Rheinhardt was aghast. Had the general lost his mind? "Herr Krieger, with all due respect," he said, "we're not building another Breendonk here, or another Sachsenhausen. Fortifying it in the way you propose would be a grave mistake, and a surefire path to failure. The Belgian partisans roam all over the countryside, searching for our armament facilities, munitions depots, hidden tanks. The last thing we need is to alert the people who spend their waking hours surveilling every German outpost in Belgium that there may be something of such enormous consequence at Zvart that it requires not only a new electrified *wall*, but *hundreds* of additional armed guards. News of it will be in London by supper. Look how they've been bombing our facilities in Hamburg. They will bomb Zvart Haus before Saul can crush his first batch of ore."

"Are you joking?" said Krieger.

"I'm not known to be a humorous man, sir," said Rheinhardt.

"Why are you allowing such partisan lawlessness under your watch?" Krieger exclaimed. "You're in charge of Antwerp security, Rheinhardt. Why aren't you doing anything to stop it?"

"Because it would mean going to war with Belgium," Rheinhardt said. "I can do it—but not under my own authority."

"I can't tell Himmler any of this," Krieger said. "He is fearful and suspicious as it is."

As if they had so many other *viable* options, Rheinhardt thought, darkly amused at his internal choice of words. "We must weigh the extraordinary opportunity presented to us against the possible security risks," he said. "The Zvart lab has operated in plain sight since 1942, and has been neither bombed nor discovered. Even I, who pay an excessive amount of attention to precisely these details, knew nothing about it until just days ago. I believe under the current concealment plan, we could safely continue our mission at Zvart for the next fourteen weeks."

They drove the rest of the way in agitated and apprehensive silence.

The convoy slowly crossed the city and pulled up to the landing area in front of *La Fortuna*. The ship stood bow in, listing slightly to one side in the tidal river. It was six in the evening.

As they got out of the car, Rheinhardt appraised the ship. *La Fortuna* still flew its Portuguese and Congolese flags, but the homemade flag of the yellow narcissus was gone. It must have blown away. Out on the cobblestones, Hubner paced frantically in front of the guards, but Rheinhardt could hear right away that the boiler had not been ignited. The ship was silent.

"Why isn't it up and running?" he said to Hubner. "You couldn't get Firmin?"

"I couldn't get him to help me, no, sir."

Rheinhardt counted the guards on duty. "Why only twelve here? Where are the rest?"

"Just a small mix-up with the switchover at three, sir—some bureaucratic confusion. I'm assured we'll be back on track by next change at eleven." Hubner didn't look directly at Rheinhardt and appeared sweatier than usual. He looked positively drenched.

"What's wrong with you?"

"Nothing, sir, just—"

Rheinhardt turned to Krieger. "I had twenty men posted here."

"It doesn't matter," said Krieger. "An hour from now the ship will have nothing worth guarding."

Rheinhardt nodded, taking a breath. "Probably more than an hour," he said. "Sixty heavy barrels."

"Look at our boys," Krieger said. "They're strapping professionals. Don't worry. Even with a manual winch, they'll manage." He motioned for the dozens of Liège soldiers to begin their preparations.

"If you come aboard with me, Herr Krieger, we can open the hold and get everything ready. I want to show you where they've hidden it. Credit where credit is due—it's really quite ingenious."

Rheinhardt and Krieger walked down the finger wharf jutting out into the Scheldt and climbed the gangplank to the open deck of the ship. Rheinhardt pulled up the O-ring on the cargo hatch to reveal a vertical set of stairs. "Be careful, General," he told Krieger, going first. "The stairs are steep."

They descended the stairs into the cargo area just below deck.

"The ship sailed light except for the birdseed?" Krieger asked.

"Oh, no, no—the ship was filled to the brim with nearly a thousand crates. We emptied it, searching for the seed."

Krieger nodded approvingly. "You're something else, Rheinhardt."

"Thank you, sir."

It was still light out, and the sun drifted pleasantly through the portholes, streaking the floor in bands of flaming gold.

"Look at this floor, General," Rheinhardt said to Krieger. "The planks are smooth. Not a single notch anywhere. It took me days to find it. I almost gave up." He led Krieger to the bow of the ship where he'd marked off with some cigarette ash the nearly invisible indent of the hidden latch.

"I don't see it," Krieger said. "There's a secret door, you say?"

"I know, mein Herr. Believe me." Rheinhardt took out his knife, jammed the tip into the groove, and began to ease the square hatch up from the floorboards.

"It's frankly astonishing that you should find this, Rheinhardt," said Krieger. "You are a remarkable man. What dogged perseverance! I would've never even thought to look."

Rheinhardt needed no extra praise from Krieger—but he quietly welcomed it. He wasn't about to tell the SS general that he, an officer of the Third Reich, had spent hours crawling on his hands and knees like a blind, boneless silverfish, scuttling over the planks, splintering his hands, feeling, believing, *knowing* the door had to be there. It simply had to be.

Perhaps Krieger was right. No one but he, in his pale obsession, could have suspected it, let alone found it.

"Thank you, sir," he said, with false humility.

"Truly, how clever of you," Krieger kept repeating, as Rheinhardt thrust aside the hatch door and shone a flashlight down into the crypt below.

The crypt was empty.

The sixty barrels of uranium were gone.

PART III

Santa Fe

"Molon Labe."
"Come and take them."

Leonidas to Xerxes, Plutarch

46

Flies on the Castle Wall

"Fletcher, wake up! Please, Fletcher!" Charlie whispered from their perch high in the battlements of Het Steen Castle, as she peered through the crenellations. She shook him. "We came here for this, you need to see—wake up!"

Fletcher was unconscious beside her, his head tucked against her leg. Charlie didn't know how she was still awake herself.

Running on fumes, that's how.

But now—alive with exhilaration. By three o'clock, they had returned to Antwerp, half-mad with fatigue, and took cover in the crumbling ruins of the castle, taking a reckless chance just to witness the moment Rheinhardt opened the hold and saw what was missing.

She shook him again. "Come on, Fletcher Gray. You'll be sorry you missed it."

At last he jolted upright. Blinking hard, he muttered an apology—"Couldn't stay awake"—and twisted around to peer through the narrow stone slit.

Rheinhardt had just stepped out of a long, gleaming Maybach sedan. He strode confidently across Glaskaai and spoke to a dozen guards and to his lieutenant.

"When did he get here?" Fletcher asked.

"Just a few minutes ago," she whispered.

Accompanied by another high-ranking SS officer, Rheinhardt walked down the wharf and up the gangplank to the deck of the ship. The other man followed close behind. Their boots echoed sharply across the boards. They descended the ladder into the cargo hold and disappeared below.

"My God, I wish we could see his face," Charlie whispered.

"Listen to them—can you hear it? They're chuckling."

They heard a faint voice, speaking German. Another replied, smooth, complimentary.

A minute passed.

Then—the sound of the lower hatch being thrown open. The cover slammed against the wood.

Charlie grabbed Fletcher's hand. Neither of them breathed.

Then: silence.

Her heart was pounding so loudly she thought they'd hear it on *La Fortuna*.

"I can hear your heart, Charlie," he whispered.

And she wanted to say, can you *really* hear my heart, Fletcher? But before she could, deranged laughter echoed from the hold, broken up by a man's caustic voice in German: "Well, well, Herr Rheinhardt, you're certainly going to achieve your immortality now, aren't you."

Charlie's taut face broke into an open-mouthed grin. She gripped Fletcher's hand tighter. Or did he grip hers?

"What did he say?"

Charlie translated.

Fletcher shook his head in disbelief, the smile ear to ear, his deep-set violet eyes joyous.

The sound of Nazi boots pounded frantically across the planked floor of the cargo hold.

"That's more like it," Fletcher whispered. "It's the only way we like them—in a helpless frenzy."

"Come this way—stick your head in with me. I've got a clearer view."

He leaned toward her until their heads were touching, and through Charlie's crenellation, they finally saw what they'd been breathlessly waiting for.

Rheinhardt, ashen, stricken, his visor fallen, clawed his way up to the deck from the hold, arms flailing. He looked weakened by shock. He bolted across the deck and stumbled and tripped down the gangplank.

"He should be careful on that gangplank," whispered Fletcher. "It's so easy to lose your footing."

Silently, Charlie laughed, giving him a light shove.

Rheinhardt kept himself from falling over, and ran full speed down the wharf. His boots clattered on the cobbled quay. His hand was on his pistol.

He stopped in front of his lieutenant and the guards, gasping, trying to speak—but no words came.

The guards looked terrified. His lieutenant raised both hands in supplication, trying to calm him.

Rheinhardt rushed to the edge of the dock, pitched forward over a bollard, gripped the pylon, and vomited into the river. For long minutes he retched, long after there was nothing left. Fletcher and Charlie stared down at him, listening to his impotent heaving, giddy with joy.

He stood in the middle of Glaskaai, undone. Sweating through his collar, tearing at his hair, he ripped at the buttons of his greatcoat, clawing it open, and spun in all directions, desperate to act, paralyzed by panic. Incomprehension and shame—they were his guards now, standing at attention beside him.

Days earlier, Charlie had watched him pace this quay with a different posture, a different presence. Same boots. Same street.

But now he was a man unmade.

Beaming, Charlie threw her head back and laughed—inaudibly. Fletcher still held her hand. He was laughing too, pressing his fist to his chest.

Mute and overflowing, they turned to each other, their eyes locking in delight, in wordless triumph. He searched her face. She opened her mouth to say—*what?*—but before she could speak, he pulled her in, tilted his head, and kissed her.

His mouth was soft and urgent, his stubble rough against her skin. It stunned her, jackknifed her heart, lurched her body into his, left her breathless.

They were on their knees behind the crenellations, pressed together.

He wrapped his arms around her.

She wrapped her arms around him.

"Oh, Charlie."

"Oh, Fletcher."

They kissed as deeply as they felt, their elation, their relief, their love—newfound, but not new—flooding into that long, open, endless embrace.

47

Sixty Barrels

"Charlie," he called out to her. "Do you hear that?"

"No, what?"

"The bell. Do you not hear? Isn't that Omloop?"

Faintly in the distance, the Waltrude bell tolled, slow and heavy—three times. It paused, then tolled three times again.

"He's knock-knock-knocking, Charlie," Fletcher said. "Quick, let's go see what he wants."

Now Fletcher was running, sprinting through the woods ahead of Charlie. She couldn't keep up. "Fletcher," she kept gasping, "Fletcher, wait."

Out of breath, Fletcher burst into the Lillehaven clearing. "Men, women, children, medics, we're up. Eyes open. Heads high. It's today." Panting, he scanned his circle of warriors. "We've got a shot, but we've got to move, and I mean *move*. It's today or never. We have thirteen hours to figure it out." Fletcher locked eyes with Ngomo. "I don't know how, but tonight, one way or another, we're getting the cargo off that fucking ship."

Ngomo shot to his feet. "What are we waiting for?" he said loudly. "On your feet, soldiers!"

"What about us?" Brigitte said.

"Didn't I also say women?" Fletcher said. "You girls are indispensable to the mission. Without you, we won't be able to do it."

Brigitte beamed. "I'm going to help you, Belvy," she said, glowing.

"I'm sure you'll be a tremendous asset," said a grumbling Belvedere.

Ngomo came to stand by Fletcher's side, his dark eyes shining. "Yesterday you said . . ."

"That was yesterday," said Fletcher, trying to forget their bleak walk through the poppies. "Today is a new day."

"The guard at *La Fortuna* has been pulled off!" Omloop said to Fletcher and Charlie an hour earlier that morning, when they reached him on foot and climbed to join him in the belfry of Saint Waltrude. "They've been reassigned. Yours is not to question the gifts—only to figure out what to do with them." During the seven o'clock shift change, the twenty-man team had been replaced with just two. The crates of grenades and machine guns were loaded onto the truck along with the men. No rotation followed. No replacements arrived. Now, only two armed sentries paced Glaskaai. "More important," Omloop said, adjusting the eyepiece of his field glass, "they're not Gestapo. Which means they're not Rheinhardt's men. They're Belgian." Even the unflappable Omloop sounded excited.

"That's a start," said Fletcher. "But what about Rheinhardt himself?" Yesterday, during the recon at Het Steen Castle, he had seen the man on the quay, consumed, obsessed, pathological.

"And here's your second miracle," Omloop said. "Dory told me that at seven this morning, Rheinhardt's adjutant, Hubner, signed out an SS sedan for his commander." Omloop paused for emphasis. "Until 1800 hours Saturday."

Charlie rolled her eyes. "I can't believe Dory actually gave you something useful. Now he'll never let us forget it."

"Charlie, Charlie," Fletcher said, his mind roaring like an engine on race day, vibrating with the thrill of possibility. With Rheinhardt gone, and the battalion reduced to just two, they had a real chance to pull it off. Twenty men was a pitched battle. Two wasn't even a fight.

"We're going to get the barrels off the ship!" Fletcher exclaimed.

"Barrels?" said Charlie. "You said it was a bomb."

"I said it's the makings of a bomb—in sixty little barrels."

"Florent, tsk-tsk," Omloop said. "You and I discussed this. Get them off the ship—and then what?"

Once again Fletcher blew past the question. "The barrels are heavy but dense. They don't take up much room. It won't be easy, but it's doable. We'll load them onto Alder's trucks and hide them in the woods. Near Lillehaven. Or other woods, if Charlie objects."

"Charlie objects," said Charlie.

"Omloop also objects," said Omloop.

"Fine. Wolski will find us a cave somewhere. Belgium has woods. Belgium has caves. What's the problem?" But even as Fletcher said it, a piston in his overeager brain misfired. He needed to slow down. "Charlie, what's the load rating on your father's trucks?"

"The *Berceau* can carry one small boy and one wounded Congolese officer," she said. "The rest, I don't know—ask my father. Maybe a ton."

Another piston misfired. He had 18,000 pounds of ore spread across sixty barrels. He'd need *nine* of Alder's flower trucks to carry it—not counting the weight of the men and their gear. Ten, to be safe. "How many trucks does your father have?"

"Four," said Charlie. "Really three, if you don't count *La Berceau*."

And just like that, another piston. The revving in his head slowed. *Nicely, done, Fletcher.* He was dismantling his own plan before it had fully formed. Alder's trucks weren't strong enough to carry that weight. Not even into the woods. He didn't need to talk to Alder or Ngomo. He had eight tons of uranium. If he staggered the runs—load four, drive out of Antwerp, find a hiding space, unload, return, repeat—he'd double the length of the operation. Hell, probably triple it. Something unforeseen always happened. He would quadruple the risk of getting caught. And driving nine or ten trucks through Antwerp checkpoints? A recipe for failure, even with infinite time.

Parking ten trucks near Glaskaai? Unwieldy. Impossible.

"Why can't we move these barrels to another part of the ship?" Charlie asked. "Hide them someplace else—like the boiler room, or the engine room, or the captain's quarters? Just move them around. Then you won't need any trucks."

"Charlie may have an idea," Omloop said.

Fletcher nodded slowly. "The man we watched for an hour yesterday, Charlotte," he said, "did he look to you like someone who wouldn't search every millimeter of that ship? How did he find the barrels to begin with?"

"How would I know? This is the first I'm hearing of some barrels."

"Ngomo told me the vault was nearly impossible to find. Only a madman could've found it. That man would not walk away from *La Fortuna*. The ship would be the first place he'd search. It's where *I'd* start."

Omloop and Charlie waited while Fletcher turned it over. "And we can't hide them in the warehouse across the quay, where the rest of *La Fortuna*'s crates are. That's the next place he'd look. The goal isn't hide-and-seek. The goal is to take them and hide them somewhere *he can't find them*."

"If you want safe, the woods are definitely not the place," Charlie said. "They're crossed a thousand times a day by civilians and Germans alike."

"Yes, and time is not unlimited," said Omloop. "Rheinhardt is coming back by 1800 Saturday at the latest. Everything has to be offloaded and hidden before he returns."

"What about another warehouse?" Charlie asked.

"He'll search each one in Antwerp until he finds it," Fletcher said. "If they have dogs that can sniff out human beings, they have dogs that can sniff out the metal in these barrels."

"What if we drop them into the river?" Charlie said.

"The river is ten feet deep at low tide," said Fletcher. "Maybe fourteen at high tide. But also—that'll be the *second* place he looks. Ship first, river second, warehouses third."

Omloop and Charlie opened their hands as if to say, *we're out of ideas.* But Fletcher just had to think. He studied Omloop, as if the answer to his predicament lay in the old man's face.

Suddenly he smiled. One of the misfiring cylinders in his head revved back to life. "Omloooooop," he said, drawing out the name affectionately.

"Oh, no you don't," Omloop said. "I'm seventy-two. I ain't carrying no barrel on my back."

"As always, it's dear Uncle Omloop for the win," said Fletcher.

"I don't know what you're on about. I'm too old and my truck's too small."

"True. Your truck is too small." Fletcher had to repeat it because Omloop clearly didn't hear him correctly. "*Your* truck is too small."

Omloop blinked.

Fletcher jostled the old man good-naturedly. "My grandfather was a bellsmith, remember. And even in his semi-retired capacity, he drove a truck capable of hauling extremely heavy loads. And it was compact. Heavy bells ride best when there's reinforced steel underneath for ballast."

"You want me to involve some poor unsuspecting schlub in your shenanigans?"

"No," said Fletcher, pulling out another pouch from his inner pocket.

"Please, no more cash," Omloop said. "You ain't got enough to cover this. This isn't filling up a drunk tank. It's something else entirely."

"I don't want you to *involve* him," Fletcher said, extending his hand. Two rough-cut diamonds lay in his palm. "I want you to borrow two trucks from him—for 24 to 48 hours. We need them immediately."

"And for this he gets *two* diamonds?" Omloop looked offended.

"No. He gets one," Fletcher said. "You get the other."

"That's better." Omloop took one of the rocks.

"Don't get the trucks from anyone in Antwerp," Fletcher said. "That's the fourth thing Rheinhardt will look for: heavy trucks that could bear the weight. Get them from Brussels. From someone who forges and delivers cathedral bells. The trucks are relatively small, but their loadbearing capacity is enormous. That's what we need. Two four-wheelers with reinforced bottoms from one of your friends in Brussels."

"How much do these barrels weigh?" Charlie asked. "Ten, twenty kilos?"

Fletcher took a breath. He didn't want to tell her. But the time for being coy about it had passed. "One hundred and fifty kilos."

Charlie nearly shrieked. "What are you *talking* about?" She laughed at the absurdity. "*I* don't weigh a hundred and fifty kilos!"

"I never said we didn't have our work cut out for us, Charlotte," Fletcher said, all his cylinders hammering back on. "But the first thing is the trucks." He gave Omloop five minutes to come up with a name. It was after nine in the morning. The night shift began in fourteen hours.

"I have someone," Omloop said. "Adrian Vervaet. Thirty years ago we worked together. But he's not involved in—" He waved his hand vaguely, indicating Belgium, war, occupation, resistance—everything. "He helps me now and again. Reluctantly. He's too successful to get caught up in it. He's not in Brussels, though. He's in Bruges."

"I don't know where that is," Fletcher said. "How long will it take us to get there? Can we walk or bike?"

"It's 120 kilometers," Omloop replied. "Can you bike that?"

"Probably not today," Fletcher said. "Okay, Charlie, let's move." He took her by the wrist, holding it for a moment before letting go. He liked feeling the warm thump of her pulse under his thumb. "We need to run—tell the others. Then you can drive us to Bruges." Leaving Omloop to contact Vervaet and arrange the handoff, Fletcher and Charlie sprinted flat-out for three kilometers back to Lillehaven.

The first priority was to figure out how to disguise the origin of the trucks to protect Adrian Vervaet. After some brainstorming, they came up with two ideas. Fletcher sketched the designs in his notebook. They renamed one truck "*Reichgesundheitsamt—Abteilung Mückenschutz*," or "Reich Health Office—Protection against Malaria and Epidemics." Underneath, in alarming yellow: "**Caution! Chemical Sprays.**" They planned to douse the truck with vinegar and castor oil, to create an intensely unpleasant odor that would be instantly repellent to anyone tempted to inspect it. Hildi even said she'd bring a container of ammonia to multiply the stench.

The other truck became "*Wehrmacht Feldküche—Besteck & Geschirr*"—"Wehrmacht Field Kitchen, Cutlery & Mess Kits." Below that: "Distribution and Repairs," and beneath that, in bold black: "***Eigentum der Wehrmacht. Unbefugte Nutzung Verboten*.**" ("**Property of the Wehrmacht. Unauthorized Use Forbidden.**")

This one was Brigitte's idea. Distribution and repairs made it sound like they handled both new and salvaged equipment—the girls said they'd even scatter old tin mess kits full of forks and spoons around the truck for sound effects, to complete the illusion. Belvedere looked almost proud. Brigitte beamed.

Because the trucks had to be returned to Vervaet immediately, they couldn't paint the logos on with anything that would be hard to remove. Fletcher wanted no complications—no kerosene to scrub off oil paint, no large amounts of water to wash off limestone pigment.

Hildimar came up with the idea of making cardboard stencils, and Maxine suggested sewing together large sacks of burlap for each truck. They would nail the stretched burlap to the wooden sideboards and stencil the fake Nazi signs directly onto it. When finished, they could rip off the burlap, leaving Vervaet's trucks unmarked. No paint would ever touch the wood, and the canvas could be burned to ash without a trace.

Fletcher smiled approvingly at Charlie.

"Why are you smiling at *her*?" Maxine said. "What did she do? We're the ones who had all the best ideas!"

"She was smart enough to find you, wasn't she?" said Fletcher.

Margot didn't want her twin to be the only one praised. "I assume the trucks aren't going to be parked right outside the ship?"

"Correct," said Charlie. "We'll park them behind the castle. We don't want any curious drunks wandering down and spotting them on the quay."

"How are you planning to transfer the barrels from the ship to the truck?" Margot asked Fletcher.

"Well, since they're barrels, Margot, we're probably going to roll them," said Fletcher with a wink.

Margot nodded. "Thought so. Since you're so clever, tell me—have you ever rolled anything across cobblestones? No? Didn't think so. Because I have. Imagine a metal drum full of rocks being dragged down a stone staircase."

Fletcher hadn't thought of that. "Right. We need something absorbent, like felt, to dampen the noise." He looked at her. "Were you just naming problems or do you have a solution? Do you have access to some fabric, Margot?"

"How much would you need?" Margot asked.

"Fifty meters," said Fletcher, checking the calculations in his notebook.

"Fifty!" said Margot. "No. That's too much."

"Maman can get it, Margot," said Maxine. "I'll go ask her—"

"I'll do it," Margot snapped. "You go play with your burlap."

"Fletcher, how could you possibly know how many meters we'd need?" exclaimed Charlie.

"What do you think I was doing yesterday up in the castle?" Fletcher said. "I wasn't just sitting there, listening to the gulls and telling jokes."

"You definitely weren't telling jokes," said Charlie.

"I was calculating. Feel a little sheepish now, don't you, for making fun of me?" He smiled.

"Like a negligible amount," said Charlie.

They had other important things to consider.

"What are we doing with the two guards?" Briggs asked.

"Killing them!" Hawk sounded unnervingly enthusiastic.

"No, Hawk," Fletcher said. "Not time for that yet."

"I'm with weird-eye boy on this," said Briggs. "We *should* kill them."

"Not killing them gives us more flexibility," Fletcher said. "Dead guards—especially if they're hidden—will trigger panic. The army could mobilize. They might close the checkpoints before we can get out."

"So what do you propose?"

"I propose letting Louise do her magical thing."

Where was Louise?

"She went to bring lunch to some professor," Rafael said. Charlie seemed aggravated about it, but Fletcher had no time to ask. When Louise returned, around two, they filled her in on the key details.

"By my *magical thing*," Louise said, in a great mood and completely indifferent to Charlie's irritation, "do you mean you want me to flatter them with chat?" She flipped back a lock of her golden hair.

"This may involve several layers of your magic, Lou," Fletcher said. "While you're doing what you do, Rafael and I will immobilize them from behind. That's where we need you too."

"To immobilize them from behind?"

Fletcher smiled. "No. To get us something from Sister Collette. I'd ask Dory, but Charlie doesn't want me to."

"That man's done enough," Charlie said. "He needs a rest from doing so much."

"What do you need?" Louise asked.

"Something to put them to sleep."

"Permanently?"

"I have a way to put them to sleep permanently," said Hawk.

"Let's start with temporarily, Hawk, and go from there," Fletcher said, using his most soothing voice.

They turned their eyes to Belvedere.

"Scopolamine," Belvedere said, once Rafael translated it.

"What's that?"

"A general anesthetic," Belvedere said. "We use it for field amputations. Aside from pain relief and sedation, it has the added benefit of amnesia. Could be useful, if we don't want them to remember Louise bewitching them in the middle of the night."

"Scopolamine," Fletcher echoed. "Excellent. How is it administered?"

"Syringe into the thigh or deltoid," Belvedere said. "But it has to be front of thigh, for best absorption. Back of leg, and you risk hitting bone. Deltoid's safer—but it might not work. Too much tunic, not enough precision. Be prepared for a fight, though. They'll thrash before they pass out."

"To flirt with two guards, we'll need two girls," Louise said.

"I'll do it," said Brigitte.

"No," said Charlie. "I'll do it."

A hush fell over the women.

"Are you *sure*?" Brigitte said.

"Shut up," Charlie said.

A hush fell over Fletcher too. "Are you *sure*?" he echoed. For reasons he didn't want to delve into, he didn't want her to do it.

"Of course," she said, frowning slightly. "If something goes wrong, I can kill them. Can Gitta?"

She was right, of course. They moved on.

Ngomo wasn't sure if the winch on the ship worked without power from the boiler. They gathered all the knotted twine they'd spent the last week braiding and splicing. Worked-over twine had many uses in loading and unloading cargo.

Fletcher and Charlie told everyone to be packed and ready to board by 1800. Yes, that would mean sitting and waiting in Antwerp until 2300, but fake Nazi trucks filled with mess kits and fumigators couldn't be pulling into the port late on a Friday night without arousing suspicion. It was true, Charlie did occasionally drive her *Berceau* into the city later than that, but her truck was small, unmarked, barely noticeable. Vervaet's trucks were bound to attract more attention.

They got their marching orders and set to work.

Wolski was reassigned to emergency twine-braiding duty. Fletcher didn't think they had enough. Zeus helped him. Belvedere got busy with his medical kit, making sure everything was in order. He counted out the little tins of Stitchless Seal he'd prepared for the team.

"For idiots," one tin was labeled.

"For arteries," another.

"For Rafael."

"Not for Gray."

Briggs huddled beside Mireille and helped her with the stencils. He did a good job. His lettering was a little uneven, but his swastika was pretty good.

Hawk cleaned his spotless rifle for an hour, then quietly helped Hildimar flatten and stretch the burlap.

"Do we need an extra pair of hands?" Charlie asked Fletcher.

"Why? Do you think we should ask Omloop to assist? Or your father?"

Charlie smiled. "I was thinking Fitz."

They eyed each other anxiously. That was too much quagmire for Fletcher. Not only was there the Louise–Rafael complication hanging over Fitz, but Alder, so excited his unwelcome guests were leaving, would almost certainly object to his only son, barely sprung from the clink, being roped into such a perilous undertaking.

"Guess you're right," Charlie muttered even though Fletcher hadn't said anything. "Probably best to let Fitz be. We all would do better to follow my motto, don't you think? *Mission before feelings*. I learned that the hard way."

Fletcher learned that the hard way too. "After you're done with the prep, pack up your things," he said, turning to his team. "We're clearing out."

"We're not coming back here after?" said Rafael.

Fletcher didn't know the answer. What if there was no after? But even if things went swimmingly, Fletcher was sure of one thing: Rheinhardt wasn't going to wash his hands of the uranium and say, *Oh well, I tried*. There would be an aftermath—whatever it was.

"No," he told his men. "We're not coming back."

On the way to Bruges, Fletcher and Charlie discussed the important things. "Did you ever see a spider trap and eat a fly?" she asked.

Fletcher, chewing at his fingertips, was running a thousand permutations in his head—about all the things that could and would and should go catastrophically wrong. Was it any wonder he couldn't make small talk? He barely remembered his manners, let alone his French. "What?" he said slowly. Then he tried. "Tell me about the spider and the fly."

"I saw it in action for the first time in May," Charlie said. "On the windowsill in my kitchen. I'll never forget it as long as I live. The spider was a cellar spider. Harmless-looking like a daddy-long-legs, but tiny. And the fly was ten times the spider's size."

"Did the spider *lure* the fly into its web?" Some could almost mistake Fletcher's tone for flirting.

"It *had* no web," Charlie said in a dark voice. "It was a jumping spider. The fly was buzzing in the corner, minding its own business, and the spider just *leapt up* and stabbed it with its *claw-horns*. Fly kept buzzing, but the venom had paralyzed it. The spider retreated—waited!—then leapt and attacked again. Fangs! Venom! Fly motionless but still buzzing! Spider stabbed it again.

Over and over it did this, at least twenty times in two minutes. It kept circling the fly, jabbing it all around. The venom didn't just immobilize it—it liquefied its insides. And once its prey was still, this tiny thing stuck its fang inside and sucked up the melted organs like soup through a straw." Charlie shuddered. "It took the spider days to finish feasting, and when it was done, nothing remained of the fly but a thin crumbly husk."

"Hmm." Fletcher measured his response. "In this metaphor . . . am I the annoying jumping spider or the dumb buzzing fly?"

"Neither," Charlie said neutrally, keeping her twinkling eyes on the road. "That exasperating man Louise delivers lunch to apparently won't stop talking to her about spiders, and I forgot to remind her to tell him that spiders aren't these cute little silk-weaving creatures he makes them out to be, but venomous carnivorous beasts that paralyze you, and then make you watch yourself die as they slurp up your liquified guts and turn your carcass to ashes."

"Yes, and Louise seems like just the gal to deliver that message," Fletcher said dryly.

They fell into an intimate silence as she drove through Flanders, past Geel, past Oostkamp, and through the soft hills near Tielt.

"Wait till you see Bruges," Charlie said. "It's a beautiful city. Sometimes I wish I lived there."

"Herentals is no slouch either," he said, watching her behind the wheel. "Do you want to tell me a story about it that doesn't involve arachnids?"

"Fine," she said. "But then you have to tell me a story about wherever you're from."

"I don't know if I have anything as colorful as what you just told me," said Fletcher.

"Somehow, *John Fletcher Beauregard Du Soleil Gray*, I don't believe that for a second."

"Okay," he said, "but we'll leave that story for another day." *Possibly, for another life.*

Charlie opened up to him, not so much about herself as about Herentals. It was founded in the eleventh century by a band of exiled monks, she said, who were cast out of Ghent during a purge of heretical sects.

"Were they actually heretics?"

"Yes," Charlie said. "The monks dared preach the Doctrine of the Compassionate Sword."

"I don't know it."

"They said righteous violence *could* be sanctified to protect the innocent or to stop great evil. They believed something had to stand between the lamb and the wolf. The Church called that heresy because to them, sword meant *conquest*.

"The monks said no. Sword meant *burden*—the terrible weight of choosing to *act* when no one else would. To them, action meant *freedom*, not submission. They accused the Church of falsely claiming to serve Christ while stripping away the free will that Christ insisted upon. And so it went."

"Sounds a lot like your spider story, to be honest," said Fletcher.

"Most stories in life are a lot like my spider story, don't you agree," she said with a chuckle, a cigarette in her mouth, her eyes on the road. "The monks fled into Kempen Forest and built a wooden abbey on the first dry patch of land they found," she said. "They called the abbey *Heren Thal*—the Lord's Hollow. In the thirteenth century, the Black Plague destroyed everything, and the town never recovered. It was a hard place, and it stayed that way, proud but isolated." Charlie gripped the wheel. "We named our fields Dead Man's Flats and Saint *Lament*. We have wells no one drinks from after dark. Children are told not to whistle after midnight, for fear that the Monks of the Hollow will whistle back. We don't walk through the woods without reciting Saint Hubert's prayer. But despite everything, we've remained here, for a thousand years. No king has ruled this land for long. No country ever truly claimed it. Flanders is in Belgium, yes, and near Holland, but not *of* either, really. It belongs to itself. And Herentals is a walled town within it."

You're talking about the town, right? he wanted to say. For a moment, a grateful Fletcher forgot his earthly cares, gazing at her as she drove. He wanted to touch her. He wanted to press his mouth to the inside of her warm wrist to feel her beating heart with his lips. He wanted to press his mouth to other things. "Herentals is a beautiful place," he said, turning to the road. "Can't imagine Bruges will be prettier."

But it turned out Bruges had a lot going for it.

The cobbled streets shimmered with old rain, and the air smelled like stone and smoke and snapdragon. To Fletcher, it looked like a city painted from memory. The artist had suddenly fled, leaving the canvas drying, the brush still wet. The war had passed Bruges by, not realizing it was even there.

"Florent would like to live here," he said, keeping the longing out of his voice.

"Told ya," said a smiling Charlie.

The moment he saw them, Fletcher knew they were exactly what he'd been looking for. Adrian Vervaet's trucks were workhorses bred for war.

Size-wise, they were no bigger than Alder's flower trucks—boxy delivery vans—but as soon as Fletcher stepped near them, he could feel their weight.

Each one had been refitted by Vervaet himself. Steel-framed and heavy-sprung, they carried cathedral bells on their fortified chassis.

Fletcher crouched near the widened rear axle, running his hand along the grimy frame. Double-thick leaf springs. Cross-bracing welded over the original rails. Vervaet told him he'd salvaged the steel from German scraps dumped outside Belgian factories. With those heavy German discards, the bellsmith rebuilt his fleet to bear enormous cast-iron bells. The trucks were the mules of machines. They were ugly and sat low to the ground. They'd win no prizes for speed. The brown-gray paint on the wooden drop-sides was dull, the canvas canopy patched and fraying. The wheels were crusted with mud, each tire thick-treaded and steel-banded.

They were threadbare nondescript behemoths, Citroen 45, common in Belgium, authentically Wehrmacht.

They were perfect.

The fuel situation concerned Fletcher. One tank wouldn't be enough to get to Antwerp and back—certainly not if they also had to drive elsewhere to hide the barrels. There was no gasoline allowance for civilian use, zip zero zilch, and even Nazi allocations were heavily rationed. German guards choked every fuel point.

Charlie told him not to worry. "If I had to rely on my father's meager fuel vouchers to ferry the children, Zeus would still be in Charleroi." She took a breath and didn't say what Fletcher himself was thinking: *Maybe Charleroi would've been a safer place for the boy, the way things were going.* "Adrian can sell us a few jerrycans if we're really stuck," she said. "Right, Adrian?"

"I gave him a diamond," Fletcher grumbled. "Maybe he could throw in the petrol for free."

Vervaet told them, almost as a boast, that he'd once used his truck to move the gargantuan south bell of Saint Michel, in Brussels: twelve hundred kilos of alloyed bronze. Barrel-chested Vervaet looked like a man who could lift the bell himself if given a good breakfast.

Ngomo described each metal barrel as about two feet tall and a foot in diameter. They were tiny, but packed a punch. Fletcher had worked it out in the notebook Charlie kept mocking. Thirty barrels came to roughly fifty cubic feet. One of Vervaet's trucks could hold ten times that. Thirty barrels would barely fill a corner. The trucks would creak, grunt, and groan—but they were strong enough and plenty big enough to carry the uranium.

"If they barely fill a corner," Charlie asked, "then why don't we just use one truck? One's much less risky. Easier to get in and out."

"That's true," said Fletcher. "But even Vervaet's Herculean truck won't support eight tons in weight. It'll snap in two. Two trucks is the risk we will have to accept." He studied her a moment. "I know you don't want to leave the *Berceau* here in Vervaet's lot," he said. "But it'll be all right for one day."

"Earlier, you couldn't assure your men you'd be coming back to Lillehaven," said Charlie. "You don't know if anything's going to be all right. Not even for one day."

For authentic detail, Hildi, a German speaker, would drive the *Gesundheit* truck, and Louise, who also spoke German, would take the one with the canteen supplies, though Rafael offered to drive in her place.

"Good thing he speaks no German," said Briggs. "I wouldn't trust that man behind the wheel. Tell them, Fletch. Rider thinks gearshift means go faster. Remember Italy?"

"I also remember who hotwired a German motorbike with a spoon," said Rafael, "drove it off and returned it to the Krauts with the top box full of C4. So pipe down, cowboy."

Before they set off for Antwerp, Fletcher gathered his five men, Charlie and her six women, Ngomo, and Zeus in front of him. He looked at each of them in turn, searching for the right words. His gaze lingered on Charlie a moment longer. He didn't know how to make speeches. But before he could rally the troops, he owed them the truth. They had to know what was inside those barrels.

He spoke for fifteen minutes. The Congo, uranium, the King, the bomb. Not *a bomb*, but *the bomb.*

Some of it, he knew, they wouldn't understand. Jonathan Reed told him—even smarter men couldn't grasp the apocalyptic power of splitting the atoms of enriched uranium. But if it all went south, Fletcher needed his band to know what they might be dying for.

"This isn't Normandy," he said, nodding to Rafael. "There's no backup. No air support. If we fail, no one will ever know what we tried to do. And if we succeed, no one will ever know that either." He paused, cleared his throat. "But it matters. Every part of it. So—eyes up. Stay tight. Make no noise. And don't screw up."

A beat.

"Let's go."

They slipped into Antwerp through two different checkpoints without hassle. No guard even wanted to glance at Hildi's papers, the stench from her truck was so strong. Louise's truck bore the words *Property of the Wehrmacht*, and no one wanted to mess with that either. They met at the pre-arranged alley and parked on the far side of the castle, tucked between a crumbling wall and an overgrown maintenance shed, well out of sight. Everyone piled into the truck that didn't smell like something had died in it. They had hours to wait. The men slept. The women sat and watched them.

Ngomo did not sleep. He sat upright against the sideboards, his black eyes wide with blinkless anxiety. Beside him, Zeus was awake too, curled in the crook of his arm, gently patting his chest every few minutes. "Maybe you should stay in the truck, Zeus," Ngomo whispered.

Zeus shook his head. "I don't want to stay by myself."

"I'm worried about you out there."

"Don't be," Zeus said, taking a breath, continuing to pat Ngomo's chest. "My name wasn't always Zeus. I was born a Zachary. But my mama renamed me. She made me promise to keep the new name forever. She said that Zeus was the name of some god, and gods didn't die, so as long as I was named Zeus, I wouldn't die." They sat in the silence. Somewhere a distant bell sounded. "Okay, Ngomo?" the boy whispered. "I'll be good, I promise. I'll be fine. I'll help."

"You've already done more than you'll ever know, little man," Ngomo said softly, giving Zeus a squeeze, his eyes catching Fletcher's, who also couldn't sleep. Who could sleep when your life was on the line?

At 10:00 p.m., everyone was awake—silent, alert, tense.

At 11:00 p.m., they left the truck and took their positions. Charlie and Louise peeled off and wandered down Jordaensstraat, careful not to let their boots echo on the stone. Fletcher and Rafael moved into a shadowed doorway of Het Steen Castle, syringes of scopolamine in hand, knives unsheathed at their waists. The rest took cover behind stacked crates, in stone alcoves, among broken columns. Zeus hid inside a rusted munitions cart, curled up small, his hand wrapped around the hilt of the trench knife Rafael had given him.

For a few more minutes they waited.

Fletcher stood still and tried to silence the roaring in his head.

This was it.

This moment was the reason Jonathan Reed had flown across the Channel to find him. The moment that had yanked him out of the bloody surf and dropped him here, on this cool, damp Belgian night, crouched in stone, waiting to alter the direction of something too big to name. If they failed—if they missed their mark, if the guards shouted, if the trucks were discovered—they would all be killed.

And more importantly, the uranium would stay in Rheinhardt's hands. If that happened, the world could turn in a different direction entirely.

This wasn't just a mission.

It was a fulcrum.

Fletcher's hand tightened around the syringe. He looked at Rafael, who didn't move, didn't blink. Nearly inaudibly, Rafael whispered, "I got you, Commander. It's going to be okay."

How do you know? Fletcher wanted to say. Was Normandy okay? Was Pointe du Fuck okay? Was Lucas?

At 11:15 p.m., Charlie and Louise—sporting red dresses over their workwear, long enough to cover their boots—turned the corner and meandered arm in arm down Glaskaai toward *La Fortuna*, boozily giggling to each other and swigging from a bottle of cheap Slivovitż. Fletcher and Rafael crouched in the doorway of the castle, twenty meters away.

"You girls out lookin' for trouble?" one of the guards called in French. Charlie and Louise sauntered over.

Louise, even pretend-drunk, never forgot her secret power. *"Mais non, Inspecteurs!"* she chirped with a dainty hiccup, though anyone could see the guards were just plain brigadiers from Garde Civique, the local police force. "We ain't lookin' for trouble—we're bringing it with us."

"Don't you know it's well past curfew?"

"Oh, yeah?" Louise smiled. "What's the penalty for breaking curfew?"

"Does it involve handcuffs?" said Charlie. The girls giggled. Their clothes smelled of alcohol. They were twinkly and red-lipped. The guards, newly on duty and staring down seven more hours alone on the docks, began flirting to pass the time.

Positioning themselves in front of the sentries, the girls stuck out their hands and introduced themselves. The guards relaxed. One laid his MP 40 on the ground; the other slung his over the shoulder. One bent toward Louise's hand—of course. "If the dock catches fire tonight, I'll know who to blame," he said to her.

The other let Charlie clutch his arm, as if to steady herself. "I like my *Inspecteur* in uniform," she said, chuckling and patting his tunic.

From behind, like silent tigers, Fletcher and Rafael closed in. Grabbing one brigadier by the shoulder, Fletcher drove the syringe to the hilt into the man's upper leg. Rafael did the same to his. Startled, the men staggered and cried out. They whirled around, flailing. One clawed at Fletcher's face, the other grabbed at the syringe buried in his thigh. Rafael had already scooped up the machine gun from the ground and leveled it at the guards. Fletcher held his target firm, gripping the man with both hands. They used force, but didn't make a sound.

Within moments, the guards weakened and collapsed to the ground. A few minutes later, they were unconscious. The others quickly approached, circling the two men. "That should last them a good ten hours," Belvedere said, evaluating them at a glance. "But tie them up. We don't want any surprises."

Briggs and Rafael dragged the pair into a storeroom of the nearest warehouse. They stripped off their uniforms and weapons, bound their wrists and ankles and gagged them.

A complaining Margot and a game Maxine put on the discarded brigadier uniforms and slung the Schmeissers over their shoulders. They needed to maintain the illusion of two men standing guard, in case anyone spotted them from a distance.

Charlie backed up one of the trucks as close as possible to the ship, positioning it across the quay next to the warehouse. The second truck stayed hidden—for now. Mireille and Louise, helped by Zeus, rolled out the red felt "carpet." It stretched from the back of the truck, down the ramp, across Glaskaai, along the finger wharf, up the gangplank, and across the deck to the cargo hatch. They had just enough.

It was dark, and the moon was new. They'd brought crank flashlights but turned on only three: one in the secret hold, one to guide the barrel from the gangplank to the truck, and one inside the truck itself. A yellow streetlamp flickered half a block away. They had a night of grueling work ahead, and it would be in near-darkness. But at least it stopped raining. The men laid down their rifles in the corner of the deck, and jumped into the cargo hold below, with Ngomo leading the way.

"Look what that fanatic had to find," he said to Fletcher, holding the flashlight low over the planks near the bow.

"Where? I see nothing."

"Exactly," Ngomo said. "Who would ever find this?"

With Fletcher's knife, Ngomo caught a corner of the hatch, lifted it and tossed it aside. The two of them descended through the narrow opening, down the smuggler's ladder, into the crypt. Briggs peered down after them. "This hatch is a joke," he said. "I've seen rabbit holes with more clearance."

Ngomo turned to Fletcher. "Are you ready?"

"I don't know." That was the truth. Fletcher held his breath.

Ngomo flicked on the crank light.

In the corner, the small stocky barrels stood dense and black, five wide, six deep, two high. Fletcher stared at them. They were mute but alive. A chill passed through him, though it was warm inside the lightless crypt.

"Do you want to touch them?"

"No."

Ngomo ran his hand over the top of one and down its side. "I was so scared I'd lost them," he said, sounding both grateful and relieved. It wasn't even close to what Fletcher was feeling. Reluctantly, Fletcher placed his hand on one—and pulled away. It didn't feel right, the warm, lethal smoothness under his fingers. He slipped on the leather work gloves Alder had given him. They all got a pair—mismatched, old, good enough. Even Zeus. "Shall we?" he said. It was 11:35.

He tried moving one of the barrels on his own. He couldn't even tilt it. "Holy shit, Ngomo," Fletcher said.

"I know. I told you."

"That's not heavy, that's a concrete fucking building."

"We can do it. The two of us."

"Let's move the first one," Fletcher said. "I'll time it, see how long it takes us to get it from here to the truck. On three?"

They grabbed it by the recessed handles and heaved together, straining, muscling it inch by inch above their heads. If Fletcher *imagined* it would be tough—deadlifting a 300-pound barrel—the reality was worse. He and Ngomo wrestled with it in the cramped space, grunting and swearing, sliding their palms under the base, trying to angle it up the narrow ladder as it teetered and wobbled. The side handles were useless in these tight quarters. Above them, Briggs and Rafael, on their knees, reached in, grabbed it and hauled it into the cargo hold, both swearing like, well, like soldiers.

It was like lifting a car, or a church bell. "Why didn't you make it a hundred barrels and put less in each one?" Fletcher said to Ngomo. "We're going to have to deadlift these fucking things sixty times up a ladder?" He climbed out to watch the barrel's progress from the ship to the truck. Briggs and Rafael rolled it across the felt-lined cargo area and raised it up to the deck, where Belvedere and Wolski knelt waiting to receive it.

"Ngomo," Belvedere said, "if you're intent on reopening your chest wound, by all means, continue doing what you're doing."

"I don't have much choice," Ngomo said. "But afterward you'll fix me up, won't you? Belvy's magic seal and all that?"

"Get out of the way," Briggs said. "Men are working here." He and Wolski took over. They rolled the barrel across the deck but couldn't carry it safely down the narrow gangplank. Another plan had to be quickly devised and improvised. They looped two braided ropes through the welded handles and eased the barrel down ahead of them as they walked slowly down behind it—Briggs first, Wolski next—keeping tension in the ropes to slow its descent.

Watching from the deck rail, Fletcher said, "A little faster. Let it move. Lean back more to steady it. Like a brake."

"You want to do it?" said Wolski.

"Steady as you go," Fletcher said. "But *go*." He checked his watch.

"Clock me now," Briggs said on the wharf, throwing off his workman's tunic and leaving himself in his black tank, "but by barrel 10, someone's going to cry and someone's going to puke—and both are probably going to be me."

Zeus, skipping along the wharf, said to Charlie, taking her hand, "Why can't they just let it roll? It'll go faster. Like a sled on a hill."

"But what if it rolls across the wharf and falls into the water, Zeus?"

"What if Zeus falls in?" said Rafael. "Tell the boy to stop skipping so close to the edge, Charlie."

She grabbed the boy and glared at Rafael. "Thanks for keeping an eye on what *I'm* doing, Sergeant."

"I don't care about *you*," Rafael said, "but I'd like Zeus to stay in one piece tonight." He saluted the boy.

Louise and Charlie, with Zeus running alongside, push-rolled the barrel down the finger wharf. Brigitte and Margot managed to lift it a few inches over the short curb. Mireille and Hildimar came to help, and the four women slowly rolled it across Glaskaai to the loading ramp at the back of the truck. Hawk and Maxine helped roll it up the ramp.

Inside the truck, Charlie and Louise upended the barrel and stacked it in the corner against the cab. Charlie gave a short quiet whistle to Fletcher on deck to signal completion.

He checked his watch.

Eight minutes.

Four hundred and eighty seconds.

Paling, he sank onto the planks, quickly doing some unwelcome math in his head.

Eight minutes per barrel.

Fifty-nine more barrels.

Seven hours and fifty-two minutes.

Nearly screaming, he leapt to his feet.

It was 11:46. The shift change was coming at 0700. They needed to be done by six at the latest to clean up and get out before being seen.

They were almost two hours short. Fletcher jumped down into the cargo area and frantically relayed his calculations to Ngomo. "What are we going to do?"

"What are we going to do?" said Ngomo. He had also taken off his outerwear and stood perspiring and large in a sleeveless black vest. "First we're going to stop counting, and start lifting. While you were adding shit in your head, Briggs and I raised barrels 2 and 3 into the cargo hold. You're up. Let's go."

"I didn't think it would take this long," Fletcher said. Jumping down into the vault, he and Ngomo grabbed the fourth barrel. "I budgeted five minutes for each."

"Let's stop talking and see if we can make your plan work," Ngomo said. "On three." They grunted and lifted.

Barrel 4 took *nine* minutes. The red felt got bunched up at the top of the gangplank. Rafael tripped, and lost his grip on the rope. Good thing Hawk was behind him. They had to go slower.

"We're going to get less efficient, Ngomo," Fletcher said, wiping his forehead. Like the rest of the men, he stripped off to his tank. "Each barrel is going to take longer."

Ngomo stopped moving and placed both his heavy arms on top of Fletcher's shoulders. "Listen to me, Commander," he said. "There is no way out. Not over it, not under it, not around it. This is the only way—through it. Let's fucking go."

"We're going to need more rest between barrels," said Fletcher.

"I don't need any rest." Ngomo grabbed the next barrel. "On three."

But Fletcher needed *sixty* before he could go on *three*.

After barrel 6, they swapped out. Briggs and Rafael took over below, while Fletcher and Ngomo fiddled with the mast boom, setting up the winch and the pulley, to at least help raise the barrels from the cargo hold to the deck. It spared the men's arms, and shaved a few seconds off the time.

But no winch or pulley could help them with one intractable, irreducible fact: to get the barrels out of the crypt, two men still had to deadlift 300 pounds of uranium six feet up a vertical ladder.

"Next time we rob a ship," Briggs said, sweat pouring off him, "let's steal iron ingots. You know—something light."

The reinforced twine threaded through the handles helped at every stage. The men in the cargo area now grabbed it by the ropes and yanked it up from the vault.

On barrel 8, the rope shredded. Good thing they had more.

"You need a deadman's knot at the top to hold the two ends of your twine together," Hawk said quietly. He looked too delicate to even perspire. "The kind that won't break. Want me to show you?"

Hawk was right. It was better, but it took time.

Barrel 10.

Barrel 12.

It was claustrophobic, narrow, heavy, bulky. Hard going. Slow going.

Deadlifting the uranium out of the vault was the hardest physical thing Fletcher had ever done. He thought resting between lifts was an impossible delay—but soon, even a few minutes weren't enough. His arms trembled before he touched the next barrel—number 13.

To save their arms and keep up the pace, the men rotated out of the crypt every three or four barrels. But the rest wasn't a cakewalk. In the cargo hold, each barrel had to be secured, fitted into the net, the pulley hook had to be securely attached, and the weight of two men was needed for ballast. It was incapacitating after a few rounds.

The swearing from the sweat-soaked Briggs never stopped. "Ready?" he kept saying, wiping his face with the crook of his arm. "Fucking ready?"

When Fletcher, to give his arms a short break, checked on Charlie, she told him the girls were having a hard time keeping up the pace. Half a dozen barrels were piling up on the quay, waiting to be moved. "Fletcher," she said, "look at me. I'm trying to kick a barrel that weighs double what I do."

"You don't have to kick it," Fletcher said. "Just roll it."

"I can't roll it," she said. "It's a rock. It doesn't roll."

All the girls helped. Hildi, whose strength was wildly disproportionate to her minuscule weight, never stopped moving, kicking, rolling. Brigitte was slower but no less spry. "Splendid form, Bree-ghee-tah," said Belvedere from the deck. "If only we had a dozen of you, we'd be finished by now."

Like Briggs, Ngomo was a giant among men. He looked and behaved like a man who'd hauled some heavy fucking loads in his life. They both worked tirelessly, but even they couldn't deadlift more than five barrels from the crypt before needing to swap out with another two-man team. "Fuck, Ngomo," Briggs kept saying.

And Ngomo would agree. "Fuck, Briggs."

"My shoulders are dislocated and my ribs have cracked," Briggs said.

"On *fuck*, Briggsy," said Ngomo, his hands around the next. "One, two, *fuck*."

The indefatigable Zeus ran up and down the wharf and across the quay ahead of each barrel, flattening the felt to keep it from catching.

"Zeus *pour la victoire*," said Belvedere, patting the boy on the head as he and Hawk eased another barrel from the gangplank to the wharf.

Charlie was right. The women had a hard time steering the barrels over cracked and broken cobblestones. Even with four girls shoving and pushing, it wasn't fast enough. And the rope kept shredding. Standing at the top of the ramp inside the truck Charlie and Louise pulled while Margot and Maxine pushed the barrels up the steel ramp. Even so, one of the men often had to come and help.

Arranging the barrels in the truck so they wouldn't move in transit meant constant tugging and adjusting. Belvedere and Hawk took turns helping Charlie, but by barrel 20, none of the men were available for anything but the deadlift, the winch, and the gangplank.

There was a moment—at barrel 23, not even halfway—when Fletcher looked over his team silently struggling, quietly swearing and thought, *We're not going to make it*. He was afraid to glance at his watch. Afraid to count the minutes left.

Worse—he didn't think *he* would be able to make it. And when he looked at Rafael's perspiring, drained face behind him, he saw that his sergeant was thinking it too.

"Fuck, Rider, what are we going to do?"

"Thank God *I'm* not the fucking commander. This was your grand plan. What are our choices?"

"Work faster."

"Or . . ."

"Work even faster than that."

After barrel 33, they took a ten-minute break to switch out the trucks. Even that, Fletcher thought, was a time-wasting indulgence.

By barrel 36, Fletcher started making bargains with himself, like a drowning man. He wondered if they *really* needed to remove *all* the uranium from the hold. Wasn't the point to get out as much as possible—not *all* of it? What time was it? *Don't look, Fletcher, don't look!* Maybe he could crank up his radio, shoot a quick message to Jonathan Reed in London, ask if they could leave some of it on the ship.

He started getting angry with Rafael—for resting too long. But Fletcher himself started taking too long between barrels—shoulders slumped, breath ragged, arms gone—until, to his shame, it was Rafael who said, "We gotta get moving, Fletch. We're running out of time." They were easing a barrel down the gangplank.

"Nope," Fletcher said. "We can't be running out of time. We've got 22 more to go." At least that was a step in the right direction. Instead of counting up, he was now counting down. Not how many they carried, but how many were left.

"What are you two waiting for—a lullaby?" Briggs roared. "Let's fucking move! You've got two more behind you, waiting for you to finish your coffee klatch."

"Briggsy," Mireille called up from the wharf, *"Avec les jambes, pas le dos!"*

Without missing a beat, Rafael translated. "She says lift with your legs, not your back."

Briggs groaned. He staggered upright with the next barrel, arms shaking. "My fucking legs died at barrel 30." To Mireille, he flashed a breathless grin. *"Bien sur, ma jolie."*

"Barrel 41, Commander," said Ngomo, rolling it across the deck. His wound was seeping blood into his vest, but he didn't stop. "Zeus," he called quietly, "careful on that plank. Please. I can't have you falling in."

"Why not?" Zeus said. "*You* fell in."

"I didn't fall in, Zeus," said Ngomo. "I jumped in."

Everyone who understood French was quiet for a moment—then resumed.

"Zeus, where are you off to?" Charlie called. The boy had strayed a few steps on the quay, peering into the darkness. "Come back, we need you. Look at the felt—it's all bunched up." Zeus returned to her side. "What were you doing there?" she asked, putting a hand on his shoulder.

"Nothing," he said, uncertainly. "I was trying to find the spot where we found Ngomo."

At barrel 44, the steel ramp at the back of the truck split in two.

Four women tried to lift one into the truck bed without calling for the men. The barrel slipped out of their hands, fell off the felt, and slammed into the cobblestones, making a terrible noise. Fletcher and Rafael ran to help. Even with all of them, they barely managed it. Fletcher looked at Charlie, full of desperation and helplessness. "It's okay," she said. "We'll do better next time. Sorry. Bring the next one."

Belvedere walked over to assess the situation. "Girls," he said, looking only at Brigitte, "if that thing lands on your foot, kiss it goodbye. You'll crush every bone from the ankle down. There'll be no putting it back."

Fletcher translated, thinking how fitting it was that uranium—refined or raw—had only one purpose: to destroy human beings.

At barrel 48, the last of the twine shredded. At barrel 49, the last net tore apart. The pulley was now useless. Each barrel had to be deadlifted four times on its backbreaking journey to the truck: from the crypt to the cargo, from the cargo to the deck, over a curb, and from the quay into the truck.

"I'm going to die," said Wolski.

"I have some morphine to help with that," said Belvedere.

Ngomo and Hawk said nothing, but the pain was etched on Hawk's ghostly face. The sky had turned blue, then pink at the edges. The sun would soon be rising over the northeastern Scheldt.

Fletcher found Charlie crouched on the wharf at the foot of the gangplank, hands on her knees, breathing hard. He'd just guided the barrel down, and was panting himself.

He crouched next to her, his gloved hand patting her shoulder. "You okay?"

"I'm great," she said, rising to her feet. "You okay?" She looked wrung out.

"I'm great," he said. Before he turned back to the gangplank, she pressed a dented canteen into his hand. "Here, or you'll drop."

"Hope it's brandy."

"The strongest kind."

Fletcher asked how the women were doing, how Zeus was doing, but he asked reluctantly, afraid she'd tell him the truth—that they couldn't keep going. That they needed his help.

He couldn't help them. He could barely help himself.

While everyone else was trembling, Briggs was heaving like an ox with fire in his blood. He stopped speaking, joking, grumbling, even swearing. He had nothing left for words. Everything was going to the barrels. He manhandled them as if they infuriated him.

The barrels weren't going to break Briggs.

He was going to break the barrels.

Fletcher started griping at Ngomo to relieve his tension. After all, the weight of every barrel could be pinned directly on him. In the Congo, it was Ngomo who decided how much each barrel should hold and how much two men could lift.

"Leave him alone, Fletch," said Rafael. "He was probably measuring by the strength of the men he had, not by the strength of skinny white boys like you."

"Fletcher is right," said Ngomo. "You're right, Commander. That one's on me. In my country, I was made strong by food and sun. I had many men, and they were big and strong too."

"Sounds like I'm the one who's fucking right," Rafael muttered.

"We worked in daytime, in heat, yes, but we had plenty of breaks. We worked in leisure. It was a slow marathon, not a sprint like this. Two of us lifted 140 kilos no problem. I placed an order for sixty barrels, custom cast to my specifications. And three months ago, when we loaded them into the ship's vault, I had fifty men doing the work. Not seven."

"What about women, Ngomo? Did you have any women doing it?" said Louise.

"Definitely not, Miss Louise." Ngomo smiled.

"What about Zeuses?" said Zeus. "Did you have any Zeuses doing it?"

"Absolutely not, little man. I think you would've helped me a lot in Matadi. Like you're helping now."

Zeus kept kicking and shoving a barrel a few inches at a time down the cobblestones. Fletcher went to help the boy. "You're strong, buddy," he said, ruffling his hair. "You've got grit. You're a good boy. And we're so close."

Everything was close. The sunrise. The shift change. The waking city.

"While you men are lollygagging, pointing fingers over whose fault this fiasco is," said Louise, "the women are still rolling barrels. Where's your famous stamina, Rafael Canario?"

"Who said anything about stamina, baby? I'm for short hops only." He grinned but went to help her with her barrel—number 53.

Painfully, slowly, arduously, the men of Easy Red and the women of *La Ligne*—plus Ngomo from the Congo and Zeus from Charleroi—continued to empty *La Fortuna* of its priceless cargo.

And in defiance of natural law, when they got down to the last five barrels, their speed doubled, and their time halved. They almost stopped feeling the weight.

The last two barrels took them less than three minutes each—to hoist, roll, lift, roll again, plank, roll again, lift again, and finally, heave inside the truck.

Fletcher and Ngomo raised the last barrel into place. For a moment, they leaned into each other, saying nothing, breathing hard, and shared a short, fierce clasp of the hands.

It was 5:59—a new day.

"Fuckin' A," said Briggs.

They had sixty seconds for a celebratory smoke before it was time to close up and clear the fuck out.

While returning the uniforms to the unconscious guards in the warehouse, Ngomo led Rafael to a crate of olives—stashed in the cargo Rheinhardt had pulled off *La Fortuna*. They took a dozen gallon cans for themselves. Ngomo found some coffee, too. They took that. "It's the best coffee you'll ever have," he said. "From the Kivu region in the Congo."

"Yes, yes, so we hear," Fletcher said. "Everything's the best in the Congo. Maybe if it wasn't so top rate, we wouldn't all be here killing ourselves for the best uranium. Let's go. It's 6:19."

Before they left, they untied the guards, ungagged them, dropped the uniforms in a heap at their feet, and took their weapons and spare clips. They doused the men with Rhum du Kasai—a crushed sugarcane cachaca liquor—leaving the empty bottle next to them. They took a crate of the rum for themselves, too, on Ngomo's recommendation.

"Don't tell me, Ngomo," said Fletcher. "Is the cachaca also the best?"

"Better than anything you've ever tasted."

"Of course," Fletcher said. "Men, women, Zeus—ready? Great job everyone. You're all miracle workers. Now, let's get the hell out of here."

Right before they left, Ngomo scaled the mast, seized the flag of the yellow narcissus and tore it down with one brutal yank.

48

The Crossing

Without Charlie, they couldn't have done any of it. How did Jonathan Reed know such a person existed in Belgium? The woman who knew all the streets and roads, the alleys and bridges, the passwords and routes. She was implacable, unshakeable—the only one who could lead them out of Antwerp. The woman who listened to everything, planned for everything, had an answer for everything. The woman who worked the barrels, who never complained. Who would not be rattled.

And yet, even this remarkable woman could misjudge by three centimeters. She had the old city of Antwerp memorized—every winding road and medieval alley—and she used the map in her head to drive her *Berceau* without being stopped or spotted. But with Vervaet's trucks, she forgot to account for the physics.

The narrowest street: 177 centimeters.

The width of the truck, mirrors included: 180 centimeters. Vlaeykensgang—a medieval alleyway with twisting stone paths.

Three centimeters too narrow. The trucks scraped against the buildings.

Burlap signs tore. Side mirrors snapped. The racket echoed down the alley.

Without saying a word, Fletcher got out. He picked up the mirror housings. Fixed up the torn signs. Got back inside. Said nothing.

But his mood worsened.

All of them were squeezed into the back of one truck. The other one smelled too horrible from all the chemicals they'd doused it with. Hildi drove it. Hawk went with her. Louise was behind the wheel of theirs, Rafael riding shotgun.

Fletcher leaned against the warm barrels, the rifle in his hands. He was shattered. He fought to stay awake, knowing that if they were stopped and inspected because their signs were torn or their mirrors were missing, they'd have to shoot their way out.

"I misjudged," Charlie said glumly, seated on the floor next to him.

"I know," Fletcher said. *Three* centimeters! He was too tired to even put his arm around her or reassure her it was going to be okay.

It was 6:30 a.m.

They parked off Oude Steenweg, in a defunct tram repair shed, its iron gate half-hanging. Charlie went ahead on foot, to recon the rickety canal crossing at Kiel and Hoboken to make sure it was unmanned before they plowed through.

When she returned, there was no mistaking the bad news on her face. The crossing was patrolled by German guards. "Must be new orders," she said quietly.

Fletcher woke Rafael, and they stood in the covered railyard away from the others and discussed their options. Rafael wanted to tear through the checkpoint. Charlie wanted to wait for the shift change.

Fletcher was inclined to agree with Rafael. Every minute in Antwerp meant increased risk. At *La Fortuna*, at the 7:00 a.m. switch, the morning guards would immediately see the night guards were missing and raise the alarm. Charlie said both men were being ridiculous. They couldn't drive in a convoy—"a mosquito truck and a spoon truck"—through a crossing guarded by actual fucking Germans!

Rafael said they had no choice. They'd have to shoot them all and blow past. Charlie said no. She insisted on waiting. She knew the Belgian guards who usually came on shift on Saturday mornings. If she was right, they'd be able to pass without incident.

"And if you're wrong?" said Rafael.

"Then you can shoot the Germans," said Charlie.

"Why wait? Let's shoot them now."

"You can't wait twenty minutes to shoot somebody, Canario?"

Both their heads jerked toward Fletcher. His exhausted brain whirred slowly forward, gears barely catching. To wait invited danger. But to shoot the guards would trigger panic at Central Command and would also invite unwelcome witnesses.

"Omloop and I use this crossing all the time," Charlie said. "The Belgian *Polizei* are loyal to the resistance. We just have to wait. We'll know in nineteen minutes. Let's argue some more to pass the time."

Nerves fraying, Fletcher reluctantly sided with Charlie.

"You're agreeing with her for all the wrong reasons," Rafael said, storming off. He couldn't stay angry for long. He fell asleep in seconds next to Louise.

Almost everyone else was out too, except for Wolski, who sat smoking in the corner of the rail depot, hunched over a map of Belgium. Maxine and Margot sat next to him. After a short smoke, Fletcher and Charlie climbed in with the rest.

It was so hard for him to find the right words. And he could see it was hard for her too. "We did okay," he finally said.

"We're not done," Charlie said. "Not nearly."

"I know. But we did the hardest thing." He didn't know how they'd done it. It seemed impossible even now just thinking about it.

"The *hardest*, really?" she said. "What about the praying mantis pacing up and down Glaskaai, staring down the ship like he's in a duel with it? He's going to use his entire SS to turn Belgium inside out looking for these barrels. And I don't need to remind you, do I, that here they still are, on the borrowed trucks—the ones we have to return to Vervaet *today*. And we have nowhere to hide them."

"I know," Fletcher said, and nothing else. Because he didn't have anything else. He'd kept pushing the moment off, to Omloop, to Charlie, kept saying he'd cross that bridge when he came to it. Well, the bridge was here, ready for a crossing, and the barrels were here too, and Fletcher still had nothing. He tried to joke his way out. "Maybe we could just drive them west," he said. "Straight to Normandy."

"Are you joking?"

He stopped smiling. "Yes." He lowered his gaze to his rifle.

"It's not funny, Fletcher," she said. "And on top of everything else, we still have to unload them." She groaned.

Reaching out, he placed his palm on her forearm, squeezing gently, to comfort her, to calm her. He stared at her profile, her downcast, exhausted face, trying to catch her eye.

Near him, he heard Zeus's voice. "Why are they fighting?" the boy asked Ngomo.

"Because everything's on their shoulders, little man," Ngomo said. "The rest of us are told what to do, and we do it, and then we sleep. And if things don't work out, it's not on us. But everything is on *them*. And you know what they want to do right now? Sleep. Like Brigitte and Belvedere, like Mireille and Briggs. But instead, they're having to figure out how to save this mission. They're so far from putting their heads down."

Receiving no response, Ngomo glanced down.

Zeus was asleep.

Moving the boy off him, Ngomo inclined toward the pair.

"Fletcher, Charlie," he said. "Listen to me."

Fletcher and Charlie stopped bickering. "What, Ngomo?" Charlie said. "Can't you see we're busy?"

"I see everything. Go see Robert Capelle, Charlie. He will help you. He's the only one who can. He will give you the name of a place we can take the barrels."

Charlie let out a short, frustrated laugh. "I told you, I went to see him last week. He walked the market surrounded by an armed posse. I couldn't get to him then, and I won't be able to get to him now. I wanted to let him know the boys were coming. I couldn't get within twenty meters of him, much less converse with him about where to hide ten tons of uranium. It's impossible."

"Fletcher, tell her it's not," said Ngomo. "We just did the truly impossible. Three hours ago, none of us thought it could be done. What we did was harder than finding a way to Capelle, Charlie."

"Ngomo is right," Fletcher said thoughtfully. "Capelle's not walking through a park, is he? He's walking through a market—which means he's buying things."

"So?"

"So," Fletcher said slowly, "why don't you go *sell* him something he might buy, daughter of a florist?"

"You mean apply for a stall? Pay for a stand?"

Fletcher nodded. "Name your price. Contact with Capelle is our only objective."

Charlie turned her face away.

"Your father literally owns a flower farm," Fletcher said quietly. "Just bring a few bushels of daffodils or yellow tulips and sell them to Capelle. But *yellow* is key."

"Yes, thank you. I figured that part out—*jonquille est morte* and all that." She scoffed. "Floral ignorance doesn't help soldiers say smart things, though. The daffodils came and went in April. Tulips too."

"No yellow flowers bloom in June?"

She didn't reply.

Fletcher nodded. "So . . . *lots* of yellow flowers bloom in June?"

"I don't want to talk about it."

The smile stayed on his face.

"I don't know why you're grinning," Charlie said. "Where's *La Berceau*, Fletcher? Bruges, right? And where's my father? Herentals, right? And we have *two* trucks filled with *your* men, my women, and your splintered bombs. And these trucks are where at the moment? In a shed here at Antwerp, right? The market at Jette, two hours away, opens at nine. You have a plan for all that?"

"What time does Capelle usually go to the market?"

"You mean the two times I've seen him there? Around noon."

"So what you're saying is we have five hours to get it done?"

"You're impossible," she said.

"But right, too?" He nudged her lightly, and when she didn't coil away, he knew what to do. He put his arm around her and brought her close, speaking comfort into her ear in a singsong voice as they huddled in the truck. "It's going to be okay. You'll see. We'll do it together. I'll help you. It's almost seven. Go and scope out the crossing, see if your guys are on shift. If they are, we'll drive to Bruges and leave the trucks and the boys at Vervaet's. They can sleep and guard the bomb. Ngomo has to stay out of sight anyway. And you and I will take your *Berceau* and do the rest. Together. While you're at the market, I'll hide in the truck, rack out for a bit. How does that sound?"

The expression on Charlie's face, so taut with tension just moments earlier, had eased.

It was even more relieved after she returned from scouting the crossing. She was almost smiling.

"It's our men," she said. "Thank God. Now we can leave quietly. Good thing you listened to me, Fletcher, and not to that trigger-happy sergeant of yours, or we'd have half the German forces pursuing us to Jette. Loosha, wake up! We have to move. Remember the call and response?"

Louise could barely open her eyes. *"The bell rings in the holy place,"* she muttered.

"And the faithful walk unharmed," said Charlie.

49

Azali

"Ngomo, if I do manage to get close to Capelle," said Charlie at Vervaet's, before she and Fletcher left for Lillehaven, "how can I tell him you're all right? When I spoke to him last, you were in such bad shape. And he can't ask me. Is there a way for me to let him know? Then he can pass it on to the King."

"Thank you, Charlie," Ngomo said, his voice catching. "Just say *Azali*. Sneak it into whatever else you're telling him."

"What does that mean?"

"In Lingala, it means *he lives*," Ngomo said. "Capelle and I worked together. We were close. I hope he can keep his composure."

"He's a count, Ngomo," Charlie said. "They're raised from birth to keep their composure. Not like us." Not being a countess herself, Charlie thought she'd done pretty well in that department, all things considered.

It was a good thing she and Fletcher had picked so many flowers, because Charlie's overflowing tented stand at the Bonaventure Market in Jette drew a great deal of attention from both the bees and the shoppers. Who wouldn't be drawn to that splash of abundant sunshine arrayed under the canvas? Tall spikes of wild loosestrife. Joyful five-petaled coreopsis, cheerful as daisies. Buckets of black-eyed Susans—sunflowers in miniature, with black centers. Fragrant yellow roses. And the superstars: the yellow flag irises, heavy with wet, stunning elegance, drooping over their buckets, dripping water and sparkling in the sun.

If it weren't war—if her country hadn't been occupied for four years, if the land from border to border wasn't on the verge of becoming another Waterloo, another muddy bloody Passchendaele, and if eight thousand kilos of something terrible weren't waiting in two trucks by a stranger's fence while the

Nazis were about to burn Belgium to the ground to find it—then it might have been a perfect Saturday afternoon.

Friendly customers browsed her table, praising her flowers, giving her coins, wishing her well. Someone was playing a guitar nearby, and the sun was warm on her face. She wore a wig of long brown braids, thick-rimmed fake glasses, and red lipstick. She even put on a floral dress for disguise. Everything was in order.

Except Robert Capelle was nowhere to be seen, and her profusion of yellow flowers was dwindling with every sale. If she didn't slow things down, the flowers might be gone before he ever appeared.

She saw Capelle's Gestapo escort first. They blocked her view of him with their gray-green uniforms, black caps, pistols and those heavy ugly boots. Her heart jumped, but her hands stayed steady as she gave change to a stout woman, keeping half an eye on the circle of Nazis. *Please notice my yellow flowers*, she cried inside. *La trompette jaune. La trompette jaune.*

"Fresh flowers!" she yelled. "Get your fresh *yellow* flowers right here! Yellow coreopsis! Yellow black-eyed Susans! Yellow *azali*!" It sounded like azaleas—the fact that yellow azaleas didn't exist didn't stop her. She had to get Capelle's attention, that's all there was to it.

At last, he sauntered over, thank Christ. She'd been helping a few women with their selection, but the moment they saw the platoon of Gestapo, they fled.

"Merci beaucoup," she muttered dryly in the direction of the posse. "Kill my business too, why don't you?"

"You gonna buy something or not?" one guard said to Capelle, who was inspecting the vivid roses.

Count Robert Capelle was a lean aristocrat in a tailored dark wool suit, even though it was mid-June and warm. His pocket handkerchief was folded into a razor-edged white square. His shoulders were like a coat rack; his hips were slim. His white hair was swept back under a gray felt hat.

"These are *ravissante*," he said, touching the yellow roses with his long, veined hands. He didn't seem to recognize her, or at least acted as if he didn't—understandable, since they'd met only once, and under dire circumstances. He barely raised his gray eyes to her. "Only yellow today? No reds or blues?"

"Not today, sir," Charlie replied. "Only *yellow* today." That was as pointed as she could make it. "Blame my father. The *yellow* seeds were on sale last spring. Now he's got fields of *puntwederik*." She smiled. Capelle glanced up briefly and quickly lowered his gaze.

"We had the most beautiful *jonquilles*, but the season for them just ended, sadly."

"That *is* unfortunate. I do like the *trompettes jaunes*."

"Yes, sir. When they're *vivante*, they're breathtaking."

"Indeed. Did I hear correctly—did you say you had some *azali*?"

"Yes, sir. I had some *azali* earlier, but they've all been sold."

The slightest pause followed. A damp blink. "Well, good for you," Capelle said. "Never mind. I'll make do with what you've got left." He bought all of Charlie's remaining irises and roses. "How beautiful it must look—a field full of yellow flowers," he said.

"The fields do glow a bit, especially when the skies are clear—like this morning," Charlie said, desperately afraid Capelle would take the flowers from her and walk away, never actually giving her what she came here for. "But do you have a *place* to put all these beautiful flowers you're buying? I know I wouldn't have enough room in *my* house for all of them."

Capelle nodded. "Of course I do." He made a nostalgic click of his tongue, half turning to one of his guards as if inviting him into the conversation. The officer remained utterly indifferent.

"When I was a little boy," he said, addressing mostly Charlie but also, pointedly, his tormentor, "my mother once took me to an abbey near Tremelo—Sancta Maria in Silvis Sacris. Saint Mary of the Sacred Wood. I'll never forget the irises and roses blanketing their gardens, swaying in the breeze." His mouth twitched. "Yours bring it all back. Yes, indeed—they're going to beautify my entire house."

He put his money on the table as she finished wrapping the flowers.

"Irises and roses are hardy perennials," Charlie said, laying out the bouquets for him one by one. "They bloom every year. They're probably swaying there as we speak. Perhaps you can visit the abbey again one day."

"Perhaps," Capelle said with veiled hostility, addressing not her but the guard beside him.

The guard misinterpreted the "perhaps" just as Capelle had intended it—a rebuke for his captivity. "Enough chatter. Have you paid?"

Charlie took the money—three times what the flowers were worth. "*Merci beaucoup*," she said. "What a successful day. I must come to this market more often."

"Next time, bring something other than yellow," Capelle said. Picking up a wrapped bouquet, he turned sharply to his guard. "Are you going to stand there, or are you going to help?"

Grumbling, the guards each picked up a giant bouquet of freshly cut flowers. It was astonishing the way even the Gestapo made space for him, respected him.

"Why'd you buy so many?" one Nazi said as they were walking away.

"My wife and I are celebrating our wedding anniversary next week," said Capelle. "They're a gift for her."

"I didn't know you had a wife," the Nazi said.

"You don't even know what you don't know," said Robert Capelle, casting one last grateful, weighted glance at Charlie, standing near her empty buckets, her fists clenched at her sides.

The Abbey of Sancta Maria in Silvis Sacris. Finally she had a place, and a name—and what a name it was. She felt such relief. First thing tomorrow, they would drive to the abbey. It was only right that they should seek sanctuary in a holy place on a Sunday morning. But tonight, Charlie and Fletcher had a rendezvous in Het Steet Castle, overlooking the site of their greatest triumph. Like flies on the wall, they would watch for the praying mantis to return to Antwerp and take his evening constitutional by the old docks of the mighty river, where an empty *La Fortuna* stood waiting for him.

50

Vandepole and Blomme

Rheinhardt had a feeling of unreality—not seeing the thing he knew must be there.

Next to him, he dimly heard Krieger's devastated voice. "*Mein Gott*," the general said. "Do you have any idea what you've done?"

Rheinhardt blinked furiously, certain his eyes were deceiving him—blinked so hard, it felt like a seizure. He didn't reach for the wall. He wouldn't give Krieger the satisfaction of seeing him stagger.

Where could it have gone? Where could it possibly have gone?

For half a minute, all life faded to gray. Then blood surged back through his veins. His face flushed. His lungs filled with fury. Without waiting for the general, Rheinhardt climbed up the smuggler's ladder and out of the cargo hold. He raged across the deck, down the gangplank, and made straight for Hubner. One look at his aide's expression and his raised, pleading hands told him that something had gone drastically wrong, and Hubner had kept quiet about it.

"Sir, I can explain . . ." But Hubner was whispering. He couldn't find his voice.

"So explain, Hubner," said Rheinhardt, who still had his.

"When I arrived this morning and rushed to the ship to turn on the boiler, as you requested, I found only two guards on duty . . ."

"What time was this?"

"Around noon."

"Why?"

"I don't know, sir. They weren't ours. And there was no one to ask—"

"Then where did these dozen men come from?"

"Belgian brigadiers from *Garde Civique*. I ordered them here on your authority, sir. I had to step on a few toes . . ."

Rheinhardt stormed toward the captain in charge, De Swaef. He had to compose himself before he spoke. Krieger followed at his shoulder, in mute shock. His silence was worse than shouting. De Swaef's eyes darted between the two SS men. He flinched at the sight of the general's black collar tabs.

"Who were the men you replaced at 1500 hours?" Rheinhardt demanded.

"Mine, sir. Frick and Metz," said De Swaef.

"And they were here since . . ."

"Seven in the morning, sir."

"And whom did *they* replace? Also yours?"

The captain floundered. His mouth opened, but no answer came.

"Whom did they replace, Captain?"

"Yes, two of my other brigadiers, sir," De Swaef said with a small sigh.

"Vandepole and Blomme."

"The best of the best, were they? Were they here all night?"

Pause. "Yes, sir."

"Were they or were they not here all night, Captain De Swaef?"

"They were . . . *here*, sir." The hesitation in his voice, on top of everything else, was enough to drive a teetotaler to drink.

"Captain," Rheinhardt said, as slowly as he could, "I will have you arrested and charged with insubordination if you don't immediately explain why you're playing word games with me."

"I'm not playing games, sir. We had a small incident—but everything was quiet. I promise you, nothing was disturbed. The chief of police came at 1600 hours and looked things over himself."

"What kind of incident?"

De Swaef shifted, visibly uncomfortable. He was trying to protect his men. Finally, he admitted that Vandepole and Blomme had been absent at shift change at seven and were found later, half-naked and drunk, sleeping it off in a nearby storeroom. He offered more detail than necessary, as if deciding a lurid story was safer than a suspicious one. "It almost seemed as if they'd found some action on a Friday night, sir. Maybe got bored, picked up some women—had too much fun . . ."

"They were passed out in a storeroom?"

"Yes, sir."

"Naked?"

"Half-naked, sir."

"And their weapons?"

This is where the story cracked—and the captain knew it. His gaze dropped. "Well, uh," he stammered, "their weapons were . . . unfortunately taken, sir."

"So you're telling me that your men—trained by you, I assume—decided to leave their post, sneak into a locked warehouse—we don't know how—get drunk with two women, pass out, and have those women walk off with their weapons?"

De Swaef didn't reply.

"Did they have their wallets on them?"

"Yes, sir."

"Was there any money in the wallets, Captain?"

"Yes, sir."

"So these *good-time girls* relieved your brigadiers of their submachine guns, but left their cash? That's your story?"

"Sir, sir," De Swaef said quickly, "I see that you're angry. But I beg you to understand. Vandepole is the son-in-law of none other than Helmut Drechsler, the Wehrmacht commander."

"Do you think being related to the chief of Antwerp entitles your brigadier to abandon his post? Or is that still punishable by court-martial—regardless of who his father-in-law is? Or maybe, just maybe, he and Blomme did not *wander off* at all. Maybe they were *subdued. Drugged*, even. And *removed*. By someone who needed the quay to be empty of oversight?"

"But there was no trouble here, sir, none whatsoever!"

"How would you know, Captain?" Rheinhardt roared. "Your armed guards were passed out!"

He turned on Hubner, still hovering at his elbow. "I had twenty men posted here when we left yesterday morning," he said through his teeth. "Who ordered my men to be removed? Please tell me you managed to learn at least *that* while you were running around trying to cover my ship with this man's incompetent detail."

"Drechsler, sir," Hubner whispered. "Helmut Drechsler."

Krieger spoke for the first time. "This is bad news, Rheinhardt. Very bad news indeed. Wehrmacht and SS do not mix well."

Fucking Drechsler.

He removed the sentry precisely when Rheinhardt left Antwerp—his first real absence in four years. If Rheinhardt had remained in Antwerp, he would have noticed the absence of the guards. Had he left, but his platoon of twenty remained, the ship would not have been left unsecured. If only one of those things had happened, the uranium would still be there.

Which meant someone had to have been watching him—and, more important, watching his men. Someone had to have known the men had been pulled off *and* that he had signed out a car for two days.

Who watched him, the ship, and the movements of the troops *so closely* that during one brief eight-hour night shift—when the roads were empty and the city lay quiet—someone had managed to steal *eight tons* of uranium from an invisible crypt? Rheinhardt's hands shook, his legs trembled.

Who knew the barrels were there?

Who knew what they held? What they were worth?

Who was prepared, had a plan, had men to execute it?

Who could have done it?

Whoever it was drugged the soldiers and dragged them into the storeroom; drugged them, but didn't kill them.

Could have killed them.

But didn't.

Why?

To give himself more time. That's what Rheinhardt would've done. Drunk and derelict men wouldn't trigger an immediate search—not like two murdered *Polizei* would.

This someone was clever.

But not cleverer than Rheinhardt. Whoever took the barrels didn't just erase them from existence.

Maybe they didn't even move them. Dragging the barrels across cobblestones would wake the dead. How do you move heavy metal canisters without the whole city hearing?

Rheinhardt ordered De Swaef and his men to search the ship from top to bottom, while he stormed off toward Groenplaats to confront Drechsler.

As an afterthought, Rheinhardt invited Krieger to accompany him. The general said nothing, but followed.

On the way, Rheinhardt barked instructions to Hubner. "On my SS letterhead, write this out—don't type. Block letters. Write it word for word: *By order of SS-Sturmbannführer: no freight vehicles or trucks are to exit the Antwerp district without full inspection. All cargo manifests are to be cross-checked. All barrels, crates, and drums must be opened. Any resistance is to be met with immediate detainment and escalation to SS-Sicherheitspolizei.*"

"Immediately, sir."

"Make a hundred carbon copies. Sign them as me. Send by courier to all bridges, crossings, *Feldgendarmerie* posts, customs at rail sidings and all *Garde Civique* stops on roads out of town."

"Immediately, sir."

"No truck of any size gets out of Antwerp."

He didn't know where the uranium had gone—yet. It could be in the river. It could be in the warehouse across the street. But if it was still in the city, he would trap it. And if it wasn't, then someone had moved faster than he could bear to imagine.

"Understood, sir."

"Where are you going, Hubner?" Rheinhardt said as his aide peeled off.

"You just told me to . . ."

"Stay with me until I finish with Drechsler."

Krieger caught up with him. "You're planning to confront Helmut Drechsler during military drills?"

"There is no time like the present, sir."

"I strongly advise against it. The Wehrmacht doesn't take kindly to SS men telling them their business."

"He undermined the business of the Reich. This concerns him too—unless he's not a German."

"Last thing we need is—" Krieger lowered his voice. "If Himmler finds out we lost the birdseed—"

"Your advice is duly noted, *sir*. Let's keep this out of Berlin—until we can't." Rheinhardt sped up.

Krieger couldn't fathom what was happening. Fanatically devoted to following orders, he lacked the imagination even to be a good German. And Rheinhardt was not going to be the one to break Krieger of this lifelong habit.

Groenplaats, the wide stone square below Antwerp's towering Gothic cathedral, had been cleared for drills. Drechsler's men marched in formation along the cathedral wall. Hands clasped behind him, Drechsler stood at the Rubens statue, barking orders. Rheinhardt headed straight for him.

51

The SS, Wehrmacht, and Firmin

Drechsler faced Rheinhardt on the plinth under the statue of Rubens. "What the devil are you talking about? What men?" The northern sun flickered through the stone facade. "I didn't order your men off the quay. I gave a general order through the Antwerp Security Council to reinforce the perimeter. We had twenty-four men killed last week at an outpost off Saint Lament—they had to be replaced."

"With *my* men?"

"With the men who were babysitting a fishing boat instead of guarding a vital port for the Führer, yes."

Rheinhardt narrowed his eyes. "I thought you didn't know what men I meant, Herr Drechsler."

"I meant I didn't want to talk about it with *you*," said Drechsler. "Of course I knew what men. Herr Brandt and I discussed your incomprehensible activities at length. I have full operational command over all military personnel in Antwerp—including yours, Rheinhardt."

"My SS men are independent of the Wehrmacht."

"Not when there's a clear and present threat of invasion."

"Why wasn't I consulted?" Rheinhardt said. "Or notified?"

"I was told you'd left for two days—gone God knows where, without *notifying* anyone. Meanwhile, two dozen of my men were wiped out."

"My men were guarding classified cargo," Rheinhardt said, "essential to the war, to the Reich, and to Herr Hitler himself."

Drechsler sneered. "What are you guarding now, Rheinhardt? Herring? Or obscene novels?"

Rheinhardt glanced sideways to find Krieger, who was as far away as possible from the public standoff. He was going to use Krieger's name, but by the general's demeanor, he wasn't certain he could count on Krieger to vouch for him. "A top-secret matter far above your authority, Herr Drechsler," he said instead, raising his voice. "You had no clearance. You had no right to pull my men. You've compromised the operation. This is a security failure of the *highest* order!"

Drechsler raised his voice in return.

"This is going to stop *right now*! Do you know the British are at Caen? Their tanks and planes are headed for Berlin. I'm responsible for garrisoning this entire city and once again you're bothering me like a fly with your *verdammt* bullshit!" He voice cracked in anger. "Was the herring also classified? What about the sex albums—were those top priority too?" Sputtering, he jabbed the air with his finger. "Why would I allow twenty armed men, working in three shifts, sixty men in all, to stand guard on an empty dock, where no one walks or goes, next to a dormant ship whose captain is *dead* and whose owner has *fled*? And this while I'm dealing with real logistical nightmares, troop movements, and a garrison of men murdered in their beds!" His voice rose to a roar. "I didn't know you were siphoning soldiers to support your own obsessions, but you're out of your fucking mind, Rheinhardt, if you think I would *ever* allow it!"

"You have no control over my men," said Rheinhardt.

"I have full control over the defense of Antwerp!" Drechsler was purple. His voice boomed through the stone square. His men stopped marching and stood motionless, backs against the wall, while Rheinhardt and Drechsler faced off, shouting for all to hear.

"I don't give a fuck about your ship, Rheinhardt, but I assure you: the Allies cannot and will not enter Antwerp! Not on my watch. The port must be held—and it will be held. There is no *your* men and *my* men. They are all German men, called into action. Your hysteria about who was pulled from your pitiful little detail is of no concern to me. Your indignation is irrelevant. You don't understand war or strategy or preparation—*nothing*. You have always been a dullard and a paper pusher. I've told Brandt for years—you've been stationed *far above* your level of competence. If it were up to me, I wouldn't let you file the manifests. Even that is above your station. For years, you've menaced me with these false alarms. Get out of my sight. That's an order, Rheinhardt—get off my plinth and out of my fucking sight."

Without waiting for a response, Drechsler spun around and gave Rheinhardt the back of his head. "Why have you stopped?" he shouted at his men. "Are you ducks waiting to be shot? *Go! Forward! March!*"

"The ship was left undefended," Rheinhardt said through his teeth, trying to contain his fury.

"It wasn't undefended," Drechsler said, without turning around. "Brandt left two men on overnight detail. One of them happens to be my son-in-law. I vouch for him myself."

"Your son-in-law was drugged and thrown into a storeroom," Rheinhardt said. "His weapons were taken. Germany's most valuable cargo was stolen in the middle of the night—because of *your* actions."

Drechsler didn't turn around, but he hesitated. "If you don't like the way I run my city, take it up with Falkenhausen in Brussels. Tell him to have me removed. Until then, leave me the fuck alone. You have a problem? Bring it to Brandt. I made no specific request to your office. *He* gave me your men."

Rheinhardt's shell was stone. Drechsler might as well have been shouting at the river, or the ship, or the sky. Nothing on Rheinhardt's face moved—not even to acknowledge that he had heard Drechsler's attack. Not in public. Not in front of SS officers, Wehrmacht soldiers, city *Polizei*. Not in front of Hubner, standing nearby, looking decimated.

Not within earshot of Sieg Krieger—second only to Himmler—pacing at the outer edge of the courtyard, chain-smoking, listening, refusing to intervene.

Rheinhardt backed down and stepped away.

The SS and the Wehrmacht could not be at war in Antwerp.

If anything happened to Drechsler, the political fallout would jeopardize the only thing that mattered.

The *uranium*.

Finding it stood above pride, above insult, above vengeance. It was Von Rheinhardt's sole imperative.

Yes, the Wehrmacht general was untouchable.

But he knew who *wasn't* untouchable.

The man who had given away his guards without warning. The man who had sabotaged him. The man who had made him look like a fool.

The indifferent, malevolent, criminally stupid *Otto Brandt.*

Krieger returned to Liège later that evening, leaving Rheinhardt with only two directives. "Drechsler is off-limits." And: "Do nothing else until you find the uranium." As if Rheinhardt had to be told.

The checkpoints in and out of Antwerp were locked down by 8:00 p.m. that Saturday night. His men began interviewing every guard who'd been on duty between 11:00 p.m. Friday and 7:00 a.m. Saturday. But there were many checkpoints, many guards, and it took time, the one thing Rheinhardt was desperately short on.

De Swaef's immediate search of the ship and of the nearby warehouses proved fruitless. Obviously a closer look needed to be paid, but at the moment neither held any clues. And that's all Rheinhardt was hoping for. A small nod to know which way to turn. Because he knew how heavy the barrels were and how impossible they would've been to move, part of him almost expected them to be found in the warehouse right across Glaskaai. That would have required *some* effort, but with wheelbarrows, it could be done. He scraped every cobwebbed corner of that vast space; he had his men open every crate. They found nothing.

He spent Sunday morning questioning Vandepole and Blomme, separately and together. It was all just a litany of "Please, sir, I don't remember," followed by a lamentation of "I'm sorry, sir, I wish I could be more helpful." They had just come on duty, both told him. Blomme looked at his watch and said, "It's 23:10. Only six hours and fifty minutes to go." Vandepole said, "I hope it's not going to rain the whole fucking night." And that was it. There was simply nothing else, until they opened their eyes on the floor of the stockroom the next morning. No matter which way Rheinhardt came at them—fill in the blank, multiple choice, true or false, or just plain conversation—they were a dead end. Except each had a fresh purple circular bruise on the upper part of his leg that he couldn't explain.

For the rest of Sunday Rheinhardt paced the old city. He walked the docks, the alleys, the narrow lanes, hunting for patterns. He found scraped plaster, shattered mirrors, a strip of burlap with half a white marking, the paint still tacky. One wall was gouged deep—a truck or trucks had forced their way through, tearing off mirrors, scouring stone. Looked like standard trucks, by the clearance. The trail ended at a crossing near Hoboken—the only checkpoint close enough to matter. Two Belgian *Polizei* saluted stiffly. He questioned them. They revealed nothing.

Was looking at trucks another dead end? An ordinary truck couldn't carry thousands of kilos of uranium without suffering permanent structural damage. Which meant its frame had to be reinforced.

And why would a truck have a reinforced frame?

Because it was already being used to carry something heavy. What was heavy that was regularly being transported in and out of Antwerp?

What a ridiculous line of reasoning this was. Rheinhardt was flagellating himself into airless corners.

What *wasn't* heavy?!

Bricks, lumber, cement, ammunition, furniture, glass, pottery, bollards, anchors, rivets, steel poles, you name it. *Everything was fucking heavy.*

Nearly seven hundred industrial trucks entered the city on Friday, June 16, 1944.

More than half were heavily reinforced.

What was he going to do, search every single one?

He focused on the warehouses.

Teams of Gestapo men searched the dockside depots up and down Glaskaai and on Jordaensstraat behind it. Every failed attempt only put another block, another street, another kilometer of distance between Rheinhardt and his uranium.

Belatedly, he was realizing how many mistakes he had made. He was so focused on *La Fortuna*, he had let the search for the black man wane. He didn't think it was as important. The man had been badly wounded and could be dead. All his colleagues were dead. Could he have escaped with Miguel Silva? Were they the ones who stole his uranium?

Rheinhardt had made a terrible error of judgment in not searching exhaustively for the Congolese man, and was now paying for it every hour, every minute, every second his barrels were in the wind.

He examined the cobblestoned quay. He examined the room where the men were found without their uniforms. He examined the wharf, the plank, the deck, the broken winch, the shredded nets, the cracked boom on the mast, the cargo hold, and the crypt.

He stood motionless in the empty vault for so long that if someone were watching him from the outside, one might conclude he'd gone mad—and was expecting at any moment to find the misplaced barrels sitting in front of him.

The vault smelled like the sweat of men. Like the herculean exertion of men who had to deadlift many *tons* of uranium ore two meters straight up.

But so what? Obviously there was sweat. The uranium didn't vanish from the depths of the ship by black magic.

There was something Rheinhardt was missing.

Something he wasn't seeing.

On the deck he stood and smoked, looking up at the ruins of the castle above him.

He heard the sound of boots rattling the wooden gangplank. It was Hubner, who came and stood beside him.

"Nothing yet, sir?"

"Would I be standing here if there was something, Hubner?"

Hubner fell silent.

"If whatever it is you're looking for is still in Antwerp, sir, we'll find it."

Antwerp was a crowded port city of a half-million people. Second in size only to Brussels. "Oh, really?" Rheinhardt said. "You couldn't find it before, on this ship thirty meters long by twenty wide. But you're certain we'll find it now, in our eight hundred warehouses and depots?" He took a breath. He couldn't do without Hubner, but sometimes the man's thickness was maddening.

"Herr Brandt stopped by Baert Haus again, sir," Hubner said. "Third time today."

"And did you tell him I didn't want to see him?" Rheinhardt paused. "Did you tell him," he said, "that I will *never* speak to him again?"

Hubner shrugged. "Not quite, sir. I told him you were busy and could not be disturbed. He repeated that he'd like to offer an apology and a truce. He said he truly believed it was overkill to have so many men on Sector 7 for no apparent reason. He said you should've told him about how important it was."

The Scheldt could freeze under Rheinhardt's gaze. "And how did you respond to this?"

"I believe my exact words were, *I will be sure to relay your full message to Herr Rheinhardt*," Hubner said.

Rheinhardt nodded his terse approval.

But Hubner didn't leave. He stood there, as if he had more to say.

"Will there be anything else?" Rheinhardt said.

"Perhaps there was a witness?" Hubner said, almost whispering. "Someone on the docks who might have heard a noise? Seen an anomaly?"

"At three in the morning during strict curfew? *Think*, Hubner."

"Have you considered talking to that Firmin fella, the boiler room expert, sir?"

"Who?"

"You suggested him yourself, sir. In Liège. You said he could help me light the boiler."

Hell has emptied and all the devils are here. "And. Did. He. Help you, Hubner?"

"No, sir, he refused—"

"So why would he help *me*?"

"Because he lives in Shed 19 near the rail spur, as you yourself told me. It's a little way from Glaskaai, but perhaps he went out for an unapproved wander during curfew. The way drunks sometimes do."

Rheinhardt stared at Hubner for a moment. Then he turned, clattered down the gangplank, and strode off down Glaskaai toward the rail spur, gathering speed as he went.

"Mückenschutz!"

Rheinhardt found Firmin outside his hovel, sitting in a rocking chair, or to be precise, a chair that was rocking. His hands shook so badly he couldn't light his cigarette. The man needed a long pour of schnapps, not a Revel. When Firmin saw Rheinhardt looming over him in a gray coat and SS visor, he began to shake even harder.

There was nowhere for Rheinhardt to sit, and asking Firmin to stand was like asking the chair to stand. So they remained off-balance—one tall stoic officer and a convulsing gnome in a metal chair.

"Firmin," Rheinhardt said, "do you remember who I am?"

"Yes, sir—no sir—I'm not sure, sir, but I think so, I believe so."

Fear really did make idiots of people.

"I won't take up too much of your time," Rheinhardt said. "I need to know if you were out and about last Friday night, anytime between midnight and six in the morning."

"I go out a lot, sir," Firmin said. "It's hard for me to pin an exact time . . ."

"I'm not here to discipline you for a curfew infraction, Firmin. I need to know if you went out walking in the middle of the night. Looking for more drink perhaps? In the trash receptacles out on the docks."

"Sometimes, sir. I'm not proud of it. But I consider it a service—I clean up the messes other people make. Quietly. Diligently. I don't bother no one."

"Were you out on Glaskaai on Friday evening?"

"It's hard to tell, sir. I don't want to make a mistake in my answer. I may have been. On the other hand, I may not have been."

"On any evening last week, while you were out and about on Glaskaai, did you notice anything unusual?"

"Unusual like what, sir? Things not cleaned up? Broken glass?"

"I don't want to put words in your mouth," said Rheinhardt. "Did you see anything that caught your attention for any reason?"

Firmin's eyes sparkled a little. "I don't think it was Friday night, but I did see a fascinating thing, yes! Beautiful women were walking a red carpet!"

Rheinhardt held his breath on "fascinating"—and released it bitterly on "women."

"What are you talking about?" Rheinhardt was so tired. So very, very tired.

"Beautiful young ladies, blonde and brown, wearing hats and lovely dresses. They were walking across the quay like they were in a fashion show! It was breathtaking!"

"Where were they walking?"

"Across Glaskaai, back and forth. And a little boy was running in front of them, throwing rose petals at their feet."

"A boy. Really."

"Yes, sir. Small."

"And this red carpet, Firmin—was it long?"

"Very long, sir. And the beautiful Nazi ladies glided across it like swans. Absolute swans."

Rheinhardt held his breath again. "Why do you say they were Nazis?"

"Because their truck was a Wehrmacht truck, sir."

Slowly and quietly, Rheinhardt spoke. "*What* truck?" When there was no response, he tried again. "Was there a name on the truck, Firmin?"

"Yes, sir, a Nazi name! I can't recall all the words, but I believe they were Nazi fumigators."

"The beautiful women were Nazi fumigators?"

"Yes, sir. And the name was something like *Insect Control, Nazi division*. Or *Mosquito Control, Aryan division*."

"Insect control."

"Ah, yes, sir! *Mückenschutz!*"

That was the first word Firmin uttered when Rheinhardt had approached him.

"The boy saw me, sir. He started walking toward me—until the lady called him back."

"And what did she call him?" Rheinhardt could not have felt more wiped out. Days without sleep had fried him to the core.

"Oh, I can't remember, sir. Something fancy. Or ancient. Not Belgian. Or Aryan. Or French. Something else."

"What do you think it was, Firmin?"

"*Perseus*, maybe? *Sophocles*, perhaps? *Xerxes*?"

Rheinhardt turned sharply on his heels and stormed away, dragging Firmin's useless revelations behind him like barrels of stone.

Into his back, he heard Firmin joyfully exclaim, "Zeus, sir! It was Zeus!"

52

Abbey in the Woods

Fletcher was up before dawn on Sunday. They'd spent the night in the shed behind Vervaet's workshop, the trucks fenced in under the trees, the men rotating sentry duty.

"On your feet—men, women, Zeuses."

Zeus was the first one up.

Charlie moaned. "Fletcher, have mercy, it's not even five."

Louise sat up beside Rafael, still wrapped in her coat. They'd slept on burlap sacks at the back of the workshop—he splayed on his back, she curled against his side. "Rafa, wake up, your lieutenant is calling."

"Hell with him," Rafael muttered.

But when Fletcher was in command mode, he was an immovable force. Fifteen minutes later, with fuel tanks filled from the jerrycans, they were up and rolling in convoy toward Tremelo, bound for the Abbey of Sancta Maria in Silvis Sacris.

Louise drove. Charlie was squeezed on the pull-down seat behind Wolski who insisted on riding shotgun and narrating every kilometer. He was like a talking map—half in French, the rest a scramble of Polish and English. It was maddening. He wouldn't shut up, and all Louise wanted was to tell Charlie about Bruges. Yesterday with Rafael was the first time she had ever been. But Wolski!

"Wolski," Louise said, exasperated. "Just tell me when to turn. I don't need a meter-by-meter commentary."

"While you berate me, you miss turn," he said.

Charlie leaned forward between them. "What do you want to tell me, Lou? You want to talk to me about Bruges? I know all about it. I hope there aren't any canals or bridges or checkpoints on these roads you're taking us on, Wolski."

"I don't know about checkpoints," said Wolski. "But there's rut ahead that cuts right. If Louise doesn't ease left, we lose suspension."

Louise eased left, but her mind was still on Bruges, the magical place the Nazis forgot. She and Rafael had spent a few hours there yesterday, with the others. They walked into town from Vervaet's shop. It was overcast and cool, and the air smelled like rain and bread. They shared a bitter beer and a small roll with jam, then wandered the canals of a city as silent as church. Behind them, a man walked, playing the squeezebox like a holy choir. Another followed him on the violin. Beside her, Rafael sang a tune she didn't know, in a language she couldn't place.

The water in the canals was still as glass. Only the little pontoon boats disturbed it. They went for a ride in one, just barely big enough for them all. The rest of the world fell away. Only Rafael remained. Rafael and Bruges.

The stepped gables of the old merchant houses were among Bruges' most unforgettable sights—tall, narrow brick facades that rose in perfect verticals, then broke into stair-step rooftops like teeth or ladders, silhouetted against the sky. Toward evening, the fading light caught on their sharp edges and they looked as if they were carved from paper. They lined the canals in rows, their forms mirrored in the still water below. As evening fell, the canals gathered the glow of the streetlamps and stretched it out like gold. Rafael gave her his arm, and she took it.

Bruges, doubled, upside down.

Like Louise.

"I want to tell you about Bruges, Charlie," said Louise with an aching sigh.

"You don't have to, Loosha," Charlie said. "I know."

The road ran low and level for hours, bordered by open fields, pastures lined with crooked fences, and hedgerows clipped by wind. But as they crossed into Flemish Brabant, the land began to roll gently. The trees thickened—in rows, clusters, then in whole woods. Birch and beech, dense and quiet, stood like sentinels. The air cooled.

Near Tremelo, the hills steepened, and the forest swallowed the road. The landscape felt older here. Charlie herself had come to Tremelo only once, in 1943, to pick up three children from a safehouse chateau. Without Wolski, she wasn't sure if they would've found the final turn at all. The narrow forest road wound downhill for half a kilometer, gravel popping under their tires, before the abbey emerged—half-built into the hill, cloaked in ivy and shadow.

The sacred woods rustled and chirped with morning life, but the stone monastery made no sound at all. The Abbey of Sancta Maria didn't rise from the ground—it sank into it. Canopied by forest, tucked into the slope, stone-walled and ivy-bound, it looked centuries old, and as if it pretended to be inconspicuous. Built from thick dark stone, its outer wall faced Charlie like a fortress. No windows, no cross, no sign of welcome. Just a single door, set deep under a square lintel.

To one side, a belltower rose high into the trees. It looked like it might have been a turret once. To the other side, blooming in half-shade, against logic and laws of floriculture, was a sprawling garden, clustered with foxglove, valerian, bleeding heart, and early delphinium—wild, bright, almost careless beauty. Charlie wondered if this was the garden Capelle had meant when he bought her flowers yesterday and offered her a sanctuary for his king's cargo.

They hopped down onto a flat stone forecourt, their boots thumping over weed-laced cobbles, and stretched their cramped legs. Fletcher approached her. "Abbey?" he said. "Or fortress?"

"A fortified monastery," said Charlie, tucking the hair away from her face and buttoning her tunic up to her throat to make herself more appropriate. She would've put on her dress, but it was *red*. "Full of Cistercian nuns who've probably never seen soldiers. Put your weapons behind you. You don't want to scare them. And stand to the side. Don't let them see you through the door slit. Let me handle it."

The heavy wooden door loomed. Charlie took a breath and knocked three times. Only as the metal hatch began to slide did she realize she didn't know the password. Or even if there was one. A wary eye stared out at her from the small opening. "Sancta Maria in Silvis Sacris is a cloistered house," a woman's gruff voice said. "Who speaks at our gate?"

Charlie had nothing prepared. Who was she supposed to say she was? She tried the password for the resistance. "*The bell rings in the holy place*," she said.

Silence was her only response.

"*La jonquille est vivante*," she said.

Nothing.

"Robert Capelle sent me here."

"It is *not* Robert Capelle who sent you here," the woman said. "It is the Lord, thy God. And I don't know who Robert Capelle is." The hatch snapped shut.

Charlie cast a flummoxed glance at Fletcher. "No, no," he whispered.

"You were doing so well. Please continue."

Rolling her eyes at him, she knocked again. The hatch reluctantly opened again. "This is a holy house," the nun said.

Charlie, mistaking it for a password, replied with, "And the earth is full of His glory."

"We do not play games here. We do not repeat phrases like parrots. You cannot come in—not because you don't know the right words, but because you are not the right person. What do you require?"

"Crux sola est nostra theologia," she said. The Cross alone is our theology.

"Your Latin is not going to help you here," the woman said, sighing. "Wait here. I shall go get the Abbess."

"You mean that *wasn't* the Abbess?" Fletcher whispered behind Charlie. "Then why the hell was she torturing you?"

"Shh! Don't say *hell* or we'll never get in."

"That's the least of what they'll hear from us soldiers," said Rafael. Charlie wished she could snap the hatch shut on him.

A few excruciating minutes later, the metal plate slid open. "I am Abbess Verene," a woman's deep, serious voice said. "What is the name?"

"I am Charlotte Fontaine," said Charlie.

Verene sighed. "Not *yours*, child."

"Oh—Count Robert Capelle."

The lock made no turn in the heavy door. "Is the *jonquille morte ou vivante*?" she said.

"La jonquille est vivante," Charlie replied, breathing a long sigh of relief. *"Mais son ombre est mortelle."* But its shadow is deadly.

"As ever," said the Abbess, finally unlocking the door but only partially opening it.

Charlie stood with her hands together. The Abbess appraised her—dirty, oily clothes, muddy boots, face streaked with sweat and dust. Charlie, in turn, appraised the Abbess.

Mother Verene was small and hard as a prayer book. Her face was weathered, finely lined, and looked like it hadn't cracked a smile since 1910. Her voice was low and in charge—when she spoke, you obeyed. Charlie wished she had a voice like that. Verene was in full Cistercian black and white habit. A wrought-iron crucifix hung low from her neck on a black iron chain.

"Have you come with the Kivu coffee?"

"Kivu? Uh—yes, yes, I have."

"The coffee is heavy?"

"Very."

"How much have you brought?"

"Sixty barrels."

"Does it take up much space?"

"No."

"I see two trucks."

"Because of weight, not volume."

Verene nodded. "Are you planning to carry it in yourself, or are the rest of your unkempt compatriots hiding outside my doorway?"

Charlie lowered her head.

"Bring them into the light where I can see them. How many?"

"Sixteen."

"All women?"

"Seven women. Seven men. And one boy."

The Abbess flung open the door. "I have been waiting since the start of the war," she said. "The King's officer—is he here?"

Ngomo stepped out of the shadows. Zeus clutched his hand.

"Hello, Ngomo," said Verene. "You certainly took your time."

"I almost didn't make it."

"Well, come in, come in. You should've told your Flemish compatriot the password. It's your name."

"I did not know this," Ngomo whispered to Charlie, as the rest of the men and women stepped forward. Admittedly, they did not look their best. The Abbess's face was a study in barely concealed disapproval. She scanned them all, her eyes resting on Louise longer than the others. Of course. She turned to the only thing she could comfortably turn to—the child. "And what is your name, little one?"

"Zeus."

"What a wonderful name," she said, giving him her hand and leading him inside.

"Can we come in too?" Charlie asked.

"Do I have a choice?" said the Reverend Mother.

Inside was not like outside—as many things in life, Fletcher was realizing, were not.

Outside was a fortress. Inside, a sanctuary. Austere, yet green. Simple, yet comforting. Spiritual, yet practical. In a small Gothic chapel in the north-east corner, seventeen nuns who lived and worked here began their day. One abbess, two senior nuns, eight middle-aged sisters, and six novices, all under thirty. Brigitte stage-whispered that the younger nuns might be in direct competition for their precious men's attention—and possibly even some of the middle-aged nuns too.

"The Abbess is the only one you really have to worry about, Gitta," said Louise. "Didn't you see? She had her eye on Belvy the moment we walked in."

"You're just teasing!" Brigitte said.

"Charlie, am I teasing?"

"Never," Charlie said. "Louise has no sense of humor, she never teases."

"Oh, isn't that the pot calling the kettle black?" said Louise. "Rafa, does Charlie have a sense of humor?"

"Charlie is as funny as a court martial," said Rafael. Then he caught Fletcher watching him—arms folded, expression flat. "I meant," Rafael said quickly, "Charlie's comedy gold. She could make a court martial sound like the Folies-Bergère."

Sister Therese quickly became everyone's favorite by offering them a hearty breakfast of tomatoes, eggs, and warm bread. They were starving; they ate gratefully. There was even some ersatz coffee—terrible, of course, but Rafael brought in a can of Ngomo's Kivu coffee as a gift. The Abbess said, "You're giving us *Kivu coffee* as a gift? No, thank you." Rafael took great offense—until Ngomo explained.

"You should've picked a different code word for your stone poison than delicious coffee," Rafael muttered.

After breakfast, the men got to work, while the women were ushered to the laundry room to bathe in the heavy stone washing troughs. A dozen nuns stood guard outside to protect the women's honor.

Fletcher was impressed by the small, crypt-like room the Abbess offered for their concealment needs, behind the cool and dry wine cellar. It was a crypt behind a crypt—and nearly as difficult to access as the secret hold on *La Fortuna*. It was going to be a long haul to get the barrels inside.

A stone path, covered with moss and lichen, led around the side of the abbey to an arched door used by the nuns to toss compost and carry firewood. The assembly line wasn't as efficient as it had been on the ship, but it didn't need to be. This time, they had all day.

Fletcher and Rafael rolled the barrels down the truck ramp, held back with twine in a controlled descent. Briggs and Ngomo deadlifted one barrel at a time into the wheelbarrow they'd borrowed from Vervaet. The barrow had a solid oak, steel-reinforced wheel and could probably carry two barrels at once, but they didn't want to risk it. If the wheelbarrow broke, they'd have no way of getting the rest into the cellar. Better to take twice as long to get there than not get there at all.

Inside the abbey, past the side door was a narrow, slightly sloped corridor that led via a stone ramp to a partially underground cellar. Another stone ramp led to the small cellar behind that. There were moments—during the *ten hours* it took them to get the uranium inside, barrel by barrel—when they all begged Fletcher to let them load up two at a time.

Fletcher said no. The job was the job. There was no cutting corners.

Amid the rolling, lifting, and grunting, Rafael decided it was the perfect time to talk to Fletcher about Louise. And Fletcher, bound to him by their pairing, couldn't stop him.

"I think I love her," Rafael said.

Fletcher rolled his eyes. "Don't you say that about all your girls? Hold the wheelbarrow steady—don't tip it."

"I'm serious, man."

"Okay, Rider. What would you like me to do—applaud?"

"No, just be a friend and listen. Then, you may offer advice, if you've got any."

Fletcher sighed. "How is this different from everyone else?"

"Well, because I feel different, for one."

Fletcher didn't know what to say. On three, they lifted the barrel out of the cart and shoved and nudged it against the cool stone wall.

"I'm telling you this not just to shoot the shit," Rafael said, "but because we can't stay here."

"Because you love her, we can't stay here?" Fletcher stopped and stared at him.

"You heard me."

Fletcher didn't even know what his next question should be. He wiped his forehead. "Why not?" he said, instantly stepping on the answer with his own follow-up. "Where do you suppose would be *better*?"

"It's an abbey, man. An *abbey.* You get what I'm saying?"

"I get what an abbey is, yes."

"They don't go for that sort of thing."

"Love?"

"Yes. Physical, vocal, ceaseless expressions of love."

Fletcher exhaled. "And you propose what?"

"I don't *know*! That's why I'm talking to you."

"Let's go get the next one, they're waiting," Fletcher said. As they walked down the hallway, he added quietly, "Rider, we don't have many good options here." Any good options, he wanted to add.

"There are always options. Let's go back to Bruges. It was a real nice place. We could get some rooms, get a bit of R&R—a few days' furlough . . ." Rafael's handsome face was awash in the imagining. "We deserve it."

"Rafael . . ."

"Fine. Then let's split up. We're done after this, right? Your German is never going to find these barrels. What did Reed tell you about after?"

"After this, we have another mission. And frankly, I'm not sure we're done with this one yet."

"Why?"

"I don't know why. Just . . ."

"Wait, what other mission?"

Fletcher spoke carefully. "I have to take Ngomo—and I guess Zeus, too—out of Belgium."

"*Out* of Belgium? The fuck you are. Where?"

Back at the truck, they paused their conversation as they deadlifted another barrel into the barrow, and returned to the path.

"It's not my decision," Fletcher said. "They tell me what to do, and I do it. The King of the Belgians wants Ngomo out of the country. He's not safe here."

"Where the fuck is he safe? The Congo? What's the plan—get him a crown and a motorcade?"

Fletcher shrugged. "Get him to Spain, maybe across the Strait of Gibraltar into Africa."

"You're headed back to *Africa*? Across the frontline that is Europe? You're insane, man."

"Orders are orders."

"And Zeus?"

"I'll try to get him to Lisbon."

"When do you plan to do this?"

"Don't know yet. When this is done."

"*This* meaning the barrels? So tonight? You're leaving tonight?"

"No. *This* meaning when I think they're safe. A week. Maybe two."

"You plan to stay *two weeks* in this abbey?" Rafael shook his head, horrified. "As God is my witness, I can't do it. I'll get thrown out, and all of you with me."

"You can't control yourself?"

"For *two weeks*? You think any of the others are going to control themselves? Briggs? Wolski? What mortal man could? Maybe you. But then again, you're not human."

"I'm human, Rider," said Fletcher. "I just . . . have control over myself."

"Spain!" Rafael muttered. "Unbelievable. And you want us to come with you?"

"No. I don't think seven men traveling together is the level of clandestine I need," said Fletcher.

"So who's going with you?"

"Wolski, obviously. Maybe Hawk. Maybe you, too."

"So . . . everyone but Briggs?"

"Briggs and Belvedere."

"You're not bringing the medic with you on a 2000-kilometer trek through *five* enemy-occupied countries? Brilliant, Fletch. Fucking brilliant."

"Didn't you say your father is from Spain?"

"I did not," said Rafael. "My father is Basque. Born in France. That's why I'm French, you see. *Not* Spanish."

"Didn't you once tell Lucas your father was a Pyrenees tracker?"

"Fletcher, I'm not going to Spain with you."

"You think you have a choice, Canario? If that's where we have to go, that's where we go."

"Without Louise? Without Charlie?"

"Of course without them! What the hell are you thinking?"

Rafael had stopped moving and stood, staring at Fletcher. "Didn't you hear a word I said?"

"Loud and clear. You need a room in Bruges. But that's not a plan, Rafa. It's a fever dream. Fantasy. Mirage. Delusion."

"Make it happen, Fletch. Don't deny us our fun in the sun. Especially if we're all splitting soon."

"I'm a soldier at war, not a damn innkeeper."

"I need a bordello for my body."

"You have an abbey for your soul."

"My soul," said Rafael, "also wants only one thing. I need to conjoin my flesh with hers, just as the good Lord himself commanded."

"Rider, for fuck's sake! You're going to get us thrown out of God's house before we spend one night here! Go pray on it. Services are every two hours in the courtyard chapel."

"Praying is maybe the fourth or fifth thing I'd like to be doing on my knees." Distracted, Rafael nearly rolled the barrow off the ramp.

"Watch where you're going!"

After securing barrel 30 in the cellar, they switched with Briggs and Belvedere and went into the woods for a smoke.

"When you say you love her . . . do you mean love or, you know—*love*?"

"Fletcher, don't you think I, of all people, know the difference?" Rafael said. "My woozy feelings are diluting my other, less noble impulses. They're painting even my lust in rosy hues." He smiled. "I need love to elevate the mundane to the divine."

"Not in this abbey," said Fletcher.

"Then I leave it in your capable hands. You know what you must do, innkeeper."

They smoked.

"Sometimes," Fletcher said, his tone almost confessional, "I feel it's indecent for a man to love hopelessly."

"I know you do, Fletch," said Rafael, patting his shoulder with fond sincerity.

"We've talked about this in Italy, me, you and Lucas. Yes, you've had a shit example of what love should be. But despite what you think, most people are not Paquito Pellerin and your Aunt Vivienne. Me, I'm full of impassioned virtue, trying to raise my life out of the mud and into the hills. That's what she's doing to me." He inhaled deeply.

Fletcher didn't react. He wanted to but simply couldn't talk to Rafael about his feelings for Charlie. Couldn't talk to anyone about it.

Rafael made a face of genuine sympathy. "I can't help you with your predicament," he said. "That's between you and Charlie. You're both closed up. Whether you and she can open, that's up to you. I'm telling you about me. I'm a flawed, complicated, passionate man," he said. "And I happen to have fallen in love with the most beautiful girl. And she appeals to me not just because of her outward comeliness, which is unmatched, but I love *her*. Even Mother Verene might approve that I wish to have found the fountain of life and the door to paradise. But Fletcher, I'm saying this as plainly as I can—one way or the other, Rafael Canario is turning on that fountain and opening that door."

"The abbey is not the place," Fletcher muttered, out of all argument. He himself also desperately wished to open the door to paradise.

Rafael slapped him on the back. "You have twenty-four hours to figure it out," he said, stubbing out his cigarette. "Let's go. Barrel 31 isn't going to roll itself."

Fletcher watched Rafael head down the slope. He glanced up, as if turning to the heavens for guidance. The leaves overhead barely stirred. The trees stood like sentinels, motionless in the late afternoon light. The abbey crouched below. He had a sudden, bone-deep sense that everything was waiting. Not just Charlie and Louise. But also the trees. The stone walls. Even the air. He stood a moment longer, then picked up his gloves and followed Rafael.

In the early evening, after all the barrels were finally offloaded and Fletcher had bathed and shaved, he was ready to speak to the Abbess. "Mother Verene, can our men and women stay here?" he asked. "Zeus too, of course."

"That wasn't part of my discussion with Capelle," she said.

"You didn't discuss sanctuary for the men and women who helped him?" This surprised Fletcher, irked him slightly. "Reverend Mother, most humbly," he said, "Charlotte and I must return the trucks to Bruges tonight, and it's too late to find the rest of my team another safe haven."

From the corner of her critical eye, Verene appraised the men and women in her courtyard. Fletcher followed her gaze. He fought the impulse to roll his eyes. Mireille sat too close to Briggs on the bench by the vegetable garden, and he was draped over her like a bear over a honeypot. Brigitte was practically in Belvedere's lap, and Wolski was flanked by Margot and Maxine, who were making him laugh far too loudly. As for Rafael and Louise, they only thought they were hidden by the cucumber supports, but nothing could hide the fire raging in that corner of the courtyard. Only Hildi and Hawk remained civilized, weeding side by side in silence, just their arms touching. The men's weapons leaned against the inner wall of the courtyard, their kits, packs, helmets, and gear sprawled across the ground in plain sight. All of it clearly distressed not only Mother Verene but her seventeen sisters of mercy.

She reluctantly allowed the band to stay—with strict conditions. Men and women would be housed in separate quarters on opposite sides of the abbey. Lights out was right after compline, and there was to be no movement until lauds at 5:00 a.m.

Fletcher agreed. What choice did he have?

All sixty barrels of uranium were securely stacked in two short rows in the back of a cellar behind a cellar, behind a retaining wall, wooden pallets of wine, and some crumbled stone.

They were as secreted away as ambergris at the bottom of the deepest ocean.

53

Silver Hart

It was almost nine in the evening when Charlie and Fletcher returned the trucks to Vervaet. They paid him extra—with cash and a gold coin—shook his hand and drove the *Berceau* into Bruges. The streets were empty, the few open restaurants ready to close.

"What do we do," Fletcher said. "Go back?"

Charlie demurred. "We wouldn't get back to the abbey till nearly midnight. The Reverend Mother won't like it. She's probably been in bed since compline."

"You sure know a lot about monastery schedules," Fletcher said teasingly.

"Always good to know when the gates close," she replied in kind.

"So, where to for us, then, if not the abbey? Should we return to Lillehaven?"

Charlie shook her head. "We'll get stopped if we're on the road after curfew. I used to get stopped all the time, but that was just between Antwerp and Herentals. What am I doing near Bruges at eleven at night?"

"So what do you want to do?" Fletcher asked. "Sleep in the *Berceau*?"

"We could," she said slowly, really wishing he'd get there on his own. She sighed. "Or . . . we could find a room somewhere."

A beat. "If you think that's best," Fletcher said in a neutral tone.

They tried three inns. All were full. Finally, they found one vacancy at a small, timeworn guesthouse called Het Zilveren Hert, the Silver Hart. A silver antler hung above the door, and the walls leaned inward from age. Charlie wore her long-haired wig and a pair of spectacles as disguise. One set of her forged papers named her as Charlotte Maes from Vorselaar, a teaching assistant. And Fletcher was her cousin Florent, already and conveniently from Bruges.

The innkeeper barely glanced at the documents. She took the cash, handed over the iron key, and muttered, "Cousin? And I'm the King's sister," with a snort that Charlie only understood when they got upstairs and with sharp disappointment she saw the room: no bigger than a storage closet, with one creaking, undersized twin bed.

Before she could so much as react to the room's obvious unsuitability, there was a knock on the door. It was the landlady, holding a tray with a small crockpot, a carafe, and two place settings. "I figured you must be hungry," she said gruffly, "and everything's closed now. Here."

They sat side by side on the bed and ate ravenously, shoveling food into their mouths. Every last bite was gone before they spoke. "What did I just eat?" Fletcher said.

"Rabbit stew with potatoes and onions," said Charlie.

"I don't know about you, but that was the best thing I've ever had." The wine was weak and red. They guzzled that too.

Charlie took off her wig and stood to walk across to the washbasin. Someone instantly pounded from below with the tip of a broom handle. "Keep it down up there!" a female voice screeched. "Decent people are trying to sleep!"

Charlie and Fletcher had no choice but to comply. There was tension between them—the physical charge of two people bound by their undeniable connection, and by the small and the large of the life they were living. There was also deep exhaustion. Charlie's whole body ached with the need to be horizontal, and she meant this *almost* without double meaning.

She peeled the rough woolen blanket off the bed and gave it to him. "This bed is only marginally more comfortable than the floor," she said, kicking off her boots.

"Does the bed smell like onions? Because the blanket does."

"Not lavender and heather?" She eased onto the narrow mattress, careful not to jostle the frame. It creaked anyway. She lay on her side, facing him.

He settled beside her, curled on the crook of his arm. The floor groaned under him.

"Don't move," she whispered.

"That's one I haven't heard before," he whispered back.

"Fletcher!"

The broom handle banged into the floorboards.

"I'm just breathing," he said.

"Breathe quieter."

It was the first time they'd been alone since last night at Het Steen Castle, and between that electric, unforgettable moment in the stone parapets and now lay a year's worth of anxiety, tension, activity, duress, and titanic exertion, not to mention the constant company of others, all of them as full of longing as they were.

"Comfortable?" he asked.

"Like a princess," she said. "You?"

"Like a prince."

Fletcher's breath had already slowed. What an amazing creature was an exhausted man, Charlie thought, reaching down and touching his hair, brushing back the strands above his temple. Her fingertips slid to his stubbled cheek. What an amazing creature was man.

He moved.

She started to pull back, but his hand came up and found hers. Without opening his eyes, he brought it to his lips, kissed it, and lowered it to his chest, holding it there.

He turned on his back and stared up at her from the floor. She lay with her cheek pressed against the mattress, staring down into his face. My God, he was so beautiful. "Perhaps if you lean over and kiss me quietly," he whispered, his arm already reaching for her head, "the broom downstairs will never know."

Charlie leaned down and kissed him quietly, and the broom downstairs never knew.

She stayed awake longer than she wanted to, lying on her side in the dark, watching his sleeping body. Fletcher. *Fletcher.*

I wish I could find the words to tell you that though yesterday began early and finished late, and though it had in it stress and hurry, heart-stopping anxiety and relentless worry, though it contained the tasks of Sisyphus and the labors of Hercules, and had discord and chaos, what it didn't have was fear. That was a first for me. I was never afraid—because whatever happened, I was with you. And all the hard things we did, we did together.

What I'm trying to say, Fletcher Gray, is yesterday was one of the best days of my life.

The throbbing in her legs gave way to something deeper, an ache that had nothing to do with tired muscles. Were they out of danger?

She hoped so. That the worst was behind them, and maybe, just maybe, before he left her to fight the rest of his war, the two of them could find a great golden feasting place without limit or restraint.

She laid her trembling palm on his sleeping heart.

She feared she hadn't made enough deals for this version of her dreamed-of life.

54

Mad Jesuit Monk

When Charlie and Fletcher returned to the abbey the following afternoon, they found the holy mother even less amenable than the night before, and she'd been barely amenable then. As she opened the door to let them in, one of the bells in the tower tolled once, and then echoed.

"Who rang the bell?" Charlie asked.

"No one," said Verene. "There used to be a bell in the tower that never rang when struck, so it was set aside. Seven new bells, large and small, were added to the belfry over the years, but no *klokkenmaker* ever came to service them. The bells have not been rung deliberately for fifty years."

"But one just tolled now," Charlie said.

"Sometimes the bell rings of its own accord," the Abbess said. "That spooked my nuns, so to steady their nerves, I removed the tongue ropes. But for reasons I can't explain, the bell still tolls sometimes—as it did just now."

"Which bell?" Charlie asked, exchanging an uneasy glance with Fletcher. "The ancient one, or one of the seven new ones?"

"I cannot say," the Abbess said. She took them to her private office, sat them down, and explained—firmly, impatiently—that even though the men and women had followed her rules, the atmosphere of secular and corporal joy they had created stirred her nuns away from the deep spiritual discipline required to conduct their daily tasks. "We are Cistercian nuns," Verene said. "We allow no frivolity, and only minimal singing."

"Was there frivolity?" asked Fletcher.

"Was there singing?" asked Charlie.

"There was both," said Verene. "And often at the same time."

Charlie and Fletcher said nothing.

"We're an austere order," Verene said. "We live our days by manual labor, self-sufficiency, prayerful silence. We make honey. We grow turnips. Your request to stay here seems to be open-ended."

"That is true, our next steps are yet to be determined," Fletcher said, sounding less like himself, Charlie thought, casting a sideways glance at him. He sounded *less polite.* He maintained a neutral face, but his violet eyes deepened.

"You brought weapons into our sanctuary," Verene said. "This is a holy place."

"It's also a hidden fortress, Reverend Mother," said Fletcher.

"That was a long time ago," Verene said. "We live a different life now."

They were being told to leave! Charlie scrambled for options. *Think, think.* Where was Wolski when she needed him? "Abbess," she said, "I had some business once with a house around here, a halfway home for refugee children who'd lost their families?"

"Ah, you must be talking about Kasteel de Velde," said Verene.

"Yes!"

"No reason to get excited," the Abbess said. "It is true, Kasteel de Velde is not far from here, maybe a kilometer over the hill through the woods. But as far as I can tell, only one of you is a small Jewish child, and Baroness Mathilde doesn't make exceptions or take permanents. Her limit is two weeks—even for the children.

"If it helps," Verene continued, "I will keep the women. And Ngomo and Zeus, of course. But the rest of the men must leave."

Charlie had no way of telling the Abbess she was worrying about the wrong sex. The men at least were *trying* to be gentlemen.

"I would like to keep the blonde one," Mother Verene said. "She is born of fire."

"What do you mean—keep her?" Charlie asked. How did the Reverend Mother peg Louise so quickly? What could've happened?

"To protect her," said Verene.

"No, you can't keep her," Charlie said. "We're quite fond of her ourselves."

"We live a hidden life here," said the Abbess. "You come in with your words and wants and all I feel is trouble brewing. For all of us."

"We just need sanctuary, Mother Verene."

"It's okay, Charlie," said Fletcher. "We'll find another way."

"Your lieutenant is right," Verene said. "This abbey used to be a fortress. It was built at the bottom of a haunted wood. In the seventh century, a Merovingian noblewoman was led here by a white stag. Pursued by men who meant to kill her, she collapsed under the ancient oaks and claimed the Virgin Mary appeared before her, holding a sprig of red berries in one hand and a flame in the other. She survived the men. And the winter. And when spring came, she summoned the Christian families nearby to build a shrine on this holy ground."

"So can we stay here or no?" said Fletcher.

The Abbess's face held no expression. "In the eleventh century," she said, "the shrine became a Benedictine monastery, ringed with protective walls so thick no sound from outside could reach the cloister. The abbey was laid siege to during the Feudal revolts. The abbot at the time, Don Anselme, stood on the parapets in his white vestments, clutching a relic said to be a splinter of the True Cross. And somehow the attack was miraculously repelled. The marauders ran screaming, claiming the forest had erupted in flames."

Fletcher leaned to Charlie to whisper something in her ear, but she shoved him away, worried that he might say something to make her laugh. If Verene saw it, she did not react. She went right on speaking.

"So yes, this place has known awful conflict. But not in the last hundred years."

"Yet its design, aged and impregnable, speaks of divinity and defense, Abbess," said Fletcher. He spoke like a soldier.

Verene shook her head. "I understand, but I cannot allow it. Some of my nuns don't even know there's a war going on, an occupation. They live inside these walls as if nothing else exists."

"But other things *do* exist, Reverend Mother," Fletcher said, sounding like he was losing his patience. "The King of Belgium has been taken to Germany against his will. His kingdom desperately needs help. Families are forced onto trains and taken to places from which they do not return. A tyrannical enemy has taken over your country. With all due respect, this is no time to be neutral."

"I'm *not* neutral," Verene said. "I am deeply afraid for my own small tribe."

Fletcher got to his feet. "What's more important, Mother Verene, victory over evil or continued oblivion?"

"You have your priorities," she said, also rising. "And I have mine. I have done what the King asked of me. I have given sanctuary to the things he wanted hidden. And I will keep his officer if he wishes to stay."

"With respect," Fletcher said, "there may be more danger in the hidden things than in anything else you're worried about."

"I know that," Verene said. "But those things are out of my control. This is not."

Fletcher shook his head, mutely and regretfully. Charlie yanked on his sleeve. Verene pointed at the door. The audience was over.

"Why did you pick a fight with her?" Charlie asked Fletcher, as they hurried to collect their team and their things. "She judged you critically, Fletcher. Like a saint might."

"Saint or executioner?" said Fletcher.

Outside, the bells remained silent, but Charlie felt their quiet like a held breath. The abbey would not save them. They would have to find another place, another refuge.

Ngomo said no to a sanctuary that was for him and Zeus only and chose to stay with the rest. Charlie sent Fletcher and everyone else but Louise on foot through the woods to find Kasteel de Velde. Wolski was in his element, leading the way with map and compass in hand, two ladies on his arm.

She and Louise took all the gear and the weapons in the *Berceau* to Baroness Mathilde's house.

"Lou, what the hell happened there yesterday?" Charlie asked. "What did you do?"

"Nothing," Louise said.

"Now that does *not* sound very convincing. We got kicked out! Were you *bad* with your wild creature?"

"I'm never bad with Rafael, only degrees of amazing."

"Yeah, yeah. Did you and he do anything that could've been construed as bad by the Reverend Mother?"

"Not a single thing."

"Louise!"

"Why are you yelling?"

"Because you're playing with me."

"You're wrong. The Abbess took a real shine to me." Louise examined her nails. "Clearly, she must have internalized my youthful longings, because yesterday after you and Fletcher left, she wouldn't leave me alone for a moment. She made us all go to church. Like, literally all and, like, literally church. Compline. In the chapel."

Charlie laughed. "Did you *all* like that?"

"It was quite beautiful, I admit."

"And after services, did you, um, go to sleep?"

"If only," said Louise. "*Then*, she didn't let me so much as wave goodnight to Rafael. She ushered me—bodily—into my room and tucked me into bed like she was my mother. She read to me from the Good Book, said another prayer over me—a hundred prayers—kissed me goodnight, and then sat in the corner of my room, waiting for me to fall asleep!"

Charlie was infinitely amused. "Next time I see your mother, I'll tell her you let another mother-figure tuck you in."

"You think being tucked in by an abbess is something I *want*?" said Louise. "She asked me if I loved him."

"I hope she meant Jesus."

"I don't think so. I told her I thought I did, but I haven't been with him long enough to truly know. She said she saw bigger things for me than mere love."

Charlie raised her eyebrows suggestively, and Louise slapped her on the arm.

"She said I was restless." Louise chuckled. "That I had a restless soul. I told her that was because I was still in the process of becoming and didn't yet know what I was supposed to be."

"And she said . . ."

"She told me to aim high."

"Why couldn't you just promise her you wouldn't get up?"

"I did! Nothing worked. To calm me, she told me the prophecy of Brother Severin and the Ashen Bell. Did she tell you the story of the abbey?"

"She did, but Fletcher upset her so much, she must've stopped before we got to Severin's prophecy."

"*Fletcher* upset her? That man doesn't know how to upset a nun."

"Oh, he obviously does." Charlie smiled into the steering wheel. She felt liquid heat flow through her heart and body when she so much as thought his name.

"You want to hear it?" The woods they were driving through were perfect for a prophecy—cool, shadowy, summery. Louise adopted the Reverend Mother's deep, sonorous tone. "During the Reformation, the abbey was abandoned and the forest consumed it. But in the late 1600s, a mad Jesuit monk named Brother Severin stumbled upon it, while wandering the woods in search of a place he'd seen in his nightmare—the oak trees bleeding sap the color of blood into the ground that was chanting and moaning in elegy."

"Did he, like, write his nightmares down or . . ."

"Yes! His journal, believed to have been long lost, was found in a crumbling wall by a novice nun at the turn of the century."

"Was that when the bells stopped ringing?"

"What bells?" Louise continued. "Most of the journal was illegible—except for a few pages, written in a strange mix of Walloon and French. Some of it was written in what appeared to be . . . dried blood."

"Dried blood, no kidding."

"Severin wrote about the vision that compelled him to leave the comfort of Bruges and seek out this strange, forbidding place. He died shortly after, his face frozen in a kind of rapture."

"Who'd want to leave Bruges?" Charlie muttered, half in reverie herself.

"Ready? *The Ashen Bell will ring*," Louise intoned, "*when blood is carried in barrels of flame, and ravening wolves in iron skin shall hunger for it.*"

"And Reverend Mother wondered why you couldn't sleep," Charlie said. Wasn't Fletcher's mission called *Santa Fe*? Operation *Holy Fire*. "Was that Severin's nightmare or his prophecy?"

"Both," said Louise. "The tower will fall when the *girl with fire in her hand* comes near."

"What girl?" said Charlie, snapping to attention.

Louise shrugged. "Sometimes the girl wears a soldier's coat, Verene said. And sometimes a white veil. She is surrounded by shadow, but the shadow does not touch her."

"Severin said this, or Mother Verene?"

"Yes," said Louise. "She made me repeat the last part three times. *One shall rise, one shall fall, one shall betray with a whisper, and the Ashen Bell will toll when the hour comes not to save the world, but to choose what must burn.*"

55

Red Line

Late Tuesday night, Otto Brandt's corpulent body was fished out of the shallow Willemstad dry dock, found decomposing, bloated, and drowned. He was in full uniform—SS Eagles and insignia still affixed to his lapel. An empty bottle of Remy Martin Louis XIII floated beside him in the dirty water. The dry dock was surrounded by office buildings and businesses. There was constant foot and vehicular traffic around it. It looked like nothing more than a nasty accident, and foul play would've been ruled out, but the body was found a block and a half from Daisy Lane.

Everyone in the SS knew of the years-long enmity between Rheinhardt and Brandt. Naturally, Rheinhardt fell under suspicion—until he produced an iron-clad alibi. In the hours immediately preceding the discovery of Brandt's body, he had been seen by at least fifteen witnesses, playing chess at Café Ruben, an upper-floor salon thick with smoke and retired Flemish military officers, all collaborators. He appeared in good spirits and more relaxed than he'd been in months, the men later said.

Everyone had a good time that evening, the Belgians testified.

Especially Rheinhardt.

His record—135 straight chess victories since 1940—remained unbroken.

"I may be disgraced, Herr Krieger," Rheinhardt said during his private audience with the general, who returned to Antwerp just *after* the investigation into Brandt's death was closed, as if he wanted nothing to do with it. "I may be disgraced, but I'm not aimless. If I'm allowed to expand the command of my port and my men, I will find what we're looking for. You know better than anyone how little time we have. I need all available resources for a proper search of the city and the region."

"And what am I supposed to tell Himmler?" Krieger said. "How long do you think I can keep equivocating?"

As long as it takes? Rheinhardt wanted to say. Instead he replied, "Tell him I'm a loyal servant of the Reich, of Germany, of Herr Hitler. I will stop at nothing to help us win this war." There was no "please." No real explanation. Just a declaration. *This is what I need, Krieger, and you are going to give it to me.*

"Listen, Rheinhardt," Krieger said, "you know we wanted to promote you. I recommended it myself. But frankly, you've been nothing but an embarrassment. The uranium is gone!"

"I will find it."

"And your superior officer is dead!"

"An unfortunate accident."

"Strange how fate favors you, Rheinhardt," said Krieger. "Especially when it comes to dead higher-ups."

Rheinhardt took a beat. "If fate really favored me, Herr Krieger, perhaps it would have disposed of Herr Brandt *before* he reassigned the men guarding Germany's most precious resource—not after."

Even Krieger gave a sharp breath of disbelief at such brazen remorselessness. "How can I possibly reward your failure with a medal and a promotion!" he exclaimed.

"Because to find what was stolen from us, I need full operational authority." He told Krieger precisely what he needed: to be made the SS commander of the Port of Antwerp. To have complete authority over the Gestapo, the SS, and the Belgian *Polizei* in northern Belgium. Unrestricted rights of search and seizure. Special dispensation for enhanced interrogation without oversight. "Nothing less than the security of our German nation is at stake."

"You've had operational authority," Krieger said. "And look what it cost us."

Rheinhardt didn't respond. "Have you been in touch with Saul Grunfell, sir?"

Krieger rolled his eyes. "I regret ever giving that man my number. Can I give him yours instead? He rings me five times a day, asking when the birdseed is coming."

Rheinhardt nodded curtly. "We need to begin work immediately on the power and exhaust upgrades to Zvart Haus, as discussed," he said.

"You want us to expand his power grid? We don't have the uranium!"

"When we get it, everything needs to be in place. New power generators. The expanded exhaust pipes. And all the copper we can get our hands on." When Rheinhardt saw that Krieger remained unconvinced, he pivoted to another, more ruthless tack. "The upgrade to Zvart Haus is a good and plausible reason you can offer Herr Himmler the next time you two speak. You can tell him we cannot begin the actual work until the expansion is done. That we're working as fast as possible. Assure him it's only a matter of time."

Krieger snickered, but there was unease in it. "That's some misplaced confidence, Rheinhardt. You want me to lie to Heinrich *Himmler*?"

"If we begin the power grid renovation, it would not be a lie, would it, sir? It would be the actual truth."

"And if you don't find it?" Krieger stayed sardonic, but his throat was dry. The words came out croaky. "We will both be executed. You understand that? It's not just your neck. It's mine too."

"Oh, I understand all too well, sir." Rheinhardt gave a slight nod. "That's why I'm asking for enhanced powers."

Krieger shook his head in nervous disbelief. "You've got some balls on you, Rheinhardt. Some fucking balls. What makes you think you'll ever see your uranium again?"

"Trust me, mein Herr. You yourself said how extraordinary it was that I found it in the first place. It's somewhere in Belgium. All I need is freedom to act."

"Needle in a haystack."

"A needle in a lump of hay a few grass blades deep."

"And those who took it from you?"

"Will be brought to swift and final justice, mein Herr."

"I thought you told me you would not start a war?"

"I was wrong," said Rheinhardt, cold as the reaper. "I will."

Rheinhardt finally had almost everything he wanted—and all it had taken was a public humiliation akin to a quartering. He was promoted to *Obersturmbannführer*—the SS equivalent of a lieutenant colonel—with full authority over all SS and SD operations in Antwerp and its vicinity. It wasn't *Standartenführer*, as he'd been promised in Liège, but it was good enough.

Upgrades at Zvart Haus began immediately: additional high-voltage lines to feed the cyclotron; new piping laid and buried underground to carry chemical fumes to the factories along the Olen canal; every system expanded to process the Congolese uranium—when it was found.

But despite the confident words Rheinhardt had thrown at Krieger, despite his blustering bravado, the red line remained unfaded—the uranium had vanished, and Rheinhardt had no idea where it was or who took it.

After another fruitless week, a despairing Rheinhardt decided to pay a visit to Grunfell. He made the trip to Zvart Haus alone, leaving Hubner to manage the flood of bureaucratic and political bullshit that had proliferated like fungus since his promotion. When Brandt had been in charge, Rheinhardt had rarely seen this side of operations in occupied Belgium.

But the Germans had deliberately constructed a labyrinthine, impermeable administration, with departments within the same division reporting to different ministries in Berlin. The SS, the Gestapo, and the secret Field Police all reported separately, rarely collaborating, and depending heavily on the Belgian *Polizei* to do most of their grunt work. Partnerships were discouraged. Actions were duplicated. And when things went wrong, the finger-pointing never stopped. It was everyone's fault, and no one's. Everyone was responsible—and no one. Rivalries bloomed where coordination should have. One team would arrest suspected partisans only to have the other unit release them for lack of paperwork—then arrest them again days later so they could claim the credit.

Now that he was in charge, Rheinhardt saw the insanity clearly and wanted no part of it. His loathsome duties had multiplied, while his nonexistent leads had all but vaporized. And every afternoon, Krieger called to ask if there was anything new to report, any good news he could bring Himmler.

Under Rheinhardt's direction, the Gestapo was searching every home where there'd been even a whisper of clandestine activity. They tore through basements, sheds, storage facilities, trucks, barns and back rooms. The official justification for such a widespread irrational sweep was Jews. Hitler's orders were clear: the Jewish question must be resolved—even in Belgium.

But Rheinhardt's efforts were proving fruitless.

There were no Jews. There were no African men.

And the trail to the missing barrels was cold.

How hard was it to find a black man in Belgium?

Impossible, as it was turning out.

How hard was it to find eight tons of uranium?

Even harder.

Even the Jews were absent.

So Rheinhardt made a decision—if he could not catch the thieves by their faces, he would catch them by their shadows. And for that, he needed Saul Grunfell.

"Oh my goodness, what happened to you?" a shocked Saul said by way of greeting when Rheinhardt entered his study and took off his coat and visor.

"I don't know what you mean," Rheinhardt said. But he knew. He must have lost ten kilos in the last few weeks.

"What happened to your hair?"

"Oh, that." Yes. There was that. Rheinhardt had gone prematurely and completely gray in the time it took to connect Saul to more power, in the time it took *not* to find the uranium. "It's of no consequence," he said, keeping the grim sigh out of his voice. "Tell me about the upgrade work. Is it proceeding well?"

"They're almost finished. But what use is it?"

"It'll be of use shortly. You've waited for this long. Be patient." *All of you have to be fucking patient*, Rheinhardt wanted to say, *while you sit here and watch me as I do all the fucking work.*

"Patient? Aren't we on the clock?"

"No one knows that better than me, Saul."

"But you still have no leads?"

"This isn't something you need to worry over." *Or that I wish to speak to you about.*

"I told you, I need fourteen weeks to make it happen."

"Yes, *yes*, you've *told* me." Rheinhardt felt each passing day like a stab wound. Every sunrise marked another Allied breakthrough in France, another meter of German retreat, another chance slipping away. Another day Grunfell wasn't working on the one thing that might still change the course of the war. "This brings me to the real reason I came," Rheinhardt said. "I need your Geiger machine."

"No," Grunfell said.

"Excuse me?"

"I said no. Ask Krieger for one."

"You know he doesn't have one."

"Maybe he can get one."

"Are you insane?" Rheinhardt said. "Do you want me to find the uranium or don't you? To find it, I need the Geiger. What do you even need it for? You've got nothing to do."

"Nothing to *do*?" Grunfell's tone was blistering. "My work hasn't stopped just because you haven't held up your end of the bargain. I'm still trying to leach yellowcake from the pissant uranium from Czechoslovakia."

Yellowcake. He remembered the flag of the yellow narcissus from the mast of *La Fortuna*. "Why is it called *yellow*cake?"

"Um . . . because it's yellow?" When Rheinhardt stared him down, Saul added flatly, "Bright yellow is the color uranium turns after oxidation. You saw it yourself in your marbled rock."

"Yes, yes." Rheinhardt became thoughtful for a moment. "And you can't work with your Czech ore without using the Geiger?"

"Are you joking?"

"Why would I be joking?"

"We use it constantly, to make sure we don't get contaminated."

"Are you *really* in danger of contamination with your one percent ore?"

Grunfell stared at him in disbelief and contempt.

"Yes, Rheinhardt," he said slowly. "Every day. Every minute. All of us who live and work in this house—especially down in the lab—are in danger of contamination from radioactive ore. The Geiger tells us when to scrub, when to shower, when to isolate. Dismiss it at your own peril."

"Duly noted—and duly dismissed," Rheinhardt said coldly. "You know as well as I do that without the Congolese uranium your so-called work is worthless. And without the Geiger, I can't find it." He stood. "So sit and relax, Grunfell. Take a load off. Read a book. Get some sun. You're looking a little gray yourself, frankly. And as you've just explained to me, you're nothing without your health." He put on his coat and waited. When Saul brought him the machine, he took it without a word, carried it to his car, and left.

For days afterward, Rheinhardt stood guard at the main checkpoint into Antwerp, waving the Geiger wand over every truck that entered, and every truck that left.

From morning till night, he walked through all the warehouses on Glaskaai. He drove with Hubner and a Gestapo contingent to every business that used fortified trucks—every farm, every house, every barn, every stable—Hubner hauling the generator-powered transformer, and Rheinhardt sweeping the wand in slow, furious arcs, hoping for a single irregular reading, a single jump of the needle.

But the needle remained unmoved.

Ten more days passed.

And then fourteen.

56

Tremelo

The woods gave way without warning, opening onto a gold meadow stretched across the flatlands. At its edge stood a long stone estate with weather-blackened shutters and a hipped slate roof. Its tall windows reflected the deep green of summer.

"It looks a little haunted," said Louise.

"No, no. The Baroness is a lovely woman," said Charlie.

"I'm not talking about the Baroness. I'm talking about her abode."

Even before they hopped out of the *Berceau*, the front door opened and a slender regal woman in her sixties stepped out, waving.

"I like that she's waving," said Louise. "Already seems more hospitable."

"Baroness Mathilde," Charlie said, stepping forward. "*Bonjour*."

"I know you," said the Baroness. "You came to me once in 1943." She smiled. "I never forget a face." She looked past Charlie into the *Berceau*. "Have you brought me more children?"

"No, Baroness," Charlie said. "But this is Louise."

"You introduced me like *I* was the child," Louise whispered sideways, elbowing Charlie. "Thanks a lot."

"A pleasure, ladies. How can I help you? Would you like to come inside? It's a balmy day for Belgium." She fanned herself. "Is it just you two?"

Charlie cleared her throat. "No, Baroness." Across the meadow, Fletcher and the others emerged from the trees. Zeus was running ahead.

Mathilde squinted into the distance. "Are they *all* with you?"

"Yes, Baroness."

Mathilde was quiet for a moment. "What happened?" she said dryly. "Did Verene kick you out?" Her mouth curved in a wry half-smile. "The Abbess is a tough old broad. But her heart is true. She's very protective of her nuns. And

I see men with you, young men with weapons—there's your whole problem in a nutshell."

Charlie offered a noncommittal shrug. They were about to ask this woman for shelter—best not to argue with her.

"You had business with the Reverend Mother?" Mathilde asked.

"We did," replied Charlie, and offered no further.

"Where are you girls from?"

"Herentals."

"Beautiful church there. Saint Waltrude. Why not go back home if you need a place to stay?"

"We need to be close to the abbey for a few days, Baroness."

"Why, is there some kind of trouble?"

"No trouble, Baroness," said Charlie. "Just a precaution."

"A precaution that needs sniper rifles and machine guns?"

Charlie said nothing.

"You can stay with me," the Baroness said. "But promise me you won't bring the war to my house. I've got trouble enough."

Why did everyone keep saying this to Charlie lately! War was everywhere. There was no getting away from it.

"Of course, Baroness."

"Stay as long as you need," Mathilde said, her mouth twisting. "I have room now. Before, I had hundreds of souls passing through. Not anymore."

"Here's one," said Charlie, extending her hand to Zeus, who'd run ahead of the others and now stood next to Charlie, disheveled and panting, his curls damp against his forehead. "This is Zeus."

"Hello, Zeus," said Mathilde. "I have three children with me at the moment. Two girls and a boy. Would you like to meet them?"

Zeus nodded, glancing at Ngomo, who was crossing the forecourt. "It's all right, Zeus," Ngomo said. "You go ahead. Go meet some kids."

Mathilde's brows lifted slightly at the sight of Ngomo. "Not quite what I expected," she said. "But all right."

"He's from the Congo," said Zeus. "That's in Africa."

"Ah. Well, *that* explains it," Mathilde said, though it explained nothing. She looked over the perspiring crew that trudged toward her. "How many of you *are* there?"

"Fifteen, Baroness."

"And Zeus makes sixteen?"

"Zeus makes fifteen," said Zeus.

"Half my house is shut off," Mathilde said. "I don't use it anymore, it's too big for me. The furniture's under sheets, and the place needs sweeping, but you can bunk there. You're welcome to use my kitchen, though I can't vouch for what you'll find in it." She took Zeus's hand, glancing over at the men and women standing close. "The boy can stay on my side of the house—with the other children. But I only have five bedrooms in the unused wing." She shrugged, then paused at the door. "I ask one thing—no radios," she said. "Not in the house, not near it. German DF trucks sweep the countryside daily. If you must transmit, walk three kilometers into the woods." With that, she left with Zeus.

The band stood in the forecourt—sweaty, hungry, sun-dazed. But for the first time, Charlie thought, they weren't unwelcome. No Alder Fontaine screaming at them. No Mother Verene weaponizing the Divine Office against them. No sawdust sleep at Vervaet's workshop. No single bed over a groaning floor—the only thing groaning in that tiny Bruges room. Her whole face lit up. The knot loosened inside her. She turned to Fletcher and smiled.

"*Kasteel* de Velde?" said Fletcher, smiling back. "I expected a proper castle—the name rather oversells it. Where are the battlements? The turrets? The moat?"

Why did she flush red? That was almost like flirting, right?

"Charlie, do you think there's a dungeon?" said Brigitte, leaning into Belvedere. "I'd like to be in the *cachot* with him."

"Behave, Gitta," said Rafael. "Or I'll translate it."

"*S'il vous plaît*—every word." She squeezed Belvedere's arm.

"Rider, where did she say she wants to be with me?" Belvedere asked.

"In the dirt, Belvy. In the dirt."

"But seriously—what the fuck," said Briggs. "Fourteen of us across *five* beds? That's not even nice. It's vaudeville with a tragic ending."

"Not just vaudeville," said Rafael. "It's Moulin Rouge. But with a tragic ending." He laughed.

"Briggs, a minute ago, you were going to six services in the abbey chapel," said Belvedere. "And now you're complaining you've got half a castle to yourself? Typical Yank. Never satisfied."

"Maybe we can rotate through the beds," said Rafael. "After two weeks, we switch. I call dibs on bedroom one." His grin at Louise was insuppressible.

"Who the hell do you think you are to call dibs on anything, Sergeant?" said Belvedere. "We have a commander. He assigns your sleeping quarters. By rank, I hope."

"Not by size?" said Briggs, and guffawed.

All eyes turned to Fletcher. He looked so uncomfortable, Charlie almost wanted to throw her arms around him. To hide his embarrassment, he put on a mock serious face. In English and French he said, "Why don't we take in the lay of the land before we duel to the death over beds."

"There's *nothing* I'd rather duel to the death over," Rafael said.

"Hear, hear," said Briggs.

"Hear, hear," said Belvedere.

"Belvedere!"

Bien dit, thought Charlie, her hooded gaze narrowed on Fletcher.

The house was dignified and large, its bones old Flemish nobility. Ivy clung to the exterior wall of the west wing and drooped over the windows. In the great hall stood a grand piano.

Hawk dropped his gear, dusted the bench with one swipe and lifted the fallboard. As soon as his fingers touched the keys, he began to play the most exquisite melody.

Wolski gaped at him, tears forming. "Who are you?" he said, coming to stand near Hawk, watching his hands. "Why are you playing me Chopin?"

"Um—because it's one of the most beautiful melodies ever composed?" said Hawk. "Nocturne in C sharp Minor."

"Where did you learn to play like that?" asked Wolski.

"It's out of tune," Hawk said. "It sounds terrible."

"You mean sublime. I thought all you knew how to do was shoot Germans."

"He has many gifts," said Hildi. It was the first time she'd spoken all day.

Fletcher, as it turned out, was right to delay the duel over five beds. In her count, Mathilde forgot to include the maid's quarters, the guest rooms, the caretaker's wing, and the groundskeeper's room. These rooms were plainer and smaller, tucked on the first floor instead of the second, and not as well appointed, but still, they were rooms. With doors. With locks. With beds.

They made a home of it fast, working with great purpose. They stripped the sheets off the furniture, swept away the dust, stacked coal by the stove, coaxed the old furnace back to life. Wolski got the hot water running, Rafael made a ring of stones for a firepit out back. Charlie found a pantry with jars still sealed, a wheel of cheese, four potatoes, some old bread, and a cellar full of bottles of red. Briggs went to chop firewood. Mireille tagged along, just to tell him how strong and brave he was. Every time she cooed, he chopped harder and faster. "Briggs will clear the entire forest if she doesn't stop egging him on," said Charlie. "Mireille! Enough out of you! There isn't enough wood in all of Belgium!"

There was a beat of silence. Fletcher and Rafael exchanged a grin. "Those two should really focus their efforts on other things," said Rafael.

"Let Briggs chop wood," said Louise. "There'll be no Mireille left if he gets to her in the state he's in."

Lucky Mireille, Charlie thought.

They ran the bath as hot as the old pipes would allow. It took a while to fill, and while the other girls bathed, Charlie took Fletcher and Wolski to find the black market. Mathilde sent them to a tavern keeper in Tremelo who sold eggs, cheese, bread, and cigarettes—even salt cod. She told them they could have milk from her goat in the mornings. She had one goat, two apple trees, four hens, and some potatoes. "*And a partridge in a pear tree*," Fletcher said in a singsong tone, and Charlie said, "What?"

"Never mind. Doesn't seem like enough food. How does the Baroness feed herself and the children without ration books?"

Charlie explained that Mathilde traded her heirlooms—jewelry, linens, silverware; the remains of her aristocratic life—for food. She knew everyone in Tremelo: the smuggler, the baker's cousin, the woman who secretly kept pigs.

"I wouldn't mind a pig," Fletcher said.

"I'd kill a Nazi for a pig," said Wolski. "Hell, I'd do it anyway. But I would love a pig."

Two hours later, they returned with the goods. Charlie was famished. She looked forward to building a fire outside, opening a bottle of rum from the Congo, maybe even grinding some of *La Fortuna*'s actual coffee beans from Kivu. Smoking for pleasure, not panic. Their first proper evening together, all of them, without the shadow of the impossible task, or Rheinhardt's henchmen. They could sing, joke, tell stories. The job was done. For now, they had a semblance of peace. She was really looking forward to the night around the fire.

But back at Kasteel, there was no one in sight to partake in Charlie's ideal evening.

It was only eight, not even dark yet.

"Where is everyone?" Charlie said, losing some of her good humor.

"Best not to ask," replied Fletcher.

"What—everyone?" She got indignant. "What about food?"

"Probably the last thing anyone's thinking about."

"Well, *I'm* thinking about it," Charlie said. Wow. Just wow.

"Hmm."

"Why did we go all the way to Tremelo if no one wants to eat?"

"I imagine they'll be hungry later."

"I'm going to eat all the food," she said in a huff. "The whole wheel of cheese. I won't leave them any. That'll show them."

"Yes," Fletcher said evenly. "That will certainly show them."

She turned to ask Wolski to build a fire, but he had vanished.

"Even Wolski abandoned us?" Charlie said. "Nice."

"I guess it's just you and me tonight, Charlotte," said Fletcher, lowering his voice a few notches.

"Just great," she said. Seeing the look in his eye, she wished she could say she wasn't as hungry herself anymore. But who was she kidding. She was *starving*. They hadn't eaten since morning—right before being expelled from a house of God.

Fletcher built the fire, while she built dinner. There was cheese and bread and some cod. He opened a bottle of rum *and* a bottle of red. They drank wine from thick porcelain cups she found in the kitchen and traded stories about all the things they used to eat in abundance in their separate corners of the world and wished they could eat again. He talked of elk steak with sage and juniper berries. She talked of chocolate. "Belgian chocolate is the best," she said.

"Oh, sure," he said. "Everything's better in Belgium." He smiled. He was lying on his side by the fire, looking up at her, a cup of rum between them on the stone patio. She sat cross-legged near his head.

"We haven't had chocolate in years," Charlie said. "The Nazis eat it all now."

"The bastards."

They drank from their common cup.

"I have chocolate," Fletcher said.

"No, you don't."

"I do," he said. "It's in my pack. Part of my K-ration. It's up in the room. Should we go get some?"

She swooned. Rum and wine and fire and Fletcher were heady stuff. He was so handsome, his deep purple intoxicated, intoxicating gaze blinking so purposefully at her. "Are you trying to lure me to your room with chocolate, Fletcher Gray?"

"Yes?" he said, like a question.

"Okay, let's go."

They didn't move. The fire was warm, and he was lying on a blanket, resting his head on his hand. He reached up and caressed her face. "Technically," he said, nudging the cup of rum aside, "I don't have to try that hard, right? Because I already kissed you. Twice."

"Technically, yes," she said, rocking toward him. "But the first time doesn't count."

"Our first kiss doesn't count?"

"No, because up in *that* castle you used *Schadenfreude* as seduction."

"And that doesn't count? What about in the Silver Fox?"

"It was the Silver Steed, and there I kissed *you*."

"It wasn't Steed," he murmured. "It was the Silver Heart."

"Not Heart," she said.

"No?"

She nearly groaned.

He edged closer. His breath smelled of red wine and smoke.

His face was nearly at her folded knees. "So I have to start from scratch is what you're telling me?" His eyes were overflowing with tenderness and rum lust. Overflowing with everything a girl who hadn't been touched in years would want a man's eyes to be filled with when he gazed up at her by the firelight.

She pitched forward to kiss him and toppled, falling over him. Her breasts swiped his face. He caught her and held her to him. "If I speak your name with all the feeling I can muster," he whispered, slurring slightly, his fanned-out palms pressing her to him, "will you give yourself to me?"

His lips found hers. Falling into each other, they kissed by the fire.

"I will give myself to you even if you say nothing," said Charlie.

57

Behold, the Man

Upstairs, in the corner room Fletcher had claimed for them, the bed was the biggest Charlie had ever seen. All her life she'd slept on singles—and, in the last few years, on the ground in the woods, and in old mills. In sheds and barns, in railcars, in Herentals, behind the stores, at Omloop's shop, in the *Berceau*.

Even a narrow mattress was a luxury during the occupation.

This bed was fit for kings.

And princesses and runaways and refugees and queens.

It was so soft, so white. The coverlet was itchy, but the quilt underneath was made of hope—that thing with feathers.

She lit two candles and set them on the side table, then threw off the coarse cover, took off her clothes, and fell back onto the down.

"Fletcher. . . ?" she whispered, raising her arms above her head. "Where are you? Come to me."

When he undressed and climbed over her, naked, and she put her palms on his bare chest and felt his steaming body over hers, she thought someone had pushed her off a cliff.

Their first time together, they barely spoke, except to say *yes*, and *please*. She moaned quietly, as if she didn't want to be either improper or impolite. She cried out into the pillows, her muffled ecstasy contained. The windows were open, and a cool June breeze blew over her parched thighs.

"I wasn't waiting for you," she said.

"I know."

"I wasn't."

"I believe you." He was kissing her face, her wet clavicle bones.

"I wasn't starving for you or longing for you or thirsting for you."

"I know." He bent his face to her breasts, his lips on her so soft, so gentle.

"I wasn't hoping for you with every breath in my soul."

"I know, Charlie," he said, his mouth on her stomach, his hands caressing her thighs. "Nor I for you."

"I *know*," she said, and tried very hard not to let him hear her cry.

"I like you more because you didn't instantly fall for me," Charlie murmured, stroking his chest, his stomach.

"Funny, I like you less for the same reason—ouch!" Fletcher said when she pinched him. He tickled her lightly. "How do you know I didn't instantly fall for you? You don't know. Maybe I was just playing it cool."

"Were you?"

"You'll have to keep guessing, won't you? A boy doesn't kiss and tell."

Pause. "How do you know *I* didn't instantly fall for you?" Charlie asked.

"Did you?" He sounded delighted.

"A girl doesn't kiss and tell."

"Oh, yeah? Can the boy get it out of the girl?"

"Well, she is certainly open to him trying."

And afterward, sweltering, gasping—"You call that trying?"

Charlie didn't want to admit it to him, not even during their rupturing love, but she did fall in love with him a little bit when she first saw him walking up to her—his face camo'ed with greasepaint, his clothes bloody, his boots full of marsh and grime, a helmet on his head, a rifle in his hands.

She'd been so upset with him for upending her carefully wrought plans that she didn't want to confess—even now—how her heart pounded at the sight of him searching for someone like himself and finding someone like her instead.

I've been alone so long, she whispered.

"Sometimes by accident you fall upon grace that turns out to be the only place you belong," he said, his head pressed into her stomach.

I saw you, Charlie thought, and the ground shifted under my feet. And now—no ground at all. *Am I falling or flying? Am I drowning or swimming?*

Charlie and Fletcher. Neither good at letting go. Both quiet. Serious. Self-contained. Wired for strategy and silence, self-preservation, defense, protection.

Until the barricades broke.

"The tenderness is supposed to come *after* the fire," she said.

"For us, just the opposite," he said. "The fire has come after the tenderness."

Her lips grazed the rough stubble of his jaw.

"Don't do it," he said. "I'm already helpless."

Everything was beautiful. His body, a lived-in thing covered in cuts and scars, soft in the tips of his fingers, soft in his lips, in his hair, in his liquid lavender eyes—and hard everywhere else.

She moved down his lean torso, the skin below his navel taut and warm, the centerline of dark hair tapering, summoning her trembling hands.

"I'm already yours, Charlie . . ."

"Tell me something about you."

"Tell me something about *you*."

"I had a happy childhood," he said, pausing slightly, as if holding a part of it back. "I had a good life. My parents loved each other. I was close to them both—and close to my grandfather, my mother's father. My siblings and I had years of endless outdoor adventures, fishing, hunting, swimming."

"What were their names?"

"Evelyn and Nate." He paused again. "And my cousin Stella." Taking a breath, he went on. "The four of us helped run the ranch, learned to shoot, rode horses, took care of animals. Played a lot of games."

Charlie held him closer. "Me too," she said quietly. "Until the Germans came, growing up on a flower farm was a blessed life. Even my now absentee mother was a wonderful mother back then. I know it must seem to you, to everybody, that Louise is a happier person than I am, but honestly, Fletcher, I'm only miserable because I once had so much, and it was all taken from me.

"But Lou suffered. She was an only child and extremely close to her father. When he died, it devastated her. She was left with her grieving, inward mother, and when they moved to Herentals, she didn't know anyone. Her mother worked all the time, and Louise was left fatherless and alone. When we became friends, she spent more time in Lillehaven than she did at her own house."

"She's like your sister."

"Yes," said Charlie. "She is like my sister."

"Did Louise love Fitz?" Fletcher asked.

Now that she'd seen Louise with Rafael, Charlie knew the truth.

"She did not." Why had it taken her so long to acknowledge such a simple but bitter truth? Because Charlie resented Louise for not returning her brother's love. She could have married him. They could have been sisters.

Next to her family, Charlie loved Louise most in the world.

No wonder she felt such hostility toward Rafael. He showed Charlie—in the starkest terms—that Fitz and Louise could never be.

"So it was just you, Fitz and Louise?"

And just like that, Fletcher's question refocused her on all the wrong things, even when naked in bed with him.

She took a breath. "It was me, Fitz, Louise, and Paolo."

"Paolo?"

"My older brother."

Fletcher didn't speak. His arms tightened around her.

"He was two years older. All of us were two years apart. Paolo was born in 1917, me 1919, Fitz 1921, and Louise 1923."

"Do you want to tell me about him?"

"Not really," she said. "It'll make me sad, and I've been sad for too long. I just want to be happy for a few precious seconds."

"I hear you," he said, kissing her. "But maybe if you tell me, your sadness will be halved."

"I don't think mine will be halved," said Charlie, her hand curling into a fist before she could stop it. "But yours might be doubled."

The furious fields raged with rattling wind, rumbling wild with thunder and the threat of bloodshed. The fields weren't safe for orphans like Louise and stray children like Charlie. The whole country wasn't safe.

The docks strained with the mud of violence.

Another train was pulling out of Mechelen.

Sleepless hours passed.

Their love was wordless, an iron cauldron, lid rattling from the percolating heat. There was almost an unbearable silence before release.

The nights were so short in June in northern Belgium. Astronomical dawn, nautical dawn, civil dawn—then actual cursed dawn would be too soon upon them.

She whispered his name when she thought he was drifting away from her.

"I'm not asleep." But his eyes were closed.

"John Fletcher Beauregard Du Soleil Gray," she whispered, creeping up to his throat, putting her mouth on his warm and pulsing skin, "I will always choose you."

"And I will always choose *you*."

She could hear his heartbeat.

She took his head and gently laid it against her breast so he could hear hers.

"I always hear your heart, Charlie," he whispered. "I heard it from the start."

"You don't want to talk to me, Fletcher?"

He was quiet. "I'm so happy right now. Sometimes I don't know what to say." He shrugged, stretched out his body, lit a cigarette. "There have been times in the past, with other girls," he said, "when I believed love was the language of weakness."

She thought he was joking. "Really?"

He didn't reply at first. "Yes. Sometimes."

"Do you think so with me?" she asked in a whisper. She didn't want an answer. Not a truthful one anyway.

"I don't know," he said, in the voice of a man who didn't know how to lie and didn't want to learn while in bed with her.

"Do you come from a long line of people who've been made weak by love, Fletcher Gray?"

"Let's just say I come from a line of people who do things you wouldn't think lovers do," he said. "Or perhaps shouldn't do. Or perhaps," he added, "they do things that are so outrageous, that it doesn't seem like love at all."

Charlie held her breath. "What did they do?"

Fletcher didn't reply. "Nothing," he said at last, stubbing out his cigarette and turning to her. "The same way you don't want to talk about Paolo, I don't want to talk about this." He ran his fingers down the length of her body, his hand gliding over her bare hip, fondling her buttocks. "You're so supple," he whispered. "You're like a soft panther." He fondled her breasts, lowered his head, kissed her nipples.

"Maybe this is what they did," she said, herself weak from his love. "Maybe this is what led to all the other things."

"Maybe." He kissed her.

"Is that what *you're* afraid of? Losing control?" Their bare bodies lay fused together in the damp warmth.

"A little bit."

She didn't want it to be true. She wanted him to lose all control with her. She turned her face away, fought back tears.

"Charlie," he whispered, "I'm really happy we got to have this. That you gave me this. Gave me yourself."

"Me too, Fletcher."

"And we'll always have Bruges."

"Yes, no one can take Bruges and the onion blanket away from us."

"Or the boat ride we took on the canal in the morning."

Smiling, wiping her face, she threw her arms around him. "Fletcher, you funny lovely boy, you can't be already feeling nostalgic about Bruges! We took that boat ride just this morning."

He laughed, nuzzling her neck. "I'm just afraid it will never come again," he whispered.

They had held hands and sat close, watching the city drift by. As the ride was ending, the boatman said to her, *When a man takes you on a boat ride through*

Bruges, he might be in love with you. But when he takes you on two dozen boat rides, he might be in love with Bruges.

She'd melted into a soft puddle of joy at the time, but now wondered if she had misunderstood. Was the boatman saying the man by her side was the first kind—or the second? And tonight, when she dared ask him, Fletcher brought her to him and murmured, "Choices, choices, why can't both things be true?"

The exquisite night was ending.

Charlie couldn't save herself from his hold on her—and didn't want to. Unlike him, she had lost all control. *He* was the holy one. He was the angel. The earth wasn't safe for him.

But when he was with her, she felt safe.

Because that's what angels do, she heard herself whisper into his chest. *They fly through the clouds. Even broken angels.*

"I'm not broken," he said. "Well, maybe a little. Like you."

They said almost nothing during, and usually not much after.

But once, here is what he said in the afterglow: "Do you know how hard it will be to get Zeus to Lisbon via the Comet Line? It's two thousand kilometers. And I don't even know if we'd be able to go from Brussels to Paris—I don't know our troop locations. If we have to go around France, south to Marseille, that'll probably add two hundred kilometers. How far can we expect to move in a day? Twenty kilometers at most? Thirty if by train. But to walk through the Pyrenees? Much slower. It'll take me 220 days to get Zeus to Lisbon. Seven months! And the Congo? Seven months to get them to safety. January 1945. Could the war be over by then?"

"Fletcher," she whispered, "are you leaving me and going to Lisbon?"

"No," he said, closing his eyes. "Not yet."

She was nearly drifting in bliss, deep in his arms, when she heard him murmuring above her head. He must have thought she'd fallen asleep.

She'd fallen all right.

Late have I loved you, he whispered.

I hungered and thirsted for you.

You touched me and set me on fire.

You cried out to me and shattered my deafness.

You were radiant and resplendent, you put an end to my blindness.

Late have I loved you, so old and so new.

You were fragrant, I drew in my breath.

I tasted you.

Late have I loved you.

58

The Road to Louise

Louise sat naked in Rafael's lap, flush against him, breast to chest, his back pressed hard against the headboard. Pillows and blankets were everywhere. She was burning. His hands caressed her bare back from her neck to her thighs while his mouth was at her throat. Her entire self was swallowed up—by his legs, his arms, his mouth, his eyes, his heart, his soul, his *everything.*

And God, was there everything.

"I recognized a fellow traveler when I laid my eyes on you," he murmured.

"Why didn't you warn me how dangerous you were?" she whispered.

"I saw with my own body that you are the rarest of all things: *a whole sex, condensed into one form.*"

He melted her flesh and liquified her bones. They were both gasping.

He clawed at her like he wanted to tear her apart.

And then he was *out.* Unconscious on the white sheets, naked, splayed on his back, taking up the whole bed like a child making angels in the snow. She lay on her side, tucked into his arm, her eyes open, her body humming. She didn't feel safe. She didn't feel saved. His hand rested on her hip, heavy and warm. She didn't move away from him. Outside, a steam train wailed faintly, a long, mournful cry. Inside, a door creaked and footsteps passed, followed by a low male voice and a tittering female one. Wolski with Maxine. Margot never laughed.

Louise floated into unconsciousness herself. The evening breeze rustled the curtains, cooled the room.

After she came to, she softly kissed his pulsing neck, nuzzled his stubbled cheek. He didn't stir. She leaned over him and bounced her heavy breasts into his face, pressed her soft flesh into his mouth. A few seconds later, he moved his head so he could inhale. "Loosha," he murmured, his hand on her hip repositioning her. "I need one minute . . ."

"You shan't have it," she said. "Did you come here for rest and relaxation or did you come here to take no prisoners?"

They remained in their room for days. They crept out at night, when everyone else was tucked away and they could sneak down into the kitchen of the cavernous Gothic love-drenched house and find something to eat.

"It's like a bordello in here," Louise murmured to him back upstairs in their room. "How do you think Mathilde feels about it? That every room in her house is flooded with carnal impropriety?"

"I'll show you carnal impropriety," he said, lifting her off her feet.

All the air in the room had been exhaled by her moans.

"Why do you keep me at arm's length?" he asked in the afterglow.

"I don't know if we can be any closer, Rafa."

"But why do you want to resist me, Lou?"

"How can I," she said, "when you use that caressing voice on me. When you graze me with your lips and set me on fire."

"I don't think you love me," said Rafael.

What are you talking about, she wanted to say. Can you not see who I am when I'm with you?

"Would you love me if you thought the world were ending tomorrow?" asked Rafael.

"No," Louise said.

"You wouldn't love me then without limits or restraint?"

"No," she repeated. *Restraint?*

"You wouldn't give me everything?"

"No."

"I knew it. But I'd give you everything."

"I wouldn't take it." She was lying. She just wanted to protect herself the only way she knew how. Through pretense.

They stared at each other. "I wish the world were ending tomorrow," he whispered.

"No, you don't," said Louise, raising her arms over her head. "You want this to be all we'll ever have?" She gave herself to him. What else could she do? He came at her, with song and guns blazing, crushing her against walls and floors, pinning her down between rocks and hard places. His body entered her body. His heart entered her heart. She had no choice but to wave her white flag. He left no other possibilities for her.

He seduced her with his words first.

And then he seduced her with the rest of him.

"I did not seduce *you, mon amour*," he said, tangled in her limbs and lips. "*You* have the dark powers. You summon the angels *and* the devils, beautiful girl. You've taken my free will from me. I have no choice but to be in your thrall."

"I was on the road to Louise," he said, "and I didn't know it. I thought it was just woods. But it was a road that led me to you." He kissed her. "As if you were my fate."

He whispered her name, like he was making love to it while he was making love to her. *Loosha. Louise. You're full of dazzling grace.*

She didn't fall for him like a feather drifting down. She fell like a Molotov dropped into a bone-dry field, fanned by the southern wind.

Come into me, she whispered, sobbing.

Blessed angels!

When he entered her, it was like he opened a door to another life.

Am I blessed or cursed? I'm so inflamed I can't even tell.

"Love me," Rafael whispered.

She held him inside her body.

"Give yourself to me."

"I'm here."

"No. *All* of yourself to me."

"I'm yours, Rafael."

They had become holy in their daily acts. She thought even Mother Verene would be proud.

"Do you want to know about me?"

"What else is there to know, Rafa?" she said. "I know everything. You're beautiful. You're kind. You make love to me with a hunger like you just learned to love. You make me feel brand new."

"Do you want to tell me about you?"

"There's nothing to tell," she said. "I'm only twenty years old. I've barely lived. I'm still with my mother. I'm an only child. I wanted to go to university, but then Germans, and Charlie, and . . ." She caressed his face, touched his lips. "I came of age during the war," she said quietly. "I haven't learned yet what I'm supposed to be. Some women become what they were born for. And some never get a chance to."

"I really hope you get a chance to, Loosha," he whispered.

"Me too, Rafa. Me too."

He gave me himself. Louise was breathless on their bed. And I knelt down and took it. Who wants to tell me I'm wrong? Go ahead. Go live your perfect loveless life. And I will live my imperfect life, full of love. *They might both be equally brief,* Louise whispered, bending to him, *with one* big *difference. I have you, and you have me, and we walk hand in hand among the lilies.*

59

Sisyphus

A desperate Rheinhardt sat in his office, door ajar, sliding his loaded Luger back and forth across the desk. He slept with the gun now. Walked the streets with his fingers curled around the grip.

A cool draft slipped through the window frame. Hubner had taped the corner last week, but the wind found its way in. A filing cabinet got stuck every time it opened, swollen from damp. Baert Haus was warping.

Everything was.

Very soon, Erich von Rheinhardt would have no moves left to make.

That time was coming.

A shadow appeared in the doorway.

"What do you want?" Rheinhardt said without looking up.

"Sir . . . please let me help you."

"You don't have enough to do? Did you review the sabotage reports from the rail lines? Reroute enough diesel for the generators at Zvart? Make sure our field generator is cranked to run the Geiger? We'll be going out again in a few minutes. You're full up, Hubner. Get to it."

Somewhere outside, a pane of glass shattered. The sound of running boots. Then nothing.

"Please, sir." Hubner stepped inside, uninvited, and crossed to the desk. "Tell me what you're looking for. Maybe I can approach it from a different angle."

Rheinhardt knew he must look a fright—lips white, hands unsteady, uncombed white hair damp with sweat. He hadn't shaved in days—a lapse that once would have humiliated him. He'd begun to notice, with some horror, the sour odor of his own body. He who had prided himself on his fastidiousness. Even the pistol gleamed too brightly in his hands, as though it had replaced him as the keeper of order.

Baert Haus, once silent and sharp-edged, now stank faintly of liniment and ozone and—he inhaled—something else. An acrid smell of smoke. A week ago, he'd spent the entire afternoon breathing in what he swore was burning wood, certain that something in the walls was smoldering. Hubner smelled nothing. "There's no such odor, sir," he had said gently, his tone containing something worse than denial—pity.

Rheinhardt didn't mention it again.

But tonight it was unmistakably there again.

Yet to *that*, Hubner was oblivious.

"You know what your *problem* is, Hubner?" Rheinhardt said. "There are many, but this is the heart of it. You think you're always one lucky insight away from solving everything—one Eureka moment from changing your fate. I've watched you do this for ten years, and I'm here to tell you—you are mistaken. Let *that* be your lucky insight. Your fate is to be unlucky." *And mine too.*

Hubner inclined his head. "My goal is to serve you, sir. Always. I have no other ambitions. That you allow me to help you at all means I have been quite lucky indeed." He didn't move. After a few moments, he pulled up a chair and sat. "What are you looking for?" he said quietly. "Tell me. What was taken from you?"

The question hung suspended between them.

Hubner—faithful, irritating, ever-present—with his constant expression of solicitude and sympathy. Rheinhardt had carried the secret alone for so long. The loss of the barrels had become so excruciating, his spine was splintering under the weight of his failure.

He didn't realize he was speaking until minutes had passed, and he heard his own voice unspooling into the room—Ngomo, *La Fortuna*, uranium, Grunfell, sixty barrels—and saw Hubner's stunned, pale face.

For a few loaded minutes, neither of them moved or spoke.

"I'm trusting you with my whole life, Hubner," said Rheinhardt.

"And I won't let you down. Now—tell me about the reinforced trucks we've been searching. The ones we've been testing with the radiation wand. In them lies the answer, sir, I'm sure of it. We just haven't found it yet."

"No shit," said Rheinhardt. What a relief it was to have shared his burden. He felt thirty barrels lighter.

Hubner began to pace, moving like a pendulum across the room.

Rheinhardt watched him—blinking, blinking . . .

60

Oars in the Water

The summer days and nights in Tremelo stretch long and golden, a story lived, not a story told.

Hawk plays aching piano for hours, and Hildimar sits next to him on the bench, watching his long fingers pound and glide through chords and intervals, interludes and adagios, diminished majors and augmented minors. Chopin, Schubert, Shostakovich, Schumann.

And while he plays, Brigitte puts on a red dress from a pile of old clothes she has found at the Kasteel, and makes Belvedere dance with her in the great hall. He grumbles he has four left feet. She doesn't care.

"We're in public," he says. "All civilized beings should care."

Rafael translates: "He loves you. Says there's no one else like you. He wants to take you upstairs."

Brigitte grabs him by the hand and leads the way.

"Why—is it something I said?"

"Yes, Belvy," Rafael calls after them, Louise on his lap, listening to Hawk render the love of Liszt in a largo. "It's something you said."

In the stream where they swim and wash, fish dart among the rocks in the crystal cold water. Immediately, the men devise a game. Each gets a line and worm. No hook, no rod. Who can catch a fish the fastest? The girls watch the boys struggle for an hour, and finally, Brigitte has had enough. She throws herself into the water and grabs the fish with her bare hands—no worm, no hook, no line, no problem.

"That's how she caught you too, Belvy," says Briggs.

"Unfortunately, and rarely for you, correct," says Belvedere with a mock sigh.

* * *

Charlie watches Fletcher teach Zeus how to play chess. He is so patient. Ngomo sits nearby, too—absorbing, just being. It's clear he likes being out in the sun. He doesn't often get that chance here. Charlie wants to tell him to get back inside—*Hide Ngomo, hide*—but she feels so bad for him. He's always hiding. It must be so oppressive. He watches Zeus with an expression that makes Charlie look away. There's so much affection and anxiety in his face. She turns her attention to Fletcher. Much simpler—happier.

"Pawns don't look like much, Zeus, but they can win you the game if you know what you're doing," says Fletcher.

"But I don't know what I'm doing," says Zeus.

"Yeah, they probably won't win you the game, then," Fletcher says, ruffling the boy's head. "Control the center," he explains, pointing to the board. "Own E4 and D4, and you own the game."

"How do I know which is E and which is D?" asks Zeus.

"That's one of the things you'll have to learn." And then: "Knights out first."

"The things that look like horsies?"

"Horsies—exactly. Develop the horsies, while the bishops wait. Open with purpose."

Zeus scrunches his brow to show he has purpose. He takes Fletcher's pawn and looks up, proud.

"Very good, Zeus. Keep going."

He's seducing her with softness, gentle humor, compassion. *Don't you know what you're doing to me?* Charlie wants to yell. *Why are you being like this?*

She wakes from a nightmare. He takes her into his arms, brings her to his chest, against his beating heart. "Still here," Fletcher says. "Still real."

None of this is real, she wants to say. *Just a sleight of hand. Don't you feel it, too?*

In the morning, she steals his military vest and poses in front of the mirror, naked, brushing her hair. The vest barely covers her high hips and is open in the front, revealing her to him fully in the reflection—the freckles between her breasts, the large brown nipples, the long strong legs. Hers is a body of a woman, yes, but a woman who has not stopped moving since 1940.

Fletcher stares at her like she's undone the laws of physics.

"You want it back?" she says, smiling.

"Never."

Fletcher stands alone at the window, staring out at the woods. The sun has just set. She comes up behind him, wraps her arms around his waist, rests her cheek on his back. "Don't go quiet on me now," she whispers.

"I'm saving all my words for later," he says, squeezing her hands.

"Ha," she says. "Later, you speak even less."

"I think I'll have to go soon," he says. His voice is so sad. "Take Ngomo and Zeus. Wolski won't be happy to leave Maxine and Margot. They adore him."

"I know how they feel."

He turns and embraces her, his long, strong arms holding her close. "I can't explain everything, Charlie," Fletcher says. "But I'm constantly afraid someone's going to catch a glimpse of Ngomo. Or that the Baroness will slip up to one of her friends, or the other kids will find new homes and casually mention a black man lives in this house. *Something*." He looks acutely uneasy. Outside, cicadas click in the grass, a static, electrical rhythm whirring beneath the quiet.

"I know," she says, swallowing hard before forcing herself to add, "You should go."

He relents. "I'll stay a few more days. I'll ask Ngomo not to go into Mathilde's part of the house."

"Teach him how to play chess, Fletch. He wants to learn. He can play with Zeus when you're on the road."

"That'll take me some time. To teach them both."

"So stay a few more days. To teach them. Then go."

"Okay," he says. "But just a few more days, Charlie."

"Yes, Fletcher. Just a few more days."

They lie on a blanket under the trees, not speaking. It's sunny, it's warm, so unlike Belgium. She jumps to her feet.

"Charlie, where are you going? Just sit. For a second." He holds her wrist.

"We've sat for two hours."

"It's been literally five minutes." Fletcher laughs. "Did it *feel* like two hours, Charlotte Fontaine?"

She laughs too.

"Go," he says, covering his grin with the crook of his arm. "I can't with you."

"And I can't with you too," she says, crouching down and kissing his face before running off.

Ngomo comes and perches by Fletcher's side. They watch Zeus play tag with Wolski, Margot, and Maxine. Zeus is fast. "Maybe if Wolski put down his map, he'd catch him," says Fletcher.

A flicker of a smile crosses Ngomo's face, then vanishes.

"Fletcher," he says. "Wolski tells me you're planning to take me somewhere else soon?"

"It's not safe here for you, Ngomo. You know that."

"Oh, I know," Ngomo says. "It's not particularly safe out there either. Long journey. Treachery. Enemies. Danger."

Fletcher sits up and lights a cigarette. He can't talk to Ngomo about this lying down.

"You plan to get me and Zeus to Lisbon?" Ngomo says. "Take Wolski and Rafael? Hawk too, for protection?"

"Yes," Fletcher says, extremely reluctantly.

Ngomo finishes his cigarette before he speaks again.

"Here's the part that must be unclear to you, Lieutenant Gray," says Ngomo. "I know that your commander Jonathan Reed must have made me your mission—your secondary mission, I hope. But I, Ngomo Kasonga, also have a commander. And I also have a mission. I serve the King. Only he or his emissary can change my mission objectives."

"Ngomo, Leopold has made his wishes extremely clear. To Churchill, no less! He wants you out."

Ngomo shakes his head. "That was before. When he thought the uranium was in German hands. Circumstances have changed. I'm still on duty. I won't leave until I know his cargo is safe."

"Is there a timeframe for this knowledge you hope to acquire?" Fletcher says. "What if the war goes on for years? And if they continue to search for you, then it's only a matter of time before they find you. It's not if. It's when, Ngomo."

"Am I a grandmother knitting on a porch?" says Ngomo. "I am a soldier in a king's army. In fact, in your own military terminology, I happen to be a lieutenant colonel. As such, I'm a member of the Allied Expeditionary Force. Same as Wolski, same as Rafael."

"Are you pulling *rank* on me, Ngomo?" Fletcher almost smiles.

"You are the commander of this mission," Ngomo says, tilting his head in deference. He pauses. "But as long as the primary mission remains, your secondary mission must wait."

A long look passes between them. Fletcher can't explain why he's so determined to get Ngomo out of Belgium, and Ngomo looks as if he wants to ask him about it but doesn't. Both men exhale, retreat. Somewhere behind them, Zeus laughs. "Ngomo, Ngomo . . ."

Fletcher watches Ngomo run toward the boy and chase him to the river. His heart hurts.

They play games to fill their days, fierce competitive contests—because they're soldiers and their women are fighters.

Charlie suspends a potato on a rope from a tree branch, nudges it into motion, and from ten meters away, they each get three tries with Fletcher's trench knife. The soldiers shred the potatoes with their lethal throws. Afterward the potatoes are boiled, fried, devoured.

Ngomo doesn't join in. He watches from the side. Next to him, Zeus, who wants desperately to try, doesn't even ask. He says instead, "Maybe someday I can learn to do that?"

"Better to learn to play chess," says Ngomo.

"Your wound's healed nicely," says Zeus, gently touching upon the brutal knife fight that brought them all here. "Your scar looks like Belgium."

Ngomo ruffles the boy's head and continues to watch.

"Bet you could beat him," Zeus says, pointing to Rafael, who never loses the knife toss.

"I don't know, little man," Ngomo says, squinting lightly. "His blade flies like it's got built-in coordinates."

Rafael's knife doesn't wobble, doesn't spin wrong. Shirtless, cigarette in mouth, olive-skinned, muscled, joyously grinning, Rafael stands with his back to the swinging potato, throws the knife behind him, and somehow manages to pierce it in two. Everybody mock-claps, groaning. Louise throws her arms around his neck.

Hawk times himself disassembling and reassembling his rifle. Hildimar times herself sharpening her blade. Next to Rafael, she is the second-best knife thrower, a skill that's gone tragically underused during her years with Omloop and Charlie.

Finished, she slides the knife toward Hawk. He takes it, tests the edge, nods. They sit on a bench, elbow to elbow, weapons between their legs. He offers her half his bread. She offers him a swig from her canteen.

Rafael watches them from his blanket, then picks up a handful of pebbles and throws them at Briggs's head. Briggs is taking a nap. He's exhausted. He spent two hours trying to catch a fish and failed. "Hey!" Briggs brushes the rocks out of his hair.

Rafael points to Hawk and Hildi under the poplar. "Why can't you be like them?" he says to Briggs. "Have those two asked me—even once—to translate anything?"

Fletcher, lying on the grass by himself—because Charlie can't sit still under any circumstances, including being in love—comes in for the vanquishing. "Hawk hasn't asked," Fletcher says, "because he speaks French."

Briggs and Rafael gasp in astonishment, then jump up and barrel toward Hawk. They grab him, lift him off the ground, and shake him. He lets them and doesn't even ask why.

"Hawk, you glass-eyed, silent bastard! You speak *French*?"

"*Oui*," says Hawk. "Put me down."

They drop him to the ground and loom over him. "Why the hell didn't you say so?"

"You never asked." Calmly, he gets to his feet, dusts himself off.

"I've never heard you squeak a syllable of French," says Rafael.

"Never needed to. You boys did all the talking."

"But I've never heard you say a thing to Hildi either!"

"What's there to say? When we need to, we communicate. Quietly. Privately. The way all communication should be. Brief. To the point."

Perched on a nearby stool, drinking hot tea on a warm afternoon, Belvedere claps. "I never thought I'd say this about a Yank," he says, "but I fucking *love* that man. Bravo, Hawk Turner. Bravo."

"I know he can be a little bit . . ." says Brigitte, while discussing Belvedere with Louise.

"Infuriating? Exasperating? Impossible?"

"Maybe." Brigitte smiles. "But you forgive him." She squeezes an unsuspecting Belvedere's cheeks between her strong fingers. "You forgive him everything." She leans in and kisses him. "Look how cute he is."

Belvedere bristles. "I'm *mignon*? Bloody hell. Hawk—come here! Tell her I'm not cute and little. I'm ruggedly handsome."

"Thanks so much, Commander Gray," says Hawk, walking away from them and translating nothing, "for your unsolicited revelations."

Mireille is teaching Briggs to say "*Coeur*."

"Core? Or Corps?" Both sound exactly the same.

"*Non. Coeur.*"

He tries again. "Cur?"

She sighs and looks around for Rafael.

"You said *liver*," Rafael translates from the hammock, where he's nestled with Louise. There's only one hammock, and the band fights every morning for the right to lie in it.

"Tell her I love her with all my liver," says Briggs, grabbing Mireille and kissing her.

Rafael jumps out of the hammock and saunters over. "Briggs, I don't know what you've been doing at night without me."

"Somehow, we've managed, brother." Briggs grins.

"What if she says to you, *faster*?"

"Easy," Briggs says. *"Plus vite, Briggsy."*

"And slower?"

"Doucement, Briggsy."

Rafael smiles. "Harder, harder?"

"Plus fort, plus fort." Briggs beams. "Usually she just says, *Continuez, s'il te plaît.*"

The elegant, graceful Mireille looks up from her stitching. "Are you two talking about me?" she says, shining up at Briggs. "I don't say anything of the sort. He does what he wants. All I say is *parfait. Tu es parfait. Formidable. Encore, encore. Et je t'aime.*"

"I je t'aime you too," says Briggs.

They play ghost, even Ngomo, even Zeus. Everyone loves that game. Only Margot sits it out. She says it's pointless to play games because she never wins. The sentry is blindfolded, and the rest have to sneak up on him without being heard and tag him.

Rafael is the best sentry. "Because I have supernatural hearing," he reminds everyone. They all boo theatrically—they've heard it a thousand times.

Briggs is always caught—he's built like a windmill in corduroy. Zeus makes it all the way to Rafael once, then sneezes before he can tag him. Fletcher plays the game like chess—all timing and angles.

Charlie is the best ghost. She's not just quiet. She's ghostly.

At the end of the game, only Charlie and Rafael are left: her silence against his gifts.

She wins. She's standing right in front of him, and he still hasn't heard her approach.

"Are you even moving?" he calls out. "We're supposed to be playing a game. Did you walk off? I swear to—"

"Boo," she says. He rips off the blindfold. She tags him and crosses her arms.

Rafael gives a grudging bow. "Where'd you learn to do that?"

"What can I say—I got very good at disappearing," says Charlie, with twitching regret. "Didn't I, Fletcher, my Rebecca in the sky?"

Fletcher blows her a kiss from the sidelines. "You're a shining beacon, my Eureka on the ground," he says. "I saw your light all the way from Holland."

At night by the fire, they play "Make Belvedere Laugh." He sits in a chair, arms crossed, legs crossed, cigarette in one hand, teacup in the other—the very personification of British disdain—and they throw gems at him, each one better than the last.

"Doctor says to the patient: I have good news and bad news. The bad news is, you have short-term memory loss. The patient says, oh no! What's the bad news?"

"Doctor says, I have to give you a transfusion. What's your blood type? Patient says, B positive. Doctor says, I'm trying, buddy, but you lost a lot of blood."

"What did I do to deserve this?" Belvedere mutters, not cracking so much as a twitch.

Rafael gets up, grabs the mug from Belvedere and, with his own half-smoked cigarette, crouches on the patio, affecting Belvedere's posture and accent in pitch-perfect imitation. "Just bloody splendid," Rafael says, stitching with an imaginary needle. "Another Yank split like a half melon because the word *duck* is not in his vocabulary. Do you not know what it means to take cover, Briggs? Were you hoping bullets would just bounce off your bravado? Hold still—no, *stiller* than that." Rafael fumbles around for Belvedere's glasses, which the medic hates to wear. "Where are those damn glasses . . . can't see a bloody thing—hold still I said! I can't stitch a moving target. This isn't a county fair, Briggs." Rafael takes another puff, another sip, adjusts the lenses on his nose. "And before you ask, no, there's no morphine left. You burned through the last of it with your delightful grenade-in-a-bucket maneuver."

A beat.

"Honestly, Briggs," says Rafael, channeling his inner Belvedere, "I should just stitch in a zipper instead. Would save us all time."

When he stands and looks over, Belvedere is laughing. Reluctantly. Soundlessly.

But definitely laughing.

Rafael has taught Louise a poem in English, and now she skips around, reciting it under her breath, glittering with amusement.

"Do you even know what you're saying?" Charlie asks.

"Of course not," Louise replies. "But it's called 'The Owl and the Pussy-Cat,' and Rafa says I'm the pussycat. He says when I memorize the whole thing, we're going to put on our finest finery and dance in the great hall."

"The what and the *what*?" says Charlie.

Giggling, flushed with mischief, Louise nods profusely. "*Le Hibou et la Chatte*."

"Louise!" *La Chatte* is far naughtier in French than in English.

"I know! Isn't he *délicieux*, Charlie?" Louise presses both fists to her heart. "Isn't he simply *délectable*?"

She learns it in no time.

In the early evening, Rafael dons his combat black, and Louise wears a long red dress and brushes out her fine blonde hair. Hawk plays a jaunty, waltzy tune, and they glide in circles across the parquet—a *pas de deux* of word and deed.

Rafael: "*Dear Pig, are you willing to sell for one shilling,*
Your ring?" Said the Piggy, "I will."
Louise: *So they took it away, and were married next day,*
By the turkey who lives on a hill.
Rafael: *They dined on mince, and slices of quince,*
Which they ate with a runcible spoon.
Louise: *And hand in hand, on the edge of the sand . . .*
Together: *They danced by the light of the moon,*
The moon,
The moon,
They danced by the light of the moon.

As their time spools on, they all linger longer by the fire, staying up well past last embers.

"When the war is over, and we're old," says Fletcher, after a shared bottle of rum, "what will we say about these summer days?"

Rafael replies, raising the last of his Congolese cachaca. "We'll say we were happy once—and in Belgium."

61

Reinforced Steel

"What trucks have we already inspected with reinforced axles and suspensions for heavy loads?" Hubner said. He hadn't stopped pacing, still lost in thought. He'd been at it for hours.

"We've been through this, Hubner." Rheinhardt was impatient. "Bricks and masonry. Lumber. Coal. Ingots. Machinery. Engine parts. Lime. Ammunition. Rail ties. Stone. We've run the Geiger wand over them all. No click, no hum, no whirr, nothing."

From a few blocks away, the cathedral bells began to strike six.

Hubner stopped sharply and turned to Rheinhardt, a spark of epiphany in his eyes. He didn't speak until the bells stopped.

Rheinhardt waited. *Please*, he thought, gripping the Luger. *Please tell me what I've missed.*

"Bellsmith, sir!" Hubner exclaimed, his arm miming a bell's swing. "Their trucks carry *cast-iron bells*. Extreme weight concentrated over a reinforced frame. *Klokkenmaker* trucks!"

Rheinhardt jumped up so fast he knocked over his chair. He knew Hubner was right. It had the feeling of breakthrough. "Hubner," he said, grabbing his coat and his visor, "you're a genius." A wide, awful grin stretched across his teeth.

"Sir, let's not get too excited. I may not be correct."

"Don't talk down your own brilliance, Hubner." Rheinhardt holstered his weapon and motioned for Hubner to follow. "We're going for a ride," he said. "You drive." He stopped and returned to the office. "But first, let me get cleaned up, shave, change my clothes. Five minutes. Go start the car."

The new ride was a Mercedes-Benz 770, worthy of Hitler himself. Massive, black, sleek, unmistakable, and polished like a coffin lid. Double SS flags were mounted on its fenders. It was registered under Rheinhardt's name, commensurate with his new title and responsibilities. All his fuel exemptions were approved by Berlin. Nowadays, Rheinhardt came and went as he pleased and no rat-bellied clerk knew what hours he kept.

"Where am I headed, sir?" asked Hubner. "To pay a visit to our old friend Omloop the *klokkenmaker*?"

"You better believe it." They raced to Herentals.

"He's never going to talk, you know," Hubner said.

"Leave that to me. Did you bring the generator?"

"Of course."

"And the Geiger itself? In my haste, I forgot."

"It's always packed and ready in the trunk. Did you want to stop at headquarters and get some officers to accompany us?"

"Why?"

"Well—in case of *resistance*?"

"Hubner, the man is an enfeebled seventy-two-year-old with a shaking disorder. I think you and I can handle him."

"We're going to have to shoot him. He won't break, sir."

"Maybe. He dies either way, so it doesn't matter to me. If he talks, good. If he doesn't, that's all right too. Omloop didn't carry sixty barrels of uranium on his palsied back. This robbery took many men—who knows who else was involved. I don't even care at this point. It's true, Hubner—you don't believe me, I see that on your face, but it's true. I don't care, because I'm not doing this to arrest the transgressors or imprison the robbers. I'm doing this because at all costs, sparing no effort, we need to find the uranium. Grunfell must begin his work. Only after we get back what's ours will we deal with the scum, each and every fucking one of them. Right now, we have a different objective—to overwhelm and confuse them, by swindle or complication. To trap them into making a mistake by our relentless aggression."

Right before they entered Herentals, Rheinhardt said, "I can't tell you what a relief it is to talk to you about this, Hubner. I'm a different man. I feel my old self again."

Omloop was in his shop under the trees near the church. When Rheinhardt flung open the door, Omloop, who'd been hunched over the brass lathe, looked up calmly. "Hello, sir," he said. "To what do I owe this unexpected pleasure?"

"Where is your truck?"

"Around the corner, on the side, but—?"

Rheinhardt was out the door before Omloop could finish.

Hubner cranked up the generator. Rheinhardt turned on the Geiger and raised the wand over Omloop's truck. The needle stayed still.

"Fuck," said Rheinhardt.

"This truck's too small to hold sixty barrels of uranium, sir," Hubner said quietly.

Rheinhardt turned around. Omloop stood behind him, watching.

"*Holy, holy, holy,*" Omloop said, letting his apron fall to the ground.

In *der Raum*, the special interrogation shed in the back of the overgrown rear garden at Baert Haus, Rheinhardt had a small bell suspended from a reinforced hook in the ceiling, tuned to the highest note.

The gendarme sat Omloop in a chair. Per Rheinhardt's orders, they left him untied. They pierced steel hooks under his fingernails, into the tendons of his fingertips. The hooks were attached to fishing lines in a tension wire system tied to the tongue of the bell. The slightest tremor or movement from Omloop caused the bell to ring, and the reverberating sound triggered the next pain cycle—each chime sent a heat shock of pain straight into Omloop's hands. He had to sit perfectly still or suffer more.

Rheinhardt thought this was the ideal motivation for a man who couldn't stop himself from moving. "Omloop, I'm not going to ask you any questions—at first," Rheinhardt said. "I'm just going to sit here for a few minutes and watch the instrument you revere betray you. You're going to become a prisoner of your own craftsmanship. This isn't about breaking you, Omloop. It's about desecrating your sacred craft."

"Well, you are a master at that," Omloop said. "Have at it."

They sat, facing each other, Omloop on a rickety stool, Rheinhardt in an elegant leather captain's chair, one elbow resting on the armrest as he smoked.

Omloop didn't speak.

But he also never shook, Rheinhardt noticed, with unhappy surprise.

"How are you managing to stay so still, Omloop? You couldn't light a cigarette in the courtyard without a half dozen tries. And now look at you."

Omloop said nothing.

Rheinhardt almost felt a grudging respect for this fragile, unbreakable gnome of a man who would not betray his thieves. "Give me one word," Rheinhardt said. "One. Tell me where it is, and I'll put you out of your misery."

"I don't know what you're talking about."

"Where is it?"

"What are you looking for?"

"Who took it off my ship?"

"Took what?"

"Where are they now?"

"Who?"

"Where are all your accomplices? Where's that nephew of yours? Is he part of it?" Rheinhardt said. "I notice he's not around to help you anymore. He'll probably want to know what's happening to his uncle. Where does he live again—Bruges? Give me his address."

"He's not there anymore," Omloop said. It was the only time he had expanded his answer. "He went to visit relatives down in Virton. Near Luxembourg. I'm expecting him back any day."

"Give me his address in Bruges. I'd like to pay his family a visit."

"Don't know the exact address," Omloop said, not a stitch of him moving.

Rheinhardt had had enough. He picked up a metal rod, raised his arm and struck the bell over Omloop's head.

The bellmaker's screams lingered in the room long after his voice gave out.

"This is what happens when seventy-year-olds decide to engage in young men's work, Omloop," Rheinhardt said. "Resistance isn't for the old."

"Holy, holy, holy," Omloop whispered, his breathing shallow and uneven.

"I don't know what that means," Rheinhardt said, lifting the metal pipe again. "I'm going outside. In three minutes, I will be back and I will strike the bell again. Harder. Use that time to consider your next move."

"I will, sir. You can be sure I will," Omloop said between ragged breaths.

When Rheinhardt returned, Omloop was dead. He was slumped in the chair, head bowed, the hooks still attached to his fingers, his arms crossed in front of him as if in prayer.

62

The Bells of Flanders

Just after dusk, as they cleared their dinner plates and were about to build a fire for their nightly song and dance, Charlie heard a bell begin to toll in the distance. Low. Measured. Hollow. Then another. And another. She paused at the sink, the dishcloth clenched in her hands. *Please no*, she thought. *Please. No.* Toll by toll, the sound filled the entire countryside. Louise came to stand by Charlie's side. Mireille and Brigitte and Maxine and Margot stepped to the window too. Only Hildimar remained near Hawk, both mute.

Fletcher, standing frozen beside Charlie, looked so stricken that she was baffled. He couldn't know what it meant, could he?

"Something terrible has happened to one of your own," Fletcher said.

Ah—so he did know what it meant. "It's telling us to take cover," said Charlie.

"We can't take cover," said Fletcher. "Until we know what happened."

"It probably has nothing to do with us," she said in a small voice.

"Yes," he said. "Or everything."

They spent a dreadful night with no fire, no love, no songs, no relief. In the morning, she and Fletcher took the back roads to Herentals under false names. The town had gone quiet again. The bells had stopped. But the weight of something awful hung in the air.

They hid the truck on the outskirts and carefully made their way to the town church, staying away from main roads. At Saint Waltrude, Father Bavo met them behind the sacristy, his cassock still dusted with ash. His cracking voice was barely audible when he told them what happened.

Fletcher was right. It had everything to do with them.

In the morning as the sun rose and the townspeople began their day, they found Omloop hanging from the belfry, small and broken. The desecration of the man and the church spoke louder than any words possibly could from the people who killed him, and who remained silent.

By sundown, they had taken Omloop from the belltower and carried his body through Herentals, not in a coffin but in their hands. Everyone knew Omloop. And before the hour was out, the bells began to toll. First in Herentals, low and slow, a mourning chime. Another in Vorselaar. Then in Lier. And in Mechelen.

Soon all the bells of Flanders were ringing. Not pealing, not chiming, but tolling in sorrow and rage, a chain of mourning stretching from steeple to steeple to warn the living.

The sound passed like smoke through windows and attics, across rail yards and river crossings, through monastery chapels and safehouse beds.

The bell rings in the holy place.
One of ours is dead. It's not safe.
And the faithful pray for mercy.

And just like fog through a field, all the good evaporated from the grasses and stones of Kasteel de Velde.

"Okay, okay," Charlie kept repeating, her voice as ghostly as her face. She kept smoking and shivering, wiping her eyes. "Our Omloop would never say anything." She stifled a sob. "He'd never talk."

"Under torture, even the strongest break," Fletcher said.

"But he didn't know anything that mattered!"

"Omloop knew you, your father, your brother—and Adrian Vervaet. He knew about the ship and the cargo. He had his entire resistance operation to give up, all *your* women. Louise, Louise's mother. Omloop was connected up and down this region. There's a lot he could have given Rheinhardt."

"He wouldn't have," Charlie said weakly, less certain.

"You need to go see Mother Verene," Fletcher said. "I know it's late. But go. Warn her. Hawk will go with you."

"Why? I mean—warn her about what? Omloop didn't know Verene or her abbey."

Fletcher didn't speak. The house, the fields were deathly still.

"It's only a matter of time, Charlie."

"Before what?"

"Before Rheinhardt finds us."

"That's not true!"

"He killed Omloop because he found something out. He is on the trail, and he's getting closer. You have to warn the Abbess."

"It's not true!"

Fletcher didn't speak.

"Fletcher, just take Ngomo and go," Charlie said, trying hard to stem her tears. "I'll keep Zeus with me. Take your men—all of them. Take the Comet Line out of Belgium. The partisans will help you. Go south to the Pyrenees. Fitz will get you the papers you need. Whatever you want, he'll get for you. Fake papers, different identities, clothes, wigs, everything. You have money, you have weapons—just go, my love."

They blinked at each other mutely. She couldn't say one more word or she would break down.

"You know we can't go now, Charlie," said Fletcher.

The unspoken hung between them like a painting scraped in ash and blood.

"Besides," he said. "You know Ngomo will never part with Zeus. Whatever happens."

"Or Zeus with Ngomo," whispered Charlie.

He took her into his arms.

After they made love in the cool night and lay entangled under warm blankets, she heard his voice. "Once the hound is on the scent, he will not stop until he finds what he's looking for," said Fletcher.

Rheinhardt was just getting started.

"Hubner, Omloop's nephew Florent was definitely from Bruges, wasn't he?"

"I believe so, sir. I wasn't there for your meeting with him, but that's what you told me. So what? Florent was another fake, most likely. Why else would Omloop refuse to give us the boy's address?"

"Of course," Rheinhardt said, "but Florent was the only time that tiny pebble of a man got flustered and provided more information than I asked for, instead of less. On the off chance the boy is actually a bellsmith, find me the names of all the foundries in Bruges. We'll pay them a visit." He frowned at Hubner's skeptical expression. "To eliminate every possibility, Hubner. We know it's not a bellsmith in Antwerp, and we know it wasn't Omloop. But it had to be someone Omloop knew. Maybe it was this Florent fellow. So let's keep at it."

They didn't find a Florent, but they found an Adrian Vervaet, who at least looked like a bellsmith—unlike Omloop, that hunchbacked horse jockey with a spine of steel.

Rheinhardt saw immediately that despite Vervaet's hefty size, this man's spine was cobbled together with cotton wool. He stood, wobbly and sweating, flinching at every word.

"You are being arrested on suspicion of sabotage," Rheinhardt said. "Any clandestine activity is sufficient grounds for arrest and interrogation. *Ample* grounds, even."

"I've done nothing!" Vervaet cried.

To be fair, Vervaet had more reason to be afraid than Omloop. Because as soon as Rheinhardt cranked the generator, turned on the Geiger, and stepped toward Vervaet's Citroen trucks, the needle jerked across the dial, and the sensor came to life, tripping and rattling.

The *rat-tat-tat* that followed was one of the happiest sounds Rheinhardt had ever heard.

Finally—an answer.

Before he approached the terrified Vervaet, already flanked by a squad of Gestapo, Rheinhardt shook Hubner's hand. "Credit where credit is due, Franz," he said quietly. "Look at what we've accomplished together."

"Nothing yet, sir," said a grateful but solemn Hubner. "But I agree, we're close."

In *der Raum*, a small table was put in front of Vervaet with a black notepad, a fountain pen, and a metronome. On a chair next to Vervaet lay a metal tray, and on this tray was a pair of industrial-size pliers.

Rheinhardt asked Vervaet to write down all the details he knew.

"Sir, I'm just a bellsmith. All of Bruges can vouch for my work."

"Write down everything, Vervaet," Rheinhardt repeated, starting the metronome with a click. Vervaet stared at the device in horror.

"You have ten minutes," Rheinhardt said. "When I come back, I expect the notepad to be full of information."

When he returned, the notepad was blank. Without any preamble, Rheinhardt ordered the guards to hold Vervaet down, picked up the pliers and yanked off one of Vervaet's fingernails.

Vervaet screamed.

Rheinhardt replaced the pliers on the tray, wiped his hands with a clean white rag, and restarted the metronome. "You have ten minutes," he said to Vervaet, "to write down what I need to know." Upon his return, Vervaet had vomited, but the notepad was filled with words, as Rheinhardt had expected. Yes, most of it was illegible, but at least now they could have a real conversation.

Clutching his mangled hand in a towel, Vervaet tearfully told Rheinhardt many things. As a favor to Omloop and for a small fee, he had lent his trucks to a man and a woman on June 16, a Friday. They never told him their names and he never asked them or Omloop what they needed the trucks for. He said he didn't want to know. They returned to his foundry on Saturday, but kept the trucks locked and with them for an extra day. There were maybe a dozen men and women in total. They were all in their twenties. They spoke French. Vervaet wasn't sure, he said, but he thought he caught a glimpse of a black man hiding inside one of the trucks. It was memorable because he'd never seen a black man before.

Rheinhardt pounded the desk when he heard this.

Fucking Ngomo Kasonga. So the bastard didn't die.

"Did you say there were women with them too?"

"Yes, sir. Many women. Oh—and one small boy. On Sunday, they all left before daybreak. The man and the woman returned the trucks to me empty and clean on Sunday night."

Rheinhardt swirled sharply to Hubner. "Get two officers at once—go seize Firmin." So that drunk idiot was telling him the truth about some women and a boy named Zeus? Unfathomable. "Run, Hubner! Run."

When Hubner returned to Baert, he said Firmin was missing.

"What does that mean, *missing*?"

"Gone from the shed, all his belongings, even the metal chair."

They stared grimly at each other.

Was Firmin one of them too? Was he the one who—unobserved by all—reported on Rheinhardt's activities, and on the troop movements around *La Fortuna*? And when interrogated, he told Rheinhardt the truth because he knew Rheinhardt would never believe him?

Rheinhardt was disgusted, revolted by the dreck he had to live among. "Is there no drunk who's just a drunk?" he bellowed. "No *klokkenmaker* who's just a *klokkenmaker*? Is it all sabotage and ambush? Everywhere I turn, criminals and fools try to do me harm. If you can't trust a homeless drunk on the docks, Hubner, whom can you trust?"

He left his men to finish with Vervaet, while he went for a walk and a smoke to calm down and clear his head. He had to think.

Ngomo Kasonga.

He was there at the beginning. And he was there at the end.

Rheinhardt cursed himself. He should have started not with a clue but with a theory.

Well, it wasn't too late. If Rheinhardt could find out who brought the uranium *into* Belgium, he could find out who had stolen it and stashed it.

Besides the African man, who else in Belgium would know about uranium mines in the Belgian Congo? Who had sole authority over the sales and export of uranium, one of the rarest and most sought-after minerals in the world?

Erich von Rheinhardt knew of only one such man. His Majesty, Leopold the Third, King of the Belgians, Duke of Saxony, Prince of Saxe-Coburg and Gotha.

This theft wasn't local.

It was sovereign.

63

No One Knows But Us

"We need Fitz's help," Fletcher said.

Under his breath, Rafael groaned. Louise too. And Charlie too! Why her? Fletcher wondered.

"We need more ammo," he went on. "With Omloop gone, your brother's the only one who can get it for us."

"Fitz could be hiding in a dozen different places," Charlie said, equivocating. "I wouldn't know where to start."

"He'll be in the Golden Rooster, Charlie," said Louise. "He loves that alehouse. It's his second home."

"Thanks heaps, Lou," Charlie said, with a headshake.

While Charlie raced off to Herentals, Fletcher had a word with Rafael.

"Rider, I'm not telling you how to live your life," he said. "But we're asking Charlie's brother for some serious fucking help, and without him, we're sunk. So please don't make things harder."

"You don't have to tell me twice, Fletch," Rafael said with a half-serious salute. "You can count on me. But eventually—when this is over—will we be allowed to tell him then?"

"You can invite him to your wedding then, for all I care," said Fletcher.

Rafael talked to Louise. When Charlie returned to Tremelo with Fitz, Rafael and Louise could not have stood farther apart on the back patio. They acted as if they'd never been introduced.

"Hello, Fitz," said Louise, her usual and smiling self.

"Hello, Louise. How have you been?"

"Fine, thank you. Was I right, Charlie? Was he in the Golden Rooster?"

"I was. You know me so well, Lou," said Fitz, bitterness, irony, and sadness flickering in his forced smile.

But Rafael separating himself from Louise made all the difference in Fitz's attitude, as Fletcher knew it would. Whatever Fitz still felt, he buried it. He was needed, and he came through. He became what Fletcher hoped he was and what Charlie told him her brother was—a fearless resistance soldier who would lead them to the caches of Wehrmacht supplies, stashed across the countryside. After studying the map with Wolski, Fitz told Fletcher there was a mixed-goods supply dump in an old barn west of Schriek, about five kilometers away. "Think Lillehaven for Nazis," said Fitz. "Quiet, overlooked, nothing but farmland and meadows."

"Probably heavily guarded, though?" said Fletcher.

Fitz shrugged. "I don't think so. It's too out of the way, and from what I'm hearing, the Wehrmacht has moved most of its regional troops into Antwerp. The site will probably be guarded by collaborators."

Fitz went on recon, taking Wolski and Hawk with him.

They were gone five hours—some of the longest of Fletcher's life.

But when they returned, they had good news. "Looks like the Germans put guns in the hands of teenagers plucked from the streets," Fitz said. "Four young bucks are stationed there."

"Four guys is not nothing," Fletcher said. "Shift change?"

Fitz shook his head. "I saw no signs of active rotation. They're not guarding, they're squatting."

Wolski agreed. "These four are entrenched. No vehicles nearby, no radio antennas. They have makeshift stove, stacked wood, crates of food, wine bottles, cigarettes. They stood their rifles against wall. Some guards! Two of them lay on grass playing cards. One of them sleeping. One standing, yes, but daydreaming. Three hammocks under trees. Yeah, Fitz right. They live on site."

Fitz offered to stay, to help, to be another frontline gun, but Charlie said no. If something happened to Fitz, it couldn't be at her hand. Her father would never speak to her again. She drove him back to the Golden Rooster. Tearfully, the Martin twins, Margot and Maxine, said goodbye to Wolski and returned to Herentals with Charlie. They were their mother's only support.

At dawn the next day, the entire band walked through the woods to Schriek. Only Zeus and Ngomo stayed behind. "We could really use Ngomo," Rafael said quietly to Fletcher. "There's going to be a shitload to carry." But Fletcher said no. They would have to make do without him.

That was a reckoning still waiting to happen, but it couldn't happen today.

At Schriek, Hawk shot one Belgian collaborator, standing guard. The other three, still sleeping in their hammocks, they dispatched with knives. One rifle shot could sound like an exhaust misfiring. Two or more was unmistakable gunfire.

Briggs forced the barn doors open with a shoulder. The smell hit Fletcher first—oil, cordite, dust, gasoline-soaked canvas. Morning light cut across the crates stacked hip high. He let out a single, satisfied breath. "Well, I'll be damned."

"Christmas come early!" said Briggs, going straight for the cigarettes. "Weapons and ammo are survival. But tobacco is life."

Inside was a treasure trove of war, organized with fanatical care. Ammo crates stamped with Reich markings, tins of grenades, mortar rounds sealed with waxed cloth, boxes of fuses, coils of det cord, flare tubes, water canteens, and medical satchels with red crosses painted on them, neat as scripture. And yes, metal tins of cut leaf tobacco, bundled with small paper booklets for rolling, and wooden matchboxes. "Admit it, Lieutenant Gray," said Rafael, mock-serious, throwing his arm around Fletcher, "You're more impressed by the order than by the contents."

"Fuck you," said Fletcher amiably. But he did like the order.

They loaded fast, taking what they could carry. Ammo came first. Med supplies next. Then grenades, flares, and fuses. Rafael tried not to load Louise down, until Charlie said, "Stop coddling her, Rafael."

"You can coddle me all you want, *mon amour*," said Louise, her eyes twinkling.

On the way out, they booby-trapped the barn with German mines, Fletcher carefully marking the location of each one. He needed to return to the arms dump the following day and didn't want any nasty surprises.

On the return trip, they moved in a staggered line through the woods like war mules—bred for burden, not speed. Crates of sniper ammo, of .45 rounds for Rafael's Thompson, boxes of 9mm rounds and 8mm Mauser belts for the heavy machine gun lashed across Fletcher's back. They said, "Fuck" with every breath. Belvedere was bursting with gauze, field dressings, morphine, splints, and a thick roll of surgical tape no one wanted to look at. Charlie carried a fuse crate in her hands, the det cords looped around her waist like a bandolier. Brigitte and Mireille hauled a crate of grenades; Hildi all the knives she could find; Louise the box of bouncing Betties and TNT.

When they returned to the Kasteel and laid out their bounty on the back patio, Charlie was horrified. To her, it looked like overkill a thousand times over. Incredulously, she tried to catch Fletcher's eye, hoping he would agree this was insanity. Instead, he lit a cigarette and said, "Brigitte, Mireille, go into the cellar and bring up all the empty wine bottles you can find. We need to start making the Molotovs."

"Molotovs?" Charlie exclaimed. "The fifty grenades you've got isn't wildly excessive?"

"Not nearly," he said. "Tomorrow when Hawk and I return to Schriek, if it's still abandoned, we'll get more."

"Why would you go back to Schriek?"

"Um—to get *more*?" He called for his men. It was time for a battle plan.

Louise put a sympathetic arm around Charlie. "It's crazy, I know," she said. "But the boys just want to be prepared. Nothing wrong with that."

"There's not a crumb that can lead Rheinhardt to the abbey," Charlie said. "Besides us, no one else in the world knows where the barrels are. No one."

Fletcher, overhearing her, straightened up from the boxes of ordnance and turned. Their eyes locked. His mute gaze conveyed more to her than all the shouted words in French ever could. Crushed, Charlie tried not to look away.

"No one knows but us," said Fletcher. *"And Robert Capelle."*

64

Yellow Flowers

A number of impediments stood between King Leopold and a middle of the road Nazi like Rheinhardt. For one, Rheinhardt knew he didn't have the power—couldn't even be given the power—to interrogate a king. Even Hitler had been unwilling to use the King's family to leverage more from Belgium—more troops, raw materials, cooperation on the Jewish question.

And two, even if Rheinhardt were somehow given this unprecedented authority, he didn't know where the King was at the moment. Since 1940, he'd been a prisoner of war, confined to his palace outside Brussels, but since the invasion there'd been talk that he and his family had been relocated out of Belgium.

"Here's your chance to inquire into the possibility of speaking to King Leopold, sir," Hubner said, holding out a folded letter. "A courier arrived from Brussels this morning. You're to attend a meeting with Alexander von Falkenhausen—immediately."

"Really?" Rheinhardt said. Rubbing his chin, he read the letter. "What's this all about, you think?"

"Probably something to do with the *klokkenmaker* hanging from a church belfry, sir. The Belgians are apparently quite unhappy about it."

"Fuck the Belgians," said Rheinhardt. "We wouldn't be in this position if they hadn't gone behind our backs to steal our uranium."

"Absolutely. Should I get the car ready for the drive to Brussels?"

"Yes, I suppose we might as well get it over and done with," said Rheinhardt. "It'll give me a chance to inquire into the King's wellbeing."

Alexander von Falkenhausen, the military Governor of occupied Belgium, was no friend of the Belgians, Rheinhardt knew, but he was not a Nazi. He was

Wehrmacht. And they did things differently in the German army. They liked to go by the book.

"You and I haven't yet had a proper introduction, Herr Rheinhardt," said the much older Falkenhausen when the two men met in the governor's study in Hotel Astoria—the most luxurious hotel in Brussels, requisitioned by the German military as both headquarters and residence during the occupation. "You should have come to me last month, after your promotion to SS Commander of Antwerp. I invited you to a reception in your honor, to celebrate your momentous achievement."

"I was busy, sir." Rheinhardt's reply was clipped. He had neither time nor appetite for pleasantries.

"Busy with matters other than hanging Belgians from belfries?"

Rheinhardt was right to be curt. This wasn't a friendly meeting. "The man was a saboteur and a criminal," he said.

"I understand," said Falkenhausen. "He was seventy-two years old, well regarded in Flanders and held in high esteem by the Bishop of Mechelen. That is not how we conduct ourselves as Germans in Belgium."

"It had to be done."

"Herr Rheinhardt," said Falkenhausen, "we've lived a certain way for four years, and quite deliberately. Belgium has been indispensable to the Wehrmacht in its industrial and agricultural production that arms and feeds our troops. As Governor, I don't wish to intensify the persecution of Belgians when Germany desperately needs their cooperation at this crucial stage of the war. I don't want to demoralize them, or do *anything* to dampen their efforts on our behalf. Your ruthless tactics damage our cause and our standing with the Belgian people. I hear you've been going into their homes without a warrant and searching their property with barely any pretext. You know this is forbidden. It's against military law. Again, we want to avoid provoking them—anything that could slow the juggernaut of Belgian production for Germany."

Von Rheinhardt listened to Falkenhausen but couldn't help feeling that the man was exhausted by the fight. He no longer had the stomach to do what had to be done.

"Governor," Rheinhardt said, "I disagree with you *most* strongly. The Belgians have been taking great advantage of our deep regard for the rule of law. We've been too lenient. This has allowed them to operate with impunity. They're killing our soldiers, cutting communication lines, filling exhaust pipes with cement, slashing tires, undersupplying food, and switching rail tracks, causing massive collisions." Rheinhardt's voice rose with each fresh offense. By the end he was nearly shouting, using his controlled anger as leverage. "Does that sound like an acceptable level of cooperation to you, Herr Falkenhausen?"

"There's always been a *certain* degree of sabotage," Falkenhausen allowed.

"An unacceptable degree," said Rheinhardt. "And that was before. Now that we're fighting for our very existence, we cannot allow anything to derail us from victory."

Falkenhausen sighed.

"Governor, it's not enough that you look the other way," said Rheinhardt. "I need full cooperation from Brussels. I need some of your Gestapo men reassigned to me so I can intensify the search of insurgents' homes. I don't have enough men for the task ahead."

"Ahead? What are you planning?"

Rheinhardt stayed silent.

"You're not a military man, are you, Rheinhardt?"

"I am, sir. I served four years in the Wehrmacht from 1930 to 1934, first as a reservist, and then as a captain. I resigned my commission when I transferred to the Gestapo under Heydrich and then to the SS under Himmler. I lived and worked in Berlin until 1940, and have been here in Antwerp for the last four years."

Falkenhausen was quiet. "I'm also seventy-two years old, just like the man you killed. My health is not what it used to be."

"We must see this through," Rheinhardt said with barely hidden disdain. "We're not done fighting, or protecting our fatherland. Just one more push to find what we need, and then we shall overcome the enemy."

"What are you even looking for, Rheinhardt?"

Inwardly, Rheinhardt was a tight coil of electrical wire, plugged in and rumbling. He wanted to scream, to throw things, to punch this man. The defeatist attitude was not for Rheinhardt; this resigned manner was anathema to him. But he spoke calmly. "Sir, I'm working on a matter of the most urgent national security—something that could potentially conclude the war in our favor. Would it be possible for me to speak directly to the King of Belgium? I have just a couple of questions for His Majesty. I need five minutes."

"Leopold?" Falkenhausen shook his head. "He's not here. He's been transferred to Germany."

"Ah," Rheinhardt replied, disappointment plain in his voice. "Shame. His family, too?" he added, carefully. "They have been moved with the King?"

Falkenhausen scoffed. "You want to speak to Leopold's wife? His children? Who do you think will help you most with your mission to ensure the Reich reigns supreme?"

Rheinhardt emitted a mirthless scoff in reply. "Of course, mein Herr. No, I was merely wondering whether any of the King's private staff remained in Brussels. Any of his adjutants, assistants, bookkeepers, counselors? Anyone from the Belgian government who had been close to him, perhaps?"

"The government, as you're well aware, is in exile in London. Who are you looking for?"

"Anyone who is still in Belgium who was close to the King."

"That's easy," said Falkenhausen. "That would be Count Robert Capelle."

Rheinhardt wished Robert Capelle were Jewish so he could have him arrested on the spot. The man was more infuriating than Drechsler and Brandt rolled into one—upright, haughty, and impervious to questioning. He clearly considered himself not only royally but morally superior to Rheinhardt. He acted as if Rheinhardt had interrupted his pleasant afternoon of tea and reading, and Capelle wasn't about to let him get away with it.

He was an aristocrat, like that damn Falkenhausen. They were birds of a feather, and perhaps that was why Capelle's extracurricular activities were being overlooked—by the very man charged with guarding him for Hitler.

"To what do I owe this unexpected visit?" Capelle said, standing by the window in his drawing room, one hand holding a cigar, the other resting on the back of an estate chair. The house was spotless, elegant, well furnished. Dove-gray damask wallpaper, muted green Aubusson carpet, a grand piano in the corner. Everything gleamed with understated luxury. If this was exile, it was first class all the way.

A bronze bust of Cicero, greened slightly with age, stood on a pedestal by the fireplace. Real, not a reproduction. *Of course* it was Cicero—like a thinly veiled critique of tyranny, Rheinhardt noted contemptuously.

Above the mantle hung a vast seascape painted by Ivan Aivazovsky—also real, not a reproduction. A solitary listing ship, its sails torn and mast snapped, adrift at night in a luminous stormy sea. The room overflowed with crystal vases of resplendent faded flowers—all yellow. The painting stirred an old, useless ache inside Rheinhardt. But the yellow flowers triggered the nerve-fire under his skin. And Capelle's supercilious demeanor incensed him. Rheinhardt was a pressure vessel, sealed tight.

"What's the occasion, Count Capelle?" he asked, gesturing brusquely toward the profusion of yellow blooms. "I've never seen so many flowers in one room."

"My wedding anniversary," Capelle said. "Is this what passes for urgent business for the SS nowadays—floral arrangements in Belgian households?"

Rheinhardt straightened, acutely aware of the coarseness of his leather gloves, the stiffness of his new SS-issued boots. "I'm investigating—among other things—a disturbing rise in local partisan activity," he said.

"I cannot be of help," Capelle said, exhaling a voluminous puff of smoke. "I'm confined to my house, as you're well aware."

"But you do go out from time to time, do you not?"

"Not to meet the partisans," Capelle said. "I go out for walks with my wife.

I go to the local alehouse. When the King was here, I would walk to Laeken Castle to visit him. I'm constantly surrounded by the Gestapo—except when I'm in my private quarters. But even then, the signal truck is parked in the forecourt—as you must have seen when you pulled up next to it. My house has been thoroughly searched. I have no contraband, no radios, no antennas. No way to communicate with any of the partisans, or even with the King."

Rheinhardt was being shut down. In one minute, his audience would be over and he wouldn't have asked any of his key questions. "Do you know a man named Ngomo Kasonga?"

"Of course," Capelle said without hesitation. "Many years ago he was the head of the King's security detail when the King was still a prince and living in the Congo." He asked no follow-up question—no, *why do you ask.*

"So he was an officer in the Congolese army?"

"He was the head of the King's security detail," Capelle repeated.

"At the end of May," Rheinhardt said, "a man named Ngomo Kasonga came to see me, presenting me with a shipping manifest from a Congolese ship called *La Fortuna*. He did not introduce himself as a military man, such as the one you describe, but as a civilian—a first mate."

Capelle said nothing.

Rheinhardt realized he hadn't asked a question. "Do you know anything about that?"

"I do not."

"On whose authority did this high-ranking officer pose as a seaman, and what possible reason would a Congolese man have to sail into Antwerp days before the enemy invasion of Normandy?"

"I have no idea." Nothing moved on Capelle, except the cigar he kept puffing on, held between fingers as steady as a surgeon's.

"You're saying it had nothing to do with you?"

"I'm saying I have no idea what you're talking about."

"How well did you know him?"

"He was the head of security for Prince Leopold—decades ago, in another country, on another continent." As if that settled it.

"How well did you know him?" Rheinhardt repeated.

"We didn't have afternoon tea together, if that's what you mean," said Capelle. "He did not drop by unannounced," he added pointedly, the unspoken *like you* hanging between them.

"When was the last time you saw or spoke to him?"

"Kinshasa, 1932—or Matadi, that same year."

"You stayed in the Congo with Prince Leopold until then?"

"I was his private secretary, so yes. I served at his pleasure."

"But you remained in the King's service even after he was detained in 1940?"

"After he became a prisoner of war?" Capelle said. "Yes. I remained with my king."

"And you have no idea why Ngomo Kasonga would suddenly sail to Belgium in 1944?"

"No idea."

Rheinhardt stepped closer, but just half a step. "I don't think you're telling me the truth, Count Capelle."

"Please," said Capelle, "I'd like to hear more about what you think."

"I think you know *precisely* why the Congolese officer was here and why the ship was here."

"Thank you for obliging me."

Such impertinence! "I know this because no high-ranking officer loyal to the King would ever undertake such preposterous actions unless he received a Royal order—either directly from Leopold or perhaps . . . from his chief advisor."

"And you know this how?" said Capelle. "Because you yourself know what it means to be loyal to a king?"

Rheinhardt didn't know whether to move forward or stagger away. He held his ground, but one of his knees nearly buckled. A dry panic rose behind his sternum. He was losing control of the exchange. He had come looking for his barrels, hoping for facts, for missteps, for a thread to pull—and Capelle had given him nothing but glacial disdain. Rheinhardt's gaze broke away, eyes darting around the room, to find anything to look at but the man by the window calmly smoking his cigar. The painting of the broken ship nearing the cliffs afflicted him in ways he didn't care to name. He turned away from that, too. The suffocating presence of the abundant flowers drew him in again. He'd already asked about them, a conversational opening pawn. But now they pressed on his mind like a finger on a bruise, sharp, electric, insistent. There had been too much *verdammt* yellow in his life of late.

"Why all yellow?"

"What?"

"Your flowers, Count Capelle," Rheinhardt said slowly. "Why are they all yellow?"

"It was all they had."

"Who's *they*?"

"Whoever sold them to me."

"Who sold them to you?"

"I don't remember."

"You don't remember where you purchased dozens of extravagant yellow bouquets?"

"It was weeks ago. They need to be thrown out. During my walks, I pass a number of flower sellers."

"Which ones?"

"A dozen places."

"Name one."

"The fruit and flower orchard near Dieleghem Fields," Capelle said without missing a beat.

"That's it? Just one?"

"Nothing else comes to mind." He stubbed out his cigar and folded his hands. "Well, I don't want to keep you. You must be a very busy man."

Rheinhardt was being dismissed.

And what was he going to say—no, I'm not busy? This is the only thing on my agenda today, to interrogate a stranger about flowers?

He straightened his visor and clicked his heels. But before he turned to go, he said, "The ship Ngomo Kasonga sailed into Antwerp on, *La Fortuna*, bore a custom-made flag on its mast—of a *yellow* narcissus."

Capelle finally looked at Rheinhardt. His gaze was like ice. "The narcissus is an exceptionally attractive flower," he said. "But if this ship was from the Congo, as you say, then it probably wasn't a narcissus. More likely, it was an African yellow hibiscus. Large golden petals, a deep maroon center. A stunning flower. No wonder you noticed it."

He didn't even offer to see Rheinhardt out.

And he still hadn't used his name. Not once. Not Herr Rheinhardt, not *Obersturmbannführer*. Nothing.

To walk stiffly out of the drawing room—past the yellow bouquets, past the broken ship—to keep his posture upright, his shoulders squared, took an extraordinary effort. It was excruciating, knowing he was being watched by that arrogant, audacious man.

As soon as Rheinhardt was out of Capelle's view, he exhaled and dropped his shoulders. His whole body sagged. He stood still for a few moments, breathing hard, gathering himself. But he wasn't letting the yellow flowers go. They were the only crumb he'd found in an otherwise wasted visit. On the way out, he stopped by the office of the Gestapo captain assigned to Capelle's manse.

From him, he learned that Capelle indeed frequented many local sellers, though he was never alone. Since June 6, he had been in the constant presence of a Gestapo contingent.

But once a week—every Saturday without fail—encircled by the guards, Robert Capelle went to the large open market on Bonaventure Street in Jette.

65

Dossin Floral

Rheinhardt headed straight for the administrative office of the Bonaventure Market and requested the vendor records for the past six Saturdays. He was looking for the name of anyone who could've sold Robert Capelle yellow flowers. One name stood out, a late entry—a florist from Mechelen. All the export papers were stamped and all the permits were proper.

The date on the permit application was Saturday, June 17, 1944.

The day *after* the uranium was stolen.

Rheinhardt was breathless, speechless.

He was *so close.*

He would drive to Mechelen immediately.

But then the name on the license caught his eye.

Dossin Floral.

He frowned, the wind taken out of his sails. As in *Dossin* Barracks? The old military compound in Mechelen that had been converted into a transit camp for Jews, before they were loaded onto freight trains and sent east?

He slumped in the back seat of the Mercedes, elation turned to defeat. He didn't even need Hubner to drive him past the address to know there was no such place as Dossin Floral. Hubner did so anyway.

And of course there wasn't.

This wasn't forgery.

It was mockery.

Whoever had forged that name knew what Dossin was.

It was someone with a stake in the game.

But what did Dossin Barracks have to do with Robert Capelle?

One insoluble Diophantine equation at a time, Rheinhardt thought.

First he would solve Dossin. Then, Bonaventure Market. And then, Robert Capelle.

Back at Baert Haus, he called Hubner into his office.

"Hubner, I've been asking you for weeks to bring me Kurt Vogel. Why haven't you done so?"

Hubner hesitated. "It's not for lack of trying, sir. Vogel has vanished."

"What does that mean?"

"*Off the face of the earth*, sir."

"Has anyone looked for him?"

"Of course."

"Has anyone reported him missing?"

"He wasn't married and had no children, sir, so no. He had a sister in Boom, but I hear they were estranged."

"Hubner, I can't explain to you how little I care about Vogel's biography. What do you suppose happened to him?"

"No one knows. He went out one morning and disappeared."

"SS officers don't *disappear*, Hubner, not even Flemish ones. Who went with him?"

"That one time, unfortunately, he went out alone." Hubner nodded. "Not advisable, I know. The corporal assigned to him had died a few weeks earlier, so Vogel went without him—obviously."

"He went out alone—and vanished?"

"Yes, sir."

"There are a lot of unusual incidents in that department, Hubner," Rheinhardt said. "More than the standard amount of death and disappearance, particularly for a division that hunts Jews and partisans."

"Yes, sir. I'll be sure to mention it to the chief of police."

"Why hasn't anyone looked for his vehicle? What was he driving? An Olympia Opel?"

"Yes, sir, normally, but someone had vandalized the tires on it, so on that last day he took one of our BMW motorcycles."

"Death, disappearance, vandalism—are they even SS over there? Has the motorcycle disappeared along with Vogel?"

"No, sir. It was found parked in the back of headquarters."

"It was where it was supposed to be, but with no sign of him?"

"That's right."

"As if he'd returned it, and vanished afterward," Rheinhardt said thoughtfully.

"Exactly, sir! That's why the investigation has stalled."

"Where were the keys?"

"Right in the ignition."

Rheinhardt hit his desk. "That's how you know it was foul play, Hubner," he said. "No SS officer, even a Flemish one, would leave the keys in the ignition of an expensive motorcycle, not with the current level of partisan disruption. Get me his personnel file immediately. And a copy of his last itinerary. Why have you not brought me these things already? I'm surprised at you, Hubner. Find his schedule. Now."

A few hours later, combing over the written details of Vogel's brief career, Rheinhardt confirmed what he half remembered: Kurt Vogel had begun his Flemish SS commission in 1942 as an overseer at Dossin Barracks in Mechelen.

Was that a coincidence too? The name Dossin Floral and Vogel's vanishing?

The officer had been missing for weeks. And he had disappeared around the time of the massacre on *La Fortuna*.

How were these events connected? *Were* they connected?

Rheinhardt checked the date on Vogel's last handwritten log.

It was Sunday, June 4, 1944.

Barely a day after the discovery of the bodies on the ship.

Even before he saw it, Rheinhardt *knew* there would be a flower vendor on Vogel's schedule.

And there was.

Lillehaven Flower Fields.

Owned by an Alder Fontaine.

Rheinhardt slapped the folder shut and stood.

It was time to pay Monsieur Fontaine a visit.

66

Alder Fontaine

Rheinhardt had Hubner drive him to Lillehaven, bringing another two officers along—just in case. Falkenhausen had warned him, and Rheinhardt was willing to give the old Wehrmacht warrior his due, what with Vogel's unexplained disappearance and all. It was no longer safe to make house calls alone.

Located just outside Herentals, Lillehaven was four smallish fields stitched together with hedgerows and low stone walls, bordered by forest. The farmhouse looked recently expanded—clearly this Fontaine was doing well for himself.

Why did everything keep happening in and around Herentals? Until last month, Rheinhardt had never even heard of Herentals—now it was all he heard. A fake *klokkenmaker*. An ambush in Saint Lament. A missing SS officer. And today, this flower farm. Why had this tiny town suddenly become a bastion of inopportune rebellion?

Hubner stopped the car in the clearing in front of the farmhouse. Rheinhardt stepped out, smoothing his greatcoat, adjusting his visor.

No one came to greet him.

A few minutes later a man emerged from the fields, dusty, perspiring, wearing a wide-brimmed hat and work overalls.

"Just one moment," the man said, walking to a tall water pump to wash his hands and face. He dried himself thoroughly, removed his apron, and only then did he turn to face Rheinhardt. His movements were deliberate, almost orchestrated.

"I'm Alder Fontaine," the man said. "These fields are mine. I saw you inspecting them—can I help you find something?"

"Erich von Rheinhardt, the SS commander for Antwerp and the region."

"The entire region?" said Alder. "I'm surprised we haven't met till now."

"You've heard of me, I'm sure."

"I have not," said Alder.

Rheinhardt blinked. Was this peasant insulting him? What was it with the Belgians these days? They were becoming positively insubordinate.

"But no matter," Alder continued pleasantly. "There are so many of you—I could've heard your name and forgot. I'm terrible with names. What can I do for you?"

"I'm looking for three things, Fontaine. First—yellow flowers."

Alder gestured to his four quadrants. "As you can see, I don't have any. Alas—they're my favorite, too. But I'm sold out. I do have some beautiful pink peonies, and *ravissante* white lisianthus. Will those work for you?"

"No," Rheinhardt said. His hackles were up. Capelle having *only* yellow flowers was as suspicious as this man not having any. Both things were out of the ordinary. Not a single yellow flower in sight?

"Someone was selling yellow flowers recently at a market in Jette."

"Who was it? By all means, try them. Perhaps they still have some left. I do not."

"I need to know if they were *your* yellow flowers. Did you have someone selling them for you there? The signature on the vendor form was illegible."

"Where—in Jette? Brussels?" Alder shook his head vigorously. "No, no. Even if I had yellow flowers, I'd never go all the way to Brussels. My business is here, or in Antwerp."

"Mechelen, too, perhaps?" Rheinhardt said.

Alder blinked. "Not much business there, no."

"Indeed," Rheinhardt said. "But a Mechelen florist's name was on the vendor list at the Jette market."

Alder spread his hands, nodding agreeably.

"Dossin Floral," Rheinhardt said. "Do you know it?"

"I do not, but Mechelen's not far from here—"

"I know where Mechelen is, Fontaine. I didn't come here for directions."

"Why *did* you come here, sir, if you don't mind my—"

"This brings me to my second question, regarding a superb officer of the Belgian SS named Kurt Vogel." Rheinhardt didn't take his eyes off Alder's face, not even to blink.

Alder didn't blink either. "I know him, of course," he said. "But what does Vogel have to do with a florist in Mechelen?"

"I was hoping you'd tell *me*."

Alder shrugged. "Haven't seen him in weeks."

"I shouldn't think so," said Rheinhardt, scanning Alder's expansive fields. "He's vanished."

"Pity," said Alder with no inflection. "Perhaps he's in Mechelen." Smooth and unfazed.

"Why would he be there?" Rheinhardt asked, furling his brow.

"I don't know. Why would he be here?"

"You're not keeping him tied up in your house, are you?"

Alder scoffed faintly and pointed toward the house. "You're welcome to check. But why would I tie up Herr Vogel?"

"I don't know *why* you would tie him up, Fontaine," Rheinhardt said. "But I also don't know why he would vanish." Rheinhardt waved his arm across Alder's fields. "Perhaps you killed him. Buried him in your garden, and are using him as compost, to help grow the flowers you deliver to the homes of our finest Nazi families. The Germans love freshly cut flowers." Rheinhardt didn't say *we Germans*, he said *the Germans*—as if Deutschland's famous love of flowers had nothing to do with him. "Your business must have exploded since we came to your country. Perhaps you derive a perverse pleasure in having the body of a Nazi officer fertilize the very flowers you arrange in their vases." He stretched his lips over his teeth in a chilling smile.

"That sounds extremely personal, Herr . . . Rheinhardt, did you say?" said Alder. "Doesn't sound like a vanishing. Sounds more like vengeance."

"Perhaps you were upset he was a collaborator with the SS."

"There's only one of me, and there are so many collaborators," Alder said. "I have a business to run. A family to take care of. I don't have time to hunt Belgian men who serve Nazi Germany."

"Perhaps it's even more personal than that, then," Rheinhardt said—and waited.

Silence met silence.

"Are there any Jews in your family, Fontaine?"

"No," said Alder in a clipped voice. "Why do you ask?"

"Kurt Vogel began his work for the Belgian SS at *Dossin* Barracks at Mechelen," Rheinhardt said.

"So?"

"Were you aware of that?"

"No, but how is that *my* business?" said Alder. There was something in his tone that caught Rheinhardt's attention. He had interrogated enough people to know when he had landed on something personal. The snag on *my business* held him there.

"I don't know *how*," Rheinhardt said, zeroing in on Alder's face. "I'm asking *why*."

"I'm just a flower farmer, Herr Rheinhardt," Alder said. His face stayed a mask, his voice flat. "I do my work, keep my head down, obey the law."

"Except Vogel's been missing for weeks," Rheinhardt said, stepping away.

"I cannot begin to guess why," said Alder.

Something was definitely happening here, but Rheinhardt would be damned if he knew what it was.

What did this abrupt, unshakeable Flemish farmer have to do with Dossin Floral—and Robert Capelle—and Rheinhardt's uranium?

"Why did you do it, Charlie—*why*?"

Alder was fear personified, pacing the kitchen while Fletcher, Charlie, and Fitz stood grim in the farthest corner, out of his way. After Rheinhardt left, Alder immediately went to Fitz and told him to find his sister and bring her back to Lillehaven.

Fletcher watched everything unraveling and didn't understand why, didn't get the subtext of it. But he knew they shouldn't have come. Curfew was soon, and they couldn't risk getting stopped on the road. And they certainly couldn't stay in Lillehaven, not with Rheinhardt quite literally knocking on Alder's door.

"Why couldn't you leave it alone?" Alder said. "Isn't my life ruined enough?"

"I'm sorry, Vake," said Charlie, her head bowed.

"Paolo didn't have the sense God gave a rock! You didn't have to name your fake business *Dossin* Floral. You didn't have to kill Vogel. Oh, my God, you didn't have to do *any* of it." He covered his face with both hands.

"Vake, please . . ."

He turned away in anguish. His shoulders shook.

Fitz and Charlie stared helplessly at one another. "Go help him," she whispered to Fitz.

"*You* go help him," Fitz whispered back. "You're the one who did it."

"What am I supposed to do now?" Alder said to his children.

Charlie exchanged a glance with Fletcher, who nodded to spur her on. "You have to leave Lillehaven, Vake," she said.

"I have to leave my house?"

"Yes. You can't stay here."

"And where do you suggest I go?" He flung his arms out. "Nazis to the west of me, Nazis to the east, every direction I look is filled up to *here* with fucking Nazis!"

Charlie didn't speak.

"And Elke?"

She and Fitz both rolled their eyes. "I suppose you should take her," Charlie said. "After all, she's nine months pregnant."

"And your brother?"

"I'm going to be fine, Vake," Fitz said. "I'm underground. I couldn't stay here with you anyway, not after what happened to Omloop."

"And what about your mother?"

"Obviously you should take our mother," said Fitz.

"Just perfect." Alder spat out his words. "Your mother, to whom I'm still married, my mistress, to whom I'm not married but who's having my child, and me, all running away together to God knows where, because your sister had to write fucking *Dossin* and shoot fucking Vogel."

"He had to die," Fitz said.

Alder didn't argue with that. "All I've done these last four years is help you two with your crazy endeavors—hide them, move them, feed them, bandage them, drive them. I've given you my trucks, my flowers, my fields, my farm, my *life*! And this is how you repay me?"

"Take one of your trucks, Vake, pile what you can in it, and go." Before her father began shouting again, Charlie cut in with, "Maman's brother, Uncle Willem lives in Sterksel, just across the border, in Holland. Not far. Near Eindhoven. Go stay with him. His house is big enough. Maman will stay out of your way. You won't be in danger there. And soon the Americans will come."

"The Americans have already come," Alder said, stabbing his finger at Fletcher. "And look at the result. But you know what—I can't even blame *them* for this. You did this, Charlotte. If you hadn't written fucking *Dossin Floral*, he never would've found us. Why did you write it, why?"

"She's been using the same name since 1942, Vake," Fitz said, coming to Charlie's defense. "It's never been an issue."

"It was an issue yesterday!"

The father and his children hung their heads.

"Excuse me," said Fletcher, finally speaking. This concerned him too—his mission, his men, Ngomo, everything. "Why does it matter what fake name is on the fake papers?"

There was a breath between words.

"Tell him, Charlie," said Alder.

"I don't want to talk about it," said Charlie. "It's not the time."

"It's literally the *only* time," said Fletcher. "There is no other time. And what does it have to do with the dead Vogel?"

Desolately, Charlie, Fitz, and Alder stared at each other.

Fletcher widened his eyes. "Charlie, *please* don't tell me that the killing of a random collaborator wasn't actually random."

Not the father nor his children spoke.

Fletcher was without words. He was furious with himself. He had let his guard down. He had let love enter his heart, just as Rafael said he should.

Look at all the love they made.

Look at all the mess they made.

With everything he had, Fletcher put away the havoc inside him to shake Alder Fontaine's hand. "Your children are right, Alder. You must leave," Fletcher said. "You're not safe."

"Are my children safe?"

How could Fletcher tell this man the truth?

"Alder," said Fletcher, "Rheinhardt is going to come back tomorrow morning and bring dogs with him who are trained to find human remains. I don't want to know, but if you've actually buried Vogel on your property, he will find him. You have to take your wife, your mistress, anything of value, and leave. When he comes—and he will come—he will arrest you, and he'll make you talk. Through you, he will find Fitz, and he will find Charlie. You are in terrible danger. If you want your children safe, you must run."

Alder was white. "Leave *tonight*?" he whispered.

"Tomorrow will be too late."

In the *Berceau*, racing back to Tremelo, Charlie said, "Once my father's in Holland, we'll be okay. Right? If Rheinhardt can't find *him*, he won't be able to find us?"

Fletcher kept his grim gaze on the road and didn't answer.

"Fletcher?"

"Charlie, if your father is here when Rheinhardt comes and finds Vogel's body, he will take your father. But if your father is not here when he comes, and the entire farm is abandoned, what do you think Rheinhardt will deduce from that? A man with nothing to hide doesn't run. Rheinhardt doesn't care a whit about Vogel. All he cares about is finding the uranium. Your father's presence will condemn us, just as much as his absence will. Do you know what we call this position in chess?" Fletcher said. "Checkmate."

"But Rheinhardt doesn't know where it is!" she cried.

"That's just chronology," Fletcher said. "As in, it's only a matter of time."

67

All Aboard

Back in Kasteel de Velde, in their bed, neither of them could speak.

"You have to tell me what's going on, Charlie," Fletcher said at last.

"Okay," she said quietly. "If that's what you want."

"I need to understand. Why did Rheinhardt come to your father's farm? Looking for Vogel, yes, but also for yellow flowers. Think how specific his details were. He knew the exact day we went to Bonaventure Market. He knew you sold *yellow* flowers. How could the word *Dossin* bring him this close to you?"

"Let me tell you about my brother Paolo."

"What does he—"

"Just let me tell it and then you'll know."

Fletcher fell quiet. She clasped her fingers like she meant to break them.

"Paolo was the original partisan," said Charlie. "He's the one who got the rest of us into it. My father is right—Paolo always had more guts than sense. He joined the resistance when it was a newborn thing—just foolish boys on bicycles handing out flyers. He was helping Omloop while the rest of us were still growing flowers.

"At first, he ferried messages. Then he started retrieving dead drops. Taking pictures. Omloop saw Paolo's knack for forgery and made him his primary counterfeiter. All the best fake papers we have are because of him. He taught Fitz to do it too.

"Then, Paolo branched out—sneaking ration cards to Jewish families, bringing them black market food when the rations weren't enough. I helped him with that—and got Louise into it, too. She's still doing it. But it wasn't idealism or righteousness that motivated Paolo. It was a Jewish woman named Mina Blumenfeld."

"The woman who worked for you?"

"Yes."

"Why? Was he in love with her?"

"Yes. But in secret. She was five years older than him. And she'd been with us since we were kids, she looked after us in the fields. We were all good friends with her, even Louise. Then Mina got married, had babies, but she never stopped working for us. Not until 1942."

"And Paolo never stopped loving her?"

"No."

"How did Mina's husband feel about that?"

"I don't know if he ever knew. He died in an industrial accident at the docks in 1940," Charlie said. "A boom from a crane hit him."

"Paolo wasn't the one operating the crane, was he?"

A corner of Charlie's mouth lifted. "He made a joke like that once too. My father nearly strangled him. Never joke about another man's death, he said."

Fletcher said nothing.

"After her husband died, Mina and Paolo became close. So you can imagine how he felt when she received her summons to report to Dossin Barracks for a transfer east. The summons itself was chillingly bureaucratic," Charlie said. "'*Arbeitseinsatz im Osten*.' Labor deployment in the East. The deportation order looked like standard paperwork. 'Report to the Emigration Office.' 'Bring a blanket and identity papers.' 'You are being resettled.'

"Mina told Paolo she didn't believe anything bad would happen to them. She was assured she'd be working in factories or on infrastructure projects to support the war effort. Everyone on those trains was fed the same words. It was all so ordinary. She was told to bring food for a few days of travel, some personal belongings.

"She and her children were required to report to Mechelen Transit Camp at Dossin Barracks on September 10, 1942."

"How old were her kids?"

"The girl was five, the boy four.

"One of Omloop's plants at the administrative headquarters in Mechelen learned the destination on the transport manifests. The trains were all headed to the same place: Auschwitz, in Poland. At the time, Auschwitz meant nothing to us."

"Yes," Fletcher said, his voice falling.

"By then, nine trains had left Belgium for Auschwitz. Mina's was the tenth.

"But Paolo went berserk. He didn't believe it was nothing. He said the Nazis lied about everything—why would this be any different?

"So he forged identity papers for him and Mina, declaring himself to be her husband, and the children theirs. He called himself Luc Van Laar; she was Anne-Marie. It was a last-minute gamble—she was already on the train when he came running down the platform, waving his documents, shouting that a terrible mistake had been made. He said he was a family man—they'd been returning to Brussels and had become accidentally separated. He insisted that his Belgian wife and children had to be let off at once.

"The train was held up while the police investigated.

"The officers checking the papers saw right away they were a forgery. But Paolo wouldn't budge. More Gestapo came to examine them. Fitz, Louise, and I could only watch, helpless, like everyone else on the platform, waving goodbye to their loved ones. Even after he was seized and accused, Paolo refused to reveal his true identity, to say who he really was. He kept insisting he was Luc Van Laar, Anne-Marie's husband. His wife and children were on that train. He demanded to be reunited with them.

"The SS said their records showed that Mina's husband was dead.

"'Do I look dead to you?' Paolo shouted. 'You have the wrong woman,' he kept saying, 'the wrong children. That woman is *not* Mina Blumenfeld. She is Anne-Marie, my Belgian wife.' They kept saying to him, 'Tell us who you really are, and we'll let you go.' But he would not."

Charlie could barely continue. "The SS officer in charge refused to separate families. He said that was not the German way, not the Belgian way, not the Nazi way. Resettlement kept families together—per Hitler's orders. Husbands with wives. Children with parents. He told Paolo, 'Either you tell us who you are, or you get on that train. You're her husband, you say? Well, there is your wife, waving to you from the window. Your children are waiting for you, Luc Van Laar. *All aboard.*'

"Mina *was* waving at Paolo. She was screaming, 'No, no. *No*. Do *not* get on the train.' The SS officer said it wasn't her choice to make. Families stayed together. Hitler decreed, and it was final." Charlie's breaths came shallow. "Fitz, Louise, and I could do nothing. We stood on the platform with the rest and watched it happen." Charlie wouldn't look at Fletcher. "We couldn't say goodbye to him. We waved goodbye to him." She fell mute.

"And so it was that my brother boarded Train Number Ten on September 15, 1942—bound for Auschwitz."

"Oh, Charlie." Fletcher reached for her, but she didn't want to be held.

Pushing away, she curled into the far corner of their bed.

"That's a catalytic wound, Charlie—for your parents, for all of you." He spoke the words from deep within, as someone who knew what a catalytic wound was.

"Yes," Charlie said. "Devastation for everybody. At least we still had each other, but Mina's whole family was destroyed. She was originally from Charleroi. Only her parents managed to escape, but that's because they left the country in 1938, before it all started. But the Germans took everyone—her grandparents, her sister, Esther, her brother-in-law, and Esther's two children, Benny . . . and Zeus."

There was a silence.

Fletcher blinked.

"Zeus?"

Charlie gave the smallest nod.

Fletcher sat up against the headboard, trying to catch his breath. "Jesus, Charlie. But how did he. . . ?"

"The family separated to survive. The father hid with the older boy. Esther took Zeus. They lived in somebody's cellar for months. He was eight when they found them. He escaped. I spent nearly a year and a half searching for him. Found him in a Carmelite monastery near Charleroi."

"How did you know he might still be alive?"

"We knew the mother boarded the train alone, so we kept searching."

"What about the father and the other boy?"

Charlie shook her head.

For a long time, Fletcher said nothing.

Only her ragged breathing and his light *shh, shh* broke the silence.

"I remember the date of Train Number Ten quite vividly," Charlie said, "because it was my birthday, you see. September 15, 1942. I turned twenty-three. The last time we celebrated my birthday was the year before, in 1941. I've been like a dragonfly in amber, Fletcher. My real life ended when I was twenty-two. And the new one hasn't yet begun."

He pulled up behind her and spooned her. "Charlie . . ." he whispered into the back of her hair.

"Do you have to ask? The Belgian SS officer who put my brother on Transport Number Ten and sent him to Auschwitz was Kurt Vogel."

68

Checkmate

Paolo Fontaine.

Charlotte Fontaine.

Fitz Fontaine.

Alder.

His wife Gretchen.

Fragments of these names littered Vogel's handwritten notes, going all the way back to September, 1942.

And one of these Fontaines had been at Bonaventure Market, selling yellow flowers to Robert Capelle.

It probably wasn't Paolo—according to Vogel's entries, he'd been deported to Auschwitz, for reasons unclear.

Floristry was women's work. A man would have drawn too much attention in an open-air market. That's why Alder stayed in the fields, while his women drove the trucks and sold the flowers.

Either the mother or the daughter was communicating with Capelle and listing *Dossin Floral* as the name of their business.

It was the realest fake name Rheinhardt had ever seen.

When he returned to Lillehaven early the next morning and found the farm abandoned, and the trucks and the people gone, he knew he was *this close* to finding his barrels.

He didn't go back to Antwerp. Gripped by terrible purpose, he told Hubner to drive with all deliberate speed to Robert Capelle's house in Jette. Not to interrogate Capelle again—Rheinhardt knew he'd get nothing from that scoundrel. But the Gestapo who guarded him could—and would—be broken.

Upon arrival, he went straight to the captain in charge of the sentry detail and asked to speak to every officer who'd been with Capelle three Saturdays ago at the market in Jette.

It took time to check the logs and round up the ten men.

While he waited, Rheinhardt reviewed the pieces again—and began to put them together.

Someone working with Ngomo Kasonga—who was working with Robert Capelle—stole the uranium off the ship and used Vervaet's trucks to drive it out of Antwerp. But they had nowhere to hide it—not yet. Rheinhardt knew this because Vervaet told him that the trucks had stayed locked in his yard all day Saturday—the day either Charlotte or Gretchen went to see Robert Capelle. Whatever the woman got from Capelle, it was enough. The trucks left again early Sunday morning—before Vervaet was awake. They were gone all day, and were returned that night—by the same man and *young* woman who'd taken them in the first place.

Charlotte Fontaine.

They paid Vervaet in gold and diamonds.

The gold coin was a *British* sovereign.

Rheinhardt wanted to tear the walls down.

Who were these people?

Capelle himself had been very clear: after the invasion of Normandy, he was never left alone for a second. He was always surrounded by a police contingent.

Which meant Charlotte Fontaine knew this and knew enough to lure Capelle to her table with yellow flowers—like *yellowcake*, like the narcissus on the *La Fortuna* flag—and in the span of a five-minute sale, extract from him where to hide the uranium.

How did she do it?

Rheinhardt was going to come at the King a different way, he decided.

He would corner him with his lowliest pawns.

Once he isolated the ten men who had gone to the market with Capelle that Saturday, he sat them down and asked each of them to recount every syllable Capelle had said to the young woman who sold him the yellow flowers.

The officers—in true pawn fashion—remembered nothing.

No amount of prodding could get them to recall what they either didn't hear or couldn't recall.

Rheinhardt stared at them—ten men in black uniforms, blank-faced, slack-shouldered, eyes flicking between each other like schoolboys at the front line. They were useless. Dolts. They were the reason operations failed. Men—incurious, oblivious, unworthy of the ranks they wore.

"I'm asking for a word," Rheinhardt said. "One word."

They shifted in their upholstered chairs. One of them scratched the back of his head. Another dared reach for a cup of tea, as if this were a briefing and not a tribunal.

Rheinhardt turned to Hubner. "If one more man touches anything on that table, shoot him."

Silence dropped like a guillotine.

Now they sat frozen, brains paralyzed. Not one of them could utter a single meaningful syllable.

"What I need," Rheinhardt said, "is a noun. A name. It doesn't have to be unusual. It can be the most ordinary thing—a market, a street in Brussels, a person, a warehouse, a cave, a farm. Any proper noun spoken that day by the man you were assigned to guard in order to ensure he would not do precisely what he did—under your noses—while you stood around twiddling your thumbs and counting butterflies."

They gave him details about the flowers. The price. The length of the girl's hair. How long they had loitered at the stall. How carefully she wrapped each bundle. One man described how hard they were to carry. One remembered the types: coreopsis and black-eyed Susans.

Rheinhardt slammed his hand against the table.

"God in heaven—you remember *petals* but not places? Are you even men?"

A long silence.

Finally, one of them spoke.

"Abbey," he said.

"What?"

"It was a throwaway line," the guard said. "Capelle mentioned some abbey he used to visit as a child with his mother. Honestly, the way that man prattles on about nonsense, I paid him absolutely no mind."

"What was the name of the abbey?"

The officer chuckled. "I don't remember *that*."

"Do not delude yourself, Captain," Rheinhardt said. "This is not a conversation. It is an interrogation. Now—what was the name of the abbey?"

"Sir . . ."

"Where was it?"

"I have no idea. I do not know. I don't remember."

Rheinhardt stepped away from the table and exchanged a mute glance with Hubner.

One of the men, younger than the rest, twitched. When he spoke, his voice was tight. "Mein Herr . . . respectfully. The man who knows the name of the abbey lives in this very house. He's probably having his morning tea. If you need the name, surely, Capelle remembers?"

The silence that followed was Arctic.

Rheinhardt tilted his head slightly, weighing whether to dignify the suggestion with a response. Above all else, he could not allow the illusion of power to slip—not for a second. "And yet I'm not asking *him*, am I?" he said with clinical finality. "I'm asking *you*."

He placed his gloved palms on the table.

"Let me make perfectly clear what's at stake," Rheinhardt said. "If I walk out of this house without the name of that abbey, all ten of you will be sent to Breendonk and put in cells with the same Belgian men you've spent the last four years terrorizing. You'll be charged with deliberate obstruction of a war operation. I will sign the papers myself."

There was a collective stiffening.

"But," Rheinhardt said, lifting a gloved finger, "whoever remembers even part of a name—a syllable, even—will be documented as having materially advanced the Reich's most important classified mission. That means commendation, reassignment, and exemption from transfer." He let the silence drag.

From the hallway behind him, a doorway creaked.

Rheinhardt turned his head.

There, at the far end of the corridor, stood Robert Capelle, hands folded behind his back. The old fox had been listening the entire time. He did not speak. He did not blink. He simply held Rheinhardt's cold gaze with his own.

Then he turned sharply and walked away. His confident footsteps echoed down the hall.

Rheinhardt exhaled slowly and turned back to his audience. "Now," he said, "let's begin again. What was the name of the abbey?"

69

Easy Red

"When I hit the beach," Fletcher said to Charlie, "Lucas was already dead. I didn't move—I'd passed out. I was drowning in six inches of water. But as I lay there, I slowly came to and started to breathe again. Horrendous fire all around me, just the most brutal assault from the hill. The bluffs were so close. In our recon photos, they looked farther away, but we were right in front of the firing line. It was low tide, yet all we had was a few yards of sand. Then the dunes. And their fucking machine guns trained on us. We were in the open, with them above us in the hills. When I saw how close they were, I thought, *How are we getting off this beach?*

"And as I lay there pretending to be dead, I realized that we were never getting off that beach. I watched other soldiers creep in the wet sand to get behind Rommel's Atlantic Wall—a wall of steel obstacles, built to keep our landing craft, ships, and tanks off the beaches. All the way to Belgium, even. They were called hedgehogs. Large X-shaped barriers. I watched my guys creep to them, trying to hide, to get just a little cover from the fire, because without them, there was absolutely *nowhere* to fucking hide. But here's what happened: as soon as our men moved behind the hedgehogs, the Germans picked them off, one by one! Our men thought they could hide, but the Germans—as soon as they saw two men together—focused all their fire on them until they both lay dead.

"We were getting annihilated," Fletcher said. "There's no other way to put it. All the men in our boat were killed. "Nineteen of us."

"You weren't killed," said Charlie.

"No," Fletcher said. "Not me." He paused. "I could see the Germans on the shingle wall, formed naturally by the tides, and I saw the men I served with lying in the sand, not moving, and I was only spared because I played dead, bobbing beside the body of my best friend, the guy who depended on me to cover him, and I said, *How the fuck am I going to get off this fucking beach?*"

"But you did," said Charlie.

"I felt so hopeless, like there was no way out. Like I wasn't going to make it."

"But you did. You did make it."

"Because of Rafael." Fletcher nodded. "He and his commando squad came at the Germans from the flank and pulverized them. They'd landed east of us, on Dog Green, and he and a few of his guys managed to survive and make it up the bluffs. Rafael fought them hand to hand, shot them, knifed them." Fletcher almost smiled. "His knife-throwing skills really came in handy. He lost a few more of his guys. But they bested the bastards. He distracted them just long enough for me to hoist Lucas out of the water and run with him to the dunes. I laid him down in a dry patch of grass and covered his face with his helmet. Then I took his rifle and pistol and knife, and his canteen, and I ran up the hill."

"Fletcher," Charlie whispered, "are you telling me this now to show me that there's always a way out?"

"Yes," he said bluntly. "I didn't want to remember it—that it was *Rafael* coming to my rescue."

"Oh, that part I don't need explained."

"But seeing him on top of that hill? It was the best sight of my life. Because it meant, for however many minutes, I still had a little life left to live."

She got up, walked to the far end of the dark room, stayed there for a while, quietly, then came back to bed.

"Rafael told us that story a different way," Charlie said, pressing her face into his chest—into his heart—kissing his jaw, his neck, his shoulder, then tucking herself under his arm. "He told Louise and me—and the other girls. By the fire."

"Where was I?"

"Doing your Fletcher things."

"What did he say?"

"He told us about the part you forgot," said Charlie. "That after you carried Lucas's body to the dunes, you returned to the water. You ran back across the beach to pull your men out. Yes, most of them were dead. But Rafael said there were three or four wounded, and you saved them. It was a wide beach, he said. It was a long run, but you made it, carrying them on your back one by one, or dragging them along the sand. He could see the tracers whizzing by you. The Germans shot the heel off your shoe. They hit your canteen. Shot through your pack. But they never touched you. You call Easy Red your doom. But Rafael said it was your salvation."

70

The Unhappy Few

The day after they'd picked up the munitions at Schriek, Fletcher returned to the arms dump and sent a quick, desperate message to Jonathan Reed, asking for more men.

JONQUILLE MORTE STOP OUTNUMBERED STOP OUTGUNNED STOP ATTACK IMMINENT STOP REQUEST REINFORCEMENT ASAP STOP COORDINATES FOLLOW STOP

Days passed without an answer.

While his men prepared the woods around the abbey for a possible assault, Fletcher, with Hawk on cover, walked the five kilometers back to Schriek each day to set up the radio during the three o'clock communication window. Hoping. Waiting.

For four days, there was nothing.

But on the fifth day, what came was worse.

When Fletcher returned to Kasteel de Velde, his face was gray. "No one's coming," he said. He couldn't bring himself to relay the full brutality of Reed's reply.

TRIED BUT IMPOSSIBLE STOP AIRSPACE TOO HOT STOP PRIORITIZE FIRST OBJECTIVE STOP SECOND OBJECTIVE STANDS STOP FIELD DISCRETION STOP GODSPEED STOP

Fletcher couldn't raise his eyes to Ngomo.

Ngomo nodded slowly, as if he didn't have to be told.

"I thought we were supposed to get Ngomo to safety," said Wolski. "How can that still stand if we're stranded?"

Ngomo was the one who answered. "That's not quite it, Wolski," he said gently. "The second objective is Ngomo must never be captured by the Nazis. Isn't that right, Lieutenant?"

Fletcher didn't speak or nod. He just stared at the ground.

And after a long exhale, so did everyone else.

"Commander," Ngomo said quietly, "let me fight by your side. You don't have enough men. You'll need my help. And in return, I give you my word, on my sacred honor, if all is lost, I will not be taken alive."

Fletcher's throat clenched. He still couldn't look at him, not even when he nodded. Especially not then.

There was silence.

"Well. *Merde*," said Rafael.

"We're really on our own?" said Briggs.

"Just us," said Fletcher. "*The unhappy few*."

"So not only is nobody coming," Rafael said, "no one will even know we were here."

"Funny," Briggs said. "We spent all this time trying *not* to fucking die, just to run headlong into it."

"We're not *running* into it," said Wolski.

"I am," said Rafael. "Let's fucking go."

Louise burst into tears.

Louise heard Hawk playing the piano downstairs, each melody more wrenching than the last. The music was tearing her heart apart. Now Hawk was playing Schubert, the melancholy "*Ständchen*."

"Loosha, why are you crying?" Rafael said soothingly. "Don't cry, *mon amour*."

"You know why," she said into the pillow.

In the middle of the night, naked both in body and soul, they were soaked like glad rags in empty bottles, setting themselves on fire again and again. Louise was weeping; she couldn't help it.

"What are we going to do?" she whispered.

"This again," he said. "But give me five minutes."

"After this."

"There's only this."

"And then?"

"There is no then."

"Rafa, but I want there to be a then. I want there to be an us."

"There will always be an us."

"I mean forever."

"There will be an us forever," Rafael said.

Louise didn't bother to wipe her face. Her breasts trembled with every moan, and his hand moved between them. "Charlie was right."

"Charlie is never right about anything," Rafael said.

"Better for me never to have known you. Never to have felt this."

"You'd rather have nothing than have this?" He caressed her nipples, the hollow of her belly, the white of her thighs.

"Yes," she said, even as her body was curving to him. "So I'd have nothing to lose."

"Don't say that," he said, pulling away from her. "Even in jest." He sat up, stopped touching her.

"Who's jesting? *Pas moi.*"

"My mother met my father in Saint-Jean-Pied-de-Port, a town at the foot of the Pyrenees where she was spending the holidays," Rafael said. "Whatever gifts you think I have, they're nothing compared to my father's. When he was young, there was no turning away from him."

You're young too, Louise thought. And there's no turning away from you.

"My mother went into it with her eyes open. As you can imagine, there was quite a scandal—a nobleman's daughter cavorting in the mountains with a shepherd. And out of that outrage, I was born. She couldn't return to England—an aristocrat, a lord's daughter, heavy with child by a smuggler. A rakish mountain guide."

"I thought you said he was a shepherd."

"My father is many things," said Rafael. "All rebellion and wild independence. And she was all manners and restraint."

"Not *all* restraint, obviously," said Louise, wiping her face.

"That's true," Rafael said. "She gave birth to me in France and stayed with him five years—until she realized he was never going to marry her."

"He wouldn't marry your mother? Didn't he love her?"

"He did. But wild men of the Pyrenees don't get married," Rafael said.

"Ah." Louise blinked, studying his expression. "So what did she do?"

"When I was five, she left him and returned to England, where she eventually married a responsible viscount, and I became a stain on the family. And the reason I'm telling you this is because for the rest of her life, every time my mother had a bad day, she'd throw up her hands and say, '*I wish I'd never met that fucking man.*' When I was fourteen, I'd had enough of it and ran off. It was 1933. I made my way south to Pau—by train and by mule—to find my father, who continued to make quite a name for himself in the mountains. The Spanish Civil War was brewing. There was plenty to do, smuggling black market goods into starving Spain. I lived with him and worked by his side until I was nineteen."

"And your mother never knew where you were?"

"She knew. I sent her a postcard."

"What did you say?"

"*The mountain air is fine here,* I wrote. *No wonder you got so taken with it. P.S.* Aita *sends his regards. Aita* is Papa in Basque."

"You didn't!"

"I did." He sighed. "And then war broke out. I returned to England and joined the British Army."

"How did your mother react to your return?"

"I didn't stay with her for long," Rafael said. "But when she first saw me, a young man of nineteen, she said, 'Of course. *Exactly* like your father. And I don't mean that as a compliment, Rafael.'"

Louise was quiet. "Is this a warning?" she said. "That I shouldn't get too close to the son of a lawless Basque rogue?"

"No," said Rafael. "Because I'm not my father. I love you, but I don't want to hear you say you wish you'd never met me."

"Okay," she said, beckoning him to lie down with her, kissing his face, holding him close. "I won't say it again."

She closed her eyes. She wouldn't say it.

But that didn't mean she wouldn't feel it.

"What's your mother's name, Rafa?"

"Lady Evangeline Ashcombe. Evie."

"And your father's?"

"Imanol Canario. Iman."

Louise opened her legs for him and let him enter her like she was his home. Afterward, she lay in his arms. "No matter what bitterness your mother carried afterward," she said softly, "the thing that made you wasn't bitterness. The thing that brought you into this world—the remarkable, inimitable, irreplaceable Rafael Canario—wasn't hatred."

"Tell that to my lady mother," said Rafael.

"Don't carve out of my body a cross," Louise whispered. "But don't be a eunuch either. I'm so jealous of you, you know."

"You're jealous of *me*?"

"Because all you do with your body is fight and love," she said.

"But all you do with yours is love," he whispered. "Much better."

They loved as best they could, knowing it might be the last time.

"I will bathe us in the river," he whispered, "fearless, swollen with love."

She prayed to go deaf—to not hear the bells of Herentals summoning them to death. Why didn't you pass me by on your road to Louise? she wanted to say to him. You deigned to summer here. You fashioned me with your hands, hard like marble—and now look what's happening. "Once upon a time, the monks made coffins in Herentals. Did you know that?" Louise said, trying very hard not to cry again.

"Are there any monks left who still do it?"

"When we die," she said, "who's going to make a coffin for you and me?"

"Someone who can make a golden coffin, I hope," said Rafael.

He was joking with her, she knew, but nothing was funny anymore.

"When you bury me," she said, "I want to hear birds singing. I want to hear the bells of Herentals ringing."

"You're in luck," he said. "They haven't stopped bloody ringing."

"I want roses. I want to be buried in the spring."

"Spring's kind of far away," he said.

"All I wanted when I first met you was to know you a little."

"And I you, Loosha. And I you, my love."

"I didn't want you to occupy my life," she said. "I wanted your black eyes to be anonymous. Your burning hands, anonymous. I wanted you to have no name."

"But I do have a name," he said.

"I wanted roses and bells, and a golden coffin, and I wanted you, nameless, to one day dance upon my grave."

"What are you talking about?" said Rafael. "You are immortal, Louise Aubel. You will never die."

71

Force Multipliers

Hubner turned off the main road, looking for the Abbey of Sancta Maria in Silvis Sacris. The trees closed in almost immediately, the branches hung low. The path barely fit the Mercedes. Gravel snapped under the tires as Hubner drove.

Rheinhardt shifted in the back seat. "The abbey is down here?" he said. "That can't be right."

"My map says . . ."

The deeper they went, the quieter it got. No wind. No birdsong. Only the hum of the car and the crunch of the pine limbs and rocks.

Rheinhardt glanced out the window.

"How much farther?"

"I don't know, sir. The map doesn't say."

It didn't feel like they were approaching an abbey.

It felt like they were being lured somewhere.

But then there it was.

The abbey lay sunken at the bottom of the woods. Heavy stone walls, no windows, one small visible entrance. A belltower that was more sniper's perch than steeple. And above it all, the woods, steep and still and watching.

Rheinhardt didn't know what he expected. Certainly not what he found. Most of Belgium's monasteries and abbeys were in the fields, near towns, villages, out in the open. He had never come across an abbey like this: a fortress in the basin, defended by rising silence. He scanned the ridgelines. A slow dread gathered in his chest. There was no movement, but the geography was wrong, the quiet was wrong.

Everything was wrong.

Hubner turned off the car and reached for the doorhandle. Rheinhardt stopped him. "No," he said. "Don't open it."

"Why, sir? We've come to the right place."

"Oh, I have no doubt about *that*. But look at it." Rheinhardt pressed himself into the back seat, as if he wanted to disappear. "Hubner," he said, almost whispering, "start the car. Quietly. Reverse. Drive away."

"What? No! Why? We must make ourselves known."

"Do what I tell you. No questions. Smoothly. Carefully. But don't dawdle. Drive with all deliberate speed." He sank low, hiding below the glass.

Hubner did as he was told. Reversing, he eased out of the forecourt and followed the winding forest path back uphill.

Rheinhardt held his breath. The trail could be mined.

But it wasn't.

At the top of the rise, where the forest lane met the paved main road, Hubner swung left—and nearly plowed into a priest. He appeared out of nowhere, dressed in a black cassock and biretta, walking unhurriedly along the verge.

Hubner swerved hard, tires screeching, and slammed the horn. The priest didn't flinch. He didn't even turn around. He simply raised his right hand and traced the sign of the cross in the air, then kept walking, leisurely and with grace.

"Don't disturb me, Hubner," Rheinhardt said on the way back to Antwerp. "I need to think."

Why was the road not mined? Was he imagining harm where there was none?

No. Just the opposite.

Harm didn't just exist. It was free-floating between the trees and the leaves.

This wasn't just bad ground. It was a kill zone. A death funnel.

His men would've driven into the woods down an unmined road and been killed before they could get out of their vehicles. There was no cover. All the fire would fly one way: down. From the heights of the trees into the dell of death.

Back at Baert Haus, the two men sat across from each other in Rheinhardt's office.

"What happened back there, sir?"

"What happened, Hubner," Rheinhardt said, "is I realized that if anyone was guarding the abbey, and you and I stepped out of the car, we would have been killed with two shots."

Hubner swallowed dry, absorbing. "You think that was an ambush?"

"It's not an abbey," Rheinhardt said. "It's a trap. And we almost walked into it like drunken fools. It would've been suicide to open that door."

How were his men supposed to walk into that trap and walk out alive?

Why couldn't a single thing be simple? Why couldn't he get a break on anything?

"Get me Sieg Krieger on the phone," Rheinhardt said. "We're going to need his help."

"But we have our own seasoned men, sir. Loyal. Battle-tested."

"We will need more than men to take back what's ours," said Rheinhardt. "We're going to need force multipliers."

Charlie, Fletcher, and Hawk lay on their stomachs high in the hills, behind a fallen tree. Hawk's scope was set on one side of the car, Fletcher's on the other. Charlie watched the Mercedes through her binoculars. *Get out of the car*, she whispered. *Get out of the fucking car.*

"Can't get a bead on them," Hawk said. "Glass too dark. Reflection too sharp."

"Just wait, they'll get out," Fletcher whispered, barely audible.

If Hawk was breathing, Charlie couldn't tell. Nothing on him moved.

Their two rifles, steadied by the fallen tree, were motionless.

All Rheinhardt and his driver had to do was open the doors.

Instead, after a few frozen moments, the car started up again, reversed out of the clearing, and made its way back up the narrow path.

"Why are they leaving?" Charlie cried.

Hawk and Fletcher flicked their safeties on and sat up against the trunk, their lowered rifles in their hands. "He knew," Fletcher said. "He could feel it."

"Feel what?"

"Death," said Hawk.

"You think that's why he didn't open the door?" said Charlie.

"Yes."

"How could he know?"

"Look at this place."

Hawk was right about that.

"So what are we going to do?"

"We'll wait another hour," said Fletcher. "Maybe they'll come back. Okay, Hawk?"

"Anything you need, Commander."

"What if they don't come back in an hour?"

"Tomorrow or the next day, they'll bring someone else here," Fletcher said. "Someone dispensable. Rheinhardt will want to test his senses. See if he's right."

"So we're going to have to stay on patrol another twenty-four hours?"

"Or more."

Charlie groaned. "I guess it's worth it," she said. "If we can kill them."

Fletcher shook his head. "We can't shoot his decoys. That's our only advantage. He has the men and the weapons. All we have is whatever edge we can take. If we shoot the decoys, he'll find another way in—through the woods. That'll be worse for us. But if we don't shoot the decoys, maybe he'll start to doubt himself. He might think he's being played. But he also might decide he was just being paranoid. It's a small chance, but it's not zero."

"So now we're *not* shooting his decoys?"

"Correct."

"Eyes up, Lieutenant," Hawk said.

A priest in black robes was walking down the forest path, headed for the abbey.

"Rheinhardt's decoy?" Charlie asked dryly.

Hawk's rifle was already aimed and in position.

Charlie watched as the priest walked up to the heavy door and knocked forcefully three times. A few beats went by. The metal hatch slid open. "Sancta Maria in Silvis Sacris is a cloistered house," Sister Therese said, in the same cadence she had used on Charlie a month earlier. "Who stands at our gate?"

"I am Father Roland of Dieleghem Fields," the priest said. "Robert Capelle sent me here."

Charlie nearly dropped her binoculars.

"Robert Capelle did *not* send you here," Therese said.

"Yes, yes," Roland said impatiently. "It was the Lord, our God. But Robert Capelle is the vessel through whom the Lord our God sent me here. Open the door, Sister, and go get Mother Verene."

Charlie rocked back in amazement. "Who *is* this man?" she whispered. "Quick. Let's go meet him."

They picked up their weapons and hurried downhill through the dense woods.

Father Roland turned when he heard the underbrush crackling behind him. He was in his fifties, in a cassock and a plain three-peaked black biretta. His soutane fit him awkwardly, as if he had a suit of armor underneath it. He was clean-shaven and short-haired. A modest cross with no ornamentation hung from his neck. He looked like a man who'd never stopped doing whatever it was he did in his youth that gave him such gravitas and heft when he stood and moved.

He appraised the three young people coming toward him with a calm, watchful eye and said, "If this is the quietest you can be, we're doomed."

Verene opened the door. "Oh, it's *you*," she said. It was unclear from her tone which of the visitors she was referring to. Roland didn't even ask for permission to enter. He just walked past Verene, blessing her with his right hand, while motioning with his left for Charlie and the men to follow him.

"Close and bolt the door," he said to Verene.

In the courtyard, the nuns stopped their work and stood to the side of the vegetable garden, gaping at him.

"Father Roland," the Abbess said, coming around to face him. "What have they wrought?"

He didn't answer her until he'd blessed the nuns. "They're here to save our Belgium," Roland said, finally addressing Verene. "You should be more hospitable." She began to defend herself, but he stopped her. "It's too late for everything now," he said. "I'm here because the Waffen-SS are coming. We cannot prevent that. But we can try to prevent them from getting inside—where they have no business being."

"Is that why *you're* here?" Verene said. "One man against all of Germany? What do you think this is, the Battle of Yser?" Yser was the last stand of the few remaining Belgians in West Flanders in 1916, who stopped the mass of Germans from capturing the final strip of unoccupied Belgian territory.

"Yes," Roland said. "Here, we too shall create an impassable swamp made of fire."

"How'd that go for you in Yser?" Verene muttered.

Father Roland didn't mutter. "We didn't fight in Yser because we sought victory, Verene," he said in a deep, resonant voice. "We fought because we refused to be defeated."

Charlie blinked. No wonder the nuns were staring at this man with barely concealed reverence. After introductions were made, Fletcher asked Roland why he was sent.

"I'm here for several reasons," Roland said. "Like you, correct?" He took a beat to let the words sink in before opening his cassock and showing Fletcher that he was loaded with weapons back to front. "I'm here to protect the nuns. This House of God is the only sanctuary left in these woods." His gaze traveled from Hawk to Charlie. "Men and women in combat together?"

"Yes," replied Charlie.

"Are all the women fighters like you?"

"Not all of them."

"You need to bring the non-combatants here. As soon as you can. They'll be safer in the cloister. But I'm also here for Ngomo. Where is he?"

Did every single person in Belgium know who Ngomo was? An incredulous Charlie tried to catch Fletcher's eye, but he wasn't responding in kind. He looked downcast and grim. “He’s with us,” Charlie replied. “But he’s not alone anymore. He’s got an orphaned boy with him.”

“Even better,” Roland said, his unblinking gaze on Fletcher, who wasn’t responding or lifting his gaze, so Charlie pushed on.

“What *I* don’t understand, Father,” she said, “is how Capelle was able to communicate with you when he is followed by a dozen Gestapo into the privy, if you’ll excuse my coarseness.”

Roland nodded, answering her while he took off his cassock and began to unstrap the rifles and pistols holstered to him. “Indeed the Nazis intrude on every aspect of our private and public lives. However, a Catholic in Belgium is still allowed to make confession.”

“Ah.” The penitent’s booth! Omloop would be proud. Poor Omloop.

“Count Capelle has been my friend since we were children,” Roland said. “He’s been confessing to me weekly since the start of the occupation. Sometimes twice-weekly.” Roland half smiled. “Yesterday, a German SS officer came to his house. Erich von Rheinhardt? This morning he returned, and one of the guards unfortunately supplied him with the name of this abbey. So we knew we were short on time. Do you have any firepower?”

Fletcher nodded.

“Probably time to bring it close.”

“It’s already here,” said Fletcher. “Been here for days. We’ve fortified the woods. We’re as ready as we can be.”

Father Roland tilted his head appreciatively, studying Fletcher with newfound respect.

“Do you have mortar?”

“Yes.”

“Mines?”

“Yes.”

“Grenades?”

“Yes.”

“Bouncing Betties?”

“Yes.”

“Rounds?”

“Thousands.”

“Rifles? Pistols?”

“Yes and yes.”

“A heavy machine gun, by chance?”

“Yes.”

Roland whistled.

“And two TNT blocks with det cords,” said Fletcher with a small smile.

While the two men spoke the litany of war, Verene and Therese crossed themselves and intoned the litany of supplication. *Lord have mercy.*

Roland made the sign of the cross on Charlie, Fletcher, and Hawk. "Go," he said. "I will eat with the nuns, go to vespers, get some rest. You should too. Come back at dawn. But bring Ngomo to me."

"I will deliver your request, Father," Fletcher said. "But Ngomo is his own man, with his own mind, believe me. He said he wants to be out there with us. He wants to fight."

"Tell him Roland and Capelle and the King believe he's done enough fighting to last five lifetimes. This time, he truly needs to be safe."

Fletcher listened mutely. "Safe or saved?"

"Both," said Roland, walking them to the door. "Listen for the Ashen Bell," he added. "And remember, children, you weren't chosen because you were ready. You were chosen because you said yes."

72

All of Us, Then

They opened every bottle they could find—wine from the cellars, a few green bottles of brandy from the castle pantry and a bottle of schnapps someone had obviously been saving for the end of days.

They toasted each other, and then they drank.

And when each bottle was emptied, they stuffed it with rags soaked in gasoline. Charlie would wipe her mouth, rise with exaggerated care and say, "Next. And next."

What they didn't drink would burn.

"Do you think we have enough?" she said, slurring slightly, pointing to the edge of the stone patio where a hundred Molotovs stood corked and ready.

And Fletcher, in his own unsteady voice, said, "We either have way too many . . . or not nearly enough."

The wine was heavy in Charlie's blood. So was the weight of the impossible hours ahead, pressing down on her, on all of them.

For part of the night, they sat and drank and worked in gathered silence.

Fletcher lifted his glass first. "To Rafael," he said, "who never ducked, even when he should have."

"Yes, to Rafael," Briggs said, "who taught me how to say 'fuck you' in five languages." They clinked and drank.

"To Fletcher," said Rafael, "who counts paces between trees, bullets in our belts, and every one of us like we're his to lose."

"And who hasn't slept since Normandy," said Briggs.

"I can attest to that," said Charlie.

"Whoa!" yelled Louise, Brigitte, and Mireille.

Fletcher tipped his glass to Charlie, his gaze laden with the burden of everything he felt for her.

"To Charlie," he said, "for all your thankless tasks."

"To Omloop," said Charlie, "without whom we'd have nothing."

"To Omloop," the girls echoed in mournful unison, downing another.

"To Hawk," Fletcher said, "who *actually* hasn't slept since Normandy, watching over me—over us."

"And to Hildi," said Charlie, "who, even now, is watching over Hawk." Her gaunt ghostly Hildi had truly found her *l'âme élue*, her chosen soul, in that gold-eyed *faucon*. Charlie's gaze drifted to Fletcher, sitting between her and Rafael, his knees drawn up, his deep-set, midnight-purple eyes staring tensely into space. Hildi's not the only one who's found her *l'âme élue*, she thought, the wine and her love for him catching in her throat.

"To Briggs," said Wolski, "who barreled through artillery bunkers at Omaha like he was mortar shell."

"To Briggs," said Mireille, in French, "the gentlest man I've ever known."

"To Wolski," said Briggs, "who could track a ghost through smoke."

"To Belvy," said Rafael, "may you never run out of your Stitchless Seal."

"To Belvy," said Briggs, "may you live to be a hundred, drinking tea out of your tin cup and ragging on us."

"If I live to be a hundred, you'll still be idiots," said Belvedere.

Brigitte couldn't say anything. She'd had too much wine, and she was crying.

"To Gitta, for seeing the good in all people," said Charlie, her softened words sliding into each other. "And to Louise, who never ran away, though she wanted to."

"I really should've when I had the chance," said Louise, sounding like she knew she never did.

"Stick with us now," said Rafael, taking her hand. "Stick with me."

"To Ngomo," said Fletcher, "for fighting even when the fight was hopeless."

"I don't deserve a toast," Ngomo said. "I'm the reason we're here."

"Ngomo is right," Rafael said. "No toast for him. Take his wine."

"To Zeus," said Ngomo, lifting his glass. "Who saved me."

"Hey!" said Charlie.

"Who told Charlie to save me," said Ngomo, with gentle grace.

"Better," said Charlie.

The fire crackled. The wind passed through the grass.

They had come this far. They knew some of them would go no further.

"To all of us, then."

They sat for a long time sobering up by the fading fire, until the last embers flickered out.

"Qui se souviendra de mon nom?" said Louise. Who'll remember my name?

"What do you mean?" said Rafael. "I'm writing it on a grenade right now—and I'm pitching it straight into Rheinhardt's Nazi heart. It'll say *the Belle of Bastogne was here*."

From the near distance, they heard the sound of a tolling bell.

They stared at each other in the gathering silence. Charlie's heart started to pound. It echoed through her body. *Please, Fletcher*, she prayed, clasping her hands together, *don't ruin this beautiful day with your death.*

The bell kept tolling, three short, one long, three short, one long . . .

"It's Hawk," said Rafael.

". . . For victory," said Fletcher. "Like the signal lamps from the planes over Normandy." He got to his feet. "Men. Women. Ngomo. Zeus. Remember—if you can't save the mission, save each other. Now let's move."

"Let's fucking go!" said Briggs, giving Mireille a kiss and leaping up like a fortress come to life. "Rider, you with me?"

"Always, Briggsy." Rafael stood, but didn't, or couldn't, look at Louise. "Let's fucking go."

73

Sancta Maria in Silvis Sacris

Rheinhardt returned to Tremelo with an army. Flamethrowers, heavy machine guns, mortars, grenades, thousands of rounds of ammunition, and a demolition squad of Waffen-SS men.

He was determined—but he had to be careful. He didn't know exactly where the barrels were hidden. Grunfell confirmed that uranium was inert—harmless until enriched, but if the abbey collapsed, if breaching the walls took charges and craters, then access to the barrels might be lost for longer than he could afford. The walls were meters thick. A single detonation could bring down tons of stone and timber, burying the uranium for good. That was a risk Rheinhardt couldn't take. He could lose a thousand men, but he couldn't lose any more time.

And he couldn't risk sabotage. One partisan with a det cord deciding the uranium must belong to no one—unthinkable. He would make sure it never came to that.

He would destroy them all.

Gone was even the pretense of trying to win cleanly.

If he couldn't walk to the abbey doors like a civilized man without being ambushed, then he would break the resistance by terror.

Before bringing an army, Rheinhardt sent a scout team. A few expendable conscripts. They returned unharmed. No mine was set off. Not a single bullet was fired.

And that's how Rheinhardt knew for certain he was dealing with another chess master.

His opponent had left the German men untouched *on purpose*—to lure Rheinhardt down the forest road, into the bottleneck of death, into the funnel of slaughter.

For a day, Rheinhardt was outraged—livid that his men had been spared. Who the fuck was this?

But now he almost wanted to thank his foe. Because now Rheinhardt understood what he was up against. So he brought an army but forbade them from using the winding road to the abbey. Instead, he ordered the men to approach through the forest, the back way, through thick hills and brush, no matter how slow, no matter how punishing.

He sent two flanking teams ahead. He didn't know how many minions the devil had, but it couldn't be enough to cover all four sides. He didn't strike the abbey first. The first thing he did at dawn, upon arriving in Tremelo, was split his flamethrower teams in four directions. Then he ordered them to set the woods on fire.

He attacked the enemy's escape routes.

He turned their stronghold into a funeral pyre.

Little by little, the forest filled with smoke. Even his own men began to choke, and to panic. They broke from the trees into the clearing to breathe—and were cut down from above. One shot. Another. Whoever it was never missed.

Never.

Not even when the trees cracked around him.

From the main road where he was stationed, Rheinhardt couldn't see the abbey at all, only the tops of the trees, shivering in streaks of sunlight. The forest swallowed everything. Fire. Gunshots. Downed men. He might have sent an army into the woods, but once they entered, they were gone. He listened for the sound of weapons and waited for his runners.

"The smoke is overpowering my men," a captain said, running up the hill.

"Where's my spotter?" Rheinhardt asked. "I need a report."

"Delayed."

"Is that a euphemism for dead? Send another. Tell him not to die this time." He seized the officer's arm. "Do you remember my order? If you come across a black man in these hills, you are not to kill him. I need him alive. At any cost."

"My men already know their orders," the captain said, peeling Rheinhardt's fingers from his sleeve. "But I'll remind them—sir."

Rheinhardt listened for the pop of rifle fire, the roar of flamethrowers. Through the trees, he could see licks of flame, hear the cracking of branches.

What if the fire reached the abbey? What if it collapsed? Hadn't he ordered his men to stay clear of the structure? To ignite only the perimeter?

"Captain!" he shouted the next time he saw him. "Why are the flames so close to the abbey? I thought my orders were clear."

"They were, sir," the officer said. "But it's *fire*." He said this as if speaking to the feeble-minded.

"Put it out," Rheinhardt said. "Don't let it get out of control."

The flames rose, dragged sideways by the morning breeze.

One of the runners returned, gasping, eyes streaming. He passed out before he could speak.

Hubner approached from the Mercedes, parked in the underbrush across the road. "Do you want me to go down, sir? I could bring back a report."

"No!" Rheinhardt said. "Back to the car. Immediately. Try not to twist your ankle." Didn't Hubner understand what was down there? Hot hell is what it was. "Faster, Hubner. Inside the car. Stay there until I call for you." He had enough to worry about. Did he have to worry about Hubner too?

Rheinhardt hated blind combat. He had no control, and that was anathema to him. He needed maps, manifests, corridors, order. Places where men behaved predictably—like lines on paper. Like chess pieces on a board.

All he had now was the fear that something was going wrong, and no way to know what it was. How could he command if he didn't know what he was facing?

The trap had been sprung—but much too slowly.

The fire hadn't cleared the bastards from the hills. They kept killing his men.

Nothing had gone to plan, absolutely fucking nothing. Three of his trucks were on fire, their ammo was dwindling, their mortars nearly gone. Hundreds of his men were dead. And he still didn't have what he wanted.

Was this witchcraft?

Who were these fucking people?

How many of them were there?

He should've brought a rocket launcher unit. Leveled all of fucking Tremelo.

Cursing, smoking, pacing, he waited.

The battle raged against the relentless march of darkness.

It was hell at high noon.

Ash fell like snow in sunlight.

The air was suffocating.

It was the middle of the day, but the smoke had blotted out the sun. The forest had been plunged into a night-black fog. Fletcher couldn't see, and he couldn't hear. The adrenaline meant he couldn't feel his wounds, and it was just as well, for he might have faltered if he knew how much blood he'd shed. There were times Fletcher wondered if they'd already won. It was so numb and silent around him, and smoke covered everything.

He gulped from his canteen before realizing it was empty. Nearby,

Belvedere knelt in the leaf rot, hands slick with blood—Fletcher didn't know whose—glasses sliding down his nose. A tin of Stitchless Seal lay open beside him.

Belvedere didn't speak, just worked, jaw set, ripping open Fletcher's tunic, packing the miracle powder into his shoulder, pressing the hot plate into his wound. "Hold still," Belvedere said, "and try not to get yourself killed in the next twelve seconds. Think how upset Rafael would be." He counted off his Saint George's prayer, snapped the tin shut, wiped his hands and crawled away to find whoever needed him next.

They used the woods to their advantage. The fight spilled through the misty forests. An overthinker, Fletcher turned the hills into a Nazi deathtrap, laying ambushes and leveraging terrain. Rafael just tommy-gunned the shit out of anyone in front of him. Three Germans broke through the trees, rifles high. Rafael let the first one come close and shot him through the throat. The second ducked—too late. Rafael spun behind a tree and knifed him as he passed. The third turned to run. Rafael shot him in the back, reloaded, kept moving.

The abbey loomed in the background, untouched for now. Shells exploded. Trees were aflame. But the holy place stood like a silent guardian amid the chaos.

Perhaps by the time they returned to life and sound, the reinforcements might come. Fletcher thought this fleetingly. Deep in his heart, he knew no one was coming.

Godspeed, Jonathan Reed had said. *Primary objective at all costs.*

Fletcher didn't know who or what was left for *any* objectives. The leaves were heavy with blood.

Rafael and Wolski got separated trying to intercept both flanks. Fletcher didn't see either of them for minutes.

Or was it hours?

The smoke was eating at his eyes.

Demons were fighting ghosts in the sacred wood.

When his sight began to recover, he saw Charlie, braced behind a rock, firing her silent rifle, and he knew what was left.

She was left.

And up above in the tower with the seven bells, Hawk was left. Soaring above them with his sights fixed and his aim unerring, knocking down the demons one by one, giving the ghosts a chance to breathe, to live, to fight, to escape, to keep their promises.

The walls of the abbey were strong, but not impenetrable. The massive door was secure, but not unbreachable. It was the doorway of Thebes.

First, men would defend it.

And when all the men were dead, the women would defend it.

And when all the women were dead, then ghosts would defend it.

Ghosts, mere specters of humans. Like him. Like her. Like that little guy, running around, finding boxes of ammo in the black magic forest.

What was his name?

Oh, yes.

Zeus.

No quarter was given, because no quarter was possible.

There was the abbey, and hidden inside its catacombs were *barrels of flame*. And either they remained where they were, and the world was safe, or they were seized, and everything else was ashes.

To repel the column of heinous men hellbent on destruction was the only imperative left to Fletcher and his brothers in arms, the only imperative left to Fletcher and his bravest girl, crouched in the moss, firing her silent weapon from behind her stone.

Fletcher knew what Charlie did not. That after the pistols and rifles were emptied came the combat with knives—face to face, throat to throat, heart to heart. That's why there was such fury in the assault now, such rage in the effort. Because soon, the unthinkable would be upon them.

Maybe Charlie could fight, maybe she could vanquish a man or two. Maybe Hildi could. But the women hiding in the abbey couldn't do it. Louise, Mireille, Brigitte.

They wouldn't survive it.

When there was no gunpowder left, only the unspeakable would remain—the slaughter of the girls who tried to help Fletcher and his men do the impossible: fend off the strongest army in the world with rocks and guts.

Soon the close-quarter combat would make this battle collapse into savagery.

And Fletcher, despite all promises, was powerless to stop it.

Claustrophobia and despair descended upon him.

The noise of the battle broke through as he ran through the woods, dropping and firing, a sound not of this world. The weapons of warfare were nothing but pure terror. The branches they made into spears. The mines they laid around the perimeter. The hydrochloric acid Hildi poured on fucking Nazis from the trees where she hid.

Everyone, even the good guys, had to close their ears to the screaming of the ruined Germans. Thankfully, the screaming was brief. Hydrochloric acid was a swift and vicious killer.

It didn't feel like war.

It felt like the apocalypse.

And soon the ghosts would have nothing with which to fight.

Ngomo was ridiculously good at close-quarter combat. He demolished anyone who got near him.

No wonder he survived the massacre at La Fortuna, Fletcher thought. He'd been forged long before that, baptized in the brutal battles of the Congo, where death came scythe to scythe. But here in the woods, one slip over rough terrain, one lunge in the wrong direction, and Zeus would have to make it to Lisbon alone.

Zeus wasn't making it easy for Fletcher to keep his promises either. The boy kept finding boxes of ammo and carrying them to the belltower, climbing the spiral staircase and handing them to Hawk. And Hawk saying thanks, buddy, but I can't see them, the smoke is making me blind. Can you find the catch on the rifle for me and pop it open, take a cartridge and shove it up there, until it clicks—yes, buddy, just like that, perfect. Now get out of here, before Fletcher goes ballistic, and Ngomo too.

Hawk's hands were going numb. Sweat dripped into his eyes. The barrel of his rifle was so hot it was burning the hands that couldn't feel. He was running out of ammo.

He'd been running out of ammo for hours.

How can you shoot if you can't see, Hawk? Zeus would ask.

And Hawk would reply with a question of his own. Are the Germans falling or are they standing, Zeus? If they are falling, then all is well. Now go. Don't come back.

And fifteen minutes later, Zeus would creep up the spiral stairs, holding another box or two in his little hands, saying Hawk, I found you some more. Can I pop them in for you? Can you see? Belvedere gave me a towel for you, and a bandage. Want me to wipe your eyes?

Sure, buddy. Wipe my eyes, but gently. They really hurt, Zeus.

I brought some cold water. Want me to wet the towel and dab your eyes?

Sure, Zeus.

Promises made.

Here was the thing about gunfire. It made you deaf at the very moment you needed to hear better than ever.

But when someone you loved was calling for you, screaming for you, in a way that sounded not just urgent but critical . . . you really needed to be able to turn to the voice and say, *What? Can you repeat that please, but slower and louder because honestly, I can't hear a fucking thing.*

Where was Rafael with his wolf-like hearing when you needed him?

It was Charlie. At his sleeve, yanking, pointing, yelling. Fletcher couldn't hear. But he read her lips.

Hawk, her mute voice carried.

HAWK.

He followed her finger. Down below, in the smoke, where Hawk couldn't see them, where Fletcher could barely see them, two Germans who'd been hiding in the bushes (as if bushes could protect them), were running. Running. Carrying a mortar between them to a flat stretch of earth. Laying it down, angling it, positioning it. The mortar was pointed straight at the belltower. Straight at Hawk. He would've killed them, but he couldn't—because he couldn't see them.

Fletcher was charging through the bush and the underbrush, calling for Briggs the same way Charlie had called for him.

HAWK, he kept yelling to Briggs.

Briggs barreled from the hills to the clearing. He was fast, but he had farther to run.

The fucking bastards. They couldn't beat Hawk, so they were trying to ambush him the only way they knew how—through the smoke-filled ruins below.

Briggs tripped on a fallen tree and scuffled through the bushes. The hilly forest had protected him this whole time, but now it stood in his way. He fought it, racing desperately to get to them before they had time to fit a shell inside the barrel of their heaviest weapon.

Fletcher got to them half a moment too late.

Briggs got to them half a moment too late.

Briggs launched himself—plunging into them, knocking them off their feet. Fletcher shot one of them. Briggs knifed the second one in the neck.

But they got to them half a moment too late.

The shell whistled through the pink, bloody forest and hit the belfry ten feet below where Hawk stood. It ripped the tower apart and exploded, pulverizing sand, clay, and the wooden spiral stairs. As the tower collapsed, its seven bells from great to small plunged into the debris and ashes, tolling against the shattering stone through fire and smoke. Like fate itself, they rang in Hawk's requiem, falling in slow motion with the crumbling tower.

Hawk was their force multiplier, their equalizer, their rocket launcher. Their army. With him gone, the hard fight got harder. They had no one to cover them.

Yet so many promises had been made.

Back and forth, from London to Belgium, from the Congo to Bruges, promises flew like bullets and bouncing Betties.

Fletcher promised Jonathan Reed who promised Robert Capelle who promised the King of all the Belgians. *Whatever happens, get Ngomo out. Don't let him die because of me, get him out. Don't let him get captured, Fletcher.* How could Fletcher make good on the promise to the King? How could he keep his word to Jonathan Reed? Ngomo was in the shit like the rest of them. How could Fletcher get Ngomo out if couldn't get himself out? And what about Ngomo's assurance to him? He said he'd never let them take him alive. Did he remember that promise?

Ngomo, Fletcher said, when he got close enough to grab the warrior's bloodied arm in the forest, remember what you vowed to Father Roland. The fucking tunnel, Ngomo. If it all goes to hell, take the hidden door at the back of the belltower. Get inside the abbey. Run to the chapel. Find the hatch. Take Zeus with you. But close it back up, or they'll find you—and our women. And the nuns. Close it up and run. The tunnel is a kilometer through the hills. It connects death with life. It opens into another forest, another field, another mountain. There's a bunker at the end. Climb out slowly. Only if you think it's safe.

No one is safe, Commander, said Ngomo. Where is Zeus? I can't find him. And then Fletcher to Wolski, Are you listening?

No, I'm bleeding from my ears.

Go with him, Wolski. Fletcher squeezed Wolski's arm and wiped the blood from his head. You *hear* me? You're the only one who can do it. Take him. And Zeus. Get them out of Belgium.

How can I get him out? Wolski said. On train? Black man will board train? Sit at window? Present his ticket?

Figure it out. Walk if you have to.

Walk with child two thousand kilometers through apocalypse?

He's lived through worse, Janusz. And you promised him. Make good on it.

Wolski making promises to Zeus.

Buddy, he said, do you remember time we had adventure in woods? We walked thirteen kilometers?

Zeus, grimy, bloodied, trying to smile. Another adventure, Yanush?

Yes, buddy, yes, but this one little longer than thirteen kilometers. Fifteen kilometers?

Wolski saying, try two thousand kilometers.

Zeus's eyes lighting up, reflecting off the embers in the woods. Okay, Yanush. Let's get Ngomo and go.

But Ngomo was still in the forest, knife to knife in the smoke.

And now Zeus was missing.

All these promises.

Fletcher in the hills trying to find Ngomo. Yelling for Rafael, for Belvedere, for Briggs. Losing the path, the plot, the thread that tied him to his men. Chaos in his head, chaos in the hills, chaos down below.

Brigitte screaming for Belvedere who was pulling Wolski through the concealed door behind the ruined belltower. Belvedere bleeding from his torso and from a gash in his neck he was trying to hold shut. Whispering to the wounded Wolski, get yourself up, you promised the boy an adventure, I heard you myself, drag yourself inside, and I promise I'll never call you an idiot again. Except this once. You're a fucking idiot, running into that bullet.

Brigitte dragging Belvedere inside the abbey walls. The medic couldn't help Wolski anymore. Not enough blood left in his body to drag someone else to safety. Brigitte dragging them both, one by one, Belvedere first. Hiding them in the crevice of the shattered wall, holding Belvedere's head in her lap, whispering. Where's your Stitchless Seal, Belvy? Where is it?

Belvedere mouthing, *You're smothering me.* Looking up at her. Raising his hand to her cheek.

Brigitte whispering, did you use it all up, Belvy? Or did you save some for yourself, a little tin box that said Belvy on it? Brigitte, searching through his sleeves and pockets, finding a little hidden pouch at last, in the stitching of his coat, trying to pry it open with trembling hands.

And Wolski gently taking it from her, whispering, leave it, Bree-ghee-tah. He's gone, our Belvy. He's gone.

Mireille saying, where's Briggs?

Ngomo saying, where's Zeus?

Briggs seeing the boy standing beneath the belltower, staring up through the smoke, calling for Hawk.

Briggs having no time even to call Zeus's name.

Briggs leaping through the clearing, with a final roar, shoving the child hard out of the way.

The bells coming down.

Taking Briggs with them.

Father Roland saying, all of you who are alive and remain, you must get into the tunnel. The walls are about to be breached. The abbey will fall. Where is Ngomo?

They couldn't find him.

Fletcher finally stumbling upon Rafael unconscious in the woods. Shaking him, Rafael coming to, screaming in pain. Fletcher helping him to his feet, choking on smoke, staggering through the abbey courtyard, trying to find the door behind the crumbled belltower. Following the voices of the women, like clarion bells through the smoke. Louise crying *Rafael, Rafael . . .*

Following her voice over the broken stones. Charlie running out, rifle in her hands, firing into the hills. Grabbing Rafael. Both of them half carrying him inside the abbey, into the chapel. Louise catching and cradling him there, sobbing, is he going to die, God? Please, no, is he going to die? His blood soaking through her dress. Rafael lying in her arms, not speaking.

Roland saying, quick, Fletcher, get into the tunnel. Save what's left of your men and women.

Fletcher saying, I can't go. *I can't go until I know who I've left behind.*

Charlie tugging on him, rifle clutched in one hand. Everyone who's still alive is down below.

Roland pushing him. Go, Fletcher. Retreat now—and live to fight another day.

Fletcher wiping blood from his mouth, whispering, does it seem to you like there'll be another day?

Roland saying, *Always*. Blessing him. Forcing him down through the hatch.

The last defenders of Thebes at their final gate. Fletcher, last one in, after Rafael, after Louise, after Charlie.

One more sign of the cross from Roland over Fletcher's bloodied head.

"You didn't fight because you sought victory," said Roland. "You fought because you refused to be defeated."

He slammed the hatch shut.

Rheinhardt gave the nuns one final chance to surrender.

They refused.

"This is not your battlefield," the Abbess called to him from inside the abbey. "Your war is waged in the filth outside."

Rheinhardt gave the order.

"The light shines in the darkness," Verene said through the narrow metal slit, "and the darkness cannot overcome it."

"I will overcome it, Reverend Mother," said Rheinhardt.

Verene remained in the chapel, even when the battle came inside.

Rheinhardt's men planted charges at the northern wall.

"Small," he told them. "Just an opening wide enough to walk through. We don't need to turn it to rubble."

The explosion shook the foundation and cracked the arch.

"Did that seem small to you, Captain?" Rheinhardt roared.

But the wall held.

Demolition teams placed more charges.

And more.

Rheinhardt watched as part of the northern wall finally gave way and collapsed.

But the priest wouldn't let anyone enter through the smashed opening. He stood pinned against the chapel wall, firing without pause—rifle, pistol, anything he could hold. No one passed until they brought forward an infantry gun and fired a single high-explosive shell. It hit low, just left of the chapel arch. The blast took down half the chapel.

The gunfire stopped.

Just in time—for Rheinhardt was down to his last dozen men. The priest had fallen in his cassock and biretta, with no rounds left in any of his weapons.

Rheinhardt stepped into the wreckage, triumphant at last.

"Hubner," he said to his trusted aide. "Bring us the Geiger. And crank that generator."

The barrels of flame were seized.

And nothing else mattered.

PART IV

Après le Déluge, Nous

"I like it," he said, "Because it is bitter,
And because it is my heart."

Stephen Crane

74

How Many Men

Rheinhardt stood at attention in front of a grim Falkenhausen. He had no time for a dressing-down. He barely had time to dress. To be forced to return to Brussels, to stand before the governor and that ingrate swine Drechsler sneering beside him, was almost more than he could bear.

Another 300 kilowatts of power needed to be diverted to Zvart Haus. The exhaust shafts still weren't finished.

Grunfell was demanding two more subterranean generator banks. More voltage transformers. A backup diesel generator, possibly two, to ensure the cyclotron never shut down.

The sheer volume of copper wire Grunfell required would have been indefensible—unless the order came directly from Hitler. Copper was nearly as rare as uranium. A finessed phone call to Krieger—possibly even to Himmler—was overdue.

One of Grunfell's ore crushers had failed. He needed a replacement. And ten more men. More shrubbery to cover the new craters around Zvart Haus. And Rheinhardt had to requisition a grader to flatten the deep ruts gouged into the mud by the trucks hauling uranium across the countryside.

There was so much to think about.

And instead—this pointless drivel.

Drechsler and Falkenhausen couldn't be counted on to do what was right for the Reich. They clung to some antique code of military honor that Rheinhardt neither understood nor cared to.

He remained motionless, trying to ignore the heat of Falkenhausen's anger.

"Herr Rheinhardt, did you hear what we asked?" Drechsler barked. Since Rheinhardt's public disgrace, they'd barely spoken. There was nothing to say.

Rheinhardt furrowed his brow, pretending to appear engaged. "Yes, sir. The destruction of the abbey *was* unfortunate. But we gave them every opportunity to surrender—and retain both their lives and their walls."

"You gave the *nuns* every opportunity to surrender," Falkenhausen repeated slowly. "And did they take it, Herr Rheinhardt?"

The question was like spilled acid. Rheinhardt had no choice but to answer it literally. "No," he said.

"Were they engaged in armed combat with your men?"

"They weren't opening their doors, sir," Rheinhardt replied, "despite our repeated requests."

"They are not required by law to open the doors to occupying forces," said Falkenhausen. "They're not required to allow anyone in. The abbey is registered as a historic site of Belgium and is protected under both national and international law. Article 27 of the Hague Convention of 1907 states—clearly—that historic monuments, religious buildings, and charitable institutions *must* be spared."

"They must be spared," Rheinhardt said, "*if* they are not being used for military purposes at the time of the conflict."

"Were there soldiers inside the abbey, Herr Rheinhardt?"

"Yes, sir. At least one of their men was inside. He was ensconced in the belltower for hours, mowing down my men." Rheinhardt's rage still had not subsided.

"But you didn't have to enter the abbey to bring down the tower." Drechsler said. "You told us your men fired a shell from the outside perimeter."

Rheinhardt nearly stumbled. "That's correct, sir. But while we were neutralizing the threat, the partisans entered the abbey grounds."

"Did they enter for combat," Drechsler asked, "or did they enter for sanctuary?"

"We were in the middle of an hours-long battle with an armed, relentless enemy," Rheinhardt said tightly. "I did not stop to ask their purpose."

"How many men did you deploy?"

"Hundreds, sir."

"And how many men did *they* deploy?" Drechsler asked, drawing blood with his question. "Just a few, correct?"

Rheinhardt blinked but didn't falter. "We do not know. The search for bodies and survivors is ongoing." He had raked through the forest branch by branch, searching for Ngomo. Did that man escape yet again? How was that possible?

"Yes, and the fallout from what you've done is also ongoing."

"Herr Drechsler is right," said Falkenhausen. "It's a disaster. Galopin is fit to be tied." Alexandre Galopin was the governor of the Société Générale de Belgique. "We need the Belgians to increase production to defeat the Allies. And instead—"

"I am also working harder than ever to defeat the Allies—*sir*," Rheinhardt said. "Within this abbey the partisans had hidden raw materials desperately needed for Germany's military weapons program."

"What raw materials?"

"You'll have to take that up with Herr Himmler," Rheinhardt said. "It's classified."

"Did you destroy a historical and sacred religious site on orders from Herr Himmler?" Drechsler asked.

Rheinhardt didn't reply. "The partisans count on our commitment to the rule of law," he said. "They know we would hesitate before attempting action inside a monastery." He squared his shoulders. "Well, this officer of the Reich does *not* waver in the face of rank provocation. If they didn't want the abbey destroyed, they should've hidden the stolen goods inside their farmhouses. Instead, they risked the lives of nuns and priests. *They* are responsible for the destruction of the abbey. *Not I.*"

"That abbey has stood since the Middle Ages!" said Falkenhausen.

"Talk to *your* prisoner, Herr Falkenhausen," Rheinhardt said, just as forcefully. "Robert Capelle, whom you allow to walk about like a free man. He goes where he pleases. Does what he wants. He's communicating with London—*with the exiled government there*—and they in turn collaborate with Allied Command." Rheinhardt's voice rose. "I know this for a fact, because Capelle is the one who told the partisans where to hide the stolen contraband—and he did it brazenly, in front of your own ranking officers. He was thumbing his nose at you and your *laws*, and you dare reprimand *me*?"

"Your actions have caused the Belgians to stop work in thirty factories around Brussels!" Falkenhausen yelled. "Nothing is being completed—at all, never mind *on time*!"

"Offer them a bonus or a firing squad," Rheinhardt said coldly. "Their choice."

"Yes, Rheinhardt," said Drechsler. "We know all about you, how you've become as generous with dispensing death as you are stingy with preserving life."

What was intended as rebuke struck Rheinhardt instead as salve. "The Belgians can do their jobs, as they're required under the laws of the occupation, or they can be shot," he said, speaking directly to the governor. "And that's your choice, too, Falkenhausen," he added, his voice darkening. "For four years you've been criminally soft on them. Pretending you can rule an occupied land with carrots and honey instead of brute force. That's why your prisoners sabotage the German war effort. That's why the Belgian partisans have grown so shameless—because they've suffered no consequences." He could feel the blood rising to his face. "They're bombing bridges, railroad tracks, supply depots. They're stealing raw materials from ships docked in *our* harbors. They're conspiring with the enemy in plain sight—and you say we must be softer?" He sneered, both unwilling and unable to hide his contempt. "Or *what*? They might blow up even more rail yards and arms depots?"

"If we lose the war," Falkenhausen said, fighting to keep his voice even, "we will all hang for our flagrant contravention of the laws that govern armed conflict between men."

"If you two would stop *hindering* me from doing my job," Rheinhardt said, "we will *not* lose the war. *I* certainly don't intend to lose it. But you're right about one thing, General—your fate is sealed either way. The Allies won't forgive you. And neither will we."

He turned to go.

"You have not been dismissed," Falkenhausen said.

Slowly, Rheinhardt turned to face the depleted commander. "As soon as I leave," he said, his voice cool as steel, "I'm going to place a personal call to Heinrich Himmler and tell him of your impotence, your utter inability to do what must be done. I will not rest until you are replaced by a man who serves the Reich."

"You're *not* one of the Reich," said Falkenhausen. "You never were, and you never will be. Because in every Wehrmacht soldier's paybook are printed the following lines—lest we forget: '*While fighting for victory, the German soldier will observe the rules of chivalrous warfare. Cruelties and senseless destruction are below his standard.*'"

Rheinhardt stepped forward. "Who says the destruction was senseless, Herr Falkenhausen?" he said, lethally quiet.

He marched out. He never looked back.

Two days later, on July 18, Alexander von Falkenhausen was relieved of his duties as Military Commander of Belgium and replaced by Josef Grohé, a committed Nazi, who was named the new *Reichskommissar* of Belgium and Northern France.

Grohé fully embraced the brutal hunt for the resistance.

Either by accident or design, Drechsler had struck on something that continued to gnaw at Rheinhardt. He had lost hundreds of men, swallowed up in the burning forest and gunned down at the abbey walls.

Yet, in the aftermath, he'd recovered only three enemy corpses beyond the warrior priest. Two outside. One inside. None of them the black man.

Where did the rest go?

There had to have been at least a hundred partisans defending that place.

On the evening after the battle, Rheinhardt had crouched in the ruined chapel, scanning stone and ash. He was at complete odds with the reality on the ground.

You didn't suffer losses like his against *four* men.

He turned to Hubner. "Where are their dead?"

"Perhaps there's a tunnel, sir," Hubner said. "In the old days, it was common for fortified abbeys to build an escape hatch—for precisely this purpose—to escape justice. They must've prepared a retreat."

They stared at each other meaningfully.

"Don't stand there, Hubner," Rheinhardt said. "Find the fucking tunnel."

But they couldn't. Their search uncovered only broken stone and scorched beams. A sanctuary in ruins. Nothing more.

Rheinhardt's threadbare composure was fraying. His sharpest weapon—cold, clear calculation—was beginning to dull. This should have been the moment of his greatest triumph. Instead, he was being weighed down by logical—and logistical—impossibilities.

Who had moved and then defended these barrels?

He and Hubner were so intent on following the ticking trail of the Geiger counter that they were nearly ambushed by their own obsession. Rheinhardt almost missed the ankle-high tripwire stretched across the entry to the wine cellar. At the last half-second, he saw it drawn taut. He lost his balance trying to stop himself from walking and pitched forward over it, falling hard onto the stone ramp. He screamed at Hubner not to take another step. He lay there, chest heaving, blood dripping from his face. The enemy had hidden the wire in shadow, camouflaged it in the natural gloom of the gray stone corridor. The tripwire ran to two pull fuses and two charges: one embedded in the ceiling, the other set into the flank of the ramp. The TNT was designed to collapse, to bury the entrance to the barrels. To trap. To kill.

It was the closest Rheinhardt had ever come to death.

And it unraveled him.

He called for a sapper. It took another hour, desperate and slow, to trace the wire, brace the housing, block the firing pins, secure the fuses, and finally cut it. Before they dared enter again, Rheinhardt ordered the engineer to crawl every centimeter of the cellar threshold—hands, knees, chest to the stone—until he was satisfied nothing else would blow.

The twelve men he had left—filthy, shell-shocked, exhausted from hours of fighting in fiery woods against an invisible enemy—were in no shape to lift a hymnbook, let alone eight tons of uranium.

It was growing dark. He was forced to wait until morning and call for reinforcements—fifteen more SS men from Krieger's Liège garrison. Even they struggled.

They hadn't brought reinforced carts. They came with dollies and coal barrows, tools better suited for crates of wine than dense Congolese ore. The wheels on the barrows cracked almost instantly. One cart buckled after a single run. They were reduced to rolling the barrels by hand or dragging them by ropes, like oxen.

It took two full days.

The scale of this gargantuan effort—and the absence of dead bodies—confirmed Rheinhardt's assessment: this could not have been the work of a ragged few. You didn't offload sixty barrels of raw uranium from a cargo ship, load them onto trucks, smuggle them through occupied territory, and drag them—*drag them*—into a hidden crypt inside a fortified abbey without a *verdammt* battalion of men.

So where were they?

75

Scout Sniper Medic Fighter

They were a long time in the dark.

Charlie and Louise sat with their backs against the wall, barely breathing, Fletcher and Rafael bleeding between them. The stone was damp and cold. Charlie's fingers had fused to the rifle grip; she had to peel them off. Her hands shook. Her eyes burned. Inside her head she still heard the bells falling, the screaming through the smoke. *Hawk . . . Zeus . . . Ngomo . . .*

She couldn't feel her fingers. Her body was scraped raw. She could hear Louise breathing, and between them, their two men not breathing enough. Her trousers were tacky. The smell of blood and ash clung to her nose.

Above them, rumbling. Crashing. German voices dimly shouting. An explosion. A cascade of stone and wood. Then—silence. Just the sound of loss trying to find its shape. The darkness pressed in like second skin.

Fletcher . . . Charlie whispered inaudibly. *Wake up. How did it go so bad so fast. There weren't enough of us.* Shells piercing the air with their shrieking cries echoed in her head. Her throat was scorched from the smoke. She kept gulping for breath, as if she were still in the woods suffocating. *Fletcher pouring water into a rag, pressing it to her mouth, telling her to breathe through it—then vanishing like vapor.*

Fletcher, mon amour . . . tu es la?

They sat for what felt like hours, Charlie clasping Louise's hand, covering the men with their bodies.

"We have to help them," Louise whispered. "How long has it been?" Charlie couldn't tell. She heard Louise fumbling in the dark. "Didn't the priest say he left candles somewhere?"

"Good luck finding them." She jostled Fletcher. "Fletch, wake up . . . please," she whispered.

"Turn on your green light," Louise said. "You must have it on you."

Charlie had forgotten all about it. The tiny light she had used to draw Fletcher to her at Saint Lament. In the dark, Rafael stirred, groaning. "Tell Belvy I need a tin of his Stitchless Seal and one Saint George's prayer," he muttered. "I promise to never call him Enobarbus again. Just get him over here."

With Charlie's dim green light, they found the candles. Father Roland had left them, a dozen red glass votives lined up along the wall, and even a pack of matches. Lighting one of the candles made everything more bearable. Lighting two was even better.

The men's large packs lay nearby. The girls found a few canteens filled with water, some bandages, and a pair of battery-powered flashlights. "We need Belvedere's bag," Louise said. The women stared mutely at each other.

"It's out there," Charlie said, pointing up. "With him."

Rafael groaned again. "Where's Belvy?"

"Rider . . ." Fletcher grabbed Rafael's arm. "Where are you hurt, man?"

"Where aren't I fucking hurt," Rafael muttered. "You?"

"I'm fine," Fletcher said, motioning for Charlie to help him sit. It took considerable effort. She brought the canteen to him; he took a few swallows. "Light the rest of the candles," he said quietly, wiping the wet grit from his mouth. "We can't fix Rider in the dark. Roland dropped Belvy's bag in last. It's here somewhere. Move quick. The candles suck up oxygen in a closed space."

"Fix *him*?" Charlie said, peering at his head, touching him. "What about *you*?"

"Just light the damn candles, Charlie."

Charlie saw—he wasn't fine. He was still seeping blood from a head wound and a leg wound and God knows where else. He couldn't sit without groaning. His combat gear was black, but when she felt around his torso, her hands came back sticky and wet. "Oh, Fletcher . . ."

"Rider's got a bullet lodged in his fucking arm and a gut wound, so please, Charlie, let's hurry." Reaching over, he smacked Rafael. "Rider. Wake up! Sergeant Canario!"

Rafael groaned.

Louise was too afraid to cut open Rafael's tunic. First things first. Charlie helped Fletcher. She wrapped his head in gauze, and cleaned out the wound on his thigh. He said no bone was hit, but it looked awful. It needed stitching. Charlie rooted around for Belvedere's magic powder, but Fletcher stopped her. "Whatever's left, we save for *him*."

"Me? No," Rafael said. "I don't need it."

"You *just* said you needed it," Fletcher said. "You were literally begging for it."

"I was begging for Belvy," Rafael said. "What good is the seal without him?"

"Belvedere's dead, Rider," Fletcher said softly. "We're going to have to make do with what he taught us and what he left us."

A shuddering Rafael turned his head away.

Using Belvedere's forceps, Charlie removed shrapnel from Fletcher's right flank. The wounds were shallow and dirty. "You're pale," she said. "Your skin is cold."

"I lost a little blood," he said, faintly. "I'll be all right. Just pull out what you can. Then pat it with iodine. Stick some gauze on it and let's go. Hurry."

Once Fletcher was bandaged, they focused on Rafael. He had a bullet lodged in his upper arm. The round needed to come out. That was a priority. It was an infection risk. He also had some serious bruising across his ribs—either from a blast, or the way he'd landed.

"How did you know about his injuries?" Charlie whispered to Fletcher. "How could you tell?"

"I saw him get thrown," Fletcher said. "When I picked him up, he wouldn't let me touch him."

They both stopped talking, Charlie remembering trying to help Fletcher get Rafael inside the abbey. *Fall back*, Fletcher was yelling or whispering. *Fall back.*

Rafael moaned. "I need Belvy. Just when I finally need him, he's nowhere to be found, the bloody bastard. Maybe Briggs can help get me up. Where's Briggs?"

"Briggs is dead, Rider," said Fletcher.

Rafael let out a wrenching cry.

"Charlie, get him some morphine," Fletcher said.

"Don't you dare give me morphine," Rafael said, his eyes shut. "Belvy was clear—morphine only for the hopeless. I'm not fucking hopeless. Just get the bullet out of my arm."

Louise staggered back. "You know I can't do it, Rafa," she cried.

"I wasn't asking *you*," said Rafael, turning his head to Charlie and opening his eyes.

"Are you sure about that?" Charlie said quietly. "You saw what I did to Ngomo. And I liked *him*."

"Charlie!" said Louise.

"All right, all right," Charlie said. "Belvy called my stitch job an abomination. Is that what you want, Rafael?"

Fletcher intervened, fumbling for her hand. "We won't need to stitch him. We'll give him the rest of Belvy's seal."

"I don't want it without Belvy," whispered Rafael.

Morphine, Fletcher mouthed to Charlie. "We won't be able to take out the bullet without it."

"I'll rip it out with my own teeth," Rafael said, "if you bring that morphine anywhere near me. Don't let them kill me," he whispered to Louise, clutching at her. "They hate me."

"They don't hate you, Rafa, *mon amour*," Louise said. "They love you."

"Now, now," said Charlie. "Let's not hyperbolize."

"Don't ever change, Charlotte," said Rafael.

They lit all the candles and set them in a circle around Rafael. The high-powered flashlight, already flickering as if running out of juice, cast an unsteady beam. They had to work fast.

Fletcher tied off Rafael's upper arm with a tourniquet, using what strength he had to hold him down. Charlie, steady and grim, used the forceps to dig out the metal round embedded in the muscle. Before she could finish, even Rafael accepted the wisdom of a little morphine. When he was relatively calm, Charlie packed the last of Belvy's Saint Spit into the wound. Fletcher heated the metal sealing plate with his Zippo. "Now, remember what Belvy told us, Fletch," Rafael murmured, his voice dulled by the opium. "Count to twelve—then take the branding iron away quick. Do you know Latin?"

"I'll count in French. Stop talking."

"Belvy always counted in Latin . . ."

"I'll count to a slow twenty if you don't shut the hell up."

Finally, Rafael's wound was sealed—with Belvy's glorified mud pie and the prayer of Saint George who slayed the dragon. Afterward he lay in Louise's arms. "Thank you for taking care of me," he whispered tenderly, looking up into her face.

That ingrate, Charlie thought.

One of their two flashlights died. They blew out all but one candle to conserve the light.

"Are you okay? Tell me you're okay," Charlie whispered, leaning over Fletcher's head, cradling him in her arms, hoping he wouldn't see her blistered and burned hands.

"Where's everyone else?" he asked, instead of answering her.

She didn't reply.

"Is anyone left?" he whispered, turning into her chest, his voice breaking.

"Yes, *shh*, Mireille and Brigitte are here," Charlie said. "They're farther down the tunnel."

"That's it?"

"That's it."

"Hildi?"

"No one's seen her."

Fletcher groaned. And then he slept.

After time had passed, she slid out from under him and tiptoed down the tunnel toward Brigitte and Mireille. The tunnel was a meter and a half high, and she had to walk hunched over. Better than crawling, she supposed, but would it have killed the medieval monks to dig down another half-meter? "Mireille, Gitta?" Up ahead, she heard someone crying. The votive candle Charlie carried barely lit up Mireille's feet. She was curled on the ground in a fetal position.

"Why didn't you answer me?"

"Briggs is dead," said Mireille. "What's there to say?"

"Where's Brigitte?"

"Lost her mind," Mireille said. "She's headed to the end of the tunnel to go find Belvedere's glasses. He lost them when he got hit. She doesn't want to bury him without them."

Before another word could be spoken, a shadow approached. It was Fletcher.

"Fletcher, where are you—"

The last of his flashlight flickered weakly against the earthen walls as he limped past. "Brigitte, stop!" he whisper-yelled.

Charlie ran after him. They caught her stumbling blind in pitch darkness, hands groping along the walls. Fletcher stopped her. Charlie held her. "Let go of me," Brigitte said in a gutted voice. "I just want to find his glasses before we bury him."

"Brigitte," Fletcher said, holding her, "you can't go out there."

"You're not in charge of me. I'm not in your army."

"The Germans are still there," he said. "They're waiting for us to come back to bury our dead. They'll shoot you. Or worse—torture you first to make you confess. You think I want to leave him, or Briggs, or Hawk?"

"You don't care about them."

"You know that's not true," said Fletcher, keeping his voice from cracking. "But I don't want to lose you too, Gitta."

"The fucking Germans are gone," Brigitte said. "Look how quiet it is."

"It's not quiet. It's a *trap*. They've above us. Listening. Looking for this tunnel. If they hear a sound, they'll fire an RPG down here. We'll all be dead. Please."

Eventually, Brigitte returned to the others and collapsed beside Mireille, who had moved to be closer to the rest of them. "I don't want to be here anymore," she said into Mireille's sleeve.

"Nobody wants to be here," said Louise, still holding Rafael.

"Easy for you to say," Brigitte said. "You still have *him*." She started to cry.

"Shh, Gitta," Fletcher said gently, comforting her.

Charlie thought he was a better man than she was a woman. She couldn't sit and comfort anyone. Not even her comrades, her closest friends. She could barely find the stoic inside herself.

They were so far from safety.

So far from the luxury of crying, of grieving, of being comforted.

"Fletcher, what are our next steps?" asked Louise, patting Charlie's leg, mouthing, *Shh, it's okay*. Louise knew her well. "We can't stay here."

"As soon as it's quiet a little longer and Rafael can stand up, we'll head toward the exit. The tunnel is long. A kilometer."

In the fading flickering light of one candle, Louise nodded, her expression grim. "Okay, great. We'll climb out when Rafa can walk. And then what?"

"We'll pile into Charlie's *Berceau* and go," Fletcher said. "Find a place to regroup. Heal a little. Plan next steps."

Louise laughed—soundlessly.

"Louise, *stop*," Charlie whispered, moving away from her friend. She didn't want to be touched by her when she was being so ornery.

"Aww. Your sweet boy doesn't know?" Louise said.

"Know *what*?"

"There *is* no *Berceau*," Louise said. "Charlie gave it away."

Fletcher almost jumped up, wounds and all. "What's she talking about?"

"She gave it to Wolski," Louise said. "And you better hope he's far away now, not dead, because he's got Ngomo and Zeus with him."

Rafael groaned. He tried to turn his body away from Louise, away from Fletcher, just . . . away. "Scout, sniper, medic, fighter," he whispered. "Wolski, Hawk, Belvy, Briggsy. All dead and gone."

"Wolski's not dead, *mon amour*," said Louise. "I told you. He's gone. Taking with him our only mode of transportation."

"Why did you do that?" Fletcher asked Charlie in a stricken voice. "That man is fine to get anywhere in the world on foot, even wounded."

"It wasn't for Wolski," Charlie said with a tearful breath. "It was for Zeus." She couldn't speak about it. Gone was the stoic. She nearly cried.

Ngomo, like a madman, yelling "Zeus! Zeus!" tearing at rocks and debris, trying to dig the boy out—

The boy who'd been hurled away from the falling tower by the fearless Briggs.

Unconscious. Crumpled. Barely alive in the burning air.

Roland shouting for Ngomo from the side door behind the collapsed tower. "We have to go, Ngomo. Please. Or they'll find a way in."

Ngomo not replying, clawing at the stones, trying to reach the boy.

Charlie unable to watch. Grabbing Belvy's Sten gun, coughing through the black haze, running out to cover Ngomo. Shooting a German coming down the hill yelling I see the black man, take him, but alive, ALIVE—

Setting the forest ablaze hurt Rheinhardt's men more than it hurt Fletcher's. The fire made it easier for the few to hide, and easier for the few to kill the many. Anywhere they pointed their muzzles, they hit a German.

Charlie yelling, "Ngomo, they're coming for you, I can't do it anymore, I'm almost out." Standing over him, shooting at anything that moved. Unable to spot either Fletcher or Rafael through the ash-thick air.

Ngomo finally dislodging a stone—

freeing the boy.

Clutching the boy deep to his chest. Whispering, Zeus, Zeus . . . can you hear me? I have called you by name. You are mine. When you walk through the fire, you will not be burned. The flames will not consume you . . . Zeus?

Zeus not stirring. Charlie saying, "Ngomo, let's go."

Didn't he hear her? She was almost out.

And they were coming to take him ALIVE.

She didn't know Ngomo was bleeding until she saw Zeus's dusty white arms and pale face stained red with Ngomo's free-flowing blood.

Barely getting back inside the abbey. Roland about to shoot into the stone above the side door, to collapse it, to seal them inside, to give them enough time to escape into the tunnel before the wall was breached—and Charlie saying no, Roland, I have to find Fletcher. And Louise weeping, saying, and Rafael. Yes. And Rafael.

Roland saying, it may be too late. I'll take these three and try to come back for you.

Louise crying, go, Charlie, go find them. Please.

Charlie saying, goodbye Ngomo. Laying her singed palm on his bloodied arm, whispering, protect that boy. Remember what you promised Fletcher. And Ngomo saying, oh, not to worry, there's isn't much alive left.

Charlie whispering, goodbye Zeus, to an unconscious boy, pressing her lips to his sooty head.

She had parked the Berceau *out of sight—in a clearing off the Hulsbeek trail, half a kilometer from the abbey. The trailhead was swallowed by underbrush. She'd left the keys in the woodcutter's hut under a broken floorboard. If anyone could find the truck, it was Wolski.*

And without the Berceau, *neither Ngomo nor Zeus would make it.*

Charlie telling Wolski to leave Louise's bike and then drive as far south as he could.

Wolski bleeding from his ear, looking confused, half there.

Roland telling him to stay off main roads, train tracks, bridges, canals. To head southwest toward Switzerland. Find a village called Les Gras. In it a tavern—Auberge des Deux Sapins. "Ask for the owner: Pierre Perriot. Say to him, Dieleghem. *If the man replies with my name, you're in the right place."*

"And if he doesn't?"

"Shoot him and keep going."

"And if there be Germans along French border? Do I shoot them too, and keep going?"

"You stay positive and pray. You have a child with you, you have our king's most trusted servant. God will walk you through the thorns, not around them. Find the inn at Les Gras. They'll give you sanctuary. Do you have petrol? Weapons?"

Wolski saying his Sten was empty.

Roland giving Wolski two boxes of cartridges, blessing Zeus, blessing Ngomo. "Go. They're breaching the abbey walls. The Lord himself goes before you. He will not fail you or forsake you. Do not be afraid. Don't look back. Just go."

76

The Cathedral of Critical Mass

"Do you want to see the lab now, Rheinhardt?" Saul asked. His voice was light, musical, as if the weight of eight tons of uranium had made him buoyant rather than burdened. He was freshly shaved and sharply dressed, his eyes bright with purpose and something perilously close to joy.

"Not particularly," Rheinhardt said—burdened, not buoyed. "But let's get it over with."

Grunfell took him to a lower level of the house, down the crumbling back stairs near the old wine cellar, where a padlocked side door masked the lab's true entrance. A steel elevator shaft creaked as it carried them down below, to a lower level still.

The narrow stone basement stairs led to another padlocked door.

And inside that door was another world.

The lab was a cathedral-sized underground chamber, lit by harsh sodium lights, humming with magnetic energy, echoing with a mechanical roar. It was much larger than Rheinhardt had envisioned. It wasn't dank or cramped, not the crypt within a crypt he had expected, but a vast chamber with soaring ceilings. At its center stood the *pièce de résistance*, the cyclotron, a honeycomb-like, steel colossus three times the height of a man.

Around it, machines, cauldrons, furnaces, wires, gleaming steel, and copper filled every corner. And the noise—the noise. Everything was humming, rumbling, turning, spinning. Metal scraped against metal. Fire crackled. Buzzers chirped. Relays clicked.

The lab assaulted all his senses at once. Then it struck deeper, warping the internal compass Rheinhardt thought and felt with, the one he made his decisions with.

He wanted out—immediately.

But Grunfell moved through the din with an uncanny serenity, speaking calmly, as if the onslaught was having the opposite effect on him.

How soundproof these walls must be, Rheinhardt thought, *to keep contained all this fury.*

Above—silence.

Below—this.

"Don't tell me, just show me," Rheinhardt said, on edge. "I can't hear you with this racket."

"I'll talk louder," said Grunfell. He took Rheinhardt to a side room, where the ore was being ground into dust. The sound in the crushing room was like standing in the center of a forest battle. Relentless hammering. Metal screaming through stone.

"Amazing, right?" Saul patted Rheinhardt on the back—like they were old friends—and Rheinhardt let him. "I have good news," Saul said. "Great news, actually. I weighed and re-weighed the ore myself. We have just over 8,300 kilos—slightly more than we thought. That little bit extra bought us the bomb, Rheinhardt. We have just enough for critical mass."

"Excellent. Where to next?" The lab was chewing off his nerve endings.

They passed storage bays for ore and waste. Overhead, pulley carts rolled the crushed material toward its next destination: the leaching room. That room was quieter. But it stank of sulfuric acid, acrid and chemical. It didn't smell like death. It smelled like something that made death.

Next to it were spectroscopy labs to confirm isotope purity, and chemistry stations to track contamination. Grunfell pointed out the air filtration units and drainage systems. He even showed Rheinhardt the emergency showers with chemical scrubbers. Everyone wore fume hoods. Everyone but Grunfell and Rheinhardt.

The lab was studded with knobs, dials, needle gauges, control panels. The gray concrete walls were plastered with blueprints and flow charts. And on one far wall hung an enormous map of isotopic separation yields—like Krieger's war map of Europe.

"Can anyone understand these numbers, Grunfell?" Rheinhardt asked.

"Just me." Saul smiled.

They went through the lab, room by room. The ore crushing room. The leaching room. The room to filter and dry the purified ore, which also housed massive rotary kilns to calcinate the ore into yellowcake—bright powder of uranium oxide that sat in vats, waiting to be forged into black corrosive crystals for the cyclotron.

A step down from the main floor stood a smaller annex, sealed behind a reinforced steel door with a pressure valve. This was the fluorination lab, where uranium conjoined with hydrofluoric acid—a marriage so volatile, Grunfell said with an exhale of reverence, that even a pinhole leak could blind or kill whoever was inside. "It unstitches your lungs in a single breath," he said. The gas chamber was under constant ventilation and sealed by chemical lock. Inside, uranium reacted with the acid in a closed furnace heated to 400°C, producing green salt—a dense, pale-jade crystalline powder of uranium tetrafluoride—one step away from becoming nuclear bomb metal.

Next to the lethal chamber was the canister vault, where each kilogram of green salt was stored in long thin nickel containers. Saul alone numbered and tracked them, watching their weight inch up toward critical mass.

Rheinhardt fought the urge to shield his nose and mouth. The smell of scorched metal and bitter acid was overpowering. He glanced at Grunfell. The man looked fresh and flushed—like a lover strolling with his bride through the lilac beds in the Tiergarten.

Afterward, Rheinhardt stood outside in the summer air and had a long smoke. *What a feat—a surfeit—of human engineering*, he thought. That was the part he valued most: production on a massive scale, all of it concealed.

Zvart Haus had no extra chimneys, no vents, no visible stacks. Every puff of exhaust—chemical, thermal, radioactive—was funneled through an elaborate subterranean duct system and exhaled kilometers away, into the waters of industrial runoff from other refineries, other factories, disguised as warmth from ovens or steam from boilers.

Zvart Haus breathed through the bones of the countryside.

Its poisons never rose.

Instead, every plume of acid vapor, every fume of hydrofluoric gas was suctioned down into the underground arteries. No smoke, no scent, not a whiff of industry. No one could trace the chemical vapors back to this house.

It gave Rheinhardt inordinate satisfaction to know that this intricate goliath lay hidden beneath a disarming green field in the bucolic countryside—invisible to everyone, guarded by no one.

And yet—a small tick of unease pressed against that satisfaction.

Why were these cavernous cathedrals of man's monstrous ambition always buried in the cellars and crypts of the other marvelous things men had built: ships, abbeys, country manses? As if the black magic ore—dragged up against its will from the depths of the earth—longed to return. Not just because it was *less*.

Not just because it was *utterly other*.

But because soon it would reduce all other wonders of the world to ashes.

Rheinhardt didn't want to think about it. He had work to do.

77

A Day of Rain

Rafael felt warm. He barely knew where he was. They found only a little sulfa powder for him. It wasn't enough.

Fletcher was grim as a grave dug too early.

Charlie was desperately worried about what they would find above ground.

Mireille and Brigitte wanted to go home.

When Fletcher told them it was safe, they climbed out. The two men went first, wounded, barely able to hold their rifles. But they held them.

The forest was quiet except for the sound of steady rain.

No one knew how long they'd been underground. Their watches had stopped. They'd forgotten to wind them, and Wolski wasn't there to glance at the sun and tell them what time it was. There was no sun. It was wet and gray.

"We can't be out in the open dell," was all Fletcher said.

"What about Mathilde?" Rafael said weakly. "Let's go back to her. She was nice. We had a bed." He couldn't even wink at Louise.

Fletcher shook his head. "It's the only estate for miles around. For sure, his men are there."

"Maybe a tavern in Tremelo?" said Charlie. "The black-market guy we bartered with?"

Fletcher shook his head. "Second place he'll search. Offer him a big Nazi-sized reward. We'll be given up."

"I want to go back and bury Belvy," said Brigitte, not even pretending to hold it together. "I want to find his glasses."

Fletcher opened his mouth to say *no.* Charlie squeezed his arm to keep him silent—and shook her head at Brigitte, to keep her silent too.

"Let's find the woodcutter's hut," Louise said. "Wolski left my bike there."

What good was a bike for six people, Charlie thought, two of those people gravely injured.

Half aimlessly, they wandered through the woods. Charlie studied the compass, wishing for Wolski.

They found the stone hut off the covered-up Hulsbeek trail after a few hard hours. Fletcher and Louise practically carried the barely conscious Rafael inside. The cabin's walls were dark with moss, its wooden roof rotted out, its rafters snapped and sagging.

"Perfect," said Louise, lovingly picking up her bike. She was the only one who was in okay spirits.

But Charlie's *Berceau* was gone. She couldn't look at anyone. She felt something close to grief for its loss. That truck was her life. She slept in it, lived in it. She found Zeus in that truck, nearly saved him in it. And others. Paolo built the secret compartment in that truck. Paolo named it. Charlie could barely breathe.

Fletcher put his comforting hand on her back. He always found a way to see her anguish despite his own. "It's okay, *ma* Charlie," he whispered, pressing his bandaged head against hers. "Your *Berceau* will save that boy again. It's worth it. He needs it more than we do, Charlie. It's okay."

"I'm fine," she said, turning her eyes away, welling up.

"Instead of praying for Wolski," said Louise, "or wasting time mourning a truck, why don't you pool your paltry spiritual forces and pray for the fucking rain to end?"

"What difference will it make?" said Brigitte.

"The difference between Rafa burning up with infection or getting better," said Louise. "That's not nothing. The difference between you being shot or returning home. That's not nothing either."

Quietly shivering, they sat glumly in the hut as the rain pounded the wood shingles, dripping through the gaping holes in the roof.

God must have heard one of them, because in the early afternoon, the rain stopped.

Louise cleaned herself up as best she could. She took Rafael's comb, brushed out her hair, tied it up in a bow, tidied up her dress, and wheeled her bike to the entryway.

"Okay, bye!" she said, waving cheerfully. *"Au revoir!"*

Fletcher and Charlie blocked her, each holding a handlebar.

"Where do you think you're going?" Charlie said.

"I'm the only one with a plan," said Louise. "The rest of you are useless. I've never had a *Berceau*, Charlie. Always had my bike, though."

"You can't go to Mathilde's, I told you," said Fletcher.

"Okay, then, I won't go to Mathilde's."

"Where, then?"

"Herentals."

Even Fletcher laughed. He and Charlie chuckled together.

Louise, perched on the bike with her hands on the bars, didn't laugh.

"When you're done giggling like toddlers," she said, "let me through."

"Lou, you can't bike to Herentals!" said Charlie.

"Watch me."

"It's forty kilometers from here!"

"So, as far as Mechelen?"

Charlie stammered. "No," she said quietly. "Mechelen was closer."

"Maybe a little. But I used to bike from home to Leuven, near Mechelen, pick up Saul's wife's letters and his lunch, then ride all the way to Zvart Haus. And back again. Was *that* more than forty kilometers? I think so, *mon amie*."

"Louise, you can't do it," said Charlie.

"I want to hear all *your* bright and beautiful ideas," said Louise, pushing her aside, "while our options shrink and *mon bien-aimé* burns up with fever. Let go. I'll be back tomorrow morning—with help. Be ready."

"You'll be back on your bike?" Letting go of the handlebars, Fletcher stared at Louise with something like reverence.

"That would be silly of me, wouldn't it, Lieutenant?" said Louise, walking her bike down the overgrown path. "Too-doo-loo," she called back with a wave.

Fletcher exchanged an incredulous glance with Charlie.

"She's still in the same peach dress from Sancta Maria," he said. "How can there be not a stain on it?"

"It's a different peach dress," Charlie said. "She carries a spare. Just in case."

He shook his head. "Who *is* this girl?"

"A mayor's daughter," Charlie replied, adoringly watching Louise disappear down the path. "I know she don't look like much"—she smiled—"but she gets shit done."

Inside the hut, Rafael, hot but lucid, was quietly telling Brigitte about Belvedere. "When he was twelve, he won best essay at Eton," Rafael said. "But got into awful trouble for correcting the master's Latin declensions in front of the headmaster."

"He was so good with declensions," said Brigitte, not even bothering to wipe her tear-stained face.

"Tell me about Briggs," said Mireille. *"Mon Dieu!"* she cried. "I don't even know his first name."

"William Cornelius Briggs," said Rafael. "Bill Briggs. If you ever called him Billy, he'd destroy you."

"William Cornelius Briggs," Mireille whispered.

"Shh," Rafael said, suddenly alert. "You hear that? There's someone outside."

Charlie heard nothing. Maybe Louise had forgotten something and come back?

"Weapons up. Someone's coming. Fletcher! Pass me my Tommy gun."

How could he hear that? Charlie picked up her Browning, Fletcher his M1, and they crept to the opening.

78

Known Unto God

Whenever Hubner had something difficult to divulge to Rheinhardt, he stood shuffling, staring at the floor, occasionally complimenting Rheinhardt on irrelevant tasks that had been done well. It was a pantomime that tested Rheinhardt's every nerve. And today—mere days after the acquisition of the uranium, when Rheinhardt was already drowning in operations and dread—the way Hubner was twitching was simply unconscionable.

"Hubner, whatever it is—out with it. If you want to know how I'm going to take bad news, I'll tell you how: badly. What is it?"

"We had a small problem with our sentry overnight," said Hubner.

"What sentry—what problem?"

"The ones we left at the abbey in Silvis Sacris, sir."

"How many?"

"We left eleven men behind."

"Hubner, why do you make me want to ram my head into a brick wall? Not how many men. How many men was there a problem with?"

"All of them, sir."

Rheinhardt bolted upright.

"What problem?"

"They're . . . well . . . I don't quite . . ." Hubner winced. "They're dead, sir."

"Pardon me?"

"Yes. In their sleep."

"They *all* died in their sleep?"

Hubner equivocated. "They were *made dead* in their sleep, yes, sir."

"Hubner, don't make me fetch pliers and pull your teeth out one by one. What happened?"

"The morning shift change found the night sentry dead. Their throats had been cut."

"And no one awakened? No one grabbed a rifle or fired a shot? What about the guards awake and on duty? Did they sound an alarm?"

"Their throats were also cut. And they were stabbed—repeatedly."

"Verdammt!"

"I agree, sir." Hubner hesitated.

"There's *more*?"

"The bodies of the enemy, sir . . . They've been buried."

"Buried?"

"Yes. Fresh graves were dug for them. They were wrapped in linen cloths—"

"What linen cloths?" Rheinhardt bellowed.

"Perhaps taken from the abbey ruins?" Hubner said. "They were adorned with skullcaps and rosaries and buried. Crosses were fashioned for them out of branches." He paused. "And on each mound, a sign was painted on a charred wooden board—in blood. *Known Unto God*."

"Why are you saying it with such unseemly solemnity, Hubner?" Rheinhardt exclaimed. "I trust you ordered the enemy exhumed, exposed, and every sign destroyed?"

"Oh, I ordered it, sir . . ." Hubner shifted, visibly uncomfortable. "But the men opted to leave them as they were."

"Hubner! They disobeyed you?"

"Here's where our position becomes tricky, mein Herr," Hubner said. "The shift change—the ones who refused to unearth the bodies—also declined to remain at post. They returned to Liège and informed Herr Krieger. And Krieger has denied approval of additional forces. He called earlier to speak to you, but . . ."

"I was busy, Hubner," Rheinhardt said. "Busy trying to do the impossible—find another ton of copper wire for our friend at Zvart Haus. What did Krieger want?"

"He told me to tell you: not one more Waffen-SS soldier will be bled out guarding bones in the dirt. You have your birdseed, he said. We have a war to win."

"What does he think I'm doing here if not winning a war?"

"The order to stand down comes direct from Himmler himself, mein Herr," Hubner said. "Shall I get him on the phone?"

Rheinhardt sat down. He tried not to sink down.

"Eleven Waffen-SS. Throats slashed," he whispered. "Who *are* these people?"

79

A Box of Unclaimed Things

It took Louise nearly six hours to bike back to Herentals. She wore no makeup and carried only her documents and a canteen of water. She got stopped twice. Once by Flemish collaborators, and once by Wehrmacht. Both times she upranked the *Unteroffiziers* to lieutenants, then showed them her actual papers, which stated that she was the daughter of the Chief Alderwoman and had been visiting the Sisters of Saint Michael at Keerbergen. Both times, when they hesitated—for reasons she didn't understand—she used her standard line. "Please, by all means, call my mother," she said. "Unless you'd rather explain your conduct to the city council next Monday." They let her through, mumbling something about needing to be extra careful because of heavy partisan violence in Tremelo. "Yes, I saw the smoke earlier," she said. "It seemed far away. Do you think it's safe to continue, *Officer*?"

Both the Belgians and the Germans apologized repeatedly for having no one available to drive her back to Herentals. Louise laughed all the way to Saint Waltrude, reveling in the idea of being hand-delivered to her parish priest by dedicated and conscientious Nazis.

She returned to the woodcutter's hut in Tremelo just after dawn the following morning, in Father Bavo's relief mission church van. Father Bavo stayed at the wheel, while Louise made her way down the trail. "Hurry up," she said, stepping inside the cabin. "I got us a ride to Herentals. Rafael, how are you feeling this morning, my love? Fletcher, can you help him—" She stopped talking and stared in shock at the ghost of a woman, sitting in the crook of Brigitte's arm, clutching a sniper rifle with a custom scope.

"Hildi?"

Brigitte helped Hildi to her feet and led her outside to the trail.

Louise turned her incredulous gaze to Charlie.

"Don't ask," said Charlie.

"I feel I must," Louise said. Hildimar was a sight to behold. She looked more haunted than ever, was more mute than usual, and was caked with dried blood.

"The blood is dried, right?" Louise whispered to Charlie.

"Don't ask."

"Is it hers? Seems an awful lot of blood for one skeletal Hildi. I wasn't sure she even bled red."

"I don't think there's a scratch on that girl," whispered Charlie.

"So whose blood is it?"

Charlie shrugged, but her eyes were lit with awe.

Brigitte helped Hildi inside Father Bavo's van, turned to Louise and, grabbing her arm, whispered, "Hildi buried my Belvy." Her face was an intense mixture of relief and grief.

"And my Briggs," said Mireille from inside the van, with a protective arm around Hildi.

"And Hawk," whispered Hildi, tightening her grip on the sniper rifle.

Louise whistled.

"Yes, but did she find Belvy's glasses?" Rafael muttered.

Brigitte opened her fist to reveal a pair of cracked, bent frames. "She brought them to me," she said, her voice breaking. "She said I needed them more than he did."

After they were dropped off at Saint Waltrude's, Brigitte and Mireille were about to walk home when Louise asked them to come inside the church for a few minutes. She said she needed their help.

"I got no more to give, Lou," Brigitte said. But the girls dragged themselves into the nave.

Thanks to some sulfa drugs from Bavo, Rafael's fever subsided slightly. Both men limped inside and sat in one of the back pews. The girls slid into the pew in front of the men, Charlie facing Fletcher, Louise facing Rafael.

"Loosha," Rafael said, holding on to the pew, "my dearest girl, tell me quick, do you have a plan that involves a bed where I can fall down and sleep for twenty hours?"

"Yes," said Louise, leaning forward and kissing his hands. "But what would you do for such a bed?"

"I'd be careful what I was promising, Rafa," said Fletcher. "Ask for the fine print."

Louise took a breath, parsing her words carefully. "I have a place the four of us can stay," she said. "With caveats."

They waited for the caveats.

"My mother's house."

Charlie recoiled from Louise, clasping her hands in mock prayer. "Lou, no. Please—no. Honestly—better to surrender to Rheinhardt."

"Stop joking."

"Who's joking?"

The men sat quietly. "What's the caveat?" said Fletcher.

"One thing you should know about my mother," said Louise. "She does everything by the book."

The men waited. Charlie was barely listening. Her face was in her hands.

"My mother does everything by the *Good* Book," Louise amended.

"I don't know what that means," said Fletcher.

"We can't live in her house unless we're married," said Louise, kneading her hands. "But once we are, we can stay as long as we want."

Charlie laughed.

"What's funny?" Louise said. "You want a place to stay or don't you?"

"Seems like a lot for a place to stay, Lou," Fletcher said carefully.

"Really?" Louise said, frowning and turning to Charlie. "Explain your man to me. I know why *you* don't want to stay with my mother . . ."

"Because she hates me?" said Charlie.

"And I know why Rafael doesn't want to get married," Louise continued. "Because wild Basque men of the Pyrenees must be free, blah blah. But why does your Fletcher, the most polite and chivalrous of men, not want to be wed?"

"He's not that polite," Rafael answered. "Fletcher's got that Creole blood running through his veins. And in bayou country, marriage, apparently, can sometimes lead to murder." He patted Fletcher's forearm affably.

"I don't think that," Fletcher said, sounding defensive.

"He's right," Charlie said. "He thinks *love* leads to murder."

Fletcher didn't even have the strength or the presence of mind to deny it. Louise and Charlie chuckled quietly.

"Listen, jokers," said Louise. "*I* got a place to stay. I *have* a home—and a bed. So, I'll say goodbye to you right now and bike five blocks to my house. You geniuses can figure out your own sanctuary."

There was crackling silence in the cavernous old church, empty this morning except for them and for Brigitte and Mireille, huddled across the aisle, near the altar.

"We can't get married," Rafael said finally. "We have no rings."

"We can't get married," echoed Fletcher. "I haven't shaved."

"Yes, and those two are exactly the same," said Charlie.

* * *

The day before, in the sacristy, from his drawer of unclaimed things—old rosaries, single gloves, orphaned earrings—Father Bavo had pulled out a small box of wedding rings. "A widow dropped hers and never claimed it," he said. "A child was playing with one and lost it between the pews. An old man left his behind after his wife's funeral and died before he could reclaim it. I kept them all. Objects have meaning. Someone might return for them. Or someone else could need them." He pushed the box toward her. "Find four that fit, and *bonne chance.*"

Now, Louise opened it for her friends. She found one gold ring, greening with age, two dull mismatched silvers, and a brass one that fit Rafael.

Rafael took it cautiously. "*Brass* ring? Am I going for it, Louise? Taking the risk, reaching for the prize?"

"If that's what you wish, then yes, *mon* soon to be *petit mari*." Louise turned to Charlie, but before she could open her mouth to ask, Charlie answered her unvoiced question.

"You biked forty kilometers for that gold ring," Charlie said. "It's yours."

Rafael dragged Louise to the steps of the altar before Father Bavo appeared. "Even in a war wedding, things have to be done a certain way," he said. "Fletch, you coming? Bring . . ." He circled his finger at Charlie. She rolled her eyes.

Louise stood in front of the altar and Rafael struggled down on one knee before her. "You're going to have to help me up, Loosh," he said, taking her hand. His shoulder wound was seeping. His beautiful face looked exhausted. He needed a bath and a new bandage. She smiled. "Louise Aubel," he said, gazing up at her, "only a woman like you could bring a man like me to his knees. With all my heart, I beg you, will you marry me?"

Over in the corner, Charlie and Fletcher had a less ostentatious moment, though no less intimate. "Charlie, I'd rather be in the fire with you than in the flowers with anyone else," he said, taking her hands into his. His leg wound prevented him from kneeling. It nearly prevented him from standing.

"Anything you ask of me, I will do," she said.

"Marry me," he said. "The world could end tomorrow."

Charlie held Fletcher's hands as if she were holding him upright. "Fletcher, I'd marry you today even if the world weren't ending tomorrow."

"We are gathered here not in splendor but in ruin," Father Bavo said at the altar of his church, adorned in full celebrant's vestments, all freshly pressed and spotless despite the wreckage around him.

"We have come together not in feast, but in the aftermath of death. These vows are not only for love and comfort. They're for courage. Time is short. Let those who weep"—he didn't look at Brigitte or Mireille—"be as though they wept not, and those who rejoice as though they rejoiced not—but let those who are bound be faithful, unto the very end. Louise and Rafael, Charlotte and Florent, you stand in blood, and still you say yes.

"Do you, Louise Aubel of Bastogne, take Rafael Barbezat of Duffel to be your husband? Because though the world has taken much from you, it has given you each other."

"I do," said Louise.

Bavo turned to Charlie and Fletcher. "Do you, Charlotte Fontaine of Herentals, take Florent Van Acker of Bruges as your wedded husband, knowing he is your one true one, no matter how many tomorrows you have left?"

"I do," said Charlie.

"Then by the authority of the church given to me, not by law, not by Rome, but by Jesus Christ, the Lord of mercy, I declare you husband and wife. To bind you to each other, yes, but also to give you sanctuary. Pray that He shall bestow upon you the gift of many years."

Brigitte stood to the side, her shoulders shaking. Mireille held her hand over her mouth, to keep her cry from spilling out. Hildi was long gone. Louise kept her head lowered and eyes squarely on the floor. She didn't dare look over at her friends. They'd lost their men, while she still had hers, barely. They were right. It was desperately unfair. But the sun broke through the stained-glass window of the Eleventh Station—Jesus nailed to the Cross—and the stream of colored light spilled across Rafael's torn sleeve, turning the blood to gold. For a radiant moment, everything was more beautiful than Louise could bear.

At the great doors, they kissed, bruised and unbowed.

"We're a mess," Charlie said. "Look at us." It was true. They were bloodied, blackened—barely standing in the boots they had fought in.

Fletcher gave Charlie his arm before they stepped over the threshold.

"We're too filthy to be sacred," he said quietly. "And too sacred to be filthy."

"Speak for yourselves," Rafael said, raising Louise's hand to his lips. "My bride is blameless, spotless, and illumined from within. She is sacred only."

80

Hélène Aubel

"*Bonjour*, maman," said Louise, stepping into her house.

"Where have you been?" her mother called from the kitchen. "Close the door. It's bug season."

The door behind Louise closed slowly—to allow three more people to enter.

When Hélène walked out of the kitchen and saw Louise with Charlie and two bandaged men—in torn black clothes, with army packs and helmets and *rifles*—she dropped the cup of tea she'd been languidly holding.

"Maman," Louise said in a well-practiced, casual tone, as if nothing whatsoever was out of the ordinary, "you know Charlie, of course. I'd like you to meet Rafael and Florent."

Her mother, tall, elegant, pristine, put together, looked at the men and at the broken cup on the floor, the creamy beige liquid splashed on her stockings, and said, "Look what you've done." No one could tell what her mother was referring to. "Child, who *are* these people?" she cried.

"Well," Louise said, with her best no-nonsense air, "Rafael is *my* husband, and Florent is Charlie's. Father Bavo married us. This morning. At the church."

Hélène fainted. Rafael, standing closest to her, managed to catch her, keeping her from hitting her head on the hardwood.

They sat a barely revived Hélène at her small kitchen table. Louise brought her wet towels. "Maman, everything's all right," she said.

Hélène stared with horror at the people in her kitchen, but mostly at her daughter. She tried to light a cigarette, but her hands weren't cooperating. Rafael came to the rescue again, smoothly lighting it for her and leaving his Zippo on the table. He left the kitchen, and Louise heard him rooting around her house, looking for something. He returned with a bottle of cognac. He poured Hélène a short drink and pushed it in front of her.

"It's ten in the morning!" she exclaimed.

"Where I come from, when you need it, you need it," said Rafael.

"And where exactly do you come from?"

Rafael began to say, the Pyrenees, but Louise cut in. "Duffel, Belgium, Maman," she said, giving him a gentle shove. They couldn't tell her mother the truth about things yet, not unless she asked for it. Because if she didn't ask, it meant she wasn't ready to hear it.

"If it weren't for *you*," Hélène said to Rafael, "I wouldn't need it." She downed the liquor in one swallow and pushed the empty glass toward him for another. Afterward, she wiped her mouth with a sleeve like she was in a tavern. "I am the Chief Alderwoman at Herentals," she said. "I work with German occupying forces on the city council. I don't want you to tell me anything I cannot repeat. So explain to me only what I don't have to lie about. You know what a terrible liar I am, Lou."

"I know, Maman." Louise patted her mother's hand.

"Are these actually Belgian men?" Hélène asked.

Louise paused. "What would you like me to say?"

"Not the truth, obviously."

"Of course, they are, Maman."

"Why do they look like they've been rolling around in blood?"

"Got into a little skirmish."

"Charlie too? But of course," Hélène said. "Skirmish, you say? She probably started it. Did you marry them under civil law?"

"No. I told you, Father Bavo married us." She smiled at Rafael. "And beautifully, too. Didn't he, Rafa?"

"So beautifully," said Rafael.

Charlie opened her mouth to give her assent.

"Did I say I wanted to hear from *you*?" Hélène said to Charlie. "Only from my daughter. And these men, do they have papers?"

"Yes."

"Fake papers, right? So it's not a real marriage." She looked almost relieved.

"Father Bavo told us," said Louise, "a sacramental marriage requires free and informed consent, witnesses, and a priest. We had all those."

"But their names are false!"

"So? It's spiritually valid. It's real and binding in the eyes of God."

"And my name *is* actually Rafael," Rafael muttered.

"Is this why you vanished for a month? You've been cavorting with—who even *are* these people?"

"Rafael is a pulper from Duffel," Louise said.

"A pulper. I see. Pulpers need rifles?"

No one said anything.

"Florent is from Bruges," Louise said. "He's Omloop's nephew."

"Did you *see* what happened to poor Omloop?" Hélène cried. She blew her nose and pulled another cigarette from her case. As Rafael was flipping open the Zippo, she said to him, "Are you going to stand there, or are you going to pour me another drink? Louise, go get the blackcurrant Slivovitz. Charlie, get four more glasses." She looked Rafael over. "Where are you actually from?"

"South of France."

"Where's your mute buddy from?"

"Wyoming."

Hélène barely glanced at Fletcher. "Don't know where *that* is—nope, and don't care. Tell me, *Ra-fa-el*, why would you allow Fitz to make you into a pulper from Duffel? Don't you know they only make scratchy wool coats in that town? Who would believe that an olive-skinned, black-eyed Adonis would spend his days elbow-deep in cellulose? Fitz is mocking you."

"I wouldn't be at all surprised if he was mocking me, Madame Aubel."

"Mon Dieu!" Hélène exclaimed. "Does Fitz know?"

"No, Maman."

Tutting, Hélène smoked her cigarette and drank her Slivovitz. "He will be so upset, Louise." She looked up at Rafael. "Fitz loved her, you know."

"So I've been hearing," Rafael said.

"He still loves her," Hélène said.

"Obviously," said Rafael. "First love never dies." He and Louise stared at each other. He reached across the kitchen for her. She came into his arms. He groaned in pain.

Charlie watched Hélène. She actually felt sorry for the woman. Hélène moved tensely from room to room in a cloud of Gauloises, hunting for extra towels, shaking out bed linens that hadn't been touched in years, setting bread to rise as if she could smell the hunger in the walls, wondering aloud if wildflowers should be picked from the garden and a wedding supper planned for another day, asking Louise if she was hurt or cold, catching Charlie's eye and snapping, "I don't know why everyone expects me to do *everything.*"

Charlie stepped forward. "I'll go pick some wildflowers for the table, Hélène," she said. "But the boys could probably use some bandages."

"I didn't know pulping and bellsmithing were such dangerous professions," Hélène said. "Do you think I have bandages lying around?"

She found some, of course. Slowly the house filled with steam and the smell of strong soap. Each one of them had to be scrubbed like stray dogs. Louise emerged first, pink and scalded, not a splinter on her or a nail broken. Rafael left blood in the drain. Poor Fletcher had to change his water *twice*. By the time Charlie got into the bath, the water was clean-*ish* but tepid. And there were no more dry towels. Charlie soaked in the cool bath until her fingers went pale and her knees stopped shaking. The palms of her hands pulsed with burning pain. She couldn't bring herself to face her reflection in the misted mirror. From her neck to her feet, she was black and blue. Some wedding night they were going to have. What a beauty she was, blackened by the battle they had fought so hard to win, and lost. In a moment of great weakness, Charlie pressed herself naked against the cold tiled wall. She almost slid down to the floor. The only thing that stopped her was knowing she wouldn't be able to get back up by herself. By the time she struggled out and climbed slowly into bed with Fletcher, trying not to groan with pain when their bodies touched, they were too exhausted to speak. He lay with his face to the wall, and she spooned him. She had rebandaged his head, his leg, his torso.

"Fletcher," she whispered. "We're married . . ." She could hardly believe it.

"We're *married*."

"Are you tired?"

"A little." His voice cracked. "I'm so sad, Charlie."

She pressed her forehead between his shoulder blades. *I know*, she wanted to say but couldn't get her words out. *Everything will be okay*. She kissed his bare back, ran her fingers gently along his arm. "Do you want to feel better?"

Stiffly and with effort, he turned to her. "More than anything," he said, threading his arm around her and bringing her close. She groaned again, not from pleasure, alas. When he pulled back the blanket and saw the state of her body, he couldn't hide his shock. "Oh my God, Charlie," he whispered.

"It's not great, not gonna lie," she murmured back. "It'll be fine. Make love to me. Just don't touch me."

"She said to her husband on their wedding night," he whispered. "Okay, my love. I'll do my level best not to touch you when I make love to you."

Louise gazed at Rafael with the erotic gleam of a newly married bride. He was lying in her childhood bed, in her childhood room, under her ballerina-pink down quilt, his black damp head on her pink satin pillows. She sauntered up to him in a green velvet robe, sashaying her hips, flouncing her breasts, letting her robe fall open, her whole full-hipped, full-breasted body exposed to him, unapologetic and luminous.

Rafael, breathing shallow, unable to look away, put up his hands, and said,

"No no, please no. I love you. But I'm a wounded man. I'm barely alive, *ma chérie . . .*"

"Oh, you're alive, *mon amour*," said Louise, pulling back the sheets. "*Plein de vie*."

She climbed on the bed like a lynx, with wild elegance, climbed on top of him, flung open her robe and draped the crushed velvet over them both. One of his hands gripped the robe, the other her velvet hip. "I don't know where the velvet ends and you begin," he groaned. "You, the robe—everything feels the same."

"I'm going to show you a few things that won't feel the same," she murmured huskily, leaning over him. "You don't have to do anything, my husband. You lie there, like an angel in the snow. Tonight, I'll do it all."

81

A Simple Formula for Success

Rheinhardt was back at Zvart by mid-afternoon.

"I thought we'd have a late lunch. Talk through a few things," he said, coming inside Saul's study and taking off his coat and visor.

"I already had my lunch," Saul said. "And I really do need to get back to the lab. Is everything all right?"

"Herr Himmler is having a very hard time understanding how eight thousand kilos of exceptional uranium adds up to barely one bomb," said Rheinhardt, as always looking for a place to sit down.

"But you explained it, right?" Grunfell said, clearing off a chair for him.

"Herr Himmler is convinced your math is wrong." Rheinhardt perched on the edge, crossing his legs and lighting a cigarette.

Grunfell bristled. "Herr Himmler is welcome to come to my lab—as you have done, as Krieger has done—and I will walk him through it myself. I've explained it to Krieger so many times, he can teach it."

"Clearly he can't teach it to Himmler."

"We crush the ore," Grunfell said, enunciating every last consonant. "We leach it with sulfuric acid. We add ammonia to this slurry. The uranium settles to the bottom as sludge. When it dries, it turns into a bright yellow powder called yellowcake.

"We convert yellowcake into uranium dioxide with the help of hydrogen and a furnace. Then we bathe it in chlorine and carbon tetrachloride—in an oven hot enough to turn stone to vapor—and cool it into crystals of uranium tetrachloride. It's corrosive, toxic, reactive, but only mildly radioactive.

"Here's where our real work begins. We spoon these crystals into teacup-sized crucibles and place them inside the cyclotron.

"There, the crystals vaporize to gas. We strip the gas of some of its electrons, or ionize it, and the cyclotron flings the freed uranium ions through an electromagnetic field, to separate the ordinary isotope from the extraordinary. The heavy U-238 ions curve less. They're not the ones we need. We're looking for the lighter U-235 ions that bend more. The ions strike different collector plates. The heavier ions we put through the cyclotron again and again, to make sure we separate every last one. We collect the plates of U-235 and store them until we have enough for the next stage. Which is when we fluorinate the U-235 with the extraordinarily toxic hydrofluoric acid to make *green salt.*

"Now, green salt—uranium tetrafluoride—is *highly* radioactive," said Saul. "It's the last step before the enriched uranium becomes the fuel of an atomic bomb. We seal it in dry, heavy nickel canisters, a kilo at a time. We tag it, weigh it, and lock it in a vault. When we get to fifty kilos, we stop.

"And when we're ready for the final bomb assembly, we heat the green salt with calcium inside a furnace brought to 900°C. The calcium rips the fluorine away, leaving behind pure uranium. Then we pour this molten uranium into two molds, one projectile and one target. And when it cools, we have ourselves two uranium masses." Saul made a motion with his hands to show it. "An anvil and a hammer. One moves, the other waits. Ram them together fast enough inside the casing, and you have a nuclear explosion."

Rheinhardt sat back. He realized he was shivering.

"I still don't understand," he said at last. "Why is there so little final product?"

"I told you why," said Grunfell. "We don't use all the uranium, only a fraction of it."

"Why?"

Saul took a deep breath. "Because the only isotope we can use for a nuclear bomb—the U-235—makes up less than one percent of the uranium I feed my cyclotron."

Rheinhardt was astonished. *That little?* He exhaled. "Less than one percent? Almost as if nature didn't intend for us to extract it."

"Yes," said Saul. "But we're smarter than nature. From every kilo of raw ore, I yield 850 grams of yellowcake. But after enrichment in the cyclotron, that yields me only about six grams of actual bomb matter—5.92 grams, to be exact."

"That's *it*? Six *grams* from one kilo?"

Grunfell nodded.

"Himmler's not going to believe this," Rheinhardt muttered.

Saul opened his hands. "Talk to God."

"There's no way to extract more?"

"There's no way to extract more because it doesn't exist," said Grunfell. "The fact that I can obtain as much as I do is a testament to the formula that

I've spent three years perfecting. I've calibrated the cyclotron to separate out the maximum amount of U-235 in the minimum amount of time." He gave a self-satisfied smile. "Grunfell's formula for success." He recited it like a prayer. "N-235 times e to the negative E delta over BT, divided by N-235 plus N-238."

He wrote it out for Rheinhardt—but didn't let him keep the paper.

$$\frac{N_{235} \bullet e - \frac{E \bullet \delta}{B \bullet T}}{N_{235} + N_{238}}$$

"You take the number of U-235 atoms," Saul said, "and multiply it by e—Euler's constant—raised to the negative power of energy input and delta diffusion loss, divided by magnetic field strength and time. Then you divide the whole thing by the total number of uranium atoms in the sample, 235 and 238 combined."

He sat back. "It is my masterpiece, I don't mind saying so. I created it while working on the Czech ore. There was such a minuscule amount, I didn't want to leave a single U-235 ion behind. The two isotopes are wildly different, even though they're nearly the same weight. The U-235 has just three fewer neutrons—yet that makes all the difference. *Three neutrons!*" Saul himself sounded as if he couldn't believe it. "The regular uranium isotope? Stable, slightly radioactive matter. The isotope missing those three neutrons? A world destroyer."

82

Check Your Bones

Charlie was worried about Fletcher.

So concerned that she decided to talk to Rafael about it.

"Where's Louise?" said Rafael, when he joined Charlie in the garden.

"Coming back soon," Charlie said, looking him over critically. "It's nearly three p.m., Rafael. Did you just wake up? The rest of us have lived half our lives already."

"You didn't live half your *best* life if you weren't sleeping," Rafael said, stretching languidly. "Coming back from where?"

"Bringing lunch to Saul," Charlie said. "I need to talk to you about Fletcher."

"What did he do now?"

"What's wrong with him? He's like a different person."

Rafael glanced at Fletcher, by himself at the back of the garden, cranking the small generator for the radio transmitter, stopping occasionally, flipping open his notebook, feverishly making notes. "Looks normal to me."

"He's barely speaking."

"He's thinking."

"About what?"

"About *what*?"

"Okay, I get that, but . . ." Charlie's gaze didn't leave Fletcher. "This isn't grief."

"I agree," Rafael said.

"So, what is it?"

"Looks to me like he's figuring out a way to find that uranium."

Charlie nearly cried out.

"Don't know what to tell you, Charlotte. He's a man, quite literally, on a mission."

"But even if he finds it, then what? There's no one left to do anything about it."

"Well, there's me," Rafael said. "And there's him. And there's you. And there's Lou."

"I don't see the point," Charlie said.

"By all means, go tell him that," said Rafael. "There's nothing a man likes more than a woman telling him what he's doing is pointless. Go ahead. I'll be right here, listening." Getting to his feet, he waved to Louise. "Loosh, we're back here!"

She was tying up her bike by the side of the house.

"Oh, my, what happened to you?" Charlie said when Louise approached them. Her blue dress, her boots, her arms were caked in dry mud. "Did you fall off your bike?"

"Yes," Louise said. She looked miserable. "There were ruts in the road on the way to Zvart—ruts like you wouldn't believe. Like tanks had been driving through. I must've fallen four times." She looked down, flicking a clump of dirt off her ruined dress. "Look at me."

"You're still nice," Rafael said from under hooded lids.

"I even brought Saul cherries and sardines," she said. "Some lunch. He was so happy to see me, he pretended not to notice my sorry state, but—"

"Who doesn't like cherries and sardines," murmured Rafael. "Let's go inside, *chérie*. I'll run you a bath. You need a good . . . cleaning."

That put a smile on Louise's sulky face.

"My God, Rafael, it's the middle of the afternoon," Charlie said.

"I just woke up, so it's morning for me. And everyone needs a good cleaning, Charlotte," said Rafael, taking Louise's hand. "You're just mad your husband is hand-cranking. Go talk to him. See if you can distract him from his purpose."

Fletcher stood in the back of the garden with his generator, staring at them with glassy eyes, a million miles away.

"Fletcher, what's wrong?" Charlie said, walking over to him.

"Nothing."

"Are you upset?"

"No."

"Don't be upset." She tried to caress him. He let her, but stiffly.

"I'm not upset."

"You've been so quiet."

"I'm not upset."

"You're not yourself either."

"This *is* me," Fletcher said. "Quiet. But not upset."

* * *

Unable to help herself, Charlie looked through his pocket notebook when he was asleep. He kept it under his pillow.

The notebook had a title.

CHECK YOUR BONES.

In it, she found a few lines of verse, written in his precise, exacting hand, each letter made as if from a printing press:

Prairie Brown
River silver
Bleached out deserts
War-torn Italy in winter
English skies before the drop
Lillehaven burned with color.
What a shock.

And underneath: *Maybe I didn't mean Lillehaven.*

The poem buoyed her. Before the war, she used to wish she could be someone's poem. She tried again. Put more effort into it. "Fletcher," she said softly, almost cooing his name. She even borrowed one of Louise's dresses. Made herself look pretty, brushed her hair. When she wasn't naked, she remained passably pleasing. But she was so self-conscious about her slowly healing bare body. It was all the colors of the rainbow. And Fletcher, though magnetizing clothed and unclothed, now limped when he walked. The wounds on his ribs were scabbing ugly.

At the table outside where they sat, she placed a vase of pink peonies and yellow roses. She brought him a lemonade and a lemon cake Louise had made. Louise was quite the baker. Who wouldn't love her lemon cakes. "Tell me what's wrong," she said. "Tell me what you're doing."

"Nothing," said Fletcher. "That's what I'm doing. *Nothing*."

You know who didn't love Louise's lemon cakes? Charlie's new husband. Barely touched them.

"Isn't this the end?" she said.

"How can it be the end?" He sounded sharp with her. On edge.

She couldn't say, *Because you lost all your men and your objective is in Nazi hands and your second objective could be in Nazi hands; we will never know.* She hoped he didn't know what she was thinking, but judging from his hostile face, he must've read her mind.

"It's not the end," Fletcher said, getting up from the table. He couldn't sit for three seconds with her without getting confrontational. "Because our job is not done. And I haven't lost all my men, if that's what you were thinking. Rafael and I are still here."

"Is there really something left for you to do?"

"By *something*, do you mean everything?" he said. "Because then—yes. There's something left." His violet eyes turned cold black-purple.

After the peony and lemon cake fiasco, Fletcher became even more mute with her.

She couldn't tell him about the words she'd read in his notebook, words she was clearly not meant to see. Even the rest of it: formulas, equations, arrows marked with distances, a radio message he was working on, crossed out words, smudged lead, missing lines. He perplexed and troubled her.

There was something else she really wanted to ask him about.

On the last page, another poem:

In the parks where they strolled
hand in hand
was forbidden
to loiter to litter
train puppies and kittens
walk backward
plant flowers
dig holes
cut down trees—
they forgot to mention
that murder was also
a breach of the peace.

All questions, and no answers.

And finally, on the back cover of the notebook: *Indeed, there is madness.* And the author's name: *Vivienne Pellerin.*

Who was Vivienne Pellerin?

What a mystery her new husband was. Who was he in his truest heart? A lieutenant? A Ranger, an assault elite soldier? A chessmaster? Her friend, her lover? She hurt all day and all night for him, even when he was on top of her, intense, murmuring, then silent. *Fletcher, Fletcher*, she whispered.

And then he slept.

And then he was mute.

That's what happened when you married someone you loved but barely understood.

In the backyard of Hélène's house, where he spent most of his waking hours in doomsday isolation, Fletcher tried to make sense of the world turned upside down with his defeat.

But he couldn't. Not without contacting Jonathan Reed. The commander must have been going out of his mind. Reed needed to know where things stood. And he was the only one who could tell Fletcher what to do next. Fletcher had to take a chance. He couldn't wait any longer.

He sent Charlie and Louise on a walkabout around the neighborhood one afternoon, to check for any Nazi signal trucks. When they returned and said they saw none, he set up his antennas, right there in Hélène's garden, behind the poplars and elms. He hand-cranked the generator once or twice, then opened the transceiver, sat on a stump, and waited for the appointed hour.

At 3:00 p.m. sharp, he turned it on and sent out a quick message using the OTP method—scrambled letter by letter with a disposable key. Random, completely unbreakable.

TO LONDON PAD 18-2 ALL BARRELS IN GERMAN HANDS STOP UNIT KIA BUT ME CANARIO STOP ADVICE URGENTLY NEEDED STOP

He transmitted the encrypted post in five-letter blocks in under five minutes, then killed the signal before the Germans could trace it.

On the second day, the response came.

PAD 22-8 TERRIBLE NEWS STOP LOSSES ACKNOWLEDGED STOP NEW ORDERS INCOMING STOP HOLD FAST STOP

Fletcher's body was healing, but his soul was sick. During the day, he tried to hide it, but at night he'd wake up drenched in nightmares. *Was there an explosion? Charlie, did you hear things come apart? Stones crashing down? Tectonic plates shifting? An avalanche? An earthquake? What else could we have done to stop evil from getting a weapon evil should never possess?*

Everything he'd done. Everyone who'd died. Was it all for nothing?

"*Now listen here, John Fletcher Beauregard Du Soleil Gray*," his mother said before he left Wyoming. "Don't let fools distract you." Her name was Beatrice Beauregard. Everyone called her BB, even her children. "The world's thick with fools, so it ain't gonna be easy.

"Don't compare yourself to the boys you fight beside. There'll be braver men, better men, maybe even better looking. So what. There'll be stupider ones too, plenty of them. You don't need to whip out your measuring stick every time, to see how you stack up. I know you like your numbers, but that's the wrong kind of counting.

"Pay no mind to nonsense. But don't get puffed up. It's unbecoming. This ain't just your mother talking—you shine too bright sometimes. And don't go bitter, neither. Nothing's uglier in a beautiful man than bitterness.

"Don't go wasting your mind. You got a sharp, clear brain. You got that from your father's side. Don't dim it with card games, loose women, men flappin' their gums about nothin'. In war, noise gets you killed. So keep your focus. Hold your line.

"Don't let anything own you. Not drink. Not women. Not vengeance. Not grief.

"When the wind knocks you flat, you ain't broke—you're just lower to the ground, where the real work gets done.

"You get thrown, you *check your bones* and get back in that saddle. *Quietly*, like a man with pride. And don't go melting down sacred things and forging blades from bells until you're damn sure there's no other way out.

"Remember who you are when you're out there in the war. You got the bayou and the cypress in your hot Du Soleil blood—slow to stir but twice as stubborn. I see it in your jaw when you go quiet-mad. When justice don't come, you want to take it into your own hands. Don't do it. Don't let the fire of injustice eat you, *bébé*.

"Don't be like my daddy. Don't be the one who can't live past it."

83

A Wedding Feast

Fitz and Dory were coming to dinner.

That wasn't quite right.

Fitz, Dory, Brigitte, Mireille, Maxine, and Margot were coming to a dinner that was more a wedding reception, if one wanted to be honest about it, which no one did, because of Fitz.

Louise told her mother that they shouldn't even be having a celebration until things were more settled. Hélène replied that poor Fitz wasn't going to be walking around Herentals with his hands in his pockets, dreaming of Louise, while she was *ensconced* with another man.

"Why did you invite Dory, Hélène?" Charlie muttered.

"Because I didn't ask you whom to invite to my own house," said Hélène.

So—a wedding feast then, but no one was allowed to call it that, or raise a glass to Louise and Rafael, because of Fitz. The wedding rings had to come off—because of Fitz. And Louise and Rafael couldn't even sit together! At their own wedding feast!

"It's just a dinner, Lou," Hélène said. "With cake and extra flowers."

Louise nearly threw a tantrum. "Is this a punishment, Maman?" she said. "Is this your revenge because I married Rafael instead of Fitz?"

"Why?" Hélène said. "Do you *deserve* punishment for marrying a black-eyed pulper from Duffel?"

"No!"

"What would Fitz say?"

"First thing I'm going to do is ask him," Louise said. "And I'm sitting next to Rafael. I don't care what you say."

"Fitz has suffered enough," Hélène said. "You can't just spring this on him, Lou. You have to prepare him, approach him gently, use a soft, quiet voice."

"Maman, is Fitz a horse?" Louise exclaimed. "Don't spook him, Louise, don't step behind him, speak softly, offer him a sugar cube."

"He's going to be here with Dory at five. Why don't you help me make a salad, instead of being salty. Why don't you set the table outside. We'll dine alfresco. The weather might hold tonight."

"So now I have to work my own wedding reception?" said Louise.

"A *dinner*," Hélène said. "With cake."

"If it's not a wedding reception, Mother," Louise said through her teeth, "and I'm not allowed to call it that, or sit next to my husband, or raise a glass, then why are we even having it?"

"My only child got married," Hélène said. "It's proper to celebrate."

Charlie's steady hand went around Louise's shoulder. "Lou, Lou, Lou," she said, before her friend lost it completely. "It's fine. Hélène and I will prepare everything. You just go and get yourself pretty. You know how long that takes." Charlie smiled. "I'll tell my brother that Fletcher and I tied the knot. That'll soften the blow before you hit him with the real news." She made a churlish sound. "I don't know why your mother insists on inviting that bread muffin Dory, though. Doesn't he have some fines to dispense or latrine duty to assign?"

"He's the only one with a car," Hélène said. "He's picking Fitz up from Vorselaar."

"Also, he's the least important part of what's happening," said Louise.

"I know, I know," Charlie said. "But I watch for him like for a snake in your grass."

She saw Fletcher beckoning them frantically from the back of the garden.

"Come, Louise," she said, taking her friend's hand. "Fletcher needs us."

A new message from Jonathan Reed had transmitted during the 3:00 p.m. open radio frequency. Fletcher showed them the contents.

HAIGERLOCH 48.3706N 8.8050E STOP TARGET KARL WIRTZ STOP TERMINATE AT ALL COSTS STOP SANTA FE CONTINUES TO END-PHASE STOP

Instead of helping Hélène prepare for a party in their honor, the four of them sat at the table in the back of the garden; mission command.

A war council, not a wedding feast.

"*Haigerloch?*" Rafael said. "Where the fuck . . ."

"Germany," said Louise. "Way down south. Near the Swiss border."

"Why would Rheinhardt send the barrels there?" Rafael said.

"The Germans built a reactor facility there," Fletcher said. "Hidden in the caves under a church. Reed always thought the barrels would go to Haigerloch if the Germans found them on the ship."

What a reversal it was, Charlie thought, watching Fletcher. The more the rest of them slumped, hunched, coiled inward, the straighter Fletcher stood. His chin angled higher, his shoulders squared. It was as if, with those five lines of Morse code, he'd reclaimed his purpose.

Terminate Karl Wirtz at all costs. Santa Fe continues to end-phase.

This was what mattered to him.

Why did that make Charlie so sad?

"Before we start assassinating scientists in Nazi Germany," said Louise, "maybe we double-check with Dory first?"

"Don't tell that weasel anything," Charlie said. "He's always darting around, sniffing out things he's not supposed to hear."

"Would Dory even know?" Fletcher asked.

"If Rheinhardt's trucks had a manifest to Haigerloch, he might," Louise said.

"If my commander tells me that's where the barrels went," Fletcher said, "then it's good enough for me."

"Probably not the worst idea to confirm with Dory, though, Fletch," said Rafael, whipping open a map. "I'm turning into Wolski," he said. "God, I miss that bastard. Let's see. We're here . . ." He traced Herentals with his finger. "And Haigerloch, wait for it, is . . . here." He put another finger on the dot on the map. "Using the trusty scale, we can conclude, even without Wolski's exceptional skills, that Haigerloch is about 500 kilometers away." Rafael straightened up. "How do you plan to get there, Lieutenant Gray? Walk? Hail a taxi?"

"Yeah, Charlie," said Louise. "Why'd you have to give away your precious *Berceau*? We could be in Germany by now, killing Nazis."

Hélène flung open the back door.

"Is anyone going to help me?" she yelled. "They'll be here any minute."

"I'm really looking forward to this celebration," Rafael said with a grimace.

"Rafael!" Hélène yelled. "Are *you* coming at least?"

Rafael sighed, flicked closed the map, and stood.

"Coming, Hélène!" he called out, muttering, "it's like living with Mom."

"It is not *like* living with Mom," said Louise. "It's *actually* living with Mom."

"Seriously, what's the plan, Fletch?" Rafael asked, tapping the map.

"Working on it," Fletcher said, tapping his head.

"Is this next scene," said Louise, "one in which I'm allowed to write Rafael and me *out* of joining you on this new crazy quest?"

"You can definitely write yourself out, Louise," said Fletcher. "Just say the word. Mireille, Gitta, Maxine, Margot, even Hildi, they all stepped away."

"Only from us," said Charlie. "They're terrorizing German fuel depots."

"But your husband is an Allied soldier still on active duty," Fletcher continued. "He cannot leave his post."

What about me, the war bride? Charlie wanted to ask. *Am I allowed to leave my post?*

It was a rhetorical question.

Charlie knew she never would.

And he didn't offer her that option. As if he knew she never would.

"Aren't even soldiers allowed a rest from battles?" Louise said. "A wedding furlough, perhaps?"

"I feel those two things—rest and honeymoon—are mutually exclusive," said Fletcher.

"Yes, especially judging from the nightly barnstorming," said Charlie. "I swear to God, Lou, pipe down. Your mother might think it's me and Fletcher." They tried so hard to keep it down.

"She already does," said Louise, batting her eyes. "Oh, hush. What did you want me to do? I couldn't tell her it was me, could I? And she hates you already, so it was really a win-win."

"They're here!" Hélène shouted through the kitchen window. "Thanks a lot, you four!"

The celebration was muted. That was the *best* you could say about it. Mireille and Brigitte wore bright dresses and had done their hair. Mireille even wore perfume. They brought a parcel of pralines and a tiny bottle of Flemish juniper gin. "But not a sip before sundown," Brigitte said, trying to smile. She couldn't look at any of them for longer than a moment before looking away, blinking furiously. They said nothing about Briggs or Belvedere. They couldn't.

"Always a pleasure, Madame Aubel," Dory said to Hélène, like he was about to sell her a Monet forgery. "If I'd known it was going to be a celebration, I would have brought my clarinet."

At dinner he talked nonstop, saying the wrong things, as always. "To new beginnings," he said, raising his glass, smiling too wide. "Though we all know how those tend to end in wartime," he added, prompting a chorus of groans and glares. He had gained weight. When every morsel of food was rationed, Dory had somehow managed to fatten up. Why was Charlie not surprised?

"You're looking healthy, Dory," she said. "Flourishing under the occupation?"

"Better than most," he said, pouring another glass. "To victory!" He tossed back his Slivovitz. Everyone else just muttered, unsure what he even meant. Before the silence settled, he poured himself another. "To love in wartime, ain't that a thing," he said, smiling into his drink. "Never enough time to ask who else was in line." He took a sip.

"All right, Dory, sit down and pipe down," Fitz said. "Anyone else for a toast?"

No one else spoke up.

"You know what they say," Dory said. "True love always finds a way." He raised another glass. "Especially when it's just come off someone else's path."

Charlie and Fitz caught up quietly about their parents in Eindhoven and what Fitz and the others had been up to. He spent most of his time disarming charges the Germans had planted on Antwerp's cranes. Mireille was back to photographing bridges. Hildi was cutting telephone lines and spiking engines, sabotaging the infrastructure.

Meanwhile, Dory was busy sabotaging Fletcher and Rafael. "What could you boys possibly be up to these days," he asked, "that you can't help our girls out with a few things? They helped *you*." After draining the last of his drink, Dory finally went quiet. "Time to get going, Fitz," he slurred into his empty glass.

"You can't leave yet!" said Hélène, jumping up. "We haven't had cake."

While she went to fetch it, Fitz asked to speak to Louise alone. They walked down the yard, under the trees.

"I don't understand," said Fitz. "What do you mean you *married* him?"

Louise looked at Fitz, standing across from her in the long evening light, the garden shadows catching half his face. His curls needed cutting, and the scruff along his jaw needed trimming. He always looked like he hadn't meant to grow a beard, he just forgot to look in the mirror, and it happened. To catch his gaze was the hardest part for her. His eyes, bright, sea-glass blue and full of things he could never say. The expression in them—wary, weary, bruised—made him seem older than he was, and younger, too. He looked as if he hadn't quite given up all hope, even though he should have.

"We did it for the war," Louise said. "We had to do it."

"When we broke up, you told me it was because you didn't want to be with anybody," Fitz said. "War and all that."

"That was true," she said. "War. And all that. What do you want me to say, Fitz?"

"Why'd you do it, Lou?—Dory! Leave me alone for a second," he said loudly to Dorian, who was skulking in the nearby bushes, feigning a sudden interest in weeding.

"I was just helping Madame Aubel with her—"

"Go help her somewhere else."

"We really need to be going, Fitz—curfew . . ."

"Five minutes, Dory!" Fitz turned to Louise. "You were about to tell me why you married another man," he said, his voice barely composed.

"We had nowhere to go," Louise said. "They were wounded. They needed medical attention and rest. You know we couldn't just barge in, the four of us, and stay with my mother. But now, I don't know. She looks almost happy." With deep fondness, Louise gazed at her mother on the patio, raising another glass with Rafael and Fletcher. "Look what a feast she's put on." It had been a long time since her mother entertained.

"So, did you marry him because you had to save yourselves . . ."

Louise waited. "Is there an *or* after that?"

"Or," Fitz continued, "did you marry him because you loved him?"

Louise felt such affection, such pity, such empathy for Fitz, a boy whom she'd known half her life. If Charlie was like her sister, Fitz was like her brother. Perhaps that's what was wrong with them as a couple. How did Fitz not see it? She thought long and hard about how to answer him. She didn't want to hurt him with the truth. And she didn't want him to hate her.

So, as always, to spare his feelings, Louise decided to lie.

But then Fitz spoke. "I really believed after this was all over, you'd come back to me," he said in a gutted voice.

Louise couldn't look up. Charlie kept telling her to be better. *Don't dangle him on a string, Lou,* she'd tell her. *You're not being considerate. You're being selfish. Let him hate you, but free him. Free him to find someone else.*

Louise wanted to throw up her hands. All their lives hung in the balance! Fletcher was concocting plans to invade Germany! Yet other things mattered to Fitz—even while he himself was risking his life climbing cranes, removing charges. Even when it seemed nothing else *should* matter. The personal still mattered the most.

"For once in your life, Lou," he said, "just give me a true answer. Not one of your embellishments or equivocations. The whole truth. Can you do that?"

"Fitz," said Louise, "I married him because I love him. To save him, yes, to protect him, yes. But mostly because I love him."

"You once said you loved me," said Fitz, his voice cracking.

She took a breath. "Not like him. I'm sorry."

"Never? Not even when . . ."

"Never. Not even then."

Fitz didn't say another word.

84

Ambassador for Enrichment

"This Grunfell guy is the only man alive who can enrich uranium fast enough using a cyclotron. No one else has the knowledge, the instinct, and the sheer will to pull it off. With him, we might actually have a working atomic bomb. Without him, we're set back years.

"If he wants to eat Caspian caviar four times a day and drink tea from China? You're going to send a man to Persia and Shanghai to get it done.

"He needs thirty workers to regulate the cyclotron? You give him sixty. The machine cannot stop for a single second. It doesn't stop until the bomb is built."

These were Himmler's exact words. Rheinhardt repeated them to Grunfell during his near-daily visits to Zvart Haus.

A day later, Himmler called Grunfell directly to thank him. Grunfell—flattered that a man like Himmler, widely known to be a Jew hater, took such a personal interest in his work—told him he might beat the deadline. "Perhaps I can do it in *thirteen* weeks," he said.

The next day, Rheinhardt arrived with a new message. Himmler wanted two bombs instead of one.

"Not three?" Grunfell said dryly. It took Rheinhardt a moment to realize Saul wasn't being serious.

"He wants you to split the uranium between two devices. Make two smaller ones, instead of one large one."

"Oh—you're not joking."

"He says it will be more *tactically flexible*," Rheinhardt said. "Do you want to discuss it with him?"

"Every second I spend up here on the telephone and not calibrating the cyclotron," said Saul, "costs us another gram of product. The machine downstairs doesn't run without me—and up here, I count on you to be my ambassador for enrichment."

"I can't explain it to him." Rheinhardt was fed up with being the go-between. Most of his day was now spent on the telephone.

"Next time, I'll make flyers and pass them out," Saul muttered. "I'm tired of repeating the basic facts. Get him on the line." He was barking now—not just at Rheinhardt, but at Himmler himself, the *Reichsführer*, second only to Hitler. "Herr Himmler," Saul said, when the line connected, "I heard about your request."

"We need them, Grunfell," Himmler said. "No ifs, ands, or buts about it. We're getting bogged down in France."

"It's not a question of need, sir. It's a question of critical mass." Saul spoke painfully slowly. "That is—the absolute minimum amount of enriched nuclear fuel required to sustain a chain reaction to cause the bomb to explode. That amount is fifty kilos. Any less, and all you have is an expensive puff of radioactive dust." He jabbed a finger into the air. "You want to split one bomb into two? Fine. But you won't get two smaller bangs. You'll get nothing. You won't get fire. You'll get silence. Without critical mass, the chain reaction dies before it begins."

"How do you know that?" Himmler said. "No one's made an atomic bomb before. How can you know how much you need?"

"It's physics, Herr Himmler," Grunfell said. "Simple elemental physics."

When he hung up, he turned to Rheinhardt. "What happened to my Caspian caviar? Suddenly it's one demand after another."

The next afternoon Rheinhardt was back. "It's driving me crazy, too, Saul," he said, as if they were partners in crime. "You think I want to be coming here every afternoon? But I'm under orders, and you're not picking up your telephone."

"I'm not answering the telephone because I have work to do," Grunfell said. "Don't Krieger and Himmler have a war to put on? A battle to win? A tank to build?"

"They want to know if they should take your depleted uranium to Haigerloch to make plutonium there. They want to make a plutonium bomb."

"They're welcome to it," said Grunfell, with a derisive smirk. "Aside from other considerations, they'll need four to six months to process and extract the six kilos of plutonium required for such a bomb."

"What other considerations?"

"The Grunfell consideration," said Saul. "There are no free neutrons left in my depleted uranium to make plutonium. Remember my formula? I've squeezed every last U-235 ion from every batch that feeds and refeeds through the cyclotron." He shook his head. "But Rheinhardt, even if I hadn't—and even if they had the time and the heavy water in Haigerloch—what they don't have is an implosion bomb housing for this non-existent plutonium. I know *I* can't build it. I don't know anyone in the world who can. Perhaps the Americans? Maybe there's someone in the US Herr Himmler can call and ask? No? I didn't think so. So, there you have it. Scrape the plates, ion by ion, for fourteen arduous weeks, and then have a nuclear bomb—or have nothing. Quite a jam, isn't it?"

"He wants to know how close you are," said Rheinhardt, defeated and out of argument. He was depleted himself, like Grunfell's uranium, every ion of energy squeezed out of him.

"It's been four weeks!" said Grunfell. "I'm not getting any closer while I'm up here talking to you about fucking plutonium, that's for sure."

Late the next morning, Rheinhardt was back, trudging up the stairs. This time he came at eleven, just before lunch.

"You're wearing out your welcome, Rheinhardt," Saul said.

"Krieger wants to know if you need help."

"Did you tell him no?"

"He says maybe if you had help, the enrichment would go faster."

"The cyclotron cannot run any longer than twenty-four hours a day," said Grunfell. "That is its absolute limit."

"He meant . . ."

"I have all the help I need."

"He doesn't mean *hands*, Grunfell," Rheinhardt said. "He means another *scientist*. He's got a physicist at Haigerloch. Karl Wirtz. Real sharp, he says."

"I'm at peak capacity."

"Another pair of eyes might be useful. He could look over the formula. Be in charge of the poison room."

"I'm. At. Peak. Capacity. It's a matter of *science*, Rheinhardt. Not another *scientist*."

"Wirtz couldn't hurt, could he?"

Grunfell stared at Rheinhardt. "I tell you what," he said, his voice low. "Before you bring him, let me tweak my formula, see if I can increase my yield. Give me a couple of days."

Rheinhardt was silent.

"Why the sudden rush?" Saul asked. "What's happening? I thought the Germans were doing all right in France?"

"Probably less well than we'd like." A beat. "It's only because you're doing the impossible, Saul," Rheinhardt said quietly, almost apologetically. "Seeing the impossible being achieved makes people believe anything's possible."

85

Fishing with Maurice

"They want to bring in someone *else* to help me," Saul blurted to Louise, when she brought him lunch in the early afternoon and asked breezily how he was.

"Help you do what?" She smiled. "Write in your notebooks?"

"Exactly right, my dear girl. They think if I have one more physicist here with me, I'll write faster."

"Won't you?" she said. "Two people can definitely paint a room faster than one."

"What if one of them doesn't speak French?"

"You dip the paintbrush in the bucket and—*swish, swish*," said Louise. "Who needs French?"

"The paint has to be prepared," said Saul. "And only I know how to do it. The paint needs to be chemically calibrated. The impurities need to be removed. And when the temperature is slightly too hot or too cold, a completely different formula takes effect. I couldn't teach Henri Weissmann the exponential effect of the decay coefficient on the drift differential . . ."

"The drift differential of paint?" Louise said teasingly. He was so worked up today. More than usual. She was about to offer him one of the still-warm poppy cakes she'd made earlier that morning.

"Correct," Saul said, ignoring the lightness in her tone. "I couldn't teach Elias this, and he and I worked together for twenty years! I've spent a thousand days perfecting my formula. You think this Wirtz fellow they want to bring in understands the decay drift, the cascade losses? He doesn't know the answer because he doesn't even know the question! The truth isn't in the steel and copper. It's in *me*." Saul stabbed himself hard in the chest with his index finger. "Is that what I'm here for—to *teach* Karl Wirtz? And in German, no less? No." Saul shook his head adamantly. "They're bringing him in because they think they can replace me." He scoffed. "They understand *nothing*. Without *me* the whole thing is just wires and dust. I'm not the cog in the machine. I *am* the machine."

Saul broke off suddenly. "Louise? Are you all right? You've gone positively ashen. Sit, sit, I don't want you to fall. My God, you look like you're about to faint. What happened? I'm sorry I went off like that. I just got the news this morning and was still reeling. I'm so happy you came. To talk to someone other than—well. It's a comfort, that's all. And you're looking just wonderful. A little less so now." He chuckled solicitously. "Do you need a glass of water? Let me go get it. I'll be right back."

Sunk in Saul's chair by the open window, Louise sat with suspended breath, caught in suspended time, staring out at the lawn. The hedge perimeter. Two relaxed guards, leaning against the posts, smoking and joking. The dirt road behind them—the ruts and the channels flattened, graded. The overgrown brush, and the drop off to the Albert Canal beyond that.

In that last white flickering newsreel frame—between what had been and what was coming—Louise remembered her father, and the girl she once was.

When she was nine and he was three months from dying, they went fishing. They'd gone out early one morning, to the quiet stream off the Sûre River, and in the low hills and shady trees of Bastogne sat for a few blissful hours on the banks, angling for some trout. When no fish came, they stood in the shallows where the mud sucked at their ankles and the dragonflies buzzed low. Their lines kept breaking. *If it breaks, it breaks*, her father kept saying. *It means the thing at the end of the line is alive. That's all that matters.* A cigarette he never got around to smoking dangled behind his ear. She kept seeing his face in profile, eyes twinkling, him murmuring, *Just one more throw, Loosha, one more, we'll get lucky this time, I feel it.*

They walked home with empty hands and dirty legs, the basket banging against her knee.

"Now we'll have to eat your mother's cooking," Maurice said.

"Maman is making rabbit stew, Papa," said Louise.

"What did that poor rabbit ever do to deserve such punishment?" said Maurice. "I adore your mother, Lou. But that rabbit should have run faster."

They passed an inn, Auberge du Marronnier, and stopped in. They sat outside in the dust, at the table with the peeling red paint. Louise kept chipping it anxiously, half expecting her mother to come looking for them down the dry road. Maurice ordered a *citron pressé* for her and a glass of *Kir* for himself. They shared a plate of *boulettes* in tomato sauce with hunks of crusty bread. The sauce was sweet and burnt, and a drop of it stained his white sleeve.

"Look, Papa," she said, pointing to her father's shirt. "Now Maman will know."

He shrugged with a smile. "It's the mark of a man who lived well today," said Maurice, reaching across and patting Louise's hand.

When she got home, Louise went straight to Fletcher in the rear garden. "Fletcher," she said. "I know where your uranium is."

86

The Conversation

"It's not in Haigerloch," Louise said. "It's at Zvart Haus."

After the collective gasp, the *how do you know?!* the fifth *fuck*, there was silence. A sparrow nested in the hollow of the elm again, darting in and out as if nothing had changed. Fletcher's hands were flat on the table. Rafael smoked—and smoked again. Louise crumbled a poppy cake between her fingers. Charlie sat opposite them, watching all three. She was trying to make sense of it, not just the stunning information, but the actual implications.

"It can't be there," Rafael said. "Fletch, didn't you tell us it's a messy, dirty, toxic process? Lou says Zvart looks like a postcard. No smoke, no smell, just trees and grass."

Louise cleared her throat. "There was always a smell," she said. "Metallic, chemical. I knew Saul had a lab. I assumed it was just his experiments. That's why his window was always open. I bring him flowers to cover up the nasty tang."

"Pipes, generators, lab, all underground," said Fletcher. "That's how they did it in Haigerloch. Lou, didn't you say it's close to the industrial plants on the Albert Canal? They probably vent it there. To hide it. The reconnaissance photos, if there are any, wouldn't show anything amiss. No smokestacks, no plumes. No dead foliage nearby—that's an instant giveaway."

Louise told them three things. First, *Karl Wirtz*—marked for destruction by Jonathan Reed—coming to Zvart Haus to help Saul. If the uranium was actually in Haigerloch, Wirtz would never leave Germany.

Second, the ruts in the road. Deep, rain-filled, cut by trucks hauling heavy loads. They'd appeared over a month ago, just after Sancta Maria, and vanished a week later.

And third: Saul's notebook. In one quick glance, Louise saw nothing but the numbers 235 and 238 filling every page.

"Rheinhardt knows Saul?" Charlie asked. "But how?"

"Who cares how?" snapped Rafael. "That's the least important thing."

"I wonder if it's his car I sometimes see when I'm biking back," said Louise, cupping her palm around Rafael's fist—to quiet him? To comfort him? "Today I saw it on my way there. Anyone know what he drives?"

"A black Mercedes 770," said Charlie, remembering when she, Fletcher, and Hawk had it in their sights, lying in the hills above the abbey, waiting for Rheinhardt and Hubner to open the doors to their deaths.

"That's the one," Louise said. "Always coming or going."

They washed down Louise's poppy cake with blackcurrant Slivovitz—usually a cure-all for grief and joy alike.

But not today.

Rafael looked both resigned and shattered. Louise caressed his hand, kissed his shoulder. "It's okay, Rafa," she said. "I promise. It'll be okay."

"Fuck it all to hell," said Rafael.

Fletcher studied the table like it was a chessboard, and every piece was in the wrong place.

Louise reached for the Slivovitz, but stopped mid-sip, as if suddenly remembering, or realizing, something. She looked both shaken and resolute, pale and determined.

Charlie scanned her friends at the table. All eyes were averted. "What's going on here?" she said, dully. "What can you three possibly see that I'm not seeing?"

Rafael hit the table with his fist.

The invisible chess pieces must have been giving Fletcher trouble, because he too said nothing.

"Do you really not see?" said Rafael, sounding more irritated with her than usual.

"Clearly I don't," Charlie said. "Tell me."

Louise shushed him, whispering, "Shh, Rafa, be nice. Her love for me is making her blind."

"It's not making *me* blind," said Rafael.

"Maybe she loves me more than you do," Louise whispered.

"Impossible," said Rafael.

"Making who blind?" said Charlie. *"Me?"*

Getting up, Louise walked around to Charlie, leaned over and hugged her deeply. "We have no options left, Charlie," said Louise. "Saul must die."

"Agreed," Charlie said. "He's a collaborator who's doing a terrible thing—for the wrong side. How do we get this done?"

Fletcher and Rafael stayed grim and mute.

The blackcaps in the elms trilled on, their relentless cheerful melody suddenly maddening. *Shut up!* Charlie wanted to yell. *Shut the hell up!*

Sitting beside her, Louise took Charlie's hand. "I'm going to ask Hildi for a vial of hydrochloric acid," she said. "You're going to get me a horse syringe from your farmer friend at Hof Ten Bril Stables. I'm going to fill it with HCl, and I'm going to bike to Zvart Haus tomorrow or overmorrow, if we need an extra day to get ready. I'll bring him lunch, like always. We'll need to find a way to keep that bastard Rheinhardt off the premises, so he doesn't show up at the wrong moment and ruin things. I'm going to walk into Saul's study, take out my needle, and pump his neck full of acid. You saw Hildi in action in Sancta Maria—HCl is lethal and fast-acting. When he is dead, I will walk back downstairs, get on my bike, and cycle home. And then we'll have to disappear. Fitz too. Maman too."

The silence around the table was louder than any silence Charlie had ever heard.

Charlie threw back her head and laughed.

No one else laughed with her.

"Are you all *insane*?" Charlie said.

Fletcher opened his mouth to speak, but Charlie cut him off.

"I don't want to hear a fucking thing."

"Charlie," said Louise. "You think I want this? None of you even know Saul." She lowered her head. "But it's the only way."

"Not only is it not the *only* way, it's not even *a* way." Charlie whirled on Fletcher. "It's almost three. Go get your kit, crank the battery, and radio your man in London. Tell him what you've learned about Zvart Haus. Invite him to come and blow the place to smithereens. They've been bombing other places. Hamburg. Cologne. Tell him to come and vaporize Zvart."

"She's right," Rafael said. The rancor and bombast were gone from his voice. "At least ask Reed if it's possible. Before we take the shot." He didn't look up—especially not at Louise.

OTP transmission:

PAD 31-5 COFFEE FOUND STOP BEANS PROCESSED ONE MONTH STOP REQUEST IMMEDIATE FULL GRINDER SERVICE ON ROASTERY STOP COORDINATES TO FOLLOW STOP

Fletcher sent the coordinates separately and was just about to power off the set when the static sharpened.

They all froze.

A faint tick. Then another. An operator's rhythm—someone was keying in. Fletcher stiffened, headset still on. "He's never answered me the same day," he said. "Too dangerous. Too exposed." He listened to the Morse, scribbling each five-letter block in his notebook. The moment it ended, Fletcher killed the power, ripped off the headset, and began decoding, his pencil scratching the paper the only sound in the garden.

Charlie, sitting next to him, saw the first word and jerked sharply away.

NEVER.

The rest was no less chilling.

COFFEE FULLY ACTIVE STOP CONTAMINATION DISPERSION ABSOLUTE STOP FIRE = DETONATION STOP CONTAIN BY OTHER MEANS STOP COLD ONLY STOP

"Reed can't do it," Fletcher said.

Rafael dropped his gaze.

"Well, Fletcher," Charlie said, fists clenched, "if your OSS commander with his fighter planes and mighty tanks can't do it, then Louise sure as hell can't fucking do it."

"Charlie." Louise's voice was soft, almost inaudible. "I'm the *only* one who can do it."

"I'm coming with you," Rafael said.

That brought a weary smile to Louise's face. "What are you going to do, Rafa?" she said, drawing his face to hers and kissing him. "Sit on my handlebars?" Her voice was full of Lillehaven nostalgia.

His arm slipped around her waist, pulling her in. "Yes, *bébé*, that's the only place I belong," he murmured. "On your handlebars."

"You can't come inside with me," she said. "You can't even bike to Zvart with me. You're a military-age man. You can't be seen."

"I won't be seen," he said. "I'll hide somewhere only you can see me—and I can see you. So you know I'm with you, if something goes wrong."

"You can't carry a rifle," she said.

"I'll bring my pistol. Two, even."

"You won't get close enough to use them. The only place for you to hide is in the thicket across the road."

"Then that's where I'll hide."

"If you fire even once, I'll never get out of the house," she said.

"He's not going to fire," said Fletcher. "He'll be there for the just in case."

"What just in case?" said Louise.

Rafael and Fletcher exchanged a look. "Lou, trust us, we've been in enough battles," Rafael said, "to know no matter how well you prepare, something always gets fucked up."

"This isn't one of those times," said Louise. "I've literally been bringing Saul lunch for years. I bike past the front gate. Turn left at the hedges. Go to the side gate. Talk to the guards. They check my basket. I give them a cookie and a peach. I walk through the side door. I go upstairs. I sit with Saul while he eats. We talk." Her face iced over and melted at the same time, as if finally glimpsing the gruesome reality of what she was proposing. "The HCl is all I can do," she said, her mouth twisting. "I can't shoot him. Too loud. And I can't use a knife—I don't know how."

"She is right," Rafael said. "There's no easy way to kill someone quietly and up close."

"There's no easy way to kill someone," Louise whispered.

They sat.

She hugged him. "But Rafa, honestly, I don't want you to come. Please. Stay here."

"You're not doing this without me," he said. "What if you need to get out quickly, or we need to run? What if someone follows you?"

"He's right. He has to come, Louise," Fletcher said.

"There are at least *four* guards on duty there!" Charlie said.

"Rider can kill four Germans before opening his eyes in the morning," Fletcher said.

"What if there are more?"

"He might have to open one of his eyes, then."

"I'll go with them, too," Charlie said. "I'll bring your rifle."

"No," said Fletcher. "I need you and Fitz on this side—for my part of the plan."

Charlie groaned. "There's a *your* part of this plan?" She put her head in her hands.

"Yes. You heard Louise," Fletcher said. "We need to distract Rheinhardt, to make sure he stays away from Zvart. I'm going to be that distraction. And I'll need you to come and rescue me when the time comes. Can we send word to your brother? I need him too for this."

"I'll help you, Fletcher," Charlie said, steeling herself. "I'll do anything for you." Her voice broke. "Whatever you need me to do, I'll do. But don't bring Fitz into this. Please."

Fletcher shook his head. "You're my cavalry, Charlie. But I need a second man for the first part of my plan. If Rheinhardt sees me with a woman, he'll immediately know it's a trap."

"A *honey* trap?" Charlie couldn't even smile.

Rafael snorted. "Definitely not a *honey* trap."

"Shut up," Charlie said. "Why can't you just take *him*?"

"Because *him*," said Rafael, "is going with Louise."

"Please don't come, Rafa," said Louise. "I promise I'll be back in an hour."

"What, Louise, you think it's too dangerous for me?" Rafael said. "Look, it's not a discussion. If you're doing this, I'm coming with you."

Louise shook her head, looking away.

"Rider is right, Lou," Fletcher said. "In a military op, you never go alone. You always bring someone to cover you."

"You're going to kill a man?" Charlie said to Louise, incredulous and anguished. *"You?"*

"Louise is a true tactician," Fletcher said. "It's our cleanest move, and it's brilliant. In chess, we call it *mate in one*."

"In life we call it fucking madness."

"Agreed," said Rafael. "It's fucking madness."

"If there's another way, please—I'm all ears," Louise said. "You think I want to do it?" She bowed her head. "But look what he's doing, what he's got his hands on. As he said to me a thousand times—without him, it doesn't happen. He *is* the machine. Whether he's their victim or their weapon, it doesn't matter. But once he's dead, the uranium is useless to them."

Charlie was too upset to see anything clearly—not Louise, not Rafael. Not even her own dread and rage. "I can't fucking believe it," she said, pacing like a caged animal. "I can't believe that Saul's piss-poor fucking choices mean you have to be dragged into this whole goddamn mess."

Rafael agreed with Charlie, for once. "She shouldn't have to be the one."

"What, you think you two are the only ones who can do hard things?" Louise said softly.

"This isn't hard," Charlie whispered. "This is unfair."

"It's cruel is what it is," said Rafael.

"Charlie," Fletcher said gently. "She's the only move we have left."

"He's right," Louise echoed. "I'm all we have left."

"And she is enough," Rafael said, his face distorting before hardening into something like composure. "You'll see. She's everything."

There was too much to do in too little time. Father Bavo offered to help—just as he had after Sancta Maria—no hesitation, no questions. Bavo was doing Omloop's holy work as well as his own. His Caritas van was parked behind Saint Waltrude's, gassed up and ready for all six of them. Their long weapons were stashed under the floorboards, and the spare ration cards were pinned to Hélène's forged travel documents. They had changes of clothes, new identities, and a first aid kit. They agreed they would meet at the church as soon as it was done. Father Bavo would extract Hélène from the town hall and tell her nothing. With a little luck, they'd be across the Dutch border by dusk.

After a hard, tense day of planning, of getting, of doing, of talking through the possibilities and the impossibilities, the next evening, before Dory brought Fitz, Charlie said to the rest, "Whatever *you* do, don't talk details in front of the small, oily man. All he wants is to matter. And he's loyal only to Fitz. Just . . . pipe down when he's near."

That night, Fletcher and Fitz and Charlie were bent over a map of Antwerp spread across the garden table, their voices low. A single oil lantern flickered between them.

"Fletcher," Fitz said, "I'll do this for you to help you, to help my sister, but if anything happens to—" He broke off.

"Rafael's taking care of it at Zvart," Charlie said, squeezing her brother's elbow.

"That's what worries me."

"He's an assault commando," said Fletcher. "Everything will be fine."

"What if Grunfell's not there?" Fitz asked.

"Why wouldn't he be there?"

"What if he's stuck in the lab? Or is in the wrong place? What if he's not alone? Or what if he screams?" Fitz said it as if *he* were going to scream.

Behind Charlie, a boot crunched on gravel. "Shh," she said before she even turned around. It was Dory.

"Pardon me, Fitz—hate to interrupt the war effort, but I'm to get you back to Vorselaar before curfew . . ."

"You go ahead, Dory," Fitz said. "I'll stay the night."

"Right," said Dory with a chuckle. "Oh—you're not joking? But what about . . ." He waved his hand to indicate the phantom of Rafael and Louise, for the moment elsewhere.

"It's fine, Dory. You know—war effort."

As Dory was about to leave, Louise walked out into the backyard, with Rafael behind her. "What have you three been conspiring about?" she said too brightly, bending over the map. Rafael leaned over too, standing scandalously close behind her. Louise shifted, barely. Charlie watched her brother watch it all, not reeling, just standing still. Fletcher elbowed Rafael, moving sharply between him and Louise to fold the map.

"What?" Rafael said quietly, as Fitz and Dory turned to go. "He's helping us. What more do you need? Louise talked to him. He's fine."

"You don't need to rub his face in it," Fletcher said.

Charlie heard Dory catch up with Fitz as they were on their way out. "Are you *sure* you want to stay here?" asked Dory.

Fitz's gaze was fixed on the ground. "It's fine, yes."

"You shouldn't let them treat you like this," Dory said. "You and your family have done more for her than he ever will."

"Whatever. It doesn't matter. We just have to get through tomorrow."

"Why? What's happening tomorrow?"

Fitz snapped out of it, blinked, looked around, caught Charlie's frown, and changed his expression to neutral. "Nothing, nothing at all. Let me walk you out."

For a few moments before Fitz returned, Charlie and Fletcher, Louise and Rafael sat alone in the dark garden. It smelled of cut grass and warm earth, with a trace of some late blooming jasmine. For some reason the words *holy holy holy* came to Charlie, and it took her a moment to remember that's what Omloop always said when he was finished. *Holy holy holy.*

And the earth is full of His glory.

Except she didn't want it to be finished. Not yet. Not like this. What you're proposing is madness, Charlie wanted to say to Fletcher. Not just for Lou. For you too. Your part in it—it's too much. What if you don't make it out? What are we all supposed to do then? What am I supposed to do? She dug her fingers into her palms so hard she might have torn them open, if she had any nails left to gouge with.

Nobody spoke. It felt like they were all holding their breath, waiting to see who would break first.

"I suppose even *the girl with fire in her hand* needs cover." Charlie's weak voice barely carried in the dark. Her fingers trembled. She couldn't hold the glass of Slivovitz steady. Fletcher put his hand on hers—steady, strong, warm. Her stomach rolled in numbing waves, like she was being hurled off a cliff. She was afraid down to her bones—for Louise, for Fletcher, even for Rafael. Even for Louise's unsuspecting mother. For everything.

"What's she talking about, Loosh?" said Rafael.

"Mother Verene, may she rest in peace, told us a story," Louise said, full of profound love, her eyes on Charlie, her hands on Rafael. "A prophecy from Brother Severin."

"Prophecy or nightmare?" said Charlie. "*The Ashen Bell will toll when the hour comes—not to save the world, but to choose what must burn.*"

87

Sham Sacrifice

Rheinhardt had just taken a sip of his second cup of excellent coffee, brewed from rich beans out of the Kivu region in the Congo, when he heard Hubner shout, "Hey! Hey! What are you doing?" A shot rang out.

Rheinhardt crossed the room with quiet urgency, pistol in hand. He saw a young man bolting down Daisy Lane. In the dusty side drive, another man stood beside the Mercedes, hands raised. "I was trying to stop him," he said in French. "You don't understand."

Rheinhardt leveled his pistol at the man's chest. "What happened?"

"I saw them, sir!" Hubner cried. "Two of them, by your rear tires, slashing them! They had blades—tools—"

The man pointed to the intact tires. "No slashing," he said. "I thought that man was planting something."

"You were leaning over him!" Hubner shouted.

"To stop him."

"Enough," Rheinhardt said. "Hubner, go get four officers. Six, if you can find them. Two inside, four outside. They were supposed to be here already. Where are they?"

"Sweeping the docks and checking for crane tampering, sir," Hubner said as he ran off, throwing one last glare at the man by the car.

Rheinhardt didn't step closer. "Are you armed?" The man looked vaguely familiar.

The young man opened his tunic and spun once. "It's illegal for Belgians to carry weapons, sir. You know that."

"Who was the one who ran?"

"Never met him."

"Why were *you* on Daisy Lane? It's not a through street. Where were *you* going?"

"Looking for work at the docks," the man said. "Trying to cut through to Rijnkaai. I thought this street connected."

"A little late for work, aren't you? The allocations are at 0700."

"It's my second shift," the man said.

"Sure it is. Your name?"

"Florent. Florent Van Acker."

As soon as the words left the man's mouth, Rheinhardt cocked his gun. *"Florent?"* he said. "As in Omloop's gimpy nephew? Florent from Bruges?"

"I am from Bruges, yes, sir." He raised his hands higher. "Omloop was my uncle, yes. He's dead now. Very unfortunate."

"*You're* unfortunate, Florent. Did you and your friend wire the car? Plant a bomb?"

"Bomb? Not me, sir. Maybe him. He wasn't my friend."

"If you're so sure the car isn't wired, then get inside and start the engine," Rheinhardt said.

"Gladly." Florent reached for the driver's door and stuck out his other hand. "The keys?"

Rheinhardt moved to get them, then stopped cold. What was he doing—handing off keys to a ghost? What if this grub took off in his car? "That's enough out of you," he said. "Let's wait."

"As you wish."

"You don't remember me, scofflaw?" Rheinhardt said. "We met at the Herentals church. You were working with your uncle."

"Ah," Florent said. "I think . . . yes . . . I'm not good with faces, sir. Just looking for work, that's all. Been scarce these past few months."

Rheinhardt narrowed his eyes. Did this nobody really not remember meeting an SS officer? Or was he banking on the SS officer not remembering him?

Hubner returned with four Gestapo. Rheinhardt had two of them seize Florent and lead him toward the shed in the back, to *der Raum*. "Hubner, bring me the clamps and the hand-crank generator," he said. "We're going to have a little talk with Florent. See what we see." The man's bravado irritated him. Not the way a liar irritates, but the way a man who believes he's safe irritates. No one should feel safe. Not here. Not with him.

"It's not me you want, sir," Florent said. "I assure you. It's the crook who ran. I stayed, didn't I? Doesn't that tell you something?"

"You have a clubfoot," Rheinhardt said. "You knew you couldn't outrun Hubner." Florent's eyes blinked a trace of contempt at Hubner—just enough to register. Rheinhardt smirked. "Hubner, are you going to stand there and take that? The cripple thinks he could've outrun you."

"I don't, sir," Florent said evenly. "But would that I had the opportunity to try."

In *der Raum*, the man stood shirtless, arms stretched high and bound with twine at the wrists to a rusted iron ring above him. Water streamed from his head and shoulders where they had doused him. Metal clamps were affixed into the flesh of his palms.

Rheinhardt circled him slowly, studying the wiry muscles under his scars. He was too lean, too strong. "You're fit for a clubfoot," he said.

"The bells don't lift themselves," Florent said, low and flat.

"You've collected scars from some serious injuries. Shrapnel. Knife wounds. Burns. Bullets?" He came around to stand in front of Florent. For a moment, their gazes locked. But something defiant glinted in Florent's eyes that was at odds with the precariousness of his situation. Almost as if . . . Rheinhardt didn't know. Almost as if Florent was thinking of other things.

He might have to redirect the man to his present predicament. Rheinhardt turned the crank, and sent a burst of raw current screaming through the clamps into Florent's flesh.

Florent convulsed against the restraints, his teeth grinding down on a cry that still tore its way out. His mouth began to drip blood.

"I didn't know bellwork was so dangerous," Rheinhardt said.

"I ran with some bad people in Bruges," Florent said after a few moments, his words thick and slurred. "My uncle put me on a straight path. It's been tough since he left us."

"Your uncle was not a good man, Florent."

"Oh, you're wrong sir. Uncle Omloop was a great man."

"Do you know what he did?"

"Yes. He fixed bells."

"What else?"

"That's all he did."

"Indeed. Do you know a man named Adrian Vervaet?" He watched the prisoner's face closely—not just for the lie, but what might lie beneath it.

"Oh, sure," Florent said. "He was a famous bellmaker in Bruges. Big reputation. He's gone now, too, unfortunately."

Nothing. Decayed pain, but otherwise, not a flinch. He was either ignorant or well trained. Better trained than half the SS. How peculiar.

Hubner brought a dozen clocks and wound each to tick at a slightly different tempo—fast, slow, erratic. Rheinhardt enjoyed this enhancement to interrogation. He called it *clockwork madness*. When he told the prisoner, *one minute*, Florent had no way to measure it. Time was fractured. Every tick was a lie.

Another slow turn of the crank. Another full body seizure.

"It's okay, Florent," Rheinhardt said. "No one's a hero in your position. No one ever asks for more. Just tell me what I want to know. There's nothing worse than physical pain."

"I don't think that's true, sir," Florent said, panting. He spit blood onto the floor.

"No?"

Florent opened his eyes and stared at Rheinhardt, who sat behind his small table, arms crossed, smoking a cigarette. "Physical pain subsides," Florent said. "The body heals. But the suffering inside? There's no way out."

Too lucid for a *klokkenmaker*. What suffering inside? Whose?

"Let's turn that crank twice instead of once, shall we?" Rheinhardt said. "See if you're correct."

Florent screamed.

"Have you had enough yet?"

"Yes, sir. Oh, yes, sir."

"Are you going to answer me?"

"I've answered you."

"Who are you? Who are you, really?"

"Who are any of us, really," Florent said—and screamed. When Rheinhardt stopped cranking, and the pain receded, the captive said, "I know what I'm called. Florent Van Acker."

"Who in Bruges can vouch for you?"

"Hundreds of people, sir. But some of them are dead. Or in prison. I told you. Rough crowd."

"Are you an errand boy for the resistance? A courier for the partisans? A hanger-on? A wannabe?"

"I'm just a dull-eyed cripple. You said so yourself."

"I never called you dull-eyed," Rheinhardt said. If anything, he thought, those purple eyes gleamed too cold and bright for his liking.

"You know what I want?" Florent said, after the sixth round.

"I can't wait for you to tell me."

"That when I die, you'll say a fervent prayer of thanks that I'm out of the fight."

"What fight?" said Rheinhardt. "You're just a ragged *stray* with a clever tongue. And I'm not killing you, Florent. Not yet. It may feel like it, but you won't die until I've squeezed the last drop of truth out of you."

"You already have. I've got nothing left. God's honest truth."

"Which God is this?" Rheinhardt asked. "The Old Testament God of brimstone and justice? Or the New Testament God of peace and mercy?"

"The New Testament God who came not to send peace but a sword," Florent said. "*That* God."

"When did he ever say that?" Rheinhardt sneered.

"Matthew 10," replied Florent.

Rheinhardt didn't waver, but he blinked slowly. Scripture, chapter and verse, from a cripple with a talent for theatrics?

He accidentally overcranked the generator and sent too strong a jolt through the clamps in Florent's hands. The man nearly passed out. "By all means, scream louder," Rheinhardt said. "Maybe afterward I'll get another story out of you." He had to be careful, though. One or two more like that, cranked too fast, and Florent might never speak again.

After a few minutes, the vagabond recovered. "I believe there aren't that many stories in the world," he said, through his bleeding mouth. "Some say there's only one."

Something in the cadence of the man's voice stirred unease. It wasn't quite the usual peasant's babble. Rheinhardt leaned forward in his chair, stiffening. "You have ninety seconds before the next clock stops. Tell me your story, *Florent*."

Florent stared at the remaining ticking clocks, perspiring, panting. "We are all trapped," he said. "Caught inside the fisherman's net of folly and weakness. We're slaves to our passions, our cruelty, our hunger, our *hubris*."

"You have one minute to tell me your real name, bell-boy," said Rheinhardt, "before I lose my sainted patience with you." Did Omloop's apprentice really just use the word *hubris*?

"Florent *is* my name," Florent said. "But even if it wasn't, what difference, at this point, does it make? When you strip your life down to the last few things that matter, is that really the question you'll be asking yourself? Who am *I*?" He paused, getting his breath. "Not—who are *you*?"

"I'm the highest-ranking SS officer of the largest port in northern Europe," Rheinhardt said. "I'm a commander of the Third Reich. I wear a uniform. I don't stink. I look like a civilized man. I'm not a prisoner, I'm not beaten—"

"No?" said Florent.

"No!" said Rheinhardt. He was being provoked. "I'm not half naked. I'm not being electrocuted, crank by crank. I'm not chained."

"I hear a lot of self-congratulation," Florent said. "I don't hear a last question."

"When the dust settles on *your* life, and you're down to your last breath—which will be sooner than you think, the way you're going—what will you ask yourself?"

"The same question you should ask *your*self," said Florent. "What effect did the act of inflicting pain have on the mind of the man inflicting it—in this case, *you*—and the soul of the man enduring it—in this case, *me*?"

Rheinhardt took strong exception to the emphasis the prisoner placed on "in *this* case." As if, in another case, the roles might be reversed. "Your time is up, Cicero," said Rheinhardt, his hand on the crank.

Behind Rheinhardt, the door to *der Raum* burst open and Hubner rushed in, panic wild on his face.

"Yours too," whispered Florent.

88

234 Steps Plus One

Louise felt so brave and determined when she got the call from Fitz just after eleven. *"Tell your mother I found the scarf,"* he said from a public telephone. That was the code phrase. It meant that Fitz had escaped, and Fletcher was in Rheinhardt's hands. Rheinhardt was now otherwise engaged. She had two hours.

Her heart jumped. The first part of the plan was in motion. After she hung up, she and Rafael embraced. "It's time, Rafa," she said, kissing him softly. "Are you ready?"

"Are *you* ready?" said Rafael.

He didn't look ready.

And once they reached Olen, and she left him at the intersection, Louise didn't feel ready either. Her certainty began to slip. As she biked alone the rest of the way to Zvart, something unspooled inside her. "Hide your bike in the brambles," she'd told him. "Make sure they don't see it. Or you."

"You don't have to worry about me, Loosha," he said, holding on to her a moment too long. "Just mind yourself."

At the front gate, she waved to the sentries. At the side gate, she smiled as always. "Bonjour *Inspecteur, Commissaire*," she said, upranking them both above their stations.

"You're late," one of them said.

"Blame the peaches," she said. "Couldn't find any ripe ones." She lifted two from the basket and tossed them over. The guard caught one, sniffed. "Pretty good," he said. "You don't have any lemon cakes in there, do you?" He opened the lid and poked through the basket. Her heart nearly stopped.

"Not today," she said lightly. "Have a poppy cake instead."

"I really like your lemon cakes," he said. "Maybe next time?"

"Definitely. Next time."

They waved her through.

Trembling, Louise climbed the back stairs to the second floor and walked down the long hallway holding on to the wall for support. At Saul's door, she stopped. She transferred the syringe from the basket to her apron, but couldn't go in. She stood frozen in the corridor, trying to recall anything anyone had ever told her. About this—about anything. Her hand was in her apron, wrapped around the syringe.

The hydrochloric acid was loaded.

There was no going back.

Fletcher told her: don't talk to him. Don't engage him in any way. Don't spend any more time in that room than you have to. I'll keep Rheinhardt away, but we don't know who else might be in the house. You've got one job. Time for conversation is long over. Don't serve him lunch. Don't make nice. Don't give him a peach or ask about his day. Put the basket down. Pull out the syringe. Do what you came to do. Don't think. Just do it.

Plunge the needle in, to the hilt, all the way. By the time he grabs your arm, the syringe will have emptied and the acid will be filling up the veins in his neck. He won't be able to say a word. Drop the syringe to the floor. Pick up the basket and leave. Don't look at him again, not even once. Just go. Walk down the back stairs—exactly the way you came. Don't run. Don't even rush. Get on your bike. Ride away. Wave to the guards. That's it. Then you meet Rafael by his bike, and you ride as fast as you can to Saint Waltrude's. We'll all be there waiting. In three hours we'll be in Eindhoven.

What else did Fletcher tell her? By the time Grunfell hits the floor, you need to be out of that room, Louise. No making him comfortable. No apologizing. No talking. Just get close. Do what you came to do. And get out.

Louise nodded. She said she understood.

Yesterday, for hours—in between Hildi and the stables and the rifles and the forgeries—they rehearsed it in the woods. Fletcher wanted the operation to be burned into Louise's muscle memory. Grunfell at the table, buried in his numbers. Louise approaching. Him turning, smiling. Her placing the basket on the floor—like always. Straightening out. Reaching into her apron.

And plunging the needle.

They timed it. And then they measured it. The entire mission—from walking in to walking out—took no more than 45 seconds. If you counted the approach—the stairs, the hallway, the room, the exit—it was 130 seconds.

Just over two minutes.

Fletcher, who measured life one step at a time, worked it all out. He counted the distance from the back door, up the stairs, down the hall, across the room, to the chair.

It was 235 steps.

Exactly 117 steps there, and 117 back.

And one step to turn from the basket on the floor to Grunfell in the chair.

Fletcher gave Louise numbers for every phase.

Through the lower hall and up the stairs: 62 steps.

The long corridor to the study: 38 steps.

From the door to his chair: 17 steps.

One way: 117 steps.

Total: 235 steps.

One to turn.

Rafael and Charlie told Fletcher only a maniac would find comfort in counting steps. He told them they were wrong.

They practiced it. Over and over. Afternoon into evening. Walking it. Timing it.

Louise was as ready as she would ever be.

But now it was step 100—just before the door.

And she couldn't move. Fletcher hadn't counted on that. That she'd be flat against the wall, her heart beating out of her chest.

Don't think.

Just do it.

Do it.

Her fingers felt for the syringe at the bottom of her pocket.

Louise took a breath—

—and stepped inside.

89

A Matter of Utmost Urgency

In *der Raum*, Rheinhardt spoke sharply to Hubner without taking his eyes off Florent. "Who wants to see me? Can't you see I'm busy?" He raised his voice. "You know better than to interrupt me, Hubner, when I'm working."

Hubner leaned in and whispered, "He says it's a matter of *utmost* urgency."

"Yes, yes," Rheinhardt snapped, still eyeing Florent. "Everything's an emergency. Welcome to Belgium in 1944."

Hubner coughed into his sleeve. "Sir, his name is Dorian de Smet. He says it's about—"

A sudden, guttural sound burst from Florent—an animal cry of agony.

"Shut up for a second! I haven't even touched you," Rheinhardt barked. "Hubner, what?"

"It's about Saul Grunfell—"

Rheinhardt exploded from his chair. He was out of *der Raum* before the final syllable left Hubner's mouth.

Behind him, Florent shouted, "Rheinhardt! My name is Fletcher Gray—!"

But Rheinhardt was gone. Fake Florent meant nothing to him now.

He stormed into Baert Haus. In the reception area stood a doughy, twitchy man-child, wringing his hands. "My name is Dorian de Smet," the man said. "I only came to you, sir, because I respect the chain of command. That's why I brought it up the chain. Should we go inside your office? Speak privately?"

"Who the fuck do you think you are, telling me to step into my own office?" Rheinhardt said. "I don't know you. I've never met you. Open your mouth and speak. No—don't sit down. I did not invite you to sit. Did you say Grunfell?"

Eagerly, Dorian nodded.

"What do you know?"

"Sir, I just want to make sure I'm protected. Because if the people I work with find out I came here, I'm a dead man. I'm not a traitor, sir. Just a concerned citizen."

"Yes, vermin, you'll be protected. Speak—now."

"You might want to put extra security around that man, Saul Grunfell," Dorian said. "Because he's about to be killed."

"Hubner!" Rheinhardt shouted, fumbling for his coat and pistol. "Car!" He motioned to Dorian. "You. Come."

"Oh, no, sir, I don't—"

Rheinhardt grabbed him by the collar and shoved him outside. "I wasn't asking. Get in the fucking car."

As they rushed into the forecourt, Rheinhardt barked at the two Gestapo posted by the Mercedes. "Get ten more men. Dogs. Rifles. Zvart Haus. You follow us—immediately."

Hubner gunned it. In the back seat, Rheinhardt turned to Dorian. "Tell me who you are."

"He works in Port Authority, sir," Hubner said. "I've seen him. Records and filing. He's one of the copying clerks."

"I just want to be useful to the right people, sir," Dorian said. "That's all I've ever tried to be. And they say you're the sharpest mind in Antwerp—I figured you'd know what to do."

"Why are your people trying to kill Saul Grunfell? How do they know who he is? Are you sure you don't have him confused with another Jew?"

"Positive, sir. I heard it myself."

"Faster, Hubner!" And to Dorian: "Who's coming to kill him? Why?"

"There's a group of Allied soldiers working with our partisans. One of their commandos was headed there with his pistols."

"Headed where?"

"Zvart Haus, I think?"

Rheinhardt felt sick. "*Faster*, Hubner," he choked out.

"I'm at maximum speed, sir," Hubner said. "We'll be there in twenty."

"What Allied soldiers?" Rheinhardt twisted toward Dorian and also somehow away from him, as if he didn't want to miss a breath of what the man was saying and yet wanted to be as far away from him as possible. "How do you know this? Aren't you with Belgian *Polizei*? Or are you one of the partisans?"

"I'm just a clerk, sir," Dorian said. "I push paper, that's all. I'm not part of it. But I do know the woman helping the Allies. Charlotte Fontaine."

Rheinhardt gave a low, guttural groan. "Helping with *what*?"

"They know what Grunfell is working on," Dorian whispered. "They've come to stop him."

"Hubner!" screamed Rheinhardt. "Go! Fucking! Faster!"

Mein Gott.

In a moment of eviscerating weakness, Rheinhardt dropped his face into his hands.

Something terrible became clear to him.

He had fallen for the feigned sacrifice. He had been blindsided by the calculated misdirection. If it weren't for this pig-faced quadruple agent, he'd never have guessed that *Florent* was one of them. He had been so obsessed with forcing a confession from that *verdammt* conman, he missed the trap being sprung beneath his feet.

For all he knew, he was already suffering a catastrophic positional collapse.

"The Allied soldiers," Rheinhardt said in a voice he didn't recognize—something between animal and insect. "Is one of them named Fletcher Gray, by any chance?"

"Yes!" Dorian exclaimed. "He's their commander. But . . . how do you know his name?"

Rheinhardt recoiled as if from a blow.

"Faster!" he croaked, like a rider spurring a collapsing horse. "Faster!"

He could already be too late.

90

Fire in Her Hand

Saul looked up from his work, turned his head to her, and smiled. "Hi there, Lou!" he said. "I didn't think you were coming today. You were just here. Oh, what happiness. I am so hungry—I had no idea what I was going to eat for lunch. Well, come in, come in, don't just stand there. Let's see what you've got for me."

A trembling Louise took seventeen steps to Saul's table by the window. Everything on her was shaking, her knees, her hands, her lips. Perspiration was dripping down her eyelids. It made her feel like she was crying.

Maybe she was crying.

Blessed art thou O Lord, teach me thy statutes was, unfortunately, what came into her head at that misguided moment.

She dropped the basket on the floor near him. She couldn't raise her eyes. Couldn't smile. Couldn't speak or move.

Reaching into her front pocket, she groped for the executioner's blade: a glass livestock syringe. She curled her fingers around the plunger, drew her arm behind her back, and stood upright—hiding it from his view. Her face must have been a sight, because Saul stopped smiling. "What's wrong with you?" He frowned.

"Saul . . ." she whispered. She remembered her instructions. Fletcher's voice rang clear in her head.

But there was another voice there too.

She knew what she had to do. She knew how.

She was a foot away from Saul.

He sat in front of her. She stood over him.

The basket lay between them.

The syringe was behind her back.

He looked up at her—faltering now, confused by her expression, her mute distress.

"What? What's wrong?"

"Saul, I beg you . . ." Her voice trembled like the rest of her. "Don't do it." She couldn't do it. She had to try it her way.

He sat, dumbfounded. "What are you talking about?"

"Don't . . . build your bomb." It was out. There was no going back.

He shot to his feet, knocking over the chair, and staggered away. She stayed rooted by the table, her arm behind her. But he was now across the room, bracing himself against a low bookshelf. "Who *are* you?" he gasped. "What do you want?"

"You know who I am," Louise said quietly. "But the uranium you've been using—it's not yours, Saul. Rheinhardt stole it from King Leopold. The Allies are trying to get it back."

"What Allies? How do *you* know who Rheinhardt is?"

"Funny, I asked myself the same question about you. I couldn't believe *my* Saul knew who Erich von Rheinhardt was."

"I'm not your Saul," he said.

"You are," said Louise. "Don't do this for the Germans. Don't give them your gift."

"Get out." Saul pointed to the door. "This doesn't concern you." He'd recovered some of his composure, though he still looked shaken. If only he knew what was clenched behind her back.

"Why would you help the men who took your life from you, who took your family?"

"You naïve child. You understand nothing."

"You're brainwashed, Saul. Do you even know who you're working for?"

"I'm not brainwashed," Saul said. "The work is the only point. Nothing else matters."

"That can't be true," she whispered. "To work in a prison? That's slavery."

"This isn't a prison—it's my freedom."

"Did you ever ask yourself why they'd let a detained Belgian Jew control the most valuable resource they've ever found?"

"Because my work speaks for itself."

"No." She shook her head. "Because they have no one else."

"Every word out of your mouth is a manipulation."

"Yes," she said—and started to cry. "I *am* trying to manipulate you. To get you to listen to me. To stop you." *With my words.*

"What do you care what I do?"

"Why don't *you* care? The *Nazis* might win the war because of the bomb you're making for them."

"You wish you had that kind of power, don't you, little Louise," Saul said. "You think you're insulting me, but all I hear is praise." He slammed his fist on the shelf. Books toppled. "No one else can build it but *me*."

"Yes—because everyone else is dead."

"Because no one else knows how." He stood tall now—exultant, imperious, unshaken. "To rip the atom apart, and then to isolate the sliver inside it that burns brighter than the sun—that's a staggering achievement. And I've done it. *Me*. Right here in this little house in the country. I'm soaring like a bird. I've bent time and light to my will." He looked radiant with pride.

Louise filled her voice with scorn to cut through his hubris. "You want to bend time and light for the *Germans*? Do you even know what they've done to your people?"

"*My* people?" Saul said. "Look at you, my pretty little lunch girl. You've dehumanized me with that phrase alone. As if I'm some separate breed. I am *Belgian*, Louise. Just like you."

Louise's lip trembled. *Fletcher was right*, she realized. She should've never engaged with Saul. She should have plunged the syringe into his neck and run. She should've uttered no words. She felt the moment slipping through her fingers.

She couldn't undo it. Couldn't go back. She felt such regret, such anger at herself. She glanced out the window, hoping for a glimpse of Rafael across the road—just something to give her strength. But he was well hidden.

"And to answer your question," Saul went on. "No, I *don't* care."

"About what?" she asked, trying not to sound defeated. "The Nazis murdering your children?"

"Enough! Don't antagonize me." He pointed at her. "Even if the rumors are true, even if they did kill some people for being Jews—"

"*If?*" Louise said. "They deported nearly all the Jews out of Belgium."

Saul shrugged. "What did Belgium have—twenty-two, twenty-five thousand Jews?"

"The *Einsatzgruppen* are mowing down Jews all across Europe," Louise said. "That's more than twenty-five thousand, no?"

"Words. Hysteria. I don't care about being Jewish," Saul said. "I don't care about being Belgian. All I care about is finishing what I've started. It's the single most important endeavor of my life."

"Even if it means Germany wins the war?"

"I. Don't. Care. How many times must I say it? Someone has to win. And frankly? They've treated me *well*. I have food. Books. Wine. Cigarettes. A state-of-the-art lab. Anything I ask, they provide. Not a copper wire's been spared."

"And your family?" Louise said in a hollow voice.

"That's what you don't understand," Saul said feverishly. "Yes, at first, they tried to use my family to coerce me. *Do this—or your wife. Build this—or your children.* It was I who refused to have any part in that. I would not be blackmailed with love. So, I let them go. I stopped writing to my wife. I made myself stop asking about my children. I chose indifference—because otherwise, I would never be free." He gripped the edge of the shelf.

"You're building the Nazis a uranium bomb," said Louise, her voice shaking, "on the back of your indifference to your own *family*?" Her vision blurred, her hearing dimmed. *Mon Dieu*, she thought. *What have I done?*

His eyes were blank. "I forced my heart to grow cold. It was the only way I could survive."

"What about your wife, your babies? Did *they* survive?" Louise whispered. "They were taken to Auschwitz. They all went on the trains to Poland."

"That's just a lie you tell yourself to get me to bend to your will. It's not going to work. You have no idea where they went."

"Oh, but I do," said Louise, her throat dry. "Transport Number Ten. September 15, 1942. They were on the same train as . . ." She stopped. She could see by Saul's face that her tears and words were falling on deaf ears—and a dead heart. "I waved goodbye to them myself."

"You're lying."

She looked at him for a long moment. "To Paolo. To Mina," she said. "And to your children, Saul. Why do you think I kept coming to you, feeding you, talking to you? Because I knew you had no one else." She bowed her shaking head. "What a terrible mistake I've made."

"You'll say anything."

"Your children are not just words," she said. "What you're doing here at Zvart is not just words. You're building for *them* a bomb that will destroy all other bombs. All other life."

"I don't see anyone else offering me a job," Saul said. "No Americans are banging on my door, giving me a lab, a title, a blank check. But here? I'm so *close*, Louise! Do you have any idea how close I am?"

"Oh, I do," said Louise. "Three months ago, I didn't know the words *uranium, Congo, enrichment, isotopes*. I wish to God I still didn't. I used to say that anything that didn't concern me was none of my business. But somehow, Saul, you've made the obliteration of mankind my business."

"Get your basket and walk out," Saul said. "There's not a single thing you can do to stop me."

They stared at each other across the room.

Slowly, she brought her right arm forward.

In her fist she held the syringe.

Saul's eyes opened.

"What is that?" he said hoarsely. "Were you planning to . . . kill me?"

"Yes," Louise said. "I came here to kill you."

Even the gasp got stuck in Saul's throat. She must have looked so incongruous to him—shimmery, blonde, fresh and young—standing there, clutching poison in her hand.

"So why—why didn't you?" His voice was barely audible.

Tears falling, she said, "I'm the only one who could get this close to you." She grabbed the table to steady herself. "I couldn't do it. We were friends. That meant something to me."

"*Friends?* You came here to kill me!" he said theatrically—like it was happening to someone else.

"I thought I could talk to you," she said. "Use my words to sway you. To make you see the truth."

"I don't know what you're talking about," Saul said, blustering again. Despite the gleaming needle in her hand, Louise saw nothing in his eyes—no flicker of Damascus, no hint of revelation. "There is truth in science. And in my imminent success. That's the only *truth* I know."

"The Germans can't win without this weapon, Saul."

"I want to build it. That's all," he said. "I have no other objective."

"You think history will remember how smart you were?"

"I know it will."

"They won't write your name next to Einstein's," she said.

"They will."

"No," said Louise. "They'll carve it into the wall at Auschwitz. Next to Heydrich's."

"I don't know who Heydrich is," Saul said.

She cried out in disbelief. "Starving men will eat poison just to fill their bellies. That's what you are. Starving. Not brilliant. You think science is what matters? You could build them a hospital for newborns—and they'll still find a way to turn it into a slaughterhouse."

He shook his head.

"You think your genius will elevate evil hands?" Louise said. "That's not science. That's surrender. They hunted you. Marked you for death. Banished you. And what do you do in return? You build them a throne of fire so they can burn us too. The whole earth will become their crematorium. Well done, Saul. You and your million bloodthirsty spiders turning the rest of us to ashes. Yes—welcome to the new world order."

She hung her head.

For a few moments, she stood there, staring at the floor, her tears falling.

And with excruciating clarity, she saw her hopes, her dreams, her youth—her entire life—receding.

"Why are *you* crying?" he said.

"Because I'm Antigone untombed," she whispered wrenchingly. "Weeping at my own grave."

I want my mother. I want Rafael. I want to go home.

She felt unendurably alone.

And it was at that moment—when she needed it most—that she heard Rafael's primal scream.

"Louise!"

She glanced out the window. He was shouting for her, running across the road, aiming his pistols. "Run, Louise!"

Shots rang out. One hit something iron. The others dropped two of the guards rushing him. *Look at him,* she thought. *He's trying to create a diversion, to give me time to escape.* There was a commotion in the hedges, at the gate. A convoy of cars screeched to a halt. Doors slammed. Men jumped out. Was that Rheinhardt's Mercedes?

The door opened.

A tall Nazi officer stepped out.

The dogs were in a frenzy, snarling and barking, tearing at their chains. Men shouted orders in German. Soldiers raced across the lawn, rifles drawn.

They had Rafael now. Two men dragged him through the gate at gunpoint. Other soldiers stormed toward the house. She heard the front door burst open. Boots pounded the staircase.

Louise turned from the window and faced the room.

Finally, she had used up all her words. She had spoken until her throat cracked. She had laid out every truth she knew. But it wasn't enough.

"Oh, Saul," she said.

For a moment, she held the syringe upright, listening to the sound of the men drawing closer. She and Saul stared at each other.

"I was going to boil you from within," she whispered—and depressed the plunger.

A thick stream of clear acid hissed onto the floorboards between them. The wood screamed like bones dissolving. Lacquer buckled and curled from the impact, and a rancid plume of gas rose like steam, stinging her eyes.

The floor sizzled, split open. The varnish blistered. The grain blackened.

The wood bowed inward as if gutted from beneath. A jagged crater formed where the liquid had hit.

Across from her, Saul stood—speechless, motionless.

His eyes betrayed the terror of a man who had glimpsed his own brutal death.

She had shown him the abyss. And for an instant, he saw it.

She placed the leaking syringe on the table, on top of his open notebook, dense with numbers, and straightened out, squaring her shoulders.

Saul took a step toward her. "Run," he breathed out. "Take the back stairs. Take my key." He fumbled in his pocket. "Go. Hide in my lab. They won't find you there. *Run, Louise!*"

But it was too late.

She stood in the center of the study, with dripping, hissing acid warping the floorboards as Rheinhardt's jackboots crashed into the room, followed by Rheinhardt himself. Seventeen steps from the door to where Louise stood.

Fewer, probably. They were men. Their strides were longer.

"Ah, *guten Morgen, Herr Untersturmführer*," Louise said to Rheinhardt as his men surrounded her. She had deliberately called him a second lieutenant, demoting him four full ranks with one jab.

"Obersturmbannführer!" Rheinhardt barked, correcting her instinctively—then paused, realizing what he had done. And what she had done. The barely concealed smirks on his officers' faces were unmistakable. His jaw twisted like he had swallowed the last drops of acid from her needle. "You stupid girl," Rheinhardt said, flushing with rage. "Don't just stand there—seize her!" he shouted to the Gestapo.

But she had already proven her power. Even in ruin.

Rheinhardt would rather lose his dignity than let her insult stand.

As they dragged her toward the stairs, her body trembling as if with cold, she managed to hum a tune—bouncy and ridiculous; defiance wrapped in nonsense. A song she'd memorized with Rafael not so long ago.

"We dined on mince," sang Louise, "*and slices of quince,*

"Which we ate with a runcible spoon;

"And hand in hand, on the edge of the sand,

"We danced by the light of the moon."

91

With Song and Guns A-Blazing

Louise had felt so alone upstairs, in the room with Rheinhardt, Saul, and their henchmen. But the moment she was thrown against Rafael out on the lawn, she felt better. He'd been hit hard and was bleeding from a cut above his eye. She clung to him—and he to her. She wiped the blood away so he could see.

The guards pulled them apart and shoved them to the yellow stucco wall on the side of the house, their careless boots trampling the red flowers blooming along the border. Louise's chipped toenails peeked out—painted for Rafael, after the night they got married. And what a night it was.

A night to remember.

Time for another pedicure, Louise thought incongruously, still studying her feet, stepping away from the fragile flowers.

Rafael squeezed her hand. "We go out the same way we came in," he said. "With song and guns a-blazing."

"Forgive me, Rafael, my love," she said.

"There's nothing to forgive."

"I couldn't do it."

"I know," he said, kissing her hand.

"We should've never sent me. What was I thinking?"

"It wasn't fair to ask this of you."

"*Vive la Belgique,*" she said.

She watched Rheinhardt stride toward them. Next to him was Dory.

"What's Dory doing here?" she said.

Rafael swore. "Charlie was right. He really was a snake, coiled in the grass, biding his time." He tutted. "Let's not tell her she was right, okay? She's already insufferable."

"Okay," Louise said. "We won't tell her."

The dozen Gestapo men stood at attention near Rheinhardt.

"Louise?" Dory said. He looked genuinely shocked. "What are *you* doing here?"

She was about to answer him—something flippant—but Rafael pulled on her hand and shook his head. "Don't even look his way," he whispered. "He's not worth a word from you."

Dory tried to stand closer to Rheinhardt, but one of the soldiers grabbed him and pushed him down the grass and against the wall, by Rafael.

"No," Rheinhardt told his officer. "Not there. Five meters over to the left. By himself. Yes—leave him."

"Wait, wait," Dory said in a high-pitched voice. "What are you doing? I wasn't part of their scheme—not at all, not in the slightest. Herr Rheinhardt! I was the one who helped you, remember? Without me, you wouldn't be here."

"You betrayed your friends," Rheinhardt said.

"They're not my friends!" Dory yelled. "I hate that man!" He pointed to Rafael.

Rafael didn't even turn his head.

"He was never my friend!" Dory cried. "He was my best friend's enemy!"

Louise felt it twist inside her. *He did it for Fitz.* My God. Poor Fitz.

"And the girl?"

"I know of her, but we were never friends. She never liked me. It was supposed to be only him!" Dory yelled to Louise. "Not *you*." He attempted to move toward Rheinhardt but was stopped by the barrel of the guard's rifle, pinning him to the wall.

"Dorian de Smet," Rheinhardt said. "You partnered with the partisans against the Reich."

"I helped you today!"

"After today, what use would I have for someone like you? You think you can slink back into the arms of your enemies?"

"You have it all wrong!"

"For four years, you have betrayed the Reich to help *them*, and now you're betraying your friends to help *me*." There was such contempt in Rheinhardt's voice. *The pitiless Nazi judging the partisan collaborator*, Louise thought. If only Charlie could hear this.

"We will *never* tell her," whispered Rafael.

"You have bargained on every side," Rheinhardt went on. "You've whispered in every ear—traded your loyalty like a counterfeit coin." He was forced again to direct his men to keep a squealing, quaking Dory in place.

"There are no more sides left to you, Dorian de Smet. Not their side. Not my side. Not even your side. Just empty space." He fell briefly silent. "Stand still."

But Dory, in full terror for his life, could not stand still. His entire body was flailing.

Rheinhardt took out his Luger, cocked it, and shot him, a bullet to the face. Dory jerked backward and collapsed into the grass, still twitching with cowardice even in death.

Holstering his weapon, Rheinhardt turned to Louise and Rafael.

"Let everyone know," he said—loud, officious, though there was no one there but him and his men—"that this man and this woman, enemies of the Reich, have been found guilty of treason, and of conspiracy to undermine the righteous ambitions of a great nation, ascending toward its inexorable destiny.

"They have been found guilty of attempted sabotage of a military-scientific project of the highest importance to the Führer.

"Their resistance has been duly and justifiably thwarted, for the Reich does not falter at the hands of feeble men.

"The sentence is death. Swift, lawful, and deserved.

"Let history record not their names—only their abject failure." He stepped back and prepared to raise his arm. "Ready?"

Hubner stopped him. "Wait," he said, his eyes on Louise. "Perhaps a blindfold for her—for them, sir?"

Louise saw Rheinhardt hesitate. His gaze traveled up to the second floor of Zvart Haus. Saul must have been standing at the window, watching. "Would you like a blindfold?" Rheinhardt asked, skeptically—already knowing the answer.

"Fuck you," said Rafael. Quickly turning to Louise, he lowered his voice. "Look at me, Louise."

A tear fell down her quivering cheek. She said nothing.

"No, not them," Rafael said. "Look only at me."

"You're all I see," she said. "*Je vois.*"

Rheinhardt raised his arm.

The bolts clacked into place as the soldiers raised and cocked their rifles. They took aim.

Hubner took a step back and lowered his head.

Gazing at her like she was the last thing he would ever love, Rafael gripped her hand.

"Aujourd'hui," he said, *"je serai avec toi dans le paradis."*

Today, I shall be with you in paradise.

Louise opened her mouth to speak—

Rifle fire cut her short.

Von Rheinhardt never said a word.

He simply flung down his arm.

92

The Waiting

Pedaling furiously all the way from Antwerp, Fletcher, Charlie, and Fitz reached the intersection at Albert Canal, just as the trucks and sedans were pulling away. They barely had time to fling themselves and their bikes down the embankment to avoid being seen. Birds scattered across the dingy water. The dogs stopped barking. A hush fell over everything—eerie, total.

Behind a rock near the canal, they found Rafael's bike.

No one could bear to look at it for more than a moment.

Fletcher couldn't bear to think about it for even that long.

They huddled low in the sparse bushes. Hope flickered in the grim silence.

Fitz kept muttering, hollow-eyed, "Why would Dory do it? I don't understand."

"Maybe he thought only Rafael would go," Fletcher said. "He overheard our conversation yesterday—caught only part of the plan. *Rifle. Rafael. Assault commando.* Assumed wrong." Fletcher was having trouble speaking. The sliver of the straight-edge razor he'd hidden in his mouth to free himself from Rheinhardt's restraints had carved up his tongue and cheek. He dripped blood with every uttered word.

"One shall rise, one shall fall, one shall betray with a whisper," Charlie said. "*Mon Dieu. Mon Dieu.* But did she *kill* him? Did she do it?"

"I don't know," said Fletcher.

"Did they make it out?" Fitz said.

"I don't know," said Fletcher. He wiped his mouth.

"What if we missed them on the road? They could be on their way to the church already. Maybe even there. We should split up—"

"Charlie!" Fitz snapped. "Can you just sit still, for once in your life? We said we would wait. Let's wait."

Fletcher said nothing. The palms of his hands were still scorched from

Rheinhardt's device. His torso ached with every breath. One rib, at least, had to be cracked. Each inhale felt like something catching fire inside him. *Without the bike, Rafael has no way of getting to the church*, he wanted to say but couldn't speak. *And his bike is here.*

An hour passed.

On his knees at the water's edge, Fitz pressed his head into the dirt. Fletcher and Charlie helped him to his feet.

Quietly, they crept along the bank through the undergrowth and brush until they were directly across the road from Zvart Haus. Charlie found Rafael's binoculars in the bushes, the strap torn, as if he had to rip them off his neck in haste.

The dogs began barking, startling them. A German officer opened fire, spraying random bullets above their heads. They sank into the slope as the rounds ricocheted off the canal behind them, metal skipping over the water.

Fletcher spoke at last. "Fitz," he said. And then nothing.

"What?"

Fletcher took a breath. "Is that Rheinhardt's car at the gate? The car we fiddled with this morning?"

"I dunno," Fitz said. "They all look the same."

Charlie crawled over to them. "Why is Rheinhardt's car still there?" she said.

Fitz groaned. Fletcher fought the urge to close his eyes. The only thing he said was, "*Shh.*"

She handed him Rafael's binoculars. "Just look quick," she said.

"What am I looking for?"

"Anything. Anything at all."

Fletcher looked, and dropped back down. "The front lawn's empty. But I can only see part of it." Was it his imagination or were there figures at the edge of the house, shovels in hand? His heart grew numb.

"What about the second-floor window?" Charlie whispered. "Do you see anyone there?"

"Like who?"

"Grunfell," Charlie said. "Louise says he always sits by the window."

Fletcher raised himself up again, peering through Rafael's binoculars.

He dropped down—and said nothing.

The dogs barked.

The guards opened fire again.

The three of them crawled away, down to the canal bank.

"Fletcher! Did you see anything?"

Fletcher put the binoculars away.

"There was a man by the window," he said.

Charlie, who never cried, burst into tears.

"Shh," Fletcher said. "Charlie, please, we can't let them hear us."

Stumbling over roots and rough terrain, they crept back to where they'd hidden their bikes, next to Rafael's.

"Why didn't she kill him, why?"

"Let's just wait a little longer," said Fitz, barely audible. "Maybe they fled on foot and are hiding."

"She wears a white veil and sometimes a soldier's coat," Charlie whispered, her voice a faltering thread. *"She's surrounded by shadow, but the shadow doesn't touch her."*

"Doesn't it?" said Fitz.

"Nothing was ever supposed to."

They sat in the gathering dark by the brackish water, heads over their knees, and wept.

Fletcher tried to console them, but he had no words—in any language. He couldn't even take a breath. He wiped the blood from his mouth.

I'm so sorry, Rafael.

You get no credit for anything. Because you've been a servant to a queen. Your face marred by dust and blood, all you ever did was strive valiantly and spend yourself in a cause not your own. You were always King of the Ring, Rider, my friend. That's the best thing I can say about you.

Fitz lashed out, accusing Fletcher of heinous things.

"No," Charlie said, pulling them apart, trying to tamp down her sobbing. "It's not his fault."

"If he'd never come—"

"And if the Germans had never come. If they hadn't taken Paolo, if I hadn't searched for Zeus, if I hadn't been at *La Fortuna* . . . if—if—*if.*" Charlie broke off. "It's not his fault, Fitz." Sister and brother huddled together, their shoulders quaking.

"I failed," Fletcher said. "I'm sorry." *I've stumbled. I've come up short, again and again. Look what I've done.*

Charlie leaned over and embraced Fletcher. "It's not your fault," she whispered.

"It is," Fitz said. He was beyond comfort.

"It is," said Fletcher.

"He tried to fix it," Charlie said. "He couldn't fix fucking Dory. I told you about him. You never listened."

"Oh, so now it's *my* fault!"

"I didn't say that, Fitz."

"I will not rest," Fletcher said, his breaking voice barely carrying through his clenched jaw, "nor flag, nor waver, until I bring justice to that man."

"What good is justice?" Fitz said. "She's dead. And for *nothing*. The bomb maker is still alive. Toll every fucking bell in Belgium until time itself is done. That, and your justice, still won't bring her back."

They sobbed.

"We have to go," Fletcher said, struggling to his feet. If they stayed here any longer, it would be the end for them, too. It could *already* be the end.

He couldn't get back on his bike without her hand on his back.

He tried. Failed. Tried again.

Somehow the three of them steadied their wheels and, leaving Rafael's bike in the bushes, rode away into the darkness.

93

Yellow Ragwort

Twenty shots, maybe thirty.

Birds tore into the sky by the thousands.

The dogs barked like packs of howling wolves.

And then—silence.

Rheinhardt left his men and tore into the house, up the stairs, and into the study. He found Grunfell staggered against the wall near the open window.

"I really apologize," Rheinhardt said. "Security was too lax. Krieger was right. That will never happen again. The men, the dogs—they're here to stay. You must have felt such terror."

Grunfell said nothing.

"Look what she did to your floor." The planks, the carpet, the leg of the chair—eaten into hollow maws by the acid. "What a horror," Rheinhardt muttered. "Just to think—she could've killed you."

But she didn't, Saul mouthed, without sound.

"What's wrong? You don't look well. Are you in shock?"

Saul didn't respond.

"Maybe you should sit down for a minute."

When Saul didn't move, Rheinhardt tried again. "I'll have this fixed in no time," he said, pointing to the damaged parquet. "The carpenter will be here tomorrow morning."

Still, Grunfell didn't speak.

"Listen," Rheinhardt said, "there's nothing more we can do right now. Might as well get back to work."

Saul's glassy, unblinking eyes stared through him.

"I didn't even get a chance to ask—how much did you make this morning—before the whole debacle?"

"Almost two hundred grams," Saul whispered.

"That's excellent!"

Saul said nothing.

Rheinhardt hesitated. "Shall I help you downstairs? Can I get you anything?"

"No," Saul said, barely audible. Then, in full voice: "What I *want* is for you to bury them."

"Who?"

Saul didn't reply.

"No, that's not—"

"Bury them where you killed them," Saul cut in. "I don't care about the . . ." He waved his hand toward the slump of Dorian's body. "Have your men dig one grave. For the man and the girl. Don't disturb the flowers."

"Grunfell," Rheinhardt said, his voice low, his frown glacial, "who are you to give me orders?"

Saul's liquid stare did not leave Rheinhardt's face.

"I'll take care of it," Rheinhardt said. "But you're concerning yourself with matters irrelevant to your most pressing obligations."

"I'll stay here until you and your men are finished," Saul said.

Rheinhardt put his hand on his pistol. Saul didn't move. "What are you going to do, Rheinhardt?" he said quietly. "Go get a shovel. Start digging. *Auf der Stelle.*"

Rheinhardt knew when he was out of moves. "Fine. But as soon as the men are done, Grunfell—straight to the lab."

"Not the men," Grunfell said. "*You.* And yes. When you are done, I'll go to the lab."

Late that night, Saul crept downstairs. A small flashlight lit his path as he made his way to the fresh mound beside the house. He brought with him a scorched plank, torn from the floor where she had spilled the acid like her own blood.

He dipped an unsteady finger into a jar of white gesso and carefully painted words of Pericles onto the ruined wood:

HEROES HAVE THE WHOLE EARTH AS THEIR TOMB.

He planted the plaque by the tangle of yellow ragwort and sank to the grass at the foot of the grave.

You stood in a room full of monsters, Saul whispered, *and you faced them without flinching. You chose mercy not murder. Even though you knew what it would cost you. Why did you do it? Oh, Louise . . .*

He sat there a long time. Eventually he grew cold and made his way back inside—and headed down the stairs to the elevator shaft.

94

Madness

"What do we do with the man in *der Raum*?" Hubner said to Rheinhardt in the car on the way back to Antwerp. It had been a very long day.

"Nothing," Rheinhardt replied, leaning against the back of the seat and closing his eyes. "He's no longer our concern." The man had been in his grasp. His grasp. And he let him go. Left him unguarded.

"But, sir, we left him with his arms extended, tied up . . ."

Rheinhardt didn't answer. If he spoke one more word, he'd break something.

He half expected *der Raum* to be blown to smithereens.

It wasn't. It was still standing. Just empty. The shredded ropes lay on the floor.

"Where did he go?" Hubner asked, confused.

"Nowhere," Rheinhardt replied. "He's lurking around every corner." He turned on his heel. "Watch your step, Hubner—and mine. I want guards posted at all hours. Get us a proper detail assigned to Baert Haus at once. I want a full escort to and from my apartment. You as well. And listen to me very carefully—do not turn the ignition in the car unless someone else starts it first. Better yet, use a decoy. Also—don't put my name or yours on any schedule, meeting, or itinerary. We don't know what resistance network he's tapped into."

"Who, sir?"

"Florent," Rheinhardt replied. "Florent, the fucking *klokkenmaker*."

He would not say the words *Fletcher Gray* out loud. He was afraid the name would haunt his nightmares too—the way it already haunted every minute of his waking life.

Small things began to go off kilter immediately.

That evening, someone left a child's brass bell toy on the hood of the Mercedes. Its clapper had been removed.

At the 11:00 p.m. shift change, a dock guard found an actual church bell—unhinged and tongueless—perched on a gangway post beneath the looming shadow of *La Fortuna*.

And the next morning, a trail of cracked tin bells, each one of them clapperless, lined the stone path in front of Baert Haus.

The guards swore they'd seen no one near Daisy Lane all night.

And yet, the bells were there.

Before lunch, Hubner brought in a stack of port clearance forms, time-sensitive and requiring immediate signature. Rheinhardt skimmed the top page and reached for his fountain pen. Mid-stroke, he stopped.

"Is this some kind of joke, Hubner?" he said quietly.

There, listed between two auxiliary port workers:

Florent Acker. Warehouse 3. Night detail.

From that point on, Rheinhardt and Hubner no longer entered or exited Baert Haus without sweeping for tripwires. They were flanked day and night by armed men, dogs, and barricades.

And still, nothing felt safe.

Every pop of an exhaust, every train horn, every clatter of a bicycle bell felt like the thing that came *after* the voiceless bells.

The final straw came just days later.

They had driven to inspect the sluice locks at the Vossenburg crossing, a vulnerable artery in the Wehrmacht's potential retreat from Antwerp. Rheinhardt spent thirty minutes inside the engineer's hut questioning workers and checking the lock mechanism.

They were about to re-enter the Mercedes, parked exactly where they'd left it by the water's edge, when Hubner paused, scanning the canal banks and open fields. "Wait, sir. Don't get in."

Rheinhardt bristled. "We've wasted enough time—"

Hubner cut him off, signaling to a nearby soldier. "You. Start the car." He and Rheinhardt backed away toward the sluice station. The guard climbed in. Turned the key.

The explosion shook four arrondissements.

Someone had wired the Mercedes—*in broad daylight*. Rheinhardt and Hubner had been inside for less than thirty minutes.

When Krieger got word of the car bomb, his response was immediate. Rheinhardt was ordered to move operations to Zvart Haus at once. Behind its iron gates and guard patrols, they would be secure. He could conduct his business by telephone. Hubner could ferry messages back and forth. Rheinhardt protested the order—quietly—but had no choice. He couldn't explain to Krieger that Zvart Haus was the last place he wanted to be.

Hubner requisitioned them a new vehicle, a scuffed, homely, dull gray Opel Olympia, smelling faintly of kerosene and beeswax. By all the devils—was this Vogel's old Olympia? Of all the vehicles in Belgium, did he truly end up with Vogel's car?

Rheinhardt and Hubner relocated, telling themselves loudly and often it was only temporary.

But while they were relatively safe from one madman's maledictions, inside Zvart Haus . . .

95

The Delta of Drift Diffusion

Rheinhardt didn't know how to tell Krieger. He didn't know how to explain it. "What do you *mean* the output yesterday was zero?" Krieger said.

Rheinhardt tried to glide over it. "Probably just an aberration."

"What do you mean *probably*?" Krieger boomed.

"I misspoke. Definitely is what I meant."

"Wasn't he making as much as four hundred grams a day?"

"He was. More sometimes."

"So what happened?"

"He's looking into it. A glitch. He says today will be better."

But today wasn't better.

It was infinitely worse.

Because today there was also no yield.

Despite his intense misgivings about being in a house awash from top to bottom with the most lethal radioactive combustible chemicals on earth, Rheinhardt stood beside Grunfell at the cyclotron's control panel and watched him study his notebook, adjust knobs and levers and check the consistency of the crystals inside the teacup crucibles.

"That should do it," Grunfell said.

But that *didn't* do it.

Quite the opposite.

Was there a number less than zero? Because that was the number Grunfell presented for the third day in a row.

"Saul," Rheinhardt said, his words and ice-blue eyes trying to conceal his hopping panic, "what's happening?"

"I don't know," Grunfell replied. "We should be all right now."

"What about the formula!"

"I've checked and re-checked it. Must be a small misalignment somewhere in the drift diffusion. You see how complex this thing is. I think it's spinning a fraction slow. I'm going to speed it up. Don't worry."

The next day, he said, "I've overcompensated. It's spinning a fraction fast. I'm going to slow it down. That should fix it."

But it didn't fix it.

Grunfell spent all day at the cyclotron, reformulating his calculations, checking the machine, opening it, closing it. "The magnets must've come loose somewhere," he said, on the *fifth* day. "I'll need to pause production and check the coils. There must be a line tear in one of the copper wires; it's not conducting properly."

When Rheinhardt, anxiety steaming from his pores, tried to impart to Saul how imperative it was that this *not* be happening, Grunfell looked up from his notebook and stared at him full in the face. "Don't you think *I* know this?" he said calmly. "Don't you think *I* know what's at stake? I've barely slept trying to solve this. You know how important this is to me. I'm fully aware of the urgency."

"We must work faster, Saul," Rheinhardt said. "That's an order from Hitler."

Grunfell pointed to an alcove in the back of the lab where a narrow cot stood. "Do you see where I sleep these days? I even take my lunch here now." Saul paused, for reasons Rheinhardt couldn't fathom and didn't want to. "I will fix it. But what I can't have is"—he waved his hand in front of Rheinhardt's face—"a verbal harangue from you every hour. Because while I'm talking, I'm not solving the problem. Do you see?"

Rheinhardt backed away. Later, outside in the yard with Hubner, Rheinhardt lit a shaky smoke. "I don't know what's happening. We were doing so well, and I don't—"

Inside the house, the telephone rang—again. Both men jumped.

"Herr Krieger," Rheinhardt said, trying to light another cigarette while holding the receiver to his ear. "How are things going, you ask? Very well, sir. Swimmingly, you could say."

With the same hand that was holding the lit cigarette, he wiped sweat from his cold brow—and set his hair on fire. Dropping both the phone and the cigarette, he slapped himself on the temple to tamp out the smoke. Now everything reeked of singed hair. "Excuse me, please. I dropped the telephone. One moment."

After he got himself together, Rheinhardt picked up the receiver. "Sorry, sir, you were asking? Oh, yes, *how* swimmingly. Well, today has barely begun, and Saul told me he's already produced three hundred grams. That's right. Yes, sir, it *is* incredible news. He's doing stellar work for us. We are adding to our arsenal every day. Sorry, what? Can you repeat? Ah. How much do we have in total?"

Rheinhardt had been lying to Krieger for the last five days. There was simply no way he could tell the general what was actually happening. Rheinhardt knew he wasn't speaking to Krieger, not really. He was speaking to Himmler. And not to Himmler either—but to Hitler himself. Every single morning, the Führer awoke and called his most loyal, most trusted general. "How is the uranium enrichment progressing?" he would ask. And Himmler would call Krieger. Who in turn called Rheinhardt.

And Rheinhardt, in turn, descended into the uranium catacomb and asked Grunfell. And he would say, *I'm working on it, sir.*

Today, KriegerHimmlerHitler said, "Listen, Rheinhardt—we *really* need to speed up production."

Rheinhardt wanted to scream. *You fucking idiot, Krieger. You fucking moron. The machine is already tapped into half the electrical grid for the entire region.* The unreleased howl was searing a hole in Rheinhardt's throat.

"What about that Karl Wirtz you were telling me about a little while ago?" Rheinhardt said. "Any chance of getting him up here to assist?"

There was a pause, a single dry cough. "He's no longer available, Rheinhardt," Krieger said. "He was an enemy of the Reich."

"I see, sir. Of course. Well, I will check with Saul and give you my full report tomorrow."

Tomorrow came. Krieger called. Rheinhardt said, "Saul says it won't be easy—but he'll try to produce 750 grams a day."

"How close are we to critical mass?" KriegerHimmlerHitler asked.

"Well over half, Saul says."

"That's not nearly enough!"

"I'll be sure to tell him, sir. I shall go downstairs at once."

The next day, Krieger said, "Does he understand the urgency?"

"Absolutely, mein Herr."

"Ask him," said Krieger, "if it's at all *possible* to make the bomb with what we have now."

Rheinhardt's throat burned raw. "You know that's not possible, sir," he said, quiet but deafening.

"We need the bomb, Rheinhardt. Just go and ask him. No, I won't hang up. I'll wait. Put the receiver down and ask him right now."

Rheinhardt set the receiver on the desk and motioned for Hubner to make walking noises with the heels of his boots. He stood next to the telephone, his eyes closed, trying to breathe, trying to swallow.

After five minutes passed, he picked up the receiver. "Are you still there, sir? Very good. I spoke to Saul, and he confirmed what he told us before. Fifty kilos is the absolute minimum. He said he needed fourteen weeks to do it, and he's had barely six."

"We don't have fourteen weeks, Rheinhardt!" Krieger shrieked. "Don't you understand?"

"How long do we have? Perhaps I can convey—"

"We're fighting to the death just north of Paris. They've surrounded us at Falaise."

Rheinhardt waited for the rest.

It didn't come.

"If we lose Falaise," Krieger gasped into the receiver, "France is lost—and they're coming for Belgium next."

"I thought you told Saul we'd keep them fighting in France until 1945?" Rheinhardt said numbly.

"I *know* what I said! And *you* said you'd have a working bomb for me!"

"In fourteen weeks, sir."

"I'm begging you!" hollered KriegerHimmlerHitler. "I'm ordering you! We need the bomb by the end of August!"

He hung up before Rheinhardt could reply—before he could say that it *was* the end of August.

When he turned around, Hubner was standing in the hallway, staring at him with misery and pity.

"Grunfell," Rheinhardt said later that afternoon, using every tool in his arsenal to sound sane, "do you have any idea the pressure I'm under?"

"I do. Absolutely. I'm doing everything I can to get it going again. Believe me."

"Why has it stopped working?" Rheinhardt whispered.

"Just a small adjustment," Saul said. "I'm correcting the containment specimen, recalibrating the copper coils in one of the vacuums. There must have been a leak in the seal. I'm optimistic it will work. We'll be up and running in no time."

Rheinhardt staggered away.

These were the same exact words Saul had been repeating, nearly verbatim, for seven days—right down to the calm unruffled cadence.

Rheinhardt went out into the backyard and did something he hadn't done since he stepped off *La Fortuna*, having discovered his barrels had been stolen.

He retched.

96

Saul

"All is lost," Krieger said when he called next.

How does he know? Rheinhardt wondered.

"The Allies are almost at Liège," Krieger said.

Ah. That. And despite the chilling message, Rheinhardt felt a trace of relief. "That can't be, sir."

"It is. It most certainly is. Listen to me very carefully. I'm abandoning Liège and returning to Germany," Krieger said. "But I need you to bring me the uranium, Rheinhardt. Everything Grunfell enriched, everything that's left—we need all of it. The Allies cannot get their hands on it. We have facilities in Berlin. What we don't have, we'll build."

"Take the *enriched* uranium with me?" Rheinhardt said, stunned.

"Yes. You need to get it out of Zvart at once. I've already sent one of my trucks. It'll reach you within the hour. Load everything on it and get to Berlin—as fast as you can."

"Sir—" Rheinhardt hesitated. "I must return to Antwerp first—"

"There's no time! You have nothing I can't replace. The uranium is the most important thing, you know that. Load it and go."

"Just to be certain, sir," Rheinhardt said tonelessly, "you want me to take the canisters of radioactive, bomb-ready uranium and drive them through collapsing front lines?"

"How many canisters could there be?" Krieger shouted. "We know we don't have *fifty* of them—or instead of having this idiotic conversation, we'd already be *winning the fucking war*!"

"And the yellowcake, sir," Rheinhardt said without inflection.

"Every. Single. Uranium. Product. At every. Stage. Of enrichment," said Krieger. "All of it—to Berlin. Direct order from the Führer himself. Am I clear?"

"Yes, sir," said Rheinhardt. "And what would you like me to do with Grunfell?"

"Are you stupid?" Krieger said. "Bring him, of course." He hung up.

"We have to hurry, Hubner," Rheinhardt said. "Pack up. This is the end. We've been ordered to go straight to Berlin. We can't return to Antwerp."

They looked at each other for a long, loaded second.

"That's a shame, sir," Hubner said quietly.

Rheinhardt refused to acknowledge it. This wasn't the time for recriminations. "Come down to the lab with me."

Hubner vehemently shook his head. "No, sir," he whispered. "Please don't make me."

"We have to get the canisters and the yellowcake up to the loading dock. Krieger sent a truck."

"Canisters of *bomb-ready* uranium?"

"I was given an order, Hubner!" Rheinhardt yelled. "And I'm giving you one. Move."

The lab was empty—but alive, buzzing with voltage and echo. Overhead, mercury vapor lamps burned in sickly rows, casting harsh white cones across the concrete. Between them, the shadows pooled deep and strange. The usual dozens of workers were gone.

Rheinhardt didn't know how they were going to hoist the yellowcake barrels up to the truck without the crew. He walked quickly around the cyclotron, weaving between the cauldrons and vats to the locked vault in the back, where the gleaming nickel cylinders of enriched uranium stood waiting.

In front of the vault stood Saul Grunfell.

Rheinhardt and Hubner froze.

"Saul," Rheinhardt said. "Where is everyone?"

"I sent them home," Grunfell said. "They haven't had a day off in months."

"Even the guards?"

"The guards are upstairs."

"We need them down here, Saul," Rheinhardt said. "We need to hoist the yellowcake and the green salt into the freight lift."

Saul didn't speak.

"Open the vault—"

"No," Saul said.

"What do you mean, no? Is it locked? Where's the key?"

"I have the only key," Saul said. "And I'm not opening it. I listened in on your conversation with Krieger. *All is lost* indeed. Go back upstairs, get in your car, and drive to Berlin. I'm not going with you." He paused. "And neither is the uranium."

"Unlock it," said Rheinhardt.

"No."

"Unlock it this instant, or I will shoot you," Rheinhardt said, drawing his Luger and aiming it at Grunfell's head.

Behind him, Hubner began to whimper. "No, sir. Bad idea. Very, very bad idea. Don't fire down here. Please."

"Hubner, shut up," Rheinhardt said. "Saul, did you hear me?"

"Loud and clear." Saul pointed to the red button on the wall. "I've pressurized the vault with hydrofluoric gas." His voice was flat, almost serene. "Only I know how to vent it safely. The steps are in here." He tapped his temple. "So go ahead. Kill me. *Please*. But the moment you unlock this door, the vault, the lab, this *house*—along with you and your lieutenant—will be bathed in *gas*." He looked Rheinhardt in the eye. "What did I teach you about hydrofluoric acid? It doesn't burn. It melts. Liquefies your lungs before you can scream. You're not taking that uranium anywhere."

Rheinhardt's trembling hand twitched on the trigger.

Behind him, he heard Hubner's frantic whispering. "Sir, I beg you—please don't fire. We don't know how a pressurized system will react. We're underground. There's radioactive material everywhere."

"And hydrofluoric gas," said Grunfell. "Remember *hydrochloric* acid, Rheinhardt? Of course you do. How could you forget? *I* certainly can't." Taking a breath, he rested his palm on the red button. "Hydrofluoric gas is a hundred times worse. It melts glass, metal, human tissue—on contact."

Rheinhardt stood aghast, a creeping realization crawling up his spine: *his precious uranium might be lost to him forever*. "Why—*why* would you pressurize the vault?"

Saul opened his mouth to say something, then closed it.

Rheinhardt's arm trembled. "You're lying."

"Do you think so?" said Saul.

The silence that followed was total.

Like ice, Saul stared into Rheinhardt's desperate, disbelieving face. He pointed up—to the vents angled directly at them.

"Why would you do this?" Rheinhardt gasped. His arm dropped to his side. "I thought we were working together. I thought you wanted it as much as I did." *More!* he almost said. *You wanted it even more than me.*

"Yes," Saul said, his voice thick with something unnameable. "That's what I thought, too."

"I *must* take the uranium to Berlin," Rheinhardt whispered.

"No, you mustn't," Saul said. "And you won't."

"The uranium doesn't belong to you," Rheinhardt said, clinging to the last ragged fringe of his superiority. "It belongs to the Reich."

"No, it doesn't," Saul said. "It belongs to the King of Belgium."

"Let's go to Antwerp, sir," Hubner whispered, tugging Rheinhardt's tunic. "We can still get out. Look at him—he's a madman. He could press that button any second."

"Listen to your lieutenant, Rheinhardt," Saul said. "I'm a madman."

97

Daisy Lane

Even the guards had fled. Zvart Haus lay completely unprotected. In the distance, Rheinhardt heard gunfire, faint whistling, dim explosions. They piled their belongings into the borrowed Opel, and Hubner drove them back to Antwerp. There was chaos on the roads, trucks racing by, people screaming. All three checkpoints—two canal crossings and a bridge into the city—stood abandoned.

"Should we call Herr Krieger, sir? Tell him about the uranium?"

"Fuck Krieger," said Rheinhardt. "Let's get in and get out."

"But this awful ruckus . . ."

"The Allies are here."

"How can that be?" Hubner exclaimed. "They were still in France two days ago! They couldn't have moved their entire army across Belgium in *one day*!"

That was true, but the noise of an advancing colossus was unmistakable. The closer they got to Antwerp, the louder it grew. Planes roaring overhead. Wheels and engines grinding. Gunfire, grenades, the high-pitched whistling that came before the bursts of high-explosive shells. The air stank of smoke. Fire rumbled closer. It was Sancta Maria all over again—only this time with a million men. A country coming apart.

"Do you smell kerosene, Hubner?" Rheinhardt asked as they pulled up to Baert Haus and jumped out. The air was filled with it.

"Yes, sir. It's not surprising. Diesel trucks, spilled petrol, people running with lamps."

Rheinhardt was glad it wasn't just his imagination like the old days, smelling things that weren't there. "You know what to do," he told Hubner, as they hurried toward the house. "Just get the important things." Baert Haus stood locked and unlit, just as they had left it a week earlier. "I'll empty the safe. You get the identity papers and our clothes. Quick."

"Yes, sir." Hubner turned the key in the padlock. "Should we get anything from upstairs?"

"The manifests? Are you insane? We need nothing. Let's go."

"Wait!" Hubner physically stopped Rheinhardt from barging inside. "Let me get a flashlight. Just in case."

"Just in case *what*, Hubner? Do you hear that racket? That's the sound of tanks down the cobblestones. They could already be in Antwerp."

"Tripwire, sir."

Rheinhardt froze. "Fine," he said. "But quick."

Hubner brought the crank light from the car. They checked around the doorframe for signs of tampering. Nothing looked suspicious. Still, Hubner made Rheinhardt stand back before he took a breath, closed his eyes, and pushed the door open.

Nothing happened.

They burst into the house. "Change first. Then the safe," Rheinhardt said.

They stripped quickly and threw on civilian clothes. Rheinhardt crossed to the large framed map of Antwerp and tore it from the wall. Behind it, the steel face of the wall safe gleamed dully. He spun the dial—three numbers—and yanked the door open.

Hubner held the satchel wide, ready for Rheinhardt to fill it with cash and gold.

Rheinhardt reached in—and stopped.

There, beside the stacks of cash, lay a small silver bell on its side, gleaming faintly with its own cold light.

This one was *not* clapperless.

His breath caught.

He was here?

The safe had been opened. Breached.

How? Rheinhardt's hand trembled. The lock was mechanical, unbreakable.

And *still*, he had been here.

For a second, Rheinhardt thought he might be sick.

Then, with a shove that was almost violent, he knocked the bell aside, swallowed down his bile, and began working.

He stuffed the bag with bills and coin, moving fast, his hands shaking.

The front door slammed shut.

Rheinhardt wouldn't even look at Hubner. "Must be the wind," he said. "Let's hurry."

They'd been at it for barely five minutes. The windows were all shuttered, but the dim office began to grow brighter as they worked. Rheinhardt cursed himself for not bringing the contents of the safe to Zvart Haus. But why would he have? Krieger assured him they had until 1945! No one said the enemy would be in Antwerp *tomorrow.* The arrival of a full invading army didn't usually come without warning. Even hasty retreats came with weeks to prepare.

Maybe others had prepared. Maybe if they hadn't spent the last week trapped at Zvart, coaxing the cyclotron, they would have too.

Even inside the safe, the light trembled. The pictures on the walls began to shimmer.

Rheinhardt exchanged a glance with Hubner. Through the wood shutters, he could see orange embers flickering.

He smelled fire.

"Hubner, do you . . ."

"Smell something burning? Yes, sir."

"We're out of time. Leave the rest. Let's go."

The flames were licking up past the office windows. In the reception area, all four shutterless windows were aglow.

"What *is* this?" Hubner cried. "Our house is in flames!"

All those weeks Rheinhardt had sat behind his desk, smelling fire in the walls, thinking he was crazy. Was it delusion or . . . *premonition*?

They ran to the front door. Hubner turned the knob, but it wouldn't budge. Pushing Hubner aside, Rheinhardt grabbed the knob and yanked. Nothing. "It's stuck," he grunted, pulling harder. "It's hot—it's burning my hands." With a groan, he stepped away. "It's not stuck," he said, his voice unsteady. "It's blocked."

"What?"

"The house has been set on fire," Rheinhardt said, his blood growing cold in the heat. Who the fuck *was* this man? He must have waited here—for *days*, crouched in the shadows, waiting for Rheinhardt to return. To trap him inside.

To set him on fire.

Rheinhardt was speechless. And terrified. What was his choice now? To stay inside and be burned alive—or to run out into the fire and find the enemy waiting?

They bolted to Rheinhardt's closet, to the hidden door that led to the side garden.

That door, too, was jammed.

"The flames are out of control, sir," Hubner said, coughing into his sleeve, trying not to breathe the smoke seeping through the cracks in the window frames. "We can't go through the window. The escape hatch?" He tapped his foot hard against the floor. His voice sounded muffled.

"Are you sure it still works?" Rheinhardt said. Sweat streamed down his cold, rigid face. "When was the last time you checked it?"

"In '43. But what choice do we have? We have no way out." Hubner pulled the rug from under their feet and pulled up on the O-ring. The open hatch led to a narrow cylindrical tunnel—just wide enough for one man at a time to crawl through. "I'll go first," he said.

"No," Rheinhardt said. Every decision felt wrong. Which way was safest? "I have the Luger. I'll go first. You crawl behind me and push the escape bag. It's heavy."

"I'll manage. Go, sir. Quick. Be careful."

"You too, Hubner. Remind me—where does the tunnel let out?"

"Far down the street, almost to the other pier. Let's go."

The tunnel was in surprisingly good shape. It wasn't clogged with debris. It wasn't crumbling. But it was tight and hard to crawl through. The enclosure, the tunneling dread, the terror of being buried alive was suffocating him. In complete darkness, Rheinhardt crept on his stomach along the dark, damp concrete.

He couldn't see—but he could hear. Above him, the sound of flames crackled, knocking down heavy things. The stone itself grew hot.

Rheinhardt had the tunnel built years ago when he repurposed Baert Haus as his command quarters. Even back in 1940, when Germany stood astride Europe, every senior Nazi knew the rule: never post up anywhere without an escape plan. This was his and Hubner's.

"Hubner? You okay?"

"I'm fine, sir." He sounded far away.

"You have the bag?"

"I have it. You have the Luger?"

"Yes." But it was impossible to crawl with the pistol in hand. Rheinhardt tucked it away.

Ach. Finally, the end. Overhead: a round iron hatch. He would not allow himself a sigh of relief until he took a gulp of fresh air.

"Be careful, sir," Hubner called from behind him. "Look before you climb out."

"Worry about yourself, Hubner. Eyes up."

"Yes, sir."

Rheinhardt lifted the lid and poked his head out like a prairie dog—and immediately broke into a coughing fit. Down Daisy Lane, Baert Haus stood fully ablaze, a pillar of fire. The acrid stench of smoke and salt water attacked his nose. So much for fresh air. The rest of the street and the nearby Napoleonkaai were quiet. That's why Rheinhardt had always liked coming to work here. It was out of the way. Even in his raging desperation, a twinge of regret passed through him for the house in flames where he had spent most of the war.

He crawled out onto the patchy, dusty grass and sat for a moment on his knees, head down, gulping the wind off the river. "Come on, Hubner," he whispered. "Push the bag up. Hurry." Under the tree, half-hidden by leaves, sat an incongruous plastic bucket, inexplicable and unnerving.

Before he could think any more about it—

A tall silent figure all in black stepped out of the shadows.

It was Fletcher Gray.

In his right hand: a cocked Colt .45.

In his left: a military knife, its blade slick with firelight.

"Aufhocker," Rheinhardt whispered, the breath catching in his throat. "It's you again."

"I've never seen you out of your Nazi dress, Oberst Rheinhardt," Fletcher said. "I almost didn't recognize you."

Gasping, Rheinhardt fumbled for the Luger in his pocket.

Fletcher fired into the dirt near him. "I wouldn't do that," he said.

"Hubner, stay down," Rheinhardt hissed sideways, as his lieutenant began pulling himself out of the tunnel.

"No, no, Hubner, come on out," said Fletcher. "There's nowhere left to hide. We burned down your house and found your rat tunnel. Where have you two been? Away on holiday?"

"How did they find it?" Hubner whispered. He was out now. Both men were down on their knees.

"Easiest riddle of all, Herr Hubner," Fletcher said. "I knew you'd build yourselves an underground escape route for precisely this outcome. All we had to do was find the hatch. The office closet was the first place we looked. It took us less than a minute. How long did it take you to find the uranium on *La Fortuna*, Rheinhardt?"

"What do you want? Money?" Rheinhardt rasped.

"Do I want your *money*?" The derision in Fletcher's voice was so thick, he could have slapped Rheinhardt across the face with it. "You insolent schoolgirl," he said. "No, I don't want your fucking money."

"What then?"

"The spearheads for the Seventh and First Armies passed Mechelen an hour ago," Fletcher said. "Do you hear that?" He cupped a gloved hand to his ear, turning slightly toward the noise. "The roar of planes? The rumble of tanks? That's the sound of your reckoning, Rheinhardt. They're coming for *you*."

A frantic Rheinhardt saw an opening and didn't hesitate. He yanked the Luger from his coat pocket, raised it from his knees, and fired wildly.

The bullet missed, but it knocked the Colt from Fletcher's hand, wounding him. Fletcher stumbled but didn't fall. Before Rheinhardt could steady the pistol to fire again, Fletcher—grunting in outrage—flipped the knife to his right hand in one fluid motion and drew back his arm to throw.

Rheinhardt saw the blade, flat and fast, a streak of steel flying straight for his chest. Breathless and paralyzed, he wanted to move but couldn't.

Hubner moved. *"No!"* With a cry, he dove sideways, knocking Rheinhardt out of the way.

The seven-inch, full tang blade tore through Hubner's left flank with devastating force.

"Hubner!" Rheinhardt screamed, slammed backward by Hubner's collapsing body. With a wet, stunned grunt, Hubner fell, his body spasming, blood bubbling in his throat. He never made another sound. Convulsing once, sagging hard, his weight pinned Rheinhardt to the ground.

Trapped, helpless, Rheinhardt struggled under Hubner's weight, slick hands fumbling through soaked fabric, feeling the wet heat of it pulse through his fingers. The knife jutted from Hubner's side. Rheinhardt couldn't bring himself to touch it. He twisted himself free and clutched Hubner with shaking red hands, trying to hold the wound closed. But the blood wouldn't stop.

"Why did you do it? Why?" Rheinhardt sobbed. He had forgotten Fletcher. Forgotten everything. Kneeling over Hubner's dying body, he cradled his head and wept.

"Hubner . . . don't leave me. Please. Don't leave me."

His agonized cries tolled down Daisy Lane.

98

The Boy from Wind River

Vivienne Pellerin was right, Fletcher thought, as he stood coldly over a weeping Rheinhardt and a dying Hubner.

Indeed, there was madness.

Fletcher gripped the M1 in his bleeding hands, the muzzle leveled at Rheinhardt.

But Fletcher's righteous fury had lost its sharpened edge.

Hubner stole that from him.

This wasn't a duel anymore as Fletcher had planned and hoped and intended. Rheinhardt was no longer a worthy opponent. He was barely human.

Fletcher picked up Rheinhardt's Luger and the leather satchel and flung them toward the trees.

He had wanted a fight so desperately—hand to hand, brutal, redemptive. That's why he didn't wait for Rheinhardt with the rifle raised and ready. He wanted to torment him.

"Hubner is dead," Fletcher said. "On your feet, *former Oberst*."

It took Rheinhardt a full pitiful minute to rise.

In that minute, Fletcher relived the past six days—days spent with Charlie, Fitz, and the band of sisters who'd returned to help.

After the car explosion failed to kill Rheinhardt, and the man fled to parts unknown, Fletcher knew they had to move quickly. The Nazi could return at any moment.

Charlie gathered her girls. Fitz brought the explosives. Brigitte and Mireille, Hildi, even the twins, Margot and Maxine—they all came back to help. Together they laid kindling, poured kerosene, strung tripwire and TNT around *der Raum*. If anyone so much as breathed near that hell room, the place would be dust.

Hildi and Margo crawled through the tunnel on their bellies, clearing debris and oiling the hatches. Hildi found a way into Baert Haus without breaking the lock. She even brought an industrial bucket full of hydrochloric acid, "just in case."

Charlie opened the safe. Who knew safecracking was one of her gifts? "Paolo taught me," she said. "My brother taught me to shoot, to fight, to pick locks. He could do everything. Except save himself."

Fletcher had seen the gold in Rheinhardt's safe when he left the bell inside. He knew the man would come back for it. It was only a matter of time.

They finished the prep in a day. And then they waited.

They kept vigil in pairs. The women brought food, drink, and news from other towns. Things were falling apart for the indomitable Third Reich. Brussels had been liberated. Leuven was collapsing. Tanks were pushing through Lier.

Fitz reported German convoys fleeing east. A bridge outside Herentals had been rigged to blow. The resistance barely defused it in time. Nazi depots were in flames. The Wehrmacht, knowing it couldn't hold Antwerp, rigged what crossings they could and fell back to the Scheldt. The Allied advance was so swift, and the German retreat so chaotic that by the time the armored spearhead units reached the city's edge, there was no frontline left. No final stand. Just a crumbling flight.

The Nazis fled, leaving everything behind.

It was to *this* Antwerp that Rheinhardt finally returned—a man who had already lost nearly all his weapons.

And now—here they were.

But instead of the women beside him, instead of Charlie at his side, Fletcher was alone—with a dead Hubner and a simpering, broken Rheinhardt, soaked to his bones in the blood of the only person in the world who cared for him, barely able to stand, much less to fight.

He was too defeated to even die.

Fletcher hit him. He cocked him hard across the face. Rheinhardt went down.

"On your feet, former Oberst."

Rheinhardt refused to stand.

Fletcher desperately wished Charlie were here.

But she was always so bad at waiting.

Two days ago, the Germans tried to blow the Esso tanks near Kattendijkdok, a critical fuel reserve. The Nazi saboteurs hid under the storage silos. Fitz said they needed all hands on deck. So Charlie went with him.

Fletcher told her to go. He could tell she couldn't sit still any longer. She didn't say it, but he knew what she was thinking: *What if Rheinhardt has fled too, is gone for good, and we're sitting in the dirt like vengeful fools while my people are dying?*

She promised she'd be back as soon as the tanks were cleared. But she didn't come back.

Fletcher waited—for the army to arrive, for Charlie to return.

He was so sick of Erich von Rheinhardt.

"Go," he said. "Get out of my sight. There's nowhere left to hide. Scurry away like a roach. You're surrounded by enemy troops. Go surrender to them."

Rheinhardt shook his head. He looked like a man who couldn't rise if he wanted to.

"I'm not sparing you," Fletcher said. "I'm ruining you. You won't last five minutes out there. But for those five minutes, I want you to crawl through the world you made."

Fletcher had tried to kill him. But fate—in the form of Hubner—intervened.

And now he was giving Rheinhardt what little was left of his life—as punishment. Life for one more hour, in the blaze, in the night, with nothing.

"This isn't mercy, Rheinhardt," he said. "It's annihilation of purpose. But if you prefer, go ahead, sit on the ground. Because in a minute, *she's* going to come for you. Like you came for her friend. And my friend."

Rheinhardt pointed weakly toward the satchel by the trees. "My bag . . ."

Fletcher shook his head. "No bag. No gun. No money. No Hubner. *Nothing*." He stepped closer. "Do you hear the bells? They've been ringing nonstop all over Belgium. They're ringing in your end. You've got nothing left but yourself. Go. See how far you get."

Rheinhardt was mute.

Fletcher scoffed bitterly. "Maybe the Drowned Lands? Walcheren? The Netherlands?"

Rheinhardt was sobbing again.

Fletcher had failed at so much. He had hunted this man relentlessly—across cities and forests, over land and sea—and in the pursuit, had lost nearly everyone he cared about.

Rafael. Louise. Hawk. Briggs. Belvedere. Wolski. Ngomo. Zeus.

Only Charlie was left.

That would have to be enough.

Where was she?

"I'm going to have a smoke," Fletcher said. "I'm going to walk down the block and light my cigarette on the ashes of your castle. If you're still here when I come back, so be it. You can wait with me—for Charlie, or for the tanks to roll through. I made my choice. You can make yours."

With an empty heart, Fletcher watched a weeping Rheinhardt cast an anguished glance at the body of Franz Hubner.

He turned away and walked down the street to the burning house. He lit his cigarette on a singed log, inhaled deeply, stood for a few moments smoking, and then slowly returned to the clearing.

Rheinhardt was gone.

He had left his leather satchel behind.

After him, Fletcher whispered the words of Victor Hugo about Napoleon's defeat at Waterloo:

"And contemplating his legion of the dying and the dead, 'God of the armies,' Napoleon said, 'is this my punishment?' And from the snow—and darkness all around—a voice said, 'No.'"

Hours passed.

Fletcher was still there, pacing up and down Daisy Lane, waiting for Charlie, when he saw the tanks and jeeps rolling through—and voices of Allied men, shouting.

A tank rumbled past. It stopped near the burning Baert Haus, now more smoke than flame, then rolled on. A captain jumped from a slow-moving truck and ran toward Fletcher.

"We're Hellfoxes," he said, rifle in front. "The 33rd Armored Recon Battalion. What happened here? And who are *you*?"

"Lieutenant Fletcher Gray," Fletcher said. "Bradley's First Army. Second Rangers. Pointe du Hoc."

"Fletcher?" someone shouted from inside the jeep. "Holy hell—Fletcher, is that you?" It was Stuart Granger. "It's me, Fletch—it's Stu!"

"Major Granger," said Fletcher. "How could I forget?"

"Can't believe we found you. Guys, look who's here! Spano, Jinx—eyes up. Reed's gonna be thrilled. He told me to keep an eye out for you—we'll radio him, as soon as we stop for the night. Where are your weapons? Look at your hand—broken bones? Medic!" Stu yelled. "Medic to the front! Let's get you out of here. What happened? Why's the street on fire? And where's your crew—Canario, Briggs, Turner?" He paused. "Or is it just you?"

Fletcher turned back, one more time, and peered into the darkness for Charlie, as Daisy Lane, Napoleon Dock, and all the surrounding roads began flooding with Allied troops and rumbling vehicles.

Charlie, are you out there?

I will find out where you have gone,
And kiss your lips
And take your hands
And walk among long dappled grass
And pluck till time and times are gone
The silver apples of the moon
The golden apples of the sun.

He blew a kiss into the night, stuck out his good arm, and was pulled into the back of the truck.

Godspeed, my love.

"It's just me," said Fletcher.

CODA

"I am content to live it all again
And yet again . . .
. . . If it be life.
To pitch into the frog-spawn of a blind man's ditch."

W. B. Yeats, "A Dialogue of Self and Soul"

1

Mirabel

A thousand kilometers from Lisbon, Ngomo and Zeus stopped for a few days in a tiny village called Mirabel-sur-Mer before resuming their ceaseless journey.

Mirabel sat in the hills on the southeast coast of France, just above the Spanish border, on the rocky shore overlooking the Mediterranean. Zeus let go of Ngomo's hand and ran downhill to the water. He fell into the pale sand and said, "It's warm, Ngomo." He had never seen the sea. From the ridge above, the village curved into the bay like an open hand, a crescent of terracotta roofs and limestone walls, the beach the color of white gold. Even Ngomo, who had seen many oceans, had to admit the water in Mirabel was startling. It looked like someone had poured a can of blue paint straight into the clear shallows.

Old men cast nets from wooden rowboats. A chapel bell rang faintly in the hills. The smoky smell of grilled fish curled into the air.

"I want to go swimming," Zeus said. "Can I?"

"I don't know," Ngomo said. "Can you swim?"

"No," said Zeus. "But how hard can it be?"

They took off their shoes, rolled up their trouser legs, and stepped into the warm tide. "Your grandparents are waiting for you, Zeus," Ngomo said, holding the boy's hand.

"I know," Zeus replied. "But they've been waiting three years. Another couple of days isn't going to kill them."

They rented a room at Pensione Violette overlooking the sea. Madame Brac was a widow whose husband died in 1940 at Narvik. Her house had a clay tile roof and faded green shutters. The sign above the door said simply, *Chambres*. She had three of them, all on the upper floor. One smelled of apples, one of mothballs, one of salt. They took the apple room. It was the largest—and it faced the sea.

Madame Brac looked at them for a long moment that first night—not quite surprised, but thoughtful. She was odd and kind, but not blind. An African man with a Jewish boy, both speaking flawless French. It was, one could say, an anomaly.

She handed Ngomo a bowl of fish stew without a word.

"We're here for just a few days," said Ngomo. "Headed to Lisbon."

"Portugal's a long way from here," she said.

"Yes."

"How long you been on the road?"

Ngomo paused. "Ten months."

She looked more closely at them.

"My mamie and papi are in Lisbon," said Zeus.

"That's good."

"And I'm on my way to the Congo," Ngomo said.

She nodded. "Very far. Do you want some more bread?"

Madame Brac had a goat in the back and in the mornings, she brought Zeus warm milk—"for the growing boy." The goat was tan, cross-eyed, and answered only to the name *Josephine*. Occasionally Madame brought Zeus an egg. The rest of the time, it was fresh bread and lentils, stewed with tomatoes and garlic.

"It's like Bruges, Ngomo," Zeus said, stuffing his mouth with an egg. "But with a beach."

"And sun," Ngomo said, closing his eyes and lifting his face to the sky.

They slept with the windows open. In the mornings, sunrise poured in from the Mediterranean, bathing their room in pink and gold. Before even breakfast, they walked barefoot down to the shore, when the tide was still low and the water like glass. In silence they listened to the gulls wheel overhead and to the Spanish guitar of toothless Don Pepino, finger-picking the same three songs from the balcony of his yellow pensione.

For weeks, in the afternoons, Zeus never left the sea.

"It's not like Belgium," he kept saying, floating in the low tide, arms out like wings.

"No, Belgium is a lot farther north," Ngomo said. "Think of how far we've come."

"How far, do you think?"

"More than a thousand kilometers."

Zeus tried to whistle. "That's a lot," he said. "Wolski would be impressed."

"Very impressed. Should we get you a map, so you can see?"

"Yes, please." The boy paused. "Do you think Wolski made it back?"

"If anyone could, it would be him. That man could find a civet in a jungle."

Zeus nodded. "Can we get a map tomorrow?"

They bought a large map of Europe and taped it to the wall beside their table. While they had their weak *café au lait*—boiled milk poured over grounds and sweetened—Ngomo would ask Zeus to find his country, Belgium, and point to the places he'd been. Charleroi, where he was born; and Vorselaar, where he hid in a monastery; Bruges, where he rode a boat; and Tremelo, with its castle in the *velde*, its abbey in the woods, and its belltowers, where a soldier named Briggs had saved his life. Herentals, where his mother's sister Mina worked for a man named Alder and became friends with a boy named Paolo, his sister Charlotte, his brother Fitz, and their best friend Louise. And finally, Antwerp, where Ngomo found Zeus.

"You didn't find me," Zeus said, his mouth full of blackcurrant jam. "I found you. Antwerp is right here." He pointed to a dot on the map and pressed his fist hard to his chest.

The church bells rang once at noon each day, and all day on Sundays.

Ngomo found work on the beach—to earn just enough to last until he could take Zeus to Lisbon and continue on to the Congo. They spent what little money they had on the room and on bouillabaisse, on goat cheese and cheap red wine, on chestnut cakes and even some octopus grilled over open fire. For a few francs a day, Ngomo set up chairs, umbrellas, and cabanas on the sand for the beachgoers.

Zeus helped him.

A few weeks went by.

Then a month.

And another.

The war ended.

They read about it in the paper. "I guess whatever happened," Zeus said, "the Germans didn't get to build that bomb."

"Guess not, little man."

Another month went by. The man who ran the beach rentals had to return to Perpignan, and he asked Ngomo to take over the business. "We should do it, Ngomo," Zeus said.

"We have to leave soon, Zeus. We should've left already. Across the Pyrenees is a long way. What if we don't find Rafael's father, the mountain guide, who can lead us across?"

"Just for a little while, Ngomo. Come on. Until summer's over." He took Ngomo's hand.

"Okay," Ngomo said. "Just till the summer's over."

That long late June evening, as the sun was setting behind the hills and they were folding up the chairs and tents, he said, "At the end of the summer, we will have to go, Zeus. No ifs, no buts. Your family is waiting."

"Of course. We'll go then."

They kept closing *les parapluies.* Zeus said, "If we make some extra, we can buy more chairs. Maybe a cabana. Hire someone. Then we can work that beautiful hotel, Saint Martin de la Mer." He pointed to a white stone villa with a brick red tile roof and striped pink awnings on every balcony. In front of it, a woman poured red wine from a clay pitcher for fishermen playing cards in the sand. "We can even raise our prices a little. I bet the people who stay in the pink hotel would pay—especially if our chairs and *parapluies* were nice colors."

"Like pink?"

"Yes! Like pink."

Silently, Ngomo watched the boy. "What else do you think Mirabel produces?"

"You mean besides pink beach chairs?" Zeus thought about it. "Fish?"

"So much of it," said Ngomo.

"You know what they probably don't produce?" Zeus said, squinting at the shimmering sunset water.

"Uranium?" said Ngomo.

They sat side by side, watching the sea glow with fading lavender and yellows.

"And so we stay?" said Zeus.

"And so we stay," said Ngomo. "But when summer ends, we'll have to go."

"Okay. When summer ends, we'll go," said Zeus. "But first, we stay."

"Yes, Zeus. But first we stay."

2

Hurtgen Forest

"Company C this way!" Charlie shouted. "Company B! Company A! To your right—Eindhoven, Bladel, Best! Go east, go north. All roads do *not* lead to the same place! One road leads to hell—the Scheldt Estuary, Walcheren Islands, the Drowned Lands! You don't want to go that way. Men, go where I'm pointing, move, come on! I know it's muddy. I know the road is long, but look, it's sunny out. The rain has stopped. Just a few more kilometers to the Dutch border. And only seventy to Arnhem. Eighty, tops!" Suddenly she stopped and gasped. The flags fell from her hands.

"Fletcher!" she yelled. *Oh my God.* He couldn't hear her. "Fletcher!"

He was marching away in the opposite direction, swallowed by a sea of soldiers, talking and smoking with the boys. The second time she hollered, he slowed and looked back, peering into the September sun.

When he saw her, he waved, and she leapt from her rock and ran to him, pushing through the others, and flinging herself into his arms.

They embraced for a long time. They kissed. She pressed him to her, squeezing shut her eyes but pulled herself together and put on her bravest face, her most joyous face—with no penumbras etched on it, no war, no pain. Just wildflowers in Lillehaven, riding the boat arm in arm down the canal in Bruges, dancing in Kasteel de Velde while Hawk played a Schubert waltz and Hildi sat watching his fingers glide along the keys. Rafael and Louise swayed nearby, wrapped around each other. Now she *really* squeezed her eyes shut. *No* penumbras, her heart yelled. No grief, no sighs everlasting. *Come on, Charlie.*

"Charlie, I'm so happy to see you," Fletcher said, caressing her face, stroking her hair. "What happened to you that night? I waited so long."

"I know," she said. "I'm sorry. They blew the bridge at Merksem. I got caught on the wrong side, and by the time I got back to Antwerp . . ." She grimaced. "Fitz took a bad one in the leg. I couldn't leave him."

"Of course you couldn't." He gazed down at her with melting tenderness. "But you're okay?"

"I burned my arm." She showed him her bandages. "Or broke it. Or both. I didn't want to *check my bones*." She grinned. "It's a nuisance, is what it is."

"Would that you had a little of Belvy's Stitchless Seal. After the war, you and I should patent it, make millions."

She shook her head. "*It's probably banned by every medical board from here to Madagascar*," she said, quoting Belvedere.

They smiled ruefully.

"Look at you in your uniform," she said, patting him, beaming. "Don't you look pretty."

"Better than the rags Florent wore?"

She shrugged, unable to keep the joy off her face, taking him helplessly in, his dress blues and that ridiculous swagger, his jaunty cap, his clean-shaven face, his deep-set eyes blooming violet love at her.

"What happened to Zvart Haus?" she said. "Do you even know?"

"First place we went after my boys found me. I brought an army with me." He grinned. "I'm not kidding."

"I know you're not."

"An actual army."

"And?"

"Place was humming but abandoned. Not a soul left." Fletcher glanced away.

"What? Did you find Saul?"

"No. He was gone. He left a note in the lab near the uranium. Three words in German. *HF-Gas unter Druck.*"

"HF gas *pressurized*?" Her eyes went wide. "He warned the Germans not to touch it?"

Fletcher nodded. "We had to bring in Reed's chem warfare specialist. Took him four hours in a rubber suit. But he vented it safely."

"And the uranium?"

"We got it all. The yellowcake and the canisters," he said. "That bastard had enriched nearly thirty kilos. In six weeks. He nearly pulled it off."

"Good thing you got there when you did."

"Yeah. Good thing."

They couldn't say another word.

Somebody wolf-whistled. Fletcher shouted, mock angry, "Hey! That's my wife you're whistling at, buddy!"

"Those your new men?" she asked, glancing behind him. They'd been slow-walking, giving their commander space. They couldn't leave without him. Finally, they pulled off to the side of the road and waited in a scrum.

"Yes, new. Well, new and Stu."

A sergeant major waved, motioning for Fletcher to wrap it up.

"Was Reed happy with you?"

"I don't know about happy," Fletcher said with a shrug. "He wasn't thrilled I lost Ngomo. Capelle either."

"Did you tell them you didn't lose him. You liberated him."

"Tomato, tom-ah-toe. They shook my hand—eventually. Reed promised me a drink and a medal when all was said and done." He paused, chewed his lip. "Rafael is receiving the Victoria Cross," he said.

She paused too. "Probably won't mean as much to him now," she said quietly.

Whoever this Stu guy was, he was waving his arms like a propeller.

"The last act is about to begin," Charlie said, her voice breaking. "For a short while we walked it together—"

"And that was better."

"But now you and I must go forth on separate adventures." She fought to compose herself.

"When the war is over, I will come back for you," he said.

"'Course you will."

"I *promise*."

She smiled with her whole heart. "We sure make a lot of promises during war, don't we?" she said.

"That we do, Charlotte, my wife."

"I don't know who *you* are, Mr. Handsome. I'm Florent's wife." They held hands, chest to chest, face to face. "Where are you off to now?"

"They're sending what's left of the 7th Army to the Ardennes," he said.

"Ah. Bastogne?"

They shared a long mute blink of their wordless sorrow.

"Hurtgen Forest." He smiled. "Hodges doesn't think the Germans will head down south. They're too busy running back to Germany through Holland, building a new front there. But you never know."

"Hurtgen Forest is not good for fighting," Charlie said, trying to sound wise. "It's hilly. The woods are dense."

"Don't worry, there won't be much fighting," Fletcher said. "Just defending. I *promise*."

She smiled gamely in return. "Will you be done by Christmas? Or get furlough? Come spend Christmas with me. Like married lovers are supposed to. Come to Eindhoven. We'll eat cake for breakfast and put candles in the windows."

"I sure will." He gestured. "What are you doing on that rock?"

She glanced at the flags lying in the dust and flung her arm toward the fork in the road. "Rerouting Allied troops to avoid German fallback traps," she replied. "When you fighting boys need to get somewhere, who else is going to tell you where to go?"

"Well, you *are* my Eureka on the ground," said Fletcher.

"And you are my Rebecca in the sky."

They fell silent, staring at the chaos of men and jeeps and tanks, slowly pushing down an unpaved narrow road between a canal and a mud plain.

"They're all just like you," Charlie said. "Heading straight for the Nazis. I should really make a sign."

"Yes," Fletcher said. "It should say, *wrong fucking way*."

They laughed. "I'm going to write exactly that," she said with a wrenching sigh. They stood locked in a war embrace—hard and tight. His men were screaming for him.

"I gotta go," he said, pushing her hair aside and kissing her neck.

"Yeah, me too." She held his head to hers.

They kissed. And ran out of words.

"Fletcher, where's your little notebook?" she said, teasingly. "Did you calculate how long it would take you to get to Hurtgen Forest on foot? It's quite a way."

"I did," he said, patting his tunic pocket. "If we're moving this slow, it will take three weeks and four days, but if we ride a little, move a little faster, then eight days and change, depending on the rain and the road conditions, and also on how many men are marching and how narrow the road is . . ."

She smiled.

He smiled.

"I love you," he said. "Now go. Go fight your corner."

"It's the only thing us young can do," said Charlie.

Don't die in Aachen, in Ardennes. Don't be my Rafael. And I'll try not to be your Louise. Gallop out the way you galloped in. In a Greek formation, swagger out of my life, Fletcher Gray.

Charlie's face didn't move. She didn't say this to him. With everything she had, she forced herself to show him only love and joy.

"Hail, Lieutenant," is what she said. "Hail and farewell."

She was having a tough time letting him go.

"Fletcher!" she yelled. "Fletcher!" He stopped and turned.

She waved to him one last time. *"Parlez moi d'amour!"* she singsong-yelled.

"I will! You know I will! *Forever.*" He blew her a kiss and ran to catch up with his men. Encircling him, they marched down the dusty road. The sun was out, drying the ground.

At Louise's house, after they got married, Charlie told him she once thought she wanted to be a *poem*. Only after she'd met him did she realize that no—what she wanted to be was a *poet*.

And she was.

Take your empty canteen and put my tears in it and take it with you to Wind River, to your next port of call, your next air drop, your next Herentals, where other bells will ring for you.

Je t'aime. Carve that on our metal Belgian skies.

Charlie watched until the last of him faded from her view.

She wiped her face and returned to the fork in the road.

Only after he was gone did she remember she'd completely forgotten to ask him what happened to Rheinhardt. Geez. *Tant pis.*

She climbed back onto her boulder, raised the Belgian flag, the Stars and Stripes, the Union Jack, and resumed waving the soldiers toward her right. "Go this way!" Charlie shouted. "Look, I'm showing you the way! No, not *that* way—*here*! Men, I'm literally giving you a sign! Oh, for Pete's sake, tank commander, technical sergeant, captain, lieutenant, general, I'm upranking you all! Do any of you even *want* to—go *this* way and live."

That was all they got.

But my God, they got it.

3

Thyboron

Five hundred miles north, near the tip of Denmark, between land and sea, lies a tiny village called Thyboron, on the bluffs and the rocks and the dunes. In 1944, its inhabitants numbered 600. Nearly half a century later, the number rose slightly, to 662. The village has remained largely unchanged for a hundred years. Its residents were fishermen then, and remain fishermen now. They catch the fish, they clean it, they eat it. Once a month their general store is replenished with tea and cigarettes. From yeast, they make their own brew, their own bread. The men live out their lives on the windswept shore, waking before dawn, spending the day out at sea, coming back, cleaning the fish, the nets, the boats, eating, drinking, smoking, sitting with friends by the fire, playing chess. Sometimes listening to music. Sometimes even singing. They celebrate birthdays well, the rare wedding even better.

Sometimes, drifters come to Thyboron.

With reservations, the locals let them stay, for as the saying goes, if anyone stays long enough in Thyboron, they deserve Thyboron. Most migrants leave after a month or two. Some stay as long as a year.

But in 1944, a man wandered into their town and stayed for half a century. He wore rags on his body and seal skins for foot coverings.

He said his name was Erik Vang. He once was a tall man, but the weight of the years had shrunk him and stooped his back. He arrived with an overgrown gray beard, and never cut it. When he first came, he was half-dead from hunger and wasting. The villagers fed him and gave him drink. They were sure he'd leave when he got better.

He didn't.

He asked if he could help them in their daily tasks in exchange for a room and some food. He was not a fisherman, he said. Before the war, he had been an accountant. He said he was from Hojer, a minuscule border town in southern Denmark, swallowed up by Germany in the 1920s. Erik Vang said he was imprisoned in Buchenwald for the better part of the war. He looked so emaciated, the people of Thyboron believed him. He said after liberation, he returned to Hojer to find his family but learned they'd all been swept away.

Completely alone, he traveled north in search of a new life.

Some didn't believe him. After the war, many Germans dispersed over Europe, trying to escape punishment. But Erik Vang looked so beaten, even the skeptics let it go.

Once healed, he learned to wash boats, mend nets, gut fish. He himself never fished. He said he didn't like the open sea; it made him sick to sway and bob in the water. He didn't mind the cold, though, or the snow, the ice, the blistering winds.

The people of Thyboron were not trusting by nature—they were reserved and wary of strangers—but with the passage of time, the fishermen grew to like Erik, and came to depend on him, for he was nothing if not reliable, nothing if not punctual, nothing if not meticulous. Sometimes they teased him about it, and he smiled like he was in on the joke. "You keep time like a German," they said to him, and he chuckled with appreciative good humor, and sometimes even joked back. "I love a good joke," he'd say. "Please submit it in triplicate." Or he'd add, "I too can be spontaneous. Every third Monday. From 3:00 to 3:15."

The village cats liked him. In the evenings he gave them fish guts to eat.

He lived in one of the seaside shacks. The hut was hidden in the dunes and faced the bitter water. He was the first one up in the morning, when it was still dark. He trudged out in his long rubber boots and pulled the boats into the water, got them ready for the other men. He brought out the nets and the lines and the hooks and laid them in their boats. Everything was clean, polished, greased. The bait was in the buckets; the nylon lines gleamed. And after the men went out, Erik walked to the commissary to have his tea with a little bread. He listened to the radio, smoked, and read last week's papers. He went into the mess hall and swept and mopped, and prepared for the men's return. In the commissary kitchen, he cleaned the pots, and in the dining hall, he set the tables. When the men returned, he went out and cleaned their fish. Afterward, they cooked together and ate together.

In the commissary, they would ask Erik Vang to sit with them, break bread, join in. Sometimes he did. But he was a man of habit, he told them, and the routine of being by himself helped bring order to his soul.

"Does your soul really need order, Vang?" they'd ask, half in jest. "Seems like that's the only thing it's got."

Erik Vang would reply. "Terrible is the dread judgment seat before which we all must appear, my brothers. There is neither slave nor freeman, neither small nor great. We all must stand naked and face it, and before that, take heed and gaze steadfast at our own graves. So, yes. My soul needs to be brought to order."

While they continued to eat, he went out to the sea and stood at the shoreline in the watery silence, his face downcast, as if condemned. After a few minutes, he began his evening work. He pulled in the boats, tied them to the bollards, inspected them for leaks, patched them if anything was torn. He cleaned the nets of fish debris, untangled them, and laid them ready for the next day.

And again.

And again.

For fifty years.

Maybe a little slower in the later years.

As he worked, he muttered to himself, to keep company with his own words.

"*Why* did you have to do that, Franz," he kept repeating. "Why did you jump in front of me?"

One of the fishermen overheard him once. "Who is Franz?" he asked. Erik Vang shrugged. After that, he muttered more quietly, so his words didn't carry quite as far. Just to the cats who sometimes walked down to the waterside with him and, when it wasn't too cold or windy, sat by his side.

With him they watched the glassy sea as if it were a mighty mystery—as if they too mourned their lives and contemplated how best to present themselves to God, faded and grieving.

I can't understand what happened with Saul, he'd whisper inaudibly. Wherever you are, Hubner, do *you* know? I just don't get it. And you know I pride myself on my intuition. I used to have a sense about people. You said that about me. I had an uncanny ability to see through things. I had a sense about you. I can't even remember when we first met, when you first started working for me. It must have been in Berlin. Three lifetimes ago.

I'm stuck on our last days together, at Zvart Haus. I still don't know what happened to make it all go off the rails. It was going so well! Grunfell was sure of success. Grunfell-level confidence, I used to call it. All he needed to do was keep going. It was just a matter of weeks. Everything was ready. The casing for the bomb was built and waiting.

And suddenly not even a gram. What happened? I've been going over and over it. Every day, every evening when I'm here, every week, every year. I know the formula like I know your name. Everything was right. So where did Saul go wrong? Was his math incorrect? Was the period in the wrong place, did he add before he subtracted, or multiply before he divided? He was a prideful man, more prideful even than me. Erik Vang smirked. My name would never be remembered like his—linked forever with the course of history, with the shifting of all human endeavor. I offered that man immortality, handed it to him in the form of a warm glowing rock.

And he wanted it so much.

He was an unrecognized genius, Franz, and those are always the easiest to manipulate. He wanted glory more than he cared for the life of his own children. I knew it, Krieger knew it, and most important, Saul himself knew it. Knew it and was all right with it.

Where did the formula fail him, fail us?

I remember the calculation, as if he told it to me fresh this morning. Everything was precisely calibrated. *N-235 times e to the negative E delta over BT, divided by N-235 plus N-238.*

The math was solid. The formula never changed. It was remarkable and sound.

The cyclotron was working, the electromagnetic coils were delivering the right amount of power, the proportions were spot on—the math, the science, was perfect!

What happened that made further enrichment impossible? Could Saul have stopped enriching it on purpose?

To this day, I can't figure it out.

Rheinhardt kept thinking it had something to do with that lovely blonde girl with acid in her hand. He kept returning to her, circling her. Sometimes it felt that the answers to all his questions lay with her. Every day he spun around her, stood in that room as she faced him, silently, motionlessly, mutely. He couldn't fathom it.

What was he missing?

The sea was quiet that evening. The cats stayed away.

From the bottom of his tackle box, wrapped in a clean towel, he pulled out his old Luger—the only thing he took from the leather bag that infernal *Aufhocker* had dropped under the trees. He sat down heavily on the pebbled sand. For a few moments he examined it, turned it over in his hands.

I wish you were here to talk it through with me, Hubner.

I won't lie, there've been times I found it hard without you these last fifty years.

N-235 times e to the negative E delta over BT, divided by N-235 plus N-238.

Rheinhardt put the barrel of the gun in his mouth and cocked the lever. He couldn't live like this for another moment. He couldn't live caring about it—not understanding it—for another moment. *To the power of negative delta . . . N-235 plus N-238 . . .*

Where did I go wrong?

He had solved every variable but one. The girl was the missing constant.

It had been so long, he couldn't even remember her name anymore.

What was it?

Oh, yes.

Louise.

Acknowledgments

My deepest thanks to Brianne Collins, my brilliant editor, my Brianne of Tarth, whose astonishing memory, sharp eye, blazing speed, and bottomless well of kindness and patience are the reason this book exists in its finished form. She sees everything, remembers everything, fixes everything. Her hands are in every barrel.

To Kane Shepherd, unsung hero of the printed page.

To Alex Lloyd, my incomparable publisher, who continues to set unmeetable deadlines—and then insists I meet them. His relentless faith in me, and in the possibility of doing the impossible, was, in the end, exactly what this book needed.

To Vanessa Lanaway, for her diligent work on the copyedit, and to Rosemary Peers, for her thoughtful, thorough final pass.

To my agents, Jacinta di Mase and Danielle Binks, for steering the ship through all kinds of stormy weather.

To Kasia Malita, who translates my books with boundless love and devotion. Would that she could render them into all languages, not just Polish.

To my beloved family, near and far, and a shout-out to my youngest, who brings oatmeal, Nespresso, sunshine, light, and the occasional dry witticism.

And finally, to the New York Yankees—for reminding me nightly what true suffering is.

About the Author

Paullina Simons is the author of sixteen internationally acclaimed, bestselling novels, including *Tully* and the Bronze Horseman Saga. Born and raised in the former Soviet Union, Paullina immigrated to the United States with her family in the mid-seventies. She has lived in Rome, London, and Dallas, and now resides in New York with her husband, one child, one dog, and a one-eyed cat.

PAULLINA SIMONS

FROM OPEN ROAD MEDIA

OPEN ROAD
INTEGRATED MEDIA

www.ingramcontent.com/pod-product-compliance
Lightning Source LLC
LaVergne TN
LVHW100459110826
845146LV00002B/460

* 9 7 9 8 3 3 7 2 0 7 4 2 1 *